# THE
# TWO GEORGES

# THE
# TWO GEORGES

Richard Dreyfuss

&

Harry Turtledove

A TOM DOHERTY ASSOCIATES BOOK
New York

THE TWO GEORGES

This book is printed on acid-free paper.

A Tor Book
Published by Tom Doherty Associates, Inc.
175 Fifth Avenue
New York, NY 10010

Tor Books on the World-Wide Web:
http://www.tor.com

Tor® is a registered trademark of Tom Doherty Associates, Inc.

Maps by Ellisa Mitchell

Design by Michael Mendelsohn

Library of Congress Cataloging-in-Publication Data

Dreyfuss, Richard
    The Two Georges   /   by Richard Dreyfuss and Harry Turtledove. — 1st ed.
        p.     cm.
    "A Tom Doherty Associates book."
    ISBN 0-312-85969-4
    I. Turtledove, Harry.     II. Title.
PS3554.R489T96     1996
813'.54—dc20                                                    95-44902
                                                                  CIP

First Edition: March 1996

Printed in the United States of America

0 9 8 7 6 5 4 3 2 1

# ACKNOWLEDGMENTS

▾

THE AUTHORS WOULD LIKE TO EXPRESS their appreciation to Mr. Bob Urhausen of Goodyear Airship Operations, Gardena, California, for arranging for them to ride on the Goodyear airship *Eagle* and for the material he provided, all of which made scenes in *The Two Georges* involving airships more realistic than they could have been otherwise.

Special thanks to Harry Harrison for his thoughts on how a world without the American Revolution might look.

Thanks also to Anne Wenzinger for her generous assistance in all matters pertaining to railroads, especially those having to do with food.

Arctic Ocean

UNITED
KINGDOM

DENMARK

SWEDEN

FRANCO - SPANISH
KINGDOM
(HOLY ALLIANCE)

HOLLAND

GERMAN
STATES

SWISS
CONF.

Austria

PORTUGAL

ITALIAN STATES

OTTOMAN
EMPIRE

RUSSIAN          EMPIRE

British
Prot.)

PERSIA

AFGHANISTAN

CHINA
(British Protectorate)

FRANCO - SPANISH
AFRICA

INDIA
(Brit.)

BRITISH
WEST
AFRICA

ETHIOPIA
(India)

BRITISH
EAST
AFRICA

INDO-
CHINA
(Fr.-Sp.)

PHILIPPINES
(Fr.-Sp.)

ANGOLA
(Port)

Indian
Ocean

MALAYA
(Brit)

SOUTH
AFRICA
(British)

MOZAMBIQUE (Port.)

MADAGASCAR
(Franco-Spanish)

DUTCH EAST INDIES

AUS

the
World
of the
Two Georges

E. Mitchell '95

THE

# TWO GEORGES

## I

THOMAS BUSHELL BENT OVER THE LITTLE desk in his stateroom, drafting yet another report. From Victoria, the capital, it was two days by airship west across the North American Union to his home in New Liverpool. He'd taken advantage of that to catch up on his paperwork, the bane of every police officer's life.

The stateroom speaker came to life with a burst of static. Then the captain announced, "Ladies and gentlemen, we are nearing the famous Meteor Crater. Those interested in observing it are invited to gather in the starboard lounge. We'll pass it in about five minutes, which gives you plenty of time to walk to the lounge and find yourself a seat. Thank you."

More static, then silence again. Bushell glanced down at the report. He laid his pen on the desk and got to his feet—it could wait. He salved his conscience by reminding himself they'd soon be serving luncheon anyhow.

He needed only a couple of quick strides to reach the door; the stateroom's mirrored wall made it seem larger than it was. He paused a moment to adjust his cravat, run a comb through his hair, and smooth down his sleek brown mustache with the side of a forefinger. He was a compact, solidly made man who looked younger than his forty-eight years . . . until you noticed his eyes. Police officers see more of the world's seamy side than most mortals. After a while, it shows in their faces. Bushell had seen more than most policemen.

He locked the door behind him when he went out into the corridor. Any thief without a mad love for paper would have come away from his stateroom disappointed, but he was not a man who invited misfortune. It came too often, even uninvited.

The lounge was decorated in the Rococo Revival style of King-Emperor Edward VIII; after half a century, the Revival was being revived once more. Plump pink cherubs fluttered on the ceiling. No wooden surface was without a coat of gold leaf, an elaborately carved curlicue, or an inlay of contrasting wood or semi-precious stone.

Bushell took a chair well away from the chattering group who'd got there ahead of him. Even after the lounge grew full, he sat in the center of a small island of privacy; studying the ground a quarter of a mile below, he made it plain he did not welcome even the most casual companionship.

13

"Something to drink, sir?" Like any servant, the tuxedoed waiter slipped unnoticed past personal boundaries the upper classes respected.

Without taking his eyes off the approaching crater, Bushell nodded. "Irish whiskey—Jameson—over ice, please."

"Very good, sir." The waiter hurried away. Bushell went back into the little bubble of reserve he'd put up around himself. The drone of the dirigible's engines, louder here than in the staterooms at the center of the passenger gondola, blurred the conversations in the lounge and helped him maintain his isolation.

The airship's whale-shaped shadow slowly slid across Meteor Crater. The crater was about three quarters of a mile across; the shadow took the same fraction of a minute to traverse it from east to west.

Someone not far from Bushell said, "Looks as if God were playing golf in the desert here and didn't replace His divot."

"If God played golf, could He take a divot?" the fellow's companion asked, chuckling. "There's one I'd wager the Archbishop of Canterbury has never pondered."

Meteor Crater did not remind Thomas Bushell of a golfer's divot. To him, it looked like a gunshot wound on the face of the world. Murders by gunfire, thankfully, were rare in the civilian world, but he'd seen more gunshot wounds than he cared to remember in his days in the Royal North American Army. The British Empire and the Franco-Spanish Holy Alliance were officially at peace, so skirmishes between the North American Union and Nueva España seldom made the newspapers or the wireless, but if you got shot in one, you died just as dead as if it had happened in the full glare of publicity.

The waiter returned and went through the lounge with a silver tray. When he came to Bushell, he said, "Jameson over ice," and handed him the glass. "That will be seven and sixpence, sir."

Bushell drew his wallet from the left front pocket of his linen trousers. He took out a dark green ten-shilling note and handed it to the waiter. Like all NAU banknotes, whatever their color and denomination, the ten-shilling green bore a copy of Gainsborough's immortal *The Two Georges*, which celebrated George Washington's presentation to George III as the leading American member of the privy council that oversaw British administration of the colonies on the western shore of the Atlantic.

The waiter set the banknote on his tray. As he gave Bushell a silver half-crown in change, he remarked, "Exciting to think the original *Two Georges* is touring the original NAU, isn't it, sir? And it'll be coming to New Liverpool next. I hope I have the chance to see it, don't you?"

"Yes, that would be very fine," Bushell said. Ever since it was painted, *The Two Georges* had symbolized everything that was good about the union between Great Britain and her American dominions.

Bushell did not tell the waiter he would be the man chiefly responsible for keeping *The Two Georges* safe while it was in New Liverpool. For one thing, in that kind of job anonymity was an advantage. For another, he had enough work to catch up on back in the stateroom that he preferred not to think about what lay ahead till it actually arrived.

From speakers mounted in the ceiling of the lounge, the airship captain said, "Ladies and gentlemen, I'd like to remind you luncheon will be served in the dining room in ten minutes. I trust you'll enjoy the cuisine that's made the *Upper California Limited* famous all over the world."

The alacrity with which the lounge emptied said the passengers trusted they would enjoy the cuisine, too. Thomas Bushell had seated himself a long way from the exit, and in any case was in no hurry. He left a shilling for the servitor who'd brought him his drink, then followed the crowd to the dining room.

A bowing waiter escorted him to a seat. Because he was one of the latecomers, he did not have a table to himself, which disappointed him, but he was near a window; though the company might prove uncongenial, the scenery never would.

The dining room would have done credit to a fine restaurant down on the ground. Bushell's feet sank deep into colorful Persian carpets as he approached his place. Starched white linen, crystal goblets, and heavy silver flatware greeted him there.

"Fred Harvey food!" boomed the man who sat across the table from him. He smacked his lips in anticipation. "We couldn't eat better at Claridge's, sir, nor even in Paris, by God." His red, jowly face and the great expanse of white shirt-front beneath his jacket said his opinion was to be reckoned with when it came to food.

"Fred Harvey is a man of whom the Empire may be proud," Bushell answered, "and his sons and grandsons have maintained his tradition." He waved out the window to the grand aerial vista spread out before them.

A waiter handed out menus, then retired to give the diners time to make their choices. Bushell was torn between the salmon poached in white wine and the larded tenderloin of beef in Madeira sauce. At last he chose the latter because it would go well with a Bordeaux whose acquaintance he'd been lucky enough to make the night before.

"A very sound selection," his corpulent table companion said when he gave his choice to the waiter. "A splendid year, 1981, and just now coming into full maturity." He picked the salmon himself, and a pinot blanc of formidable heritage.

Far below, dust devils swirled over the red-brown desert ground. The wind that kicked them up also beat against the airship. The passenger gondola rocked slightly, as if it were a boat on a rippling pond. The sommelier arrived just then with the wine. After the ritual of the cork, he poured. The headwind made the wine stir in its goblet, but it did not come close to spilling.

"Better than traveling by sea," the fat man said as the wine steward poured his fancy white. "There they put the tables on gimbals, to keep the food from winding up in the passenger's laps. And it would be a pity to waste this lovely wine on my trousers. They haven't the palate to appreciate it." He chuckled wheezily.

Bushell raised his goblet in salute. "His Majesty, the King-Emperor!" he said. He and his companion both sipped their wine to the traditional toast heard round the world in the British Empire.

"I drink to headwinds," the fat man said, lifting his glass in turn. "If they make us late getting into New Liverpool, we shall be able to enjoy another supper in this splendid establishment."

"I shouldn't drink to that one," Bushell said. "I have enough work ahead of me to want to get to it as soon as I can. However—" He paused, remembering supper the night before, then brought the goblet to his lips. The fat man laughed again.

The waiters began serving. Conversation in the dining room ebbed, supplanted by the gentle music of silver on silver. Meals aboard the *Upper California Limited* deserved, and got, serious attention. Bushell's tenderloin was fork-tender and meltingly rich, the dry wine in the Madeira sauce bringing out the full flavor of the beef. The tenderloin was a generous cut, but when it was gone he found himself wishing it had been larger.

Across the table from him, the fat man methodically demolished his salmon. Bushell had chosen a plate of cheese and apple slices for dessert, but the fat man devoured something Teutonically full of chocolate and cream and pureed raspberries. When he leaned back in his chair, replete at last, he was even more florid than he had been before the meal.

He drew a silver case from the inner pocket of his jacket. "D'you mind, sir?"

"By no means." Bushell took out his own case, chose a cigar from it, and struck a lucifer. He savored the mild smoke. The aroma of the fat man's panatela said he was as much a connoisseur of tobacco as he was of fine wine.

Bushell savored his feeling of contentment with the world; he knew it too seldom. He leaned back in his chair, peered out the window once more. Suddenly he pointed. "Look! There's an aeroplane!"

"Where?" The fat man stared. "Ah, I see it. Not a sight one comes across every day."

"Not in peacetime, certainly," Bushell said. The aeroplane flashed by at breathtaking speed, twin wings above and below its lean, sharklike fuselage providing lift. It was gone before Bushell got more than a glimpse of the blue, white, and red roundel on its flank that announced it belonged to the Royal North American Flying Corps.

The fat man puffed moodily on his cigar. "So much speed is vulgar, don't you think?"

"Useful for the military," Bushell answered. "In civilian life, though, there's not usually much point to dashing across the continent in ten or twelve hours. You hardly have the time to accomplish anything while you're traveling."

"Quite, quite." The fat man's jowls wobbled when he nodded. "If you need to get anyplace in such a tearing hurry, chances are you've either started too late or, more likely, put less thought into your journey than you should have."

"Just so." Bushell finished his cigar and then, with a nod to his table companion, excused himself and went back to his stateroom. He knew how much he still had to accomplish before the *Upper California Limited* docked itself to the mooring mast in New Liverpool.

When he got back to his desk, he lit another cigar and plunged once more into paperwork. As much as anything could, the smoke relaxed him. In the early days of dirigibles, when inflammable hydrogen filled their gasbags, such a simple pleasure would have been forbidden as deadly dangerous. But coronium, though its lifting power was slightly less, had the great advantage of being immune to the risk of fire. Tapping his ash into a cut-glass tray, Bushell gave silent thanks to technical progress.

He had so immersed himself in his reports that he started when the captain came on the ceiling speaker and said, "Ladies and gentlemen, we shall be mooring in New Liverpool about an hour from now, just before four in the afternoon, very close to our scheduled arrival time. I hope you have enjoyed your flight aboard the *Upper California Limited,* and that—"

Bushell stopped listening and went back to work. About forty minutes later, he found himself rubbing his eyes. At first, he thought they were just tired. Then he laughed. "I'm nearly home: I can feel it in the air," he murmured. Although New Liverpool drew most of its power from electric plants far away, the valleys in which the city nestled had a way of trapping the fumes of burnt kerosene from steam cars, along with factory smoke and locomotive exhaust, until they sometimes made the air almost as bad as it got in London.

The policeman got up, stretched, and packed the reports on which he'd labored so mightily into his carpetbag. After checking to make sure he was leaving nothing behind in the stateroom, he went to the lounge to watch the dirigible land. The lounge was packed; a good many others had the same idea.

The *Upper California Limited* glided over the streets and suburbs of New Liverpool toward the airship port, a great flat expanse of macadam hard by the Pacific, south and west of the central core of the city. But New Liverpool sprawled in a way different from cities in the eastern provinces of the NAU. Because earthquakes visited the Californias so often, buildings above a dozen stories were forbidden here. New Liverpool had grown out, not up.

"Look!" someone said. "You can read the traffic commandments painted on the highways down there."

"And look at the steamers and the electric coaches," someone else chimed in. "They're tiny as toys."

Off to the north, a train, also seemingly toy-sized, rolled toward the station. Private cars were wonderful for getting about inside a town, but trains and airships traversed the vast reaches of the North American Union far more efficiently.

Down on the sidewalks, antlike people pointed and waved up to the *Upper California Limited.* They and their conveyances swelled as the dirigible continued its descent toward the airship port. Bushell spied the great silver shapes of two other airships already berthed at their masts.

The muted roar of the *Upper California Limited'*s motors lessened as it neared its own mooring mast. The airship slowed until it was all but hovering, like an enormous, elongated soap bubble. The captain let down the landing lines. A swarm of overall-clad groundcrew men—about half and half, pale Irish and brown Nuevespañolans—seized the lines and began the job of tethering the airship to the ground once more.

The *snap!* that locked the flange at the airship's nose to the collar atop the mooring mast made the immense craft vibrate for a moment. "Ladies and gentle-men, we've reached the ground at New Liverpool at three fifty-eight local time. The weather is sunny, as you'll have seen; local temperature is seventy-seven de-grees. On behalf of the entire crew, I'd like to say it's been a pleasure serving you aboard the *Upper California Limited* these past two days. We hope you'll fly with us again soon."

Along with the rest of the passengers, Bushell filed toward the exit at the rear of the gondola. As always at the end of an airship flight, the sound of run-ning, splashing water filled his ears as the ground crew pumped the ballast tanks to the very top to make the *Upper California Limited* less a plaything for the fickle wind.

A man shifted from foot to foot. After glancing around to make sure no women were in earshot, he said, "That noise always reminds me I should have gone to the jakes." Bushell smiled, but thinly; the joke had to be as old as air-ships.

While the passengers descended the wheeled stairway the ground crew had attached to the exit door, their luggage slid down a metal ramp alongside. As soon as he started down the stairs, Bushell donned the snap-brim fedora he'd car-ried in his left hand. Once on the ground, he queued up to reclaim his bags. That took a while; the Negro clerk who gave them out lived up to his race's reputation for fussy precision, meticulously comparing every claim check to the correspond-ing label on suitcase or trunk.

"Those two there," Bushell said, pointing to his pigskin bags.

"Yes, sir," the clerk replied, though his eyes said he looked at Bushell, as at everyone else, as a likely thief. "Give me your stubs, sir, and I'll just go and see if they're the proper ones." He took the stubs, compared the numbers, and let out a loud "Huh!" when they matched. Bushell took the bags, tipped him a sixpence, and carried them off toward the parking garage a couple of hundred yards away.

By the time he got to his steamer, his arms felt several inches longer. He opened the boot and tossed in the suitcases, then got behind the wheel and put his carpetbag on the seat beside him. The car had sat idle here for several days while he was in Victoria, so he'd shut off the burner under the boiler. That meant he'd have to get up steam before he could go.

He turned the key. A battery-powered sparker lit the burner. A twist of a dashboard knob brought the flame up to high. Then he had nothing to do but wait and watch the pressure gauge. He glanced at his pocket watch, wondering if he had time to go back to his flat before he reported to the Royal American Mounted Police office. He shook his head. No.

After eight or ten minutes, the pressure gauge eased off the zero peg. He re-duced flame; maintaining pressure took a lot less kerosene than starting up. He released the brake, put the steamer in gear, and drove away. The garage attendant glanced at the date stamped on the ticket he presented, said, "That'll be two pounds even, sir," and accepted the blue banknote he proffered with a word of thanks and the brush of a forefinger against the brim of his flat cloth cap.

Traffic, light near the airship port, picked up as Bushell made his way toward the heart of New Liverpool. Not for the first time, he marveled at how the sleepy

Franco-Spanish village of Los Angeles had, in the century and a third since its incorporation into the North American Union, grown into a great and thoroughly Brittanic city.

Oh, a fair number of the people in cars, on bicycles, and walking on the sidewalks showed Nuevespañolan blood. In manner and dress, though, most of them were not easily distinguishable from their Anglo-Saxon and Celtic counterparts of similar class.

Clothes didn't make the man, but they gave an experienced observer like Bushell a good idea of how he earned his bread: laborers in overalls and cloth caps; jacketless clerks, some also wearing caps, others in straw boaters; junior businessmen in wide-legged trousers and striped jackets with high, pointed lapels, generally in fedoras with snap or round brims but sometimes choosing straws; more senior businessmen in tighter-fitting pants and longer jackets of somber black or brown or blue, many with cravats in public-school patterns, almost all wearing waistcoats and homburgs or narrow-brimmed derbies. A few men showed they were on holiday with their tennis whites or cricketers' caps.

By their clothing, the Negro men Bushell saw might all have been captains of industry. Most of them, though, were undoubtedly civil servants, even if they did affect the quiet elegance of the moneyed classes.

But for those who wore the black dress and white apron that marked servants, women enjoyed more latitude in their dress than men. Age and fashion spoke louder than class. Older women's dresses still brushed the sidewalk, as they had in Victoria's day. Their daughters and granddaughters, though, displayed not only ankles but several inches of shapely calf in pleated linen skirts of bright, flowery hues.

"Irene," Bushell muttered, and gripped the steering wheel with unnecessary force. She'd been older than most women who'd adopted the daring new style a few years before, but no one who saw her in one of those short skirts would have denied she had the legs to wear them. No one at all . . .

He pulled into the carpark next to the Royal American Mounties' headquarters just as the bells of the Anglican cathedral across the street rang five. When he parked, he put the steamer in neutral, set the hand brake, and turned the burner flame down to its lowest setting, just enough to keep the steam live in the boiler and let him drive off without having to wait and get it up again.

RAMs greeted him as he got out of the car and headed for the office, carpetbag in hand: "Welcome back, Colonel!" "Hope you gave the red-tape artists in Victoria the what-for." A couple of men asked anxiously, "How does the appropriation look for next year?" New Liverpool was a long way from the capital of the NAU; everyone worried about being forgotten when budget time rolled around.

"General Bragg says we have nothing to worry about," Bushell answered, to the visible relief of his questioners. They knew he and Lieutenant General Sir Horace Bragg had been friends since their days as subalterns in the army; if the RAMs' commandant told Bushell the appropriation would be all right, you could rely on it.

Bushell went up the marble steps and into the office building. He exchanged more greetings with the men he met there, but didn't pause to chat. As he headed for the stairway, someone behind him said, "He's got his business face on already."

"No—still," someone else answered, just loud enough for him to catch.

He took the stairs quickly, and was breathing a little hard by the time he reached the third floor. That annoyed him, and made him think less kindly of the large and excellent luncheon he'd eaten aboard the airship. As if to exorcise the ghost of that luncheon, he half trotted down the hall to his office.

Gilt letters on the door stared at him as he fumbled for his keys:

COLONEL THOMAS BUSHELL, CHIEF
UPPER CALIFORNIA SECTION
ROYAL AMERICAN MOUNTED POLICE

One of these days, they'd scrape off his name and rank and replace them with someone else's. The rest of the legend could stay the same. That would save the ratepayers money.

He turned the key in the lock, opened the door, closed and locked it after him. The office was twilight gloomy, the venetian blinds closed so the late-afternoon sun only painted two rows of little glowing dots across the near wall. Instead of opening the blinds, Bushell flicked the switch by the door. A bare bulb mounted in a ceiling fixture filled the office with harsh, yellow light.

The wooden swivel chair behind the heavy oak desk squeaked as Bushell lowered his weight into it. It squeaked again when he leaned back and stared at the opposite wall. Between a tall, oak file cabinet that matched the desk and a bookcase crowded with statute books, legal tomes, and criminological texts hung a framed color print of *The Two Georges.* Just below it was a rectangular patch where the wallpaper was of a slightly darker blue than anywhere else in the office, as if another picture had hung there until recently.

Bushell looked at that darker patch for a couple of minutes, his face utterly empty of expression. Then he reached into his trouser pocket and pulled out his keys once more. They jingled; he had a lot of them. He went through them one by one until he found a short, stubby shiny one, which he inserted into the lock above the top right drawer of his desk.

He pulled the drawer open. It was not packed with papers like the rest of the desk drawers. One of the things it held was a gilt-framed picture, about the size of the darker rectangle on the wallpaper. The picture was face-down. Bushell did not turn it over. On top of the picture lay a flat pint bottle of Jameson Irish whiskey. He picked it up, pulled out the stopper, and took a swig, then another.

The smoky taste of the whiskey filled his mouth. Its warmth filled his belly and mounted to his head. He took one more pull and then, with slow delibera-tion, corked the bottle and put it back in the drawer, which he locked. He went back to staring at the wallpaper. Eventually, the darker patch would fade to the color of the rest and disappear. If only memories faded so conveniently.

Someone knocked on the door. Bushell started. The someone tried the knob, which gave Bushell a good notion of who it was. "Half a moment, Sam," he called, loud enough for his voice to pierce the thick wood. He was relieved to find he sounded sober as a judge (and wasn't that a laugh, with half of them bloody lushes!).

He used the half a moment to light a hasty cigar. Its aroma would cover that of the Jameson in the room and, more to the point, on his breath.

He went to the door and opened it. Sure enough, there stood Captain Samuel Stanley, his adjutant. "Welcome back, Chief," he said, and stuck out his hand.

Bushell shook it, then stood aside. "Come in out of the rain."

"Don't mind if I do." Stanley walked into the office. He was a round-faced, medium-dark Negro, four or five years older than Bushell and several inches taller. His hair was as closely cropped as it had been in the long-ago days when he was staff sergeant in Bushell's platoon, but the pepper hadn't been dusted with salt then.

"One thing I have to give you, Sam," Bushell said with a chuckle: "you don't dress like most colored men I see."

Samuel Stanley looked down at himself with considerable dignity. "And why the devil should I?" he asked. "I'm not a petty official trying to pretend I'm better than I am, and I'm not an undertaker, either. I'm an officer of the RAMs in a warm town, and damn proud of it."

He glared at his longtime comrade, daring him to make something of it. And indeed, his double-breasted light blue blazer and white worsted trousers with thin black stripes were not only acceptable but handsome. As Bushell had said, though, most men of his race would never have appeared in anything save black or navy, nor worn a gold silk cravat dotted with crimson.

"Good. You damn well ought to be," Bushell said. "Clothes won't matter tonight, anyway: time to hope the moths haven't eaten our dress uniforms."

"As soon as I heard you were back, that's what I came here to remind you about," Stanley said. "After all the fuss and feathers in Victoria, there was always the chance you'd lost track of the date."

"Not bloody likely." Bushell pointed to the print of *The Two Georges*. "After looking at that every day I'm here, after seeing it every time I pull out my wallet, after growing up in a house with an enormous lithograph of it hung over the sofa in the parlor, do you think I'd miss the chance to see the original at last?"

"Now that you mention it, no." Samuel Stanley chuckled. "About as easy to get away from *The Two Georges* as to flap your arms and fly to the moon, isn't it? What's that word the damn Russians use for a religious painting?"

"An icon," Bushell answered. "That's about right, too." He walked over to the small closet behind his desk, pulled the door open, peered inside. "Well, the moths seem to have left something here. You have your dress reds?" The question was purely rhetorical; Samuel Stanley, as best as he could tell, never forgot anything.

The black man nodded. "I brought them in this morning. I'm just a lowly captain, don't you know"—his voice took on the languid accents of an English milord of Oxonian overeducation—"so I don't have a la-de-da closet in my office."

Bushell snorted. "Go change, then, and meet me back here in fifteen minutes." He pulled out his pocket watch. "We're in good time. The reception doesn't start until half past eight, and the governor's mansion is only about half an hour from here. That should give us plenty of time to mingle beforehand"—he rolled his eyes to show how much he looked forward to that—"and to make sure security is as tight in the mansion as it looks on paper."

"Nothing is ever as good as it looks on paper," Stanley said with the certainty of a veteran noncommissioned officer, "but you're right; one more round of checks won't hurt. I'll see you as soon as I'm in uniform." He nodded to Bushell and left the office.

Bushell got out of his civilian clothes, hung them up, and put on the red-striped black trousers and the red tunic he took out of the closet. The tunic had two rows of seven gilt buttons down the breast, and a high stand collar that was damnably uncomfortable. The shoulderboards showed Bushell's rank with the crown of the British Empire (differenced from that of the military by the letters RAMP beneath) and two pips each.

He belted on his ceremonial sword, pulled his service cap from the shelf above the coat rail, and set it on his desk. The visor had a row of scrambled eggs along the edge, but not by the crown. That and the band of red around the cap also signified his colonelcy.

Samuel Stanley knocked on the door well before the fifteen minutes had passed. That surprised Bushell not at all; he was just glad to be ready himself. Stanley grinned when he saw Bushell. "Don't we make a fine pair!" he exclaimed.

His tunic bore a single row of buttons. On his shoulder boards were three pips apiece, and the letters RAMP. His cap was plain black, without red band or scrambled eggs. The basket hilt of his sword was plain steel, while Bushell's had been gilded.

"We'll break up the monotony of frock coats, white shirtfronts, and toppers, that's certain," Bushell said. "Nothing like a uniform to make the pretty girls notice you, eh, Sam?"

Stanley sent him a wary look. He and his wife, Phyllis, had been married for more than twenty-five years. As for Bushell . . . Stanley's eyes slid to the dark rectangle below the print of *The Two Georges*. Instead of rising to the bait, he said, "Let's get going, shall we?"

"I'll drive," Bushell said. "I enjoy it, and the steam's up in my car."

"Are you all right?" Stanley asked.

"Right as rain," Bushell answered. "I slept better in the airship the last two nights than I do in my own flat." That was true. If it wasn't precisely what his friend had enquired about, he chose not to notice.

He and Stanley went downstairs together. As soon as they left the RAM headquarters, they set their caps on their heads, almost in unison, and smiled at each other. Bushell held the passenger door open for his friend, then went around to the right side of the steamer and slid behind the wheel. He backed the car out of its parking space, shifted to the lowest of his three forward gears, and all but silently rolled away. He turned up the burner to give him more pressure in reserve when he got out onto the street.

The RAM office building was in what had been downtown ever since New

Liverpool belonged to the Franco-Spanish Holy Alliance. The provincial governor's mansion lay some miles to the west; as at the airship port, Pacific breezes helped moderate the climate there.

Sunset Highway offered the quickest, most direct route between downtown New Liverpool and the governor's mansion. The highway traversed not only settled districts but also parklands—some green with irrigation, others the semi-desert scrub native to Upper California—and citrus groves whose shiny green leaves perfumed the air.

A patch of light in a dark doorway made Bushell's head whip around as the steamer passed through an urban stretch. When he saw the doorway belonged to a tavern, he relaxed. "I was afraid that might have been a fire," he said, "but it's just a televisor screen."

"Nothing like getting together with your chums after a hard day, soaking up a pint or two while you watch the cricket matches or rugby or tennis or whatever happens to be showing," Samuel Stanley said. "Keep your eyes on the screen and you don't have to think about what ails you—or much of anything else, come to that."

They passed a trafficator whose wigwag signs gave cars on the cross street the right of way. "Do you know," Bushell remarked, "one of the airship passengers was boasting at supper last night that he had a televisor screen in his own home."

His friend turned to stare at him, incredulous distaste on his face. "You are joking, I hope."

Bushell raised his right hand, as if he were about to stand in the witness box. "Upon my solemn oath." The wigwag switched. He put the steamer back into gear.

"Why would anyone want such a thing?" Stanley said, not so much to Bushell as to the world at large. "Wireless is one thing: you can read or talk or do anything else you care to while it's on. But a televisor screen . . . if it's showing something, you bloody well have to *watch* it. Suppose you have guests? I've never heard of anything so, so vulgar in all my life, I don't think. Besides, televisors don't come cheap. What did this chap do, anyhow?"

"By what he said, he's just made a killing in pork futures," Bushell answered dryly. "What was that last street we just passed? Loring Drive? We should be very near now."

The governor's mansion occupied a great tract of land south of Sunset Highway and west of Hilgard Place. The grounds around the mansion were rolled billiard-table flat, the lawn a velvety coat of green as perfect as any in England itself—no mean feat, given New Liverpool's hot, dry weather. That splendid lawn made the untouched chaparral rising from the north side of the highway all the more wild and impenetrable by comparison.

The view across the lawn, obstructed only by statuary of marble and bronze, let Bushell see the governor's mansion clearly as soon as he passed Hilgard Place. It also let him clearly see the line of picketers in front of the mansion. One eyebrow rose. He turned to Samuel Stanley. "What the devil's all that in aid of?"

His adjutant grimaced. "I just got word of them today. They're a group of coal miners from the eastern provinces—Pennsylvania, Virginia, Franklin—here to protest the way the rest of the NAU treats them. They say the rest of the dominion can stay clean because they're so dirty."

"If they have complaints like that, why don't they take them to their own provincial parliaments?" Bushell held up a finger before Stanley could answer. "Wait, don't tell me. They came out here because New Liverpool has dirty air, too, and they figured they'd get more attention protesting far from home."

"Right the first time," Samuel Stanley said. As the steamer neared the entrance to the governor's mansion, Bushell saw there were nearly as many reporters as picketers in front of the four-story, foursquare building. Flashbulbs popped like a fusillade of small-arms fire.

He turned left onto the grounds of the mansion. A New Liverpool constable in dark blue, a billy club swinging from his belt, gestured with a red lantern to guide the steamer toward the carpark west of the building. "Just put it anywhere, gents," he said. By the way he sounded, keeping an eye on where cars parked was the least of his worries tonight.

The picketers started a chant: "Clean air, clean water, clean work! Filthy air, filthy water, no work! Clean air, clean water, clean—"

The constable rolled his eyes. "God damn me to hell, gents, if one in three of those sons of bitches don't belong to the Sons of Liberty."

"I shouldn't be surprised," Bushell said solemnly.

"Bloody fools," Samuel Stanley said. "Some people are never satisfied, don't know when they're well off. What would North America be outside the British Empire? Alone and poor, if you ask me."

"You're right," the constable said. "May you have a better time inside there with the nabobs than that rabble does outdoors. Go on and park your steamer, gents." He pointed the way with his lantern once more.

"There should be a downstairs for buggies like this one, eh, Sam?" Bushell said as he looked at the big, gleaming vehicles crowding the carpark: British Rollses and Supermarines; a low, devilish-looking Franco-Spanish Peugeot; and the cream of the NAU's automotive crop, Washingtons and Wrightmobiles and two or three battery-powered Lightnings. His own middle-aged, middle-class Henry was definitely below the salt here.

He found a space, turned the burner down, set the brake, and got out. So did Samuel Stanley. The captain grinned and pointed. "Look there, Chief, a couple of rows over. You should have parked by that one. Yours would look a hell of a lot classier by comparison."

"You're right about that." Bushell wondered what the weatherbeaten little Traveler was doing here. Then the driver's-side door to the old steamer opened. His jaw dropped. "Will you look at that?"

Stanley whistled softly. "I'll be damned. It's Tricky Dick, the Steamer King! I didn't know he was still alive."

"He must be past eighty by now," Bushell agreed. "When we meet him inside, you'd better remember to call him Honest Dick, too."

"I'll call him whatever I choose," his adjutant answered. "I remember the last car I bought off one of his lots—too bloody well, I do. How about you?"

"My luck with his machines hasn't been too bad," Bushell said. "I wonder how many people all over the NAU bought their first steamer secondhand off one of Tricky Dick's—*Honest* Dick's: there, you've got me doing it—lots."

"About half the people who weren't born to mansions of their own, is my guess," Samuel Stanley said. Bushell nodded. For the past half-century, the only way to escape Honest Dick's relentless promotion was to be blind and deaf. For most of that time, the man had been synonymous with secondhand cars. With its long, swooping nose, his profile was probably the second most recognizable in the NAU, after only the King-Emperor's. Stanley went on, "No wonder he was invited tonight. He's got more money than the Bank of England, or I'm a Dutchman."

"That you're not," Bushell replied. "He really does drive one of his old coughboilers, though. I'd heard as much, but I hadn't believed it."

"No, no chauffeur for him, and Lord knows he could afford one," Stanley said. "He's pretty spry for an old fellow, too." Although the Steamer King carried a cane and walked with a slight limp, he moved at a good clip as he made his way toward the front entrance to the governor's mansion.

Several of the picketers recognized him. They sent catcalls his way. He scowled at them from under thick, still-dark eyebrows. "Let me say this to you, young men," he said in the deep, rather throaty voice Bushell had heard countless times on the wireless. "I think you should be ashamed of what you're doing here this evening. The strength and prosperity of the North American Union depend on her coal. You have no business acting in any way that threatens our prosperity." He shook the cane to emphasize his words.

The picketers shouted back: "Go peddle your steamers, Tricky Dick!" "Keep your pointy nose out of what you don't understand!" "If we're so all-fired important to the NAU, how come nobody treats us decent?" "How'd you like to cough yourself to death before you're fifty, like two of my brothers did?"

Honest Dick ignored the jeers and kept walking. Behind him, Samuel Stanley said, "He's heard worse than that from maybe one customer in three." Bushell clicked his tongue between his teeth, as if to a naughty child, but he also nodded.

The columned entranceway was surmounted by a severely classical relief of the Hesperides, the nymphs who guarded the golden apples of the sun in their far western land. The golden apples of the sun also appeared on the green field of Upper California's provincial flag, which rippled with the Union Jack and the NAU's Jack and Stripes in spotlighted splendor out on the lawn.

Just inside the entranceway, a RAM sergeant apologetically asked Bushell and Stanley to show their identification—"I know you're really you, Colonel, Captain, but I'm checking everybody"—then lined through their names on a list he held on a clipboard.

"If you hadn't asked for my papers, Jim, you'd have been in my office tomorrow morning," Bushell said. The sergeant nodded; he knew how his boss did things.

The RAM chief and his adjutant checked their service caps. The servant who took them hung them on pegs in the crowded cloakroom. She pointed down a hall. "The receiving line and cocktail reception are in the Drake Room, sirs."

"To the Drake Room we shall go, then," Bushell said agreeably.

The hallway was paneled in gleaming mahogany and decorated first with portraits of previous governors of Upper California and then, after it had jogged to the right, with the heads of deer, bears, and catamounts some of those governors had slain. A rising tide of talk came from the Drake Room, almost enough to drown the Vivaldi a string quartet was softly playing.

Going down the reception line was like running the gauntlet: Governor John Burnett, bluff, ruddy, and florid, with a fringe of gingery beard; his wife, Stella, in a gown of mulberry silk that did not quite suit her sallow complexion; Jonas Barber, head of the New Liverpool town council, a plump little man with a shiny bald head who in formal attire lacked only orange shoes to make a perfect penguin; his wife, Marcella, several inches taller, looking elegant in a flowered print dress with a bow at the bodice and shirred flyaway sleeves; and the lieutenant governor and other six town councilmen with their respective spouses.

Thomas Bushell shook the men's hands, bowed over those of the ladies. Small talk set his teeth on edge, but no man who led a large organization could afford to be without it. At the end of the receiving line he looked for one more man, the K. FLANNERY who, documents said, headed the staff of curators and historians of art traveling with *The Two Georges*.

To his surprise, though, at the end of the line stood not a man but a woman. The dark green gown with thin, matching satin stripes in inverted V's showed off a figure which left no possible doubt of that. As soon as he saw her face, he had no doubt she was the K. Flannery in question, either. Porcelain-pale skin, high, strong, forward-thrusting cheekbones, and narrow jaw proclaimed her Irish blood, as did green eyes and red-gold hair spilling down over her shoulders in elaborately casual curls.

"Glad you're on the job, Colonel," one of the town councilmen said as Bushell moved past him. "*The Two Georges*'ll be as safe here as back at the Victoria and Albert in London, eh?"

"Good of you to say so," Bushell replied, but he'd only half heard the councilman's remark. His eyes kept sliding back toward the startling curator of *The Two Georges*. They met hers for a moment. She smiled at him. At first he thought that very forward of her, but then he realized she would have recognized his uniform as that which belonged to the local head of security. She doubtless had her itinerary, as he had his.

The town councilman wanted to blather on about a large load of cannabis the RAMs had recently captured. Bushell had written up that report aboard the *Upper California Limited*, but he answered in monosyllables till the councilman gave up and let him reach the end of the receiving line.

"You must be Colonel T. Bushell," the Irish-looking woman said, smiling again. "May I ask what the *T.* stands for?"

"If you'll tell me what the *K.* is for in K. Flannery," he answered, and added, "The same clerk must have typed both our lists."

"I shouldn't be a bit surprised," she said. "My Christian name is Kathleen. And yours?"

"Thomas," he said. She nodded slightly, as if in approval. He took her hand

and bowed over it, as he had for the other women—*overstuffed dowagers, the lot of them*, he thought—in the receiving line. He held hers a bit longer and a bit tighter, though: not enough to be in any way offensive, but plenty to convey a small message of admiration. Her eyes said she'd received it.

"Now that you're here," she said briskly, "I have leave to quit this line and take you straight upstairs to show you the arrangements we've made for displaying *The Two Georges* here tonight. Or, if you'd rather mingle for a time before you make your inspection, that would be all right, too."

"Business first," he said at once. Again she gave him that approving nod. He went on, "As part of that business, allow me to present my adjutant, Captain Samuel—who is probably S. on your list—Stanley. Sam, this is Kathleen Flannery, curator of the traveling exhibit."

"Pleasure to meet you, ma'am," Stanley said. He turned to Bushell. "I hope you'll excuse me for a bit, sir? I see Phyllis in the crowd there." He pointed. "Odds are, she's been waiting for me since half past two. She's more excited about this than I am; seeing *The Two Georges* isn't something you get to do every day. Of course, she's not here on duty, either."

"Give her a kiss for me," Bushell said, and Samuel Stanley slid through the crush toward his wife. Bushell dipped his head to Kathleen Flannery. "At your service."

"I hope I haven't been rude," she said. "If your wife is here also, don't let business get ahead of that. *The Two Georges* can certainly wait a few minutes."

"I'm—not married," he said shortly. As a single man's will, his eyes slipped, almost of themselves, to the fourth finger of her left hand. It bore no ring. He wondered why—unless he was mistaken (and about such things he seldom was), she'd passed thirty by a year or two. Married to her career, maybe? He gave a mental shrug. None of his business—and *The Two Georges* was.

As they walked to the curving stair of polished marble, he heard Honest Dick the Steamer King complaining to anyone who would listen about the "band of damned Irish hooligans parading outside. Not a one of them with an ounce of respect for the law or an ounce of appreciation for their place in society. Riffraff, the lot of them." Bushell didn't need to turn around to imagine the steamer magnate's jowls wobbling in righteous indignation.

Kathleen Flannery didn't turn around, either, but her back, already straight, got straighter. Quietly, Bushell said, "Landing the position you have now can't have been easy, not when you're Irish and a woman both."

"Thank you, Colonel," she said, and then went on, sighing, "My family has been on this side of the Atlantic for almost a hundred and fifty years, but people still judge me by my surname. I can't help that. And women have been taking jobs that require skill for even longer—ever since the typewriter was invented, I suppose."

"Ah, the typewriter," Bushell said. "If you knew how many times I've listened to Sam go on about how the typewriter made his family what it is today—"

"I shouldn't wonder," Kathleen answered.

"A lot of Negroes left the southern plantations when the Empire outlawed slavery in 1834," Bushell said, "and got the education they couldn't have in bondage. And because they were newly free and looking for work and willing to work cheap—"

"—They've been typists and clerks and petty officials ever since," she finished for him. "How did your adjutant end up a RAM instead?"

"He says the army made him realize he didn't want to be chained to a desk and a file drawer the rest of his life." Bushell let out a wry chuckle. "That only shows he didn't know much about police work when he took it on."

Kathleen Flannery left the stairs at the first-floor landing. Bushell followed her down a hall ornamented with a mural of Royal Navy steamships bombarding Franco-Spanish Los Angeles and landing red-clad marines to cement Britain's hold on it.

"*The Two Georges* is in the Cardigan Room," Kathleen Flannery said. "Here."

The two RAMs standing in front of the famous painting came to rigid attention as Bushell walked into the room. Each of them was but a stride or two from a button that would set off an alarm at the slightest hint of trouble. Bushell pointed to one of the buttons. "I presume that's been checked recently?" he asked in a voice that presumed nothing.

"Yes, sir, this afternoon," the RAM nearer that button answered. "Makes a h—"—he glanced toward Kathleen and revised his choice of words—"quite a racket, it does. And if that doesn't do the trick, we've got these." He rested a hand on the grip of the long-barreled Colt revolver he wore on his right hip.

"Are armed guards really necessary?" Kathleen asked, frowning.

Bushell understood why the notion upset her; civilians who weren't hunters rarely saw or had anything to do with firearms. But he answered, "I think they are. I have to act on the assumption that someone *will* try to steal *The Two Georges*, no matter how farfetched it may seem."

She still looked unhappy, but said no more. Bushell paced the Cardigan Room, making sure arrangements were as he'd ordained. The room had no windows, and only the one door to the hallway. There were also connecting doors to the chambers on either side, but at the moment they did not connect. To make sure they did not and would not connect, they had been reinforced and fitted with stout new locks, the keys to which resided in the RAM guards' trouser pockets.

"It should do," Bushell said grudgingly. "It should." He didn't want to admit anything of the sort. "Emergency exit—"

"There's a service lift two doors farther along the hall," Kathleen Flannery answered, as if she thought he didn't know. "Two days from now, we'll take the painting down on it, load it aboard our steam lorry, and move it to the Provincial Museum for public display."

As soon as she said that, Bushell saw in his mind a floor plan for the Provincial Museum, and began to worry about security precautions there. Things in the governor's mansion seemed safe enough, but there was so much more to plan for with the general public involved. The guest list here had been carefully screened. You couldn't do that at the Provincial Museum no matter how much more convenient it would make things. So many people wanted to see *The Two Georges*. . . .

Kathleen brought him back to the here and now: "In case of fire, there's another stairway just past the lift."

"Good," he said, nodding. "Now, about earthquakes—"

"Colonel Bushell, if in the next two days there is an earthquake strong enough to reduce the governor's mansion to a pile of rubble, I admit that *The Two Georges* is unlikely to survive," she said tartly. "In that unhappy event, however, I am also unlikely to survive, and so I shall spend very little time fretting over it."

One of the RAM guards snickered, then tried to pretend he hadn't. Kathleen could tell off his boss without getting called on the carpet for insubordination.

Bushell started another circuit of the Cardigan Room. He pulled out his cigar case; the smoke would help him think. "Do you mind?" he asked Kathleen Flannery, and reached for a cigar in anticipation of the permission that almost always came.

But she said, "I'm afraid I do. There's no smoking in this room, both to protect the colors of the painting and to reduce the risk of fire."

*Told off again*, Bushell thought. But the objection made sense. He tucked the case back into his tunic pocket. After a last look around the room, he reluctantly concluded he could do no more to make *The Two Georges* safe than he had already done. For the first time, he paid serious attention to the canvas itself.

In one form or another, he, like everyone else in the NAU, saw the painting every day. Taking a long look at the original, he realized how much about it he had never noticed. It was more than a symbol of the union of the colonies with the mother country; it was a great work of art in its own right.

A master of color and texture, Gainsborough had outdone himself on the uniforms the two Georges wore. Every fold, every crease in the crimson wool of George III's coat was marked by a subtle gradation in shading. The rough, light-drinking texture of the wool contrasted with the lace at the king's cuffs, the smoother linen of his breeches, and the shimmer from his silk stockings. Lamplight glittered from the gold buckles of his shoes and from the large sunburst of a medal he wore on his left breast.

Bowing before the king, George Washington was made to appear shorter than his sovereign. The blue coat that proclaimed his colonial colonelcy was of wool like that of George III, but of a coarser weave speaking of homespun. Not all its creases were those of fashion; with a few strategic wrinkles and some frayed fringes depending from one epaulette, Gainsborough managed to suggest how long the garment had lain folded in its trunk while Washington sailed across the Atlantic to advance the colonies' interests on the privy council George III had established.

As a portraitist, Gainsborough more often succeeded with women than with men. Both protagonists in *The Two Georges* broke that rule. Here was George III, perhaps not the most able of men but earnest, serious, plainly anxious to be doing the best thing for England and her American colonies, his small head leaning slightly forward from its perch atop his pear-shaped body. And opposite him, Washington. The colonial leader was a man to be reckoned with. In his bow,

Gainsborough had caught the strength and athleticism that informed his body. The artist also captured a look in his eyes, a set to his expression, that Bushell had seen in any number of veterans: here, without doubt, stood a man who'd known combat.

You could gather so much from any four-shilling lithograph, or indeed from any banknote in your wallet. But the devil, as always, lay in the details. "There's so *much* to see!" Bushell breathed.

Kathleen Flannery nodded. "Almost anyone who was anyone in England in the 1760s is there, regardless of whether he was really at the ceremony: Gainsborough was working to produce a piece that would symbolize unity, not just between England and the colonies but also between Tories and Whigs."

Bushell didn't answer. He was giving the background of the painting the same careful scrutiny he'd used with the figures of George Washington and George III. Some of the men in the palace chamber he recognized at once, as most subjects of the British Empire would have: there stood the elder Pitt, prime minister at the time, his face thin and intelligent-looking, dominated by a fleshy nose and intense, penetrating eyes, the ermine trim of his robe so prefectly rendered that Bushell could almost count the individual hairs; not far away, his successor, Lord North, plump and soft-faced almost to the point of effeminacy, plucked a roasted chicken leg from a serving girl's silver tray.

Benjamin Franklin stood nearby. He seemed to have one eye on the ceremony, the other on the serving girl, a detail reproductions invariably missed. And there was Samuel Adams, fleshier than Washington but with a face every bit as determined. The colonies had sent their best to London.

Kathleen Flannery waited till Bushell took a step back from *The Two Georges*, then pointed out some of the men whose names, while prominent during their lifetimes, had since faded: Newcastle, first lord of the treasury; George Grenville, who nearly gained the prime ministry; the political pamphleteer Sir Philip Francis; John Wilkes, another firebrand; and more.

"And there, off in a corner"—Kathleen pointed—"sketching busily away, is Thomas Gainsborough himself. He doesn't seem to have painted himself into the picture till the very last moment, when he realized he'd created a painting that would live forever."

"I never noticed him before," Bushell said, almost angrily, for he hated to overlook anything. "You're right, Miss Flannery: he's made himself as immortal as *The Two Georges* itself."

"Dr. Flannery, if you don't mind, Colonel." She kept her tone light, but he could tell she meant it. A man might not have stressed the title so hard, but a man wouldn't have had to go through so much to earn it—and the respect of the world afterwards—either.

"*Dr.* Flannery; I beg your pardon," Bushell said. "After I check the lift and that other stairway, shall we go back down to the reception? If you'll let me, I'll get you a drink and do my best to make amends."

She visibly thought it over before she nodded. He was glad; he hadn't warmed so to a woman on brief acquaintance since Irene. . . . But if he let himself think too much about Irene, he'd go back down to the reception and drink himself blind. He'd done that too many times before to doubt it.

Nodding to the RAM guards, he went out into the hallway and looked over the opening for the lift and the stairs Kathleen had mentioned. "Surely you'll have seen those in the plans for the mansion," she said. "You're very thorough, to want to inspect them in person."

"The same here as with *The Two Georges*," he answered. "Until you see something for yourself, you never know what you might be missing."

She studied him as he'd studied the painting. He wondered what she might find lurking in his background to point out. But all she said was, "You must be good at what you do."

"If a RAM isn't good at what he does, he should go do something else," Bushell said. "And shouldn't we go back to the reception downstairs?"

Kathleen nodded. "Yes. I ought to get back. But making sure *The Two Georges* is safe came first."

"As it should." Bushell patted the sleeve of his scarlet coat. "I'll look official and soldierly and frighten away all the art thieves with my impressive military bearing." He raised an eyebrow to show this was not to be taken seriously. As they reached the head of the stairs, he offered her his arm. She took it, and they descended side by side.

Governor Burnett came over as they reached the ground floor. "Everything as it should be, Colonel?" he asked anxiously.

"Yes, Your Excellency," Bushell answered. To his regret, Kathleen Flannery, seeing him engaged, turned aside to a waiter who carried a tray of shrimp, oysters, and marinated slices of abalone on a bed of ice. She speared a shrimp with a toothpick, popped it into her mouth.

Bushell set about reassuring the governor. He had trouble blaming Burnett for sounding nervous. The picketers in front of the mansion were chanting louder now, loud enough for their rhythmic calls to travel down the hall and penetrate the chatter that filled the Drake Room.

"I don't want trouble of any sort tonight," Burnett said, "especially not with press people and wireless reporters here from all over the NAU and from England, too."

"That's why the picketers are here, too," Bushell replied. "They want the reporters to take their protest far and wide."

The governor nodded impatiently. "I know that. It's just—" He stopped, perhaps not sure how frank he wanted to be.

"You want the story to be about how Upper California is proud to have *The Two Georges* here, not about coal miners complaining over the state of their lungs," Bushell suggested.

"Exactly!" Burnett said, beaming. But his face fell. "For all you do, sometimes the story you get isn't the story you want."

"As long as they picket peaceably, they have the right to be here." Bushell cocked an ear toward the front of the mansion. "No matter how raucous they are."

The coal miners started a new chant: "Hey, Tricky Dick! Hey, Tricky Dick! Our air stinks worse than your burners!" They seemed to like it; it got louder with every repetition.

Bushell glanced around to see how the used-car magnate was taking that. By the way he'd acted outside the mansion, Honest Dick didn't fancy being the butt of ridicule. Now he slammed his whiskey-and-soda down on the bar and growled, "God damn those sons of bitches to hell, and I hope the devil stokes the fire with their own coal. They're all full of shit—every fucking one of them, do you hear me?"

Everyone in the Drake Room must have heard him, for he made not the slightest effort to keep his voice down: on the contrary. Women looked away in embarrassment; a couple of men let out significant coughs. That kind of language might have gone unremarked over cigars and port when the sexes separated after supper, but it was more than startling in mixed company.

"*Not* a gentleman," someone murmured, a verdict which garnered low-voiced agreement from around the room.

No matter how old the Steamer King was, he still had sharp ears. "Not a gentleman?" he said (shouted, actually; Bushell wondered how many whiskey-and-sodas he'd had before this latest one). "No, I'm not a gentleman, and I'm proud of it—what d'you think of that? My father grew oranges and lemons and ran a general store. He didn't have two shillings to jingle in his pocket, and I didn't have two ha'pennies. My wife wore a plain, cloth coat till the day she died, God bless her; no fancy furs and silks for her. I worked my way to where I am with these two hands"—he held them high—"and anybody who wants to look down on me for not being some toffee-nosed toff, all I have to say is, fuck him, too!"

But for the soft strains of Vivaldi, an awful silence filled the Drake Room, which only made the miners' chant easier to hear. No one seemed to know where to look, or to want to look at anyone else.

Very quietly, for Bushell's ears alone, Governor Burnett said, "Every word of that is true, you know—about his being a self-made man, I mean."

Bushell wondered what part of Honest Dick's millions had found its way into the coffers of the governor's party. At the moment, though, that was not the point. As softly as Burnett had spoken, Bushell replied, "A man who is not a gentleman is one thing; as with Honest Dick, hard work may have kept him from having the chance to become one. But a man who boasts of not being a gentleman . . . he, in my opinion, is something else again."

"You are of course entitled to your opinion, Colonel," the governor said in a voice like ice, and pointedly turned away. Bushell realized he'd succeeded in offending another politico. He'd long since got past the point where that worried him.

He looked around to see what Kathleen Flannery was doing, and spotted her deep in conversation with Sergei Pavlov, the Russian Empire's consul in New Liverpool. When Pavlov wasn't decked out in knee breeches and dark green velvet swallowtail coat—Russian notions of formal attire being even more conservative than those of the British Empire—he was a leading wholesaler of caviar and the tasteless but potent spirit the Russians distilled from potatoes.

Kathleen said something that made him laugh. They were both speaking French, which educated Russians often preferred to their own language. Bushell could hear that, but not what they were saying. His own French was accented but serviceable; it was a useful language for a RAM to know.

He thought about joining the conversation, but couldn't see a way to do it without being impolite. Another glance round the Drake Room showed him few people with whom he did feel like talking. He drifted toward the bar. He'd just taken his first sip of Jameson over ice when Samuel Stanley materialized at his elbow.

"Everything all right, Chief?" his adjutant asked, his voice studiously casual.

That was the second time tonight Stanley had asked him the same question; he realized his hastily lit cigar back at the office hadn't fooled the other RAM. "It passes muster," he said. "Seeing *The Two Georges* from about three feet makes up for a lot."

Phyllis Stanley came up beside her husband. "Now that's something I can hardly wait to do," she declared. "Anyone who tries to slide in there between me and that painting is going to get an elbow where it will do *me* the most good."

"I wouldn't have expected anything else." Laughing, Bushell kissed her on the cheek. She was a pleasantly plump woman of about his age, slightly darker than her husband, and she carried herself like a queen. Her dress of orange beaded silk brushed the floor but left her shoulders bare.

"Anyone who tries to get between Phyllis and what she wants is going to end up trampled," Samuel Stanley said: admiration, not criticism. He went on, "Somebody must have rung up headquarters when the coal miners started getting noisy—I've seen a few more of our boys in red shirts about."

"By rights, keeping the miners in check should be a job for the New Liverpool constables." Bushell shrugged. "Let it go. I'm not about to fret over jurisdiction, not with *The Two Georges* in town."

"Just what I thought," Samuel Stanley said. "As far as I'm concerned, the more, the merrier."

Governor Burnett strode up to the podium and waited to be noticed. Bushell snuck a look at his pocket watch. Whatever you thought of Burnett for cronyism, he ran his show on time. This was when the schedule called for the guests to troop upstairs and admire *The Two Georges*—and, no doubt, for Burnett to make a speech the local papers would play up.

But before he could start, the picketing coal miners outside began yet another new chant, this one suggesting an intimate relationship between Tricky Dick and the steam dispersal pipes of the vehicles he sold.

The Steamer King had already shown nothing was wrong with his ears. "Bastards!" he growled, brandishing his cane. "I'll show them they don't have Honest Dick to kick around!" He stormed out of the Drake Room. Moments later, Bushell heard him shouting at the picketers. They jeered back.

By his face, Governor Burnett now heartily wished he hadn't invited the used-car magnate to this exhibition. He had no choice, though, but to make the best of it. "Ladies and gentlemen," he began in the rounded tones that made him a master of the wireless, "we are gathered here this evening to celebrate once more our union with the mother country, and to—"

Again he was interrupted, this time by four or five popping noises from outside. "Fireworks," someone said. "Boiler tubes bursting in one of Tricky Dick's steamers," someone else suggested, and got a laugh.

Bushell turned to Samuel Stanley. "That's rifle fire," he said in a flat voice. His adjutant didn't argue; he was already shouldering his way out through the crowd. Behind them, Governor Burnett, unaware anything was seriously wrong, resumed his speech.

The two RAMs sprinted up the hall from the Drake Room to the entrance of the governor's mansion. Before they reached it, a shrill scream brought the rest of the guests pounding after them: the cloakroom girl had gone outside to see what the popping noises were about. She stood in the entranceway now, hands pressed to her face in horror.

Bushell and Stanley ran past her. The coal miners had fallen silent. They and the RAM sergeant who'd been at the door crowded round a crumpled figure still clutching a stick. One bullet had caught Honest Dick in the neck. Another had taken him just above one eye and blown off most of the back of his head, splashing blood and brains and bits of bone all over the pavement.

# ΙΙ

▼

ALONG WITH BUSHELL AND STANLEY, THE
miners stared in horror at the crumpled corpse of the Steamer King. One of
them, his eyes wide, his mouth an O of dismay, looked from the still-spreading
pool of blood beneath Honest Dick's head to the tunics of nearly identical hue
the two RAMs wore.

Seeing those tunics, recognizing them for what they were, may have helped
him build up steam to talk. "Wasn't us, sirs," he said. "Wasn't none of us who
done him, swear to God it wasn't."

"That's right," another picketer said amidst a growing mutter of agreement.
"Wouldn't have minded breakin' the handle of my sign here over the damn fool's
head, that there's a fact. But to blow it off like this here—" He gulped and turned
away, as if about to be sick.

Two miners pointed north toward the brush-covered knoll across Sunset
Highway from the grounds of the governor's mansion. "Shots came from over
there somewhere," one of them said.

"That's correct," said one of the blue-suited New Liverpool constables who'd
been making sure the picketing coal miners didn't do anything more than march
and chant. "Tricky Dick—uh, Honest Dick—came out here to the location of his
decease and began a, well, a harangue, to which some of these here gentlemen responded, mm, intemperately. He was just commencing his reply when the perpe-
trator caused him to expire."

Another New Liverpool constable trotted toward the mansion, saying, "I'm
calling Captain Macias."

Bushell nodded to the New Liverpool constable who'd spoken first. "This is
your case, sir. RAMs have no primary jurisdiction in homicide cases, even if the
homicide is by gunfire. My adjutant and I will, of course, help you in any way we
can."

The other constable was having a tough time pushing his way into the mansion against the stream of distinguished people emerging to gape at the murder
that had been done. "Fools," Samuel Stanley said. "If that maniac is still out
there, he can pot anybody he pleases."

"Jesus God, you're right," the New Liverpool constable near him exclaimed.
He turned to a couple of his comrades. "Hank, Mortimer, go cross the highway
and see if you can flush the bugger out."

Hank and Mortimer obeyed with an alacrity that spoke well of their training and their courage. Bushell wouldn't have cared to try chasing down a man with a rifle who'd already proved he wasn't afraid to use it, not in pitch darkness and carrying nothing more lethal than a truncheon.

A newspaper photographer touched off a flashbulb next to him, then another reporter on the far side of the Steamer King's corpse used one, too. That second flash made Bushell blink, filled his eyes with tears, and left a glowing purple spot in the center of his vision. More and more flashbulbs went off; Honest Dick would have nothing to complain about over the publicity his passing would get.

"We've got to dust off the obit and bring it up to date," one of the reporters said to the photographer beside him.

"Yeah," the photographer answered, squatting to find the shot he wanted. As with policemen, his trade made him think of violent death as part of business, something to be dealt with rather than exclaimed over. "Who d'you suppose would want to do in old Tricky Dick?"

"Somebody who bought a car from him," the reporter said with a cynical chuckle. He saw Bushell's uniform and asked him, "Who *would* want to kill Honest Dick, anyhow?" He poised pencil over pad to take down the RAM chief's reply.

"I wouldn't try to guess—that's your job," Bushell said. The reporter snorted. Bushell went on, "I'm sure the New Liverpool constabulary will investigate the case most thoroughly—murder by firearm is as vicious a crime as the statue book knows."

"We've already five of 'em here this year, and it's only June," the reporter said. "What do you think of that?"

"I'm against it," Bushell answered solemnly. "I'm also against cannabis-smuggling and the white slave trade, and for motherhood, the King-Emperor, and the right of trial by jury. Go ahead and quote me on any of those."

The reporter snorted, then scraped a lucifer against the sole of his shoe and used it to light a cigarillo. When he had the nasty little cheroot going, he said, "Awright, Chief, I oughta know better than to expect a straight answer from you. Next time I will."

"Fat chance," Bushell said. The reporter laughed out loud.

Headlamps glowing, a steam lorry chuffed around from behind the mansion and rolled slowly out toward Sunset Highway. The driver stared back at the murder scene and paused to talk for a moment with the lantern-carrying New Liverpool constable at the end of the driveway before vanishing into the night.

Governor Burnett came up to Bushell. He was not used to sudden and violent death, and averted his eyes from Honest Dick's body as he asked in a shaken voice, "Colonel, what does this, this tragedy do to the showing of *The Two Georges*?"

"I don't know how interested people will be in the painting now, but you may carry on for all of me," Bushell answered. "Since the victim here was murdered from a distance, none of your guests is a suspect. I do suggest, though, that you keep everyone downstairs until the New Liverpool constables finish taking statements. They'll want to know what made Honest Dick go outside just then, what he said, things of that sort."

Samuel Stanley said, "I wish the fellow out there hadn't let that lorry leave, not that the driver would have told us anything we won't hear from half a dozen other people."

"Maybe more than half a dozen." Bushell pointed back toward the mansion. Governor Burnett's guests crowded the entryway, jostling one another to get a better view of a spectacle vastly different from the one they had been invited here to see. Moreover, servants' staring faces—like those of the laborers at the airship port, a mixture of light and dark—filled every ground-floor window. The mansion staff and the chauffeurs who had brought some of the richer guests and those more enamored of display were also getting an eyeful.

Burnett, on the other hand, still seemed unable to look at the corpse. "Someone will have to telephone his daughters," he said.

"You'll have their numbers?" Bushell asked.

The governor nodded. "My secretary will have them in his files." He turned back to the mansion, shouted, "Wilberforce!" After some delay, a tall, thin, dignified black man made his way out through the crush. Burnett explained what he wanted.

"I shall locate those numbers directly, excellency," Wilberforce said. He glanced down at Honest Dick's body for a moment, then delicately looked away. "You'll not want me to place the telephone calls, though?"

"No, no." Burnett sighed. "It's my responsibility, and I shall attend to it. I just wish to God I didn't have to." There, for once, Bushell believed him perfectly sincere. The governor clapped a melodramatic hand to his forehead. "What else can go wrong now?"

As if to answer him, a loud, insistent bell began to ring, somewhere deep inside the mansion. People looked around and stared at one another, trying to figure out where the noise was coming from and what it meant. A woman shrieked, then cried out, "Mother Mary, that's the alarm!" It was Kathleen Flannery's voice.

Bushell threw himself into the crowd at the entranceway, Samuel Stanley beside him. "Move!" they shouted. "Make way, there!" Some of the guests would have moved if they could, but everyone was too tightly packed to make that easy for anybody. Bushell knifed through the crush like a Rugby three-quarterback. He realized he's stuck an elbow in the ample belly of the lieutenant governor of Upper California only when that worthy grunted and folded up like a concertina.

At last he got past the knot of people gathered in the front door to the mansion. He sprinted down the hall toward the stairway. Though he ran with everything he had in him, Samuel Stanley passed him ten yards before the foot of the stairs. His adjutant might have carried a few extra years, but he also had longer legs.

Both RAMs bounded up the stairway two and three steps at a time. Halfway up, Bushell wondered what sort of weapon he'd use to stop the thieves. He yanked his ceremonial sword out of its scabbard. He was no fencer, but the thing had a point. It might frighten someone, if nothing more. The idea of actually having to use such a silly toy certainly frightened him.

As he ran in dress uniform down the first-floor hall toward the Cardigan Room, he thought of how much he looked like the British marines in the patriotic mural on the wall. The marines, though, had had the sense to carry rifles.

Stanley stopped dead in the doorway to the Cardigan Room. Stumbling to a stop behind him, Bushell almost ran him through. "Let me by," he panted. Silently, his adjutant stood aside.

The wall on which *The Two Georges* had hung was bare. Bushell took in that single catastrophe first. Everything else followed, a piece at a time.

One of the RAMs guards sprawled on the floor, unconscious or dead. Unconscious—he was breathing. The other guard seemed to be holding himself up by main force of will. He staggered toward Bushell, croaking in a thick, slurred voice, "Sh-sir, regret to report that—" He clutched his stomach, doubled over, and was noisily sick on the fine Persian carpet.

The stink of the vomit mixed with another odor, strong, heavy, sweetish. Bushell had smelled it before, but couldn't place it. Stanley did. "Chloroform!" he exclaimed.

"You're right," Bushell said. "I had a dentist use it to pull a wisdom tooth, years ago. That explains what happened to these poor devils, but not how." He turned to the conscious guard, who was wiping at his mouth with a pocket handkerchief. "How did they get close enough to chloroform you?" *How did you let them get that close?* underlay the question.

"We heard the shots outside, sir, and then everyone raising the most hellish commotion." The guard still spoke slowly, often pausing between words, partly from the direct effect of the anesthetic, partly because his memory was still blurred. Gathering himself, he went on, "Hiram and I, we stuck to our post here, of course. Then these three RAMs came running into the room." He grimaced ruefully. "Or men in RAM uniforms, I should say. We found out about that."

Behind Bushell, someone let out a gasp of horror. He spun around and saw Kathleen Flannery staring at the blank wall in the Cardigan Room with as much horror as the cloakroom girl had shown at Honest Dick's bleeding corpse. "Yes, it's gone," he said roughly, and turned back to the guard. "Did you recognize them?"

"No, sir." The guard started to shake his head, then stopped abruptly; it must have hurt. "But we didn't think anything of it. I don't know what went through Hiram's head, but my guess was that they were boys from out of province, here along with *The Two Georges*."

Kathleen shook her head. "We relied on the authorities in each town for security personnel. Up to now, everything had gone perfectly." She withered Bushell with a glance.

He wanted a drink—Christ, he wanted a bottle. The first interesting woman he'd met in a long time, and now she had to hate him. And, he realized, he had to suspect her.

The guard said, "We found out what they were, sir, when one of them pulled out his revolver and told us to put up our hands and freeze if we wanted to go on living. The other two went round behind us and jammed these stinking sponges over our faces. They were professionals, sir, nothing else but. We never had a chance to try and fight back, and next thing I knew, I was lying on the floor and the painting was gone. I hit the alarm button, and—" He shrugged helplessly.

A flashbulb went off behind Bushell, printing his shadow for a moment on the wall where *The Two Georges* had hung. Some of the reporters had broken away from the murder in front of the mansion, then. He turned around and said, "Boys, no more of that. This is a crime scene under investigation. No photographs in the papers."

"Why the devil not?" The photographer who'd just shot was screwing in a new bulb, and hissing between his teeth because the old one was hot. "How can photos from out in the hall here mess up your investigation?"

"Because if they're published, they'll help tell the criminals what we know," Bushell answered. "You know me, most of you. You know I play fair. I tell you what I can as soon as I can. Till then—" He gestured to Kathleen Flannery to come inside, then closed the door to the Cardigan Room in the reporters' faces.

"They won't be happy," Samuel Stanley warned.

"Too bad for them," Bushell answered. Then something new occurred to him. "Sam, go and tell those New Liverpool constables not to let anybody else off the mansion grounds, no matter what." He slammed one fist into the palms of his other hand in lieu of swearing. "What do you want to bet that lorry pulled out of here with *The Two Georges* in its bed?"

Stanley groaned. "I have the terrible feeling you're right, Chief, but just in case you're wrong, I'll go talk to the New Liverpool men." He opened the door. The hubbub outside doubled. When he closed it again, the noise redoubled, angrily.

Bushell took another look around the Cardigan Room. Close to the wall opposite the one on which *The Two Georges* had hung sat a lacquered metal box with a crank on one side and a trumpet-shaped speaker coming out of another: a wind-up phonogram, of the sort a young man and his sweetheart might take on a picnic in the country.

"That has no business being here," Kathleen Flannery said, pointing to it.

"No business of ours," Bushell said in abstracted tones; he'd seen such portable phonograms at crime scenes once or twice before. "But I know what tune the platter inside will play."

"What tune is that?" The vertical crease between Kathleen's eyebrows said she didn't know what Bushell was talking about, or care.

"An old one called 'Yankee Doodle,'" he answered, and watched her narrowly.

"God in heaven," she said quietly. "The Sons of Liberty. Our worst nightmare." The Sons of Liberty had been a tiny splinter group for more than a century, and seldom impinged on the awareness of the average citizen of the NAU, who was not only content but proud to be a subject of the British Empire. But a curator in charge of *The Two Georges* had to know extremists might want to strike at the symbol of imperial unity. No, not might—did.

If she was faking, she was a good actress. A couple of hours before, she'd just been K. FLANNERY on a list to Bushell; for all he knew, she *was* a good actress.

Someone knocked on the door to the Cardigan Room. Bushell was ready to ignore it, but Samuel Stanley called, "It's me, Chief." For his adjutant, Bushell opened the door. Stanley came in with two men: a dark-skinned fellow in New Liverpool blues, complete with a turban matching his uniform, and a graying blond man wearing a doctor's white coat with several fresh bloodstains on it.

Stanley pointed first to one, then to the other. "This is Sergeant Singh, a New Liverpool forensics specialist, and here we have Dr. Foxx, the coroner."

"We've met, I think," Bushell said to Foxx, who nodded. The RAM colonel turned to Sergeant Singh. "Can you dust that phonogram for fingerprints, Sergeant?" He pointed to the wind-up machine by the far wall. Samuel Stanley had not noticed it before. Recognizing it for what it was, he whistled softly.

"Oh my yes, I shall certainly do that," the forensics sergeant said, his words precise but his accent singsong and nasal.

Dr. Foxx stooped by Hiram, the still-unconscious RAM. "Pleasant, working on a live one," he remarked, seizing the fellow's wrist. "Makes for a bit of a change." He glanced at his pocket watch for a measured half minute, then stowed it in his waistcoat. "Pulse is a firm seventy, respiration also normal. Nothing to do but wait till he comes round, I'd say."

"Closest thing to good news I've had tonight, I'd say," Bushell answered. "They called you out to look at Honest Dick?"

"Just so." With a grunt, Foxx got to his feet. "He might have survived the throat wound; witnesses say that one was first. But the bullet to the head—" He held out his hand, fingers in a fist, thumb pointing down. "Nasty thing. Glad I don't see those every day, that I tell you."

Sergeant Singh said, "No fingerprints do I find on the outer casing, no, none."

"In that case—" Bushell took out his pocket handkerchief and covered his own fingers with it as he worked the catch that held the phonogram closed. He opened the lid. Inside, along with the labelless shellac platter he'd expected, was a sheet of cheap notepaper. He glanced to Sergeant Singh. "May I?"

The forensics man nodded. Taking care not to touch the paper with his bare fingers, Bushell unfolded it. Singh read the two-line typed message with him. So did Samuel Stanley and Kathleen Flannery, who had stood over him while he opened the phonogram.

THE COLONIES SHALL BE FREE.
WASHINGTON WAS A TRAITOR.

"Bastards," Stanley muttered, and then, "I'm sorry, ma'am; I'm upset."

"It's all right," Kathleen Flannery said, her voice quivering with suppressed fury. "They *are* bastards. To steal *The Two Georges* . . ."

"It's a blow at the Empire itself," Bushell said grimly. On his knees, he moved backward, away from the phonogram. He took out his cigar case and showed it to Kathleen Flannery. After a small, helpless shrug, she nodded. She had no reason to keep him from smoking in the Cardigan Room now.

Sergeant Singh dusted the inside of the phonogram case and the platter with a fine white powder, then used what looked like a miniature badger-hair shaving brush to sweep it away. "Also I see no fingerprints here," he said when he was done. His liquid brown eyes were gloomy. "Very careful they must have been."

"The Sons of Liberty? They're good at what they do." Bushell looked round for an ashtray. Not finding one, he knocked his ash onto the floor. Samuel Stanley ground it into the carpet with his heel.

Bushell wrapped his handkerchief around the crank and wound up the phonogram. When he released the crank, the platter began to spin. He picked up the tone arm, again without touching it with his bare skin, and set the needle in the outer groove of the platter.

"Yankee Doodle" blared out. Bushell listened to a few bars of the jaunty, hateful tune, then lifted the needle off the platter and flicked the catch that kept the spring from unwinding further.

"You didn't need to do that, Chief," Samuel Stanley said quietly. "The phonogram here, the note inside—they tell us it was a Sons of Liberty job. Even without 'em, I'd have bet it was, just from how the villains carried it off."

"Maybe I'm thorough, the way Dr. Flannery said. Or maybe I just like hurting myself." Bushell shook his head like a man emerging from cold, deep water. "That's about all we can do here right now. We'll keep this room sealed off until Sergeant Singh and our own people can go over every inch of it, top to bottom. I want to talk with this Captain Macias before I call Sir Horace Bragg back in Victoria."

"But he's just here for the mur—" Kathleen Flannery stopped. When she began again, she sounded almost accustory: "You think there's a connection."

"Between blowing Tricky Dick's head off and stealing *The Two Georges*, you mean? No, just a coincidence." Bushell's tone belied his words.

"But what if he hadn't decided to come out just then?" she asked, frowning. "They couldn't have known he would."

"They probably would have shot someone else," Bushell answered. "One of the picketers, one of the constables, one of the reporters out there . . ." He shook his head. "No, no one would have cared if they shot a reporter." At Kathleen's scandalized expression, he added, "Joke," and knew he was telling some of the truth.

Leaving Samuel Stanley to hold the fort in the Cardigan Room, Bushell went out into the hallway and fought through the mob out there toward the stairs. Photographers fired enough flashes to make him think he'd been looking straight into the sun. Reporters yelled questions at him. He tried to limit his answers to the obvious: yes, *The Two Georges* was gone; yes, he thought there was a connection between the shooting of the Steamer King and the theft; no, he had no idea where the purloined painting was at the moment.

"Do you think a group you know stole the painting?" someone asked. "Or was it somebody, say, who wanted *The Two Georges* for itself and would try to pass it off as a copy or something like that?"

"We'll be investigating that for some time," Bushell answered, wishing he thought he was dealing with a fanatical art collector.

"Are the Sons of Liberty involved?" another reporter called.

"We'll be investigating that for some time," Bushell repeated in carefully neutral tones. "Now if you'll excuse me, gentlemen—"

He had to answer the same questions from the herd of dignitaries who now would not be seeing *The Two Georges*. Men and women of wealth, power, and influence, they waxed indignant when he was no more forthcoming with them than he had been with the press. Jonas Barber shook a forefinger in his face and almost stuck it in his eye. "See here, Colonel," the little bald town council president snapped, "you have an obligation to make amends for your incompetence."

"My only obligation, Your Honor, is to get *The Two Georges* back." Bushell pushed past, leaving the politico dissatisfied.

The New Liverpool constables had cordoned off the area around Honest Dick's corpse. They did not object, though, when Bushell stepped over the tape they'd laid down to keep back curious civilians.

A brown-skinned man in a wide-shouldered, double-breasted suit of brown worsted came up to him, hand extended. "You would be Colonel Bushell?" he asked. "I'm Jaime Macias, captain of grand felonies." Macias was a handsome man in his mid-thirties—young for a captain—with black hair so thick it amounted almost to a pelt and bushy black side whiskers and mustache. He glanced up toward the first floor. "I think we are going to be living in each other's pockets with this investigation."

"I think you're right, Captain," Bushell said, shaking the New Liverpool man's hand. He glanced toward the body. "Found out anything past the obvious here?"

"As a matter of fact, yes," Captain Macias answered. He had an intonation, the ghost of an accent, that said his family had spoken Spanish in the not too distant past. "We've recovered one of the bullets."

"The devil you say!" Bushell burst out. "That *is* good news."

Macias nodded. His hair, shiny with pomade, glistened under the lights of the mansion. "We were lucky, too—it's not badly damaged," he said. He glanced down at the rubberized sheet someone—probably one of the coroner's aides—had thrown over Honest Dick's body. "Likely to be the one that made the neck wound, I'd say. A bullet hitting bone would have taken much more deformation."

"No doubt." Bushell nodded, too. When Macias didn't go on right away, the RAM chief said, "All right, you found it. What does it tell you? Spill, Captain."

"Interesting caliber," Macias remarked. "It's not a .303, which is what we thought it was when we first came upon it."

"Interesting, indeed." Bushell combed at his mustache with a forefinger. "Not a rifle from the British Empire, then."

"No, not our standard caliber," Macias agreed.

"Let me guess," Bushell said: "A .315."

Captain Macias shook his head. "No, it's not a weapon from the Holy Alliance, either. With Nueva España so close, that was our next guess."

"Well, where is it from, then?" Bushell demanded. "Prussia? One of the other German states? An Italian kingdom?"

Macias shook his head again. "It's what some people would call a three-line rifle. Do you happen to know what a line is?"

"A tenth of an inch," Bushell answered. "So it's exactly .30-caliber, is it?" He ran a finger over his mustache once more. "You don't often see a rifle from the Russian Empire in this part of the NAU."

"I've never seen one," Jaime Macias said. "Franco-Spanish stuff, yes, that comes over the border all the time. But the Russians? No."

"I don't think we worry enough about the Russians, myself," Bushell said. "The Holy Alliance is an obvious rival: France and Spain so close to England, all the wars between us and them, the long border between the NAU and Nueva España, the rivalries in Africa. . . . But the Russians aren't our friends, either. They want to dominate the Germanies, they bump up against us and the Japanese in China, they loom over India and the Ottoman protectorates, and they keep that foothold along our northwestern frontier, too."

"Alaska," Macias said.

"We started offering to buy Alaska from them back in Victoria's day," Bushell said, "but the tsars kept saying no. Russians are good at no. But why would a Russian or somebody with a Russian rifle want to gun down the Steamer King?"

The New Liverpool constable glanced up toward the first floor of the governor's mansion. He picked his words with some care: "Did I hear rightly that the Sons of Liberty may have had a hand in tonight's events?"

"You heard rightly, Captain." Bushell scowled. "And you have a point, too, worse luck. The Sons of Liberty will take anything they can get from anybody who will give it to them." He scuffed a foot on the pavement; the toe of his shoe just missed a small, drying puddle of blood. "I don't like thinking of the Russians and the Sons operating hand in glove here in New Liverpool."

"I don't like thinking of anything that's happened here tonight," Macias said somberly. "Homicide by firearm is bad enough. But *The Two Georges* on top of it—" He broke off, anger distorting his regular features. Nuevespañolan blood might run through his veins, but he had any British subject's outrage at the theft of the famous painting.

"Yes," Bushell said. "The next thing to worry about, I suppose, is what they'll do with—or to—the painting now that they have it." He twisted away, more from that thought than from Macias. "As you said, Captain, we'll be seeing a lot of each other in days to come. I'd sooner have met you under more pleasant circumstances, but—"

"If we required pleasant circumstances, Colonel Bushell, we should have chosen a different line of work, you and I," Macias said, and Bushell nodded.

He stepped out over the tape that fenced off the spot where Honest Dick had fallen. Most of the dignitaries had gone back inside the governor's mansion. Bushell went inside, too, and headed for the Drake Room: with a bar set up there, that was where people—including Governor Burnett, for whom he was looking in particular—were likely to be.

He was halfway down the hall when he spotted the governor's secretary, who would do as well as Burnett. "Mr. Wilberforce!" he called.

"How may I be of assistance to you, Colonel?" the Negro asked gravely.

"I need a telephone," Bushell said.

"Let me take you to my office," Wilberforce said at once. "You may use my private line for as long as you like." He hesitated, then drew out his pocket watch. "It will be well after midnight in Victoria, Colonel. Will whomever you call be glad to hear from you?"

"With all this? Not bloody likely," Bushell answered. "But my boss will be more angry if I wait than if I wake him."

"The proper sort of a superior to have," Wilberforce said, approval in his voice. He led Bushell to his office, unlocked it, and stood aside to let the RAM chief precede him in. The engraved ebony plaque on his desk proclaimed that his Christian name was Harrington. Nodding to Bushell, he said, "This, no doubt, is a conversation you will wish to conduct in privacy." He left the office, closing the door behind him as he went.

He was the proper sort of aide to have. Bushell wondered how fully Governor Burnett realized that. He shrugged; it wasn't his affair, and he didn't have time to worry about it anyhow. He sat down behind Wilberforce's desk and picked up the telephone.

A woman's voice came on the line. "Operator Fitzwilliams speaking. How may I help you?"

"I need to place a call back to Victoria, operator. The number I want is PLassey 4782. My name is Thomas Bushell."

"PLassey 4782," the operator echoed. "Very good, Mr.—Bushell? Do I have that right? Mr. Bushell, yes. Your call will take a few minutes to complete, sir."

"Then you'd better get busy, hadn't you?" Bushell listened to the call wending its way from one phone corporation to the next across the NAU: hisses, pops, and the faint voices of operators talking to one another over the miles. His time in the army had taught him how to wait. At last, faintly, a bell chimed in his ear.

It chimed several times before a southeastern-accented voice, sodden with sleep, mumbled, "Hullo? Bragg here."

"Mr. Bragg, sir, I have a call for you, from Mr., uh, Thomas Bushell in New Liverpool, Upper California," operator Fitzwilliams said.

As if he were focusing field glasses, Lieutenant General Sir Horace Bragg made his voice sharper. Sleep audibly fell away from him: "Yes, I'll accept that call. Thank you, operator." A click announced the woman leaving the circuit she'd completed. "All right, Tom, what's gone wrong?" Bragg demanded. "You wouldn't have called at this ungodly hour if it weren't something dreadful." He took his mouth away from the handset; rather more faintly than he'd spoken before, he said, "It's business, I'm afraid, Cecilia. Go back to sleep if you can." Then, louder again: "Sorry. I'm back."

"*The Two Georges* has been stolen from Governor Burnett's mansion, sir," Bushell said baldly. "Almost at the same time, and probably as a diversion, Honest Dick the Steamer King was murdered by rifle fire when he stepped outside the mansion to continue a quarrel with a group of picketing coal miners parading there."

After several seconds of silence broken only by the gentle hiss of the telephone line, Bragg whispered, "My God." He was not an easy man to take aback, but Bushell had done it. The RAM commandant recovered quickly. "Give me all the details you know."

"Yes, sir," Bushell said, and obeyed. He told Bragg what he'd learned in the Cardigan Room, and what Captain Macias had told him about the murder of Honest Dick.

"Never mind the late, not particularly lamented Steamer King," Bragg said when he was done. "We have local constabularies to run murderers to earth. I want you—in fact, I order you—to concentrate all your efforts on recovering *The Two Georges*. If anything happens to that painting, the NAU won't be the same."

"You're right, sir," Bushell said. On the wall to one side of the desk, Harrington Wilberforce had a fine print of *The Two Georges*. Till that moment, Bushell hadn't truly noticed it: he took its presence in any official setting altogether for granted. He went on, "That was what I was going to do, anyhow."

"Only possible course to take," Bragg said. "RAMs deal with crimes of an interprovincial nature. If the NAU has anything more interprovincial than *The Two Georges*, I'm damned if I know what it is." From his choice of words, Bushell inferred that Cecilia Bragg had gone back to sleep. Sir Horace continued, "What do you intend to do now?"

"You mean, besides slitting my wrists? Get statements from all the people here, find out where they were, whom they were with, what they saw—probably not much, but you never can tell. I especially want to talk with Hiram, the other guard who was chloroformed, when he comes around. He really may have seen something worth knowing."

"Might could be you're right." Bragg hesitated, then laughed at himself. "You know I'm all in a twitter when you can hear backwoods North Carolina in the way I talk." Bushell nodded; he couldn't remember the last time Sir Horace had slipped so. Bragg asked, "Have you telephoned the governor-general yet?"

"No, sir. You're the first call I've made; Sir Martin was next on my list."

"I'll ring up Sir Martin," Bragg said. "You sound as if you have quite enough on your hands out there as things stand."

"Thank you, sir. Please tell him I take full responsibility for the theft."

"Don't beat yourself too hard, Tom," Bragg said. "If you were perfect, they wouldn't have got away with it. You're not perfect. Nobody is. If the world were a perfect place, we wouldn't need police, and then you and I would both be out of a job."

*Easy enough for you to say,* Bushell thought. *Your career hasn't just fallen into the jakes.* But Bragg was trying to help, as best he could across close to three thousand miles. "Thank you," Bushell repeated. "If you're going to ring the governor general, I'll get back to it here."

He hung up and started out of Wilberforce's office to begin asking questions. Before he got to the door, he stopped and frisked himself. His snort was rueful. In dress uniform, he had neither notebook nor pencil. When he left the office, he was anything but surprised to find Governor Burnett's secretary waiting in the hall. He explained his plight. Wilberforce ducked into the office next to his own—"My clerk's, you understand"—and returned with two stenographic notebooks and a pair of already sharpened pencils.

"Mr. Wilberforce, you are a wonder," Bushell said.

"I do endeavor to provide what assistance I can, sir," Wilberforce answered.

Now armed, Bushell found Samuel Stanley, gave him a notebook and pencil, and said. "Let's divide 'em into two groups and run straight through it: who they are, where they live, telephone number, what they saw, and whom they saw it with. If we have a few people nobody else saw, or a small group who saw only one another—"

"Then that may give us something to go on," Stanley said. "Or it may not mean a bloody thing, depending." He hesitated, then asked. "Have you rung up Lieutenant General Bragg yet?" At Bushell's nod, he tried another question: "How did he take it?"

Bushell searched for a judicious word, and by luck found one: "Professionally."

"Could be worse," Stanley said, nodding. "Did you ring Sir Martin, too?"

"No. Sir Horace told me to get on with the investigation here—he'd telephone the governor himself."

"Did he? That's a conversation I wouldn't mind listening in on. It should be—interesting." Samuel Stanley's face bore a peculiar expression, or rather lack of expression: it didn't quite fit the prospect of the RAM commandant's having to announce the disappearance of *The Two Georges* to the King-Emperor's chief official in the North American Union. Bushell almost asked him about it, but the pressure of other matters of greater urgency and consequence drove it from his mind.

The ubiquitous and apparently omnicompetent Harrington Wilberforce found him and Stanley adjoining offices. The New Liverpool constables rounded up the picketers, the reporters, the guests, and the staff of the governor's mansion and split them into two groups, one for each RAM officer. Then the grilling started.

Hiram, the RAM guard, was the second man Bushell questioned. He was still pale and shaky from the chloroform he'd had to breathe, but eager to tell what he knew. Unfortunately, that added little to what Bushell had learned from his comrade. All three of the false RAMs had been white men. . . . Hiram managed a wan smile. "No surprise there, not if the sons of bitches are Sons of Liberty, eh, sir?"

"No." Bushell bared his teeth, too, but more in a snarl than a smile. Not only did the Sons of Liberty want North America free from Britain, they wanted it free of Negroes, Jews, East Indians, Chinese . . . everyone but the pure and original settlers of the land—or so they said. Just how they managed to want to be rid of the Red Indians, too, Bushell wasn't quite sure, but they did; one of their grievances against the Crown was that it had acted to slow white settlement of the continent and let a few Indian nations remain intact and locally autonomous, much like the princely states of East India.

Hiram said, "Sorry I didn't observe more closely, sir, but I didn't give the buggers a second thought till it was too late."

"You did the best you could," Bushell said, sighing. "Go on, get home, get some rest. Your family will be worried about you when they hear the news, I'm sure. If you're a praying man, spend a minute thanking God you're alive."

"Yes, sir, I'll do that. Thank you, sir." Still a bit wobbly on his pins, Hiram left the office.

Before Bushell questioned the next witness, he slammed a fist down on his borrowed desk, hard enough to make pain shoot up his arm. He had more for which to reproach himself than Hiram did. Sam Stanley had said extra RAMs were about. He'd assumed they'd either come from the New Liverpool office or were traveling with the exhibition. He hadn't asked any questions about them. That the guards had made the same mistake didn't excuse his own negligence.

The next person in to see him was Marcella Barber, the wife of the town council head. He threw questions at her until she snapped, "See here, Colonel, I assure you I am quite as sorry as anyone else to see *The Two Georges* stolen, but you have no cause to address me as if you were certain I personally carried it away in my handbag."

"How large a handbag do you carry, madam?" he asked, deadpan.

She stared, then laughed, but her eyes were shrewd as she said, "You'd sooner be screaming at yourself, wouldn't you?"

"Mrs. Barber, whatever makes you think I'm not?" he replied mildly. She pursed her lips, then nodded, like a judge pleased with an obscure but telling citation. Bushell finished interrogating her in a much softer tone of voice.

After her came Kathleen Flannery. He couldn't take out his anger on her; she had every right to take out her anger on him. "We're doing everything we can to get that painting back, Dr. Flannery," he said.

"I'm certain you are," she said in a tone of brittle politeness. "It should never have been lost in the first place, though."

He flipped to the next page in the spiral-bound notebook Harrington Wilberforce had given him. Scrawling Kathleen's name at the top of the page, he asked, "Where are you staying while you're in New Liverpool, Dr. Flannery?"

"I'm at the Hotel La Cienega, here on the west side of town. They've put me in room 268. It's very close to the mansion here, and . . . Why are you smiling, Colonel?"

"People in New Liverpool have a habit of using Spanish names to make a place or a business sound exotic," he answered. "They often don't care what those names mean. That one, for instance, means 'the swamp.' "

"Does it?" she said. "That is amusing—or would be, under other circumstances."

Under other circumstances, Bushell would have tried to find out where she was staying for reasons which had nothing to do with police business. As it was, he said, "I know you were part of the crowd at the entrance to the mansion when the alarm went off. I saw you there, and heard you cry out."

"That's correct," she said tonelessly.

Bushell jotted the information on the page under her name. He already knew it, but his would not be the only eyes examining these notes. He asked, "Whom did you recognize as also being there?"

She frowned in thought. "So much has happened since then—Let me see.

The lieutenant governor had just stepped on my foot, and apologized very hand-somely for it. One of the town councilmen was right in front of me, blocking my view. I don't recall his name, but he was the wide-shouldered chap with the wal-rus mustache."

"That's Lionel Harris," Bushell said, writing it down. "Was his wife with him?"

"She was in the teal, wasn't she? Yes, she was there. And I remember notic-ing the viola player from the string quartet, and thinking he shouldn't have left the Drake Room."

"I agree with you. You're certain it was the viola player?" Bushell had en-joyed the Vivaldi, but hadn't paid much attention to the musicians performing it.

Kathleen Flannery nodded decisively. "Yes—he was the blond with the hair spilling down over his collar."

"I shall take your word for it." Bushell wondered if she'd noticed the man be-cause she found him attractive. She had the right, of course. Somehow that only made the idea more irksome. "Anyone else?" he asked. "Any of your colleagues from the exhibition?"

"No, I didn't see any of them," Kathleen said, "but I resent the implication that they might somehow be involved in this, this—horrible crime."

"Dr. Flannery, you may condemn me for allowing *The Two Georges* to be stolen, or you may condemn me for being too zealous in pursuit of the thieves." Bushell held the pencil between his two index fingers, one at the point, the other at the rubber. "In logic, though, I truly don't see how you can condemn me for both those things at once."

"Logic, at the moment, has very little to do with it," she retorted. "I do know, though, that my assistants would no more harm *The Two Georges* in any way than I would."

Bushell looked down at his notes. He wished he could be sure she was above suspicion. He knew too well that he couldn't. Answering her indirectly, he said, "Many of the most infamous crimes are committed by people in positions of trust. Because they're trusted, they can do things more ordinary criminals can't."

"Not this time, Colonel Bushell," Kathleen Flannery said through tight lips and clenched teeth.

"I hope you're right, but I can't overlook the chance that you might be wrong," Bushell said. "Not very long ago, if you'll remember, you called me thor-ough. I was pleased to take it for a compliment."

That reached her. Her nod was reluctant, but it was a nod. "All right, Colonel, I understand that. As you've said, you have your job to do. It's just that—" She didn't go on, but buried her face in her hands.

She saw her career crashing in flames like a hydrogen-filled airship from her great-grandfather's day, just as Bushell did his. He said, "I—will—get—it—back, Dr. Flannery."

She looked up at him. "You sound like the Lieutenant Colonel Bonaparte, blasting the rabble away from the Bastille. He must have used that same tone of voice when he said, '*Ils ne passeront pas.*'"

"He made himself a great man in France that day," Bushell answered. "I don't care about being a great man. I just want to beat those"—the presence of a lady inhibited him in language—"individuals who are laughing up their sleeves because they got the better of me here tonight."

"That's all well and good, but what will they do with *The Two Georges* while they have it?" Kathleen asked. "If any harm should come to the painting—"

"What will they do with it?" Bushell had already started thinking about that. He rubbed at his mustache. "One of two things, I think. They may destroy it, perhaps publicly, to show what they think of the British Empire and of the NAU's being part of it." At that, Kathleen Flannery looked physically ill. Bushell went on, "Or they may try to ransom it. That might fit their sense of humor, to get some great sum of money for *The Two Georges* and then turn around and use that money to subvert the union the painting symbolizes."

"That would be—better," Kathleen Flannery said. "The NAU can defend itself; the poor painting can't." She hesitated. "The Sons of Liberty seem to have quite enough money for subversion already. Where do they get it?"

"Their political wing, the Independence Party, isn't clandestine; we're sure some party dues end up with the Sons, though we've never been able to prove it in a court of law," Bushell answered. "But they'll take money from whoever will give it to them. The Holy Alliance and the Russians both funnel gold their way now and then: if we're tied up with troubles inside the Empire, that works to their advantage."

"The Russians?" Kathleen Flannery bit her lip. Bushell nodded. She said to him, "Because you're thorough, you'll be investigating me in more detail than just these few questions, won't you?" He nodded again. She sighed. "In that case, let me tell you now that a few years ago I was engaged to be married to a gentleman named Kyril Lozovsky. He was the assistant commercial secretary at the Russian ministry in Victoria."

Bushell wrote the information down without changing expression. "You *were* engaged, you say? The marriage did not take place?"

"No." Kathleen looked down into her lap. A blush mounted from her throat to her forehead. "A couple of weeks before we were to wed, I learned Mr. Lozovsky was also engaged to a young woman back in Tsaritsin. I've heard he married her after he went back to Russia, but I don't know that for a fact."

"I—see," Bushell said. "Thank you for telling me. If Mr. Lozovsky already had a fiancée in Russia, he was less than a gentleman to acquire one here." And if something like that had happened to her, no wonder she hadn't married since. One rotten apple must have spoiled the barrel of men for her. He shook his head. Too bad. Flipping his notebook to the next empty page, he said, "I think that will be all for now. I have a great many more people to question tonight."

"I understand," she said. "I'll do everything I can to help get *The Two Georges* back."

Bushell was in the middle of his next interview, this one with a plump pastry chef, when someone knocked on the closed door to the office he was using. He frowned. "Excuse me," he told the chef, and went to the door, expecting some impatient dignitary demanding his turn at once.

But instead of an indignant politico or a wealthy baronet, he found himself face to face with Harrington Wilberforce. "I beg your pardon for interrupting, Colonel," the Negro said, "but the governor-general has telephoned Governor Burnett, and also expresses the desire to speak with you. If you will please follow me—?"

"Of course," Bushell said, and hurried with Wilberforce past the line of prominent people, coal miners, mansion staff members, and reporters outside the office he had commandeered. A couple of them called after him as he went. "Back as soon as I can," he said several times.

Governor Burnett's office was decorated and furnished in the same gaudy Rococo Revival style as the observation lounge in the *Upper California Limited* had been. It was also big enough to swallow both Wilberforce's and Bushell's offices with room to spare. The governor sat behind an oak dreadnought of a desk. He spoke into the telephone: "Here he is, Your Excellency." He thrust the handset at Bushell.

"Your Excellency?" Bushell said. "How can I help you?"

"The greatest service you can do me, Colonel Bushell, and do the people of the North American Union, is to recover *The Two Georges* unharmed, and quickly." Even across a telephone connection spanning the continent, Sir Martin Luther King's deep, rich voice was unmistakable. It made Bushell want to push the investigation even harder than he was already.

"I'll do everything I can, Your Excellency," he said. He had to fight down the urge to hang up on the governor-general and rush back to interrogating the pastry chef.

"I'm sure of that, Colonel, and I shall pray for your success." A minister before he entered politics, Sir Martin was able to imbue that sentiment with far more sincerity than most officials could have conjured up. He went on, "Lieutenant General Bragg gave me a brief summary of what happened in New Liverpool, and Governor Burnett has told me more. I want to hear the details from the man on the spot, however."

"Yes, sir." Bushell knew he was the man on the spot in more ways than one. Unconsciously, he drew himself up to attention, as if reporting to a military superior. He gave Sir Martin Luther King the same account he had to Horace Bragg, and also described what he was trying to learn from questioning the people who had been in and around the mansion: "I have no direct reason to suspect anyone here of aiding the thieves. I'm trying to eliminate indirect reasons as well."

"A prudent course, Colonel." Sir Martin sighed. "You are certain the Sons of Liberty are responsible for this—outrage?"

By way of reply, Bushell whistled the opening bars to "Yankee Doodle." Not recognizing the song from that snatch, Governor Burnett looked puzzled. Harrington Wilberforce's lean features contracted further: he knew what Bushell was whistling.

So did Sir Martin Luther King. "When Rome fell, Colonel, the barbarians poured in from over the borders," he said, sighing again. "We raise up our own barbarians inside the nation."

"That's true, Your Excellency. What comes over the border for our barbarians is money and guns," Bushell said.

"Yes, you told me they used a Russian rifle to murder the Steamer King," Sir Martin said, as if reminding himself. He clicked his tongue between his teeth. "That grasping little man courted fame all too successfully, I fear." Bushell did not answer; the governor-general seemed to be talking more to himself than to anyone else. When Sir Martin resumed, he was brisk once more: "Carry on there, Colonel. All the resources of the North American Union shall be at your disposal. And as a symbol of that and a show of the national government's concern for this horrendous crime, I, Lieutenant General Bragg, and leading members of our staffs will depart by train for Liverpool as soon as dawn breaks here, to lend you our support in this time of shock and crisis."

"That's kind of you, Your Excellency, but, between the RAMs and the New Liverpool constabulary, we have everything we need here for the time being," Bushell replied quickly.

"Good of you to say so, but my plans are already in motion," Sir Martin answered.

Bushell said the only thing he could: "Yes, sir." Without a doubt, Sir Martin would make a speech every time the train stopped. Without a doubt, he would arrange for it to stop a great many times. Without a doubt, once he got to New Liverpool he would not only make more speeches but spend the time when he wasn't making speeches looking over Bushell's shoulder. Without a doubt, Sir Horace would be looking over Bushell's shoulder, too. And, without a doubt, so would all the bright young solicitors on Sir Martin's staff and all the bright young investigators on Sir Horace's.

And, as if that weren't enough, Sir Martin's chief of staff was Sir David Clarke. Had Bushell thought Sir David Clarke would stay back in Victoria, he would have been willing to put up with the rest. But he was grimly certain Clarke would accompany the governor-general.

Sir Martin said, "I know you still have a long night ahead of you out there, Colonel, so I shan't keep you any longer. I'll see you in three days' time. Good night." He hung up. The line went dead.

Bushell hung up the telephone. "Is there anything I should know from that?" Governor Burnett asked.

"As a matter of fact, there is: Sir Martin will be coming out to lend his support to the investigation. He'll be here in three days." Bushell bared his teeth in what a wolf might have used for a smile. "Huzzah."

He found his own way back to the office he'd borrowed from Wilberforce. For some time, he became an interrogating machine, asking questions and scrawling down answers with next to no conscious thought in the process. Finally, to his exhausted surprise, he discovered no one left waiting outside to be interviewed.

Two people were still standing in front of the office Samuel Stanley was using. Bushell took one of them back into his own temporary office and grilled her. The moment she'd left, he realized he didn't remember a thing she'd said, not even her name. Shaking his head, he glanced at the notebook. No, it didn't matter. The notes were there.

He walked out into the hallway again. Now only Stanley stood there, looking as worn as Bushell felt. "What time is it, anyway?" Stanley asked. He shook his hand, trying to work feeling back into it.

Bushell took out his pocket watch. "Quarter to two," he answered. "God, what a night." The hall, the whole mansion, was eerily quiet. The two RAMs were a goodly chunk of the people still awake inside the massive building.

Stanley held up his notebook. "I didn't get anything that leapt right out at me. How about you?"

"The same, I'm afraid. A lot of people who didn't see anything much." Bushell sighed. Witnesses so often disappointed. Then, remembering, he held up a forefinger. I don't suppose you've heard this yet—" He recounted his conversation with the governor-general.

"Sir Martin *and* Sir Horace *and* their staffs?" Samuel Stanley said when he was done. He rolled his eyes. "They'll all just stand around telling us what to do, and then they'll blame us when their brilliant ideas don't work."

"You wouldn't expect them to blame themselves, would you?" Bushell said. "No help for it, either. They all outrank us." He covered a yawn with his hand. "Lord, I'm worn."

"Me, too," Stanley agreed. "Phyllis is resting in one of the guest rooms. I'll wake her up and take her home in our car. You ought to go back to your flat and get a little rest." He assumed Bushell intended to be at RAM headquarters at eight o'clock. He was right.

Even so, Bushell protested. "Then she'll have to bring you in tomorrow—your steamer's still downtown. I'll take you back there to pick it up."

"No, sir," his adjutant said firmly. "That would cost us close to an extra hour apiece before we finally got to bed. We'll be running on coffee and smoke tomorrow as is; we'll need as much sleep as we can find." He spoke with a platoon sergeant's insistence.

Bushell surrendered. "You're right." Learning when to obey your sergeant was not part of the standard officer's training course, but Bushell, like any subaltern with promise, had picked it up in a hurry. "Tell Phyllis I'm sorry I ruined her evening."

"She'll be all right," Stanley said. "The bed in there looked more comfortable than the one at home."

"That's not what I meant." Bushell's voice went bleak. "She didn't have the chance to see *The Two Georges*."

"Oh." Samuel Stanley looked down at his shoes. "We've been friends a long time now. She'll probably forgive you in eight or ten years."

His delivery was so perfect that Bushell flinched before he saw the smile his adjutant was hiding. He wagged a finger at him. "God will get you for that, Sam, and if He doesn't, I will."

"Go home and go to bed, Chief."

"Right." Bushell trudged out to the cloakroom. His uniform cap and Samuel Stanley's were the only ones still on their pegs. The cloakroom girl had long since retired to the servants' quarters. Bushell retrieved his own cap. He left a couple of shillings under an ashtray, where the girl would be more likely to find them than anyone else, and walked out into the night.

The New Liverpool constables had taken Honest Dick's body away. Only their tape and the large, dark stain on the pavement spoke of what had happened in front of the governor's mansion.

His Henry and Phyllis Stanley's little red Reliable were the last two machines left in the visitors' carpark. He got into his car, turned up the burner to make sure he had plenty of pressure for the trip home, and drove out toward Sunset Highway.

He had the road almost entirely to himself. Few headlamps besides his own were to be seen. The street cleaners and rubbish haulers wouldn't be out and about for another hour or so, while even the latest of the late-night theater crowd had for the most part sought their beds.

Bushell snorted when that thought crossed his mind. The neighborhood in which he lived had a far larger proportion of the late-night hooligan crowd than that devoted to the late-night theater. The suburb of Hawthorne, its bucolic name notwithstanding, was a working-class town not far from the airship port. He'd had a fancier residence before he came to New Liverpool, but . . .

"A single man doesn't need fancy digs," he told the black, empty street. It did not argue with him.

He parked the steamer in front of his block of flats. When he got out, he made sure the car's doors were locked. In most neighborhoods, he wouldn't have bothered, but Hawthorne abounded with light-fingered types. He'd taken a couple of steps toward the entrance when he remembered the bags in the boot. He went back and got them and carried them upstairs.

He was glad no one saw him in his dress uniform. It would have ruined his reputation among his neighbors. So far as he knew, none of them had the slightest idea how he made his living. He preferred it that way.

He set the bags down in front of his door. One key opened the cheap lock the landlord had installed. Another drew back the much sturdier deadbolt Bushell had paid for when he moved into the flat. He plopped the bags down by the door, closed it, and locked both locks. Only then did he reach up and yank the chain on the ceiling lamp near the doorway.

The furnished flat was astringently neat: a soldier's housekeeping, not a woman's. Everything was exactly and obviously where it belonged, and it belonged where it was for a reason that was practical, not decorative. The coffee table in front of the sofa and the end table by it were bare and clean, as if waiting to be shown to a prospective new tenant.

Only a wireless receiver, a phonogram, and several bookcases gave the room any individuality. They all belonged to Bushell; he'd brought them into the flat. The bookcases were bare of ornamental gewgaws. The books in them were grouped by subject (police work; militaria; history; half a shelf of Greek and Latin classics from his university days; the works of Pope, Swift, Defoe, and Boswell's *Life of Samuel Johnson* filling out that shelf; a few modern historical novels) and alphabetically by author within each subject.

Bushell opened the suitcases. He put soiled clothes in a duffel bag he kept in the hall closet. Tomorrow—no, later today, it was—he would take them to the cleaning establishment around the corner. He stripped off his dress uniform, folded tunic and trousers, and set them in the carpetbag he would take to head-quarters come the dawn. The RAMs had their own cleaning establishment for such articles of dress. He laid his sword by the bag.

Undershirt, shorts, and socks went into the duffel bag. The pyjamas he pulled from a dresser drawer in his bedroom were folded as precisely as if they, like his dress uniform, were liable to be inspected without warning.

All the patent medicines on the glass shelves below the bathroom mirror also stood in ranks at attention. He reached for his toothbrush and the red-and-white tin of tooth powder, then drew back his hand. Barefoot, he padded back out to the kitchen. The liquor bottles in the pantry above the sink were lined up in a row. He poured a hefty dollop of Jameson into a tumbler, drank it down, re-placed the bottle, washed the glass, dried it, and put it away. Then he brushed his teeth, set the loudly ticking alarm clock on the nightstand by the bed, and set-tled down for three hours' sleep.

The telephone rang. He jerked bolt upright in bed. He didn't know how long he'd been asleep. He did know it hadn't been long. He groped for the tele-phone with one hand and the nightstand lamp with the other. A call at this time of night had to be important: Sir Martin Luther King, Sir Horace . . .

"Hullo? Bushell here," he said in a voice that sounded much like his own.

"Good morning, Colonel Bushell." Whoever was on the other end of the line, he sounded indecently cheerful for the hour. That meant he was a reporter. Reporters thought they could call anyone at any time for any reason. They had stories to write, after all. "This is Ted McKenzie of the *New Liverpool Ledger*. I wonder if you could give me a brief statement on the murder of Tricky Dick"—he used the Steamer King's unflattering nickname with relish—"and the theft of *The Two Georges*."

"I can give you a very brief statement: go to hell." Bushell slammed the handset down on the hook. "Newshounds," he muttered. He turned off the light and lay down on his back, hands clasped behind his head. His heart was still pounding in his chest from being jolted out of exhausted sleep. He breathed slowly and deeply, trying to calm himself. Initial startlement faded, but not the anger at Ted McKenzie's gall. He wondered how long he would need to fall asleep now.

He was still awake fifteen minutes later when the phone rang again. This time it was a reporter from the North American Broadcasting Corporation. Like McKenzie, she put the accent in Bushell's name on the first syllable, as if it were *bushel*. He declined to give her a statement, too, though in more temperate terms than he'd used with the fellow from the *Ledger*. When he hung up after that sec-ond call, he felt more resigned than furious. This was the biggest story in the NAU for years.

The bright glow of publicity wouldn't make investigating any easier, either. He wished he could do something about that, and knew he couldn't.

The real sun would be rising too soon. Bushell turned out the bedside lamp, flipped over onto his side, and did his best to sleep. In his army days, he'd had a knack for dropping off whenever he got the chance. Somewhere, over the years, he'd mislaid it.

Even had he found it, it wouldn't have done him much good. The telephone rang twice more in the waning hours of the night: a reporter from the *New Liverpool Citizen-Journal* and another from the *Toronto American*. "I'll schedule a press conference for this afternoon." Bushell said at last, yielding to the inevitable.

Thanks to the interruptions, he'd had a bit more than an hour's sleep when the alarm clock went off beside his head like a bomb. Groggily, he picked up the telephone. "Bushell." Only when the clock kept on clattering did he realize what it was and turn it off.

He got into the bathtub and stood under a cold shower for as long as he could bear it. Emerging with the shivers and chattering teeth, he shaved, dressed, and went into the kitchen. He had tea canisters in the same neat row as his liquor bottles—Earl Grey, Lapsang Souchong, Irish Breakfast, vintage Darjeeling, blackcurrant. He ignored them all and made himself a pot of coffee with twice as much of the ground bean as he normally would have used. While it was brewing, he cut two slices from the loaf of egg bread on the counter by the stove, toasted them, and spread them with orange marmalade. He washed down each slice with a large, black cup of the snarling coffee.

Thus fortified, he picked up the carpetbag and his ceremonial sword and went out to face the day.

# III

▼

Long before he got to the RAM headquarters in downtown New Liverpool, Bushell knew what sort of day it would be. Newsboys on every other street corner waved papers with screaming headlines. The big one was always the same, regardless of the daily: TWO GEORGES STOLEN! The number of exclamation points following the head did vary, from none in the staid *New Liverpool Tory* to four in the *Citizen-Journal*.

Subheads also varied. SHAME! cried one. Another wailed, MONSTROUS CRIME! And a third declared, THE EMPIRE MOURNS! Some mentioned the Steamer King's demise (only the *Citizen-Journal* called him Tricky Dick, while the headline man for the *Ledger* was clever enough to link his murder to the theft of *The Two Georges*), while others went on talking about the theft itself.

The newsboys were doing a land-office business. Men and women crowded round them, pressing shillings into their hands. Several of the boys sold every copy they had and stood disconsolate, waiting for a steam lorry to bring them more from their paper's printing plant.

Bushell stopped and bought a copy of every newspaper. Reporters were detectives of a sort; he'd often heard things from them that he hadn't been able to find out for himself. But each new inky-smelling daily he tossed onto the front seat of his steamer was also a fresh goad to get the painting back.

In spite of his stops, Bushell pulled into the RAM carpark at five minutes to eight, as usual. He nodded to the men coming in to work with him, and to the night workers leaving their shift. Few greeted him in return, and no one seemed to know what to say.

He walked into the little kitchen down the hall from the main entrance. They had a coffeepot there, too, along with hot water for tea. He was anything but surprised to find Samuel Stanley pulling a cardboard cup from the box between the hot-water dispenser and the coffeepot. Beneath his brown skin, Stanley looked gray. He normally favored tea, as did Bushell, but not today.

"You'd better leave some of that for me, Sam," Bushell said.

"Depends on how much I need." Stanley yawned enormously. "Way things worked out, I'm just as glad Phyllis had to drive me here today. I was so deep underwater, I probably would have crashed the steamer." He poured cream into his coffee, stirred it with a wooden stick. "I haven't been that tired since the last time we had a baby in the house."

56

"When I was what they called a flaming youth, I'd stay up till all hours and be fresh the next morning," Bushell said, reaching for the coffeepot when his adjutant put it back on the hotplate. "No more."

"Lord, no." Samuel Stanley blew on his coffee, then drained half the cup. "When I was in the army, nights I got leave I'd be drinking and playing the piano and watching the sun come up. I just wanted to do things all the time. If I lose that much sleep now, I'm a dead man the next day."

Bushell didn't say anything about his own aborted tries at slumber. There wasn't enough difference between one hour of sleep and three hours' worth to talk about. You were a shambling wreck either way.

The coffee burned his mouth when he gulped it down. He didn't care. If he drank enough, he could build a brittle crust of energy over his exhaustion. That might get him through the day, and, if he was lucky, he'd go home and collapse when evening came. He poured the cardboard cup full again.

Samuel Stanley was right behind him. "What's first on the list, Chief?" he asked, as he held the cream pitcher over his cup.

"I'm going to tell the public information officer to arrange a press conference for me in the afternoon." Bushell sighed. "I'm looking forward to that. Then I want to ring up the Victoria office and get everything they have on Kathleen Flannery and the rest of the people who were traveling with *The Two Georges*."

His adjutant nodded. "Makes sense to me. The Sons of Liberty would have had an easier time of it with inside help."

"Just what I'm thinking," Bushell said. "After that, I think I'll pay a call on Independence Party headquarters—"

"They'll deny everything," Samuel Stanley said.

"Of course they will. Has to be done, though. There's always that one-in-a-hundred chance. And then," Bushell said, as much to get things straight in his own mind as to keep on talking with Stanley, "I'll pull the files on some of the Sons of Liberty and see what we can pry out of them. We'll visit them warrants in hand, I think. Every so often, they get sloppy and we learn something. Make sure we have the papers we need, will you? Judge Huygens cooperates with us pretty well."

"Yes, I've gone to him before. That sounds good to me," Stanley said. "If I may make a suggestion . . . ?" He waited for Bushell to nod, then went on, "You might do well to have me or one of our other colored RAMs along when you question the Sons of Liberty. Just because they look down their noses at us, they might let something slip that they'd keep a secret from a white man, because they'd assume we wouldn't notice it anyway."

"That is a devilish notion," Bushell said with a slow smile, "and I shall take you up on it. If the foe offers us his petard, the least we can do is hoist him on it." He drank the last of his coffee, crumpled the cup, and chucked it into the rubbish bin by the door. "And now, off to public information."

The public information officer was a young lieutenant named Robert Thirkettle. "When would you like to take questions from the press, sir?" he asked.

"When would I like to? Ten years from Tuesday strikes me as a good date," Bushell said. Lieutenant Thirkettle looked pained. If he'd had his way, Bushell would have spent so much time talking with reporters that he'd have got precious little actual work done. Sighing, Bushell said, "Set up the conference for late this afternoon—three would be fine, four would be better."

"Four won't let your remarks get into most editions of the afternoon dailies," Thirkettle pointed out.

"Oh? What a pity." Bushell strode out of the public information officer's cubicle without giving him a chance to reply.

On his way up to his own office, he paused to light a cigar. His hand quivered as he brought the lucifer up to the tip of the tobacco tube. That told him how much coffee he'd poured into himself. He got the cigar going and gratefully sucked smoke. It relaxed him and left him alert at the same time. The Jameson in his desk couldn't match that. *Pity*, he thought.

He couldn't lock the world away from him now, as he had the evening before. He set his sword on the closet shelf, took the trousers and tunic of his dress uniform out of the carpetbag, and set them on top of a file cabinet. If they were someplace where he could see them, maybe he'd remember to take them down to be cleaned if he had a spare moment.

He telephoned the RAM headquarters in Victoria and asked for Sally Reese, Lieutenant General Sir Horace Bragg's longtime secretary. "Everything's all in a twitter here today, Colonel," she said; Bushell wondered whether she'd borrowed the phrase from Bragg or the other way round. "How can I help you?"

"I assume you people have compiled full dossiers on Dr. Flannery and the others traveling with *The Two Georges*," he said.

"Oh, yes," Sally Reese answered at once. "Scotland Yard wouldn't let any colonials"—she sniffed—"get within ten yards of the painting till they'd been fully vetted."

"Good. Do you have those where you can get your hands on them?"

"Oh, yes," Sir Horace's secretary repeated. "Wait there just one minute." Bushell duly waited. He heard a faint thump, as of a thick pile of manila folders landing on a desk. Sally Reese returned to the line: "Here they are. Now what do you want me to do with them?"

"Two things," he said. "First, skim through them and tell me over the phone anything that makes you think of a connection to the Sons of Liberty."

"I can do that," she said. "It'll take a while, but I can do it."

"You're a sweetheart," Bushell told her, which made her giggle. "After you've done that, send carbons—or your originals, if you don't have carbons—to me by military aeroplane. Sometimes speed does matter. I want them here tomorrow, or next day at the latest."

Now doubt filled her voice: "Oh, I don't know about that, Colonel. It's not normal procedure at all." Sally Reese was a spinster but, like a great many secretaries, wedded to routine.

Bushell said, "These aren't normal circumstances, either. And when I spoke to Sir Martin last night, he promised me all the cooperation the NAU could give. If that doesn't include an aeroplane to carry important documents, it isn't worth much, is it?"

"I don't know . . ." Sally Reese said again. Bushell wanted to shake some sense into her, but couldn't, not across the continent. At last she said, "All right, Colonel, since it's you that's doing the asking. You and Sir Horace have been friends for so long, I know he'd want me to do whatever I can for you."

"Thank you, darling," Bushell breathed. "You're doing the right thing."

"I hope so," she answered, not altogether convinced despite the endearment. "Here, let me give you some of this over the wire now."

Bushell spent the next forty-five minutes taking notes. The pace was less frantic than it had been the night before: Sally Reese would find a tidbit, pass it on, and then continue for another couple of pages before finding another.

Not all of what she found struck him as relevant, either. That Dr. Malcolm Desmond, the Gainsborough scholar, had been expelled from a preparatory school for unnatural vice might have been important in a different case. But the Sons of Liberty despised that sort of thing far more than the authorities did. Dr. Desmond was unlikely to be one of theirs.

Dr. Walter Pine, the historian of George III's long reign, had signed several petitions protesting the conciliatory stance the NAU had taken in the latest round of border talks with the Holy Alliance. The Independence Party had circulated some of those petitions. How much that meant, Bushell couldn't say.

The scene designer (Bushell snorted when he heard that—as if *The Two Georges* needed a fancy setting for display!), Christopher Parker, had two arrests for driving a steamer while intoxicated. Sally Reese made little clicking noises at such depravity, but Bushell didn't think it was the sort of thing likely to turn a man into a Son of Liberty.

Then Sir Horace's secretary got to the dossier on Kathleen Flannery. The first thing she reported was Kathleen's broken engagement to Kyril Lozovsky. "Yes, I know about that," Bushell said. "She mentioned it last night."

"She must have reckoned you'd find out anyway," Sally Reese said, accurately enough, but in a way that irked Bushell. She flipped through pages one after another. After a moment, she let out a little hiss of almost malicious triumph. "Here's something else. She's been subscribing to *Common Sense* for the past eight or nine years. Did she mention that, Colonel Bushell?"

Bushell pursed his lips, as if tasting something sour. "No, as a matter of fact, she didn't." He wished Kathleen had told him that. *Common Sense* was as near to an official journal as the Sons of Liberty had. With Boston Irish money behind it, it lambasted the Crown and the Empire every month, but somehow managed to stay just this side of open treason.

"You want to know what I think, Colonel, I think that's a disgraceful rag, and anybody who puts down good money to buy it ought to be ashamed of himself." Sally Reese was a little on the deaf side, and spoke loudly over the telephone. She also had a harsh prairie accent that took any possible element of compromise from what she said: she sounded like a preacher sure of his own righteousness.

"You may be right," Bushell answered. Had anyone asked him he would have said much the same thing himself. But hearing it in tones Moses wouldn't have presumed to use coming down from Mount Sinai with the Ten Commandments reflexively made him want to disagree. He didn't; he couldn't afford to argue with her, not when he needed her help. "Can you arrange for those to go out by air today?"

"I'll do it, Colonel," she answered. "I'll do it right now, and take my luncheon later. We have to get *The Two Georges* back."

There he found no room for disagreement. "Thank you, Sally," he said. "Good-bye." He hung up and lit a cigar. "*Common Sense*," he muttered, shaking his head. She should have told him that. Maybe she'd assumed the RAMs wouldn't know. Or maybe she'd thought it nothing out of the ordinary. He couldn't decide which idea bothered him more.

He got no time to brood about it. Samuel Stanley walked into the office. Bushell waved him to a chair. His adjutant took out a cigar, too. When he lit it, the lucifer in his hand shook. Bushell nodded, recognizing the symptoms. "*How* much coffee have you had this morning?" he asked.

"Enough to let me live through the day—I hope," Stanley answered. "With the sort of luck we've been having, enough to keep me from sleeping tonight, so I can start the same way tomorrow."

Bushell looked up to—and through—the ceiling. "Don't listen to him, God. He doesn't know what he's talking about."

Samuel Stanley chuckled. He blew a smoke ring. "Here's hoping you're right. A couple of things I need to ask you, Chief: who's going to head up the investigation team for *The Two Georges*, and whom will you send out into the field to interview the Independence Party people and whatever Sons of Liberty we can get to in the next couple of days?"

"Me," Bushell said.

Stanley nodded. A good many years in the army had taught him to think well of officers who led from the front. But, in the reasonable tones he would have used to remind a subaltern to think things through before he started spewing words, he asked, "You for which, sir? You can't do both."

Bushell was in no mood to be reasonable. "The hell I can't," he said. "I was personally responsible for *The Two Georges*' going missing, and I am personally responsible for getting it back. I have no intention of sitting here on my arse shuffling papers at a damned desk." He looked up at Stanley, who was grinning. "Does that particular speech remind you of anyone you know, Sam?"

"You mean me?" His adjutant's brown face was a study in innocence. Nonetheless, he persisted, "If you're going to be in the field, Chief, we'll need somebody back here coordinating what everybody's doing. You won't have the time to handle both assignments at once."

That was common sense, too, and of a better sort than came out of Boston. Bushell yielded—up to a point. "All right, Sam, here's what I'll do: I'll make, hmm, Major Rhodes headquarters coordinator for the investigation. I like Gordon, and he'd be right for the job—he's patient, he doesn't panic, and he has an eye for detail. But when I'm in the office, things will go to me before they go to him."

"Yes, sir," Samuel Stanley said, as Bushell had to Sir Martin Luther King. "I hope it works out all right." That was as close to criticism as he would come.

Bushell got up from behind his desk. He walked over to a bookcase and pulled out a telephone directory: not an obvious tool of police work, perhaps, but an important one. Sure enough, Independence Party headquarters had a listing. He scrawled the address down on a sheet torn from a scribbling-block.

Samuel Stanley read over his shoulder, as he had when Bushell unfolded the note from the Sons of Liberty. That had been only half a day earlier; it seemed half a lifetime. Stanley grunted. "They're out there in the back of beyond, are they? Good place for them."

"Isn't that the truth?" The valley north and west of the central city of New Liverpool was still half given over to farming: oranges and lemons, strawberries and maize, chickens and turkeys and pigs. But more and more homes had gone up there in the past generation, and business districts to serve their needs. The people in the valley, or many of them, had a clannish streak: no wonder the Independence Party was trying to take root there.

Stanley said, "You'll be an hour getting out and another hour coming back. That won't leave you a whole lot of time for work this afternoon before your press conference."

"What a pity," Bushell said, as he had to Thirkettle. He sighed. "This once, the reporters get a fair shot at me. From now on, God willing, I'll be too busy."

"*That's* why you want to spend all your time in the field," Samuel Stanley said, with the air of a man who has had a revelation.

"Who, me?" Bushell said. "While I'm gone this morning, Sam, I want you to give your notebook from last night, and mine, too, to Gordon Rhodes. Tell him I want him to put all the pieces together by the time I get back, so we know who was where and who saw whom."

"That's a lot of work for a few hours," his adjutant said doubtfully.

"Gordon will figure out a way to do it," Bushell predicted. "He's the best-organized man I know."

He grabbed two pens, a notebook, and his hat, and was out the door and heading for the stairs before Sam Stanley could say anything else. The drive up through the Cowanger Pass was pleasant enough (Bushell idly wondered, as he had once or twice before, what Spanish name had been corrupted to give that English version). Even before the narrow, winding road reached the top of the pass, he'd left most of New Liverpool behind. Tumbleweeds and yuccas clung to the hills on either side of the road. Butterflies flitted from one plant to another. Birds pursued them. He normally sympathized with the butterflies. Today, a pursuer himself, he pulled for the birds.

From the top of the pass, the valley spread out before him. Most of it was a study in green and brown: the dark shiny green of citrus groves; a lighter shade for growing maize; gray-brown dirt not under irrigation; dark, rich earth that felt the life-giving touch of water. A grid of widespread streets carved the farm country into squares, as if it were a draughts board.

Independence Party headquarters lay on Laurel Canyon Highway, though well to the north of the eponymous canyon. It was a neat, one-story white stucco building with a red tile roof, vaguely Spanish in style, with the party's name painted above the large window that fronted the street in big black letters that might have come off a Roman inscription.

But for that name, and for the flagpole that took the place of a red-and-white striped pole, the place resembled nothing so much as a moderately successful barbershop. Bushell glanced at the flag rippling in a light breeze atop that staff. A moment later, his eyes snapped back to it. It was not the NAU's Jack and Stripes, though it resembled the dominion's flag. But instead of the superimposed crosses of St. George, St. Andrew, and St. Patrick, the dark blue canton bore a bald eagle, wings outstretched, beak agape.

He shook his head as he walked toward the doorway. There was nothing illegal about that flag. It offended him all the same.

He'd visited Tory and Whig headquarters before. This one was much like those, if smaller: women at typewriters, men and women talking on telephones, some private offices toward the back of the building for more important functionaries. The place smelled of tobacco smoke, coffee, and sweet pastries.

All the faces that looked up at him when he came in were white. That was out of the ordinary, especially in New Liverpool. Blacks here, as elsewhere, were mostly staunch Tories; people of Nuevespañolan and East Indian blood most often backed the Whigs.

"How may I help you, sir?" asked a middle-aged woman in a gingham frock.

"Take me to the chairman: that would be Mr. Johnston, would it not?" Bushell could see she was going to say the illustrious Mr. Johnston couldn't speak to just anyone. He held up a hand and beat her to the punch. "I am Colonel Thomas Bushell of the Royal American Mounted Police. I am here to investigate last night's theft of *The Two Georges*."

Everyone in the office stopped talking and stared at him. The woman in gingham had spunk: "We had nothing to do with that, and you have your nerve insinuating that we did. The very idea!" She sniffed indignantly.

"The very idea, madam, has probably crossed the minds of half the people in New Liverpool this morning," Bushell answered.

"Then half the people in New Liverpool are mistaken," a big, beefy man said, emerging from one of the offices in the back. "I'm Morton Johnston, Colonel—Bushell, was it? Come with me, if you please, sir."

"Thank you," Bushell said, and took a seat across from Johnston's desk.

The Independence Party chairman looked like a prosperous barrister or a politico: handsome, ruddy, mustachioed, his graying brown hair combed across his scalp to try to conceal a growing bald spot. He dressed the part: white shirt, wing collar, black bow tie, dark blue pin-striped suit and waistcoat; a black homburg hung on a rack to one side of the desk.

His office also resembled that of a typical barrister or politico, with one exception. Where a reproduction of *The Two Georges* would normally take pride of place, he had instead a lithographic copy of the flag that flew outside the building.

"Tea, Colonel, or coffee?" he asked. When Bushell said he wanted coffee, Morton Johnston called to one of the secretaries out front. She fetched in a cup. It was not very good coffee, but it was strong. At the moment, that counted for more. Johnston let Bushell sip for a moment, then said, "Colonel Bushell, I can authoritatively state that the Independence Party had nothing whatever to do with the unfortunate disappearance of *The Two Georges*."

"I can authoritatively state a lot of things," Bushell answered. "That doesn't make them true, just authoritative."

Johnston went from ruddy to unabashed red. "You would be hard-pressed, sir, to find a more law-abiding group of citizens than the members of the Independence Party."

"That's true," Bushell said. "You make a point of it. But I'd also be hard-pressed to find a nastier bunch of thuggees than the Sons of Liberty—and they and you are . . . how shall I put it? Half brothers, perhaps?"

"Colonel Bushell, I resent that remark," Johnston said, donning an expression of such stern rectitude that Bushell was convinced he had to make his living as a barrister. "No formal connections whatever exist between the Independence Party and the Sons of Liberty."

"None we've proved, anyhow," Bushell said cheerfully. "But I didn't come here to talk about proof. I came to talk about help. If the Independence Party is as simon-pure as you've always claimed, you'll want to do your duty and help us recover *The Two Georges.* You said yourself it was unfortunate that someone stole it. We have excellent reason to believe the someone belongs to the Sons of Liberty. We also have excellent reason to believe you're in a good position to know more about the Sons than, say, the local Tory chairman. So share what you know with us, Mr. Johnston."

Johnston licked his lips. After a moment, he said, "I'm afraid I can't do that, Colonel Bushell. I've told you what I know and what the Independence Party knows, which is nothing. You aren't interested in my guesses—"

"Who says I'm not?" Bushell broke in.

"—and, given His Majesty's statutes on slander, I don't care to make them," Johnston went on, as if he hadn't spoken. "Even if I did, they would be my guesses, not the party's. We aim to free North America from the British Empire by peaceful means, not the violence the Sons of Liberty use."

"You want to get out of the Empire," Bushell said, "but you hide behind its laws while you're in it." He hadn't expected anything else, not really, but disappointment ate at him all the same. He'd hoped for better, even from the Independence Party, in a crisis like this.

Morton Johnston stood and glowered down at him. "Good day, Colonel," he said pointedly.

Bushell rose, too. He turned and pointed to the eagle on the banner with which the Independence Party wanted to replace the Jack and Stripes. "You've chosen a good mascot."

"What do you mean?"

"That bird is a carrion-eating scavenger that makes a good part of its living by stealing fish from seahawks honest and hardworking enough to do their own hunting. I can find my own way out, sir."

He felt Johnston's eyes boring into him as he strode toward the door, but did not look back.

He was on his way to his steamer when his stomach growled angrily. It wasn't happy anyway, not with all the black coffee he'd poured into it. He looked at his pocket watch. It lacked but a few minutes of noon. There was a fish-and-chips shop a few doors down, and a Nuevespañolan-style cafe across the street. After a few seconds' hesitation, he decided on fish and chips.

The fish was Pacific red snapper, not the cod it would have been in London, but the two elderly Scotsmen—brothers, by the look of them—who ran the shop knew their business. They dipped the fillets in batter and fried them just firm, wrapped them in newspaper, and handed them to him along with a generous helping of golden-brown fried potatoes.

"That'll be ten and sixpense, sir," one of the brothers said. "Half a guinea, if you like." He laughed. A fish-and-chips shop was hardly the sort of establishment where prices were quoted in guineas.

Bushell doused the fish and chips in malt vinegar and spread salt over them from a big tin shaker. They burned his fingers through the newspaper. One of the stories that wrapped his fish was about *The Two Georges*. He was just as glad when spreading grease made it illegible.

He ate quickly, gulped yet another cup of coffee, wiped his hands on a brown paper serviette, and headed for his car, well enough pleased with his luncheon. Had the brothers' shop been downtown rather than in this backwater, he thought, they would have been well on their way to being wealthy men.

The breeze had picked up while Bushell was eating. The Independence Party flag flapped loudly on its pole. He gave it one last scowl as he turned up the burner and headed back toward the office.

When he got there, he went straight to Major Gordon Rhodes's office. As he'd expected, he found Rhodes and Sam Stanley there. The major was a few years younger than Bushell, on the chunky side, with blond hair and a face as florid as Morton Johnston's, but scholarly rather than bluff.

From somewhere, Rhodes had commandeered a big table and spread a sheet of white butcher paper over it, holding the paper down at the corners with knickknacks from his bookshelves. He'd used a yardstick to rule the paper into small squares. As Bushell came in, he was asking Stanley, "Who's next?"

Stanley turned the page on one of the notebooks he and Bushell had used the night before to interrogate the people at the governor's mansion. "Malcolm Desmond," he answered.

"Very good." Rhodes ran his finger down the names written in the left-hand cells until he came to Desmond's. "And whom did he see?"

"He was still back in the Drake Room," Stanley answered, checking his notes. "He saw Gavagan the bartender, three of the four people in the string quartet, and Mrs. Town Councilman Gilbert. Some others, he said, but he's not sure of them."

"Very good," Rhodes repeated. "We have other testimony that Jorkens was by the entranceway, so that leaves Brassman, Cooper, and Campbell, along with Gavagan behind the bar." He bent over the spread sheet. Bushell saw names at the top of the columns, too. Rhodes put marks in the appropriate columns along Desmond's row. "And I shan't forget Mrs. Gilbert, either."

The chart was already well measled with checks. Bushell studied it with nothing but admiration. "This is splendid, Gordon," he said. "We should have your sheet here photographed when you're done, and reproductions furnished to everyone working on the case."

"You were right, Chief," Stanley said. "I didn't see how he'd do it, but he worked out this scheme almost as fast as we're talking now."

"You're too kind, both of you." Rhodes had a way of taking what he did for granted, not thinking it anything out of the ordinary. Maybe that was one of the reasons he remained a major. He said, "When we're done here, we'll make a similar chart showing everyone's location when the alarm bell began to ring. Between the two of them, they may tell us quite a lot. Or, of course, if no one in the mansion was involved in the plot, they may well tell us nothing."

"Nothing else had told us anything thus far," Bushell answered. "Why should this be any different?"

"It's not so bad as that, Chief," Samuel Stanley said. "We know a Russian rifle killed Tricky Dick, and we know the Sons of Liberty stole the painting. Put those two together and we have—"

"Inference," Bushell said. "Nothing else but."

"Pretty solid inference, I think," Gordon Rhodes protested.

"I'd rather have evidence," Bushell said.

"We are working on it, Chief," Samuel Stanley reminded him. "The damned painting's been gone less than a day, after all. You ask me, even having the start of an idea about which way we're going is one for our side. Oh." He paused. "Speaking of going, we got a ring this morning from one of those coal miners who were picketing out in front of the governor's mansion. They're all booked aboard a train that heads east tonight. He wanted to make sure it's all right for them to leave. I didn't see any reason why not, but I told him I'd have to check with you."

Bushell considered. "I think we can let them go," he said at last. "As the constable in front of the mansion said, some of them are probably Sons themselves, but they weren't directly involved in the theft or the shooting, so we can't in law hold them. We might do well, though, to telegraph lists of their names back to the RAMs in their home provinces."

"I've already taken care of that," Stanley said without a hint of smugness.

"Have you?" Bushell said. "Well, good. I'm going back to the files, remind myself what the Sons have been up to lately, and pick out a few lovely chaps to question this afternoon—"

"The press conference," his adjutant broke in.

"Damnation take the press conference," Bushell snapped. But damnation would take him if he wasn't there to give it. Press and politicos would band together to howl for his head. He didn't need his elbow joggled that way, not now. And so, this afternoon, he would be questionee, not questioner. Sighing, he yielded: "I'll pick out a few lovely chaps to question tomorrow, then."

Samuel Stanley nodded approvingly. He and Rhodes went back to work on their butcher-paper chart. Bushell went down to the RAM record room, which took up most of the first floor. The musty smell of old paper wrapped itself around him as he went inside. The record room was nothing but old paper, and cabinets to hold it. It was also the only room in headquarters where smoking was forbidden: one not-quite-extinguished lucifer or a carelessly dropped coal from a cigar or pipe could spark a conflagration.

The Sons of Liberty had a couple of file cabinets all to themselves. Bushell pulled open the top drawer of the wrong one, only to be confronted by yellowing file folders and the old-fashioned typewriter letter styles and copperplate handwriting of the end of the last century. One corner of his mouth twisted. The Sons had a long and dishonorable history.

He got the right cabinet and drawer on his next try. He pulled out the half-dozen most recent folders (which, but for their fresh manila board and the more modern typefaces on their labels, looked all but identical to their centenarian ancestors) and carried them over to a table.

When he opened the first one, an unflattering police photograph of a Son of Liberty stared out at him. Peter Jarrold had been arrested the winter before on suspicion of setting fire to a synagogue in the eastern part of New Liverpool. Bushell's mouth twisted again. Jews were so thin on the ground in the NAU that only a madman could reckon them any sort of threat to anyone.

Peter Jarrold didn't look like a madman, but he didn't look particularly bright, either. He looked like what he was: a street tough in his early twenties, with a scar over one eye and another on his chin. Like a lot of the younger Sons of Liberty, he wore his hair cropped short. The Roundhead look, they called it, after the followers of Oliver Cromwell the regicide. To the Sons, that made Cromwell a hero.

Bushell flipped through the folder. Jarrold was currently starting ten years' penal servitude, so he hadn't had anything to do with stealing *The Two Georges*.

The pair of men in the next folder seemed more interesting. The year before, Titus Hackett and Franklin Mansfield had been charged with printing and distributing an obscene publication: a lampoon of the marital troubles of the grandchildren of George, Duke of Kent, the younger brother of Edward VIII. A copy was in the file. Bushell glanced at it. It had funny spots, but looked obscene to him, too. A jury, though, had disagreed, and let Hackett and Mansfield go free.

Bushell thought that unfortunate, but it wasn't what really interested him about the case. The rascals' pamphlet had got a surprisingly wide distribution around New Liverpool; they'd been able to afford to print a lot of copies. At Mansfield's house, the arresting officer had found out how they'd been able to do so: with a goodly supply of gold Russian roubles.

No one had been able to prove Mansfield came by those roubles illegally. At the time, they hadn't seemed to mean much. But when you put them together with a three-line rifle, you had to start wondering what the Russian Empire was up to in and around New Liverpool. Bushell noted Mansfield's home address, and Hackett's, and that of the print shop they ran together. Come the morning, he would have some questions to put to them.

He flipped rapidly through the rest of the folders, noting down names of other Sons—some Roundheads, some not—who had been charged with relatively recent offenses. Most of the crimes of which they'd been accused were of a simpler nature than that of Hackett and Mansfield. One Joseph Watkins, for instance, had been charged with heaving a brick through the front window of the local office of the League of Colored Citizens, but was released before trial for lack of sufficient evidence.

Looking at Joseph Watkins, Bushell would have bet he was guilty of something. He had the same tough, violent stare as Peter Jarrold and, the report noted, a large eagle tattooed on his chest and a smaller one on his right bicep. But the law couldn't prove beyond reasonable doubt that he'd committed this particular crime, and so he was free.

A couple of other Sons had stomped a Nuevespañolan man nearly to death outside a tavern. They were behind bars; witnesses had identified them beyond doubt. Another gentleman, the late Andrew Kincaid, had tried cracking a Sikh's skull with a length of lead pipe while shouting, "Go back to India, you stinking wog!" The Sikh, true to the martial tenets of his faith, had been armed with a dagger, and had let the air out of Mr. Kincaid for good.

"And we don't miss him one bloody bit, either," Bushell murmured.

When he was done, he stacked the folders in a single pile and stared at them. They'd helped less than he'd hoped. For one thing, the Sons were a close-mouthed bunch. Even when they were caught, they didn't rat on their friends.

For another, few of the locals, at any rate, seemed to have the brains to have pulled off anything like the theft of *The Two Georges*. They were bruisers, ruffians, men who couldn't succeed and sought someone outside themselves to blame for their failure. They knew how to hate, but not how to think. The thieves at the governor's mansion had been brilliantly effective.

The door to the records room opened. "Colonel Bushell?" someone called. Bushell recognized Lieutenant Thirkettle's voice.

"I'm here," he answered mournfully. "Let me refile these. Is it that time already?"

"Yes, sir, it is." Thirkettle sounded indecently cheerful, but then, he wasn't about to face a firing squad, or, worse, a pack of ravening reporters. He asked, "Can I get you anything before you speak to the press, sir?"

"A cup of hemlock?" Bushell suggested.

"Sir?" Thirkettle didn't understand. Bushell shook his head. They weren't training them in the classics the way they had in his day.

▼

Once, in the cinema, Bushell had watched wolves pull down a moose. They'd flung themselves on the poor beast and started to feed while it still lived. He'd never thought to find himself playing the role of that moose until he walked into the press briefing room and stood before the reporters and photographers from all over the NAU. They jammed it to the point where the New Liverpool fire marshal should have taken notice and ousted a third of them.

The fire marshal and his minions were nowhere to be seen. Even had they been around, throwing out a third of the reporters, however gratifying Bushell might have found it, wouldn't have done him any good. The survivors would have been plenty to pull him down and eat him alive.

A fusillade of flashbulbs greeted him when he entered the briefing room and followed him to the podium. The big tin reflectors behind the flashbulbs sent all their light straight into his face and left him dazzled. By this time tomorrow, his visage would be splashed across half the dailies in the country. His Hawthorne neighbors would no longer be in doubt about what he did for a living.

He tapped at the microphone. It was live. Whether it would help him overcome the din—*the baying,* he thought—of the press was another question. "Ladies and gentlemen," he said, and then again, louder: "Ladies and gentlemen." The din diminished, but did not vanish. After half a minute or so, Bushell concluded it wouldn't vanish. "Ladies and gentlemen, if you'll bear with me, I have a brief statement I'd like to make. Then I'll take your questions."

A rather loud quiet descended. Into it, Bushell said, "Last night, Honest Dick the Steamer King was murdered by gunfire outside Governor Burnett's mansion here in New Liverpool. Not long thereafter, an alarm inside the mansion went off. It was discovered that a gang of at least three individuals had succeeded in absconding with *The Two Georges,* which was then on private display at the mansion and was soon to have been shown to the public. At present, the perpetrators remain at large. We have had no communication from them since the painting was stolen. This morning, a spokesman for the Independence Party formally denied any connection between his organization and the theft of *The Two Georges.*"

His pause told the reporters he had finished. Hands flew into the air. Men and women shouted at the tops of their lungs. Bushell heard not a word of it. He cupped his hand behind his ear.

The racket abated. The reporter asked his question again: "The Independence Party denies involvement. What about the Sons of Liberty?"

"No spokesman of theirs has denied involvement," Bushell said dryly. That drew scattered laughs, but also calls for more detail. Reluctantly, Bushell added, "We did find at the crime scene certain things which are consistent with its being the work of the Sons, yes."

"What sort of things?" four people shouted at the same time.

"I'd rather not discuss that publicly," Bushell said. "Some people like to imitate infamous crimes or pretend they were involved, and we'd sooner have an easy time than a hard one sorting out imitators from the real Sons of Liberty." He mentally crossed his fingers. Sometimes that sort of appeal worked, but sometimes it just fanned the hunger of the press.

This time, it worked, at least for the moment. A woman in a royal-blue silk dress asked, "Are you certain there's a connection between Tricky Dick's murder and the theft of the painting?"

"As certain as I can be without interrogating the perpetrators, yes," Bushell answered. "Using a diversion is a common military trick." He spread his hands. "This time, unfortunately, it worked against us." He pointed to a man in the third row wearing a gaudy silk cravat. "Yes, sir?"

The reporter preened a moment on being recognized, then said, "We are given to understand that *The Two Georges* was taken from Governor Burnett's mansion in a lorry. Why was that lorry allowed to leave?"

"I wish it hadn't been," Bushell answered. "No, wait—I know that doesn't answer your question. When the lorry left, no one outside the mansion had the slightest notion *The Two Georges* was in it. We did know, however, that Honest Dick had been shot at long range, from the brush-covered knoll across Sunset Highway from the governor's residence and its grounds. The New Liverpool constable at the turnoff to Sunset Highway reasonably concluded the lorry driver could not have been involved in the murder, and let him go. Reasonable conditions, worse luck, aren't always right ones."

"Did the lorry go east or west after it left the mansion grounds?" someone asked.

"East, back toward the central city," Bushell said. "I personally saw that lorry leave, and I could not tell you of my own knowledge whether it turned right or left. I was concerned about Honest Dick, and paid the lorry little attention. The witnesses who did notice which way it went, though, unanimously say it turned right."

A man with a military bearing gained his attention. "Up on this grassy knoll, sir: have they recovered the cartridge casings from the rifle that killed Honest Dick?"

"They hadn't as of last night," Bushell said. "At the moment, that's all I know. I haven't had the chance to speak with the New Liverpool constables today, and they are primarily responsible for investigating the murder. Our efforts—that is, those of the RAMs—will concentrate on recovering *The Two Georges*."

"Why aren't you looking into Tricky Dick's murder yourself?" three reporters asked, while two others said, "It's part of the same case, isn't it?"

"Technically, no, it is not a part of the same case," Bushell answered. "However much we believe the murder of the Steamer King and the theft of *The Two Georges* to be related, we have not proved that to be so. And homicide without flight across provincial lines, even homicide by means of a firearm, is not a crime that comes under the jurisdiction of the Royal American Mounted Police. It falls under the authority of the constabulary of New Liverpool and of the province of Upper California." He smiled wryly. "Anyone who thinks we're not going to be working very closely with the New Liverpool constabulary, though . . ."

After that, the questions began to get repetitive: reporters were looking for new ways to say old things. Finally, one overstuffed fellow with a monocle asked, "D'you you think Tricky Dick was involved in the plot to steal *The Two Georges* and killed to keep him quiet?"

"In a word, no," Bushell said. "If you are reduced to questions of that sort, I think, the proceedings are at an end. Thank you, ladies and gentlemen." He stepped away from the podium.

Lieutenant Thirkettle rushed up to spread a cloud of politeness over the press conference. He was good at what he did. By the time he'd finished, even the reporters whose questions Bushell hadn't answered or to which he'd given short shrift were in a happy mood. They chattered among themselves as they hurried out of the briefing room to write and file their stories.

The vaults of the Bank of England did not hold enough gold sovereigns to make Bushell take over Thirkettle's job.

When the last reporters were gone, the public information officer came up and said, "On the whole, that was very nicely done, Colonel, although I do wish you'd been a touch more . . . diplomatic there at the end."

"I was patient as long as I could manage," Bushell said, meaning _as long as I could stand._ "I never have suffered fools gladly, though, and I didn't aim to start with that fat donkey."

"Er—yes." Lieutenant Thirkettle looked pained. To carry out his assignment well, he had to get along with the press, which meant getting along with a certain number of fools and donkeys, which meant not referring to them—maybe not thinking of them—as fools and donkeys. Poor sorry devil.

Bushell pulled out his pocket watch. It was afer five. Yawning, he said, "Lieutenant, with your ever so gracious permission, I'm going upstairs to see how Major Rhodes is doing. Then I am going to go home and, God willing, go to bed. Running on an hour's worth of sleep is not something I can do every day any more." He wanted to laugh at himself for implying once upon a time he'd been able to run on an hour of sleep a day.

Without waiting for Thirkettle's reply, he headed for the stairs. When he got to Gordon Rhodes's office, he was surprised not to find Samuel Stanley there. Rhodes said, "He went home about an hour ago, sir—said he was so tired, he couldn't see straight. The way he was acting, I believed him."

"I know just how he feels," Bushell said sincerely.

Major Rhodes handed him a manila envelope. "He picked these up for you from Judge Huygens. Says they're a present to be used carefully."

Bushell undid the metal clasp on the envelope. Inside were a dozen search warrants, all signed by the judge. The lines for the date and the name and place of the person to be served with the warrants were left bank. Bushell whistled softly. He asked Gordon Rhodes, "Have you seen these documents?"

"No, sir," Rhodes answered. "What are they?"

"Never mind." Bushell hadn't seen many blank warrants, not in all his years as a RAM, and he'd never seen so many together at once. Judge Huygens had indeed given him a present. If any word ever got out about what sort of present it was, though, it would be useless—worse than useless, for it would turn into a weapon against him. If you used shortcuts in the legal system very often, pretty soon you wouldn't have a legal system. But if you let yourself get hamstrung on time-wasting technicalities, you had problems of a different kind. Being trusted with blank warrants was a compliment, of sorts.

Major Rhodes was a smart officer in more ways than one. Some men would have asked questions after that "Never mind," and found out things they were better off not knowing officially. The only question Rhodes asked was, "What now, sir?"

"Now I'm going home and going to bed," Bushell told him. "If Sam threw in the sponge an hour ago, I'm entitled to do it myself. That damned train is on the way here from Victoria. It'll be here day after tomorrow, I expect, and I'll have to be at my best to deal with Sir Horace and Sir Martin. See you in the morning."

He almost fell asleep in his car, waiting for steam pressure to build so he could drive home. He drove carefully, as if he'd had too much to drink: not very fast, not very close to the car in front of him. He knew his reflexes weren't all they might have been.

The early editions of the evening papers didn't yet have his picture in them. *One more day of anonymity,* he thought. When he got home, he had to park down the street from his block of flats—everyone else was returning from work, too. He picked up his mail—a couple of bills, a couple of advertising circulars, a letter from an old friend from his army days who by now assuredly would have heard about him if not from him—and went upstairs.

He busied himself in the flat's little kitchen. After tossing a spud in the oven, he made a green salad and pan-broiled a beefsteak he took from the icebox. He also took out some ice, put it in a tumbler, and poured Jameson over it.

He had the tumbler about half empty by the time his supper was ready. The whiskey made him even more tired than he had been, undercutting the layer of alertness he'd borrowed from the coffee to get through the day. He no longer cared. "I made it," he said to the wall.

After he'd washed and dried and put away the dishes, he lit a cigar, pulled out a copy of Pope's translation of the *Iliad,* and turned on the wireless. He spun the dial, looking for news. He skidded past a pianist playing the *Waldstein* sonata, an advertisement for Bovril, some syncopated electric Nawleans music that made him curl his lip, and the postmortem of a rubgy match before he finally found some.

"In Pittsburgh earlier today, Governor-general Sir Martin Luther King again pledged every possible effort to recover *The Two Georges,* stolen last night in New Liverpool in a crime of appalling brazenness," the newsreader said.

Bushell sighed as he sat down on the couch. He'd been sure Sir Martin would say something like that. It sounded good, didn't cost anything, and didn't mean anything, either.

The newsreader went on, "In New Liverpool, however local RAM commandant Colonel Thomas Bushell stated that, while the clandestine organization known as the Sons of Liberty is believed to be connected to the theft, no specific clues as to the identity of the criminals or the whereabouts of *The Two Georges* have yet to come to light. It is to be hoped that this unfortunate situation will soon be remedied, as the disappearance of the painting has sent shock waves through both the NAU and the mother country. In London, the prime minister said—"

With a grunt, Bushell opened his book. He didn't care what the prime minister said. She was six thousand miles away and knew even less about the matter than he did himself, which, considering how little he knew, was saying something. He smiled at the elegant Augustan verse into which Pope had rendered the *Iliad.* It wasn't Homer—he'd read Homer in the original—but it was fine poetry. He wouldn't have minded a god coming down from Olympus to give him a hand in the investigation. "Why Achilles and not me?" he murmured.

Zeus didn't answer. Instead, the telephone rang. He went into the bedroom and answered it. It was a reporter. "I'm sorry I couldn't get to the press conference, Colonel, but if you'd be so kind as to tell me—" Bushell hung up. If the fellow couldn't get where he was supposed to be on time, to hell with him.

"To hell with him anyway," Bushell said. He stared down at the telephone.

After a moment, he took it off the hook and stuffed the handset in the night-stand drawer. He wasn't supposed to be out of contact with the office, but tonight he needed sleep more than anything else. Reporters were more likely to call than his colleagues, who knew how tired he was. He nodded. He'd take the chance.

He went out to the kitchen and poured himself another Irish whiskey. He drank it, washed the glass and put it away, replaced the volume of Pope on the shelf, and switched off the wireless. Then he changed into his pyjamas and got into bed. He remembered nothing more until his alarm clock jerked him head-long out of sleep.

▼

The printing establishment Franklin Mansfield and Titus Hackett ran lay about halfway between downtown New Liverpool and Governor Burnett's residence in the West End. Two steamers full of RAMs quietly pulled up in front of it. People on the street stared as half a dozen big men in red tunics piled out of the cars and gathered in front of the doorway to the shop.

A scrawny bald man in his shirtsleeves threw open the door, not to let them in but to cry angrily, "What's the meaning of this? Unless you ugly louts have a warrant, sod off and let an honest man carry on with his trade."

"I have a warrant here, Mr. Hackett," Bushell said, recognizing the fellow from his photograph in the files. He displayed the official paper. "As you see, it gives us leave to search these premises pursuant to the investigation of the theft of *The Two Georges*. Now stand aside and let us do our job."

"Just a bleeding minute." Hackett snatched the warrant out of his hands. Franklin Mansfield came out to read it with him: a beefy fellow with curly black hair and bushy side whiskers. "Bah!" Hackett said, and shoved the warrant back at Bushell. "You got your trained seal of a judge to sign it, and you have your Cossacks with you, the same as the damned Tsar would do."

"Cossacks don't bother with warrants," Bushell answered. "Now stand aside."

Scowling, Hackett and Mansfield got out of the way. The RAMs in red swarmed into the shop and began turning it upside down with the practiced effi-ciency of men who had performed a great number of searches. Franklin Mansfield spoke for the first time: "I shall make certain they're planting nothing incrimi-nating." His voice was deep and smooth and rich; but for a slight lisp, perhaps an affectation, he could have been a newsreader himself.

"What are you doing here, anyhow?" Hackett snarled at Bushell. He had no affectations, only rage. "You've got no call to be tossing the place like that." He pointed to the chaos the RAMs were making in their search for evidence. "You bloody well ought to leave us alone. That jury found us innocent, it did."

"No, it found you not guilty, which is not the same thing," Bushell answered. "As for why we're here—where did you and your partner come by those gold Russian roubles you used to spread your filth far and wide?"

"It wasn't filth—it was the truth. And we came by 'em legal, in payment for another job," Hackett answered. "We took 'em, and glad enough to have 'em. Weight for weight, their gold's as good as sovereigns or francs." The printer spat on the sidewalk. "There! You can run me in for that, if you've a fancy." He clapped a hand to his forehead. "We'll be days putting back together the rubbish heap your apes are leaving."

"If we find nothing of interest, you shall in due course receive a formal written apology from the governor-general's office in Victoria," Bushell said, knowing that was the last thing the printer wanted.

Hackett stared at him, watery blue eyes going wide. He cocked a fist in anger. Bushell hoped he would swing. Conviction on a charge of battery against one of the King-Emperor's police would put Hackett in a warm, dry place for some time to come. But, with an obvious effort of will, the printer mastered himself.

One of the uniformed RAMs, a muscular Negro named Clarence Malmsey, brought a typed sheet of paper out to Bushell. "Here's something interesting, sir," he said: "a bill paid off by seven hundred gold roubles."

"Let me see that." Bushell took his reading glasses from their case, set them on his nose. "Queen Charlotte Islands Board of Tourism?" He frowned. "I didn't think the Queen Charlotte Islands had a board of tourism. Isn't that where the imperial naval base is, up by Russian Alaska?" He frowned again, trying to be just. "But since they are up by Alaska, that may account for the roubles."

"First right thing you've said today," Titus Hackett exclaimed.

"It might be so, sir, but I didn't see anything that looked like the makings for a tourist brochure in there with the bill," Malmsey said. "What was in there, among other things, was this." Now he proffered an eight-by-ten glossy photograph.

Bushell clicked his tongue between his teeth. The photograph showed a prince's skinny, blond, estranged wife frolicking nearly in the altogether through surf on a beach in a climate much more tropical than that boasted by the Queen Charlotte Islands. He held it out to Hackett. "I take it you and Mr. Mansfield are planning to try to repeat your earlier publishing success, sir? And that you will be retaining the same barrister as before?"

"None of your bloody business," Hackett said.

"No doubt everyone will be curious to learn why the Queen Charlotte Islands Board of Tourism is so interested in this project," Bushell remarked.

"So we misfiled the bill," Hackett said. "You're a RAM, God's angel in a little red suit, so I suppose you never misfiled anything."

"More times than I like to remember," Bushell said easily, "but never such an—interesting—juxtaposition." He turned to the uniformed trooper. "See if you can find anything in there that has to do with the Queen Charlotte Islands and a tourism brochure: that, or any more of this slime." He held up the glossy photograph.

"I understand, sir," Clarence Malmsey said. "If we don't come up with any brochure, that'll mean the bill for it is some kind of blind." He hurried back into the printers' shop, calling out new instructions to his comrades.

To Bushell's surprise and disappointment, they did find photographs and copy and a rough layout for a brochure about the distant islands. Titus Hackett gloated at him. The RAM who brought out what Bushell thought of as the bad news said, "Here's another account paid in roubles," and handed his chief the bill. The fellow went on, "And here's something else we found in the same file folder."

This photograph showed a different princess, with a reputation perhaps even more scandalous than the other's, in a costume that left next to nothing to the imagination. Bushell studied it wistfully, then sighed. "Thank God the direct imperial line has better sense than the side branches of the house of Saxe-Coburg-Gotha. Must come of the real royals' having to work for a living."

"Ahh, they're all a pack of bleeding parasites, every one of 'em," Hackett said contemputously. He spat again.

"We could jail this chap and the fat one for possession of salacious material," the uniformed RAM said hopefully. By the way his eyes kept sliding back to the picture he'd given Bushell, he found it salacious—enjoyably so.

But Bushell shook his head. "That wouldn't do, I'm afraid. At the trial, their barrister would make a point—a political point—of dragging the imperial family through the dirt."

"Aye, that's right, try and hide the truth away," Hackett jeered. "Whited sepulchers, that's what the royals are. If the people knew the truth about the whores and perverts who rule 'em, they'd—"

"Mr. Hackett, shut your filthy mouth." Bushell spoke quietly, but with a snap of command in his voice. Hackett stared and said not another word.

▼

"A Russian connection," Bushell muttered to himself as the steamer rolled down toward St. Peter's docks, the harbor district of New Liverpool. He'd wondered about that since Captain Macias told him Tricky Dick had been shot with a three-line rifle. The Sons of Liberty in New Liverpool certainly seemed to be getting aid and comfort from the subjects of the Tsar—but what did that prove? Not enough.

Joseph Watkins was on the dole, and living in a dingy rooming house whose front hall reeked of hot grease and stale urine. Expecting Watkins to be out at a tavern or something of the like, Bushell served the warrant on the landlord, a ferret-faced fellow who looked imperfectly delighted to have RAMs in his building.

He unwillingly led the RAMs upstairs to Watkins's first-floor room. Raucous electric Nawleans music spilled into the hall from behind the door at which the landlord pointed. He pressed the search warrant and a skeleton key into Bushell's hands, saying, "He's all yours, mate," and made himself scarce.

Since Watkins did appear likely to be in there, Bushell had to serve the warrant all over again. He rapped on the door. Nothing happened. He rapped again, louder. He heard heavy footfalls coming toward the door. It flew open. Joseph Watkins glowered out at the world at large. "God damn it, I told you not to piss and moan about playing the wireless so—" he began. Then he realized his visitors were not neighbors complaining about the noise. The realization visibly failed to fill him with joy. "Oh. Robin Redbreasts." He spotted Clarence Malmsey. His mouth narrowed. "And a tame geechee with 'em. What the hell do you bastards want now?"

The photograph of Joseph Watkins had shown him to be a tough. It hadn't shown that he was about six foot four and wide through the shoulders, width emphasized by the strapped vest that was all he wore above the waist. He dwarfed the RAMs with Bushell, and none of them was small.

Bushell held up the search warrant. "Mr. Watkins, this warrant gives us leave to search these premises pursuant to an ongoing investigation of the Royal American Mounted Police. Stand aside and let us do our job."

Watkins studied the opposition. He glared down at Bushell. "You didn't have your bully boys with you, little man, I'd squash you like the bug you are." Bushell looked back at him, expressionless. After a moment, Watkins got out of the way.

He inhabited one room, with a tiny alcove that could be screened off and held a toilet and stall shower. Greasy newspapers on the table, on the floor, and in the waste-paper basket said he lived mostly on fish and chips. Everything in the room was nasty and cheap except for the fine crystal sculpture of a fierce-looking eagle that perched atop the mantel and almost matched in pose the tattoo on his arm. On one wall, instead of the print of *The Two Georges* that would have adorned most homes, he'd nailed a large Independence Party flag, also with a rampant eagle.

He caught Bushell looking at it. "Nothing wrong with a man wanting his country free of the bloody Crown," he growled.

"In itself, no," Bushell said. "Whether or not it's foolish is another question. And crimes remain crimes, no matter in what cause they're committed."

"Nice when you can make your own rules, isn't it, and call trying to get free a crime," Watkins retorted. His head twisted constantly as he watched the RAMs tearing the furnished room to pieces.

Watkins had a laundry hamper, but didn't bother with it. Instead, he just left his dirty clothes wherever they happened to fall. After the RAMs went through the pockets of each pair of denims and overalls and collarless workman's shirts, they tossed it into the wicker hamper. In that small way, the room got neater. In every other way, a tornado might have descended on the place.

"Watch that, you big ugly buck," Watkins snarled when Clarence Malmsey tore down his eagle flag to see if he'd secreted anything behind it. He hadn't. Malmsey smiled sweetly, crumpled the flag in his hands, and threw it on the floor. Watkins took a step toward him, fists clenched. Two other RAMs reached for the clubs on their belts. Watkins subsided, hate smoldering in his gray eyes.

The RAMs pulled out the drawers in which he stored his food, turned them upside down to dump out what they held, and peered into the spaces thus opened to make sure he hadn't hid anything in back of them. One of the men took out his billy club and poked at the plywood behind the drawers, turning his head to listen for any hollows thus revealed.

Bushell went through Watkins's reading material himself. There was more of it than he'd expected a Roundhead lout to own: Watkins might not be bright, but he was politically conscious. He had a long shelf of cheaply printed political tracts, some from the Independence Party, others out-and-out calls for insurrection. Mixed with them were back issues of *Common Sense* (Bushell reminded himself to ring up Kathleen Flannery, whose full dossier was sitting, as yet unstudied, on his desk) and several of what were politely called "novels of imagination" describing the utopia North America would have become had it long ago freed itself from the British Empire. Bushell had perused a great many examples of the genre, and had a low opinion of it. The hacks who perpetrated them were as politically naïve as they were illiterate, which was no small claim.

When the door to Joseph Watkins's room was open, it hid the only closet the room boasted. Clarence Malmsey swung the door most of the way open so he could search the closet. He tossed out trousers and shirts and jackets, creating a new pile to take the place of the one his colleagues had put in the hamper.

"You've found damn all," Watkins said in tones of injured innocence, "and the reason you've found damn all is that I haven't done a bloody thing. So why don't you bugger off and let me pick up the rubbish pitch you've made of my place here?"

"Don't you think it looks better now?" Bushell asked. Watkins scowled at him.

Once the closet was empty, Malmsey did as his colleagues had and poked at the boards of the wall with his stick. Everyone in the room heard the deeper *thock!* that came from one blow. "Well, well!" the Negro said happily. "What have we here? Somebody hand me a pry bar."

Joseph Watkins made a run for it.

Had the door been open rather than almost shut, he would have got out into the hall, and might even have escaped. As things were, Clarence Malmsey sprang out and grabbed at him just as he seized the doorknob. He needed a second to hurl Malmsey aside with a sweep of his thick arm, and the second let another uniformed RAM and Bushell pile onto his back.

Watkins was big and strong and fierce and tough, all of which availed him little. The RAMs were far from weaklings, they outnumbered him, and they had learned to fight in a school every bit as nasty as his and a good deal more skillful to boot. Before long, he lay flat on his belly, still swearing at the top of his lungs, hands manacled and ankles shackled behind him, blood from a cut above one eye running down his face and onto the cheap, already stained carpet.

"Mr. Watkins, sir, in case you didn't notice, you are under arrest," Bushell announced. He looked down at himself. In the struggle, one sleeve of his jacket had torn loose. "Damnation!"

Clarence Malmsey said, "Shall we find out what dear Joey boy didn't want us to find?" He got the pry bar he'd asked for and ripped away with a will. Boards came up with a splintering crunch and the squeal of stout nails pulling loose from wood. The RAM yanked the boards out further, reached into the space behind them.

He brought out a long, thin, rectangular package, wrapped in thick brown paper for passage through the mails. "What's the postmark?" Bushell asked.

Malmsey turned the package to peer at the blurry inked handstamp. "Place called Skidegate," he answered. "Don't know where the devil that is. Wait a moment, there're more letters here." He held the package up to his face so he could examine the mark more closely. His voice rose with excitement. "Here we are: Skidegate, QCI."

For a moment, that meant nothing to Bushell. Then it did. "Skidegate, Queen Charlotte Islands," he whispered.

One of the other RAMs asked, "What's in there? I can make a guess from the shape, but—"

The top of the package had been neatly slit open. Clarence Malmsey flipped up that end, pulled out some excelsior, and then, with a sigh like a lover's when he encounters his beloved, a rifle, the yellow wood of the stock polished till it gleamed, the barrel glistening with gun oil. "Not a model I recognize offhand," he said.

"I do," Bushell said. "It's a Nagant."

# IV

▼

$B$USHELL SAT DOWN AT HIS DESK AND slammed his fist down hard enough to make pen stand, inkwell, cigar case, and wooden IN tray jump. "God damn it to hell, Sam," he ground out, "I thought we had the case half broken, right then and there. I'd have given a thousand pounds for that, just to be able to drop it in Sir Horace's lap—and Sir Martin's—when they get into town this afternoon."

"Would have been fine, Chief," Samuel Stanley agreed. "Too bad that rifle had never been fired, let alone at Tricky Dick."

"Too bad, the man says." Bushell looked up to the ceiling, as if someone invisible up there would nod and tell him he was right. "The other question is, how many more Nagant rifles are sitting in flats and hidden away in houses, just waiting to cause us more trouble? Every time things look bad in this case, they get worse, not better."

"That's so," Stanley said. He looked better for a couple of nights' sleep. "Other thing is, of course, the Sons may just have set a lucifer to *The Two Georges* the minute they got out of sight of Governor Burnett's mansion."

"Yes, that's possible, but I don't believe it," Bushell said. *I won't believe it,* he thought. But he had reasons for doubt: "If they're going to destroy it, they'll do that publicly: smuggle it into a city square someplace, maybe, and then touch it off. I still think they're likelier to be holding it for ransom. They could bring in enough gold to keep themselves in business for years. They might even collect goodwill that way, too."

"I thought the same thing, right after the painting was stolen," Samuel Stanley answered. "But if they planned to ransom it, wouldn't we have heard from them by now?"

"That worries me, too," Bushell admitted. "It's still early, though. Maybe they're waiting for Sir Martin to get here, so they can present the demand directly to him. After all, we're just police; if anyone is the painting's patron here in the NAU, he's the man."

"Mm, there's a point," his adjutant said judiciously. "I hadn't thought it through like that. I was there when *The Two Georges* disappeared, so I just assumed the ransom note would be heading in my direction. But it ain't necessarily so." Just for a sentence, he dropped into the heavy farm-Negro patois of the southeastern provinces, a dialect his family hadn't used for four or five generations.

"Go chop your cotton," Bushell said with a snort. "See if you and Rhodes can pull any magical answers out of that fancy chart the two of you made. I've got enough of my own work to do, I can tell you that."

With a laugh, Samuel Stanley got up and went out the door. He let one hand linger for moment in a wave, then headed down the hall toward the stairs. Bushell lit a cigar. He looked longingly at the locked desk drawer. A good knock of Jameson would make him feel like a new man. But then the new man would want his own knock, and then . . . Regretfully he shook his head.

He flipped through a telephone directory until he found the number of the Hotel La Cienega, where Kathleen Flannery was staying. He dialed it, then went through the hotel switchboard to reach her room. He wondered if he'd catch her out for breakfast, but she answered the phone on the second ring: "Hullo?"

"Dr. Flannery? This is Tom Bushell, from the local RAM office." Not until he'd introduced himself did Bushell notice he'd used the diminutive for his name. He hadn't planned to do that. Shrugging in his seat, he went on, "How are you this morning?"

"I'm well enough, thank you, Colonel. And you?" When Bushell admitted he was also well, Kathleen continued, "How can I help you today? Have you learned something important about *The Two Georges?*"

"I'm afraid not. I just have some more questions for you."

"Oh." As it had risen, her voice fell. "I don't have anything much new to tell you, either. I was hoping I would. I've been ringing up some people I know in the art business—auctioneers, agents, curators, people like that—in the hope they might have heard something about where *The Two Georges* might be. But I've had no luck, and I was wishing you'd call me to tell me you had." She laughed sadly. "So much for wishes."

Bushell took a deep breath, slowly let it out. He said, "Dr. Flannery, do not— I repeat, do not—pursue any independent investigations of your own. You may muddy the waters for me, you may alert the thieves, and you may also put yourself in danger. I really must insist." *And besides, you're already an object of suspicion. Who knows what you were doing with your telephone calls?*

"I am sorry, Colonel," she said. He could all but see her green eyes going wide with surprise. "I didn't mean any harm, please believe me."

*I wish I could. I wish I could be sure of you.* Instead of saying that, Bushell struck hard: "Dr. Flannery, when I questioned you after *The Two Georges* was stolen, why didn't you tell me you subscribed to *Common Sense?*"

The silence on the other end of the line lasted long enough for Bushell to pull out his pocket watch and see ten or fifteen seconds go by. At last, Kathleen Flannery said, "How in God's name did you find that out? Next thing you'll tell me is what sort of underwear I have on."

Under other circumstances, Bushell might have been pleasantly distracted thinking about Kathleen Flannery in her underwear—or out of it. As things were, his main thought was that she was trying to distract him so. "Just answer the question."

"If you must know, Colonel, my father buys a subscription for me every year," she answered. "*Common Sense* suits his politics, not mine. I hardly ever look at it.

If you know I subscribe, you can probably find out that the cheques to the magazine are always in his name—Aloysius Flannery—and drawn on his bank."

She was right; the RAMs could do that. Bushell wondered if it was worthwhile. Probably not, he judged, at least not yet. "You were so open with your failed engagement, I wondered why you didn't mention the other."

"It didn't cross my mind," Kathleen said "Half the time I toss *Common Sense* into the rubbish without even opening it." Which meant that half the time she didn't, but Bushell held his peace. She asked, "Is there anything else?"

"Does the name Skidegate mean anything to you?" he asked idly.

He'd expected her to say no, or to ask who Skidegate was. But she answered, "That's the chief town of the Queen Charlotte Islands, I believe. The Queen Charlottes and southern Alaska are, or rather were, home to the Haida Indians. The All-Union Museum in Victoria has an extensive collection of Haida totem poles and other wood carvings. They were masters of the craft."

"Why do you say 'were'?" Bushell asked.

"White men's diseases hit them hard," Kathleen said, "and that disrupted their way of life. And a lot of the survivors were resettled to the mainland when the naval base was built there, so few of them still follow their old tribal habits. It's a pity; as I say, they produced some wonderful woodcarvers." She paused and came up with a question she might have found sooner: "What on earth does Skidegate have to do with *The Two Georges?*"

"I don't know yet," Bushell said. *And if I did, I wouldn't tell you.* Aloud, he went on, "Thank you for your time, Dr. Flannery. And please, for the sake of the painting, don't do any more investigating on your own. The odds are ten to one—a hundred to one—you'll do more harm than good. Do you understand me?"

"You make yourself very clear, Colonel. Good morning." Kathleen Flannery hung up. Bushell stared at the telephone, then uttered a pungent phrase that would have been more appropriate in the barracks than in the office of the chief of the New Liverpool RAMs; a chief, after all was supposed to maintain a certain dignity. The barracks comparison was apt in another way, too: Kathleen sounded like a soldier intent on evading an order that didn't suit him. Short of having the telephone torn out of her room, Bushell didn't know what he was supposed to do about that.

He growled the phrase again, louder this time. Just as he was about to pick up the telephone to call Captain Jaime Macias, it rang. He stared balefully at it before he picked it up. "Bushell."

One of the switchboard operators said, "Colonel, I have on the line a man who claims to have *The Two Georges.* He'll only talk to you, he says."

"Put him on." Excitement tingled through Bushell. What now? A ransom demand? A threat? A couple of clicks and the operator was off the line. "Hullo?" Bushell said, and gave his name and rank.

"Yeah, uh, Colonel Bushell?" The man talking to him, even though he'd just heard the name pronounced, put the accent on the wrong syllable. "You listen here, Colonel, you ever want *The Two Georges* back, you got to pay me fifty thousand pounds. You hear me, Colonel? Fifty thousand quid or that there painting's catmeat."

*You contemptible fraud,* Bushell thought. *A vulture and a piker at the same time.* "How do I know you have it?" he said. "What did you leave behind in the governor's mansion?"

"What did I leave behind?" the man on the telephone echoed. "Why, uh, that is—"

"Sir," Bushell said coldly, "you should be aware that all telephone conversations in this building are routinely traced. You should also be aware that seeking money under false pretenses is a felony. And, sir, you should also be aware that a pair of RAMs will be at your home within the hour to place you under arrest."

The only answer he got was a loud *click!* as the man hung up on him. Bushell laughed. He hoped he'd given the bloody fraud an anxious half hour or so. He could see the fellow tiptoeing over to the front window every so often, peeling back the drapes perhaps a finger's width, and peering out to make sure no RAM steamer had just pulled up in front of his house. If a constabulary car happened to cruise down his street in the next hour, the man might stay panicked for days.

But more calls like this one would come. Some of the liars would have brains as well as gall. Finding out what the Sons of Liberty did to mark their crimes wasn't impossible. If you knew where to look, it wasn't even difficult. As if life weren't hard enough already, it would get harder.

If Bushell called out, he wouldn't have to worry about anyone else calling in for a while. He dialed the number of the New Liverpool constabulary, and was quickly connected to Captain Macias. "Tell me, Colonel," Macias said, "is my beard black or gray?"

"You don't wear a beard," Bushell answered. A split second later, a flashbulb exploded in his head. "You've had cranks ringing you up, too!"

"Haven't I just," Macias said ruefully. "You're the third person this morning who's claimed to be you—and the first one I think may be telling me the truth. What can I do for you, Colonel?"

"You need to know there may be more Nagant rifles floating around in New Liverpool, and not among people you'd want having them." Bushell explained how his men had found the firearm in Joseph Watkins's room. "It hadn't been there long, or he'd have used it: he's that type. But how many others may have come down from Skidegate, or who has them—I just don't know yet."

"We're liable to find out, you're telling me. *Aii!*" Hit where he lived, Macias sounded for a moment like a man of Nuevespañolan blood, just as Sir Horace Bragg showed he was indeed a Carolinian. "All right, Colonel, we shall do what we can to deal with this." After the one exclamation, he sounded like a constabulary man again.

"You have anything for me?" Bushell asked.

"Autopsy report: Tricky Dick was shot," Macias answered laconically. "No, in fact, there's a bit more. The pathologist found a big enough piece of the bullet that blew out his brains to match it to the other one we recovered. They both came from the same weapon: only one gunman up on the knoll."

"That is worth knowing," Bushell said. "It doesn't surprise me. The fewer people in on a plot, the likelier it is to stay tight. But thinking something is so and having evidence it's so are different."

"So is having evidence and having suspects," Macias said, his voice mournful.

"I know." Bushell sighed. "And having, say, two dozen rifles loose in New Liverpool doesn't strike me as any too appetizing, either. Fanatics with guns could kill dozens of people over the next few years. And this used to be such a peaceful city." He sighed again. Nothing seemed good any more.

Captain Macias echoed his gloom: "Some of the people they kill will be my constables, too. We can't stand up against that kind of firepower."

"Neither can we," Bushell said. "I had to pull wires to arrange for the guards in the room with *The Two Georges* at the governor's mansion to carry pistols." He laughed bitterly. "And a whole bloody lot of good that did me. But if we went to court to let all our men wear guns all the time, people would scream for our heads, and I can't say I'd blame them much."

"I wouldn't, either," Macias said. "But that holds only if nobody does any shooting. If the villains are aiming at my men how can I send them out there unless they're able to shoot back?"

"You can't," Bushell said without hesitation. "But if it comes to that, the British Empire won't be the same place. Thanks for your information, Captain. I'll ring you up again directly I learn anything."

"Call me Jaime," Macias answered. "We're going to get to know each other very well. I said as much outside the governor's mansion the other night."

"All right, Jaime, then I'm Tom. You did say that. I remember. What I don't remember, worse luck, is being able to disagree with you."

▼

The New Liverpool All-Union Train Station lay not far east of RAM headquarters. Getting to it was easy. All the same, Bushell went there with the same enthusiasm he would have given a trip to the dentist.

Like so much of New Liverpool, the train station sprawled over a wide area to minimize earthquake damage. Its low buildings were of white stucco with red tile roofs; the old Franco-Spanish flavor of what had been Los Angeles lived on more in architecture, perhaps, than in any other aspect of modern New Liverpool. The style suited the climate better than models imported from England or even from the older provinces of eastern North America.

Reporters and photographers had already jammed the waiting area by the time Bushell got there. Since the train full of dignitaries wouldn't arrive for another half hour, they turned on Bushell instead. He understood how Canute had felt with the tide flowing up over his shoes.

He didn't think telling the reporters he believed Tricky Dick had been shot by a lone gunman would damage the investigation, so he did that. It was, however, the only piece of new information he had. The reporters complained he wasn't telling them enough.

"The more time I spend answering questions, the less time I have to ask them," he said pointedly. "The fewer questions I get to ask, the less I'll find out, and the less I find out, the less I'll have to tell you."

Some of them got what he was driving at; one or two even gave him sympathetic grins. Most of those were veterans of the crime beat. But the theft of *The Two Georges* was such an important story, more than mere crime reporters were covering it. A lot of the people shouting questions in his face didn't know grand theft from grand opera, or felonies from feldspar. They didn't understand that policemen couldn't deliver answers on silver trays like *cartes de visite*. "I don't know" seemed to infuriate them, but Bushell had no better reply to give.

Finally, to his relief, ceiling-mounted speakers blared, "The governor-general's special train is approaching the station on Track Two."

Like sheep, the reporters flocked toward Platform Two, carrying the RAM along in their midst. "I see it!" somebody called excitedly. "There's the plume of exhaust, sure enough," somebody else added. Bushell couldn't see anything except the shoulders of the people around him. A little judicious work with his elbows, though, and a few feet trod upon not quite by accident, got him near the edge of the platform, near enough to look down the track when he peered east.

Sure enough, the special train was getting close. Gray-black smoke rose from the stack. The steam whistle roared, warning anything and everything out of its path. The whistle blew again, even louder, as the train approached the platform. The brakes gripped, sparks flew from the wheels and from the track. A third blast from the whistle sent reporters stumbling away from the edge of the platform, hands to their ears. Bushell held his ground. The train stopped.

When an ordinary train came up to the platform, porters and doormen ran over to assist departing passengers and those who were boarding. Not here, not now. The last car in the short train had on its fantail a gleaming maple podium. Governor-General King had used that podium to deliver several speeches on his way across the continent. Unless Bushell had lost his instinct for such things, Sir Martin was about to use it to deliver one more.

Sure enough, he stepped out to the podium, a sheet of paper in hand. In his scarlet robe of office, he still looked like the preacher he had been a generation before. He still had the cadences of a preacher, too: hardly looking at the text of his speech, he began, "My friends, we are not met here today gladly, but in sorrow. Something precious has been taken from our lives. If we work together, and if God is kind and smiles on us, we can recover it once more."

Sir Martin's deep, rich voice was made for pulpit or podium. The reporters listened raptly. Some of them were too caught up even to take notes. Bushell would not have been surprised to hear shouts of "Amen!" ring out from the crowd, as if it were indeed a church congregation.

The governor-general's first few sentences convinced him, though, that the speech would hold little of substance. He didn't blame Sir Martin for that: with *The Two Georges* missing and clues few and far between, what was the man supposed to say? But to Bushell, the speech was not the fodder from which news was made, as it was for the press corps. It was just a waste of time, and with *The Two Georges* stolen, he did not have time to waste.

He spotted red uniforms in a coach several cars up from the one where Sir Martin was addressing the crowd of reporters. He made his way toward it; by the time he got to it, he'd broken out of the crush. He hopped up on to the platform over the coupling and rapped on the door there. A stern-looking face appeared in the window. Bushell held up his badge. The RAM inside the car nodded and opened the door.

The air on the platform had been thick with smoke from pipes, cigars, and cigarillos. The air inside the car was positively blue. Bushell took out a cigar, scraped a lucifer on the sole of his shoe, and added to the clouds.

"Tom!" Lieutenant General Sir Horace Bragg pushed his way down the aisle toward Bushell; the RAMs who had accompanied him across the continent got out of his way. "Good to see you, by God!" He stuck out his hand.

Bushell shook it. "Good to see you, too, sir," he said. "Good to see any friendly face—I've not seen many the past few days, and that's the truth. You're looking very well, if I may say so."

"I'm getting fat," Bragg said. "It's only the cut of the uniform tunic that hides it."

"Sir—rubbish," Bushell said. Both men laughed. Bragg had been complaining about his weight for as long as Bushell had known him—more than half a lifetime, in other words. Few men ever complained more with less reason. Bragg was lean to the point of gauntness, with hollows under his cheekbones that the graying beard he wore could not disguise. His face was long and pale, with dark eyes peering out at the world from under heavy eyebrows.

He quickly sobered, and set a hand on Bushell's shoulder. "This is a hell of a mess, Tom," he said. "The whole dominion's in an uproar. If we don't find that painting—" He shook his head. Lowering his voice, he went on. "There are even more complications than you know."

"Tell me, then," Bushell said.

But Sir Horace Bragg shook his head. "Not my place to do that, I'm afraid. Sir Martin will have to take care of it, either him or"—he grimaced apologetically—"Sir David Clarke."

"It's all right," Bushell said easily. "I expected he'd be coming west with Sir Martin." But, despite his casual tone, it was not all right. His pulse beat so heavily, he could feel it pounding in the veins of his forehead. Still keeping his voice light, he asked, "Does this ever-so-official railway car boast an ever-so-official railway bar?"

Sir Horace sent him a worried look; he knew the bottle could get hold of Tom Bushell rather than the other way round. Bushell looked back, smiling, open, innocent, bland—with the slightest devilment in his eyes to make sure no one took the rest too seriously. Bragg recognized that look not just from their time in the RAMs but from their army days. He threw his hands in the air, turned to one of the officers who'd sat down to let him pass. "Felix, fix Tom here an Irish over ice, if you'd be so kind."

"Happy to, Sir Horace, Colonel Bushell." The officer—like Bragg, he was in dress uniform, with the crown and pip of a lieutenant-colonel on his shoulder boards—went down to the other end of the car, scooped ice from a silver bucket into a highball glass, and poured from a crystal decanter. He brought the glass back to Bushell, presented it with a flourish.

"Thanks very much, Lieutenant-Colonel, ah—" Bushell glanced to Sir Horace Bragg.

"I beg your pardon," Bragg said. "I forgot Felix was up in Boston while you were back at the capital; he got in the day after you left. Tom, let me present to you Lieutenant-Colonel Felix Crooke. Felix, my old friend Colonel Thomas Bushell."

The two men shook hands. Crooke was stocky, pale, clean-shaven, with hair black as a Spaniard's and eyes so blue they put Bushell in mind of a Siamese cat. He had a powerful grip. "Pleased to meet you at last, Colonel," he said. "Lieutenant General Sir Horace often speaks of you."

"I deny everything," Bushell declared, sipping his drink. Crooke laughed.

Sir Horace Bragg said, "Felix is one of our leading students of the Sons of Liberty in Victoria these days. He took over when Thaddeus Bishop retired a couple of years ago."

"Ah, Thad," Bushell said. "I remember him from my days at the capital." He drank again; not all his memories of Victoria were as pleasant as those of Thaddeus Bishop. "I'm sure he enjoys going after trout more than he ever did, going after the Sons." He nodded to Crooke. "Boston, eh? Find anything you could pin on *Common Sense* and make it stick?"

"Damn all," Felix Crooke said glumly. "Their solicitors have kept them just this side of the line for years, and there's no proof they give money to the Sons. Lord, how I wish there were. That would really hurt the Sons of Liberty, more than arresting some of the bastards every now and again ever could."

"You know, they may have shot themselves in the foot, stealing *The Two Georges*," Bushell said. "The whole NAU loves that painting."

Sir Horace Bragg chuckled. "Anyone would think you'd been writing Sir Martin's speeches for him, Tom. That's one of the things he's been doing all the way across the Union: saying that whatever people who do things like that want, it can't be any good, because only people who do things like that could want it." The commandant of the Royal American Mounted Police nodded in grudging admiration. "He's clever, you have to give him that."

"Who, Sir Martin? I should say so," Bushell answered. "And when you add in a voice he plays like a church organ—" He shrugged. "It didn't surprise me when the King-Emperor named him governor-general." He knocked back the rest of his drink. He wanted another one, but the look Sir Horace had given him made him hold his peace.

"The King-Emperor, yes," Bragg said slowly. Then he brightened, as much as any man with a countenance two parts basset hound could brighten. "Here, Tom, let me introduce you to some of the other men I've brought to Upper California. You won't have met all of them when you were in Victoria."

Bushell wished he could whip out a notebook and jot down names and ranks, as if the RAMS were suspects; that would have helped him keep them straight. Except for Felix Crooke, Bragg had left most of his top people behind in the capital, and had with him captains and majors who probably had more recent active-duty experience than their superiors.

Major Michael Foster would be in charge of forensics investigation. He looked too young to be in charge of anything: he looked too young to be anything more than a university undergraduate. But he had two service hashmarks on the left sleeve of his dress tunic, so he'd been a RAM at least ten years. Bushell said, "You'll need to talk with Sergeant Singh of the New Liverpool constabulary. He did the first workup of the crime scene."

"I'll talk with him," Foster said, "but I'll go over the site myself, too." That could have meant he was eager to inspect it personally. From his tone, though, he sounded more condescending, as if wondering whether someone named Singh could possibly have done an adequate job.

Looking around the car, Bushell saw that everyone in it was white. He'd lived in New Liverpool long enough to find that noteworthy, as he had at Independence Party headquarters. Victoria didn't have the large concentrations of Nuevespañolans and East Indians that New Liverpool did, but it had a great many Negroes: with so many of them in clerical and bureaucratic positions, only natural for the capital to draw them like a lodestone.

But just because they lived in and around Victoria, Bushell reminded himself, didn't mean they had to join the RAMs in any significant numbers. Though a lot of police work was bureaucratic in nature, the RAMs were not the sort of bureaucracy to which people of cautious, conservative bent often aspired.

Sir Horace Bragg said, "And here is Captain Patricia Oliver, whose area of expertise is handwriting and typewriter analysis."

"Captain." Since this was business, Bushell stuck out his hand as he would have for a man. Smiling in approval, Patricia Oliver pumped it briskly. She was somewhere not far from forty, her light brown hair touched with gray, her skin pale under powder and rouge: like a lot of RAMs with specializations such as hers, she didn't spend much time in the sun.

"I'm pleased to meet you, Colonel Bushell," she said. "I'll want to see that note you recovered from the phonogram, match it to others we have from the Sons. I've brought along several dozen samples for comparisons. With luck, I'll be able to identify the typewriter." Her voice showed the same no-nonsense attitude as her handshake.

"I'll take care of that for you." Bushell promised, pleased with her. Few women reached captain's rank in the RAMs. She filled out her uniform tunic in a different and pleasant way. Beneath it, instead of trousers, she wore an ankle-length skirt of black wool.

He glanced at her left hand. The fourth finger bore a slim gold band with a sparkling diamond. *I might have known*, he thought. *The good ones are mostly taken.* Kathleen Flannery wasn't, but she would have been had Kyril Lozovsky proved himself something other than a bounder. Or was she not taken because she wasn't a good one? He'd have to think about that.

"Captain Oliver's husband is one of the prosecuting attorneys for the province of Virginia," Sir Horace said.

"Is he?" Bushell murmured. He wondered if Captain Oliver had met her husband while they were both involved with the same case. Or had she got her interest in police work from him? It wasn't any of Bushell's business. Politely, he said, "A prominent man."

"A busy man," she answered, looking him straight in the eye. "And because I'm also busy, I don't see him nearly as much as I'd like." After a second or two, he recognized the way she was studying him—with much the same hopeful speculation he'd used when he met Kathleen Flannery. Under other circumstances, that would have been flattering, perhaps delightfully so. As things were, he found it disturbing.

Outside on the platform, the reporters started streaming away from the car where Sir Martin Luther King had spoken. Sir Horace Bragg took Bushell by the arm. "Now that His Excellency has finished out there, Tom, we throw you to the wolves."

He laughed to show that was meant as a joke, but it held too much truth for Bushell to do anything more than skin his lips back from his teeth in the pretense of a smile. If any audience would be tougher than the press, it was Sir Martin's staff. Bushell had embarrassed their patron. To any politico's aides, that was more dastardly than murder.

None of the RAMs save Sir Horace accompanied Bushell into the next coach back. He had the idea they wanted as little to do with the governor-general's staff as they could manage. From everything he'd seen of the men who worked for politicos, he was willing to believe the feeling mutual.

The RAMs' red tunics had provided a splash of color against the earth tones of leather and polished mahogany in their car. The governor-general's men dressed like bankers and brokers, in muted grays and blues or funereal black. Bushell wondered if they did so in the hope of convincing people that they, like prominent capitalists, served a useful purpose.

His voice cool and formal, Sir Horace Bragg said, "Gentlemen, allow me to present to you my friend Colonel Thomas Bushell, commandant of the Royal American Mounties based in New Liverpool." That *my friend* took courage. Not many commanders would have publicly identified themselves with a subordinate on whose watch disaster had struck.

The governor-general's men realized as much. They came up one by one to introduce themselves to Bushell: Roy Saunders, deputy minister of the exchequer, thin and sandy and acerbic; Hiram Defoe, postage minister and Sir Martin's chief political fixer, who, if he didn't know everything and everyone, made a good game try of not letting on; Sir Devereaux Jones, NAU Tory Party chairman, his ebony face clever and closed; and a couple of others whose names Bushell missed.

In back of them, not pushing his way forward, stood Sir David Clarke.

Before long, though, the moment could be avoided no more. The governor-general's chief of staff came up to Bushell. "Colonel," he said quietly, and held out his hand.

Bushell's eyes flicked to the well-groomed appendage, then up to Clarke's handsome, craggy face. The two men were about the same age, but somehow Clarke had managed to hide ten or fifteen years where they did not show. His smile was broad and perfect, his teeth even and gleaming, the whites of his blue, blue eyes untracked by red. He looked too good to be true.

"Sir David," Bushell said. A quarter of a heartbeat late, he shook Clarke's hand.

A couple of Sir Martin's aides whispered behind their hands to the rest.

Bushell could not hear what they were saying, but he knew. He wanted to hit Sir David in those sparkling teeth, to wipe that condescendingly uncondescending smile off his face. He'd done it once. He couldn't now. He rubbed at his mustache. Sometimes the price of duty was almost more than a man could bear to pay.

He asked the question Clarke was waiting for: "I hope Irene is well?"

"Quite well, yes, thank you," Sir David answered, the picture of civilized restraint. Bushell hated him more than ever. Clarke twisted the knife a little: "When she learned I was coming to New Liverpool, she asked me to say hello for her."

"Tell her hello from me," Bushell said tonelessly. The inside of the railway car had gone very quiet; he could hear his words echoing from the walls and ceiling.

In the quiet, footsteps echoed on the platform at the rear of the car. "Here is Sir Martin now," Sir Horace Bragg said as the governor-general came in. The two men got along imperfectly well; Bushell had never imagined his old friend sounding so glad and relieved to report the arrival of Sir Martin Luther King.

The governor-general of the North American Union had doffed his robe of office before coming up into the car in which his aides worked. Now he wore a suit and waistcoat of darkest navy, so dark the eye mistook it for black at first glance. With that as background, his skin seemed almost pale; he was a couple of shades lighter than Sir Devereaux Jones.

As Sir David Clarke had, he held out his hand to Bushell and said, "Colonel." His orator's voice filled the car. Bushell found it daunting to have that voice, trained to sway thousands in a crowd or millions over the wireless, turned on him alone.

He shook the governor-general's hand and said, "Your Excellency, honored as I am to meet you, I wish it were under happier circumstances."

"So do I, Colonel Bushell," Sir Martin answered. Beneath the trained phrasing, he sounded worn. He was in his sixties, his hair and mustache graying, tired pouches under his narrow, slanting, almost Oriental eyes. Cross-country railway travel, even at its most luxurious, would tell on a man no longer young. "So do I, for more reasons than you yet know."

"Sir Horace alluded to those reasons, sir," Bushell said, glancing toward his commandant. "He said he was not the proper person to elaborate on them: that was your province, no one else's."

"He was correct." Sir Martin Luther King also let his eyes slide toward Sir Horace, just for a moment, as if granting even so much praise pained him. After a brief hesitation, the governor-general went on, "We have a need more pressing than you can imagine to recover *The Two Georges* quickly. Were you not involved in this case, you would not hear of it for some time to come."

"Your Excellency, I assure you that Tom Bushell is reliable in every way," Sir Horace Bragg declared.

Sir Martin did not answer. He did not need to answer. Had Bushell been reliable in every way, *The Two Georges* would not have been stolen, and he himself would have been comfortably back in Victoria.

"Your Excellency, if you don't think I should have whatever this information may be, don't tell me," Bushell said. "I understand secrets and the need for them."

"Well said," Hiram Defoe murmured. Several of the governor-general's aides nodded. Sir David Clarke stood unmoving. He understood secrets, too, and what they could do when they were secret no more.

"Colonel, I tell you frankly that I would withhold this information if I could," Sir Martin said. "I am far from convinced you should know it. But I am convinced you *must* know it, to appreciate the urgency of our predicament. *The Two Georges* was scheduled to return to Victoria on 15 August—two months from now, less three days. That much you already know."

Bushell nodded. "Yes, sir."

"Very well. What you do not know is that His Majesty Charles III is scheduled to arrive in Victoria on the following day aboard the imperial yacht *Britannia*, to view the painting in its colonial setting and deliver an address touching on the importance of the ties between the NAU and the mother country. Surely I need not emphasize for you the unfortunate symbolism which would be conveyed were *The Two Georges* to be missing upon his arrival."

"No, Your Excellency, you don't," Bushell said. He had as little to do with politics as he could, but he didn't have to be a fixer of Hiram Defoe's caliber to figure out what would happen if the King-Emperor gave his speech in front of a blank wall rather than before the painting. A generation might pass before London again trusted the NAU to handle anything important on its own.

"I hate it when political considerations interfere with the investigation of a crime," Sir Horace Bragg said, "but sometimes they do, and that's a fact we can't ignore."

"Yes, sir," Bushell said; Bragg might have been reciting any competent policeman's creed. Of Sir Martin Luther King, Bushell asked, "Your Excellency, would the Sons of Liberty have had any idea the King-Emperor is sailing to the NAU? Is that part of the reason why they stole *The Two Georges?*"

"That's an ugly thought, Tom," Sir Horace Bragg said before the governor-general could answer.

"It is indeed an ugly thought," Sir Martin echoed. His glance slid to Bragg once more, either in annoyance at being anticipated or, perhaps more likely, in surprise at agreeing so much with the RAM commandant. After a moment, he went on, "To the best of my knowledge, Colonel, you are the first person outside London and Victoria to be entrusted with that secret. We shall presently make the great to-do appropriate for a visit from His Majesty, but for the time being all arrangements are tightly held, the better to keep the King-Emperor safe and secure."

"If the Sons of Liberty did get word of Charles's impending visit, they got it from someone on this train," Sir Horace Bragg said. "I can't believe any of us here would violate a sacred trust in such a way. The timing of the theft has to be coincidental."

"Once more, I find myself agreeing with Lieutenant General Bragg," Sir Martin said. He spoke the words through slightly pursed lips, as if they tasted sour. "That the Sons of Liberty could have penetrated our inmost councils—inconceivable, sir, inconceivable."

"Fewer things are truly inconceivable than we'd like to believe, Your Excellency," Bushell said, "and some people know more about betrayal than they should." He was speaking to the governor-general, but looked straight at Sir David Clarke.

▼

That evening, over beefsteak in the dining room of the Grosvenor Hotel—the closest to RAM headquarters—Sir Horace Bragg said, "You did yourself no good there, Tom, pitching dirt at Sir Martin's fair-haired boy."

"I didn't give a damn," Bushell said savagely. He tossed down his Jameson and waved for a waiter to fetch him another. "That toffee-nosed bastard, standing there all smooth and smug and sweatless, looking like butter wouldn't melt in his mouth. If I had my druthers, I'd have put him in hospital for a week or two." He sliced away at his beefsteak. He'd ordered it blood rare, and wished the red juice spurting from it poured from the veins of Sir David Clarke.

"It's done, Tom," Bragg said. "No point dwelling on it, brooding over it, now."

"I know," Bushell answered. "Intellectually, I know. But it's been years now, and I can't let go of it, not for good." He cut off another bite of rare, rare meat, raised it to his mouth. The waiter, black satin cummerbund glistening in the lamplight, set a fresh Irish whiskey before him. He swallowed the beefsteak and took a long pull at the drink.

"When I learned Smithers was going to retire, I sent you out here to take his place so you would get a fresh start on life," Bragg said. He sent Bushell a reproving stare with his houndlike eyes. "That was a long time ago. You've done very well here, by all accounts and by your record. I really thought you'd managed to forget. But then today—" He shook his head.

"I'm sorry," Bushell said. "I didn't intend to embarrass you, sir. And I do forget, sometimes for weeks at a stretch. But it keeps coming back, like memories from a bad stretch of combat. And when I saw Sir David's face—"

He slammed a fist down on the snowy linen of the tablecloth. China and silverware jumped. Jameson shook in his glass, an Upper California Burgundy in Bragg's. The sudden sharp noise made people's heads turn all over the dining room. The newly arrived RAMs resolutely pretended Bushell had done nothing out of the ordinary, which made him feel worse than the civilians' stares. Only Patricia Oliver met his eyes. He thought she looked sympathetic, but had reason to distrust his own judgment.

As the hum of conversation slowly revived, Bushell mumbled, "I do apologize. Another unseemly display to put in my file."

"Oh, nonsense." Sir Horace Bragg waved that away. "You're a human being, Tom, and human beings have a way of doing unseemly things every so often." He hesitated, then added, "You might get along better if you remembered you're human a little more often. Then you wouldn't be so taken by surprise when it happens."

"Duty comes first," Bushell answered, as automatically as he would have given his name had someone asked him that. Bragg glanced up to the ceiling and said no more.

After fruit and cheese, cigars and brandy, after he paid the bill, Sir Horace yawned and got to his feet. "I'm for bed," he declared. "Everyone tells me the rumble of a train rolling down the tracks is restful, but I've never found it so. Peace and quiet suit me better. I must be getting old." He squeezed Bushell's shoulder. "See you in the morning, Tom."

"Yes, sir," Bushell said. He knew that meant he should get into his steamer, drive back to his flat, and get some rest himself. Instead, he walked into the bar next to the dining room, caught the bartender's eye, and said, "Jameson over ice, if you'd be so kind."

He drank two Irish whiskeys in rapid succession, then paused, thoughtful and numb at the same time. If he went on from here, he wouldn't stop until he fell asleep with his head on the polished wood of the bar. He'd done that more times than he cared to remember. But if he stopped at this point, all the memories would well up, and the Jameson had dissolved the shields he usually held against them. Could he bear that? If he could, why did he have the shields?

He looked around. The bar was nearly empty. If he did make a sodden mess of himself, he didn't think any of his colleagues would find out about it. Like Sir Horace Bragg, they'd doubtless headed upstairs for a good night's sleep. Most RAMs were fine, upstanding citizens. *The drunken reprobates like me are few and far between*, he thought.

He lifted the forefinger of his right hand. The bartender didn't see it. Bushell opened his mouth to call the fellow. Just then, one of the newly arrived RAMs paused at the entrance to the bar. Bushell's call turned into a cough. He let his forefinger fall.

His colleague saw him and came striding up. "May I join you?" Patricia Oliver asked. She'd changed from uniform tunic and skirt to a skirt checked in light and dark green and a light green jacket with bow, cuffs, felt, and pocket edges checked to match the skirt. The sports outfit made her look less severe and several years younger.

Bushell let his hand rest for a moment on the round leather seat of the bar stool next to him. "Please do," he said. "What can I get for you?"

"Scotch and soda," she answered as she sat down. Bushell gave the bartender the order. He did not ask for anything for himself. Patricia Oliver sent him a curious look. "You're not drinking, Colonel?"

"I've been drinking," he said. "Perhaps in a while, I'll drink some more. Right now"—he shrugged—"I'm not drinking." The bartender returned with the Scotch and soda. Bushell set a pound note on the bar, with half a crown for a tip. One more argument against getting drunk here was that it cost even more than it would have aboard the *Upper California Limited*. He took out his cigar case. "Do you mind if I smoke?"

"Not at all." Patricia reached into her handbag and produced a monogrammed gold cigarette case. She drew one of the slender white tubes from it, tapped the end of the cigarette against the bar. "Do you mind if I join you?"

By way of reply, Bushell scraped a lucifer afire. He held it out for her. She lighted her cigarette; her cheeks hollowed as she sucked in smoke. Bushell thought cigarettes harsh and acrid, but Patricia Oliver had not asked his opinion. He got his cigar going. Its savory aroma helped mask that of the cigarette.

Patricia reached out and knocked ash into the crystal tray in front of Bushell. Her lipstick had drawn a band of red around the cigarette. She raised her glass. "Down with the Sons of Liberty!" she said, and sipped.

Bushell shifted his cigar to his left hand. He lifted an imaginary glass high with his right, brought it to his mouth, and tipped his head back. "Consider that drunk to."

Her laugh exposed small, white, even teeth. "Are you serious enough to make a proper RAM? We're a sobersided lot, most of us."

He considered that—seriously. "I'm serious on duty," he said. "Off duty, I'm no more serious than I have to be." Even with whiskey in him, *sobersided* was an adjective that fit well, maybe too well, but he didn't have to acknowledge it.

"That's fair," Patricia Oliver said with a nod. "Too many people take the office wherever they go, though." She sipped her drink, staring pensively at the glowing coal of her cigarette and the thin, twisting ribbon of smoke that rose from it. After a moment's silence, she asked, "Do you think we have any chance at all of recovering *The Two Georges* intact?" No sooner had the words passed her lips than she burst out with a long peal of laughter. "There I was, mocking people who bring their work with them no matter where they are, and now I've done it myself."

"It's all right," Bushell said. "It's what we have in common, after all." He thought about the question, slowly answered, "The only way we'll see it, I think, is if the Sons of Liberty think that's to their advantage. Otherwise—" He looked down at the bar and wished the imaginary shot of Irish whiskey he'd downed had been real. "Otherwise, I'll have found a way of going down in history that isn't the one I had in mind."

Patricia Oliver's red mouth closed on the cigarette. She took a long drag and let the smoke out a little at a time, so that she sat as if shrouded in fog. "It's not your fault, or not altogether," she said.

"I was in charge. By God, I was *there*," Bushell said. "My duty was to keep that painting safe, and I didn't do it." He started to signal the bartender, but hesitated once more. Too soon since the last one, if he wanted to stay on the dry side of the slough of despond.

"It's not that simple," she answered. "It's Sir Horace's responsibility, too, but he's not losing sleep over it." That was literally true; Sir Horace had gone up to bed. Patricia continued, "Anyone who expects perfection is asking too much. The Sons of Liberty can try a hundred outrages; if they succeed with one, they come out ahead. If we fail one time in a hundred, we lose. That's not right. You can't blame yourself for not being perfect."

"I found out I wasn't perfect a long time ago," Bushell said with a rueful twist to his lips that wasn't quite a smile. "Of me as me, I expect what I can get by doing the best I know how. Of me as RAM commander here—the job needs to be perfect, even if the man isn't."

She shook her head. "No," she said, almost angrily. "Not even priests ask that much of themselves."

Bushell shrugged.

"How do you live with yourself?" Patricia Oliver wondered. He shrugged again, not sure if she was asking the question of some higher authority. She knocked back her drink with a flick of the wrist, man-fashion, and signaled the bartender for a refill. He'd been polishing the already gleaming wood of the bar for some time, and looked grateful for something better to do.

This time, Bushell, having exhausted his singles, handed the man a blue two-pound note. This time, too, he consciously noticed the reproduction of *The Two Georges* on the banknote. He grimaced and looked away; the image too vividly called to mind the original he'd seen and then lost. The bartender, mindful of his own tip, gave back a pound's worth of change in a jingle of silver. Bushell left one gleaming coin on the bar and scooped the rest into his trouser pocket.

Patricia Oliver said, "Are you going to drink another imaginary toast with me?" Her eyes challenged him.

Sighing, he dug out the change he'd just put away, and more besides. The bartender brought him a shot of Jameson and then went back to plying his cloth.

"Anyone would think you were a Son yourself, drinking Irish whiskey like that," Patricia said, one eyebrow quirking up.

"I like it," Bushell said. "I got a taste for it in my army days, maybe even before I'd ever heard of the Sons of Liberty. It doesn't taste like medicine, the way Scotch does for me." He sipped; Jameson was the medicine he needed, all right. "And I wish to God I still hadn't heard of the Sons."

"I don't blame you." She set her hand lightly atop one of his. He looked up at her face. He saw sympathy and—something else? He wasn't sure. She went on, "You're blaming yourself enough as is. This must be hell for you."

"Now that you mention it," he said, "yes."

The weight of her hand on his grew slightly. Her skin was warm and very smooth. She said, "If it weren't for the Russians and the Holy Alliance, the Sons would long ago have dried up and blown away for lack of blood—I mean, money."

"Not much difference between the two, not when it comes to politics," he said, nodding. He told her of what he'd uncovered while the special train was traveling west from Victoria: the Nagant rifle posted from Skidegate and the scandalous pamphlet commingled with accounts paid in gold roubles for the travel brochure about the Queen Charlotte Islands.

"*Russian* money," she said with a quick indrawn breath, "and Russian guns, too. No telling how many more Russian guns are loose in New Liverpool, either."

"I had that same happy thought," Bushell agreed. "Of course, it doesn't necessarily prove anything: men who aren't Russians can lay hands on gold roubles, and on Nagants, too, I suppose, though that would be harder. But it gives us a place to start looking, and in a case like this—"

"We're grateful for any place to start," she finished for him.

They spent the next considerable while talking about the case, and about other things. But for them, the bar was dead quiet: a slow weekday evening. Bushell had another drink, and then another. He nursed them instead of leaping headlong into them as he had before. He knew they were in him, but somehow they lacked the power over him whiskey sometimes seized.

With a yawn, the bartender sat down on a stool in the far corner of his little domain. He leaned against the wall, giving every sign of being about to fall asleep. Bushell pulled out his pocket watch, "Good heavens," he said, staring at it. "How did it get to be a quarter to one?"

"For me, it was the pleasant company," Patricia Oliver said.

Pleasant company was all very well. Bushell was thinking he was most of an hour from home, most if not all of another hour back to RAM headquarters, and not enough hours of sleep sandwiched in between there. Having gone through a day on no sleep a short while earlier, he did not want to do it again. "I think I'll go over to the office and put my feet up on my desk," he said. "I've done that before, a time or two."

"Why don't you come up to my room instead?" Patricia said.

He looked up from his glass to her. She met his eye with the same directness she'd shown in the railway coach. "What sort of invitation is that?" he asked slowly.

"Whatever sort you want it to be," she answered. The pink tip of her tongue lingered between her teeth for a moment before she drew it back once more. "I hope you find the idea . . . inviting."

That told him what sort of invitation it was. He had not been a monk since his marriage to Irene exploded, but this . . . "Mrs. Oliver—" he began.

"'Mrs. Oliver'?" she echoed, her voice still low, but mocking. "Not Patricia, not even Captain Oliver, but *Mrs.* Oliver? What on earth has this"—she held out her left hand: even in the muted light of the bar, the diamond on the fourth finger sparkled—"got to do with anything?"

"Quite a lot," he answered quietly.

She laughed out loud. She remained very much in control, so as not to rouse the bartender (whose eyes had fallen closed), but she was also very much amused. "How could it possibly matter?" she exclaimed. "My husband is on the other side of the dominion, and what dear Roland doesn't know will never, ever hurt him. I'm sure I don't know a great many things of his doing, and I've not lost a moment's sleep over any of them."

"Mrs. Oliver—" Bushell said again.

"Stop that!" Now her eyes sparked. "If you do it again, you will make me angry. Don't tell me you're not interested. I've been watching you for hours. I know better."

"I wasn't going to tell you that," he answered. His face felt wooden; getting each word out took a separate effort. "But what I am interested in doing and what I do are not necessarily one and inseparable."

She stared at him. "What on earth?" she said in honest bewilderment. Then her gaze happened to fall to the ring she'd displayed a moment before. "Don't tell me this bothers you?" she said. When he nodded like a machine whose mechanism needed oiling, she took it off and put it in her handbag. "There! Is that better?"

He shook his head, as jerkily as he'd nodded.

"A man of scruples!" she exclaimed in wonder. Bushell had always thought of himself so, but not in the way she said it. From her red lips, it sounded foolish, outmoded, useless. She cocked her head to one side, studying him like some strange biological specimen. "You shan't even let me seduce you?"

He discovered the Jameson he'd taken on board was still with him after all. It had just been lying low. Without it, he never would have replied as he did: "Mrs. Oliver"—he stared at her, through her, so fiercely that she did not correct him—"were that ring not on your finger, I should like nothing better than taking you upstairs and"—not even the whiskey could make him say to a woman *fucking your brains out*, which was the thought uppermost in his mind—"making love to you. You may forgive me for declining or not, as you see fit, but I have a"—he hesitated again before coming up with the right word—"a horror of adultery."

He waited for Patricia to say something else cutting. *How quaint* was what he thought most likely. But she was a RAM, and a good one, or she wouldn't have been in New Liverpool, and she had a police officer's itch to know. Very quietly, she spoke one word: "Why?"

He wanted another drink, wanted it with a sweaty passion not much different from lust. But the Irish whiskey already in him kept his tongue loose in his mouth. "I used to work out of Victoria myself, some years back now. Once, I finished a piece of business up in the Oregon country a couple of days sooner than I'd thought I would. I didn't telegraph or telephone—I thought I'd come home early and surprise Irene."

"That's enough," Patricia Oliver said, looking not at him but down at her hands. "You don't need to tell me any more. I don't want you to tell me any more."

Obediently, he fell silent. But he did not need to tell the rest of his story to have it unwind in his head as if played on a cinema a finger's breadth in front of his eyes. He'd opened the front door, set down his bags, and heard some small noise in the bedroom that told him Irene was there. He'd walked in quietly and . . .

She'd been naked, straddling Sir David Clarke, sliding up and down on his thick, hard tool, her head thrown back in abandon, little whimpering noises coming from her throat. Then she'd gasped, and then he had, and then, as they'd slowly begun to come back to themselves, they'd noticed Bushell standing in the doorway.

"You never know for certain where anyone is until you actually see him," he remarked, not so much to Patricia Oliver as to Irene back in the days when he'd thought he was a happy, lucky man.

Patricia had grit. She slid the wedding ring back onto her finger. Then she raised her eyes to his face and said, "I hope this won't interfere with our working together."

"Captain Oliver, if I can work with Sir David Clarke—I'm not giving out any great secrets there; you'll hear it from others if not from me—I can work with you."

She nodded at that, and then again to show she'd noticed him using her title. "I am going up to bed now," she said, sliding off the bar stool. "Good night, Colonel." He dipped his head in return. Formality was a grease that could help people from grinding against one another.

Bushell rose, too. He reached into his pocket, pulled out a couple of shillings, and set them on the bar: quietly, so as not to disturb the dozing bartender. He walked out into the lobby. Patricia had already disappeared; catching a lift upstairs at this hour must have been easy.

Under the glow of electric lamps, the streets were almost deserted. Every now and then, a steamer rolled past, nearly as silent as the rest of the night. A couple of women who probably were not ladies stood on a streetcorner, talking in low voices. Here and there, in shadows where the streetlamps did not reach, men with no better place to stay slept curled in ragged blankets or wrapped in newspapers to hold chill at bay. Some of them clutched the bottles that were at once their solace and ruination.

A tavern just a few doors down from RAM headquarters was an oasis of light and noise. Flickering images from the large televisor screen at one end of the bar showed a London soccer match that had to have been filmed a couple of weeks before. As Bushell walked past, one of the teams scored a goal. The tavern erupted in cheers, as if the action itself, not a faded, tardy simulacrum, had taken place before the eyes of those who watched it. Bushell rubbed at his mustache, marveling that so many people confused with reality what the televisor showed.

Televisor or no, he thought about going in, and even took one step halfway in the direction of the door. *Another drink, or two, or three? Why not?* But even as the temptation formed in his mind, he forced it to dissolve. He knew why not, all too well. Another drink, or two, or three, another drunk, or two, or three, and he might find himself one of those broken men on the sidewalk, a bottle in hand, oblivion all he craved. He shuddered and walked on.

The sergeant at the duty desk nodded to Bushell when he strode in. If he found anything in the least unusual about his chief's appearance there in the wee small hours of the morning, he did not presume to show it.

A Nuevespañolan janitor sweeping the hall in front of his office did give Bushell a curious glance as he went in, but said nothing. Bushell locked the door after himself, took off his shoes, loosened his tie, and sank down in his swivel chair. He put his feet up on the desk, as he'd told Patricia Oliver he would, and did his best to sleep.

But sleep would not come. Despite weariness, despite Jameson, behind his eyelids he kept seeing Irene's white buttocks clench and loosen, kept hearing her moans of delight, kept smelling her sweat—and her lover's. The images came to him all too often, even now, but seldom with such force as tonight. "Damn that Oliver woman," he muttered, shifting in the chair as he searched for some spot that was comfortable, or at least restful.

The bells of the Anglican cathedral chimed two. He did not hear them chime three.

▼

Bushell's chin came up off his chest. Light was leaking in through the closed venetian blinds. He pulled out his pocket watch: a quarter to seven. Four hours' sleep would get him through the day. He snorted. If he'd managed on one, he could manage on four.

His head throbbed dully. It wasn't a hangover, not quite, but it wasn't the way he cared to start the day, either. He jerked open the middle drawer of his desk, unscrewed the lid from a bottle of paracetamol tablets, and dry-swallowed two. When he got out of the chair and stood up, he discovered his head was not the only part of him that ached. In his army days, he'd slept on hard ground as if it were a feather mattress. His army days, he had to keep reminding himself, were well behind him. He hoped the paracetamol would start working soon.

He looked down at himself. Sleeping in a swivel chair had done nothing for the press of his suit. If he left it on, he'd look like a derelict in secondhand clothes. He rubbed his chin. Whiskers rasped under his fingers. They'd only add to the impression of seediness.

Then he looked to one of the file cabinets across from his desk. On it, still neatly folded, lay his dress uniform. He'd never found time to take it to be cleaned, but it was in far better shape than the clothes he was wearing. Without hesitation, he got out of his suit and put on the red tunic and striped trousers. Some of his men would raise an eyebrow at seeing him in uniform, but not so high as if he'd stayed in the suit.

He telephoned the duty desk. "This is Colonel Bushell. I've been, ah, working up here all night. Could you fetch me up a razor and some shaving soap?"

"I'll send them directly, sir," the sergeant at the desk said. "I heard you were in the building, so I thought you might be wanting them."

"Thank you," Bushell said, and hung up. The night man had warned his replacement, then, Some things didn't change from the army to police work.

The RAM who brought him the shaving implements did indeed blink to confront him all gleaming in crimson and gold, but held his incredulity to the one blink. Bushell was certain that, by the time he came downstairs, the entire headquarters building would know how he'd chosen to dress.

He walked into the lavatory, turned on the hot water at a faucet, lathered up, and scraped the straight razor across cheeks and chin and throat. He nicked himself a couple of times; the blood matched the red wool of his tunic. That tradition went back more than two thousand years to the Spartans, who hadn't wanted their clothing to betray their wounds. He dabbed at the nicks with a paper towel, then surveyed himself in the mirror. His eyes were redder than they should have been, the hollows under them deeper and darker, but he'd do.

The RAMs he encountered ostentatiously ignored his uniform as he made his way to the little kitchen not far from the duty desk. There he almost bumped into Samuel Stanley, who was fixing himself a spicy-smelling cup of Earl Grey. As an old friend, Stanley enjoyed—and took advantage of—the privilege of staring.

Bushell took a waxed cardboard cup and advanced on the coffeepot. He poured steaming coffee into the cup, drank it down hot and black and bitter. "All the rankers from Victoria are in their fancy dress, so I thought I'd match them," he said. The explanation did not sound especially convincing, even to himself.

"Uh-*huh*," Stanley said, which meant he hadn't convinced his adjutant, either. Stanley went on, "Chief, you're going to kill yourself if you spend all your time here, and you won't do the case any good if you're too worn to think straight."

"I know," Bushell said, "but I was so busy talking with the people from Victoria last night that time got away from me." That was even true, though he didn't mention what he and Patricia Oliver had been talking about. He went on, "I thought I'd get more rest here than by driving down to my flat and back."

"Mm, maybe." Samuel Stanley watched him gulp another cup of coffee. "However much rest you got, it wasn't enough."

"It's never enough," Bushell answered. "I'll make it up after we have *The Two Georges* back." When he said it, he believed it. By the way Samuel Stanley swallowed wrong and started coughing, he didn't. After a moment, neither did Bushell. Something else would come up, and he'd push himself just as hard for that. And then there would be yet one thing more. . . . "If we don't push ourselves every day, we don't belong in this business."

"Can't argue with you there," his adjutant conceded. He cocked an eyebrow at Bushell. "I suppose Lieutenant General Sir Horace Bragg and his band of merry men are certain they'll have the case wrapped up in tinsel and string by about day after tomorrow? That's the way it usually goes when they deign to come down from their mountain and do some real work."

"You're a cynical soul today," Bushell said. "Anyone would think you were a police officer, or something similarly disreputable." He and Samuel Stanley both laughed. The humor had a bitter edge to it, though, for Stanley had spoken unvarnished truth—and any police officer with more than a year on the job was steeped, indeed pickled, in cynicism. Learning what your fellow man was capable of all too often failed to endear him to you.

Stanley lowered his voice: "The other thing is, Chief, that if you say that too loud, somebody besides me will hear you."

"Me? What about you, Sam? Why, if you weren't dead right, I'd have to speak sharply to you about lack of proper respect for those illustrious enough to work out of Victoria."

Bushell did not bother to keep his voice down. Sir Horace knew his views on the ivory tower—or perhaps the whited sepulcher made a better comparison—that was Victoria. And if Sir Horace hadn't known them, Bushell wouldn't have cared if he heard. His commandant had done him a favor in more ways than one in getting him out of the capital after his marriage so spectacularly collapsed.

Samuel Stanley said, "Well, I'd better get back to it. And so had you, or the redcoats from Victoria will land on your back, knock you over, and kick you while you're down."

"It's not the redcoats I worry about. After all, they're policemen, too, after a fashion." Bushell chuckled, both at his adjutant's scandalized expression and his own wit, but he wasn't more than half joking. He went on, "The ones who scare me are the politicos. They want the rabbit pulled out of the hat right away, and if the rabbit's not there to begin with—" He spread his hands, palms up.

"Watch yourself, Chief. That's all." Stanley hurried out of the little room.

After a moment, Bushell left, too. He was only slightly surprised to find Sir Horace Bragg talking with the sergeant at the duty desk. Sir Horace might not have gone into the field for a good many years before this, but he worked hard at whatever he did. More than brilliance, dogged, unyielding persistence had got him the lieutenant general's uniform he wore today.

He spotted Bushell in turn and hurried up to him. "Good morning, Tom. I was just asking your man there where I could get myself round a cuppa. I gather you had the same notion."

"I just got myself round two coffees," Bushell answered. "Now that I've topped up the boiler, I'm ready to hit the day head-on."

"You're ahead of me, then." Bragg raised one of his bushy eyebrows. "In uniform, are you? Not on my account, I hope. Unless I'm no more senile than I think, I don't recall you being much one for such fripperies. Or did you sleep in your office and put on the only fresh things you had?"

"Sir, you know me too well," Bushell said with rueful admiration. "Tomorrow you'll see me in civilian clothes again, I expect. You'd better, because if I'm still in uniform then, the sky will be falling."

Without waiting for a reply, he bounded upstairs to his office. As long as he had the coffee surging in him, he intended to take advantage of the energy it lent. He tore through paperwork, then telephoned down to Gordon Rhodes to see if any fresh evidence or leads had come in while he snatched sleep. The call, unfortunately, proved a waste of time: Rhodes had heard nothing new.

A RAM came into Bushell's office and dumped the morning mail delivery onto his desk. He had a secretary next door, but made as little use of her services as he could: he was better at doing his job than at handing off parts of it for others to do. He rapidly sorted through the envelopes. Some went into the wastepaper basket unopened. Others got a quick skim and then joined them there. After a few minutes, only half a dozen items were left. He set them aside to be dealt with individually.

One was from the New Liverpool constabulary, the detailed report on the autopsy of Honest Dick the Steamer King. Bushell glanced through it, then put it away for detailed consideration later—it didn't offer any immediately obvious clues to the murderer's identity.

Most of the remaining envelopes held forms he had to complete for the budgetary process back in Victoria. On any other day, those would have taken priority. They might still, but Bushell, after examining them, shoved them aside. Hard as it was to believe inside the bureaucracy that bound together the greatest empire the world had ever known, budgets were not always the be-all and end-all of a man's career.

"And then there was one," Bushell said, picking up the last envelope, a large manila. His name, title, and address were neatly typed in the center of the envelope: the upper left-hand corner bore no return address. The manila envelope did not bend when he picked it up.

His letter opener was in the shape of a cavalry saber, and as sharp as one of the swords it mimicked. He slit the envelope and drew out two sheets of cardboard and the photograph they protected.

He stared at that photograph for a long time. One of the people who'd sent it obviously knew how to develop film himself; it could hardly have been entrusted to a commercial developing service. It showed *The Two Georges* leaning against a blank plaster wall, with a hand and arm thrusting into the picture the front page of a newspaper whose headline screamed of the theft of the painting.

Bushell set down the photo, picked up the envelope, and looked inside. Sure enough, it held a note-sized sheet of paper he hadn't seen before. On the paper, typed by a machine different from the one that had addressed the envelope, was a note:

IF YOU WANT THIS STINKING PAINTING BACK, YOU WILL PAY US
£50,000,000 BY 15 AUGUST. OTHERWISE, THE SYMBOL OF
OPPRESSION WILL BE CAST INTO THE FIRE OF LIBERATION.
INSTRUCTIONS ON HOW TO PAY THE RANSOM SO WE CAN SAFELY
RECOVER IT WILL REACH YOU. OBEY THEM. DO NOT THINK YOU CAN
KEEP THIS A SECRET FOR YOUR OWN TREACHEROUS ENDS--COPIES
ARE GOING TO THE NEWSPAPERS. AMERICA SHALL BE FREE.

# V

▼

M AJOR MICHAEL FOSTER'S BOYISH FACE
was petulant, as if his mother had forbidden him a hoped-for sweet. "Nothing,"
he said glumly. "Not a fingerprint anywhere except your own, Colonel Bushell.
Not on the photograph, not on the ransom note, not on the cardboards. There
are prints on the envelope itself, of course, but a hopeless jumble of them: it went
through the mails, after all. But I would wager any amount you care to name that
none of them will prove in any way connected to the Sons of Liberty."

"You're only too likely to be right," Bushell answered. "The Sons are all too
good at what they do. But have you by any chance examined the stamps? There,
if anywhere, some significant fingerprint might be lurking: a Son would have
bought them at a post office, would he not? He probably wouldn't have worn
gloves for such a purchase, not in summertime."

The forensics specialist from Victoria respectfully dipped his head. "Well
reasoned, Colonel. But take a closer look at the stamps." He pointed to the envelope on the conference table. "Notice how the top edges are imperforate. That
means they came from inside a booklet, whose outer covering could be handled
by any number of Sons of Liberty without our being any the wiser from the
stamps themselves."

Bushell ran a forefinger across his mustache. He wanted to express his detailed opinion of the criminal competence of the Sons of Liberty, but was inhibited in his choice of language by the presence of Patricia Oliver, who sat next to
Major Foster. "Captain, are they using a familiar machine?" he asked, curious to
see how she'd react after the previous night's scene.

"As far as I can tell on hasty first examination, no," she answered coolly. "I
hope further study will show I'm wrong there. If we can identify the typewriter,
we'll have a start on knowing where the ransom note was composed. It was
posted locally, of course, but that doesn't have to mean anything."

"My guess is that the photograph isn't local," Bushell said. "I brought all the
New Liverpool dailies the morning and afternoon after *The Two Georges* was
stolen, and I don't remember any headline from them exactly matching the one
we see there. It's something to research, at any rate."

"So it is." Sir Horace Bragg rested his chin in his hands. His expression was
dolorous. "We have so much to research, and so few answers."

"Have you spoken with Sir Martin Luther King yet?" Bushell asked. "Would

His Majesty's North American government pay ransom to the Sons of Liberty to get *The Two Georges* back?" If one such theft is paid, how many more would come in future?

"Were it up to me, I'd not give them a counterfeit ha'penny," Sir Horace said. "What Sir Martin will choose to do, however, who can say? And I did find the timing of the ransom deadline . . . intriguing. Wouldn't you agree, Tom?"

"*Intriguing* is a good word for it, sir," Bushell said slowly. "*Disturbing* is another one that springs to mind." The Sons of Liberty had threatened to destroy *The Two Georges* if they didn't get their fifty million pounds by the day before that on which Charles III, King of England, Wales, Scotland, Ireland, the North American Union, Australia, and New Zealand, Defender of the Faith, Emperor of India and the African Possessions, Lord of Gibraltar, Malta, and Cyprus, Protector of the Ottomans, the Chinese, and the Hawaiians, was scheduled to arrive on his state visit to Victoria. Coincidence? Bushell didn't believe in coincidence, not in a case like this.

The rest of the RAMs in the room looked curiously from him to Bragg. He realized they hadn't yet been told of the King-Emperor's impending visit. He also realized that, if the Sons of Liberty knew about it, they must have heard from someone who did know: either someone from London or, more likely, someone close to Sir Martin Luther King. He took out a cigar and, after a nod from Patricia Oliver, struck a lucifer and lit it.

He'd already known she didn't mind smoke, of course, but he was doing his best to pretend—perhaps to himself as much as to the outside world—their encounter had never happened. By the casual, practiced way she responded to his silent question, she had plenty of experience with like pretenses. That eased his mind and saddened him at the same time.

Sir Horace said, "Matters of timing notwithstanding, we have our preliminary lines of inquiry laid out for us. Seeing if we can match the typewriter's typeface and identify the newspaper whose headline is being utilized here will—or at least may—give us some notion of the locality in which this demand originated. We should also investigate the local post office from which the missive was actually sent, in the hope that a clerk will recall the person who handed him the envelope—if it was handed in rather than dropped into a letter box, that is. And, of course, I shall have to convey the ransom demand to the governor-general for his response." A twitch of his shaggy eyebrows showed how much he looked forward to that.

The RAMs who'd accompanied him from Victoria rose and left the conference room. So did most of the officers from New Liverpool with whom they'd be working. After a couple of minutes, the room held only Bragg and Bushell.

When Bushell made no move to go, Sir Horace looked at him in some surprise and said, "Is anything wrong, Tom?"

"Oh, not much," Bushell answered, a sardonic bite to his voice. "I just wanted to thank you for coming and taking the investigation right out of my hands. 'We need to do this. We need to do that. I'll tell Sir Martin.' Thank you very much, Lieutenant General Bragg, sir."

Bragg held up a placating hand. "Take it easy, will you, please? For now, I'm the senior officer on the scene, that's all. In a few days, a couple of weeks at most, I'll be back in Victoria and the case will be yours again."

"When an admiral comes aboard a ship commanded by a captain, that doesn't make him ship's commander, not unless he's been ordered to take over," Bushell said stubbornly. "Either this is my case or it isn't. And you may go back to Victoria, sir, but that doesn't mean you won't be running things by telephone and wire. If you're going to do that, please give me formal orders so I know where I stand. Sir."

"You can be most exasperating when you're nominally most obedient, do you know that?" Sir Horace said.

Bushell stood mute.

Bragg sighed. Just for a moment, as he exhaled, his hollow cheeks filled out and made him look like a well-fleshed man. Then they sagged again. He seemed older, more tired, than Bushell had ever seen him. "What am I supposed to do with you, Tom?" he asked quietly.

He hadn't intended that as a question to be answered; he'd started to say more. But Bushell, given the opening, charged into it: "Stand back, get out of the way, and let me do my job."

"It's not as simple as that." Now Sir Horace sounded almost pleading. "Don't you see? This isn't just a criminal case—it's a political one, too."

"I don't give a damn about politics," Bushell said. "Find the painting and all the political nonsense goes away, anyhow."

"If we rescue it, yes," Sir Horace Bragg said. "If, on the other hand, we cause it to be destroyed, Sir Martin Luther King—to say nothing of everyone else in the NAU and the mother country—will be looking for a scapegoat. Do you really want everyone looking straight at you?"

Bushell's eyes widened. "Of course I do. Hell, I'll be looking at myself, too, and pointing a finger at my face in the mirror."

"You mean it." Bragg shook his head. At first Bushell thought that was wonder; after a moment, he realized it was more resignation. Sir Horace went on, "It's no good arguing with you. I've known that for years, just as I've known you truly don't care a fig for politics. I've always thought you were more able than I am, Tom, but not caring about politics is a fatal flaw for a man in public service. It's why I am where I am today, and why you are where you are."

Would changing his nature be worth a lieutenant general's crown and crossed sword and baton? Would it be worth a knighthood, with the hope of a patent of nobility upon retirement? Bushell shrugged. The questions were irrelevant, since he could no more change his nature than the shape of his face. He said, "I suppose I'll have to live with that, sir. Now, who is running this investigation?"

"I didn't come to New Liverpool to take it away from you," Bragg answered.

"No, sir. But it seems to have worked out that way." With a quick-snapped salute and a precise about-turn, Bushell strode out of the conference room, leaving Sir Horace Bragg staring at his back.

▼

The telephone jangled. Bushell made a typographical error. Muttering a low-voiced curse, he spun his chair around so he could pick up the phone. It was not the first such interruption he'd had today. "Bushell," he said.

A woman's voice spoke into his ear. "I have a long-distance call for you from New Orleans, Colonel, uh, Bushell." She hesitated over his name, but pronounced it correctly.

"Go ahead," he said wearily.

"Go ahead," the operator echoed, and a man came on the line: "Good afternoon, Colonel; I am Chauncey Dupuy, of the *Herald-Leader and Picayune*." He sounded like a New Orleans man, with an accent that at first hearing sounded more nearly northeastern than southern. "I wish to ask you some questions about this outrageous ransom demand for the return of *The Two Georges*."

"Go ahead," Bushell repeated. He knew what the questions would be before they were asked, and answered them with mechanical competence. Yes, he had received the ransom note. Yes, the photograph appeared genuine. No, he couldn't say anything more about it than that. Yes, fifty million pounds was, as far as he knew, the largest ransom demand in the history of the NAU (Dupuy was thorough; not all the newshounds asked that one). Yes, the demand had been passed on to Sir Martin Luther King. No, Bushell didn't know whether Sir Martin intended to meet it.

"What would you do if it were up to you, Colonel?" Dupuy asked.

"Go on with my work without having to answer some reporter's questions every half hour," Bushell answered. "Good day, sir." With that, he hung up.

He turned the swivel chair back toward the typewriter. After he'd erased his error, though, he hesitated, then spun around to the desk again. He picked up the telephone, rang up the RAM switchboard. He told the operator who answered, "Direct any more calls for me from reporters to Lieutenant Thirkettle, if you'd be so kind. He can tell them as much as I can."

"Very good, Colonel," the operator said sympathetically. "I'll pass the word on to the rest of the crew. Shall we brief the next shift in the same way?"

"Probably a good idea," Bushell replied after a moment's thought. "I'm liable to stay on after you've gone home." He was liable to fall asleep in his chair again, too. He thought about ordering a cot sent up and installing it in his office. If things got worse, he would. *How could things get worse?* he asked himself, and was afraid he might find out.

He knew brief guilt at dumping the reporters in Lieutenant Thirkettle's lap. But what was a public information officer for, if not to give the public information? And reporters, as they themselves like to brag, were part of the public.

Conscience thus assuaged, Bushell rang the Hotel La Cienega and asked to speak to Kathleen Flannery. After a moment's silence, the hotel operator replied, "I'm sorry, sir, but Dr. Flannery checked out earlier this morning."

"Thank you," Bushell said, and hung up. He hadn't told Kathleen she couldn't leave town; he'd had no reason to justify telling her anything of the sort. But she'd be in transit for the next two or three days if she was going back home to Victoria, and so hard to reach. He supposed he could track down which train or airship she'd taken and wire ahead to one of its stopping points, but a moment's thought told him it wasn't worth the effort. All he'd wanted to know was her view of ransoming *The Two Georges*, and her view wouldn't count. That decision rested on the shoulders of Sir Martin Luther King.

Now that he'd given Thirkettle the joy of dealing with reporters, he had some small hope of catching up on the paperwork the reporters had been interrupting. He turned back to the typewriter and plunged ahead. Just as he was beginning to concentrate on the report in front of him, someone knocked on the frame of the open door.

He looked up with a snarl, ready to rend whoever had the temerity to break in on his thoughts at the exact moment when he was starting to accomplish something. Lieutenant General Sir Horace Bragg, however, was not rendable, not by a mere colonel. "Sorry to bother you, Tom," Bragg said, as if they had not quarreled a few hours before, "but Sir Martin had summoned both you and me to a meeting in his suite at the Grosvenor to discuss our proper response to the demand you received this morning."

"I wasn't the only one who got it," Bushell answered. "As best I can tell from the telephone calls I've got, word of the ransom demand went out to every newspaper in the civilized world except maybe the *St. Petersburg Iskra*. I've not had a call from Russia, at any rate."

As he spoke, he covered the typewriter and got to his feet. The governor-general had the power to bind and to loose. If he wanted to see Bushell, Bushell would indeed go see him. And if that meant Bushell didn't get any paperwork done the rest of the day, he bloody well didn't, and that was all there was to it. No denying the subject Sir Martin wanted to discuss was an important one—*the* important one, at the moment.

"Let's go," he said. With luck, he might even turn the meeting to his own ends.

▼

Sir Martin Luther King was staying in the Royal Suite at the Grosvenor Hotel. So far as Bushell knew, the suite had never actually been occupied by royalty, but, as the King-Emperor's direct representative—essentially, viceroy—for the NAU, Sir Martin came close to that exalted status.

Only Bragg and Bushell represented the RAMs at the meeting. Sir Martin had with him but a single civilian aide: Sir David Clarke. Bushell nodded coldly to the man who'd taken Irene away from him.

"Thank you for joining me this afternoon, gentlemen." The governor-general pointed to a sideboard atop which sat a silver tea and coffee service. "Please help yourselves. We'll stand on no ceremony here, and the presence of servants would be not only distracting but possibly disastrous."

Sir Horace Bragg poured himself a cup of tea—English Breakfast, Bushell thought it was, a safe choice whatever the hour. Sir Horace also picked up a couple of biscuits and set them on the saucer's outer rim. Bushell took coffee. He looked at the biscuits but decided he didn't care for anything sweet.

He and Sir Horace set their saucers on the mahogany table in front of the couch where Sir Martin and Sir David were sitting, then brought up velvet-upholstered chairs. Bushell didn't like the arrangement—it smacked of civilians vs. police—but could do nothing about it. He sat down. The chair's upholstery enfolded him, almost like a lover's embrace.

Sir Horace Bragg laughed. "We'd best get down to business, Your Excellency, because if we sit quietly here for long, these chairs are plenty comfortable enough to sleep in." Having put his fundament at the none-too-tender mercy of a hard, wooden swivel chair the night before, Bushell could only nod.

"The business is simple, but unpleasing," Sir Martin Luther King said. "Do we pay the Sons of Liberty their ransom, or do we say be damned to them? Neither course seems appetizing."

"Were it up to me, I'd not give them a farthing," Bushell said. Bragg sent him a surprised look; he seldom threw his opinion out with such reckless abandon.

"You'd let *The Two Georges* be destroyed?" Sir David Clarke said, shock in his voice. He put a little too much shock there, like an actor overemoting on stage. Bushell had been sure Sir David would oppose him—and sound shocked doing it—no matter what he said.

He answered, "Yes, I would. Why not? It would show the Sons of Liberty up for what they are: a pack of bloody-minded know-nothings who care only for themselves, not the NAU. As for *The Two Georges*, it's very fine, but there's more to bind the NAU to England than a stretch of oil paint on canvas. People know it, too."

"You have no understanding of symbolism," Clarke said.

"Maybe not, but I understand what giving the Sons of Liberty fifty million pounds will do. I understand that all too well." Bushell leaned forward in his chair, even though it did not seem to want to let him go. "And if you make one more smart crack, you'll regret it for a long time."

Sir Horace Bragg held up a hand. "Gentlemen, please—this is not quite an either-or proposition. We can negotiate with the Sons of Liberty for the picture's safe return while we keep on trying to find it. Should our investigation prove fruitless as the deadline approaches, we can then decide what we ought to do next."

"However attractive that may seem, it may also prove impracticable," Sir David said. "Suppose the Sons of Liberty demand, as a condition for the safe return of *The Two Georges*, that we cease our search for it until the ransom be paid? Such a proviso, I fear, strikes me as all too likely."

Bushell waited for Sir Horace to knock that into a cocked hat. When his superior sat silent, he gave Sir David Clarke his own answer: "Bugger the Sons of Liberty and what they want."

Sir Martin Luther King had let the other men wrangle; he'd listened, fingers steepled, face inscrutable. Now he spoke for the first time: "Come what may, investigation into the theft shall continue. The Sons of Liberty would assume we made any pledge to refrain under duress, and that we would clandestinely break it whenever opportunity presented itself. They would not, in my judgment, hold such investigation against us despite their rhetoric to the contrary."

"There is that, of course," Sir David said. Flexible as a stem of grass, he bent to his chief's opinion, whatever it might be.

"I can tell you one thing I'd like to see investigated, Your Excellency," Bushell said, "and that's how the Sons learned the King-Emperor was coming to the NAU. It can't be a coincidence that the date they set for their deadline is one day away from the one on which His Majesty reaches Victoria. If we pay the ransom then, our humiliation is at its peak. If we don't pay, they'll greet Charles III by destroying the painting. *How did they know?*" By the way he scowled at Sir David Clarke, he had one possible answer in mind.

Clarke glared back. "See here, sir," he said angrily, "I find your demeanor insulting." Bushell folded his arms and said nothing, relishing the moment. Dueling was illegal in Upper California, as it had been in every province of the NAU for many years. Nevertheless, it did happen now and again. If Sir David said one more word, it would constitute a challenge. As challenged party, Bushell would choose pistols—and blow off Sir David's handsome head.

"If we fight among ourselves, gentlemen, the only gainers are the Sons of Liberty," Sir Horace Bragg said. "If it suits Your Excellency, I will take personal charge of finding out how—or *if*, if you'd prefer, Sir David—the Sons learned His Majesty was sailing to this side of the Atlantic on that particular date."

"Please do, and I thank you," Sir Martin said. "As you rightly pointed out, personal animosities serve no helpful purpose here."

"You're right, of course, Your Excellency," Bushell said. "I apologize to you for the inconvenience I may have caused." He did not apologize to Sir David Clarke.

"I have but one reservation, and that purely hypothetical, in regard to Sir Horace's undertaking this investigation," Sir David said. "If he is the guilty party, he would naturally be able to suppress that fact."

Bushell sprang to his feet. Had the table not stood between him and Sir David, he would have gone for the bigger man's throat. *Easy*, he told himself. And it would be easy, all too easy, for the real hatred he bore Sir David to turn on him and wreck everything he'd been trying to do here. *Use the rage, don't let it use you.* "Listen to me, Clarke," he hissed, all but spitting the unadorned surname, "you've already done your worst as far as I'm concerned, but if you start smearing tar on my friends, I'll give you a thrashing to make the last one you got seem like a pat on the cheek. Do you hear me?"

"For God's sake, Tom, sit down," Sir Horace Bragg said, reaching out to take his arm and restrain him at need. "I'm not insulted, and there's no call for you to be insulted on my behalf. Sir David said he was speaking hypothetically. He would be failing His Excellency if he didn't examine all possibilities."

"Quite," Sir Martin Luther King said, his voice icy. "Please sit down, Colonel. You are most definitely out of order."

Like a dirigible unable to stay airborne because of a leak, Bushell sank slowly back into his seat. He knew what he had to do next. And if it was to be done, it had to be done well. Looking Clarke in the eye, he said, "Sir David, I apologize for my violent, intemperate remarks." Every word came out burning like vitriol.

"Let it pass," Sir David Clarke said. "We are not friends, and we shall not be friends: I understand that. Your loyalty to a man who is your friend deserves nothing but commendation."

If anything, giving Sir David the chance to be magnanimous at his expense hurt worse than apologizing. Sir Horace Bragg pulled the meeting back toward the purpose for which it had been called: "Your Excellency, let us suppose it draws near the middle of August. His Majesty the King-Emperor is on the high seas, sailing nearer to Victoria day by day. Despite our best efforts, we have not succeeded in recovering *The Two Georges*. What then? Do we pay what the Sons of Liberty demand? Or do we cast defiance in their face?"

Bushell knew his answer. He'd already given it. But then he'd proceeded to discredit that answer by his own conduct, just as the actions of the Sons of Liberty discredited what they called patriotism. That was more humiliating even than Sir David's magnanimity. As Sir Horace had said, a public servant should have a certain rudimentary feel for politics.

Sir Martin Luther King looked unhappy. No politico enjoyed being put on the spot. But no man of sense—which Sir Martin certainly was—faced the future without a plan. Reluctantly, the governor-general said, "If worse comes to worst, Sir Horace, my thought is to pay the ransom, recover the painting, and then bend every effort toward capturing those responsible for the theft and regaining the money. They may get their ransom, but they shall not employ it."

Sir David Clarke beamed as if his favorite football club had just won the All-Empire Cup. Sir Horace Bragg, by contrast, was utterly expressionless. "I shall conduct myself according to your decision, Your Excellency," he said, his voice empty.

"And you, Colonel Bushell?" Sir Martin asked. He was justly proud of his powers of persuasion, and wanted everyone to be happy with his choices once he'd made them.

"Your Excellency, you represent His Majesty in North America, so of course I shall obey your orders," Bushell said. Even now, though, he would not leave well enough alone: "If you're asking my personal opinion, however, I believe you are making a dreadful mistake. If you once treat with these bandits and murderers, you and your successors will have to do it again and again for the next hundred years."

"Thank you for expressing your views so forthrightly, Colonel." Sir Martin's tone was anything but grateful. He got to his feet. "I think everything that needs saying for the moment has been said." Bushell would have bet he thought a good deal more than needed saying had been said. The formalities as the meeting broke up were perfunctory at best.

Walking back to RAM headquarters, Sir Horace Bragg sadly shook his head. "You do look for new and different ways to stick your foot in it, don't you, Tom?"

"If you mean I won't say chalk is cheese just because someone wants me to, you're right," Bushell said. "You didn't seem any too happy with the notion of ransom, either. What policeman would?"

"Even if we have to pay it, it may work out all right." Bragg sounded like a man trying to convince himself. "One thing's sure: if the Sons start spending sterling like a sailor home from six months at sea, they'll every one of them be wearing the broad arrow in short order."

"That's so," Bushell said, "but if they were stupid enough to do that, they'd not be the problem they are." He walked on a few paces in silence, then changed the subject: "Just how long do you expect to be heading up the investigation here in New Liverpool, sir?"

"A fortnight or so at most, as I said before," Sir Horace answered. "Why?"

"Just wondering, sir," Bushell answered innocently.

▼

At a little past nine the next morning, Bushell walked into Major Gordon Rhodes's office. That he'd had a decent night's sleep was shown by the gently steaming cup of tea he held in his hand. He was unsurprised to find Samuel Stanley huddled with Rhodes over their charts. Both men glanced up as he came in and shut the door behind himself.

"Uh-oh," Stanley said. "I don't like the look on your face, Chief."

Bushell could not see the expression he was wearing, but had no trouble figuring out what it was. "I don't like it, either," he said. "Now, gentlemen, I want your promise that what I'm going to tell you will not go beyond this room."

Stanley nodded at once, Rhodes after a moment's hesitation. Bushell did not think ill of him for that pause; he was visibly deciding whether he could in good conscience make such a promise. "Go ahead, sir," he said at last.

"I met with Sir Horace, Sir Martin, and his chief of staff yesterday," Bushell began, unwilling even to name Sir David Clarke. He explained what Sir Martin had decided to do, and also how long Sir Horace was likely to stay in New Liverpool to head up the investigation.

When he was through, Samuel Stanley's face twisted. "Paying ransom," he said, as if someone had dropped a large, dead, stinking fish in front of him. "You just can't do anything worse than that."

"You're right, Sam," Rhodes said. "You beat me to it, that's all."

"You both knew it, and I know it, and Sir Horace knows it, too, but the politicos don't know it, and that ties Sir Horace's hands, and that ties ours," Bushell said. "The only thing I can think of to do is to make sure *The Two Georges* is safe before the deadline gets here. I can't do everything I would be doing to make sure we recover the painting, because Sir Horace will be doing most of those things himself. I am not going to let myself be taken out of this game, either. I'm responsible for *The Two Georges'* going missing, and I'm not about to sit on the shelf while it's being found."

"What will you do, Chief?" Stanley asked. "What *can* you do, in a fix like that?"

Bushell's smile was half predatory, half beatific. "For some reason or other, Sir Martin's chief of staff and I had a disagreement yesterday. I don't think Sir Martin is happy with me for that, or for saying I didn't want to ransom *The Two Georges*. If I suggest that I go off investigating at places far, far away from New Liverpool, I doubt the prospect will break His Excellency the governor-general's heart. In fact, I think he'll leap to say yes before I change my mind. And that, by God, will get me out from under Sir Horace's thumb."

"And let you do what you wanted to do all along," Stanley said admiringly. "Tell me, did you pick the fight with Sir David on purpose?"

"Who, me?" Bushell said, as if in surprise. "But he is a piece of work, that one. He even had the cheek to insult Sir Horace, for no better reason than to bait me." Scowling, he shook his head again, then turned to Major Rhodes. "When I go into the field, Gordon, the weight of coordinating the investigation will fall even more heavily on you. You'll be Sir Horace's prop, that's certain. You may have to be his brains as well; I have no notion of how good he is at casework these days."

"I can see where you might be worried, sir, but I think I can handle it," Gordon Rhodes said, without arrogance but also without false modesty. He would have been doing most of the job under Bushell; now he might be doing more still, but his shoulders seemed wide enough to carry the weight.

Bushell clapped him on one of those shoulders. "Stout fellow!" He resolved to do something to get Rhodes a promotion when this mess finally ended. What with the political odor he was in at the moment, the best thing he might be able to do for the up-and-coming major was to stay as far away from him as possible. Well, he was taking care of that.

Sir Horace Bragg had been installed in an office not far from Rhodes's; the two captains who had shared it were now squatting with a couple of other officers of similarly unexalted rank. "Good morning, Tom," Bragg said, looking up from a copy of the *New Liverpool Tory*. Like all the other dailies, the conservative newspaper headlined the Sons' demand for fifty million pounds. Bragg neatly folded the paper and set it on his desk. "What can I do for you?"

"You can say good-bye, sir, and wish me luck," Bushell said.

Behind his reading glasses, Bragg's eyes widened. He peered over the rims of the spectacles to see Bushell clearly. "My God, Tom, you're not so upset about yesterday that you're quitting on me?" he said, something like horror in his voice.

"Quitting on you? No, sir," Bushell answered. A great many things had passed through his mind since *The Two Georges* was stolen, but resigning from the RAMs was not among them. He explained what he did have in mind.

Sir Horace took off his glasses and set them atop the *Tory*. His usually doleful expression grew even more so. "I know why you want to leave, but please reconsider," he said. "If you go gallivanting off into the wilderness, it will be like cutting off my right hand here."

"I'm sorry, sir, but I don't see it that way," Bushell answered. "With you here, I don't have either enough work or enough responsibility to make staying worth my while. From where I stand, I'm not your right hand now; I'm put away on a shelf. I can't bear that."

"Then I'll go back to Victoria," Sir Horace said, getting up from his chair as if he intended to start walking that very instant. "I'll stay in overall charge of the case from the capital, but the day-to-day search here will be in your hands."

"That's—extraordinarily generous of you, sir," Bushell said, touched at the confidence his old friend and present superior vested in him. But, gently, he continued, "It's impossible, though, and you know it as well as I do. After yesterday afternoon, Sir Martin would never let you go away and leave me at the top of the tree here—and if the thought even crossed his mind, Sir David would talk him out of it."

"I'll speak to Sir Martin—" Bragg's voice stumbled and faltered. He didn't imagine he could change the governor-general's mind, either. He glared at Bushell. "I'm sorrier than I can say that you feel the need to do this, Tom. I would have stayed home had I thought my coming here would make you want to leave. But since you do, I wish you Godspeed and good luck." He stuck out his hand.

Bushell took it, squeezed hard. "Thank you, sir. I'll bring that painting back." Without waiting for Sir Horace's reply, he turned and left the office. He hadn't even got to the hall before a wide smile spread over his face. He'd been difficult, he'd been stubborn, and he'd got away with it.

▼

He hadn't been up in his own office long before someone tapped on the door frame. He looked up from paperwork to find Lieutenant-Colonel Felix Crooke standing there. "Yes?" Bushell asked, wondering if Sir Horace had sent up the expert on the Sons of Liberty to try to change his mind.

"Lieutenant General Bragg tells me you'll be leaving New Liverpool to pursue your investigation of the theft," Crooke began. Bushell nodded cautious agreement, still not sure what the RAM from Victoria had in mind. Then Crooke's very blue eyes kindled. "Would you be so kind as to consider letting me accompany you, sir? When I bearded Sir Horace about it, he didn't look happy, but—"

"—Then again, he never looks happy," Bushell finished.

"Well, yes," Crooke beamed. "In the end, he gave his permission: said he would have told me no if he could, but he didn't see the way to do it."

"He told me very much the same thing, but he didn't find a way to say no to me, either," Bushell answered. "There's a certain freedom you find when you defy authority and pull it off, isn't there?"

"Yes, sir," Felix Crooke said enthusiastically.

"I'd be delighted to have you along," Bushell said, warming to that enthusiasm. "Do you have the gear you'll need? We may be going into rugged country now and again, and I aim to leave New Liverpool tomorrow, by airship if possible. I've no idea how long we'll be gone."

"What I don't have, I'll beg, borrow, or buy when we get where we're going," Crooke replied. He hesitated. "Where are we going?"

"First stop I have in mind is Skidegate," Bushell said. Crooke nodded; he remembered where the little town was. Bushell went on, "From there, I have no idea. With luck, either we'll find leads there or more will turn up here to give us our direction." Without luck, he'd be stuck on the Queen Charlotte Islands utterly devoid of ideas, a notion he found too depressing to contemplate.

Felix Crooke must have felt the same way. "Capital!" he exclaimed. "I shall have to lay in a mackintosh, then, or something of the sort. I didn't think I'd need one, coming to New Liverpool in June."

"I expect we'll be able to fit you out with one here at headquarters," Bushell said. "It does rain in New Liverpool, though not in June. I have one question: did you bring a weapon with you?"

"A weapon?" Crooke stared at him as if he'd suddenly started speaking Finnish. "Colonel, I tell you honestly, the thought never once crossed my mind."

"Well it bloody well should, for this jaunt," Bushell said. "The Sons killed Tricky Dick with a rifle. They've been shipping more rifles into New Liverpool, how many God only knows. One of the men who actually lifted *The Two Georges* menaced the guards with a pistol. These are not chaps who play by the rules."

"You're right, of course, and I thank you for reminding me," Crooke murmured. "The need would never have occurred to me if you hadn't. Even the Sons don't, or rather didn't, commonly go in for firearms. Can I draw a revolver from your armorer?"

"If you can't, we'll have a new armorer this time tomorrow."

Felix Crooke smiled. "Capital!" he said again, and looked excited, from which Bushell concluded he'd never been under fire. "Where do I find the gentleman?" Bushell gave him directions. He set off with a spring in his step. Bushell envied him his innocence.

The RAM chief was pounding away on the typewriter when another knock made him spin in his chair. Samuel Stanley had already stridden into the office and now shut the door behind him. Bushell studied his face, then said, "All right, Sam, what's gone wrong this time?"

"Sir, I have a favor to ask of you." Stanley sounded so solemn and formal, dread grew to flower in Bushell's heart. He didn't remember the last time his adjutant had called him *sir*, as opposed to *chief*, when the two of them were alone together.

"Whatever you need," he said expansively. Only after the words were out of his mouth did he remember the trouble Herodotus said Xerxes the Persian king had found for himself with a similar rash promise. The trouble with a classic education was that you commonly didn't remember the wise precepts you'd picked up till it was too late to use them.

But Samuel Stanley, instead of asking for the moon, the stars, or something equally unattainable, said, "Sir, when you go after *The Two Georges*, please take me with you."

"You're the second one to ask me that in the past couple of hours," Bushell said, bemused. "I just said yes to Lieutenant-Colonel Crooke, but why you? I'd counted on your staying here to help Gordon Rhodes keep things running steady while Sir Horace is at the helm."

"Sir, I'd be just as much spare baggage under Major Rhodes as you are under Lieutenant General Sir Horace Bragg."

"I'm sorry, Sam, but that doesn't strike me as reason enough," Bushell said. "There'll be plenty down here for you to do, and—forgive me—you're not having your command taken away from you, as I am."

"Oh, I understand all that, sir." Stanley looked as miserable as Bushell had ever seen him. "I don't really know how to explain the problem to you."

"You'd better try. Forgive me again, but you're not making much sense now."

"I know, sir. Part of the trouble is, you and Sir Horace, you've been friends a long time, and you and I, we've been friends a long time, too. But it doesn't follow from that—" Samuel Stanley turned away. "Forget I ever asked you, sir. I shouldn't have come up here. I see that now."

"No, wait—don't go," Bushell said. His adjutant halted with obvious reluctance. Bushell said, "It doesn't follow that . . ." His voice trailed off, though not in the same way Stanley's had. He'd just been thinking about classical allusions. Classical logic had its place, too. "It doesn't follow from my being friends with you and Sir Horace both that you and he are friends with each other. Is that what you're saying?"

"Yes, sir," Stanley answered unhappily.

"Well, I can see that," Bushell said. "His family used to be aristocrats some generations back, to hear him tell it, but he's the first Bragg in a long time to amount to much. In his own fashion, I suppose, he's been almost as driven to make good as old Tricky Dick. It never much bothered me, but I can see how it might set your teeth on edge. Is that what's troubling you?"

"That's—some of it, Chief." When Samuel Stanley used the more familiar title, Bushell knew a good deal of relief. After a moment's hesitation, Stanley added, "Most people now, they've let go of those plantation days. Sometimes I think Sir Horace wouldn't mind seeing them back."

"If he has a successful term as RAM commandant, he may end up with a patent of nobility to pass down to his eldest son." Bushell had a sudden burst of insight. "That's probably one of the reasons he's so worried about this case. If *The Two Georges* is gone for good, he'll never be a baronet, much less a baron."

"As may be, Chief. But I wouldn't be doing all I should for the case if I stayed here. A lot of people can fill in for me with Major Rhodes. You, Chief, you're going to need all the help you can get."

"God knows that's true." Bushell stabbed a forefinger out at his friend. "What will Phyllis have to say about your taking off for parts unknown for only heaven can guess how long?"

"Phyllis knows about the trouble I have with Sir Horace," Stanley answered quietly. "She'll understand why I need to do this."

"Which is still more than I do," Bushell said. Sam Stanley sounded very sure about his wife's views, which surprised Bushell; his adjutant usually left work behind at the office. If he'd been talking about Bragg with Phyllis, the RAM commandant was indeed on his mind. Bushell threw his hands in the air. "All right, Sam, you've argued me down."

"That's first-rate, Chief," Stanley said. "Now: details. Do you want to go by train or airship?"

"Airship's faster, at least up to Wellesley on the Puget Sound," Bushell answered. "I've been making inquiries, as you'll gather. They won't fly dirigibles north of the Puget Sound: the winds make safe passage too risky. We go by train up to Prince Rupert and then by ship across to Skidegate. There's an airship leaving for Wellesley at eight o'clock tomorrow morning, so I'll see you at the port then. I'll call and book another stateroom for you."

"Very good, Chief. That'd be the *Empire Builder*, wouldn't it?"

"Yes, as a matter of fact, it would." Bushell paused and gave his adjutant a suspicious stare. "You've been checking up on this yourself." He laughed at how accusatory he sounded.

"Guilty as charged," Samuel Stanley said, laughing, too. He abruptly grew serious again. "You're going to want us to go armed, aren't you?"

"I'm damned glad you think straight, Sam," Bushell said. "Felix Crooke gaped at me as if I'd just grown a second head when I suggested that he draw a pistol from the armorer. After he thought for a bit, he conceded the need, but he never would have seen it for himself."

"Not an army man, then," Stanley judged. "You get shot at once or twice, you don't want the other fellow to have himself a gun when you're without one. I wish I had a rifle to bring along; going up against a Nagant with a revolver isn't my idea of a pleasant holiday, either." He shrugged. "At a pinch, I suppose we can borrow longarms from the navy chaps."

"I hope it doesn't come to that." Bushell reached for the telephone. "Go on, get out of here now that you've had your way with me. I'll book that stateroom—and I'll see you in the morning."

"Right you are, Chief." Stanley closed the door behind him as he left.

Bushell called Sunset Airships, Ltd., and confirmed a stateroom for Samuel Stanley. Then he leaned back in his seat, put his hands behind his head, and laced his fingers. He took a deep breath, let it out. Almost for the first time since *The Two Georges* was stolen, he had a moment to think of something else.

After a few seconds, he sat up straight again and unlocked the upper right-hand drawer of his desk. He picked up the pint of Jameson, looked at it, and set it on the floor by the desk. Then he turned over the framed photograph of Irene.

Her black-and-white image smiled sunnily up at him: dark hair, light eyes, wide, happy mouth in a pleasantly plump face. Her hair was cut in the shingle bangs that had been the height of style ten years before, when the photograph was taken. Even after he came out to New Liverpool, he'd hung her portrait on the wall below the print of *The Two Georges* until, at last, he could bear to look at her no more.

"Why?" he asked the flat, blank, dead photo.

Getting no reply, he turned it facedown once more. He picked up the whiskey bottle, yanked out the stopper, and gulped down a long harsh swallow. Then he closed it and stuck it back in the drawer, which he locked. The whiskey burning in him, he went back to work.

▼

The airship port was cool and foggy. The sun might not burn through for several hours yet. The rolling mist now revealed, now hid the dirigibles at the mooring towers. The leviathans of the air reminded Bushell of the great whales of the Pacific, yet were vaster by far than any creatures of mere flesh and blood.

He pushed the baggage cart he'd hired for a florin toward the *Empire Builder*, which, by luck, was moored at the tower closest to the garage where he'd parked his steamer. Men and women were already ascending the stairway to the passenger gondola. The airship would depart in less than a half an hour.

A Negro clerk carefully examined Bushell's ticket and checked his name off on the passenger list. "You'll be in stateroom twelve, sir," he said. "Stateroom twelve is on the starboard side. Turn right once you go up the stairs, then left at the first hallway. Your stateroom will be the third one on the left. Here is your key—yes, this is number twelve. I hope you have a pleasant flight."

"Thank you," Bushell said, smiling a little at the man's fussy precision. He handed his bags to a muscular fellow with green eyes, carroty hair, and a face full of freckles.

The loader started to haul them up the ladder to the baggage compartment, then stopped and looked back at Bushell. "You're the chap trying to get *The Two Georges* back, ain't you, sir?" he asked.

"So I am," Bushell said. He was glad no reporters had got wind of his imminent departure.

"Hope you find it, sir, and catch the ones what took it, too," the loader said. "Right bunch o' bastards they are, you ask me." His large, knobby-knuckled hands curled into fists. Bushell sent him a grateful smile; he was always delighted when such an obvious Irishman showed his loyalty to King-Emperor and country.

The Negro clerk, however, sniffed and said, "Please don't vex the passengers with conversation, O'Leary." The loader brushed a forefinger to the bill of his cap to show he'd understood and would obey.

"I wasn't vexed," Bushell said. The clerk looked through him as if he hadn't spoken. Plainly, the fixed policy of Sunset Airships, Ltd., took precedence over the whim of any one traveler.

The brief delay let Felix Crooke come up to join Bushell. He was carrying his bags himself. "Bloody fog!" he said. "The cabby I hired lost his way twice. I was afraid you'd have to depart without me. This isn't the weather for which New Liverpool is famous, you know." He looked at Bushell as if holding him personally responsible.

"It's often like this in June," Bushell answered. "By the way, Sam Stanley, whom you will have met, is accompanying us on our flight north." He turned to the clerk, who was droning through the formalities of Crooke's finding his stateroom. "Could you tell me if Samuel Stanley is abroad the airship yet?"

The Negro made a point of finishing his business with Felix Crooke before deigning to consult the passenger list for Stanley's name. At last he said, "Yes, sir, that gentleman has checked in." He made it sound as if the admission had been forced from him by a clever barrister in a court of law.

One after the other, Bushell and Crooke climbed the detachable stairway to the passenger gondola. A Nuevespañolan steward in a morning coat stood at the entrance to make sure they did not stumble.

"I'm going to my room," Crooke said. "How about you, sir?"

"I like to watch takeoffs from the lounge," Bushell answered. "Probably won't be much to see today, what with this mist, but you never can tell."

Signs led him to the lounge; as on the *Upper California Limited*, it lay on the starboard side of the gondola, though some airship lines preferred to put it to port. As he'd expected, Bushell found himself alone in the hall that led to the lounge entrance. Watching gray tendrils of fog swirl around the *Empire Builder* as it rose was not a pastime which held mass appeal.

But he would not be alone in the lounge: he realized that as he neared the door. Someone was playing the piano in there—quite well, too. Bushell set his jaw before he went in; "I Remember Your Name," a sentimental favorite from two decades before, had been the song he and Irene always thought of as theirs. Whenever he heard it now, it was a dash of salt in the wound that never quite seemed to close.

"I Remember Your Name" came to a sudden, jangling halt when Bushell walked into the lounge. Samuel Stanley sprang up from the piano bench, guilt and worry on his face. "I'm sorry, Chief," he said quickly. "Been too long since we've flown together, dammit. I forgot you've got the lounge habit, too."

"It's all right," Bushell said. "Go ahead and play it, Sam. You might as well take it all the way through to the end. I know how it goes."

"But—" Stanley bit his lip. Now he was wrong whether he finished the song or he didn't. At last, unhappily, he sat back down and hurried through the last part of it. His mind wasn't on his playing; he made more fluffs in those few bars than he usually did in a week, and finished with obvious relief.

Bushell sat down on a rattan chair. In keeping with its name, the lounge of the *Empire Builder* had an East Indian theme. The furniture was of rattan and teak, with bright, intricately patterned cushions. Carpets from Armritsar and Bangalore covered the floor, some with elaborate Urdu calligraphy. On the walls, British soldiers in pith helmets and red uniforms of bygone days rode to battle atop war elephants.

A middle-aged man, an elderly woman in the black dress and veil of mourning, and a young man in checked trousers came into the lounge one by one. Politely reserved, they sat well apart from one another and from Bushell and Stanley. The young man asked the woman whether she minded him smoking. When she waved permission, he lit up a meerschaum.

Bushell drew out his pocket watch. At seven minutes of eight, the pumps began draining the airship's ballast chambers. Less than a minute later, the middle-aged man hastily left the lounge. Sam Stanley caught Bushell's eye. Neither of them laughed or even smiled, but each enjoyed the other's amusement.

At two minutes of eight, the airship's motors started up. The low roar filled the lounge. The overhead speaker crackled to life: "This is your captain, ladies and gentlemen. We will be taking off momentarily, and I advise you to find a seat if you'd be so kind. The nose of the airship will rise a bit, which means the floor will tilt until we reach our cruising height of fifteen hundred feet. Thank you, and I hope you'll all have a pleasant flight with us today aboard the *Empire Builder*."

A snap Bushell felt as much as he heard announced the release from the mooring tower. For a moment, the dirigible simply floated in the air. The motors began to work harder. Mist swirled away as the *Empire Builder* began moving through it. As the captain had warned, the floor did tilt, but not to any great degree. Soon Bushell could see only gray all around; the airship might have been packed in dirty cotton batting.

After a few minutes, the rate of climb leveled off. A steward came around with tea and coffee. Bushell chose Darjeeling, Stanley Irish Breakfast. The steward said, "We shall be serving breakfast in the dining area beginning at a quarter of nine, gentlemen."

"Nothing but fog today, I'm afraid," Stanley said, waving at the gloomy prospect outside the observation windows. "You might as well have gone to your stateroom." By his tone, he wished Bushell had gone to the stateroom. Then he could have played "I Remember Your Name" without embarrassment.

"It doesn't matter, Sam," Bushell answered. He didn't know himself whether he meant the mist or the song. After a moment, he lowered his voice and went on, "For the rest of this trip, I think I'd best be just Tom and Lieutenant-Colonel Crooke Felix. Too many people have heard my rank and surname, and maybe yours and his, too."

"Incognito we shall be—Tom," Stanley agreed, and laughed at the hitch he'd put in what should have been a smooth sentence. "I'll have to work to remember that," he added seriously, his face full of concentration. "The habit of subordination is hard to break."

"True enough," Bushell said, taking out a cigar. "I've known Lieutenant General Sir Horace Bragg what seems like a thousand years now, and I count him a good friend even if you don't. But whenever we talk, on duty or off, he's always *sir*, and whenever I talk about him he's *Sir Horace* or *Lieutenant General Bragg*, not plain old *Horace*."

Whatever Stanley thought about Bushell's friendship with Sir Horace, he kept it to himself, saying, "Ah, but you have it easiest here—Tom." He paused again, and ruefully shook his head at the blunder before continuing. "Superiors can call inferiors by their Christian names, but not the other way round. You're used to going *Sam* and *Felix*, but we aren't used to *Tom*."

"By the time we finish this case, I expect you will be," Bushell answered.

When he'd smoked the cigar down to a short butt, he stubbed it out and went with Samuel Stanley to the airship's dining room. Felix Crooke was already there, holding a couple of seats against the polite protests of the waiters. "Good thing you came to my rescue, sir," he said to Bushell. "I was beginning to fear they'd heave me over the side."

"Can't have that," Bushell said gravely. "Now as for this *sir* business—" He explained his notion to Crooke.

"Very sensible," the RAM from Victoria said at once. "The less public we can keep the investigation, the better it will go and the happier we all shall be." Courteously, he turned to Stanley. "Don't you agree, Sam?"

"Absolutely, Lieu—uh, Felix," Stanley said, following the flub with a muffled "Dammit!" All three RAMs laughed.

"Good to see you gentlemen in such fine humor this morning," a waiter said, coming over to their table with pencil poised above notepad. "And what would you care to have for breakfast?"

"Eggs Benedict for me, please," Bushell said. "Since I'm here, I have every intention of enjoying myself."

"An excellent notion," the waiter said. He nodded to Samuel Stanley. "And you, sir?"

"I want four rashers of bacon cooked very crisp, with toast and marmalade alongside."

"Very good, sir." The waiter wrote it down, then looked a question to Felix Crooke.

Crooke coughed a couple of times. "I don't see it on the menu, but could you grill me a bloater and serve it up with mashed potatoes?"

The waiter almost lost his professional impassivity at that emphatically proletarian choice, but said, "I shall enquire of the chef, sir. We do endeavor to satisfy every taste." He was shaking his head as he walked back toward the kitchen.

"I like bloaters," Crooke said defensively. "I've been eating them since I was a boy, and I still do, every chance I get."

"I didn't say a thing," Bushell replied. "Did you say anything, Sam?"

"Me? Not a word," Stanley said solemnly. "Felix, if fancying bloaters for breakfast is the craziest thing you do, then you're one of the saner men I've met."

"He doesn't say *present company included*, mind you," Bushell put in, pointing to himself, "but he's thinking it, never fear. Your adjutant is like your valet: he knows you too well to give anything near the amount of respect you think you deserve."

"I like that, by God." Felix Crooke made silent clapping motions. "Given half a chance, I expect I'll steal it. I tell you openly, you see, for I'm a brazen thief."

"That's how you got to be our chief student of the Sons of Liberty, is it?" Bushell shot back. "They set you after them because they know you thought the same way?"

Samuel Stanley struck an injured pose "The two of you are going at each other so hard and fast, I didn't get to say I thought Tom was spouting rubbish."

"Your mother trained you up right, Sam, and taught you not to interrupt," Bushell said. "Now you're suffering for it." All three men were smiling broadly. Bushell hadn't known how Crooke would fit in with Stanley and himself, but a man who could take banter and give it back promised to be easy to work with.

The waiter returned with three covered plates on a tray. "Your eggs, sir," he said, setting one in front of Bushell and removing the metal lid with a flourish. Bushell smiled in anticipation as the poached eggs, smothered in rich hollandaise sauce and topping ham and muffins, were revealed. The waiter gave Sam Stanley his bacon and toast, then turned to Felix Crooke. "Here is your bloater and mash, sir. I am told the chef does keep them on hand, as several of our engine mechanics have a fondness for them."

*So there*, Bushell thought. Crooke might as well not have heard the waiter's editorial remark. He gazed on the large, lightly smoked herring with pleasure unalloyed. Steam rose from it and from the large mound of fluffy potatoes with which it shared the plate. He sprinkled the potatoes with salt and pepper, then dug in.

The bloater's strong odor distracted Bushell from his own more delicate breakfast, but only till he took the first bite. After that, nothing short of the airship's falling into the sea could have made his attention waver from the food.

▼

The *Empire Builder* reached Drakestown just past one in the afternoon, within a few minutes of its scheduled arrival. By then, the sun had long since succeeded in burning away the morning mist. It sparkled off the little waves in San Francisco Bay, which somehow had not changed its name when Upper California passed from Franco-Spanish to British possession.

The bay was full of ships, not only those of the Royal Navy and Royal North American Navy but also merchant vessels flying every flag in the world and a great multitude of ferryboats traveling back and forth between Drakestown and the smaller cities on the eastern shore of the bay.

Bushell watched the ferries for a while, then turned to Samuel Stanley and asked, "Do you think they'll ever bridge the bay? They've been talking about it since I was a boy—do you remember the drawings in the supplements to the Sunday papers?"

"As if you were looking down from an airship, with all the steamers on the bridge as tiny as ants?" Stanley said, nodding. "I think everyone remembers those. A few years ago, I would have said it might happen. But after that last earthquake? How would you like to be *on* a bridge going across the bay when the ground started shaking?"

"No, thank you," Bushell said. "Getting through an earthquake while you're on solid ground is bad enough, if you ask me. I suppose you're right; and the ferryboats do a good enough job, by all accounts. Still, a bridge that size would have been grand to see, don't you think?"

"For as long as it stood, yes." Listening to Stanley, anyone would have pegged him at once for a veteran sergeant or a police officer. He had a deep and abiding faith that things would go wrong.

The *Empire Builder* dropped its mooring lines. With the help of the ground crew at Drakestown's airship port, it locked itself to a mooring tower to disembark some passengers and take on others, along with fuel and water for ballast. By half past two it was airborne again, swaying a little in a crosswind from the west.

Before sunset, it crossed from Upper California into the larger but more sparsely settled province of Oregon. "Are we scheduled to stop at West Boston on the way up to Wellesley?" Felix Crooke asked.

"On the Columbia, you mean?" Bushell said. "Yes, I believe we are. It's a nice enough town; I've been there once or twice." The last time had been the mission from which he'd decided to come home early. To keep from thinking about that again, he went on, "Did you know it was almost called West Portland? The first settlers were Massachusetts men, and they spun a shilling, or so the story goes, to see after which of their towns they'd name this one."

"I looked at the itinerary in my stateroom," Samuel Stanley said. "We're supposed to stop at West Boston from ten o'clock to just before midnight. We get into Wellesley at a little past four tomorrow morning." He rolled his eyes to show what he thought of that.

"Good," Bushell said, which made both the other RAMs stare at him. He explained: "God willing, at that heathen hour all the reporters will be sleeping peacefully in their nice, warm beds."

"At that heathen hour, I want to be sleeping peacefully in *my* nice, warm bed," Felix Crooke said feelingly.

Bushell sought his own nice, warm bed not long after supper. He was far enough behind on sleep not to mind going to bed early, especially when he knew he'd have to rise early, too.

The captain's voice from the ceiling speaker woke him from a dream in which *The Two Georges* had somehow stolen Sir Horace Bragg and was holding him for ransom: "Ladies and gentlemen, I am sorry to do this to you, but I have to let you know we will be arriving in Wellesley in half an hour. Please do prepare for departure. Thank you." A hiss of static, and the speaker went dead.

Bushell yawned, knuckled his eyes, and groped for the light switch beside his bed. He found it, clicked on a lamp, and sat up, blinking against the sudden glare. He was pulling off his pyjamas and putting on a suit of dark gray wool when a steward pounded on the door and said, "Landing soon, sir. Are you awake in there?"

"No," Bushell answered as he buttoned his fly.

The steward paused, coughed, chuckled, and said, "Sorry to disturb you, but it has to be done on these early-morning arrivals." He went down the corridor to rap on the next stateroom door. Despite the captain's announcement, despite the stewards' diligence, Bushell was sure somebody would still be sleeping when the *Empire Builder* locked itself to the mooring mast at the Wellesley Municipal Airship Port.

A cup of English Breakfast tea, so strong it was almost bitter, helped him face the prospect of being alert at four in the morning with something like equanimity. Stanley drank English Breakfast, too; Felix Crooke opted for black coffee.

The three RAMs were among the first passengers off the airship once it was safely moored. Before Bushell had taken more than two steps on the ground, a fusillade of flashbulbs went off in his face. "Why are you in Wellesley, Colonel?" somebody shouted. Somebody else yelled, "Will you be staying here?" "Where do you go from here, Colonel Bushell?" a woman's voice bawled.

"I'm sorry, but I have nothing to say," Bushell answered, and repeated that again and again as he and his colleagues claimed their bags and headed for the cab stand at the kerb a couple of hundred yards from the airship. The reporters followed. Some, like cats, followed the RAMs in front of them, and complained almost as bitterly of trod-on toes as of the lack of satisfactory answers for their questions.

Among them, Bushell, Stanley, Crooke, and their gear filled to overflowing the steamer they hired. "Can you get us to the train station without having that pack of vultures on our trail?" Bushell asked, pointing back to the reporters, who were wrangling over who would take which of the other cabs at the stand.

"Do my best, sir," the cabbie answered, and put his vehicle in gear. Bushell leaned back in the seat, aghast at how many reporters had come to meet him and how persistent they were. He'd known the case would be conducted in the glare of publicity, but he'd hoped to be able to escape that glare every now and again. The Sons of Liberty were going to know his every move almost before he made it.

The cab driver, to his great relief, did escape before the pursuit got properly organized. By the time his steamer reached the station—a huge, half-timbered building that resembled nothing so much as a Tudor palace—approaching sunrise was lightening the gray, overcast sky in the east. Bushell tipped him a green ten-shilling note, which sent him on his way with a smile on his face.

Inside the station, a ticket agent confirmed the reservations Bushell had made over the telephone. A stout porter took charge of the RAMs' bags. The police officers went into a small cafe across from their departure platform and ordered breakfast. "I don't want to be sitting out there in the open for those blasted reporters to see," Bushell said. "That would make me a perfect target."

Sure enough, a couple of reporters did come wandering by. One of them even poked his head into the cafe. Bushell kept his own head down and escaped unnoticed.

He and his companions boarded the train as soon as it pulled up to the platform. Samuel Stanley stared in surprise at the informational brochure he pulled from a box mounted on the door near the entry. "Bloody roundabout way of getting from here to Prince Rupert," he said, pointing to a map on the back page of the brochure. It showed the route looping through half the province of Vancouver. "I thought we'd just go straight up the coast."

"Mountains in the way, with no good passes," Bushell said. He read over his adjutant's shoulder as Stanley unfolded the brochure. "When luncheon comes around, I want to try the fish chowder they're talking about. If it's half as good as they make it sound, you can walk on water once you've eaten it."

The chowder—simmered haddock and salt pork with potatoes, onions, and garlic in a broth of rich cream and fish stock—might not have been good enough to serve as a prelude to miracle-working, but it was tasty and filling. The spectacular mountains and pine woods through which the train passed made the long trip worthwhile. A bear pawing at an old stump looked up as the noisy locomotive rolled by, then went back to grubbing for mice or honey or whatever it was after.

They pulled into Prince George, the gateway town to Vancouver province's northwest, about seven that evening. The sun was still high in the sky; at fifty-four degrees north latitude, summer days lingered long. But Prince Rupert was still 450 miles—nine long hours—to the west.

"Another four o'clock arrival," Samuel Stanley said mournfully. "Shame to get into a town at a time when you can't do anything useful there."

"And after that, another six hours by ship to Skidegate," Felix Crooke put in.

"We've had all this time to plan," Bushell said. "When we get there, we go into action." He could hear—he could all but taste—the eagerness in his own voice. To be out and doing—that was why he'd become a RAM in the first place. His last chance might be here now. He intended to make the most of it.

# VĬ

▼

WELCOME TO PRINCE RUPERT, THE HALIBUT CAPITAL OF THE WORLD, said the sign in the train station. A faint fishy odor that persisted through steam and coal smoke and tobacco made it plain that was no idle boast.

So did the bill of fare of the station cafe, which had opened to receive early-arriving passengers while the rest of the town slept on. Along with the usual eggs and sausage and bacon and hot and cold porridges, all quite dear not only because the cafe enjoyed a clientele with few other choices but also because Prince Rupert was as far from where processed foods were produced as any place in the NAU, the menu featured fried halibut, poached halibut, dried and salted halibut, smoked halibut, halibut croquettes, and halibut balls in cream gravy.

Bushell had never before breakfasted on poached halibut, but it was far from bad. "You order this in a fancy restaurant in New Liverpool, it would set you back six or eight quid, not seventeen and a tanner," he said.

"It's good smoked, too," Felix Crooke said. His choice—the nearest thing to a bloater available—did not surprise Bushell. Samuel Stanley, a resolute conservative, worked his way through fried eggs and saveloy sausages.

Twilight brightened as the three men ate. The sun rose early, as it had set late. The cafe boasted a large, west-facing window. From Kaien Island, on which the town of Prince Rupert sat, Bushell looked across Prince Rupert Harbor to Digby Island, which shielded the island from storms. Fishing boats were already putting out to sea. Clouds of gulls wheeled and swirled above them, hoping to scavenge some of the day's catch.

Bigger ships also sat in the harbor: merchantmen to carry coal and grain and lumber brought into Prince Rupert by rail, the ferry that would take Bushell and his comrades across the Hecate Strait to the Queen Charlotte Islands, and several lean, gray frigates and corvettes with four-inch guns, a reminder that Russian Alaska lay not far to the north.

It was about half a mile from the train station down to the harbor, and a light rain was falling. Bushell hired a cab for the journey; walking so far through drizzle carrying heavy bags did not strike him as an appealing prospect. "Going across to the Queen Charlottes, I'll lay," the driver said. "You must have some work with the Royal Navy, eh?"

"You might say that," Bushell answered.

122

"I knew it," the cabman said smugly. "I'm right clever about such things, I am." He was clever enough, apparently, to be one of the few human beings on the face of the earth who did not recognize Bushell. Happy in momentary anonymity, Bushell said not a word to enlighten him.

The ferry, the *Northern Lights*, was smaller and more elderly than the shiny, modern boats that plied the San Francisco Bay. Only a handful of Bushell's fellow train passengers boarded the *Northern Lights*. Most of the men on it wore the bell-bottomed trousers and dark caps of the navy; many of them were muffled in sou'westers or duffel coats against the rain. Their expressions showed them to be less than ecstatic at the prospect of returning to Skidegate.

"To them, Prince Rupert must be bright lights and the big city," Felix Crooke said.

Bushell looked back at the halibut capital of the world. "Poor devils," he said with feeling.

Several of the crewmen of the *Northern Lights* had coppery skins and black, black hair. Every now and then, as they chattered back and forth with one another, they'd use a word or a phrase that didn't sound like English. Bushell wondered if they were some of the Haida Indians of whom Kathleen Flannery had spoken. He also wondered what Kathleen was doing. He hoped she'd gone back to Victoria and, when the latest issue of *Common Sense* arrived in her mailbox, had thrown it straight into the wastepaper basket.

The ferryboat let out a deafening blast from its steam whistle and then, black coal smoke pouring out of its stacks, pulled away from the pier. It steamed around the southern tip of Digby Island and then west across the Hecate Strait toward Skidegate.

Most of the sailors went below; for them, the ocean was a place to work, not something conducive to sightseeing. A couple, perhaps men who had indulged too strenuously in the fleshpots of Prince Rupert (if such there were), leaned far over the lee rail and rid themselves of what ailed them. The passage did not strike Bushell as particularly choppy. He'd expected worse in the northern Pacific.

As the morning advanced, the sun began to break through the low clouds. Samuel Stanley pointed northward. "Look, there's an aeroplane," he said.

One of the ferry's crewmen said, "Nothing to be surprised at, sir, not up here. You'll see 'em all the time, coming back from patrol off the Alaskan coast. They have a field on Digby Island, and another not far from Skidegate, too."

"Ever see any Russian aeroplanes?" Bushell asked as the biplane Stanley had spotted buzzed away toward the east.

"I haven't myself, sir," the sailor answered, "but I hear tell they've landed at our fields a time or two, when they had engine trouble and couldn't get home. They fly patrol same as we do, after all; I reckon our flying machines have used their fields every once in a while, too. Up here, the wind and the ocean are worse enemies than the Russians and us are to each other."

*That's what you think.* Bushell, Stanley, and Crooke met one another's eyes, each with the same thing in his mind. None of them spoke.

Luncheon was more halibut, baked or steamed. Not long afterwards, the

Queen Charlotte Islands came into sight in the west: a low, gray-green line rising up between sea and sky.

"You can see both the biggest islands from here," a seaman said. "That's Graham—where we're going—to the north and Moresby to the south. Just looks like one, though, because Skidegate Inlet narrows down to a narrow little channel between them. You don't want to sail there unless you have charts and you're with someone who knows the local waters. It's never the same twice, on account of the tides."

Bushell had no interest in sailing narrow tidal channels, nor indeed in sailing of any sort. As far as he was concerned, ships were utilitarian conveyances designed to take him from hither to yon when yon happened to lie across more water than he felt like swimming. But he let the crewman rattle on; policemen soon figured out that you couldn't tell in advance when you'd learn something useful.

The fellow pointed ahead. "There's Skidegate Village, where a lot of the Haida live." He chuckled. "One of my great-grandmothers was Haida, though you wouldn't guess it from my blue eyes. If you look sharp now, you can see a couple of totem poles standing in front of the houses. Skidegate proper's at the end of the spit of land, a mile or so south of the Haida village. You can spy the navy ships at anchor there."

"Yes, I see them." Bushell nodded. "I'd think they'd base them in the far north of the island, to keep watch on the Russians."

"There's torpedo boats and such up at Masset," the crewman answered, "but the harbor there's not deep enough to let large warships come in."

Next to the corvettes and the looming bulk of an armored cruiser, the *Northern Lights* seemed even smaller and dingier than she really was. As the ship tied up at the dock, Navy men shouldered duffel bags and resignedly queued up by the gangplank, then filed off the ferry. Struggling with their luggage, the three RAMs followed.

"Where now?" Samuel Stanley asked, setting down his bags with a grunt of relief.

"Hotel first, or whatever passes for one here," Bushell said. "Then the local constabulary—there won't be a RAM station—and then the naval commandant. And after that"—he let out a long breath of anticipation—"the post office."

Getting to the Skidegate Lodge proved no problem. Cabmen fell with glad cries on everyone not wearing navy blue who disembarked from the *Northern Lights*. The driver who took the RAMs to the hotel chattered on about the theft of *The Two Georges*, and seemed indignant when his passengers replied only in monosyllables. "Up here, by heaven, we care about our country, we do," he declared. "Down south, you ask me, they take it for granted."

"God save the King-Emperor," Bushell said, and still would not talk about the case.

Skidegate, he saw as the cabby took him and his companions through it, was a town whose principal function was to serve the local Navy base and to separate sailors and Royal Marines from their money as enjoyably as possible. It abounded in grogshops, dance halls, and, for those who had already spent their money but still had other chattels, pawnshops. Most of the people on the sidewalks wore navy blue, and most of the rest Marine khaki; the cab rolled past several detachments of truncheon-toting military policemen in white armbands. The truncheons notwithstanding, the redcaps always seemed to travel in groups of two or more.

The Skidegate Lodge was apparently *the* hotel in town. A stuffed bald eagle glared at Bushell with eyes of amber glass from its perch on the registration counter. His first thought was of the Independence Party flag, which made suspicion flare in him. But a great many eagles soared majestically over Skidegate and rooted, less majestically, in the rubbish pitch at the edge of the naval base. He decided he was overreacting—the bird did make a splendid trophy.

Seeing him eye it, the desk clerk asked, "Will you be going hunting, sir? Game laws say you can't shoot an eagle within five miles of the town limits, and they're strictly enforced."

"Thanks for the warning," Bushell said, not directly answering the question. "Have you a town telephone directory I might see?"

"Certainly, sir." The clerk reached under the desk and pulled one out. He passed it across the polished cedar surface to Bushell, who had to hide a smile as he took it. He was used to the New Liverpool directory, a book thick and heavy enough to make a good bludgeon. By contrast, a skinny little pamphlet served all of Skidegate's needs.

It did not, however, serve his. After going through it, he said to the clerk, "Could you give me some help, please? I see no listing for a local constabulary."

"No, sir, you wouldn't find that," the clerk said. By the wary look in his eye, he didn't much care to have anything to do with anyone interested in finding it, either. But, after a moment's hesitation, he condescended to explain: "The Navy, sir, deals with such matters all over the island. Only fair, I think, seeing as Navy men cause most of our trouble. When the swabbies or the bullocks"—by which he meant the Royal Marines—"have nothing to do with it, they ship the villains across to Prince Rupert to let the civil courts handle things." He had the air of a man who knew from experience whereof he spoke.

"Who is the commandant of the Navy's—what would I call it?—security detachment, then?" Bushell asked.

"That would be Commander Hairston," the desk clerk answered. "His offices are in the Naval Administration Building, close by the docks."

"Back the way we came," Bushell said with a sigh. "Well, I suppose we'll get settled in here before we go pay him a visit." He glanced over to Stanley and Crooke, who both nodded agreement. Bushell turned back to the clerk. "One last question: is the post office close by?"

"Just around the corner here and then down Carlotta Street half a block. You can't miss it," the clerk said, with the sublime optimism all locals show when strangers ask directions. The desk clerk shook his head in bemusement. "I get asked about bear and deer and salmon and eagles all the time, but never till now about constables and patrollers and post offices. Why'd you gents come to Skidegate anyhow, if you don't mind my asking?"

"To hunt," Bushell answered. Smiling grimly, he and his companions went up to their rooms, leaving the clerk scratching his head.

▼

As the clerk had promised, the Skidegate post office was easy to find. That being almost the first thing that had gone right with the investigation, Bushell cherished it. He, Crooke, and Stanley took off their hats and unbuttoned their coats when they went inside; it might have been the beginning of summer, but Skidegate was cool and shrouded in mist and drizzle.

A plump, bald, red-faced man looked up from behind the counter. "Help you gents?" he said. He swept away what Bushell thought was a book of word puzzles; business at the post office did not seem brisk.

"I'm looking for the postmaster," Bushell said.

"You're not only looking for him, my friend, you're looking *at* him," the red-faced fellow answered with a chuckle that was half cackle. "Rob Pratson's the name. Now what can I do for you?"

"Mr. Pratson, I hope you're not given to gossip," Bushell said, displaying the badge that identified him as an officer of the Royal American Mounted Police. Sam Stanley and Felix Crooke followed suit.

Pratson's watery blue eyes got wide. "Ain't never seen one of those up here before, 'cept in the cinema, and now here's three all together. Ain't that a thing and a half?" He remembered Bushell's question. "No, sir, I don't gab, not me. You can't do it, not if you're postmaster in a small town and you want to have friends."

"Good," Bushell said. "Not gossiping may involve your neck, not just friendships. Do you understand that?" At Pratson's nod, he went on, "Now, do you remember receiving one or more packages, shaped about like this"—he used his hands to draw a long, thin rectangular solid—"to be posted to New Liverpool?"

"Oh, that I do," the postmaster answered. "We've had a good many of those go through, past six months or so."

"Have you?" That was the last thing Bushell wanted to hear. He didn't tell Pratson what the packages contained; the fewer who knew of such things, the better. Instead, he went on, "Who's sending them?"

"I've had packages like that from three or four people, sir, I have," Rob Pratson said. "Don't rightly recall none of their last names; they just go by Geoff and Patrick and Elgin and . . . what the devil's that other one called? I ain't seen him but once or twice." The postmaster snapped his fingers. "Benjamin, that's it! I think that's it."

Stanley and Crooke both had out notepads and were scribbling down the names, just as Bushell was. "Do these four men live in Skidegate?" he asked hopefully. Maybe, just this once, something would be simple and straightforward.

But Pratson shook his head. "Oh, God bless you, sir, no they don't. They're up at Buckley Bay, they are. Far as I know, they're the only four people up at Buckley Bay."

"Where the devil's Buckley Bay, and why are these four chaps the only people there?" Sam Stanley asked. By his tone, he was as sick of complications as Bushell was.

"Buckley Bay ain't nothin' these days—hasn't been for years," Pratson said. "Used to be a logging town over on the west shore of Masset Inlet, right about in the center of the island here. But ain't nobody done any logging there since I was a sprout, and that goes back a deal of years, don't it just. Till them four moved in, the buildings, they just got left to themselves to fall to pieces one bit at a time."

"What do these four men do there, then?" Bushell demanded. "How do they make their living? How long have they been there?"

The postmaster shrugged. "Been there two, three years, I guess—that's how long they been comin' into Skidegate, anyways. They mail their packages, buy a few things down to the grocer's shop or the ironmonger's, head on out again. Dunno just how they get by. Hunting and fishing, I reckon, and I hear tell they take sightseers around sometimes, show 'em the best spots for salmon and I don't know what all. Whatever they do, nobody ever said they was lackin' a quid they had need of."

"Why does that last observation not surprise me?" Felix Crooke said.

Pratson would not have known a rhetorical question had one come in to buy a stamp of him. "Dunno, sir, why don't it?"

"Never mind," Bushell said. "Thank you, Mr. Pratson—you've been very helpful. Let me repeat that you'd be wise to keep this to yourself. If you're a married man, don't even tell your wife."

"Sooner or later, Myrtle will find out someways, and then I'm in the soup," Pratson said resignedly. "But I won't blab. Still and all, I wish you'd tell me what this here's all about. What have them four fellers gone and did?"

"I don't know yet," Bushell said. "But I promise you: I'm going to find out."

▼

Commander Nathan Hairston was a big, bluff man with muttonchop whiskers and a walrus mustache. "Pleasure to meet you gentlemen—pleasure," he said as a sailor hurriedly brought a couple of spare chairs into his office. "Haven't seen RAMs here since Hector was a pup. What can I do to help you?"

Bushell explained. By the time he was nearly through, Commander Hairston's mouth had fallen open in amazement. He finished, "Do you know these men? Geoff, Patrick, Elgin, and Benjamin the postmaster called them. He didn't recollect their surnames."

"I don't either, I'm afraid. I know the men you mean, or know of them, rather—so far as I was officially aware, they'd never given anyone a moment's trouble." Hairston shook his head like a man coming out of a showerbath. "Colonel, to be frank with you, the civilians hereabouts are mostly dull as dust, except every once in a while when they've had too much to drink. To think of this sleepy, godforsaken place involved in what has to be the most outrageous crime since the Duke of Philadelphia's daughter was kidnapped fifty years ago . . . I tell you, sir, I can hardly believe it."

"Not much room for doubt, Commander," Samuel Stanley said. "Tricky Dick was killed with a Nagant to distract us while the Sons stole *The Two Georges*, and people here are posting Nagants down to New Liverpool. That would want looking into even if we left the painting out of the bargain."

"It certainly would," Felix Crooke said. The expert on the Sons of Liberty went on, "This is a smuggling avenue about which we haven't had to concern ourselves before. Have you had much trouble along those lines?"

"Smuggling, you mean?" Hairston said. "Never firearms, at least never that I knew till now. We do have men with small boats sneaking down from Alaska every now and again, but we've never caught them with anything worse than Russian vodka, the kind that's strong enough to kick off the top of your head. I suspect they pass off more of that to fishermen on the high seas, too, but it's all bloody difficult to prove, as you must know."

"Commander, I am not accusing you of being derelict in your duties," Bushell said quickly. "This plot must have been a long time hatching, and closely concealed." His lips twisted in a bitter smile. "It certainly took *me* by surprise."

"Mm, yes." Hairston sent him a sympathetic look. "I asked you once in a general way, but now I'll be more specific: what can I do to help you?"

"Do you have one particular judge likely to issue a speedy search warrant?" Bushell asked. He still had the blank but signed ones he'd got down in New Liverpool, but he wanted to save those if he could.

Commander Hairston surprised him by throwing back his head and letting out a Jovian laugh. "My dear fellow, the Queen Charlotte Islands are in their entirety a military reservation, under the direct jurisdiction of the Royal Navy and Royal North American Navy. If we do something altogether outrageous, the judges in Prince Rupert will quash it, but you seem on most solid ground here."

"The next time I feel on solid ground in this case will be the first," Bushell said. "Most criminals are bloody stupid." Hairston and both RAMs nodded at that. Bushell went on, "Whoever's behind this theft, though, he's no fool. But never mind that. All right, Commander—you have the jurisdiction." The desk clerk at the hotel had told him as much; he should have thought through the implications. "What help can you give me?"

"How would you like a couple of squads of Royal Marines first thing tomorrow morning?" Hairston asked. Seeing Bushell's flabbergasted expression, the Navy man laughed again. "Colonel, this isn't supposed to be a fair fight. If we've got four villains out by Buckley Bay, the idea is to make them give up without a fight or make damned sure we win it. Good heavens, man, did you even bring weapons with you from New Liverpool?"

"We have three pistols," Bushell answered. "If we needed anything more, we expected we'd be able to draw it from you."

"Good for you, then," Commander Hairston said. "From what I've seen of a lot of civil police, they forget the nasty chaps can get very nasty, indeed."

"I would have," Felix Crooke said. "Colonel Bushell didn't let me." He smoothly made the change back to formal address. Bushell sent him an approving glance. Crooke hadn't had to admit his own naïveté, but he'd done it—a man of integrity.

"If you want rifles, you may certainly have a couple of ours," Hairston said. "I wouldn't care to carry anything less, I'll tell you that."

Bushell and Stanley both nodded right away. Crooke said, "It's been so many years since I had a rifle in my hands, I expect I'd be more dangerous to my friends than to the villains. I'll stick to my revolver, if it's all the same to you; I'm familiar with it, which counts."

"However you like, Lieutenant-Colonel," Hairston said with a shrug of his wide shoulders. He got up from his desk and stood beside the large-scale map of the Queen Charlotte Islands on the wall behind it. "How do you gents have in mind getting to Buckley Bay? There are no roads on the western shore of Masset Inlet. No reason to have 'em—hardly anybody lives there. You can go by road to Port Clements, here on the eastern side of the inlet. From there, the road up from Skidegate heads due north to Masset."

"We don't want to take a boat straight across the inlet to Buckley Bay, I shouldn't think," Bushell said. "If they saw us coming, they'd just fade back into the woods, and then your Marines might have a hard time running them to earth."

"I'm afraid you're right about that," Hairston said mournfully. "If they've been living as trappers and hunters, they'll know the land in that area better than my men will. How's this, then: suppose you sail across the inlet from Port Clements to a point, oh, five miles north of the old logging town? Your men won't think anything's amiss even if they do see the boat. You can move down to Buckley Bay and nab them at your convenience."

"That sounds good to me, Commander," Samuel Stanley said. "Coming at villains from a direction they don't expect is always a good idea."

"I agree," Bushell said, and Felix Crooke nodded again. That Stanley thought well of the plan was in itself recommendation enough for Bushell. Ever since his army days, he'd had reason to admire his adjutant's tactical sense.

"We'll do it that way, then," Hairston said. "Have you brought along clothing and shoes that will stand up to a five-mile hike through woods and brush?"

"I haven't," Crooke said. "I took clothes suitable for New Liverpool when I came out from Victoria. I'm afraid the Queen Charlottes are both cooler and damper than I was prepared for."

"Yes, they would be, if you came from New Liverpool." Nathan Hairston glanced at Bushell and Stanley. "You two have what you need? I'm impressed. Lieutenant-Colonel Crooke, we'll send you off to the quartermaster and outfit you as a Royal Marine. You gents are out at the Skidegate Lodge? I'll send a driver round for you at half past four, then."

Samuel Stanley looked martyred. "After three mornings in a row of getting up ungodly early, I should be growing used to it. But I'm not—all I'm growing is old, too bloody fast."

"Think of it this way, Sam," Bushell said helpfully: "if you're awake all the time, you'll seem to live longer." By Stanley's expression, that offered insufficient consolation.

Crooke went off to be outfitted, and returned to Hairston's office a little later with khaki tunic and trousers, a rubberized cape of the same color, a webbing belt in Royal Marine red, stout boots with rawhide lacings, and a slouch hat. "Thank you very much for your help, Commander Hairston," he said.

"My pleasure," the Skidegate security chief answered. "I'll give you chaps a lift back to the Lodge, too. Colonel, Captain, we'll have the rifles waiting for you here when you set out, if that's all right. You won't want to have to explain how you came by them when you walk through the lobby."

"That's true," Bushell said. "In fact, if you can get a bag—a civilian-style bag—for that uniform, it would help. And I hope you'll take us to and from the hotel in civilian steamers. We don't want word of who we are and what we're about getting to Buckley Bay ahead of us."

"I like the way you think, Colonel," Commander Hairston said with a brusque nod. "Just being in this business makes us take a good many chances. You don't seem to take any you needn't."

A young sailor, grinning from ear to ear at the chance to wear mufti, however briefly, drove the three RAMs back into Skidegate in Hairston's personal steamer. "Here you are, sir," he said to Bushell as he pulled up in front of the Skidegate Lodge. "Now to get back before the commander figures I've wrapped it around a tree." Still grinning, he sped away.

"What say we go up to our rooms and then meet in the lobby for supper?" Bushell said. "The Haida Lounge attached to the hotel looked—interesting. They say New Liverpool has every sort of restaurant in the world, but there are no Haida Indian eateries there."

"They say the same thing about Victoria," Felix Crooke said, "but it hasn't got any, either. I'm game for something new. Just let me stow my kit here"—he hefted the bag that held the Royal Marines uniform—"and I'll be with you directly."

The Haida Lounge was a smoky place. Bushell had been in any number of smoky taverns and restaurants in his time, but without exception their haze sprang from tobacco. Here the smoke was an integral part of the decor; the chef worked at a grill over an alderwood fire in the center of the room. Fans sent some of the smoke toward an opening in the ceiling, but not all.

Bushell had expected to find venison and halibut on the menu, and was not disappointed. Sealmeat steaks, salmon cheeks, and dried herring eggs on kelp, however, made him raise an eyebrow, and a couple of items left him altogether at a loss. "What the devil *is* a fiddlehead?" he said to the waiter.

"No reason for you to know, if you're a stranger here." The waiter himself looked to be Haida, at least in good part; his English, while fluent, held a hissing, guttural undertone. "Fiddleheads are the shoots of sword ferns. They curl around on themselves at the tip, like the end of a violin's neck. We serve them boiled, with butter or with hollandaise sauce."

"I'll try some, then—with butter, I think—and for my main course I'll want the seal." Bushell reflected that both butter and hollandaise were imperfectly authentic additions to native Haida cuisine, but he hadn't come here to quibble. "I'll start with the island salad here, the crabapples and fireweed and cow parsnip."

"Very good." The waiter nodded, perhaps pleased by his sense of adventure, then turned to Sam Stanley.

"The venison and wild rice for me," Stanley said, "and a bottle of your Caribou Ale to wash it down."

"Yes, sir." After writing down his order, the waiter looked expectantly to Felix Crooke.

"I'll have the herring eggs and kelp," Crooke said, "and the wild rice to go with them. I might almost be eating in a Japanese restaurant."

"Interesting you should say so, sir," the waiter remarked. "We sometimes get Japanese here, buying fish or timber. They often order those same dishes. And would you also like an ale?" At Crooke's nod, the young man turned to Bushell. "And what will you have to drink, sir?"

"Have you got Jameson Irish whiskey?" Bushell asked. The waiter's blank look said they didn't. Bushell shrugged. "In that case, bring me one of these Caribous, too." As the young man hurried off to fetch the ales, Bushell turned to his companions. He raised a quizzical eyebrow. "Damned if I know what sort of wine goes with seal meat, anyhow."

The seal steak was richly marbled and had a somewhat fishy flavor, no doubt because of the seal's diet. The fiddleheads tasted nutty; Bushell enjoyed them. The well-hopped ale complimented the meal better than any wine he could think of; he patted himself on the back for a good choice.

Sam Stanley demolished his cut of venison and looked ecstatic doing it. And Felix Crooke ate his dried fish eggs and kelp with every sign of relish. "You'd pay thirty pounds in Victoria for a meal like this," he said.

"I wouldn't," Stanley said. He was proud of his conservative tastes.

"Our Haida sweet is whipped soapberries," the waiter said as he gathered up supper plates. "It's surprisingly close to ice cream. Would any of you gentlemen care to try it?"

Bushell and Crooke nodded. Sam Stanley said, "Soapberries? No, thank you," and ordered another Caribou Ale instead. Conservatism had its own punishment; the berries, despite their off-putting name, were sweet and delicious.

After a cigar, Bushell said, "I'm turning in. We shall be busy boys tomorrow."

"Busy boys early tomorrow," Stanley added. "I'm going to ask the desk clerk to ring my room at four." His sigh was long, mournful, and heartfelt.

"Ask him to do the same for Felix and me, too." Bushell blew a smoke ring up toward the ceiling. It soon thinned and vanished, reminding him all too much of most of the leads they'd had in the case.

▼

When the dreaded telephone call came, Bushell dragged himself out of bed and climbed into the denim trousers, plaid wool shirt, and hooded anorak he'd brought up from New Liverpool and set out before he went to sleep. Then he put on a pair of stout shoes a constable might have worn walking a beat. They weren't as good as military boots, but they were the best he had.

To his dismay, he found the Haida Lounge closed when he went down to the lobby. Stanley joined him a couple of minutes later, similarly dressed and similarly distressed because he wouldn't be able to get some tea or coffee to make his heart start beating. "Maybe the Marines will have a vacuum flask," he said hopefully.

Felix Crooke was already wearing his rain cape when he came downstairs. Bushell wondered at that for a moment, but then realized it let the RAM carry his revolver on his belt unseen.

At exactly half past four, a steamer pulled up in front of the Skidegate Lodge. The three RAMs stepped out into light drizzle and piled into it. "Have you back at the base in just a moment, sirs," the sailor behind the wheel said, and took off with speed enough to push Bushell back against his seat.

The steamer stopped behind two large lorries with khaki canvas tops. Waiting next to the lorries were Commander Nathan Hairston and his promised two squads of Royal Marines. "Good morning," Hairston boomed blithely when the RAMs got out of the motorcar. He looked from Bushell to Stanley, back again. "Yes, for civilian gear what you have isn't bad at all. Now, you'll want rifles, you said." When the RAMs nodded, a Marine lieutenant fetched a couple of Lee-Enfields and handed one to Bushell, the other to Stanley.

The weapons had their magazines attached. When Bushell checked, he found a cartridge in the breech. "Good," he said approvingly, flicking on the safety. "The best way not to have trouble is to be ready for it." He slung the rifle over his shoulder. By the time the day was done, he feared he'd be walking with a list. He hadn't carried a rifle since his army days.

"Speaking of readiness," the lieutenant said, and handed Stanley and him four five-round boxes of ammunition apiece.

Bushell stowed them in the outer pockets of his anorak. The weight had already started to grow, and he wasn't carrying anything like full kit, as the Royal Marines were. He said, "Thank you very much, Lieutenant, ah—"

"Colonel, let me introduce to you Lieutenant Morton Green and his NCOs, Sergeant Fuller and Corporals Johnston and Wainwright," Hairston said. He did not present the Marine privates. "They know their task is to assist you and your companions in apprehending the four men of whom we spoke yesterday and any of their confederates who may be with them. For this mission, they will treat your RAM ranks as if those obtained in the Royal Marines."

"That is a high honor," Bushell said. Lieutenant Green saluted smartly. He was about thirty, of medium height but very fit, with features that seemed both tough and intelligent. His sergeant, Fuller, was a few years older, and had eyes that missed nothing. Although he was blond and ruddy, his air of unhurried competence put Bushell in mind of Samuel Stanley. Corporal Johnston was tall and Corporal Wainwright short—or perhaps it was the other way round.

As for the rest of the Marines, what struck Bushell like a blow was how young they were. Had the soldiers he'd commanded as a lieutenant been that young? Very likely, but he'd been young in those days, too. Now he felt almost grandfatherly. He saw the Marines studying him, too. *Wondering if I can keep up on a hike through the woods,* he thought. He wondered the same thing. One way or the other, he'd find out.

"No sense standing around here making chitchat," Commander Hairston said. "You have your job to do, and I wish you only success with it."

Lieutenant Green waved at the Marines, who swarmed aboard the lorries. Those were troop transporters identical to the ones the army used, with six inward-facing seats on each side of the bed. With the drivers and two more men on each front seat, there was room and to spare for the twenty Marines, their four leaders, and the three RAMs.

"Good luck," Hairston called. As if that were a signal, the lorries rolled away. They seemed to have no dampers; whenever a tyre went over a stone or into a pothole, everybody aboard felt it. The kidney-shaking ride took Bushell back across half a lifetime. By the way Samuel Stanley smiled to himself, he was remembering long-ago lorry trips, too.

The few civilians up and about in Skidegate didn't give the lorries a second glance. They were used to military vehicles passing through for one reason or another. From Skidegate, the road swung north along the eastern coast of Graham Island through the Haida town of Skidegate Village and then up toward Tlell.

Bushell, Crooke, and Stanley, having got on last, had seats near their lorry's rear gate and could see, if not where they were going, at least where they'd been. Bushell had noticed the totem poles of Skidegate Village as the ferry came in to Skidegate itself. Now he got a better look at the houses those poles fronted.

Some were of various imperial styles, like those the British had built in Skidegate. Others, though, preserved the native Haida way of doing things: long houses built of red cedar and roofed with cedar bark. The beams of the roofs—there always seemed to be seven—projected out several feet from the walls at front and rear, perhaps to offer space where people could get dry before going inside. A couple of the long houses had smoke rising from a vent hole in the center of the roof, an arrangement the Haida Lounge must have borrowed along with its name.

Skidegate Village was no larger than its name implied. In moments it fell away behind the lorries. The road ran north just inland from the beach, against which the waters of the Hecate Strait slapped gently. The beach was strewn with driftwood. Along with the wood, Bushell spied a couple of large glass globes that puzzled him until he realized they were floats for fishing nets. He wondered how many miles and how many years they had drifted before finally washing ashore. Gulls and other shorebirds flew up in squawking clouds when the lorries went by.

"They don't seem used to having people about," Felix Crooke said. "I wonder how much traffic this road gets."

"Not much, by the look of it," Bushell answered. "Haven't seen any steamers behind us since we got out of Skidegate Village, and I haven't noticed any coming southbound past us, either."

He looked inland. Every so often, a dirt trail would join the north-south road. Most of those trails were overgrown, and a lot of the buildings to which they led were weathered and abandoned, their broken-out windows staring like blind eyes. Making a go of it here on the edge of nowhere was anything but easy.

Every so often, though, someone managed it. A couple of farms looked prosperous, with shaggy cattle grazing in the meadows. Bushell pointed to one of them. "There you go, Sam. That's probably where last night's venison came from."

"Colonel, you have a low, nasty, suspicious mind, and it wouldn't surprise me one bloody bit if you were right," Stanley said.

"We've spare water bottles for you and your friends, Colonel," Lieutenant Green said, "and St. Mary's Spring is a good place to fill them. The water's always good there, and you can't say the same for the streams running into Masset Inlet. It'll be coming up in a couple of minutes, if you'd like me to stop the lorry for you."

"Yes, do that, please," Bushell answered. *No tea*, he thought with a mental sigh. "Could we beg some rations from you, too? We left the hotel without breakfast."

"I expect we can do something about that, sir," Morton Green said. The Marines donated tins of stew, some hard crackers, and a jar of jam that smelled something like pineapple and something like methylated spirit. Felix Crooke sniffed at it and shook his head; like the jouncing ride of the lorry, it took Bushell back to his younger days.

St. Mary's Spring ran cold and clear. Bushell filled his bottle, screwed on the top. Then he dug into a hasty breakfast. The stew would have been better hot (it wouldn't have been good no matter what anyone did to it), but he could eat it cold, and he didn't have time to waste. Along with Stanley and Crooke, he chucked the empty container into a rubbish bin by the spring and climbed back into the lorry.

They got into Tlell about forty-five minutes after they'd left the Skidegate naval base. The little town lay between tree-covered dunes and the Tlell River. The lorries didn't stop, but rolled over the Tlell River Bridge. The road swung inland after that, running northwest toward Port Clements. About halfway to the town on Masset Inlet lay Mayer Lake, not quite a mile north of the road. As the gulls on the coast had done, loons and other water birds flew up in alarm when the lorries went past.

Port Clements was bigger than Tlell, though Bushell doubted it held as many as five hundred people. It boasted a doctor's office, but not a post office. A sawmill was much the largest building in town.

A couple of men—loggers, by the look of them—glanced curiously at the lorries as they headed for the wharf. "Except for the cutter crew, we don't—the Navy doesn't, I mean—come here all that often," Lieutenant Green said.

"That's not so good," Sam Stanley said quietly. "We're liable to be blowing our cover."

"I thought of that, too, but I'm not going to worry about it," Bushell answered. "If Buckley Bay's been abandoned for the past sixty years, our chums over there aren't likely to have a telephone to let someone here ring them up and warn them we're on the way. As long as the Navy keeps boats here tied up at the wharf for a couple of hours after we leave, we should be all right."

"Good enough," Stanley said, and leaned back in his hard, uncomfortable seat.

Bushell, the other RAMs, and the Royal Marines scrambled out of the lorries as soon as they stopped moving. The cutter, the HMS *Grampus*—a miniature corvette about seventy feet long, with a two-pounder for a deck gun—already had her engine running; stinking fuel-oil fumes fouled the cool, damp air.

"Permission to come aboard?" Lieutenant Green called at the foot of the gangplank.

"Granted," said the lieutenant commander who looked to command the cutter. "You've given the lads and me something out of the ordinary to do with our morning, I'll say that much for you."

"How far is it across the inlet, Captain?" Bushell asked the officer in charge of the cutter. He peered west himself, but mist and cloud obscured the far shore.

The naval officer beamed at having his functional title given rather than the rank he wore on his cuffs and shoulder boards. "It's about ten miles to where Commander Hairston told me you want to be left off." He stuck out his hand. "I'm Edward Woodbridge, by the way."

"Tom Bushell." Bushell introduced Crooke and Stanley.

"Pleased to meet you, gentlemen," Woodbridge said. "I'm told this has somewhat to do with The Two Georges' going missing. Never would have expected any such thing here—the Queen Charlottes are mostly quiet as the tomb, not to put too fine a point on it—but we'll do everything we can to help you get it back. Love that painting, I do." He looked around. "Are you all aboard? Yes? We'll cast off, then."

The rumble of the engine grew louder and deeper. The cutter pulled away from the wharf and onto the still, smooth waters of Masset Inlet. One of the sailors came up to Bushell. "We have a small galley, sir. Would you fancy a cup of tea?"

"Would I, by God!" Bushell exclaimed. "I've been wanting some all morning." The sailor brought it to him in a thick china mug. It was hot and strong and sweet, but had no milk in it. He wondered about that, and asked, "Haven't you got an icebox in your little galley?"

"That we do, sir, but no milk in it, I'm afraid," the man answered. "Sailors up here in the Queen Charlottes, we mostly drink our tea Russian-style, with sugar and nothing more."

"Alaska's close by," Bushell observed.

"Yes, sir, that's part of it, I suppose. The other side of the shilling is, it stays hotter longer without pouring milk into it. In the chill and the wet hereabouts, that's not the worst thing in the world."

Bushell walked to the bow of the cutter. Port Clements was already hazy behind him, the far shore of Masset Inlet not yet visible ahead. Two sailors at the bow stared intently down into the water of the inlet. "What are you looking for?" Bushell asked.

"Deadheads, sir," one of them answered without turning his head. "All sorts of logs drifting just below the surface. Sometimes, for no reason anybody can figure, they'll bob up into the air—or into your hull, if you're not watching out for 'em."

"I see," Bushell said. That watch no doubt also explained why the Grampus wasn't making a better turn of speed: you didn't want to be going too fast to stop or swerve if you spotted a deadhead. He checked the time. They'd been a little more than an hour on the road from the Skidegate naval base to Port Clements. It still wasn't close to half past six. *Not bad*, he thought. The sun, already high in the northeastern sky, was trying to burn through the clouds that hung over the Queen Charlotte Islands.

A bald eagle flew low across the inlet, chasing an osprey with a fish in its talons. The osprey dropped the fish and flapped off, screeching furiously; the eagle flew away with the prize. "Damned thief," Bushell muttered. As far as he was concerned, that the Independence Party and the Sons of Liberty revered the bald eagle said more about them than it did about the bird.

Because of the watch for logs, the cutter took most of an hour to reach the western shore of Masset Inlet. She glided to a stop about a hundred yards from the muddy beach. "Lower the boats!" Lieutenant Commander Woodbridge said. The sailors went about it as if they'd done it a thousand times, which they probably had. Drill was bloody dull, but it paid off.

One boat held a dozen men, the other eight. The Royal Marines got down into them with the same practiced ease the sailors had shown. A couple of Navy men joined them in each boat. Scrambling down a rope with his feet against the side of a rolling ship was nothing Bushell had practiced, but the Marines grabbed him and helped him ease into the larger boat.

They also aided Samuel Stanley and Felix Crooke. "Thank you, gentlemen," Crooke said. "For a moment there, I felt like the pendulum in a grandfather clock." The Marines grinned, proud of the skill they'd shown.

From the deck of the *Grampus*, Ted Woodbridge called, "I've never seen bullocks and RAMs in the same boat till now." The Royal Marines hooted at him. His grin got broader. "Good hunting, my friends. I'll see you off Buckely Bay at noon."

The Marines seized the oars in the bottom of the boats and made short work of the stretch of water between them and the shore. Mud and sand grated under the boats as they rowed them up onto the beach. The Marines leaped out. Rather more slowly, the three RAMs followed. "I'm already feeling old, and we haven't even started hiking yet," Bushell said. Sam Stanley nodded agreement.

The sailors rowed the boats back to the cutter to pick up the Royal Marines who hadn't been able to fit the first time. When everyone was ashore, Lieutenant Green turned to Bushell and said, "I expect you'll want us to go inland a bit before we move on Buckley Bay, eh, sir? If we just come straight down the beach, the chaps we're looking for will be able to spy us a long ways off."

"Can't have that," Bushell said. "Until we get there, Lieutenant, I'm going to put myself in your hands. You know this country better than I do." He waved at the trees—cedar and spruce, pine and fir—that came down close to the beach. The land rose up more steeply here than it had on the eastern side of the inlet; he'd seen that much from the cutter. What it would be like when he got into the forest, he couldn't begin to guess. Most of his military experience had been on the border with Nueva España, hot, dry country as different from these woods as the mountains of the moon.

"Come on, then," Green said, and led the men inland from the beach.

Bushell felt as if he'd stepped into a cool green cathedral, with God the architect rather than man. The sun had come out, but was rarely able to penetrate the canopy of dark green branches overhead. The air was moist and full of the tangy, resinous scent of the trees all around. He wanted to gulp down great lungsful of it and take them with him when he went back to New Liverpool.

"We'll form a skirmish line, man on the left close enough to the edge of the woods to see the inlet," Green said. "If you get separated, steer southwest by the sun and you won't go far wrong. If the sun goes behind the clouds again or you're in amongst growth too thick to let you see it, remember that your compass needle will bear a bit northeast, not true north. We're close enough to the North Magnetic Pole for the deflection to matter."

"Now there's something I never imagined I'd have to worry about," Samuel Stanley said. He took a compass from a pocket of his anorak and gave it a thoughtful look. "Can't tell that it's lying to me." Shaking his head, he put it back. Bushell kicked at the red-brown needles underfoot; he hadn't thought to bring a compass.

They set off toward Buckley Bay, each man only a couple of yards from the fellow to his side. Ferns pushed up through the dead needles: bright splashes of green against the dun ground and tree trunks. Here and there, moss found a hold on some of those trunks, and on boulders as well. Bushell suspected that if he stood still for a couple of hours in the cool moistness of the forest, moss would start growing on him, too.

Something screeched *jeep! jeep!* right above his ear. He had his rifle off his back and halfway to his shoulder before he heard a whir of flapping wings and got a glimpse of a dark blue bird streaking away. "What the devil was that?" he asked. "It scared me out of a year's growth."

"Just a jay, sir," the Marine on his left answered. "Noisy buggers, aren't they? I'd sooner run across one of them than a bear, though."

"Right." Bushell kept his voice under tight rein. He wondered how many RAM investigations had been halted because a wild beast devoured the investigator. Most of the time, he worried only about dangerous men. Adding wild animals to the mix struck him as unfair.

Every so often, he had to leap over or splash through a little stream; from everything he'd seen, the Queen Charlotte Islands had more water than they knew what to do with. Before long, his feet were soaked. He envied the Royal Marines their tall boots. "Hope you don't pick up any leeches, sir," the Marine beside him said helpfully. He gave the pup a dirty look and kept slogging along.

To his right, Sam Stanley was also making good progress. *Not bad for a couple of old men*, Bushell thought. Felix Crooke was years younger than either of them but already starting to pant. "I've been behind a desk too long," he said. "If I fall behind, just shoot me and carry on."

Stanley made as if to unsling his rifle, then seemed to think better of it. "Can't do that, sir, I'm afraid," he said. "The sound would carry too far."

"I'm so glad you have my welfare in mind," Crooke said with a rasping chuckle.

After two or three miles, they came to a river too wide to be easily forded.

"There's a log bridge a couple of hundred yards upstream," Morton Green said. The party gathered together to find it and crossed a few at a time.

Bushell looked down into the clear water to the stream's gravel bed. Fish hung motionless above the pebbles and small rounded stones, or else dashed off to snap at insects on the surface. Some of the shining green creatures were as long as his arm. As his knowledge of fish before they were cooked was on the theoretical side, he asked Lieutenant Green, "Are those salmon?"

The Marine nodded. "Yes, sir, and trout, too. They all make fine eating when there's time to fish." He walked over the bridge with a sigh of regret. So did Bushell. The fresher fish was, the better, and how could it be fresher than just pulled from a river? He thought it a pity his water jar held only water and not a good white wine, a Meursault perhaps, or a Vouvray, or a Rhine wine from the Palatinate.

Not long after they'd crossed over the river, they came out of forest into a stretch of saplings and weeds and brush running for several hundred yards: logged-over land that hadn't yet regrown. Bushell said. "This can't date back to the days when Buckley Bay was a going concern."

"It doesn't," Lieutenant Green answered. "From the height of those young trees, I'd say it was cut about ten years ago: the trunks would have been rafted across the inlet to Port Clements and dealt with there. By the time it's sat idle sixty years, it'll be ready for another round of cutting."

Bushell was beginning to feel his years when one of the Royal Marines said, "Hold up—pass the word." Inside a few steps, everyone had stopped. A moment later, the reason for the halt came down the line: "You can see the old settlement through the trees."

"How are we going to proceed?" Lieutenant Green asked. "If it were a purely military operation, I'd send some men through the woods beyond Buckley Bay and approach from all sides at once to prevent any possible escapes. If, however, you'd sooner just tramp up and rap on the front door, we can do that. Consider me and my men at your disposal."

"Normally, we would just rap at the front door," Felix Crooke said.

"Normally, we wouldn't be carrying these." Bushell reached over his shoulder to touch the barrel of the rifle slung there. "For that matter, I don't know which front door in the settlement belongs to the men we're looking for. We'll use the military approach here."

Crooke still looked doubtful, but Samuel Stanley nodded emphatic agreement and said, "Villains with rifles aren't the sort of people whose front doors I care to rap on."

"Good enough." Green gave swift orders to his men. Sergeant Fuller and Corporal Wainwright led one squad off on the flanking maneuver Green had described. Corporal Johnston and the rest of the Royal Marines stayed behind with Green and the RAMs. Green said, "Let's spread out along the treeline, not showing ourselves, and see what we can see."

What Bushell saw, from behind a cedar whose trunk was thicker than his body, was the ghostly ruin of what once had been a thriving little town. Overgrown streets made a grid centering on a small square. More than his lifetime of storms and rain and wind and sun had peeled every speck of paint from the buildings and bleached almost white the boards of which they were made. The windows were all blank and vacant, with not a shard of glass anywhere. Here and there, ferns grew on rooftops; beards of moss and lichen hung from eaves.

A couple of trees over, Sam Stanley let out a soft hiss. "Do you see it, sir?" he called to Bushell. "That place on the east side of the square with the big window in front, looks like it was a grocer's shop once upon a time. There's smoke coming up from the chimney."

"I see it," Bushell answered. It wasn't a lot of smoke, just the wisps that came from a low fire, but it stood out like a flag (an *Independence Party* flag, Bushell thought) in a town otherwise slowly being reclaimed by wilderness.

Lieutenant Green saw it, too. "Is that where our suspects live, sir?" he asked Bushell.

"Either them or the Ladies' Aid Society," Bushell answered. "How long will your other squad of Marines need to get around to the far side of Buckley Bay?"

"Let's give them fifteen minutes, unless we spy them advancing out of the forest there sooner," Green said. "I am correct in assuming you wish a stealthy approach to the target building?"

"That might be a good idea," Bushell agreed dryly.

Felix Crooke said, "Surely they'll surrender when they realize we represent the law and the military power, and that we have them outnumbered and surrounded."

"Don't think of them as ordinary villains, Felix," Bushell said. "Think of them as soldiers. They're playing for keeps." Behind a spruce, Crooke nodded. Bushell did not like that nod. It looked more as if it came from dutiful obedience than from conviction.

Fifteen minutes passed, then a couple more. Just as Bushell was beginning to get itchy, several men in dark khaki that made them hard to spot burst out of the woods on the far side of Buckley Bay and sprinted toward the lesser cover of saplings, tall clumps of fir, and scattered boulders. As soon as they had flopped down in their new places of concealment, the other half of the squad Sergeant Fuller led ran past them into other hiding places closer to the abandoned town. It was as pretty an example of move-and-support as Bushell had ever seen.

"Now we can start," Lieutenant Green said softly. "Corporal, you and the odd numbers forward, if you please."

"Sir!" Corporal Johnston said. He and half the squad ran forward forty or fifty yards and went to ground in the cover they'd chosen for themselves.

"Even numbers and gentlemen of the RAMs," Green said. Bushell realized he should long since have figured out where he was going to run when the time came. He hadn't played this game in too long, too long. He spotted a fallen tree that for whatever reason hadn't been dragged away after it went down. It had lain there a long time; sword ferns grew in profusion atop it. Crouching almost double, he ran for it and dove in behind it hard enough to knock half the wind out of him.

Sam Stanley came down behind a moss-covered rock. He mimed wiping sweat from his forehead, but the way he panted was no joke. Southwest of Buckley Bay, Sergeant Fuller's squad was moving up again. Behind Bushell, Corporal Johnston called, "Odd numbers move." His half of the squad sprinted past the RAMs.

This time, Bushell had picked in advance the spot to which he would go. When Lieutenant Green ordered the even numbers ahead, he streaked for the corner of a building on the very edge of Buckley Bay. He crouched, gasping, behind it. Streaks of rust from old nails bled down the boards and gave them their only color.

Corporal Johnston's demisquad worked their way into town, too. "Now we move forward until we are noticed," Green said quietly, "at which point, command returns to your hands, Colonel Bushell."

"Right," Bushell said. He slithered through the heather and ferns that choked what had been one of Buckley Bay's main streets, making for the open square on which stood the building the men he sought were using. He could smell the smoke from their fire: not just wood but roasting meat. The odor made his belly rumble and spit rush into his mouth. *Come on, boys, you be hungry, too,* he thought. *Watch the joint get done cooking or sit around eating it up, don't pay a bit of attention to what's going on outside, and we'll scoop you up neat as you please.*

No sooner had the thought crossed his mind than a shout made him, his RAM comrades, and the Royal Marines freeze in place: "Who the devil's sneaking around out there? Whoever you are, you'd better clear out, or you'll be sorry."

"Who are you?" Bushell called back. "Is this the residence of four gentlemen named Geoff and Patrick and Elgin and Benjamin?" The formalities had to be observed: there was the one-in-a-milliard chance he was wrong.

"Who wants to know?" that same voice yelled from inside the old shop.

To Bushell's horror, Felix Crooke broke cover and stood up, saying, "We are members of the Royal American Mounted Police and the Royal Marines. We have you outnumbered and trapped. Come out with your hands above your heads and you shall not be harmed."

"Get down, you damned fool!" Bushell shouted, a split second behind Samuel Stanley. Crooke started to shake his head—afterwards, Bushell was almost sure of it. But an element of doubt always remained, for at that moment a rifle shot rang out. Crooke went down then, but not of his own will; he crashed to earth as if all his bones had suddenly turned to water.

Bushell stared in disbelief and horror. He'd warned Felix Crooke to think of the men they were after as soldiers, not ordinary criminals, but he hadn't thought of them that way himself, not down deep where it counted. He'd never fired a weapon in the field in all his years as a RAM, and never dreamt of being fired on himself. That was something Russian *Okhrana* men worried about, or inquisitors of the Holy Alliance. The game was played by different rules in the British Empire.

No. The game had been played by different rules.

"Come on, the lot of you, and you'll get what he got!" The man inside the grocer's shop sounded fiercely exultant, as if he had done something good and true and noble, not shot a man down in cold blood.

Shock at the unexpected gunplay held Bushell frozen, just for a moment. To the Royal Marines, though, gunfire was anything but unexpected. They opened up with a fusillade that sent bullets flying through the empty window frame from which the shot had come and made chips fly off the timbers of the building with the smoking chimney.

That great racket of riflery got Bushell moving. All at once, he wasn't a RAM any more, but a subaltern with troops pinned down amid mesquite and chaparral not far from the Rio Grande. As he had then, he knew what wanted doing now: getting his wounded out of further harm's way.

He dashed out into the square to Felix Crooke. A bullet cracked past his head closer than he cared to think about: the Marines' barrage hadn't silenced the Sons of Liberty. He slung Crooke across his back and, staggering under the weight of the bigger man, carried him through an open doorway into a shop or home that perhaps had not known the tread of human feet since before he was born.

He set Crooke down and groped for a pulse. He found none. Crooke's eyes were wide and staring. Frantically, Bushell pulled off the khaki cape his fellow RAM was wearing and ripped open his tunic. The bullet—*without a doubt, a three-line bullet,* the clinical part of him reported: *a bullet from a Nagant*—had struck just to the left of Crooke's breastbone. He'd been dead, he must have been dead, before he hit the ground.

Cold and terrible anger filled Bushell. Later, when he had time, he would mourn. Now . . . Now he flicked the safety off his own rifle, heaved it to his shoulder, and fired at what he thought was movement back behind the abandoned shop Geoff and Patrick, Elgin and Benjamin had taken for their own. The kick from the Lee-Enfield was like the touch of an old friend: it had been away for a long time, but was immediately familiar. He worked the bolt. An empty brass shell casing flipped out of the breech and landed beside his feet with a small, metallic *ting*. A fresh round in the chamber, he peered out, waiting for a target.

After the first hail of lead, a lull came over the firing. A couple of Marines were down, one ominously still, the other twisting and writhing in pain. The rest had pulled back into the buildings across the overgrown square from the shop. Bushell couldn't see Samuel Stanley. He couldn't worry now, any more than he could mourn. Finishing this dreadful business came first.

"Give yourselves up!" he called across the square. "You'll have a fair trial."

"Not bloody likely," came the reply—a different voice from the one that had spoken first. He fervently hoped the owner of that voice was dead. "We'd swing, and you bloody well know it. You want us, you stinking redcoat, you come get us and pay the price." As if to punctuate his words, he fired at the spot from which he thought Bushell's voice was coming. The bullet slammed into the back wall ten feet or so from where the RAM stood.

Several Marines blazed away at the muzzle flash. A mocking laugh told them they'd missed their target. "Covering fire, sir, if you'd be so kind," an unruffled voice said: after a moment, Bushell recognized it as Sergeant Fuller's.

"Covering fire!" Lieutenant Green shouted. The Royal Marines banged away at their foes. Bushell emptied the box of ammunition in his rifle. He pulled another magazine from his pocket, clicked it into place, and shot again. The Sons of Liberty seemed to have plenty of cartridges. He was painfully aware he didn't.

Sergeant Fuller and half his squad raced across the street where the square ended, to try to flank out the villains. Someone inside the building where the Sons of Liberty sheltered was screaming now, a high, shrill sound of torment that made the hairs on the back of Bushell's neck try to rise. But firing kept coming from the building, and from a couple of others nearby. The Sons were not making it easy for anyone.

Charging straight across the square at them was nothing but a grandiose way of committing suicide. Flanking them out, as Fuller had realized, gave better odds. Bushell crawled to the rear of the building where he'd brought Felix Crooke, groped in gloom for a back door. His hand closed on something cold and wet and slimy that writhed as he squeezed it: a slug as big and thick as his forefinger. He made a choking sound of disgust, wiped his palm on the thigh of his denims, and at last found the latch he'd been seeking.

The door didn't want to open. He got to his feet, hoping no one could see him from across the square, and slammed a shoulder against it. It gave all at once. He stumbled out into the overgrown alley behind the building.

Motion there made the barrel of his rifle automatically jerk toward it. He checked himself and exclaimed in glad relief: "Sam!"

"Chief!" Stanley had been swinging his rifle toward Bushell. "How's Felix?" he demanded. Bushell gave a thumbs-down. Stanley grimaced. "Damn the bastards!" he said. "I figured our best chance at winkling them out was sliding round to one side."

"Same thing I was thinking," Bushell said. Together they trotted north past the edge of the square. Getting close a street at a time was different from running across the open space straight at the enemy's guns.

"Had enough of coming under fire in my army days," Stanley said. "Never thought it would happen to me as a RAM."

"Neither did I," Bushell answered. "Just because we're up near Russia doesn't mean we're *in* it."

They wrestled another back door open. The brass latch had turned green over the years, but was still strong. Brushing aside cobwebs, they went out to the front of the building and peered through a window. Bushell paused a moment to catch his breath. He could still smell the cheerful odor of the cookfire and faintly, beneath it, the reek from the rubbish the Sons of Liberty had discarded over their years here.

He looked at Stanley, who nodded. They yanked open the front door and dashed for the buildings on the eastern side of the street.

A bullet kicked up dirt a couple of feet away from Bushell. He dove straight through a window as bare of glass as a skull's eye socket was of flesh. "Oof!" he said as he landed on a hard floor, but he bounced to his feet. Sam Stanley sailed through the window next to the one he'd chosen, and came to earth no more gracefully than he had. He too, though, quickly got up again.

The back door to this building opened without a squeal or a groan, for which

Bushell was grateful. Lee-Enfield at the ready, he stepped out into the alley. Samuel Stanley came right behind him. "Watch yourself, Chief," Stanley said, his eyes flicking every which way. "The buggers have been moving about—"

"Don't I know it." Bushell too was scanning every building, every window, every doorway. The inside of his mouth felt dry and rough. His heart pounded. Breath whistled in and out of his nostrils. He'd forgotten what combat did to a man.

The firing picked up again off to the north, this time from the flank. "That Fuller, he knows what he wants to do and how to do it," Stanley said, now sounding intensely satisfied. Bushell nodded, unsurprised at the way his adjutant responded to an NCO's professional competence.

From the south, a young man came dashing round the corner. He wore a bushy beard, but the hair atop his head was cropped Roundhead close. He carried a rifle in his right hand.

"Hold it right there!" Bushell shouted, at the same instant as Samuel Stanley screamed, "Drop that gun or you're dead!"

Instead of dropping it, the man started to raise it to his shoulder. Bushell and Stanley fired together. The rifle flew from the young man's hands. He let out a grunt, a sound more of startlement than of pain. One finger started to move toward a hole in his wool plaid shirt, as if wondering how it had got there. Before the motion was more than well begun, he crumpled amidst the ferns.

Bushell ran to him. The fellow had fallen facedown, which let Bushell see the exit wounds in his back. He was still breathing, but more feebly with every moment that passed. "He's not going to make it, Sam," Bushell said.

"Not with one in the chest and one in the belly, he won't," Stanley agreed. He knelt beside the Son of Liberty. "We have to try, though. Cover me while I work on him—wish I had a proper wound dressing here; this'll cost me my vest." He shrugged out of his anorak, unbuttoned his shirt, and peeled off the white cotton vest beneath it.

Bushell trotted up toward the corner, sprawled behind a long-abandoned barrel. From there, he could pick off anyone who tried to come by. The firing by the old grocer's shop had died down again. He heard running feet. His finger tensed on the trigger.

No one came into sight. From around the corner came Sergeant Fuller's nononsense tones: "If that's you, you RAMs, give me your names."

"Bushell and Stanley," Bushell answered. "We have one of the villains down here, Sergeant."

"He's gone, Chief," Stanley said. He rubbed his hands on the ground, then reached for his shirt and anorak.

"We have two dead, one wounded further south," Sergeant Fuller said, showing himself now. "That should be the lot." His face went grim, or rather, grimmer. "Good riddance, I say."

# VII

▼

BUSHELL PULLED OUT HIS WATCH AND looked at it. When he saw the hour was just past nine, he shook his head in astonishment. The fight with the Sons of Liberty seemed to have lasted for hours, not bare minutes. He'd run into that before, down on the Nuevespañolan border. *One more thing about combat I'd managed to forget,* he thought.

"What now?" Sam Stanley asked. "The cutter isn't due back till noon."

"We search the area and we question the prisoner," Bushell said. "I wish Felix hadn't bought his plot. He was the one who knew the Sons backwards and forwards." He turned to Fuller. "What were your casualties, Sergeant?"

"Not counting your comrade, sir, two dead and four wounded," the noncom answered. "None of the wounds seems likely to prove fatal, but one of the lads will be on a stick for a long time to come, I'm afraid: took a bullet in the ankle."

"I'm sorry," Bushell said. "I never dreamt it would come to—this." Few criminals in the NAU had firearms, few of those who had them used them when the forces of the law caught them up, and none who did resort to firearms fought with such determination. None had, at any rate—not till now.

"In what sort of shape is the one you captured?" Stanley asked.

"Bullet in the shoulder, through-and-through flesh wound in the leg." Sergeant Fuller spat in the dirt. "Bugger'll live to hang. Waste of good rope, I call it, but what can you do?"

"Can he answer questions?" Bushell said.

A murky light kindled in Fuller's eyes. "If he doesn't, by God, we've ways to make him sing."

Two things flashed through Bushell's mind: *Sam would never say such a thing* and then, a moment later, *Thank heaven the military stays out of police work most places.* He kept that to himself; Fuller had put his life on the line to bag the Sons of Liberty. What he did say was, "Take us to him. We'll see what he tells us."

"Yes, sir." Sergeant Fuller led them back toward the grocer's shop. They passed several two-man teams of Royal Marines methodically going through the abandoned businesses of Buckley Bay. "I set them searching, sir," Fuller said, noting Bushell's glance. "We don't know for a fact there were only the four of them, do we?"

"No, we don't." Bushell took a tighter grip on his rifle; he hadn't thought of that. His soldierly skills, at least in the field, left a good deal to be desired these days. He hoped he'd made up for that loss with what he'd learned as a RAM. Given the way *The Two Georges* had vanished from under his nose, he had no proof of that, either.

No more gunshots rang out, from which he presumed the Marines found no one new to flush from cover. Lieutenant Green and a couple of other men crouched on the ground beside a fellow who, from his looks, could have been a cousin to the Son of Liberty Bushell and Stanley had shot. He had a bandage on his shoulder and another on his leg, both stained with red.

Green looked up. "Here he is, Colonel. Says his name is Elgin Goldsmith. Past that, he's kept mum, except to say he wants to speak to a solicitor."

Bushell glowered at the prisoner. "To hell with him and to hell with what he wants. Your men are more important to me, Lieutenant. How are your wounded? Sergeant Fuller says they should pull through."

"Seems that way, yes," Green said, nodding, "though poor Metcalf took a nasty one. Do you want to see what you can get out of Mr. Goldsmith here?" He made the title one of contempt.

"What I want is to drag him into the woods and let the bears have him," Bushell said savagely. "If I do that, though, I sink to his level, which isn't a place I care to go." He squatted beside Lieutenant Green. "All right, Goldsmith, you may as well talk. It can't make things worse for you, and it might make them better."

Pain twisted Goldsmith's face, but his pale eyes blazed at that. "Don't make me laugh," he said. "You'll fucking try me and you'll fucking hang me, whether I nark or not."

Since that was true, Bushell didn't bother arguing it. "Where did you get the rifles you were posting down to New Liverpool?" he asked. Goldsmith set his jaw and said nothing. In a conversational tone of voice, Bushell remarked, "I wonder what would happen if I hit that shoulder of yours with my rifle butt—purely by accident, of course."

"Chief—" Samuel Stanley began in worried tones. He hadn't cared for Sergeant Fuller's suggestion either, then. The sergeant, though, grinned from ear to ear. Bushell would not have cared to be on the receiving end of that grin.

Elgin Goldsmith started to shrug, winced, and stopped halfway. "Go on, then, you damned *Okhrana* man, if you're about to. Couldn't make me hurt no worse than I do already."

"Oh yes, he could," Sergeant Fuller said, sounding as if he looked forward to the prospect—and also as if he knew what he was talking about.

Bushell turned his head away from the prisoner before he sighed. One of the things he'd learned was that, unfortunately, courage did not reside only in the hearts of those who were by his standards good men. Villains had their share of it, too: and, of course, no man was ever a villain in his own eyes. Goldsmith no doubt reckoned himself a martyr to the cause of liberty. To him, the cause justified gunrunning, murder, and whatever other crimes he'd committed.

To Bushell, no cause justified crimes. While he might threaten torture, he would not inflict it. "How many rifles have you sent to New Liverpool?" he asked. Goldsmith said nothing. Bushell tried again: "Who pays you to send the rifles, and how much?"

When Goldsmith still refused to talk, Sergeant Fuller said, "Why don't you walk out into the woods, Colonel? I'll get your answers for you, and you won't have to know how I did it." Noncommissioned officers did many useful things for their superiors in that fashion, but Bushell shook his head. He might not see what Fuller did, but he'd know.

The Marine sergeant shrugged; his was not to argue with a colonel. Elgin Goldsmith visibly gloated. That came closer than any of Fuller's suggestions to making Bushell want to let the Marine loose on him.

Instead, he turned away himself. "Let's see what we can find in the building where they were living," he said to Samuel Stanley. "Maybe that will tell us what our charming friend won't."

"Maybe," Stanley said. As they walked toward the grocer's shop, he added quietly, for Bushell's ears alone, "For a second there, Chief, I thought you really were going to knock that bugger around."

"The only time I was tempted was when he sneered at me," Bushell answered. "If he'd caught me instead of the other way round, he wouldn't have thought twice." He stepped into the gloom inside the shop. "To hell with that. What have we here?"

As his eyes adjusted, he saw dark stains on the rammed-earth floor. A trail of blood led toward the back and, when he followed it, out into the alley behind the grocer's shop. Maybe he hadn't fired at an imaginary target back there after all, then.

Behind him, Samuel Stanley whistled softly. "Will you just look at this, Chief?"

Bushell had followed the blood trail into the back room without paying attention to anything else there. Now he ducked back inside and turned around. He sucked in his breath in what was almost a gasp: a couple of dozen Nagant rifles hung on nails that had been driven into the boards of the wall. On the floor were piled wooden chests. The top one was open, and half empty. He reached in and picked up a metal five-round box magazine of slightly different shape from the one that fed his Lee-Enfield.

"They had all the ammunition they needed, didn't they?" Stanley said.

"Enough to fight a small war," Bushell agreed. "All of it Russian gear." He looked north, toward Alaska. Stanley nodded, understanding that huntsman's gaze without a word of explanation.

Next to the wooden ammunition chests stood a smaller one made of painted metal. A lock held it closed. Bushell attacked the chest with the butt of his rifle, venting some of the fury he hadn't let himself turn on Elgin Goldsmith. The lock was made of stern stuff; it did not yield. After a few strokes, though, the hasp that held it to the chest broke off.

Bushell lifted the lid. For a moment, he just stared. "Lord have mercy," Samuel Stanley said softly. "How many roubles d'you reckon there are?"

"A great bloody lot of them," Bushell answered. Even in the dim light of the back room, the gold coins gleamed and sparkled. Next to English sovereigns, they were little things, each one worth two shillings, a penny ha'penny. Enough of them, though, added up to a good sum of money. There were more than enough here for that.

"I wonder how often those four shipped roubles out of here along with rifles," Stanley said. "The money and the guns all ended up in the wrong hands."

"I know one set of hands that closed on the money," Bushell said: "that printer I raided. He got paid in roubles for sightseeing brochures about the Queen Charlotte Islands, and spent them on those obscene pamphlets about the princesses."

"You'd have the devil's own time proving it before a magistrate," Stanley said. "A smart barrister would talk about circumstantial evidence and reasonable doubt until a jury couldn't tell right from Tuesday." He quoted Shakespeare, something he was fond of doing: "'The first thing we do, let's kill all the lawyers.'"

Normally, Bushell would have joined him for a round of cursing at men whose principal task, as he saw it, was keeping villains out of the gaol cells they deserved. Here, though, he kept his equanimity. "I don't care about barristers and judges. I know what I know. The Sons of Liberty here got the Nagant that killed Tricky Dick, and they got the roubles for Titus Hackett to spread his filth around. That means those two are connected here, even if neither one knew what the other was doing."

His adjutant nodded. "It also means both operations were getting their money from the same place." Now he turned his head toward Russian Alaska.

"We'll have a day of reckoning," Bushell said. "First, we need to put our own house in order. Once we get *The Two Georges* back, we'll be in a better position to ask questions of Duke Orlov in Victoria—and also of Sergei Pavlov back in New Liverpool."

"Indeed we will," Stanley said with a certain anticipatory relish. "One always assumes Russian consuls are spies. Now we'll have evidence to ship Sergei back to St. Petersburg. And speaking of evidence, let's see what else we can come up with here."

Before continuing the search, Bushell lowered the lid to the little metal chest, lest a Royal Marine find temptation stronger than duty. The trouble with gold was its very anonymity; any banker anywhere in the world would give you two shillings, a penny ha'penny for every gold rouble you handed him. Away from a setting like this, the coins weren't evidence, they were just money. As Stanley had said, a barrister would have no trouble establishing reasonable doubt about the provenance of the printer's roubles. Up here near the border, a lot of Russian gold would be in circulation, just as a good many British sovereigns were apt to be floating around in Sitka and Kodiak.

But for the rifles and money, the interior of the grocer's shop yielded little in the way of evidence. Geoff, Patrick, Elgin, and Benjamin had apparently whiled away some of their time with tracts full of hatred similar to those Joseph Watkins had had in his flat, but those, however distasteful, were not against the law. The traps and lines stored in the front room said the Sons of Liberty truly had made part of their living hunting and fishing, as they'd claimed.

"This place is too bloody neat," Samuel Stanley complained. "It's almost as if they knew they were going to have visitors, but we made sure they hadn't a clue."

"Just because we haven't found everything doesn't mean it's not here," Bushell said. He snapped his fingers. "For instance—where's their rubbish pitch?"

Stanley's eyes lit up. "We haven't smelled it much, so it'll be downwind from here: by the water, I'd guess, unless they've gone and heaved everything straight into Masset Inlet."

"There's a grim thought," Bushell said. "But you wouldn't chuck everything into the inlet. If some of your rubbish started turning up at Port Clements, that might bring the *Grampus* by to give you a caution. They wouldn't want to draw notice to themselves."

"Let's look about," Stanley said.

Looking didn't find the rubbish pitch; their noses did. As soon as they'd gone a little more than halfway toward the edge of Masset Inlet, they got wind of the stink. "*That* way," they said together. After a moment, Bushell added, "It's a wonder we haven't spied a great flock of bald eagles quarreling over the refuse. That would have told us where they kept it."

When they reached the building where the Sons of Liberty stowed their rubbish, they found a grid of slats nailed over its windows, perhaps for the very purpose of keeping away the eagles. The door also bore a stout padlock. "Bears," Stanley said, and Bushell nodded.

This time, hammering at the lock with a rifle butt accomplished nothing. "Back in a moment," Bushell said. When he returned, he had Lieutenant Green in tow, and was carrying all the keys the Sons of Liberty had had on their persons. One of those proved to fit the lock.

"Phew!" Green said, as opening the door released a wave of stinking air. "I'm damned glad this place never has hot summers."

"Well—yes." Bushell went first into the rubbish-filled room. The stench here wasn't as bad as it might have been, but it was pretty bad. Cockroaches scurried round his feet; slugs would have scurried had they been able to move faster.

The midden inside reached more than halfway to the ceiling. An archaeologist could have studied the festering pile for weeks, going through it layer by layer. Bushell, however, was uninterested in the geologic past. He snatched papers off the front and top of the mound, figuring they were the most recent. Gasping and fighting his stomach, he carried a double handful outside.

"My turn," Stanley said, and plunged into the reeking room. The papers he brought out, like those in Bushell's hands, carried the reek with them. They were crumpled and torn and stained with tea leaves, coffee grounds, grease, and other less easily identifiable substances. As soon as Stanley emerged, Bushell went back inside.

Lieutenant Green watched them with genuine admiration. "You couldn't make me do that every day," he said, "not for a hundred thousand pounds a year."

"Most of the filth we go through is metaphorical," Bushell said, setting down another stinking load of what might have been evidence and might have been only wastepaper. "Every now and then, though—"

Samuel Stanley brought out a few more papers. "I think that's the last of them, unless we want to go digging," he said, and then, "Phew! They won't let us into the Skidegate Lodge tonight, not smelling like this they won't."

"We'll worry about that later." Bushell turned to Morton Green. "Have you stripped the bodies of the Sons of Liberty? We'll want any papers you find on them, and on the live one, too—Elgin, that's his name." As long as he concentrated on what needed doing here, he wouldn't have to think about Felix Crooke, now growing cold and stiff inside a dead house in a dead town.

"We've searched the prisoner, sir, but, except for those keys, we haven't gone over the effects of the dead men," Green answered. "I'll tend to that straightaway."

He started to leave. Before he could, Bushell said, "If you have someone with a sack, have him bring it here so we can load this"—he groped for a word, but found only a vague gesture—"into it." Nodding, Green took off at a trot.

That left Bushell having done everything he could for the moment. "Jesus God, Sam, what have we stumbled into?" he groaned, his face a naked mask of pain. "Poor Crooke told the buggers who we were, and they shot him down like a dog. Like a dog." His shoulders sagged, as if, like Hercules, he'd taken the weight of the world away from Atlas for a moment.

"He was stupid, Chief, and you know it," Samuel Stanley answered. "We told him what these villains were liable to be like, but he stood up and gave them a clean shot at him. He didn't believe you, he didn't believe me, he thought everything would be cricket no matter what we said—and he paid for it."

"Thinking everything will be cricket shouldn't get you killed," Bushell said.

"No, it shouldn't—but sometimes it will." Stanley sounded very much like a veteran sergeant talking with a young lieutenant after his first action. "If everything were cricket all the time, there'd be no work for the likes of you and me."

"He should have stayed behind his desk," Bushell said. "He knew what he was doing there."

"*The Two Georges* should have stayed on the wall in the governor's mansion," Stanley said. Bushell grimaced, then nodded.

▼

Lieutenant Commander Edward Woodbridge got out of the larger of the two boats his sailors had rowed from the *Grampus* to the shore. Nodding to Bushell, he said, "Good morning—no, excuse me, good afternoon, Colonel. I trust you have the villains in captivity?"

Bushell gestured wordlessly. The Navy man followed him to what had been the Buckley Bay town square. The oarsmen tagged along after them. There, faces covered by rain capes, lay Felix Crooke, the three dead Sons of Liberty, and the two dead Royal Marines. With them were the wounded prisoner and the four wounded Marines.

Woodbridge stared in disbelief at the carnage. Before he could speak, one of the sailors behind him burst out, "Lor' love a duck, wot the bleedin' 'ell 'appened 'ere?"

"Silence, Montague!" Woodbridge snapped automatically. But he said nothing more after that: Montague's question was the only one that made sense. Bushell himself was damned if he could see how better to phrase it.

As baldly as if he were dictating an after-action report—something he would have to do all too soon—he described the morning's events for Woodbridge. When he was through, he asked, "Could a boat have slipped out of Port Clements after the *Grampus* sailed, to warn these men here?"

"No, sir," Woodbridge answered decisively. "Not possible. I've been on the wireless back to the port several times since we disembarked your party. No untoward action of any sort."

"That makes sense, Chief, much as I hate to say it." Samuel Stanley looked as unhappy as he sounded, but went on, "They wouldn't have yelled out 'Who are you?' the way they did if they'd known what we were about."

"You're right, and I'm grasping at straws." Bushell slammed a fist into his open palm. "It just—went wrong." He turned away.

Lieutenant Commander Woodbridge said, "Let's get everyone aboard ship. We'll stow the prisoner in the brig and the other wounded in sick bay; we have a pharmacist's mate who can tend to them there. Not that you haven't done well with your first aid, I'm sure, but—"

Bushell nodded, cutting him off. "That would be splendid. Would you see to it?" He started to walk away, to be alone again, but duty pulled him back and made him ask, "When we get back to Port Clements, have you a telephone there I might use?"

"Certainly, Colonel," Woodbridge answered. "Would you care to wireless a message ahead, so one of my men might relay it for you?"

After a moment's thought, Bushell shook his head. "No, I'll tell the RAMs myself. I know the details." That said, he did walk off. He'd never set himself a task he relished less.

"Sir, I shall also need to ring up Commander Hairston," Lieutenant Green said to Woodbridge.

The Navy man nodded. Then he turned to his sailors and ordered them back to the *Grampus* for stretchers to transport the wounded—and the dead—to the boats. "And bring Hartnett with you when you return," he added, explaining to Bushell, "That's the pharmacist's mate I mentioned."

"Very good," Bushell said wearily. He took out his water bottle and drank from it. It wasn't as cold and sweet as it had been when he filled it at St. Mary's Spring in the early hours of the morning. He didn't care. Water wasn't what he craved. Enough whiskey to find oblivion at least for a night . . . that would be sweet. But he couldn't even drink himself into a stupor, not now, not with so much still to do.

Transferring everyone back to the *Grampus* took far longer than anyone would have imagined before the familiar world of law exploded in gunfire. The Royal Marines would not let the sailors load their fallen comrades onto the stretchers or carry them to the boats. "We tend to our own," one of them said, pride in his voice. Bushell understood that; he and Stanley set Felix Crooke's body on its stretcher. Royal Marines also put the dead Sons of Liberty on stretchers, dumping them down onto the canvas as if they were so many chunks of wood.

Hartnett fixed a fresh splint to the leg of the Marine with a shattered ankle, but otherwise pronounced himself satisfied with the treatment the wounded had received. Lieutenant Commander Woodbridge said to Bushell, "By your leave, I can wireless ahead to Port Clements so Dr. Lansing can meet us at the wharf."

"Yes, go ahead," Bushell said. He wished Woodbridge—and the entire world—would leave him alone: this even though he knew work, in the absence of whiskey, was the best anodyne he would find.

At last the unwounded living went back aboard the *Grampus*. The cutter backed away from the shore, turned, and, skirting the little tree-covered island not far from Buckley Bay, sailed east across Masset Inlet toward Port Clements.

Bushell stood at the stern, staring back toward the abandoned town. Once Woodbridge made as if to approach him. He did not turn his head, he did not move in any definable way, but he made it plain he did not want anyone near. Woodbridge's shoulders slumped, ever so slightly. He went back to his duties.

Perhaps ten minutes after that, Sam Stanley came up. Bushell projected the same signal by body wireless. Taking advantage of long friendship, Stanley ignored it. He stood beside Bushell, leaning his elbows on the rail and propping his chin in his hands. "Brooding about it won't make it better," he observed. "Won't make you better, either."

"Go away," Bushell said without turning his head.

Instead of leaving, Stanley reached into the hip pocket of his trousers and pulled out his wallet. From it he drew a purple five-pound note. He held it in front of Bushell's nose, so close that Bushell's eyes had to cross to focus on the small reproduction of *The Two Georges* on the banknote. "This is what it's all about, Chief," he said quietly. "Shall we start looking over the evidence we picked up? Woodbridge has given me a little compartment we can use."

He waited. When Bushell didn't answer, he sighed and went off. After a moment, Bushell followed him.

Work did prove a pain reliever almost as potent as Jameson. Seated across a steel table in a tiny, metal room painted grey and garishly lit by a bare bulb mounted in the ceiling, Bushell and Stanley sorted through the pile of papers they'd snatched from the rubbish heap the Sons of Liberty had built up in Buckley Bay.

"We'll do envelopes first," Bushell declared. "They'll have dates and postmarks on them, so we'll know when the villains got them and where they came from."

"Right, Chief," Samuel Stanley said, so enthusiastically that Bushell suspected he'd have got loud agreement had he suggested sorting papers by the size and color of the stains they bore. But he was functioning again, and when he functioned, he functioned well.

"Thanks, Sam," he murmured without looking up.

"For what?" his adjutant asked. "Here, you take this bunch while I'm going through the rest." He pushed filthy, crumpled papers at Bushell.

Some of the envelopes were from commercial establishments in Skidegate. Bushell set those aside for the time being, since they'd been discarded unopened. Then curiosity got the better of him. He slit one—and pulled out an advertising circular. Even in the back of beyond, such worthless tripe got posted.

The rest of the envelopes proved more interesting. "They had friends all over the bloody place, didn't they?" Stanley remarked.

"That they did," Bushell said somberly. Just looking at the postmarks made him see the spiderweb of conspiracy the Sons of Liberty had spun across the NAU. The threads were thin and normally all but invisible, but no less sticky and dangerous on account of that.

He'd expected to find envelopes posted from New Liverpool, and he did. To his disappointment, none of them came from Sergei Pavlov. And he knew the Sons of Liberty were strong in Boston and Pennsylvania: *Common Sense* came out of the one, while the harsh lives the coal miners of the other led inclined them away from the status quo. But one envelope he discovered left him shaking his head. "Will you look at this, Sam?"

"What have you got?"

Bushell passed him the envelope. It was franked not with the usual one-florin stamps of the NAU, but with one that bore a lightning bolt, the legend HENO THE THUNDERER, and, in larger letters, the words THE SIX NATIONS. The postmark read *Doshoweh*.

Stanley clicked his tongue between his teeth. "If that's not the strangest place from which to post something to the Sons of Liberty, damn me if I know what is."

"Just what I was thinking," Bushell answered. The Six Nations that made up the Iroquois Confederacy controlled the land just west of the province of New York, and did so for the most part under their own laws, though the NAU had charge of their dealings with foreign powers. The relationship, though (like much of the Empire's constitution) never formally defined, had continued for more than two centuries, and satisfied most people on both sides of it.

"Doshoweh's that town not far from Niagara Falls, isn't it?" Stanley said.

"That's right—capital of the Six Nations. And, as you said, a bloody odd place for the Sons of Liberty to be operating." The liberty to which the Sons dedicated themselves was reserved for them alone, and emphatically did not include the Indians who had inhabited North America before the Sons' fathers crossed the Atlantic.

"It might be a brilliant piece of cover," Stanley said, passing the envelope back to Bushell. "I don't think we've ever looked for the Sons of Liberty inside the Six Nations—who would? They could do just about whatever they pleased there, so long as they kept quiet about it and didn't draw the notice of the local authorities."

Bushell examined the postmark more closely. "Whatever they've been doing, they're still at it. This was sent less than a week ago. Eighteenth June, the date is."

"Is that a fact?" Stanley said. "Then it won't have got to our villains much before we did. I wonder if we can find the letter that came in the envelope."

They went through the papers they'd collected from the rubbish heap. To their frustration, none of them proved to bear the requisite date. Then Bushell said, "Maybe one of the villains still had it on him when the fighting started."

Those papers were separate from the ones plucked off the midden. Instead of stains from tea leaves and coffee grounds, some of them were brownish-black with drying blood. Bushell carefully unfolded one. "Here!" he exclaimed. "It's dated 18 June—no address, though, worse luck. Just the message—listen to this, Sam: 'Stop sending rifles at once; repeat, at once. No point to drawing unwanted attention to ourselves.' And it's signed, 'Joe.'"

Stanley slammed his fist down on the tabletop. "We're on the right track." He looked up to the bare bulb as if it were the naked face of God. "At last."

"Amen," Bushell said: it was, for him, an answered prayer.

▼

Bushell approached the telephone in Lieutenant Commander Woodbridge's office in Port Clements like a man walking to the gallows, each step more difficult than the one that had gone before. When he sat down at the desk, he felt as if the hangman had slipped the hood down over his head.

He picked up the phone, and in his mind heard and felt the trap fall out from under his feet. To the operator, he said, "I'd like to ring the offices of the Royal American Mounted Police in New Liverpool, Upper California, please. The number there is BLenheim 1415, and my name is Thomas Bushell."

"Sir, your call will need a little while to put through," the operator warned, surprise in her voice.

He'd expected that. He wondered how long it had been since anyone in the Queen Charlotte Islands had telephoned New Liverpool. "Do whatever you need to do," he said, and settled down to wait, the telephone handset against his ear.

The Port Clements operator relayed the call to Skidegate, the Skidegate operator to Prince Rupert across the Hecate Strait. That connection took a while to make; listening to the clicks and pops in his ear, Bushell wondered if the call was going by wire or swimming over the waves. At last Prince Rupert acknowledged the existence of Skidegate, but then had to pass the call on to Prince George. From Prince George, probably by a roundabout route paralleling the railroad tracks, it reached Wellesley on the Puget Sound.

After that, as if relieved to be returning to civilization, the call moved rapidly south. Almost twenty minutes had passed before the Port Clements operator told the RAM switchboard, "I have a long-distance call for you from Mr. Thomas Bushell."

"Yes, have him go ahead," the RAM operator said, and then, to Bushell, "How may I help you, Colonel?"

"Is that you, Jonathan?" Bushell said. "Put me through to Lieutenant General Sir Horace Bragg, please."

"I'm sorry, Colonel, but I can't," Jonathan answered. "His train departed for Victoria this morning."

"What's that?" Bushell said. "He told me he was going to stay in New Liverpool for a couple of weeks, maybe longer."

"Yes, sir, that's what he'd been saying up until yesterday," the RAM operator answered. "But Sir Martin Luther King and his staff headed back for the capital last night. I don't know this for a fact, sir"—Jonathan's voice went low and conspiratorial as he shared his gossip—"but they say Sir Horace was going on about not letting Sir Martin and some of the people who work for him out of his sight for any longer than he could help."

"Was he?" Bushell replied with interest. Sir Horace had suspicions, then; Bushell wondered how closely they marched with his own. "Get me Gordon Rhodes, then."

"Colonel Bushell! I'm so glad to hear from you," Major Rhodes exclaimed when the call went through. Before Bushell could answer, Rhodes went on, "We've finally tracked down the newspaper whose headline the Sons of Liberty used in the photograph they sent us and the press along with their ransom note."

"Have you?" Bushell said. That was important enough that he needed to know it, so he held off giving his own news, most of which he was less than eager to pass on in any case. "Tell me."

"Yes, sir." Rhodes took a deep, portentous breath. "It's from the *Doshoweh Sentinel,* the chief English-language newspaper in the Six Nations. Isn't that remarkable? Who would have thought the Sons of Liberty had penetrated the Iroquois chiefdom?"

"Up until an hour ago, no one," Bushell said. That discovery fit all too well with his own, and had been won at far less cost.

Full of his own concerns, Rhodes failed to pay close attention to his superior's reply. He continued, "It's a pity Captain Oliver had to return to Victoria with Sir Horace. She did some outstanding work for us here, identifying that headline, and I want to be certain she gets the credit she deserves."

He sounded so enthusiastic, Bushell wondered whether Patricia Oliver had been as outstanding off duty as she had while at RAM headquarters. He scowled down at Lieutenant Commander Woodbridge's desk. It wasn't his business. Better he didn't know, in fact.

Gordon Rhodes said, "And how are things up in the Queen Charlotte Islands, sir? Do you know, I had to check in the *Times Atlas of the British Empire* to be sure where you and Captain Stanley and Lieutenant-Colonel Crooke were going."

"So did I, before we set out," Bushell answered. Once he'd said that, though, he had to tell the rest: the Sons of Liberty shooting Felix Crooke as he tried to persuade them to surrender, the gun battle that followed, the casualties among both the Sons and the Royal Marines.

"Good God, sir!" Rhodes said when Bushell paused in the dismal narrative. "A RAM gunned down like a bandit down in the Nuevespañolan mountains?" He sounded shocked to the core. Bushell did not blame him. He was shocked, too; he'd seen it happen instead of hearing about it over fifteen hundred miles of wire. When the news spread, flags would fly at half staff in front of every RAM office in the NAU.

Mechanically, Bushell went on to summarize the evidence he and Samuel Stanley had found after the shooting stopped. "We need to notify the RAMs in

Doshoweh at once," he said. "I doubt *The Two Georges* is still there—the Sons would have moved it as soon as they posted their pictures—but we may be able to keep them from operating out of the Six Nations any more."

"I'll take care of that, sir," Gordon Rhodes said. "We'll have to deal with the local Iroquois constabulary, too; the Six Nations being as they are, we have rather less authority there than elsewhere in the Union."

"That's right," Bushell said. *One more thing to complicate my life* ran through his mind. "We'll have to manage as best we can, that's all. Oh—when you call Doshoweh, tell them one more thing, will you?"

"Whatever you like, sir," Rhodes said, and waited expectantly. When Bushell didn't answer right away, he asked, "Er—what is it?"

"Tell them Sam and I are on our way."

▼

Getting off the Queen Charlotte Islands wasn't as easy as Bushell had hoped. He and Lieutenant Green both spoke to Commander Hairston by telephone from Port Clements, but, in a case with half a dozen men dead by gunfire and more wounded, that was not of itself an adequate response.

"I'll need formal depositions from you and Captain Stanley, Colonel," Hairston said. "I want to wrap up the case against this Goldsmith so tight, there'll be not a chance of his wriggling free of the noose."

"But, Commander, Captain Stanley and I have to go back to the mainland to follow the leads to *The Two Georges* we discovered," Bushell protested.

"No, sir," Hairston said. "That case is a theft. This one is a homicide, so it takes precedence. You and your adjutant are not going back to Prince Rupert till you tell me everything you know about what happened at Buckley Bay. The faster you do that, the faster you get what you want."

He was right. After a moment's anger, Bushell realized as much. He also realized it wouldn't have mattered had Hairston been wrong: the man had the authority to hold him here, if not indefinitely, then long enough to play havoc with the investigation. He sighed. "All right, Commander. When we get back to Skidegate, we shall be at your service."

The drive back to Skidegate was made in mournful silence. Along with the lorries that had made the trip north from the naval base came a flat-bed machine driven by one of Lieutenant Commander Woodbridge's sailors. In the staked bed, covered by a large canvas tarpaulin from the *Grampus*, lay the bodies of Felix Crooke and the slain Royal Marines and Sons of Liberty. Dr. Lansing, the Port Clements physician, drove some of the wounded to Skidegate in the town ambulance. Another sailor drove the rest—including Elgin Goldsmith—in Lansing's private steamer.

It was nearly four o'clock by the time the sad convoy reached the naval base. Redcaps took charge of Goldsmith, and of the dead; Navy doctors saw to the injured Marines. The flatbed lorry, ambulance, and motorcar steamed back toward Port Clements.

Commander Hairston met the returning RAMs and Royal Marines with half a dozen yeomen, each poised to record witness statements tachygraphically. Four of the six clerks were Negroes; their predilection for bureaucratic slots seemed to hold good even in the Navy.

Bushell spoke mechanically, as if someone had wound up a platter and were playing it through his mouth rather than a phonogram. A yeoman's pen raced across sheet after sheet of paper, covering the pages with arcane pothooks. Hairston sat in a chair off to one side, listening like a man carved from stone.

When Bushell had finished, Hairston spoke to the yeoman: "Thank you, Washington. Now go transcribe that; I'll want Colonel Bushell's signature on the fair copy before he leaves Skidegate." Saluting, the colored yeoman departed. Hairston turned to Bushell. "You got your tail in a crack, didn't you, Colonel? God in heaven, what a mess."

"God in heaven," Bushell repeated dully. He shook his head, still having trouble believing how things had turned sour so fast. "Everything was going just as it should, and then—" He didn't go on. He didn't need to go on.

"Not your fault, Colonel, I shouldn't think," Hairston said. "You and your party did everything right, up to the very last minute. For whatever it may be worth to you, you have my sympathy."

"I don't want your sympathy," Bushell said. "I want to—" *To get drunk and blot out everything that happened today.* But he couldn't say that. Worse luck, he couldn't do it. Haltingly, he continued, "I want to get on with the investigation. I want Felix still to be alive, and your Marines, too." He couldn't have that, either.

In a room not far away, a typewriter started tapping. After a while, another joined it, then another and another. The clattering keys and the warning bells as the machines reached the ends of lines were normally sounds of purposeful activity. Now they reminded Bushell of the other, more violent activity they were setting down on paper, magically transmuting terror to evidence.

Hairston said, "I'm afraid the afternoon ferry will already have sailed for Prince Rupert, Colonel. You'll be laying over here another night."

"Yes, I know." Bushell kept his temper under tight rein—as well he was sober. Rationally, he knew the local security chief was doing his job, and doing it properly. Rationality had nothing to do with the way he wanted to storm forward after *The Two Georges*—and escape the Queen Charlotte Islands as fast as he could.

"Will you take charge of Lieutenant-Colonel Crooke's body?" Hairston asked. "I'm sure you RAMs have your own procedures for comrades killed in the line of duty."

Bushell covered his face with his hands. Wish as he would, he couldn't escape what had happened. "I'll see the body across to Prince Rupert, at any rate," he said. "I'm sure we do have procedures for such a case, Commander, but I'm damned if I know what they are. I don't remember when the last RAM was shot dead attempting to make an arrest. It's been years—I know that."

Yeoman Washington brought in a typed version of Bushell's statement. Bushell skimmed it, scrawled his signature, and thrust the papers at Hairston. The security chief took them, then reached for the telephone. "I'll get you and Captain Stanley a driver to take you back to the Skidegate Lodge," he said.

The ride to the hotel passed in almost complete silence. The sailor at the wheel of the steamer knew what had happened up at Buckley Bay. His mute outrage blended with those of Bushell and Stanley; the men understood one another without need for words.

"Evenin', gents," the clerk who had registered them the day before called from behind the desk. He suddenly noticed that, while he'd registered three men, only two were walking into the hotel. "Where's your friend? The fish catch *him?*" He laughed at his own wit.

Bushell crossed the lobby in half a dozen long strides. Eyes blazing, he seized the clerk by the cravat and dragged him forward across the registration desk until the two men were nose to nose. The clerk let out a strangled squawk and tried to break free, but Bushell slapped his arm aside.

Samuel Stanley hurried up, set a hand on Bushell's shoulder. "Let him go, Chief!" he said in a low but urgent voice.

As if throwing a piece of garbage, Bushell pushed the clerk back to his place. The man stared at him, popeyed. "I'll have the redcaps on you," he gasped.

"Our friend is dead—shot dead," Stanley said. "So are two Royal Marines. So are three villains. Aside from those small details, the world's a lovely place."

The clerk's eyes got wider. Bushell watched the process with a certain abstract interest; he hadn't thought it possible. "I—I'm sorry," the fellow stammered. "I didn't know—"

"Why does this not surprise me?" Bushell turned on his heel and strode toward the stairs. Stanley followed him. As they climbed to their rooms, Bushell said, "We have a lot of planning to do, if we're going to find the fastest way to get to Doshoweh from Prince Rupert."

"Isn't that the truth?" His adjutant started ticking possibilities off on his fingers: "Train back to Wellesley and then airship—or airships; I don't know the routes offhand—to Doshoweh; train all the way from Prince Rupert; or train partway east from Prince Rupert to Doshoweh and then pick up an airship. Which one's fastest is going to depend on what sort of conditions we can get and the layovers we'll have to make."

"We can't find out what we need to know, not here in this one-lung town," Bushell said. "We'll learn more in Prince Rupert—at the train station, or else from the RAMs: they'll have to do a good deal of traveling, I expect."

"Yes, Prince Rupert's a long way from—anywhere, when you get down to it," Stanley said. "For tonight, what say we wash up and eat some supper in the Haida Lounge?" He paused, then added cautiously, "And maybe we could have a couple of drinks, too."

"Now you're talking," Bushell said with such enthusiasm that his adjutant looked at him in alarm. He patted Stanley on the shoulder. "Relax, Sam. I don't have to be functional till tomorrow afternoon. When the ferry comes, I'll be ready to meet it."

"All right, Chief." Stanley still looked dubious. "See you downstairs in, oh, half an hour?"

Bushell nodded and went into his room. He spent most of the time in the showerbath, with the water as hot as he could stand it. Scrub as he would, though, he couldn't wash away the feeling that Felix Crooke's blood still stained him.

In the Haida Lounge, he ordered salmon cheeks. Samuel Stanley surprised him by picking the dried herring eggs on kelp. He started to ask Stanley about it, then held his peace: his adjutant had found his own way to memorialize their fallen comrade.

Both men chose Caribou Ale. Bushell resolved to stick to that. Getting drunk on ale took application; it wasn't as easy as it was with Jameson. After the third bottle, the tip of his nose began to go numb, a sign the brew was starting to have its way with him. After the third one, though, he also had to visit the jakes, and he sloshed when he got up to do it. Dedicated drinkers of ale and beer could put away vast amounts of their chosen beverage, but he hadn't developed the knack. After five ales, he was logy and yawning and ready for bed. Samuel Stanley beamed with well-hopped approval as the two of them, none too steadily, headed up to their rooms.

▼

The headache with which Bushell woke soon yielded to a couple of paracetamol tablets. He called the hotel's housekeeping service and gave them the clothes he'd worn the day before. A couple of hours later, a young woman returned the garments. "I'm sorry, sir," she said, "but you can still see the stain on your anorak from the deer or whatever you killed. We did our best, but—" She spread her hands.

"Thanks for trying," Bushell said, and tipped her ten shillings. After he shut the door, he wadded up the anorak and threw it into a corner of the closet. If one of the cleaning men wanted it, he could take it, and welcome.

He jumped when the telephone rang. It was Commander Hairston. "We'll have Lieutenant-Colonel Crooke's body at the dock in a Navy coffin to meet the ferry. I've rung up the Prince Rupert RAMs, too, let them know what's happened. Someone will be waiting for you there when you make port."

"I'm grateful for your help," Bushell said, though he dreaded spending hours having to bear the silent reproach of the plain pine box and what it bore.

He and Stanley took a cab to the harbor—by chance, the same cab that had taken them to the Skidegate Lodge when they reached the Queen Charlotte Islands. As the desk clerk had, the driver said, "Weren't there three of you gents before?"

Unlike the clerk, he wasn't being snide, merely curious. After a moment of awkward silence, Samuel Stanley answered, "Our friend—will be waiting for us there." Bushell bit his lip.

A long queue of happy sailors bound for leave waited for the ferry to board passengers for Prince Rupert. A couple of minutes after Bushell and Stanley arrived, a Navy lorry pulled up at the dock. Half a dozen redcaps lifted the coffin down from the bed of the lorry. The sailors stared.

Commander Hairston got out of the left side of the driver's compartment and walked over to Bushell and Stanley. "I'm sorry it turned out this way, gentle-men," he said heavily. "That's all I can tell you."

When the crew of the *Northern Lights* moved aside the light metal gate from the dock end of the gangplank, the sailors stood aside to let the military police carry Felix Crooke's body aboard the ferry. Some of them took off their caps in token of respect for the dead. They would have heard about what happened up at Buckley Bay; that story must have gone through barracks and ships at the speed of light.

Bushell stood by the bow rail most of the way across the Hecate Strait, as if he did not want to look back at the islands he was leaving. Once or twice, sailors started to come up to him, whether to ask questions about the gun battle or to of-fer their sympathies he could not guess. None actually got close enough to speak to him; as he had on the *Grampus*, he made it very plain he wanted to be left alone. On this journey, Samuel Stanley respected his privacy, too. Stanley, no doubt, did not want sailors importuning him, either.

The sun still stood high in the northwest when the *Northern Lights* got into Prince Rupert a few minutes past eight in the evening. On the docks waited six RAMs in dress reds—*more pallbearers*, Bushell thought—along with another, older man in civilian clothes. After the sailors streamed off the ferry, the RAMs boarded and came up to Bushell and Stanley, who met them beside Crooke's coffin.

"Colonel Bushell?" The man in mufti held out his hand. "I'm Major Win-ston Macmillan, commandant here. Commander Hairston rang me up this morning. Terrible thing." His eyes flicked to the coffin. "I can't believe it."

"Thank you for your help, Major." Bushell was sick of saying that. He didn't want to be the object of anyone's help; he just wanted to get on with the business of cracking his case. But what he wanted and what he got had swung away from each other in the old logging town.

"I gather you'll want us to take charge of arrangements for transportation of the body and such." Macmillan again glanced down at the box that held the mortal remains of Felix Crooke.

"If you'd be so kind."

"We are at your service, Colonel—and at Lieutenant-Colonel Crooke's." He looked at the coffin once more. His voice went heavy and full of grief: "He's one of ours, after all." After a moment to collect himself, he continued, "If you two gentlemen will be so kind as to accompany me? No matter what has happened here, of course, your duty does not cease. *The Two Georges*—" As he had before, Macmillan murmured, "Terrible thing."

By the size of the headquarters he commanded, Macmillan had been hard-pressed to collect half a dozen men to bear away Felix Crooke's coffin, though he had responsibility over an area the size of Upper California. He did, however, possess an abundance of railroad and airship schedules, and pored over them with Bushell and Stanley.

"The train rolls out of here at half past five tomorrow morning," he said. "That's the one fixed point amongst the variables. It's bound for Wellesley, of course, and would put you there late tomorrow evening. The next airship out of Wellesley wouldn't be till the morning after, though. You could change trains in Prince George and go east over the Rockies that way. From Regina, you could take an airship to Astoria on Lake Michigan and make your connection for Doshoweh there. If all goes well, I believe that is your fastest route to the Six Nations."

"Let me see the schedules once more," Bushell said, and he and Stanley spent the next hour or so in calculation. At some time during that interval, roast-beef sandwiches on sourdough bread appeared as if by magic. Bushell had his two thirds eaten before he fully realized it was there.

"Going to be very tight, Chief," Stanley said. Bushell looked for him to complain about having to rise early yet again to catch the eastbound train, but he was all business. "We don't have much time to get from the train station to the airship port in Regina, or from one airship to the other in Astoria. If we run even a little late, we lose half a day, and you know what they say about the Astoria airship port."

Bushell did know. O'Hare Airship Port was the busiest one in the NAU. Astoria, being centrally located, lay at the heart of several airship companies' routes. Delays there were legendary.

"Safer just to take the train all the way from Regina," Stanley went on. "We could just as easily get into Doshoweh later as earlier if we gamble on the airships."

"You're right—it would be safer," Bushell said. His adjutant started to brighten, but then he went on, "All the same, we'll gamble. If we're late, we're late, but I want the chance to be early." He turned to Major Macmillan. "Have your people make the arrangements."

"Yes, sir," Macmillan said, in the tone of voice juniors use to betoken obedience to their superior's foolish orders. Samuel Stanley said nothing, but the expression he wore was eloquent. Bushell didn't care. He felt all too acutely time's hot breath on the back of his neck. Anything he could do that might wring out a few more precious hours in which to pursue *The Two Georges*, he would.

He and Stanley waited at the headquarters building until their travel plans were set up. Then Macmillan, as if washing his hands of them, had them motored to the Highliner Inn. It was after eleven, but through scattered clouds twilight remained bright in the west and north. As it did at any other hour, the air smelled faintly of halibut.

▼

Over halibut balls in the train-station café the next morning, Bushell plowed through the *Prince Rupert Register*. The banner headline told of the gunfight at Buckley Bay and the death of Felix Crooke. He was, an enterprising reporter had discovered, the first RAM killed by gunfire in fourteen years.

Samuel Stanley had a copy of the *Register*, too. When he finished his eggs and bacon, he slammed the paper down and growled, "Why don't they just wire the Sons of Liberty what we were up to there? Every bloody rag in the whole bloody NAU will have printed this by tomorrow."

Tomorrow, the two RAMs would, if everything went well, be getting into Regina and making their airship connection for Astoria. Worrying about that was enough for Bushell at the moment; he stayed philosophical about the newspaper. "Could be worse," he said. "The story doesn't mention our names."

"Huzzah," Stanley said sourly. "The whole bloody Empire already knows we were headed up this way. The trouble with the Sons is, they're smart enough to remember that and make the connection."

"Damn all we can do about it," Bushell said. A tinny speaker announced the imminent departure of the train bound for Prince George and Wellesley. He gulped the last of his Irish Breakfast, slammed the cup down on the table, and hurried to the platform. Still grumbling, Samuel Stanley followed.

The nine-hour trip back to Prince George was like watching a film run in reverse. Bushell felt bored and useless. On most journeys, he used his time wisely, bringing along plenty of work to occupy him while he was traveling to ready him for whatever he had to do once he arrived at his destination. All that mattered now was arriving, for he couldn't do anything useful till he got to Doshoweh. The thought of climbing into the open cockpit of a military aeroplane and whizzing across the continent at a couple of hundred miles an hour seemed less foolishly extravagant than it had when he'd laughed at it in the dining room of the *Upper California Limited*.

He fell asleep in his seat, lulled by the rhythm of the rails and by a long succession of short nights. The squeal of the train's brakes as it pulled into Prince George woke him. In the aisle seat beside him, Samuel Stanley seemed ready to snore all the way down to Wellesley.

Regretfully, Bushell shook him. "We change trains here, Sam."

Stanley's eyes flew open. "I wasn't asleep," he said indignantly. He looked out the window and saw they were at the station. A sheepish grin spread over his face. "Oh. Maybe I was."

They went back to the baggage car and made sure a porter transferred their cases to the platform where the train that would take them to Regina waited. Bushell slipped the fellow a ten-shilling note and, after a moment's hesitation, half a crown to go with it. Far from home, he was willing to pay to ensure things running smoothly.

The *Northern Rockies Special* pulled out of Prince George at twenty past three, ten minutes late. Although the delay would be inconsequential when set against the nearly daylong journey to Regina, Bushell fretted nonetheless. He knew he was gambling, and knew that if he lost his gamble he would have done better not to make it.

"I wish Edmonton had airships going out of it oftener than every third day," he muttered to Samuel Stanley.

"So do I, Chief—uh, Tom—but I can't do anything about it," Stanley answered. "Might as well wish the Rockies were flat, so we'd make better time through 'em. We do the best we can with the hand we've been dealt, that's all."

They were approaching the Rockies when they went to the dining car for supper. Bushell ate steak and kidney pie, Stanley Helvetian steak with mushrooms. When they'd finished, they returned to the sleeping compartment they were sharing and watched for a while as the mountains grew all around them. Yellowknife Pass, through which they'd traverse the Rockies, topped out at less than four thousand feet, but great steep piles of granite and basalt, cloaked with conifers on their lower slopes and snow and ice above, reached high into the sky to north and south.

"Pretty country," Stanley remarked after a while.

Bushell grunted. He had his nose in a book by then: a scientific romance he'd taken from the Sons' shelter in Buckley Bay. It was called *The United Colonies Triumphant* and seemed typical of the breed: it showed an independent North America coming to the rescue of England in a great European war against, not the Holy Alliance or Russia, but, of all improbable things, a unified Germany.

"Damned foolishness," Bushell growled, tempted to fling the poorly written tome across the compartment. "As if the British Empire wouldn't be the mightiest in the world even without North America."

"Why do you wade through the tripe if it annoys you so?" Stanley asked.

"I keep trying to understand how the Sons think—'know your enemy,'" Bushell said. "But this is just foolishness. The book is set now, more or less, and in this mythical world North America is an even greater center of manufactures than it is in truth, but it still keeps Negroes and Indians in bondage as farmhands. The author is too ignorant to see how machines would take the place of slaves."

Stanley's mouth tightened. "Even so, that does tell you something about the way those people think."

"Something, yes, but nothing pleasant—and nothing I didn't already know." Bushell paused to light a cigar, then picked up *The United Colonies Triumphant* once more. "'Scientific romance' my arse—no science and no romance to it that I can see: just someone who doesn't write very well proving it at great length. A world that never could be, not in a thousand years." He let out a noise half snort, half guffaw. The book was too preposterous for words.

A large sign by the railroad track announced that they were passing out of the province of Vancouver and into the province of Albertus. A few hundred yards farther on, a series of several smaller signs extolled the virtues of a patent shaving soap. Bushell found the foolish jingling verses on them badly out of place when set against the brooding majesty of the mountains.

Shadows pooled and lengthened. After a while, the train was running in deep twilight while the mountainsides above still blazed with light. Some of the mountains' flanks were covered not merely with snow but with ice; near the little town of Jasper, one glacier came down almost near enough to touch out the window, or so it seemed.

"Beautiful scenery," Bushell said; *The United Colonies Triumphant* wasn't nearly interesting enough to keep him reading at a steady clip. "But it's a cold beauty, and it makes me cold looking at it."

"If that Swedish fashion for sliding through snow with boards on your feet ever caught on in the NAU, this is where they'd come to do it," Samuel Stanley said. "Skiing, that's what they call it. I'd almost forgotten."

"I never knew," Bushell said. "Where did you learn that?"

"The army, a couple of years before I was attached to your platoon," Stanley answered. "If you ever have to fight on snow, you can go a lot faster on those skis than you can on snowshoes. The Russians have skiers in Alaska: a couple of regiments of them, they said at my training center."

Bushell had a disquieting vision of regiments of Russians with boards on their feet and Nagants on their backs gliding across the frozen northern reaches of the NAU one winter, not stopping till they came to the icebound shores of Hudson Bay. He knew the vision was absurd; no matter how mobile they were, a couple of regiments of troops wouldn't go far, and a lot of land lay between the Alaskan frontier and Hudson Bay. But he'd had Russians on the brain lately.

To keep from thinking about Russians and ski troops, he went back to the scientific romance again. They worried about Germans there. That was laughable by anyone's standards. Germans were good for music, beer, heavy food, heavier philosophies, and squabbling among themselves. Bavarians were jolly, Austrians haughty, and Prussians inclined to be dour (who could blame them for that, when they were stuck next to Russia?), but they weren't forces to reckon with, nor was any other German kingdom, principality, duchy, archibishopric, or free city. The idea of all of them behind a single malign ruler was . . ."Absurd," Bushell said with another snort, and plowed on.

After a while, he surprised himself in a yawn. The book made a soporific to rank with Jameson. He set it down and got into his pyjamas. After his earlier nap, he didn't think he'd be able to sleep, but surprised himself again by dropping off almost at once.

▼

"Get down, you damned fool!" Bushell shouted. A shot rang out. But instead of watching Felix Crooke fall, he felt an explosion of light in his own head.

His eyes flew open. A morning sunbeam had stolen through the slats of the blinds and was hitting him in the face. "Jesus," he muttered. The dream had been terrifyingly real.

He groped for his pocket watch. It was a little past five. The dining car wouldn't be open for breakfast yet, and he'd wake Sam if he did a lot of moving around. That meant going back to *The United Colonies Triumphant.* He turned on the reading lamp in his bunk. The book was better than his nightmare—but not much.

Samuel Stanley woke up less than half an hour later. He blinked to see Bushell already among those present, then let out a wry chuckle. "We must be getting used to climbing out of bed at these appalling hours. I didn't think that was what the papers meant by a fate worse than death, but I could be wrong."

Bushell dogeared the book with a grunt of relief and slid out of bed. When he pulled up the blinds, he grunted again, this time in surprise, and gave back a pace from the window. The train might have been transported to a new and different world while he and Stanley slept. The Rockies that separated Vancouver from Albertus had vanished behind them. Instead, the *Northern Rockies Special* rolled through flat farmlands, punctuated here and there with low, rolling hills.

"Are those *wheatfields* out there?" Stanley also seemed startled at the overnight transformation of the world.

"More likely rye or barley," Bushell answered. "We're still pretty far north."

"Mm, maybe so." Stanley also got up. His mind quickly went to more immediately relevant matters: "What time do you suppose the diner opens?"

"Six if we're lucky, seven if we're not." Bushell unbuttoned his pyjama tops. "I intend to find out how lucky I am."

His luck was in. He and Stanley systematically demolished their breakfasts, then sat at the table while they fortified themselves from a strong pot of English Breakfast tea. "Damned if I know how the Russians take it without milk all the time," Stanley said, pouring a generous white stream into his cup.

Bushell quoted Herodotus: " 'Custom is king of all.' They're used to it that way, so for them it tastes right." He wondered if custom was all that bound the NAU to England. Had the American colonies broken away all those years ago, would they now think of their independence as natural and right?

He shook his head. It wasn't the same thing.

The train pulled in to Regina at half past one. The airship was due to leave for Astoria at 2:05. "We're not going to make it," Stanley said as they recovered their bags and flagged a cab.

"The hell we're not." When the driver opened the boot of his steamer for their baggage, Bushell told him, "Ten quid—no, fifteen—if you get us to the airship port in time for the flight to Astoria."

The cabbie touched a forefinger to the brim of his cap, then pulled out his pocket watch. He whistled softly. "Won't be easy, gents, but I'll do my damnedest. Hop in."

Afterwards, Bushell decided Regina's constables slept on the job. If they hadn't, they would have cited the cab a dozen times, maybe more. He wondered if he was going to live through the wild ride to the southwestern outskirts of town. But the cab pulled up to the waiting airship at seven minutes of two. "I will be damned," Samuel Stanley said reverently.

Over and above the fare, Bushell handed the cab man a green ten-pound note and a purple fiver. The fellow helped them carry their bags to the airship and gave them to the handler while a supercilious clerk declared, "You gentlemen are lucky this flight did not depart without you."

"Don't you take that uppity tone with us," Stanley snapped. Had the clerk been white, he would have flushed. As it was, he stamped their tickets with altogether unnecessary force, thrust their stateroom keys at them, and pointed to the ladder without another word.

As soon as Bushell and Stanley climbed aboard, that ladder was moved away from the passenger gondola. Pumps were noisily sucking water ballast from the airship. "Welcome to the *Prairie Schooner*, gentlemen," the steward said. If passengers arriving at the last possible minute upset him, he didn't show it.

"Thanks," Bushell said. "Is the bar to port or starboard?" The steward pointed to the left. To Stanley, Bushell added, "I'd say we've earned watching takeoff from there this time."

Stanley swept off his fedora and bowed. "Motion seconded and passed by acclamation. First round is on me, too—I never thought we'd get here on time."

"O ye of little faith," Bushell said.

"If I had little faith, I never would have got in the cab with that madman. Come on."

They'd just walked into the bar when, light as a feather, the *Prairie Schooner* floated away from the ground. The floor developed a list. Once on a stool, though, his feet resting on the brass rail, Bushell felt altogether at home. "Here's to getting into Astoria at six tomorrow morning, and out again an hour later," he said, lifting his glass of Jameson high before he drank. Stanley joined him in the toast.

The bartender raised a grizzled eyebrow. "Good luck, gents," he said in a gravelly voice. Both RAMs ignored him.

Bushell watched prairie go by under the *Prairie Schooner* till it was time for supper, and then till it got too dark to see. The land was green and flat and dotted with lakes and ponds of every imaginable size and shape. "There must be ten thousand of them down there," Stanley said.

"Easily," Bushell agreed.

He went to bed in his stateroom reveling in the prospect of being able to sleep undisturbed till half past five. And, sure enough, at exactly that hour, a burst of static announced the ceiling speaker coming to life: "Ladies and gentlemen, this is your captain. We're about thirty-five miles outside of Astoria, on our final approach to O'Hare Airship Port. I regret to have to inform you, though, that wireless traffic tells me all mooring masts at the airship port are currently occupied, and several airships are already floating above the port, awaiting their turn to land. Because O'Hare is so busy, these things do happen from time to time. We regret the inconvenience. We'll get you down on the ground just as soon as we can, I promise you. Meanwhile, enjoy a little extra sleep. Thank you."

The speaker crackled again, then fell silent. Bushell got out of bed with an oath. He dressed fast enough to satisfy the most irascible training sergeant and dashed for the lounge. Sam Stanley burst in not thirty seconds behind him.

The newly risen sun shone off farmland and forest, and reflected brilliantly from Lake Michigan. Astoria's never-sleeping factories threw columns of smoke into the air. A light breeze from out of the east brought the harsh smell of industry to the *Prairie Schooner*. With it came a barnyard reek; along with its factories, Astoria was a great livestock center.

As the airship neared the port, Bushell spied half a dozen fat cigar shapes hanging in the sky, decked out in the varying bright colors of their airship lines. He wished desperately for them to disappear.

A steward approached with two pots and some cups on a silver tray. "Would you like tea or coffee?" he asked the two RAMs.

"What I'd like is to land," Bushell said. "Have you got that in a pot?" The steward beat a quick retreat.

Land the *Prairie Schooner* did, at twenty past seven. By then, another handful of airships had queued up behind it. As soon as their feet hit the ground, Bushell and Stanley rushed for the transfer agent, who'd set up a podium near the tail of the dirigible. With his longer legs, Stanley got there first. "Do we still have time to catch the *Six Nations Special?*" he gasped, panting.

The transfer agent gave him a bright, meaningless professional smile. "I'm afraid not, sir," she said. "The *Six Nations Special* is the airship that departed from this mooring mast so the *Prairie Schooner* could land."

Bushell and Stanley looked at each other in dismay. They would be late to Doshoweh after all.

# VIII

▼

THE AIRSHIP COMPANY AND ITS REPRESEN-
tatives did everything they could for the RAMs. Later, Bushell would have admitted as much. At the time, converting airship tickets to ones for the railroad,
making his way by cab from the O'Hare Airship Port to the La Salle Street Station in the middle of the morning rush hour, and then settling down to wait until the train pulled out at a quarter past twelve all aggravated his liver.

After loading his pockets with so much change that he jingled when he
walked, he telephoned the RAM office and local constables in Doshoweh to
warn them he'd been delayed. Making long-distance calls from public phones
was an exasperating process at the best of times, too. You stood there drumming
your fingers against the glass of the booth, waiting for your call to be transferred
from one operator to another. Calling into the Six Nations added a new layer of
frustration, for some of the operators seemed to have only an imperfect grasp of
English. But at last he managed to leave his messages, one after the other. He fed
shillings and florins and heavy silver crowns into the public telephone until the
local operator pronounced herself satisfied.

The *Twentieth-Century Limited* rolled through the provinces of Tippecanoe
and Miami. Doshoweh lay ten hours away. As soon as Bushell left the dining car
after a luncheon of chicken pot pie and apricot and almond custard, he pulled
out his pocket watch, glowered at it, and said, "If we'd caught the *Six Nations Special*, we'd be there by now."

"I know," Samuel Stanley said, and wisely let it go at that.

Bushell sat down and stayed in his seat, making himself hold still though he
wanted to get up and pace. Every so often, the train rolled through another industrial town with smokestacks vomiting forth the waste of the factories that
made the NAU one of the marvels of the world. To compensate for that smoke,
almost every motorcar on the roads was a clean electric.

Stanley noticed that, too. "Good thing towns are packed so close together
hereabouts," he said. "Electrics are fine for the short haul, but steamers have it all
over them when it comes to going a long way." He looked out the window,
drummed his fingers on the table. "If it weren't for all the electricity from the big
grids in the coal-mining provinces, this part of the NAU would be too dirty for
anyone to want to live here."

167

"That's true," Bushell said. "But Pennsylvania and western Virginia and eastern Franklin are filthier than they would be otherwise, to make up for it."

After cutting across the neck of the Huron Peninsula, they reached Toledo on the shore of Lake Erie a little before six o'clock. From then on, they had the lake on their left hand as they steamed east toward Doshoweh. After a brief pause there, the *Twentieth-Century Limited* would swing inland through the Six Nations and then into New York province, pulling into New York City twenty hours after leaving Astoria.

For supper, the dining car offered a lobster à la Newburg that would have done a Boston seaside restaurant proud. Cream and sherry and noodles and sweet chunks of lobster meat helped soften Bushell's resentment at being delayed. When he lighted a cigar afterwards, he was, if not at peace with the world, at least willing to declare a temporary cease-fire.

Thanks to the lobster, the very good Le Montrachet that went with it, and, most of all, what seemed like an endless stream of days on the road, Bushell was yawning when the train pulled to a stop in Doshoweh a few minutes after eleven. The conductor announced the stop not only in English but also, reading from a card, in the Iroquois language. Most of the people who got up to leave the train along with Bushell and Stanley had straight black hair and coppery skins, though they dressed like anyone else.

In most respects, the train station was a train station, and might have been in any part of the NAU or, indeed, in any part of the British Empire. But underneath the English-language signs directing passengers, people waiting to pick up passengers, and visitors were what Bushell guessed to be their equivalents in Iroquois.

Samuel Stanley nodded toward one of those signs. "Doesn't seem quite right," he remarked, his voice so low only Bushell heard him. "They're part of the Empire; they should use English."

"So long as they're loyal, I don't think the King-Emperor cares what language they speak," Bushell answered.

"Can't fault 'em for that. The Iroquois Scouts rank right up there with the Gurkha Rifles," Stanley said: a soldier's assessment. His mouth twisted as he went on, "They aren't like the Frenchies in Quebec, giving aid and comfort to the Holy Alliance every chance they get. Good thing the Sons of Liberty can't stand the idea of Frenchies in their new, ever-so-free country; if the Sons would have 'em, they'd sure as hell join, and make our lives even more miserable."

He left off grumbling then. Two white men and an extraordinarily well dressed Iroquois stood together talking; one of the whites was holding up a cardboard sign that read, TOM & SAM. Bushell nodded approval as he walked up to greet them: his last name had been bandied about in the newspapers altogether too much lately. Tom and Sam, though, might be anyone.

The two white men were local RAMs, a captain and a lieutenant named Sylvanus Greeley and Charles Lucas. Greeley, who wore a mustache waxed to handlebar perfection, said, "And let me introduce you to Major Shikalimo of the Doshoweh constabulary." He noticed Bushell's surprise at being presented to a local major instead of the other way around, and added, "Shikalimo here is nephew to Otetiani, the Tododaho—the Grand Sachem, you might say—of the Iroquois."

As far as Bushell was concerned, that explained why Shikalimo had made major at such an early age—he couldn't have been much past twenty-five—but not much more. The Iroquois, though, accepted the order of the introductions as if he'd imagined nothing else.

He was gracious enough, saying, "Delight to make your acquaintance, gentlemen," in an accent that shouted Oxford or Cambridge and made Bushell feel decidedly—and unexpectedly—colonial. Yet despite the cool elegance of his speech, his black homburg, and his pinstriped suit and waistcoat, he had a twinkle in his eye and a smile that flashed all the brighter because of his dark skin.

"You chaps will be about done in, I expect," Greeley said when the introductions were done. "We've booked you into the Hotel Ahgusweyo, which is conveniently close to our headquarters, and also to the constabulary station."

"The Better Hotel, you would say in English," Shikalimo said, flashing that dazzling smile again. "We leave it partly in our language to make it seem exotic for sightseers. We get a good many here, some curious about us, others about Niagara Falls. If you like, gentlemen, I should be delighted to drive you to the hotel."

"If it's no trouble—" Bushell began.

Shikalimo waved that aside. "It would be an honor, not an inconvenience. We of the Hodenosaunee—the Iroquois, as you call us—take the theft of *The Two Georges* most seriously, I assure you; it is a blow at us no less than at the white citizens of the North American Union. Any assistance we can render in its safe return will be a privilege, not a duty." His face went grim. "I was outraged to learn the Sons of Liberty may be secreting the painting here. That our land was used to abet this crime in an insult that cries out to be avenged."

Bushell would not have wanted Shikalimo interested in taking vengeance on him. He had a florid way of speaking, but seemed a fine figure of a man all the same. Bushell decided to take him up on his invitation: "If you're sure it's no bother, I thank you very much."

"No trouble at all." Shikalimo pointed toward one of the exit doors. "If you bring your baggage there, I'll go reclaim my steamer from the carpark and meet you in a moment." Without waiting for a reply, he hurried away.

"He's bloody sure of himself, isn't he?" Samuel Stanley remarked when Shikalimo had got out of earshot. "By his manner, you'd think he was the Grand Sachem's son, not just his nephew."

Sylvanus Greeley and Charles Lucas exchanged glances. "My dear sir—" they began together, and both laughed. "Go ahead, Charlie," Greeley said.

"Thanks, Captain," the younger man replied. He turned to Stanley and Bushell. "The Iroquois, they do things differently. Captain Greeley and I, we've been here a while, and we're used to it. Sometimes we forget outsiders aren't. The Iroquois, they reckon descent through the mother. The Tododaho's sons, they aren't of his clan: they belong to the one his wife is in. But the Sachem's sister's son, now, he's—"

"He's the heir, you're saying," Bushell put in, fitting the puzzle pieces together. "Well. No wonder he acts as if he's someone, then. He *is*."

"Yeah, and we'd better not keep him waiting, either." Samuel Stanley picked up a suitcase. "Come on."

No sooner had they stepped outside than Shikalimo pulled up in a Supermarine saloon so low and rakish, it looked ready to spit fire. The Iroquois nobleman—or so Bushell classified him—didn't seem unduly impressed with his own importance: he helped the RAMs load their luggage into the boot and held the passenger-side doors open so they could get in.

The Supermarine glided away from the kerb. Shikalimo was an expert driver, going through the gears so smoothly, Bushell had trouble noticing the shifts. He wasn't paying a great deal of attention to such things in any case. He'd never been in the Six Nations before, and wondered how Doshoweh differed from the town it might have been had Englishmen built it.

He couldn't see much difference. The people on the street—not many, at an hour marching toward midnight—wore clothes that wouldn't have been out of place on a warm summer night in New Liverpool, although he wouldn't have spotted men wearing earrings there. The buildings looked like buildings, not wigwams. Only the bilingual signs really told him he was in an unusual part of the NAU.

Shikalimo said, "I want you to know, Colonel, Captain, it's an honor for me to be working so closely with you. I expect to learn a great deal from this. Your techniques are a model of what investigation should be. If we here had access to facilities like yours in Victoria—" He let out a long, envious sigh.

Bushell realized that, while he was trying to isolate what made the Six Nations unique, Shikalimo was looking out from his limited perspective toward the wider, more cosmopolitan world of the NAU as a whole, which Bushell took as much for granted as Shikalimo did the narrow view from Doshoweh. What you wanted to see depended on where you were standing.

He said, "We'll cooperate with you in any way we can, Major. Having someone so prominent in the community here working alongside us will help make witnesses more willing to talk."

To his surprise, Shikalimo lifted one hand off the steering wheel, then angrily slammed it down again. "Greeley and Lucas are good enough fellows in their way, but they talk too bloody much," he said. "I hope you will not be offended when I say I have noted this flaw regrettably often in white men."

"Doesn't offend *me* one bit," Samuel Stanley said with a chuckle.

"A distinct point, Captain Stanley." Shikalimo laughed, too. But he quickly grew serious again: "I wish your fellow RAMs had not gone into detail about my social rank here, as opposed to that in our constabulary, because I want you to think of me as a colleague to be judged like any other colleague. Social rank and ability do not necessarily go hand in hand."

"Seems to me your people are doing things the same way the royal family does," Bushell said. "Give the heir something worthwhile to do before he gets stuck with the top job and he'll generally handle that one pretty well, too."

Shikalimo glanced over to him. "That is precisely the paradigm my uncle cited, Colonel," he said, respect in his voice.

Otetiani sounded like a sensible chap. Bushell couldn't figure out how to say so without seeming to make too much of himself. He covered his brief confusion with brusqueness: "To business. You've had a couple of days now to search for the Sons of Liberty here. Any luck?"

"None to speak of, unfortunately," Shikalimo answered. "Somewhere between a fourth and a third of the populace of Doshoweh is white. With such a large haystack to sift through, we've yet to come across our poisoned needle."

"Have a care as you sift," Samuel Stanley warned. "If you want to learn from us, for God's sake learn that. The Sons will hurt you badly if you run up against them unprepared."

"For this word of caution I thank you, and I shall convey it to my comrades and superiors," Shikalimo said. He pulled to a stop in front of the Hotel Ahgusweyo, which, unlike the other buildings Bushell had seen, did have the look of a longhouse writ large, in stone and concrete rather than wood and bark. Shikalimo remarked, "Sightseers expect certain things of us. We make an effort to satisfy them, even if their expectations do not always match modern reality."

A servant came with a cart to take the baggage from the boot of Shikalimo's Supermarine. Recognizing the driver, he nodded deferentially and murmured something in his own language, to which Shikalimo responded. Bushell concluded not all the old ways of the Iroquois had fallen into desuetude.

As had that of the Skidegate Lodge, the lobby of the Hotel Ahgusweyo tried to show the traveler he had came to someplace out of the ordinary. Colorful dried ears of maize were displayed on the walls, along with war clubs, tobacco pipes, and baskets and medicine masks of dried ash splints. A dugout canoe hung from the ceiling on stout chains.

When he got up to his room and flipped on the light, the first thing he noticed was a large print of *The Two Georges* hanging over the bed. It surprised a snort of laughter out of him. "What is funny, sir?" the bellhop asked, setting his suitcases down on the floor.

He pointed to the print. "That. Anywhere else in the NAU, I would have expected it. But here—"

"George Washington is very important to the Hodenosaunee, too, sir," the bellhop said, sounding indignant Bushell had doubted it. "Those of us who follow Hawenneyu, the Great Spirit, and not your Christian God"—with a slight motion of his hand, he included himself among that number—"we say Washington is the only white man who has joined Hawenneyu in his heaven."

"The rest of us are in hell?" Bushell asked, bemused.

But the bellhop shook his head. "No, sir. Hawenneyu takes no notice of you, for good or ill. But Washington was such a noble man, the Great Spirit smiled on him no matter what his color."

"Is that a fact?" Bushell said. It wasn't a fact, of course; it was a theological opinion, than which nothing was less susceptible to proof. But it was a theological opinion that stuck his fancy. He tipped the bellhop a pound, twice the going rate. The man bowed and slipped away.

On the wall across from the bed hung a smaller print, this one of a man with dark, Red Indian features and extraordinarily intelligent, probing eyes. There were letters underneath the print. Walking up to it, Bushell saw that they spelled out what looked like an Iroquois name: Sosehawa.

He wished the bellhop hadn't left. Most bellhops knew where the good restaurants were or how to find a companion for the evening if you were so inclined. This fellow had seemed well informed about other matters as well.

Bushell shrugged. Shikalimo would know who Sosehawa was. All that could wait till morning. He unpacked his pyjamas, put them on, and went to bed.

▼

Samuel Stanley stared at the breakfast menu with a dismay Bushell found incomprehensible. "Hommony cakes!" Stanley exploded. "In this day and age they expect people to eat hommony cakes—and pay hotel prices to do it? They won't get 'em from me, by God!"

"What the devil *are* hommony cakes?" Bushell asked, once the offending item was identified.

"Hommony is maize treated with lye to hull it and then ground into flour. You can make it into cakes or you can serve it up as porridge—but you'd better not, not if you want to keep your Negro trade," Stanley said.

"Sorry, Sam—I'm still not following this."

"Hommony was slave food. It was cheap, it would keep a man going . . . it still will, come to that, and poor people in the southeastern provinces eat it to this day. But for a Negro family that's come up in the world, as most of us have—" Stanley shook his head. "My folks got some in the house just once that I remember, when I was about fourteen. They served me up a big bowl of the porridge and made me eat it all. My father said my grandpa had done the same for him, and so on as far back as any of us remember. He called it knowing what we'd got away from."

Bushell had been curious about the hommony, but after that impassioned speech he decided he'd be wiser leaving it alone. He chose griddlecakes from good old unabashed wheat flour instead, and maple syrup to go with them. Sam Stanley ordered bacon and eggs, with chips on the side.

Their breakfasts had just arrived when Bushell stiffened as a waiter led a new patron to a table. He caught Stanley's eye. The adjutant followed his gaze. A forkful of eggs halted halfway to Stanley's mouth. "What do you know about that?" he said softly.

"I don't know a bloody thing, but I'm going to find out." Bushell rose from his seat and strode over to the woman who had just come into the dining room. "Won't you join me for breakfast, Dr. Flannery?" he said with an ironic courtesy that masked the anger and suspicion he felt.

Kathleen Flannery looked up in surprise that rapidly became alarm. "Why, Colonel Bushell," she said. "How . . . pleasant to see you again." Color rose from her throat to her cheeks to her forehead.

"Won't you join me for breakfast?" Bushell repeated. It was phrased as a request, but not meant as one. She bit her lip, nodded, and rose. Bushell paced beside her, as if to make sure she didn't cut and run. He pulled out a chair for her. "I'm sure you also remember Captain Stanley?"

"Of course," Kathleen answered, nodding. "How are you this morning, Captain?"

"Curious," Stanley said bluntly. That made her look down at the linen tablecloth in confusion—or was it embarrassment? Bushell couldn't tell.

A waiter came to the table where Kathleen Flannery had been seated. He scratched his head for a moment, then smiled when he saw her sitting with Bushell and Stanley. "Ah, you have friends here," he said. "How nice."

"Yes," she answered, her voice brittle. When he expectantly poised pencil above pad, she ordered the hommony porridge with a small pitcher of cream. Bushell waited for Samuel Stanley to detonate once more, but his adjutant put on a poker face instead. Stanley knew when not to show his cards.

Bushell waited till everyone had finished eating before he lighted a cigar and asked, "And what brings you to Doshoweh at such an, mm, opportune time, Dr. Flannery?"

Kathleen had recovered her spirits. "I don't have to answer your questions, Colonel," she said, and started to rise. "If you will excuse me—"

"Sit down." Bushell's voice was very quiet; no one two tables over would have heard him. But he'd learned, first in the army and then in the RAMs, to put the snap of command into what he said. Kathleen Flannery returned to her chair before she quite realized she'd done so. Bushell went on, "Would you sooner discuss this at the Doshoweh RAM headquarters? They're around the corner, I'm told. Or perhaps the local constables would be curious to know why you came into Doshoweh only days after *The Two Georges* did."

She stared at him. "Then it's true," she breathed. "It *did* come here." She reached out to set her hand on his. "Have you got it back?"

"No, we haven't got it back," Bushell said roughly, and she took her hand away. "My best guess is that it's not here now." He grimaced, wishing he hadn't told her even that much. Covering annoyance by pouring himself more tea, he continued, "How the devil did you know it was in the first place? What are you doing chasing it after I told you to stay out of the case?"

Kathleen answered the second question: "I'm not your servant, Colonel, no matter what you may think, and I am not obliged to act on your say-so. Serving as curator for the traveling exhibition of *The Two Georges* would have been a highlight of my career, something to build on for years to come. Having the painting stolen while touring—Think what that does for my prospects."

Bushell thought about it. She would carry the same sort of black mark on her record as he. "That doesn't tell me what you're doing *here*," he said. "It took a lot of police work—it took a man dying, for God's sake—to get us here . . . and we find you in Doshoweh ahead of us. How did you know *The Two Georges* was here?"

"I don't know anything about police work," she said. "I don't know what you found or where you found it. What I know is art. Every time a major painting is stolen, there's always a flood of rumors about where it's gone and who has it. This time we know who has it, and—"

"—And they made sure there wouldn't be any rumors about where it was," Bushell interrupted. "So what are you doing here, Dr. Flannery? Answer me, please."

"I am trying to answer you," she said. Now the color that rose to her cheeks was anger, not embarrassment. "It's much more difficult for me to do so when you keep breaking in."

"Go on, then," he told her.

"Thank you so much," she said icily. "As I think I told you during one of your interrogations in New Liverpool, the All-Union Museum has an extensive collection of Red Indian artifacts. Our associate curator of Iroquois art, Dr. Gyantwaka, recognized that the headline the villains showed with *The Two Georges* came from the *Doshoweh Sentinel*. Actually, he wasn't quite certain, but I decided to take the chance and see what I could find here. And so I arrived day before yesterday."

Bushell and Samuel Stanley conducted a short conversation that consisted entirely of twitching eyebrows, lip corners moving up and down, and small hand gestures. "It could be," Bushell said at last, delivering the verdict with obvious reluctance. "Let me ask you another question, then: once you learned this, why did you go haring off on your own? Why didn't you pass on what you'd learned to the RAMs in Victoria?"

Her green eyes widened slightly. "You mean you didn't know? Surely, with RAMs from all over the NAU, some of them would have noticed the same thing Dr. Gyantwaka did."

"We don't have a lot of Iroquois in the RAMs, I'm afraid," Stanley said, his voice grave. "No one recognized the headline as coming from his hometown newspaper. We had to dig the information out the hard way. We didn't discover the source ourselves until a couple of days ago."

"Oh, dear," Kathleen Flannery said. "No wonder you were surprised to see me."

*Surprised* wasn't the word. *Mistrustful* was. Everything Kathleen Flannery did or said seemed perfectly innocent, and everything required checking. Bushell supposed he could ask Major Shikalimo about Dr. Gyantwaka; if Shikalimo didn't know him or know of him, he'd know somebody who did. Very likely Gyantwaka would check out fine, as the other things Kathleen had said proved for the most part to be as she'd said them. But that everything needed checking bothered Bushell no end.

So did the simple fact of her presence here. "Dr. Flannery," he said, "don't you know that an amateur can—"

"—Evidently discover some things about as fast as the entire corps of the Royal American Mounted Police? Is that what you were going to say, Colonel?" Kathleen smiled at him. It was a very sweet smile. It also had razors in it.

Bushell opened his mouth. He closed it again. Damn it, she *had* found out that *The Two Georges* was in Doshoweh as fast as the entire corps of the Royal American Mounted Police. He glanced over to Samuel Stanley for support. Stanley was looking down into his teacup. Bushell thought he was trying not to chuckle. That didn't help him muster the crushing reply he was looking for.

Kathleen Flannery didn't give him much time to gather his wits, either. "You were about to say, Colonel?" she prompted, smiling again with that sweet ferocity.

He recognized the interrogation technique. If you hurried somebody, made him respond to you instead of picking his own pace, you seized the initiative. He'd used the technique himself, hundreds of times. It worked. It was working on him now. That smile made it all the more devastating; it made him want to tell Kathleen everything she wanted to hear. Too bad that was a variant he couldn't use against villains, few of whose pulses quickened at the sight of his pearly whites.

Kathleen tapped her long nails on the tabletop in obvious, and irritating, impatience. That made Bushell want to laugh; if she hadn't got the gesture from the cinema, she truly was an inspired amateur. And if she was—

"Here's what we're going to do, Dr. Flannery," he said, as if he'd had it in mind all along. "You have done better than I thought you could back in New Liverpool. I admit it. Congratulations."

"Thank you," she said, but she now sounded more wary than relieved. Samuel Stanley also looked puzzled, though he was doing his best not to show it. Bushell wasn't in the habit of giving in so tamely.

He didn't intend to give in now, either. Doing his best to match Kathleen's smile, he said, "Since you've proved yourself such a fine amateur detective, Dr. Flannery, it's only right that you move up into the first division and join the professional team. If you're going to look into the theft of *The Two Georges*, you can lend your talents to Sam and me and accompany us on our investigations." *That way we can keep an eye on you all the time*, he didn't add, not aloud. "What say you?"

Kathleen Flannery might have been headstrong, but she was anything but a fool. Her eyes sparked angrily as she saw the trap Bushell had set for her. "What happens if I say no, Colonel?"

"Most likely, you'd be investigated as a material witness," Bushell answered. "I expect the questioning would be *most* thorough. You'd certainly have to leave off chasing *The Two Georges*."

Her lips silently shaped a word he would not have used in her company. She had sand, though. "My solicitor would prepare a brief for a barrister to take to court to stop this harassment."

"Harassment?" Bushell's eyes were large and round and innocent. "You *are* a material witness, Dr. Flannery. Finding out what you know and how you know it may well prove relevant to this case." That was all too true, any which way. "As for any court action, well, you can't do much investigating while you're testifying."

She looked as if she hated him. She probably did. Somewhere back in his mind, that hurt, more than he wanted to admit even to himself. He was used to ignoring that kind of hurt, though, ignoring it and going forward. Getting *The Two Georges* back came first. If you didn't do your duty, you didn't deserve the privilege of citizenship in the British Empire.

"Very well, Colonel," she said at last, her voice wintry. "If this is the only way you will permit me to do what I should be doing, I must agree." The expression on her face told how happy she was about agreeing.

Bushell sent her a thoughtful look. She too took the concept of duty seriously. To him, that was one in her favor . . . for the moment. Elgin Goldsmith and his comrades had fought as bravely as any soldiers for what they saw as their duty, too. Maybe duty, like an electric torch, needed to be pointed in the right direction before it could illuminate the path one should take. He shook his head, unhappy at the thought. Duty should be simple, straightforward.

"What's first on the list for today, Chief?" Samuel Stanley asked. "Shall we visit the RAMs or Major Shikalimo?"

"Shikalimo, I think," Bushell answered after a moment's thought. "One thing Dr. Flannery has done for us is show us that we RAMs don't know everything we should about what's going on in the Six Nations. If anyone does, it'll be the local constabulary."

"I saw a public telephone just outside the restaurant," Stanley said, pointing. "Let me go ring him up. How soon do you want to see him?"

"As soon as he'll see us," Bushell said.

"Right. If you'll excuse me . . ." Stanley hurried out of the room. When he came back a couple of minutes later, he said, "Half past nine. And I have exact directions on how to get there—it's about a five-minute walk, they say."

"Good enough." Bushell dipped his head to Kathleen. "Shall we meet in the lobby at nine-twenty, then?"

"Of course," she said. He winced at the distaste she packed into two words.

▼

As he and his companions walked to the Doshoweh constabulary station, Bushell watched the Iroquois watching them. He drew no special notice himself; a fair number of white men were on the streets. But Kathleen Flannery's auburn hair made people give her second looks, and several frankly stared at Samuel Stanley.

That amused Stanley more than it annoyed him. Chuckling, he said, "Not a whole lot of Negroes in the Six Nations, looks like. Maybe I ought to do a little dance, to give them something to remember me by."

Some of the locals spoke English, others their own purring tongue. Newsboys hawked papers in both languages. Now that it had been brought to his notice, Bushell saw that the typefaces the *Doshoweh Sentinel* used were like those on the photograph the Sons of Liberty had sent with their ransom demand. He slapped his hand against the side of his leg. If only someone had noticed earlier!

The constabulary station was a nondescript four-story building of muddy yellow brick. Bushell's first thought was that it would fall down in an earthquake. Doshoweh, though, didn't need to worry about earthquakes the way New Liverpool did.

Some of the constables inside the station were using the Iroquois language. Bushell noticed that. A lot of Spanish-speakers lived in Upper California, but

English was the universal language of government there. But the affiliation of the Six Nations to the NAU was looser than that of ordinary provinces.

Major Shikalimo met them in the lobby. When he saw Kathleen Flannery, he looked a question to Bushell. After introducing her to him, Bushell said, "Dr. Flannery has been conducting her own independent investigation of the theft of *The Two Georges*. Now that we've run into each other here, we've decided to join forces." He spoke in carefully neutral tones, hiding both his annoyance that Kathleen hadn't listened to him and her resentment at being forced into an alliance.

"I see," Shikalimo said in a voice just as neutral, and then, as if reminding himself, "Well, this is an unusual case in almost every way." He knew Bushell hadn't told him anywhere near the whole story, then. When he saw he wasn't going to get any more of it, he gave half a shrug and went on, "If you'll come with me to my office, I'll show you what we've been doing here the past few days."

His office was bigger than the one Bushell had back in New Liverpool, but Bushell wasn't the chief's nephew, either. On the wall opposite Shikalimo's desk was a large print of *The Two Georges*; on the wall in back of his desk hung a copy of the same portrait of Sosehawa as the one in Bushell's hotel room.

He pointed to it. "By the way it's displayed, that picture is as important here as *The Two Georges* is all over the NAU. Who was Sosehawa, if I may ask?"

Kathleen Flannery stirred, as if she knew the answer. But Bushell had aimed the question at Shikalimo, and she left the reply to him. He said, "He was the man who made my people what we are today. He went east, into the province of New York, in 1821, and there he had a—well, you might call it a religious revelation."

"He was a prophet, then?" Bushell had already heard that some of the Iroquois still followed their Great Spirit, so it stood to reason that they'd had prophets.

But Shikalimo smiled. "Only in a manner of speaking. Sosehawa saw all the new things brewing in New York province: the steamships in New York harbor, the very beginnings of the railroad, things like that. He realized we of the Hodenosaunee did not even know how to smelt iron. If we needed guns to defend ourselves, we had to buy them from white men, for we could not make them ourselves. We were living on the white man's sufferance, for if whites wanted to brush us aside, they had the power to do it."

"And Sosehawa changed all that?" Bushell said.

"Exactly. Thanks to him, schools went up all through the Six Nations. We brought in smiths and craftsmen of all sorts, and learned from them all we could. It did not happen overnight, but in a couple of generations' time we took our place beside the white man as full equals, and no longer had to beg scraps from his table."

"What's finest about that is how you've kept your own traditions, too," Kathleen Flannery said. "You've taken what you found useful without throwing away everything you had before."

"That's what we've tried to do, at any rate," Shikalimo said. "It's not always easy. With so many more of you people, with your books and films and wireless, we sometimes feel swamped. But we can speak of history another time. On to the matter at hand."

Bushell leaned forward in his chair. "Good. What have you done since you learned the Sons of Liberty have been operating out of Doshoweh? How do we go about discovering who they are and where in the city they might have concealed *The Two Georges?*"

"That is the question," Shikalimo said, with an intonation that left no doubt he was quoting from *Hamlet.* He spread his hands. "So long as they stab *sub rosa,* it's—difficult. What we've begun to do is look close at those white men named Joe and Joseph and even Josiah who have let their distaste, shall we say, for the Iroquois become obvious to us. Things would be easier if your letter writer had a name less common among you."

"Don't I know it," Bushell said. "That is a place to start, I suppose, but the Sons, at least the ones involved in this crime, are liable to be too clever to give themselves away so readily."

"I am assuming as much," Shikalimo answered. "I don't look to find them among the men who are outspoken in their scorn. But like associates with like. Some of the men who loudly hate us will have quiet friends who are more dangerous."

Samuel Stanley glanced over at Bushell. He nodded slightly. Bushell nodded back. Sachem's nephew he might be, but Shikalimo thought like a police officer. Kathleen Flannery was looking out the window at Doshoweh and missed the bit of byplay. Shikalimo didn't. He said nothing, but glanced down at his desk as any well-bred man might have on finding himself praised.

He said, "I gather from your colleagues, gentlemen, that you RAMs identified the headline in the newspaper pictured with *The Two Georges* as coming from the *Doshoweh Sentinel,* and that is what brought you here."

"In part, yes," Bushell said. "Dr. Flannery made the identification independently, with help from an associate of hers, Dr. Gyantwaka—I hope I'm not pronouncing that too badly."

"You're understandable," Shikalimo said: faint praise. "Yes, Gyantwaka is from my clan. We're all very proud of him, though he and I are only distantly related." Bushell felt the triumphant smile Kathleen sent his way. Before he could respond to it, Shikalimo went on, "That photograph, by the by, was *not* sent to the *Sentinel,* or to any other part in Doshoweh."

"As I said, the villains here are clever," Bushell answered. "They tried to delay recognition of the headline for as long as they could."

"Yes," Shikalimo said, drawing the word out into a thoughtful hiss. His eyes suddenly came to intent focus on Bushell—he had the makings of a formidable interrogator. "You say you came to Doshoweh in part because of the headline from the *Sentinel.* The rest would have involved your discovery of the note signed by the man named Joe?"

That led to Bushell's recounting yet again the story of the gunfight at Buckley Bay, and of finding the envelope postmarked Doshoweh and the note among the rubbish the Sons of Liberty had thrown away.

Shikalimo clicked his tongue between his teeth, not quite in the same way a white man would have. "Not only clever men, but terribly in earnest," he observed. That intent look returned to his long, high-cheekboned face. "Did you bring the envelope with you when you came here? Perhaps by studying the postmark, we can learn from which part of the city it was sent."

"Major Shikalimo, I was hoping either you or the local RAMs would say something like that." Bushell reached into the inner pocket of his jacket. "Here you are." He handed the Iroquois constable the envelope.

Shikalimo looked at it for a moment, then set it on his desk and picked up the telephone. He spoke rapidly in his own language, paused to listen, spoke again, and hung up. A couple of minutes later, another Iroquois whose neat queue contrasted oddly with his spotless white laboratory robe came into Shikalimo's office. The major's guests might as well not have been there for him; he had eyes only for the envelope. Carrying it with the care another man might have given the Holy Grail, he departed.

"If it can tell us anything, Ganeodiyo will make it speak," Shikalimo said.

"Shall we invite Captain Greeley and Lieutenant Lucas here, so they can learn whatever your man finds out?" Bushell said; he was not about to try to pronounce the name of the Iroquois technician on one hearing.

"Very well, since you ask," Shikalimo said, and rang the local RAM offices. When he got off the telephone, he glanced Bushell's way in some amusement. "You seem surprised at my hesitation."

"Not at all," Bushell said, though *astonished* would more accurately have described his feelings. Anywhere else in the NAU, constables would have leaped to seek help from the RAMs.

Shikalimo spoke to precisely that point: "Within our borders, Colonel, the Six Nations *are* autonomous, and we take that seriously. From time to time, officials of the Crown, no doubt with the highest of motives"—an eyebrow-twitch showed irony—"have tried to lessen that autonomy. As might not surprise you, we've also been training lawyers since Sosehawa's time."

They made idle chitchat while waiting for Greeley, Lucas, and Ganeodiyo. Bushell said, "I heard last night that Washington"—he nodded toward the print of *The Two Georges*—"is reckoned the only white man to reach your heaven." When Shikalimo nodded, the RAM went on, "How did he earn such a literally singular honor?"

"Not least by enforcing, for a while at any rate, the ban on white settlement west of the Appalachians His Majesty's government had laid down in 1763," Shikalimo answered. "Eventually, of course, even King Canute couldn't have held back the tide, and the ban was lifted. But the thirty-five years it was in force enabled us to consolidate as a nation, and set the stage for Sosehawa's reforms. Washington could have turned a blind eye to the ban; it would have been a popular thing to do. But he upheld the law. We honor him for that."

It occurred to Bushell that the Iroquois no doubt viewed the spread of British settlers and provinces in a light different from the one shone on it during his school days. Who could say which perspective, if either, was the true one?

Sylvanus Greeley and Charles Lucas arrived just then, making him lose that train of thought. "Thanks for including us," Greeley told Shikalimo; he recognized he was here with the Iroquois's permission. Both local RAMs accepted Bushell's introduction of Kathleen Flannery with what he thought of as polite horror. Since he outranked them, though, they had to make the best of it.

Ganeodiyo returned a couple of minutes later, triumph lighting his solemn features. "Deohstegaa district, on the lakeshore," he declared. "Now we know where to focus our efforts."

"Good work," Shikalimo said in English,. and then added several sentences in the Iroquois language. Then Sylvanus Greeley spoke in the same tongue, not with great fluency but plainly making himself understood. Ganeodiyo answered; they went back and forth for a minute or so.

Greeley turned to Bushell. "I'm conveying our gratitude."

"Thank you," Bushell said. He was impressed the local RAM could do so in the language of the Six Nations. He'd picked up a fair amount of Spanish since coming to New Liverpool, but Spanish came easy to a man who spoke French and had had Latin drilled into him since boyhood. Acquiring Iroquois struck him as an altogether more difficult undertaking.

"That will help us narrow down our search, as Ganeodiyo said." Shikalimo spoke with great satisfaction. "We shan't neglect the rest of Doshoweh, but we will concentrate on men with homes or businesses in that part of the city."

"The Great Spirit has guided our hunts for longer than the memory of our people reaches," Ganeodiyo said. "He will smile on our work again." With a nod to Shikalimo and a grudging one to Sylvanus Greeley, he left the office.

"Forgive him," Shikalimo murmured to Bushell. "He thinks those who don't speak our language are slightly less than human. He might almost be an Englishman in that regard."

The major had a knack for coming up with quietly devastating asides. Having got in the way of one, Bushell felt like an airship with a punctured coronium cell. Rallying, he said, "How can we help you in sifting through whatever evidence you have about white men here who aren't fond of you Iroquois?"

"Colonel, meaning no disrespect, but that would be difficult for you," Shikalimo answered. Bushell was irked to see Sylvanus Greeley nodding agreement. Shikalimo went on, "Most of it is not evidence in the proper sense of the word, certainly none that would stand up in a court of law. We know some of the whites who despise us. We'll ask around in the Deohstegaa district and undoubtedly uncover the names of more. All that, of necessity, is work for our local constables. My people would not be nearly so forthcoming for white men—or even for the charming Dr. Flannery." He smiled at her.

That irked Bushell, too, partly because she was a suspect in his mind and partly because he didn't want anyone else trying to charm her. He made himself stick to the business at hand. "Very well, Major, you have a point."

"I'm not putting you out like maize to parch, I promise you that," Shikalimo said. "Once we have an idea of whose associates may be involved with the Sons of Liberty, we'll need to avail ourselves of your expertise in picking our most likely targets." He laughed. "We of the Hodenosaunee have been trying to understand the white man, and the Englishman in particular, for several hundred years now, with results decidedly mixed."

Bushell got that punctured feeling again. For the most part, Shikalimo behaved like any well-educated subject of the British Empire, but showed now and then that he was at bottom the product of a very different tradition. He seemed to enjoy showing that, rocking Bushell back on his heels and making sure he himself was not taken for granted.

An exceedingly decorative young Iroquois woman in a calico tunic and blue broadcloth skirt, both elaborately embroidered with beadwork, came into the office and smiled at Shikalimo as she set some papers on his desk. Several pairs of male eyes followed her when she swayed away. Charles Lucas laughed. "Ah, Major, it's a rough duty you have here."

"What?" For a moment, Shikalimo obviously hadn't the slightest idea what the RAM was talking about. Then he snapped his fingers. "Oh. I understand. You mean Dewasenta. She is pretty, isn't she? Till you alluded to it, though, I'd never thought of her that way. She's of the Turtle clan, you see."

He spoke as if that explained everything. It evidently explained enough to Lucas, who nodded and subsided. Once again, though, it gave Bushell the feeling that, although Shikalimo spoke impeccable English, he used it to convey alien thoughts. Coughing a little, he said, "Excuse me, Major, but—" He paused, unsure how to go on.

Shikalimo got him out of the predicament by laughing out loud. "But you haven't the slightest idea what I'm talking about, you mean. We Hodenosaunee divide ourselves into eight clans, in two groups of four: the Wolf, Bear, Beaver, and Turtle on the one hand, and the Deer, Snipe, Heron, and Hawk on the other. I am of the Bear clan; men of the Bear clan from all the Six Nations are my brothers, and so, in lesser degree, are Wolves, Beavers, and Turtles. And the women of those four clans are my sisters. We do not marry our sisters any more than you do, Colonel."

Kathleen Flannery nodded along with Shikalimo; she'd known what he was going to say. Bushell hadn't. Eliminating half the women of your nation struck him as unduly narrowing your choices . . . until he remembered that, with all the women of the NAU from whom to choose, he'd picked Irene. A man could be dead wrong under any circumstances.

Samuel Stanley asked, "Do boys and girls from the wrong clans ever fall in love and run away from the Six Nations to be married?"

"It happens," Shikalimo admitted, sounding unhappy about it. "Our laws and customs go no farther than our own borders, while the ways of the rest of the NAU seep in. I blame your romantic wireless shows and especially the cinema for many of the troubles of our young people."

"I blame them for some of the troubles of *our* young people," Bushell said.

Shikalimo blinked; maybe he'd been expecting an argument. "Will there be anything else, Colonel?" he asked, with a glance toward the papers Dewasenta had brought him.

Bushell wished he could answer yes. No matter what Shikalimo promised, he worried that the Iroquois would put him on the shelf. But, in the end, he had to shake his head, get up, and go.

▼

To preserve his sense that he was doing something useful while waiting for Shikalimo to call, Bushell spent a good part of the next three days on the telephone. He rang Major Gordon Rhodes, who had nothing much new to report. He'd grilled Titus Hackett and Franklin Mansfield, but the printers denied any connection between the gold roubles they'd received from the Queen Charlotte Islands and the four Sons of Liberty who'd lived at Buckley Bay. So far, no one had managed to unearth evidence they were lying and bring it to any of His Majesty's prosecutors.

He rang Jaime Macias, but the New Liverpool constabulary captain had even less to tell him than did Rhodes. The constables had had no luck running Tricky Dick's killer to earth, and hadn't turned up any new Nagants used in other crimes, either.

"Knives and coshes and one chap with more imagination than brains who tried to hold up an ironmonger's shop with a crossbow, but no more rifles," Macias said. "Can't say I miss them, either."

"A crossbow?" Bushell said, bemused. "There's something you don't see every day. What happened?"

"He shot his bolt—and missed." Macias chuckled. "Whereupon the shopkeeper hit him several fine licks with a fireplace poker. He'll be in hospital for a couple of weeks before they can try him, and in gaol afterwards rather longer than that, unless I'm very much mistaken."

"Here's hoping you're not," Bushell said. "You haven't helped me much, but you have brightened up the day. A crossbow!" He let out a highly unprofessional chortle.

His next telephone call went to Victoria. "Dreadful business you went through at Buckley Bay," Sir Horace Bragg said once the connection was made. "Shocking. A terrible loss, too; Felix Crooke was the best we had when it came to dealing with the Sons."

"This time they dealt with him," Bushell said with grim irony. "It'll hurt us down the line, too. It can't help but."

"Try not to take it too hard. From all I've heard, you did everything in the most proper fashion imaginable," Bragg said.

"Yes, and a crown with that will buy me a cup of tea," Bushell replied. "They don't pay off for doing things properly. They pay off for getting them *done.*"

"Doing them properly is most often the way to get them done," Bragg said. Bushell didn't answer, since that was true. Bragg went on, "Your investigations certainly seem to be leading you all over the NAU. You're in the Six Nations now? Who would have imagined the Sons operating there?"

"None of us, evidently," Bushell said. He didn't mention Kathleen Flannery. He didn't want Bragg clucking at him over his mild treatment of her; he had enough on his plate without that. "I feel I'm chasing shapes in the mist, and whenever I get close to one, it disappears. The clock is ticking, too."

"Well, I can tell you something," Bragg said in confidential tones. "At a reception at the French embassy last night, Sir David Clarke was seen talking *most* animatedly with Duke Orlov. Was seen by me, in fact; I was there. Nothing I can prove, nothing I can take to Sir Martin—as if he'd listen to me anyhow—but damn me if I like it."

"I don't, either," Bushell said. "It's a good job you went back to the capital." The idea of Sir David and the Russian ambassador to the NAU getting together for a cozy *tête-à-tête* at some formal reception revolted him. "Pity you couldn't hear what they were saying."

"My French isn't all it should be," Sir Horace confessed, "and that's the language they were using." Under his breath, he added, "It's just like Clarke to be fluent in it, too."

Bushell spoke reasonably good French himself, but he understood what Bragg meant. French was the language of people who called themselves sophisticates the world around, and a good many of the sophisticates were degenerates masquerading under the politer name—Sir David Clarke immediately sprang to mind there. And furthermore, he thought with the British citizen's almost inborn suspicion for any language not his own, French *sounded* slimy.

Bragg asked, "How are you doing there, Tom?" Bushell gave him a precis, again not mentioning Kathleen Flannery. When he was through, Sir Horace said, "Sounds like you're doing a splendid job. Keep up the good work, and by all means keep me apprised of your progress."

"I shall, sir," Bushell said, and hung up. He didn't think he was doing a splendid job. A splendid job would have meant *The Two Georges* on display back in New Liverpool, and him back there, too, and Felix Crooke in Victoria, worried about the Sons but not too much. He scowled, grimaced, and wished he had a drink.

However mildly he was treating Kathleen Flannery, he didn't trust her very far. One of the things he didn't trust her about was going off on her own and learning who could guess what without telling him about it. She'd already shown she did things like that, or she wouldn't have been in Doshoweh complicating his life.

The only way he saw to be certain she didn't wander off by herself was to make sure either he or Samuel Stanley stuck close to her all the time. He ended up doing a good deal more of that than Stanley did. He told himself that was because it was part of the case he could personally control. The explanation was true; not even the unsleepingly watchful part of him that demanded perfection could deny it.

But neither that part of him nor any other could deny that he found Kathleen attractive, either. He would have seen a good deal of her in the course of duty, had *The Two Georges* stayed safe in New Liverpool. He might well have tried seeing her off duty, too: who better to show her the sights?

He didn't know the sights of Doshoweh. The Six Nations had seldom

crossed his professional path even before he moved to the southwestern part of
the NAU. The Iroquois kept to themselves and stayed out of trouble, character-
istics he heartily favored. The only case involving them he remembered was one
where they'd asked for RAM help in keeping smugglers from sneaking rotgut into
the Six Nations without paying the hefty tax they slapped on it.

Even had he known the sights, Kathleen Flannery likely would have been
happier seeing them without him. He'd meet her for breakfast each morning in
the restaurant attached to the Hotel Ahgusweyo. The small talk, he thought
gloomily, was very small indeed. She had an Irish temper, at least when it came
to nursing grudges. He thought it unfair that she reckoned keeping her from
hurting the investigation a grudge, but she did.

Another trouble was that Doshoweh itself didn't have a lot of sights. A museum dedicated to the achievements of Sosehawa took up one day and filled
Kathleen with more enthusiasm than she'd shown lately, but left Bushell discontented.

Kathleen noticed. "He was a great man," she declared, as if he'd denied it. By
the light that came into her eyes, she was spoiling for a fight.

"Well, what if he was?" Bushell answered. "The ancient Greeks turned their
great men into demigods. From what I saw in there, the Iroquois have done the
same thing. You'd think the Great Spirit was whispering into Sosehawa's ear
every step he took."

"He's a hero to them—in the mythological sense of the word—and he's
earned it, too," she said. "Without him, they might have been overwhelmed, the
way so many Indian nations were. It's only natural for them to make him out to
be larger than life."

Stubbornly, Bushell shook his head. "Remembering the real man and his real
accomplishments is more important. Make him out to be half-magical and you
take away the chance of having more like him."

"That's a reductionist view of history." By the way Kathleen said it, she
might have been accusing him of eating with his fingers.

He spoiled that by ignoring her tone and taking it for a compliment. "Yes,
I do try to reduce things to facts. They're easier to deal with than opinions,
and more reliable." He might have said more than that, but it occurred to
him that opinions were meat and drink to the curator of an art museum. How
could you objectively decide which painting was better than all the rest? You
couldn't, but people got rich claiming they could. That was a fact, and an unsavory one.

Kathleen said, "If all people thought of when they saw *The Two Georges* was
the painting itself, the Sons of Liberty wouldn't have bothered stealing it."

"It's important because it reminds us of some facts and what sprang from
them," Bushell retorted. "The Sons have a low opinion of those facts."

"That's not what I meant." She exhaled in exasperation. "The opinion people have about *The Two Georges*—"

"—Is a fact we need to bear in mind while we investigate," Bushell broke in.
"For instance, I'll be heartily glad if I never see another reporter again, but I'm
sure I will."

She still glared at him, but now, perhaps, with grudging respect. "You are a very stubborn man."

"Thank you," he said, though he knew she hadn't intended that for a compliment, either. "Shall we head back to the hotel for supper?" After a moment's hesitation, he offered her his arm. After a longer moment's hesitation, she took it.

After supper, he spoke to the concierge. The results of the conversation were as he'd hoped they'd be. At breakfast the next morning, he said in elaborately casual tones, "I'm told the hotel operates an omnibus service up to Niagara Falls. The journey takes about forty minutes each way, they say, and gives between two and three hours for sightseeing and a light luncheon. Seems a pity not to see the falls when we're so close. Would you care to join me on the 'bus?"

She sipped at her tea before answering, "Well, why not? Since everything here is going at a snail's pace, we might as well see what we can. When does the omnibus leave?"

"Ten o'clock," he said, and risked a smile. He was glad she'd said yes, and at the same time angry at himself for inviting her. It wasn't the right way to go about things, and he knew it: too many unanswered questions still floated around her. *But if you're going to keep an eye on her, you might as well enjoy yourself doing it,* he thought. That just made him scowl down at his toast; he knew a rationalization when he saw one, even if he was the fellow who made it.

Samuel Stanley paused at the restaurant entrance to look around, spotted Bushell and Kathleen, and hurried over to them. "Good thing I was still up in my room," he said. "Shikalimo just telephoned. He wants all three of us at the constabulary building right away—says he has a list of prospects and their friends and acquaintances for us to look over."

"We'd better go do it, then," Bushell said, rising from the table. *So much for Niagara Falls* ran mournfully through his mind. Kathleen Flannery also got up. Bushell turned to Stanley. "We can go on ahead, if you want. Get yourself some breakfast."

"They'll be able to feed me something there, I expect," Stanley said. "As long as it's not that . . . hommony mush, I'll be all right." Bushell suspected he'd swallowed an uncouth adjective, or perhaps even a participle, in the nick of time.

Sylvanus Greeley and Charles Lucas were sitting in Shikalimo's office when Bushell and his companions got there. He nodded to his fellow RAMs, and to Shikalimo. He gave the Iroquois constabulary major credit for marshaling all his resources no matter how jealously he guarded his own autonomy.

Shikalimo said, "I've sent out for tea and coffee. Has anyone missed breakfast?" When Samuel Stanley nodded, he asked, "What would you like? I'll get it for you." He put his hand on the telephone but waited for Stanley's reply before picking it up.

"Anything easy," Stanley said. "A ham and cheese sandwich, say."

"However you like," Shikalimo answered, and made the call. After he hung up, he remarked, "You're a man of simple pleasures, Captain. I think I'd have chosen something on the order of strawberries in cider and fried lake clams, perhaps with waffles and maple syrup afterwards."

The proposed combination made Bushell's mouth water. Along with Shikalimo's elegant accent, it reminded him of how well the Iroquois had done as clients of the Empire and how, while retaining many of their own ways, they'd also borrowed from the British.

Stanley's mind ran in more immediately practical channels. "If I ate that much, I'd fall asleep on you. A ham sandwich is working food."

"Then let's get to work," Shikalimo said. "We've pinpointed four white men in the Deohstegaa area who, mm, have been known to be imperfectly polite in their references to the folk of the Six Nations." He coughed discreetly. Bushell could imagine for himself the racialist remarks that cough implied.

"Who are these people?" Sylvanus Greeley asked. "I presume you've never had grounds for holding any of them."

"No, we've not," Shikalimo said. "A man is free to express his opinions, no matter how unpalatable his neighbors may find them. This is a principle of your law, by the way, not our own, and I confess I sometimes wonder as to its wisdom. But I digress. The men in question—the questionable men, if you prefer—are Donald Morton, the lake-shipping magnate; Augustus Northgate, the grocer; Solomon York, who runs a printing establishment; and James Stonebreaker, who is, oddly enough, a mason by trade."

"There are printers involved with the Sons in New Liverpool," Bushell said. "York would go to the top of my list just on account of his trade."

"So far as we know, his shop has not produced anything unsavory," Shikalimo answered. "How far we know is, of course, an open question. I thought we'd agreed earlier that our likeliest targets were to be among the quiet friends and acquaintances of these men."

"Yes, yes," Bushell said.

Shikalimo sensed his urgency. "Here we are," he said, handing papers to the RAMs and to Kathleen Flannery. "I hope Dewasenta did up enough carbons of these for all of us—ah, good. I also hope that, with the resources you gentlemen enjoy, you'll be able to tell me if any of these chaps is known to be associated with the Sons of Liberty. We have nothing more on any of them than a few minor traffic offenses."

Bushell's eyes went down the list. The names were grouped by the man with whom they were linked. Donald Morton must have known a whole great raft of people, if he knew this many named Joe. Whether these Joes were friends or not was another question, one he couldn't answer. None of the names on the list was familiar to him.

"Lieutenant-Colonel Crooke, I wish he were here," Charles Lucas said.

"I'm sure he wishes the same thing," Bushell said. "But he's not, so we'll have to do it ourselves." Instead of Crooke's face, though, what came into his mind was a quart bottle of Jameson, stopper out and lying on the table beside it. He could smell the whiskey, could feel the heft and the round smoothness of the bottle in his hand, sweet to the touch as a woman's breast, could hear the gentle gurgle as he poured amber fire over ice or straight down his throat.

Someone said something. He looked up, startled. The whiskey vision had been so vivid, he'd almost lost himself in it. There was a hell of a thing. He'd been soberer than usual these past few days, but the bottle had hold of him even when he wasn't drinking.

Evidently for his benefit, Shikalimo repeated, "Does anyone see any names he recognizes?"

None of the RAMs said anything. Shikalimo looked down at his desk. His faith in the omniscience and infallibility of the NAU's top police force had just gone down a peg, or maybe two. He was a young man yet, Bushell thought. He had a lot of disappointments ahead of him yet.

Then, hesitantly, Kathleen Flannery said, "I don't know if this is the same Joseph Kilbride as the one I've heard of before, but there is a man by that name who collects art from the later colonial period, just before the days when the Union was organized."

Bushell sent her a sharp glance. He'd been wishing Shikalimo hadn't given her the list. If she saw on it someone whose name she knew, she could easily keep quiet about it and alert him. Now she'd identified somebody. He didn't know what to make of that. Maybe she was sincerely trying to help the investigation. Recovering *The Two Georges* would put her career back on the rails. But if she put suspicion on the wrong man, the right one could carry on unhindered.

Sylvanus Greeley had a more basic question: "What does his taste in art collecting have to do with the case?"

Shikalimo shifted in his seat. As clearly as if he'd shouted it, Bushell could read what he was thinking: *this man may be a RAM, but he has no imagination.* He was thinking the same thing himself. But he let Kathleen explain. She, after all, had raised the issue.

By the tone she took—rather like a teacher explaining fractions to a room full of restive trade-school students—her estimate of Greeley's candlepower was also none too high. "In the 1760s, there was quite a bit of tension between the mother country and the colonies, and talk of their breaking away. The Sons of Liberty still think that would have been a good idea. It might have happened— or might have been tried, anyhow—if His Majesty's government and the leaders of the colonies hadn't worked out a *modus vivendi*."

"I still don't see—" Greeley began, but then he held up a finger. "Oh, wait. Maybe I do. You're saying that anybody who's interested in art from that time would be interested in other things, too, like us breaking off from England."

Greeley wasn't an idiot after all. A muttonhead, perhaps, but not an idiot. "And a half plus a half really *is* one," Bushell muttered under his breath. "God save the King-Emperor."

Kathleen sent him a curious look, but then nodded to Sylvanus Greeley. "That's my idea, anyhow—or that he may be interested in those other things, too. For that matter, I don't know whether this is the Joseph Kilbride who collects art. It's not the most common name, but it's not precisely a rare one, either."

"I can find out this Kilbride's avocations, I expect," Shikalimo said. He too looked toward Bushell, silently asking whether the track was worth pursuing. Bushell sent back an almost imperceptible nod. He didn't like relying on Kathleen, but he didn't see that he had much choice. Had she named Joseph Kilbride after someone else had proposed a different target for investigation, he would have thought a red herring more likely.

Shikalimo picked up the telephone. He spoke into it in his own language, but every now and then a name or phrase in English would come through: Joseph Kilbride, colonial art, Sons of Liberty. Hearing them embedded in the throaty Iroquois language bemused Bushell. When Shikalimo hung up, he returned to English to say, "I'll have four or five people checking on that. We should know soon."

Sure enough, the phone rang in less than ten minutes. Shikalimo listened, murmured, "Oh, jolly good," and laid the handset in its cradle. "Hasanoanda gets things done," he said with a smile. "He rang up the *Doshoweh Sentinel*, as being most likely to know what hobbyhorses a white man might ride. Sure enough, this is the Joseph Kilbride of whom Dr. Flannery has heard."

"Now we're getting somewhere," Samuel Stanley said.

"I propose we get over to Mr. Kilbride's residence and ask some questions of him," Sylvanus Greeley boomed, as if he'd found out about Kilbride through his own skill at detection. Since the move was so obvious even a proved muttonhead could see it, Bushell forbore to argue.

# IX

$S$HIKALIMO'S SUPERMARINE SALOON HELD himself, the two local RAMs, and the three travelers. The backseat made a tight squeeze, but Bushell minded less than he might have, for he was pressed up against Kathleen Flannery. As good manners demanded, they both pretended to ignore the close contact. Bushell, though, was very much aware of what he affected to disregard. He wondered if Kathleen was, too.

As he had when he picked up Bushell and Stanley at the train station, Shikalimo drove the powerful Supermarine as if he were in a road race. "Have a care, there," Charles Lucas protested feebly when he shot around a lorry and then swung back into the lane it occupied so abruptly that his passengers slid from side to side as much as their cramped quarters would allow.

"Haven't had a wreck yet," Shikalimo said gaily. He changed lanes again, for no purpose Bushell could see other than horrifying Lucas.

With three large men in the front seat and only the roadster's small side windows to look out of, Bushell didn't see as much of Doshoweh as he would have wanted. He did note that, once they got away from the center of the city, it stopped looking quite so much like any other town of similar size in the NAU.

For one thing, except in scattered districts, signs written in English almost disappeared. As they were speeding through one such district, Shikalimo remarked, "A lot of whites here." The houses bore him out: they were clapboards and half-timbered Tudors that wouldn't have looked out of place in New England or New York.

Away from the white parts of town, though, houses as he knew them largely disappeared. Instead, long, narrow buildings of bark and timber framing stretched on and on, sometimes for fifty or sixty feet, sometimes for twice that. Children too young for school played around them, while women cultivated maize and beans and squashes in gardens that replaced lawns.

Shikalimo said, "Some of our people live in the *ganosote*, the bark house, because they can afford no better. Others, though, prefer our traditional homes for other reasons: they enjoy the sense of community the *ganosote* gives them. I mean that literally as well as metaphorically; more often than not, all the families in a bark house will be of the same clan."

Bushell thought of the block of flats in which he lived. People came and went almost at random. He knew only a handful of his fellow lodgers by name. "Maybe your people have the right idea," he said.

"Sometimes differences are just—different," Shikalimo answered with a shrug. "When I went off to university, I wondered how you whites managed to live as naked individuals, so to speak: without the clan structure I'd taken for granted, and with even your families pale things by the standards to which I was accustomed. But, after some years of that life, coming home to the Six Nations was a shock of another sort. What I do, whom I see are dictated more by my position in the clan than my own choice. It sometimes has the feel of a straitjacket—rather a loose-fitting one, but a straitjacket nonetheless."

"Isn't that partly because you're the Sachem's nephew?" Samuel Stanley asked.

"Partly, but less than you'd think," Shikalimo said. "Among us, your place in the clan dictates possibilities no matter who you are." He chuckled in wry amusement. "I daresay I have more sympathy for the scandalous princesses on the odd branches of His Majesty's family tree than the rest of you might. Their kicking over the traces so thoroughly makes me jealous."

"It also makes them fine targets for the scandal sheets the Sons of Liberty turn out," Bushell said.

"I wonder what sort of scandal I could essay," Shikalimo murmured. Bushell wouldn't have been more than half surprised to find he meant it seriously.

Deohstegaa lay northwest of the center of Doshoweh. The shore of the lake the Iroquois called Doshoweh Tecarneodi and the English-speaking world Lake Erie was rocky thereabouts, but quays running out into the water made for a fine harbor. As Shikalimo raced past that harbor, Bushell saw that most of the men working there were of the blood of the Six Nations.

Perhaps catching his gaze in the mirror, Shikalimo said, "We really are part of the twentieth century these days, Colonel."

"If I were you, I wouldn't be so proud of it," Bushell answered.

The house in front of which Shikalimo stopped was in an enclave of British-style homes that spoke of wealth despite being close to the docks. Had the lawns in front of it been a vegetable garden, the crops it yielded might have fed a fair part of Doshoweh. When Bushell pressed the button by the door, chimes played the opening bars of Beethoven's Third Symphony, the *Fallen Innocents*, which the radical composer had dedicated to those who fell to Bonaparte's guns in the ill-fated French uprising against Louis XVI.

Bushell raised an eyebrow. "If this chap's not a Son of Liberty, his doorbell doesn't know it."

The door opened. A butler in black tie and frock coat peered out at the group on the porch. If he was impressed, he hid it well. "Yes? How may I help you?" he asked, in tones that implied, *How may I help you off the property?*

Bushell displayed his badge. So did Samuel Stanley. So did the two local RAMs. So did Shikalimo. Kathleen Flannery took something official-looking from her handbag and held it up, too. For all Bushell knew, it entitled her to visit the washroom at her museum. When flashed along with so much highly intimidating and highly genuine tin, it passed muster.

"Where's Kilbride?" Bushell growled, like a cinema ruffian.

The butler's mouth worked. For close to fifteen seconds, nothing came out. At last, in strangled tones, he managed, "Mr. Kilbride is not here at present."

"No reason he should be. I'm sure he's a busy man," Samuel Stanley said smoothly. He and Bushell had played nice guy, tough guy at scores of interrogations; they did it now almost without conscious thought. "Can you tell us where his place of business is?"

"You don't understand," the butler said, his voice losing culture and hauteur at about the same speed. "I don't mean he's not at home. I mean he's not in Doshoweh right now."

"Where'd he go?" Bushell demanded, still sounding tough. "When'd he leave?"

"He's in Pennsylvania," the butler answered. "I don't know anything more about it than that, honest I don't. He packed up and took off day before yesterday. Nobody knew he was going to do it till he had Foyt drive him to the train station." He gamely tried to recover his professional persona: "It has thrown the household into rather a muddle." The persona crumbled again, for he expanded on that, saying, "Everything's gone to hell in a handbasket, as a matter of fact."

"Whereabouts in Pennsylvania is he?" Bushell said, at the same time as Sylvanus Greeley was asking, "When will he be back?"

"Don't know," the butler replied. He said no more; the answer was evidently intended to be comprehensive.

"Somebody tipped him," Stanley muttered in disgust. The butler's face made a fascinating study. Bushell wouldn't have minded turning Gainsborough loose on him as he tried to figure out what his master might have done.

He agreed with his adjutant: someone had to have warned Kilbride to make himself scarce. And if that was so, Kathleen Flannery really had uncovered a villain—unless this was all an elaborate feint to throw him off the scent. He didn't find that likely: plans so elaborate had a way of breaking down. Which meant—probably meant—Kathleen was trustworthy.

It also meant they needed to run Joseph Kilbride to earth as fast as they could. "Give me your master's business address and telephone number," he told the butler. "Maybe they'll know there why he's left town and just where the devil he's gone."

The butler plucked a card from a silver box on a table close by the door. "Here is the information you require, sir."

Bushell put on his spectacles to read the engraved typography on the business card. JOSEPH J. KILBRIDE, PURVEYOR OF FINE FOODS AND SPIRITS, the card declared, and gave the telephone number and an address on Gawehga Road. "Where's Gawehga Road?" he asked.

"Not far from here," Greeley, Lucas, and Shikalimo answered in the same breath. Shikalimo added, "*Gawehga*, in case you're interested, means *snowshoe*." He gave Bushell a mischievous look. "Actually, it means *snowshoe* even if you're not interested."

Bushell turned back to the butler. "Before we go haring off to this grocer's shop or whatever it is"—he watched the fellow's nostrils flare in what might have been anger or might have been half a guffaw—"would anybody else around this shack know where Kilbride's gone? Is there a Mrs. Kilbride, for instance?"

"Sir, if I am not acquainted with Mr. Kilbride's destination, no one associated with this establishment is, of that I assure you." The butler had his fancy diction back in place. "And I am not. Mr. Kilbride, furthermore, is a widower. None of his occasional companions is likely to be informed of his comings and goings."

"Hangs about with tarts, does he?" Bushell waited for the butler's stifled snort of laughter to prove the guess good, then grinned at Shikalimo. "See if you can run some of them down when you get the chance. Never can tell what a dirty old man might say in between the sheets."

"Sir!" The butler blushed bright red. But after he glanced back over his shoulder to make sure no one down the hall could hear him, he leaned forward and said, "Not a chance, pal. The boss talks like every word costs him a shilling—and he's tight with his shillings, he is." He straightened up and became once more the image of decorum.

That sounded like the truth to Bushell. It also made Kilbride sound like a Son of Liberty, or at least like someone who could be a Son without letting on. If he was a man of that sort, they wouldn't find out where he'd gone from anyone with whom he worked. They had to try, though. "Let's go," Bushell said.

He wondered if the butler would slam the door in relief at having them gone, and kept an ear peeled as they walked back toward Shikalimo's steamer. Rather to his disappointment, he didn't hear any bang.

KILBRIDE'S FINE FOOD AND DRINK, declared the sign above the shop of Gawehga Road. Across the street was open ground, a park or possibly just a meadow. Several dozen people were gathered there, some in clothing that wouldn't have been out of place anywhere in the Empire, some in Iroquois-style skins and embroidered cloth of like cut, some mixing the two. One of them thrust a torch into a brazier. Whatever was in there burned smokily, a grey-white plume rising toward the sky. The—*congregation* was the word that sprang to Bushell's mind—chanted something in the Iroquois language and began a slow, dignified line dance.

"A prayer of thanksgiving to Hawenneyu—the Great Spirit, one would say in English," Shikalimo said. "The smoke from the tobacco wafts the prayer up to the heavens. Incense served a similar function in Christian worship at one time, I believe."

Bushell didn't know enough about such things to say whether he was right or wrong. He asked, "How many of your people have kept the old ways, and how many gone over to Christianity?"

"We're about evenly divided," the Iroquois answered. "A couple of generations ago, there was fear the worship of Hawenneyu might fade away, leaving us without an important piece of our past. Even in this twentieth century, we have long memories, as you British do. But that seems not to have happened; the balance has remained more or less constant for as long as I've been alive." He pointed toward the sign above Kilbride's establishment. "Just as well, too, I'd say, for it keeps us from seeing more things like that."

For a moment, Bushell didn't follow him. Then he realized the sign was only in English, without an Iroquois equivalent. Most businesses in Doshoweh were more likely to be missing English than the language of the Six Nations. Kilbride's choice said something about the way he thought. When you coupled that with his taste in art and the music of his door chime. . . .

Bushell's pulse quickened. Joseph Kilbride did seem to have all the mental furniture of a Son of Liberty, and he was also a capable, prosperous man. If he wassa Son, he ought to be one of high stature. And a Son of high Stature might know quite a lot about *The Two Georges.*

The bell above the door pealed when Bushell and his companions went into Kilbride's establishment. He saw at once that the *fine* in the title of the shop was not misplaced. Kilbride sold fancy hams from Virginia and the Germanies, New Scotland smoked salmon, tinned lobster meat, fancy capers, salted olives from the Ottoman protectorates, and a variety of fresh spices whose aromas made Bushell's nose twitch appreciatively. One wall held fine wines from France and Upper California, the Germanies and the Italian states, along with Russian potato spirits, Holland gin, and whiskey from Scotland and the provinces of Franklin and Tennessee. For good measure, humidors of expensive Havanas stood nearby.

Bushell took a look at some of the prices. An eyebrow rose. Everything in the place was expensive. Part of that was quality. Part of it looked to be profit.

"May I help you?" a clerk called from behind a counter.

"Is Mr. Kilbride in?" Bushell asked.

"I'm sorry, sir, no," the clerk answered, shaking his head. "What's this in aid of, if I may ask?" As those of Kilbride's butler had, his eyes grew wide when Bushell and the other officers displayed their badges. He licked his lips. "Uh, let me refer you to Mr. Whitby. He is our senior manager. Excuse me." He headed for the back of the store at an undignified lope.

When he returned, he brought with him a stout, bald, sour-faced gentleman in a suit of grey worsted whose lines tried without much success to disguise his bulk. The man thrust out a large pink hand. "I'm Anson Whitby." His voice was a rumbling bass. "Kilbride's is not accustomed to having constabulary officers inquiring after its proprietor."

"I'm not a constabulary officer," Bushell said with a bright smile. "I'm a RAM."

Whitby proved his face could express something other than glowering disapproval: he looked astonished. "Good heavens!" he said. "What on earth can Kilbride's have done to deserve this?"

"Not Kilbride's—Kilbride," Bushell said, cheery still—it seemed to disconcert Anson Whitby. "Where exactly is Mr. Kilbride, if he's not at home and he's not here?"

"He telephoned me morning before last, saying he was called away to Pennsylvania on urgent business," Whitby answered. "I asked him where in Pennsylvania and how long he would be gone, and he told me to mind my damned business. Beg your pardon, ma'am," he added to Kathleen Flannery, "but that's what he said."

"Is that how he usually talks?" Bushell asked.

"Too right it is," Whitby said. "And if he could keep his left hand from knowing what his right hand was up to, he'd do that, too." He cocked his head to one side, so that he took on the aspect of a bulldog deciding whether to bite. "What do you think he's done, anyhow?"

"I think he's done all sorts of interesting and unpleasant things," Bushell answered, not caring to give details. "I think he'll pay for them with a good many years in gaol once we run him to earth, too."

Anson Whitby stared at him. So did the clerk, in slack-jawed, round-eyed astonishment. From their reactions, he guessed neither of them was party to Kilbride's extracurricular activities, though Whitby, at least, had the look of a man who could run a bluff.

The door chime rang. Bushell half turned to see who was coming in. To his surprise, the customer was an Iroquois, an elderly man in the dark suit, waistcoat, and homburg of a prosperous businessman anywhere in the British Empire. By the way he nodded to Anson Whitby, he was a regular here. That surprised Bushell, who hadn't expected Kilbride's shop to cater to anyone but whites.

The Iroquois made a beeline for the wall of liquors. He chose a bottle of Franklin whiskey and another of potent Russian spirits and carried them to the counter. The clerk hurried behind it to ring up the sale on the register.

"That will be twenty guineas," he said. The Iroquois gentleman drew a beaded wallet from a trouser pocket. He handed the clerk a red twenty-pound note, then added a gold sovereign to make up the extra twenty shillings. The clerk put the bottles of spirits into a paper sack for him.

As the customer turned to go, he caught sight of Shikalimo among the whites in the shop. His smile was sickly as he hurried out the door. He leaped into the steamer he'd parked in front of the Supermarine and sped away.

Shikalimo sighed. "Even with the taxes we slap on liquor, our people remain too fond of it. You British have been drinking spirits for centuries longer than we have, and they still do you harm. With us, they might as well be poison."

They were poison for Bushell, too, but that didn't stop him from drinking them. His body was telling him he hadn't had enough to drink in a long time. His body, though, thought enough to drink meant drinking till he couldn't hold up a glass any more. His mind knew better . . . sometimes.

Samuel Stanley said, "You won't have a lot of drunks here, not at ten guineas the bottle you won't."

"That's the idea, yes," Shikalimo said. He turned a hooded glance on Anson Whitby. "Of course, not all establishments have tariffs quite so high as these."

"How many Iroquois do come in here?" Bushell asked Whitby.

"A goodly number, that's as much as I can say," Whitby answered. "Keeping track of our customers by race would be a gross invasion of their privacy." He seemed to wrap himself in an invisible banner of rectitude.

"What does Joseph Kilbride think about the Iroquois?" Bushell asked.

"I've never heard him express an opinion," Whitby said.

He was a tough customer. When Bushell put that question to the senior manager, he looked not at him but toward the young clerk. At Whitby's steadfast denial, the clerk stared down at the countertop and fiddled with some jars of gumdrops on it. The tips of his ears turned pink.

"You, there!" Bushell called, and the clerk jumped. "Have *you* ever heard Mr. Kilbride express an opinion about the Iroquois?"

"Me?" the clerk squeaked. The tips of his ears got redder. He glanced nervously toward Whitby, who stared back with a gaze a basilisk might have envied. "Uh, no, not really. That is—"

Bushell strode over to him. "Are you afraid of that fat tun? Don't be. The worst he can do is give you the sack, and a man who's willing to work won't lack a situation long. And if you tell us what you know, you'll be helping us track down *The Two Georges*."

He hadn't mentioned the painting till then. The clerk's eyes got big again. "Really?" he breathed, and stopped looking toward Anson Whitby. "I remember he said once that he liked having Indians come into the shop because he got their money and he got them drunk, too. I could be wrong, but I think the person he said it to was Mr. Whitby."

"It was not," Whitby said evenly. "As I told you, I never heard him express any such opinion—nor any complimentary one, either. He is, as I've noted, sparing of speech."

Shikalimo said, "Mr. Whitby, if you are discovered to be tampering with the truth in this matter, I assure you that you shall regret it." Had he made the threat in obvious anger, it would have been easier to shrug off. Instead, he stated it as if it were a simple law of nature, inexorable as night following day. Bushell would not have cared to have such a warning leveled at him.

"I regret nothing," Whitby said. "The facts are as I state them. If you prefer a clerk's word to mine, I can do nothing but conclude it better fits some theory you have already concocted."

"Thank you both," Bushell said to Whitby and the clerk, and headed for the door. Samuel Stanley followed at once, willing to back whatever play he made. Shikalimo began to expostulate, but found himself talking to Bushell's back. He went after Bushell with obvious reluctance. So did the local RAMs and Kathleen Flannery.

Out on the sidewalk, Charles Lucas exclaimed, "That fast bastard, he's lying through his teeth, Colonel. What are you doing letting him off like that?"

"Of course he's lying," Bushell said, which touched off a fresh round of protests. "So what?"

That startled the others into a moment's silence. A grin suddenly spread over Samuel Stanley's face. "'So what?' is right," he said. "Whitby's not the chap we're after, no matter what sort of villain he turns out to be in his own right."

"You've got it," Bushell agreed. "We want Kilbride. We've found out enough to know he leans toward the Sons of Liberty. All I want to do now is go to the train station, find out if he bought a ticket there, where in Pennsylvania he was going, and whether he got on the train. If he did, I'm going after him."

Shikalimo nodded thoughtfully. "You focus on the essentials, Colonel. This is worth remembering."

"I wouldn't have known Kilbride was essential if Dr. Flannery hadn't recognized his name." Bushell turned to Kathleen. "Thank you."

"You're welcome," she answered. "As I've been trying to tell you, Colonel, I really do want to get *The Two Georges* back."

"Yes, you have said that," Bushell agreed, which was not the same as admitting he completely believed her. To his relief, she did not seem to notice the distinction. That she'd spotted Kilbride's name made him more inclined to trust her, but he could not escape the nagging fear that the pursuit on which he was embarking was intended to distract him from the true trail. A drowning man, though, grabbed for any spar he could reach.

Shikalimo was busy focusing on the essentials: "When we go to the station, we should be armed with a picture of the honorable Mr. Kilbride." For a man so young, he had a nice command of irony. "I wonder if that butler could be persuaded to part with one without our having to go to the trouble of obtaining a search warrant. If he liked his master better, I should say no, but as things are—" He let that hang, continuing in a slightly different vein: "I do sometimes find the Anglo-Saxon insistence on having the proper papers even in emergencies a curious bit of superstition."

"It's a better way to do things than the one the Russians use, where the *Okhrana* can knock on your door—knock down your door—with any excuse or none," Bushell said. Shikalimo shrugged, but was too polite to take the argument any further.

They drove back to Joseph Kilbride's mansion. "A picture?" the butler said. "I can do that. Just let me nip one out from where it won't be noticed." He disappeared. From inside the house came a woman's voice (perhaps Kilbride's latest lady friend, Bushell thought, or perhaps just the housekeeper), then his, then the woman's again, louder. The butler returned, handed Bushell a photograph, and declared in stentorian tones, "As I told you before, you are not welcome here without the due legal formalities." He tipped Bushell a wink while slamming the door in his face.

In deference to the charade, they went out to Shikalimo's steamer before looking at the picture. "Lovely chap," Bushell murmured as Joseph Kilbride stared pugnaciously up from the palm of his hand. Kilbride looked more like a retired prizefighter than an art collector. He had a large Celtic face and a large broken nose. His eyes were pale and hard and shrewd.

"If they sold him a ticket, they'll remember him," Samuel Stanley said.

"Then we'll find out if they did," Shikalimo said, and put the Supermarine in gear.

Returning to the train station was almost like coming home. After you'd been on the road for a while, any place you saw twice seemed intimately familiar—and train stations were all pretty much alike to begin with. The men and women in the ticket cages exclaimed in excitement when Major Shikalimo, the RAMs, and Kathleen Flannery descended on them.

"Oh, him," a woman with a grey streak in her midnight hair said when she saw Kilbride's photograph. "Yes, I sold him a ticket." She laughed. "He tried to bargain over the price, like a man buying terrapins at the fish market."

"Where was he going?" Bushell asked.

The ticket seller frowned. "Charleroi, that's it," she said after a moment. Seeing Bushell's blank look, she added, "It's south of Pittsburgh."

"Mining town," Shikalimo put in. "But then, around Pittsburgh they're all mining towns." He sighed. "The NAU needs the coal, needs the electricity, but that's an ugly part of the world—as if someone took a lot of the ugliness from the rest of the Union and dropped it there."

"Charleroi," Samuel Stanley muttered, half to himself. "Charleroi . . . Why have I heard that name before?" He took a couple of steps back and forth, then suddenly straightened. "Some of the coal miners who were out picketing when Tricky Dick got shot came from Charleroi." He got a faraway look in his eyes as he went back over the evidence he'd gathered what seemed an age before. "McGaffigan, O'Flynn—somebody else, too, I forget who."

"Isn't that interesting?" Bushell said. "Do you think things might be coming together after all?" He laughed. "Probably something in the rules against that, but we'll find out."

"You're going on to Charleroi, then?" Kathleen Flannery asked.

"No, Dr. Flannery—we are." He'd wanted to take her to Niagara Falls, by all accounts one of the most beautiful spots in the British Empire. The Pennsylvania coal mines did not strike him as an adequate substitute.

▼

When Shikalimo dropped Bushell, Stanley, and Kathleen Flannery at the train station the next afternoon, he said, "We often look over the border and think how lucky we are." The Pennsylvania Railroad train that would pull out of Doshoweh, bound for Pittsburgh and points south, had no name. It was just a train, doing a job that had to be done but didn't seem worth commemorating in any way. Bushell took that as a symptom of what the Iroquois was talking about. Nobody much wanted to go to western Pennsylvania. Sometimes, though, you had to, like it or not.

With one exception, service aboard the train reflected its determinedly anonymous status. The upholstery and springs of the seats had seen better days. The dining car was dingy, the beefsteak Bushell ordered for supper overcooked and fatty. The stewards slapped food and dishes around in a way he hadn't seen since his last army mess hall. And yet, every so often, people would come up from the car in back of the diner with beatific smiles on their faces.

Bushell's curiosity finally got the better of him. When still another obviously satisfied soul went past him, he reached out to bar the fellow's path, asking, "What do they have back there, friend, the hashish?"

"You ain't far wrong, buddy. That's the Pennsy club car, that is," the man answered in tones of reverence better suited to discussions of St. Paul's Cathedral. The high-proof fumes he breathed into Bushell's face added their accent to his words.

After the stewards went clattering off with the last of the china and silver-ware, Bushell said to Sam and Kathleen, "Well, shall we see if that really is a proper oasis?"

"Why not?" Kathleen said. "It can't be worse than the rest of the train, and it might be better."

"Couldn't have put it neater myself," Samuel Stanley said as he got up from the table.

"Well, well," Bushell murmured when they went into the club car, and then again: "Well, well." The car was cool and dim and seemed quiet, maybe because of that—it rattled along over the rails no different from any other. But none of that was why Bushell had exclaimed.

"Will you look at the display behind the bar?" Stanley said softly. "I've seen fancy taverns that don't stock half as many kinds of hooch. You want anything at all, you can get it here."

"Amen," Bushell said. "And catch the mirror behind the bottles—it makes it look as if there are twice as many." He laughed. "Overkill."

Four men got up from the bar. Bushell and his companions slid onto three of the stools they'd vacated. He ordered Jameson over ice, Kathleen a gin and tonic, and Samuel Stanley a pint of Molson's ale. The bartender drew it from the tap with practiced perfection, stopping the flow so the top of the head reached the edge of the glass without a drop spilling over.

After he went off to serve another thirsty soul, Stanley said, "I know why the club car's so fancy even when the rest of the train's down at the heels." Bushell raised a questioning eyebrow. His adjutant explained: "If you were going into the Pennsylvania coal country, wouldn't you want someplace where you could try and forget it?"

"Many a truth spoken in jest," Bushell said. He raised his glass. "To finding Joseph Kilbride and some answers, in whichever order we come across them." They all drank. He savored the smoky taste of the Irish whiskey in his mouth and its warmth in his belly.

When Kathleen Flannery's drink was done, she excused herself for a mo-ment. Bushell ordered a second round from the bartender. When the new drinks came, he said, "Here's another toast for you and me, Sam: here's hoping we didn't leave Doshoweh too bloody soon."

Stanley sighed and nodded. "We left a lot behind, didn't we? I'd like to know more about that printer Shikalimo turned up, I'd like to have found the room where the Sons were hiding *The Two Georges*, I'd like to have done a whole lot of things. But we can't be in two or four places at once, and we don't have a lot of time. We have to follow the trail that looks hottest and remember we have other people looking in other places."

"The trail that looks hottest," Bushell repeated. "Here's one more toast still: here's hoping it doesn't look hottest because somebody set it up to look that way." Without waiting for Stanley to follow suit, he poured the shot of Jameson down his throat and signaled the bartender for another.

"You still aren't sure about—" Stanley suddenly clammed up.

Kathleen Flannery slid back onto her stool. "The two of you are pretty quiet," she said. "You must have been talking about me."

Samuel Stanley swigged at his Molson's to give himself an excuse not to deal with that one. "Men always talk about women when they aren't there," Bushell answered lazily. "It gives us the chance to—"

"—To bend your elbow, it looks like," Kathleen said, pointing to the empty glass the bartender hadn't taken away.

"To squeeze a word in without getting interrupted, I was going to say," Bushell finished.

"Were you?" Kathleen picked up her fresh drink, sipped, and peered at him from over the rim of the glass.

"If I wasn't, you'll never prove it now," he said.

"So I won't. Point to you, Colonel Bushell." Kathleen Flannery could have said that in tones of Alaskan ice, as she'd spoken when Bushell gave her no choice about coming along with him and Sam Stanley. She didn't—quite. He took that as progress, all the while wondering whether she was playing the same game as he or a different one altogether.

That was the question in more ways than one, especially when they were almost flirting like this. *Is she a suspect?* had nearly vanished from his mind, but it was still there. But he also wondered what else lay behind those green eyes. *Does she feel anything for me?* He couldn't just ask. That would break the rules of the game. He'd have to find out.

He had that drink, and then another one, and then another. Samuel Stanley nursed his second ale. Bushell wondered if Sam was going to kick him in the ankle to try to get him to slow down. His adjutant had a good deal of mother hen in him. Stanley contented himself with looking worried. Since he looked worried a lot of the time, only Bushell noticed.

Kathleen Flannery finished three drinks. She was starting a fourth when the train pulled into Pittsburgh. Streetlamps and tongues of flame from factory chimneys made the sooty air outside seem thick, almost curdled. "I've been through here in the daytime," Kathleen said. "It's worse then; you can see the smoke curling and twisting through the valleys that lead down to the rivers." She spoke slowly and carefully, pausing every couple of words to make sure they'd come out the way she wanted them.

"New Liverpool's air isn't all it should be," Bushell said, "but it's nothing like this." His speech did not show that he had considerably more liquor on board than Kathleen. Some of the learned quacks said holding your whiskey well was a sign you were too fond of it. For one thing, Bushell already knew how fond of whiskey he was. For another, he wasn't in the habit of listening to quacks no matter how learned they were.

The conductor came through the club car. "Liberty Street station!" he called. "All out for Pittsburgh!" There was a general exodus. No matter how unpleasant a place the grimy industrial city was, a lot of capital resided here, and gold drew men as a lodestone draws iron.

"Liberty Street?" Bushell raised his glass once more. "Down with liberty—

and its sons." He and Stanley drank to that at once. Kathleen Flannery followed suit, a little more slowly. Did that mean she didn't care for the toast, or just that she'd had enough to drink? Bushell rubbed at his mustache. How far to rely on her? If he guessed wrong on that— He drained his Jameson.

At some time in the past—whether ten years before or only six months, Bushell couldn't tell—the Pennsylvania Railroad station in Pittsburgh had been painted white. Now it was a streaky, dingy grey, uglier than it would have been had it not tried defying the soft-coal smoke that made the town what it was.

The train lay over in Pittsburgh for most of an hour, loading and unloading passengers. Some of the people who came into the club car had the sleek and prosperous look of businessmen. More, though, were miners and factory hands heading back to their home towns after coming into the city for whatever they couldn't get locally.

A lot of the men in overalls and boots and cloth caps and collarless shirts spoke with a brogue. Bushell glanced over to Kathleen. Her English was almost as elegant as Shikalimo's. He wondered what her father sounded like.

From Pittsburgh to Charleroi was a journey of less than half an hour, and would have taken only half that time had the train not made several stops at other industrial and mining towns along the way. The laborers who packed the club car drank with a grim intensity that made even Bushell raise an eyebrow. No men who were happy with their lot would have needed so much anesthesia before they got home.

Some of the drinkers had their hair cropped short in the Roundhead look that set his teeth on edge. Others rolled up shirtsleeves to show off eagles tattooed on forearms or biceps. He wondered how many of them were Sons of Liberty and how many just venting frustration at life in the NAU. They were fools if they thought breaking away from England would get them out of the mines and foundries. An independent North America would need coal and steel no less than the NAU did.

He shrugged and knocked back the last of his Jameson. Some people thought change automatically led to improvement. Having been through a great many changes in his own life—and ended up half drunk on a nameless train rattling south toward a grimy coal town—he wondered about that.

"Charleroi!" the conductor called. "All out for Charleroi!" He pushed his way through the club car to make the announcement in the next one back.

The train squealed to a stop. The Charleroi station hardly rated the name. It boasted a ticket booth, an awning over the tracks to keep rain off arriving and departing passengers, and not much more.

Bushell, Stanley, and Kathleen Flannery got their bags and then stood under the awning for a moment, wondering where to go next. They drew guarded looks from the miners and the women and children who came to meet them: not only were they strangers, but their clothes proclaimed them to be of a different class from the locals.

Bushell walked over to the ticket booth. "If I want a good hotel, where do I go?"

The ticket seller shifted a pipe to the corner of his mouth and answered,

"Somewheres else." When that failed to shift Bushell, he sighed and pointed south. "Down there just a couple buildings, that's the Ribblesdale House. Best we got. It ain't much, and that's a fact."

Despite its fancy name, the Ribblesdale House proved to be a down-at-the-heels building with tired wallpaper and carpeting grey with ground-in grime. "Yes, sir, we have plenty of rooms," the desk clerk said. The unspoken question in his eyes was, *Why the devil were you stupid enough to come to Charleroi?*

"Do you have a Joseph Kilbride registered here?" Bushell asked.

"I'm sorry, sir, but I can't give out that information," the clerk answered. Bushell laid his badge on the counter. The clerk's eyes went large and round. "Uh, let me check." He flipped through the registration book. "No, no one by that name here. I didn't think so."

"Well, where is he, then?" Samuel Stanley burst out. He rounded on the clerk. "Does this godforsaken hole in the ground have any other hotels?"

The young man's skin was fair enough to let Bushell see his flush. "There's the Hastings Arms," he said, with the clear implication that anyone who'd register at the Hastings Arms was a savage irremediably beyond the pale of civilization.

"We'll check it in the morning," Bushell decided. "He may be staying with friends, too. If he has any friends in this town, he deserves to stay with them, and they deserve to have him."

"Here are your keys, sirs, ma'am," the clerk said. "I've given you three adjoining rooms right upstairs on the first floor: 135, 137, and 139."

"Thank you, Mr.—" Bushell peered toward the name badge the fellow wore on his right lapel. "Mr. Devlin. Those will do nicely."

▼

The Ribblesdale House had an attached dining room. It did not come up to Bushell's standards. The eggs were greasy, the bacon overcooked, and the pot of English Breakfast he ordered had been steeped so long, it was bitter. The toast came to the table cold, but that was common practice at hotels that tried to ape those of England, so he didn't know whether to blame it on mere fecklessness or social climbing.

He and his companions stolidly worked their way through breakfast, imperfectly satisfactory though it was. He was lighting his first cigar of the morning to get the bitter taste of the tea out of his mouth when a couple of young men in suits and waistcoats paused at the entrance to the dining room. At first he pegged them for businessmen, but their lapels were too wide and too sharp, their trousers too baggy, to let them fit into most reputable businesses. He sucked in more aromatic cigar smoke. Charleroi might not have any reputable businesses.

The pair spotted him, Stanley, and Kathleen—not hard, since they were the only people in the dining room. Side by side, the newcomers walked over to stand close by the table where Bushell and his companions sat. Except to blow cigar smoke in their direction, he ignored them. Samuel Stanley and Kathleen followed his lead, save that they did not have cigars.

One of the two young men had a receding hairline. The other wore a close-trimmed, gingery beard. The balding one whipped out a notebook and fountain pen. In portentous tones, the other asked, "You're the RAMs who came into Charleroi last night?" The chap with the pen and notebook started scribbling before Bushell spoke a word.

"If you already know the answers, why ask the questions?" Bushell said mildly. *Reporters*, he thought, in lieu of a stronger pejorative. "Let's try it the other way: who are you?"

"Michael Shaughnessy," said the one with the notebook, at the same time as the bearded one was saying, "Jerry Doyle." Bushell expected them to announce the name of the Charleroi—or possibly Pittsburgh—paper that employed them. Instead, they chorused, "We're with *Common Sense*."

"Are you?" Bushell said, still not sounding very interested. "If you had any, you wouldn't be." While the two reporters were adding that up and discovering that it came out to something less than a ringing endorsement, he let his eyes stray casually to Kathleen Flannery.

She was looking straight at him, perhaps expecting that questioning gaze. "I didn't call them," she declared. "I've never set eyes on them before, I've never heard of them, and I didn't know they were going to be here."

"Did I say you did?" Bushell answered. But her quick, vehement denial rekindled the doubts that had died to smoldering embers. The edge of a headache he had from last night's whiskey got worse. He didn't let any of that show, but nodded affably enough to Doyle and Shaughnessy. "I might have known Mr. Kennedy would send out a vulture, but I didn't think he'd put a bald eagle on the train with him."

Michael Shaughnessy reddened as easily as a woman might have. "Now see here, you tyrant's slave—"

Doyle set a hand on his companion's arm. "He's trying to get your goat, Mike, and by the sound of you he has it." Like Shaughnessy, he had a vanishing trace of a brogue, almost swallowed in a flat New England accent. Turning to Bushell, he said, "We'll come to keep an eye on the monstrous waste of public money you RAMs are making of the search for that ugly daub, *The Two Georges*."

"Isn't it nice, Sam?" Bushell steepled his fingers. "*Common Sense* sends the art critics to look after us."

Samuel Stanley was too angry to enjoy irony. "How the devil did that blasted rag know to send them here? We just got here ourselves." His not looking at Kathleen was as pointed as the glance Bushell had sent her. Then he glowered up at the reporters. "Who tipped you off?"

"You don't think we'd tell you?" Jerry Doyle raised an eyebrow in well-crafted dismay. "The press is still free, not the muzzled lapdog of the Crown you'd make it if you had your way."

"Be careful who you're talking to," Shaughnessy warned, mock alarm in his voice. "For if the one here is the famous Colonel Bushell who's had his pictures in all the papers, the other must be his just as famous aide, Captain Stanley—Sam the spade." He rocked back on his heels in amusement to see how the RAMs would take that.

Stanley bit his lip. Bushell wondered how long it had been since someone sneered at him on account of his race. Such things happened more often than RAMs getting shot at in the course of their duties, but they weren't common: Negroes of a given social class were usually treated much like their white counterparts. *Why not?* Bushell thought. A man couldn't help his race, but hard work would lift him out of the class into which he'd been born.

"Vulgarians," Kathleen muttered. It wasn't meant to be overheard. That made Bushell feel better about catching it. If Kathleen didn't think well of men who would make a racialist joke, maybe she hadn't been the one who called *Common Sense*.

On the other hand, maybe she just hadn't known whom the periodical would despatch to Charleroi.

Bushell looked at the reporters as if he'd bitten into an apple and found them in there. "Do you know a fellow called Joseph Kilbride?" he asked.

He expected them to shake their heads. That was what Shaughnessy did. Jerry Doyle said, "The art collector? What's he got to do with anything? You think he has *The Two Georges* hanging in his parlor?" He laughed loud and long at his own wit.

"Stranger things have happened." Bushell got up from the table. He tossed down banknotes to cover the cost of breakfast. Kathleen and Sam rose, too. Stanley stared at the two men from *Common Sense* for a couple of seconds. He was taller than either of them, and wider through the shoulders and narrower in the hips. He didn't say anything; he didn't move toward them. They drew back a pace anyhow. He strode through the space they had vacated. You got the idea he would have gone through there whether they'd stepped back or not.

"Constabulary station should only be a couple of blocks that way," Bushell said, pointing toward the Monongehela as he and his companions left the hotel.

"We'll do better there than we have here, that's certain," Sam Stanley said, and set off for the station with the same determined steps he'd shown in the hotel dining room.

Bushell and Kathleen Flannery followed him. Just breathing made Bushell feel as if he'd smoked a dozen cigars in a room without ventilation. The air had a smoky, sulfurous tang to it. Buildings only a few blocks away seemed hazy, indistinct, yet the hot sun beat down out of a clear sky. Bushell thought longingly of the cool, crisp, pine-scented air of the Queen Charlotte Islands. He hadn't imagined he would look with longing on anything that had to do with the Queen Charlotte Islands.

His first glimpse of Charleroi by daylight left him unimpressed. The Ribblesdale House was in the middle of the downtown business district, but most of the businesses, by the look of them, would have quickly failed in New Liverpool. The mannequins in the windows of clothiers' wore garments either poorly made or overpriced or both. He'd never seen such an expanse of unpainted pine and garish upholstery as the furniture shops displayed. The profusion of secondhand shops argued that not enough people had the wherewithal to buy new goods.

Taverns, pubs, saloons, bars . . . Charleroi had far more than its share of those. Unlike the other establishments, they were most of them clean and freshly painted. They could afford such luxuries. If you didn't drink in Charleroi, what else did you have to do with your time?

Kathleen pointed ahead. "Is that the station? The building with the flag in front of it?"

Bushell's cough had nothing to do with the noxious air he was breathing. "Wrong flag, I'm afraid." In New Liverpool, Independence Party headquarters lay out in the distant suburbs. In Charleroi, the banner with the eagle and stripes flew in front of a building as impressive as any the downtown boasted. Charleroi being what it was, that didn't say much, but what it did say, Bushell didn't like.

People inside the Independence Party building were busy. Bushell watched them bustling around as he walked by. Sam Stanley also paid thoughtful attention to the party headquarters. "If we're lucky," he said, "we'll spot Kilbride in there, and make life easier for ourselves."

They weren't lucky.

The constabulary station lay a few doors past the building that housed the Independence Party. Comparing them, Bushell suspected the party had more money than the constables did. If anybody had painted the station since the reign of Edward IX, he would have been astonished.

"Help you?" the big, burly sergeant behind the front desk asked in a gravelly voice when Bushell and his companions walked in. The station was even less prepossessing on the inside than its exterior suggested. It stank of sweat and smoke and puke and stale tea leaves. Kathleen looked appalled; Bushell and Stanley had seen the like before. Bushell showed his badge. The constabulary sergeant nodded. "Come on, I'll take you back to the chief."

The sergeant's boss looked like him, but with an extra ten years and a greying beard tacked on. Like his underling, Chief John Lassiter looked as if he'd be more at home down in a mine than keeping order aboveground. He didn't seem sure of what Kathleen Flannery was doing with the two RAMs, but he didn't ask any questions about it, either. Since Bushell wasn't so sure what Kathleen was doing there himself, that was just as well.

He came straight to the point: "Chief, we think a fellow named Joseph Kilbride came down here from Doshoweh the other day. He's not at the Ribblesdale. If he's not at the—what was the name of the place?—the Hasting Arms, that's it, where is he likely to be?"

"You talk about hotels, those two are about it," Lassiter said. "We got some rooming houses, too, or he could be staying with somebody here, you know. Kilbride, eh?" He chewed on the end of the pencil he used to jot down the name. "That's liable to be tough. These micks, they stick together like nobody's business."

Kathleen Flannery sucked in a long, angry breath. Bushell stepped on her toe. Chief Lassiter's desk didn't let him see that. Kathleen glared but subsided.

Lassiter sighed. "Well, we'll do what we can for you, Colonel." He glanced over his shoulder at the print of *The Two Georges* behind his desk. "We got to get that painting back. You have a description of this Kilbride item?"

"Can't give you height or weight, I'm afraid, but here's our boy." Bushell passed Lassiter the photograph of Joseph Kilbride that the butler had given him.

"May I keep this?" the chief asked.

"Long enough to duplicate it, no more," Bushell said. "If we don't catch up with him here, we're liable to need it again."

Lassiter gnawed on the end of the pencil once more. "Mm, that's fair. Anything else you can tell me about him?" He glanced down at the picture. "Wouldn't want to meet him in an alley after dark, not with a phiz like that."

"He's supposed to be a tightwad, too, people in Doshoweh say," Samuel Stanley put in.

"All right, so we won't catch him in a saloon buying a round for the house," Lassiter said. In spite of the sarcasm, he wrote that down. "Never can tell what'll turn up useful, though." He gave the pencil another couple of gentle nibbles, then set it down. "Anything else I can do for you folks today?"

Bushell pulled out some notes. "We need addresses—records too, if they have any—for three miners: Percy McGaffigan, Michael O'Flynn, and Anthony Rothrock."

"There's four or five Michael O'Flynns in this town I can think of off the top of my head," Lassiter said. "Any way to narrow it down?"

"We want the one who went to New Liverpool to picket at the governor's mansion the night *The Two Georges* got stolen."

Lassiter thumped his forehead with the heel of his hand. "Yeah, of course you do. I'm stupid this morning—sue me. I can dig that out. You're at the Ribblesdale, I think you said? Somebody will ring you tonight. We got a lot of McGaffigans, too, but not a lot of Percys, I bet. The other one was Rothrock? Come on in the back room with me. We'll see what we find."

The back room was a miniature and rather disorganized version of the records room at the New Liverpool RAM station. Chief Lassiter seemed to know where the bodies were buried, though. He shoved aside two boxes of files to get at the bottom drawer of a cabinet.

"McGaffigan, Fred; McGaffigan, Liam, McGaffigan, Percy—here we go." He pulled out the file folder. "Last address we have for him is 39 Lantern Way." The curl of his lip said what he thought of that address. He flipped through the reports in the file. "Drunk and disorderly five years ago, public drunkenness year before that, drunk and disorderly last year—paid a twenty-quid fine for that one. Sounds like a miner, in other words."

Bushell scribbled the address into a notebook. "What about Rothrock?"

"Name rings a bell," Lassiter said. "Let's have us a look." The folder in question was in one of the boxes he'd move to get to McGaffigan's. "Here we go. Anthony Aurelius Rothrock, last address 2 Coker Drive." From his face, that was a worse place to live than Lantern Way. "Drunk and disorderly; wife beating, but his old woman wouldn't press the charge; D and D again . . . ah, here's why I remember him. Assault with intent to maim: he went after a fellow with a broken bottle in a tavern brawl a couple of years ago. Carved him up proper, too."

"Why isn't he in gaol, then?" Bushell and Stanley asked in the same breath.

"A pack of his mates were in the place with him, and they all swore up and down it was self-defense." By the way Lassiter's eyebrows climbed toward his hairline, he was less than convinced. He shrugged a constable's shrug, as if to say, *What can you do?*

"Have you got a town plan, so we can find these places?" Bushell asked.

"Come back to my office with me, and I'll get you one," the local chief said. While rummaging through his desk, he looked up toward Kathleen Flannery for a moment. "These places you're going, they might not be the sort where you'd want to take a lady."

Bushell didn't answer. He'd figured that out for himself. On the other hand, he didn't want to leave Kathleen by herself, either—no telling what sort of mischief she might get into. It was a poser.

Kathleen solved it for him, saying indignantly, "If these gentlemen"—she freighted the word with meaning it was not altogether intended to bear—"can make their visits, I think I shall be able to accompany them."

Chief Lassiter's eyebrows rose again, this time in a slightly different way. "However you like, then," he said, and ran one hand over the other in a gesture of which Pontius Pilate would have approved. "Ah, here we are," he added with a grunt of triumph, and presented Bushell a much-folded map.

"Can you find out whether McGaffigan and Rothrock are on day shift or nights?" Bushell said.

Lassiter nodded. "No point going to see 'em if you won't find 'em home, is there?" He plucked at his beard. "Let me call the colliery for you." He picked up the telephone, dialed a number without having to look it up. "Stephen? John here, down at the station. Need a bit of information from you—" He asked a couple of questions, scribbled, asked again, scribbled some more, said, "Thanks," and hung up. Turning to Bushell, he said. "They're both on days. Day shift lets off at five. If you get there at half past or a bit later, you'll catch them at home, probably before they've started supper. You'd not want to get them then, I shouldn't think."

"Too right," Bushell said. "They don't have to say a thing to us. If we get them angry, they won't want to talk."

"Don't know that they will anyhow," Lassiter said, "but that's your lookout. I'll start beating the bushes about Kilbride, and I'll track down which O'Flynn was gone from the mine when *The Two Georges* got nicked. Stephen should know, or be able to find out. I'll ring you when I have what you need."

"Why don't you give us the address of the Hastings Arms?" Samuel Stanley said. "If it's not too far, we can check it ourselves—give us something useful to do the rest of this morning."

"That makes sense," Lassiter agreed. "The Hastings is at 137 Royal Street— that's two streets north of here, down close to the river."

By the time they left the constabulary station, summer heat and stickiness were out in full force. They made Bushell's shirt cling greasily to his torso; he took off his hat and fanned his head with it. The smoke and the harsh, sulfurous tang of the air left his lungs stinging from every breath. At the end of the ten-minute walk, he felt more worn than he had during the hike to Buckley Bay.

In front of the Hastings Arms, he paused a moment to look out at the Monongahela. The river was wide and swift and should have been beautiful, but no river full of coal barges and stained with the effluents of factories uncounted could look anything but grim.

Sam Stanley's gaze followed his. "That's the water that comes out of the taps at the hotel," he said, sounding unhappy at the notion.

Bushell considered. "Best argument I've heard yet for drinking whiskey."

"Let's go inside," Kathleen said, dabbing at her forehead with a linen handkerchief. "Maybe they'll have ceiling fans working."

"And you're from Victoria," Stanley said. "In New Liverpool, they don't have this kind of muggy heat. You can stick a fork in me, because I'm baked."

No ceiling fans spun inside the lobby of the Hastings Arms. The place was almost as shabby as the supercilious clerk back at the Ribblesdale had said it would be. The potted plant that had been set up as an ornament was now brown and dead, but nobody had bothered taking it away. To Bushell's mind, two even more unlovely growths had sprouted in the lobby: Michael Shaughnessy and Jerry Doyle.

The reporters from *Common Sense* moved to cut Bushell off as he walked toward the front desk. "What took you so long to get here, Colonel?" Shaughnessy asked, as Doyle readied pad and pen to record Bushell's reply for posterity. "We've been waiting half an hour, maybe longer."

"So very sorry to inconvenience you," Bushell replied. "Had I but known you were here, I would have dropped everything else I was doing and rushed right over. I'm sure you understand that."

Jerry Doyle smiled for a moment. Shaughnessy turned an angry red. Bushell strode past both of them. He hoped they hadn't worked on the desk clerk.

Shaughnessy said, "Dr. Flannery, what are you doing coursing with the hunting dogs of the filthy, corrupt Crown?"

Bushell stiffened. So they knew who she was, did they? They might have found out from the register at the Ribblesdale, or . . . "Help you, sir?" the desk clerk asked, distracting him.

He showed the fellow his badge. "Do you have a Joseph Kilbride registered here?" he asked; since he'd left Kilbride's photograph with Chief Lassiter, he had to use a verbal description. Behind him, Kathleen Flannery was answering Shaughnessy's question. Since he was talking himself, he couldn't hear what she said.

"These guys here were asking me the same thing." The clerk pointed to Doyle and Shaughnessy. "I told them no, and I got to tell you the same thing." The register was on a plate that spun. The clerk spun it so it was right side up for Bushell. "You can see for yourself."

The pages open for Bushell's inspection showed people who'd registered at the Hastings Arms for the past ten days: a good sign the place wasn't doing much business. A look at the lobby would have sufficed to tell Bushell that, though. The register showed no sign of tampering, but he looked at some earlier and later leaves all the same. As Chief Lassiter had said, you never could tell. But he found nothing out of the ordinary elsewhere in the register, either.

"All right, the man's not staying here," he said. "Have you seen him in town?"

"Afraid I haven't, sir," the desk clerk replied, spinning the hotel register so it faced back toward him once more. "If I had, I expect I'd know it, too. You make him sound like a right bruiser, and that's a fact."

"He is, I think," Bushell said. "If you do see him, ring me at the Ribblesdale straightaway." The clerk touched a knuckle to his forehead, just below the hairline, in token of obedience. From the look in his eyes, though, Bushell figured the chance he would telephone was at best one in three. When you factored that in with a one-in-a-million chance of the man's actually spotting Kilbride, the odds of hearing from him again weren't what you'd call good.

Bushell turned away. The Jameson headache with which he'd got up still throbbed at his temples. The best cure he knew was more of the same, especially since frustration was making his head hurt more than it would have otherwise. Charleroi didn't have much going for it; even here downtown, it was a grimy, depressing place. But one thing it did have was plenty of watering holes.

A voice inside his head jeered at him: *Go ahead, drink your luncheon*, it said. *Maybe tomorrow you'll drink your breakfast, too. Maybe the day after that you'll drink your breakfast and forget you've done it.*

*Shut up,* he told the voice fiercely. *I've only done that once.* Discovering he'd had half a day carved out of his memory had frightened him enough that he'd stayed teetotal for—longer than usual when he tried laying off, anyhow.

Kathleen Flannery was saying, "Why don't you go away and quit pestering us and let us do our job?" That pleased Bushell enough to take his mind off whiskey for a while.

"It's just our own jobs we're doing," Michael Shaughnessy answered, striking a dramatic pose. "Keeping the people informed, you might say—more than the tame papers in every town do, that I tell you. And you, you're no police dog. Talk of your job, why aren't you back at your precious art museum?"

"Because something precious is missing," she said in the controlled snarl Bushell had more often heard aimed at him. "If you haven't the eyes to see that, God and the saints help you."

"But Dr. Flannery, all we're trying to do is make North America free from the Crown that—" Shaughnessy's voice rose shrilly.

Kathleen cut through his tumbled words: "Go away." She turned her back to make it plain she was taking no further notice of the man from *Common Sense.*

He kept on talking. Bushell stepped between him and Kathleen. He was older, smaller, and lighter than Shaughnessy. "Don't you think it would be polite to do as the lady asked you?" he asked quietly.

Shaughnessy turned to Jerry Doyle. "Do you hear him threatening me?" he said in a loud voice.

"I asked you to be polite, sir," Bushell said. "If you find that a threat—well, you're working for the right publication."

"Come on, Mike," Doyle said. "If we go on with it, they'll find some way to make trouble for us." Reluctantly, his colleague accompanied him toward the street door of the Hastings Arms. As they went out, Doyle fired a Parthian shot at the RAMs: "You've not seen the last of us, I'll have you know."

"Thus unlamenting let me die," Bushell said, slightly changing Pope's "Ode

on Solitude" to good effect. By then, though, the door had closed, so the reporters didn't hear him.

"Thank you," Kathleen said, turning toward Bushell. "I don't like being bad-
gered—by anyone."

"Really?" His mouth dropped open in surprise. "I hadn't noticed." Her eyes
sparked dangerously for a moment. Then she let out a strangled snort that was
evidently intended as a laugh: as if she didn't want to admit, even to herself, that
he'd amused her.

"Where now, Chief?" Samuel Stanley asked.

Bushell didn't answer till after he led his companions out onto the sidewalk: no telling what affiliations the desk clerk had. Doyle and Shaughnessy were
already a long block away, and by all appearances arguing with each other. He approved.

"Where now?" he said. "I've been thinking about that." It was a thumping
lie, but his mouth was smarter than his brain, because he came up with a good
answer: "Aside from art, what does Kilbride do? He sells food and spirits. A business trip would give him a coronium-tight alibi for coming here. If we check
some of the taverns around here, we might find someone who's seen him."

"That's a fine notion," Kathleen said, nodding vigorously.

Sam Stanley looked at Bushell out of the corner of his eye. Any time Bushell
proposed going into a tavern, he turned suspicious. Since the idea did make
sense, though, he too nodded after a moment. "Maybe one of them will have a
decent luncheon spread set out, too," he said. "I'm getting on toward feeling
peckish. You can't be sure with things like that—they might not, too, what with
so many of their customers down underground right now. Only one way to find
out."

They started working their way west along Royal Street, away from the
Monongehela. The impressively named avenue had as rich a supply of drinking
establishments as any of the other streets Bushell had seen in downtown
Charleroi. They didn't lack for customers, either, despite the early hour.

None of the bartenders and proprietors with whom Bushell spoke admitted
to having heard of Joseph Kilbride. One of them said, "Wish I had, pal. If he can
keep himself in business up in the Six Nations, what with the taxes they charge
there, I bet he's a man I could deal with."

A couple of saloons had Independence Party flags prominently displayed in
back of the bar along with sparkling rows of liquor bottles. Since that wasn't illegal—and since he hoped his barroom brawling days were behind him—Bushell
didn't make an issue of it. He garnered quite enough suspicious looks just by
walking into those places in a suit and tie and wearing a fedora rather than a
shapeless cloth cap.

"Here we go!" Samuel Stanley said when they found an establishment that
catered to a somewhat higher class of customer: it was across the street from the
Charleroi Central Bank, and full of earnest young men in somber business
clothes and young women in flowery dresses and hairstyles that had been all the
rage in New York and New Liverpool the year before. As many of them were eating as drinking. "Something better than tinned steak-and-kidney pie, with luck."

"Business first," Bushell said, but the man behind the counter (who also proved to be the owner) denied any knowledge of Kilbride. Still, the place did seem about as good as they were likely to find for luncheon. They grabbed a table. When a waitress came by, Bushell ordered corned beef and cabbage—and a Jameson to go with it.

Samuel Stanley coughed significantly. Bushell had expected that, and pretended not to hear it—Sam was his adjutant, not his nursemaid. He hadn't expected a dirty look from Kathleen, who'd chosen a bacon, lettuce, and tomato sandwich for herself.

She gave him another dirty look when the food arrived. He didn't think it was because he spread mustard on both the fragrantly steaming meat and the cabbage. In fact, he didn't see any reason for it. But when her glare didn't go away, he finally asked, "Is something wrong?"

"That," she said through tight lips, pointing to his plate. "While you're at it, why don't you give us a few choruses of 'McNamara's Band'?"

"Oh," Bushell said, and then muttered, "Hommony grits," under his breath. Stanley, who was with great gusto carving a piece off a slice of roast beef while eating another, swallowed wrong. Bushell pounded him on the back. When he decided Sam wasn't going to choke to death after all, he gave his attention back to Kathleen. "The only reason I ordered *that*"—he tapped the corned beef with his fork—"was that I figured it had better be good in a town full of Irishmen."

She studied him as if he were a painting that had come before her for authentication: was he an Old Master or just a worthless modern forgery? "All right," she said after that long, measuring stare, and then, perhaps feeling that wasn't enough, "If you knew how many times I've had being Irish thrown in my face— If I do my job well, who my father is shouldn't matter a farthing's worth."

Bushell raised his glass of whiskey and solemnly drank in salute to that. All the same, he could not help remembering that Kathleen's father—Aloysius Flannery, that's what his name was—bought her a subscription to *Common Sense* every year.

B USHELL HAD NEVER SEEN SO MANY BLACK
men on the streets in his life. The miners heading away from the mines after
their shift ended were not merely brown, as Samuel Stanley was—they were
black. *Black as coal*, Bushell thought, *and no wonder.*

They bantered with one another as they spread through the town, some going home, others hurrying to the taverns to slake their thirst. Had Bushell been
among their number, he would have had a drink, or more likely several, before
he'd have wanted to face anyone he loved. Putting in a day's work hundreds,
maybe thousands of feet underground in tunnels barely tall enough to stand up
in, never knowing when those tunnels would flood or come crashing down on
your head or collapse somewhere behind you, sealing you off from any hope of
rescue . . . The very idea made the hair stand up on the back of his neck.

But what had Shakespeare said of the gravedigger? "Custom had made it in
him a property of easiness," that was the line. It held with the miners, too. They
were raucous and cheerful, almost to a man. If they worried about how they made
their living, they didn't show it on the outside.

They were magnificent-looking men, too, despite, or maybe because of, the
coal dust that coated their bare torsos. Whatever evils that could be ascribed to
it—and Bushell know how many they were—laboring in the mines kept a man
fit—till blacklung got him, anyhow. For his age, he was in good condition, but
miners who had to be ten years older were far firmer and stronger. He felt himself
drawing back his shoulders, tightening his belly. Walking along beside him,
Samuel Stanley also held himself quite erect.

As soon as the two RAMs and Kathleen Flannery got out of Charleroi's business district, Kathleen's attention swung from the miners themselves to the
homes in which they lived. "How can we expect human beings to put up with
conditions like these?" she said, pointing. "And how long can we expect human
beings to put up with them?"

Looking down the long rows of hovels jammed against one another, Bushell
had a hard time finding an answer for those questions. The whole block of houses
on Lantern Way leaned from the vertical; doors and windows were ten or even
twenty degrees out of true. Grass grew rank on the thin strip of lawn between the
sagging houses and the street. A few houses had decrepit steamers in various states
of disrepair up on the lawn. Most, though, were without motorcars of any sort.

211

Swarms of boys played on the grass and in the street. With bats that looked carved from branches, wickets made of piled jackets, and a sixpenny India-rubber ball, a mob of them had a spirited, if disorderly, game of cricket under way. They paused in their action while Bushell, Stanley, and Kathleen walked through the makeshift playing field toward Percy McGaffigan's house at number 39. The older lads followed Kathleen Flannery with their eyes; young and old seemed to view the presence of well-dressed strangers with suspicion, for Bushell and his companions brought silence with them, the usual racket resuming behind them after they'd passed.

Only a worn path in the grass served as a walkway up to number 39. The door leaned enough to the left to be disconcerting. Bushell wanted to lean that way himself, to make the world look straight. Running into the effect without having several Jameson in him was new, but not particularly welcome.

"I feel like I'm going into one of those crooked houses they have at carnivals sometimes," Samuel Stanley said, so Bushell wasn't the only one the off-kilter door bothered.

He looked for a bell. Not finding one, he rapped on the door. A dog yapped inside the house. The door opened with a squeal; Bushell wouldn't have been surprised if it hadn't been capable of opening. A plump, pale, tired-looking woman in a cheap cotton dress of a bilious green stared at him as if he'd just dropped from the moon. Behind her, two small boys and a somewhat larger girl looked equally amazed.

"Does Percy McGaffigan live here?" he asked, showing his badge.

The woman's eyes got even wider. "No," she said quickly. "Never heard of no McGaffigans. You got the wrong house, Mister. Go away."

"It's all right, Maggie," a man's voice said from behind her. "Leastways, I think it is. These are the blokes from New Liverpool I was telling you about. Let 'em in. They're just sniffing after *The Two Georges*, nothing more."

Reluctantly, Maggie McGaffigan stood aside. She didn't look happy about it, whether because she still feared for her husband's safety or because she didn't want strangers inspecting her housekeeping Bushell couldn't have said. By the way the parlor looked, she didn't do enough housekeeping to make inspection worthwhile. The room was small and dingy, the furniture—mismatched pieces looking as if they'd been found at jumble sales—falling to bits, dirty clothes strewn everywhere. The place smelled of sweat, grease, and dog.

Percy McGaffigan squatted in a corner of the parlor with an enamel basin half full of water, a rag, and a bar of soap. His face and arms and most of his chest were pink, the rest of his chest, his ridged belly, and his back still the coal-dust black they'd been when he emerged from the mine. The rag and the water had already gone gray with the dust he'd washed from himself.

"Don't mind me," he said, lathering the soap in the dirty water. "Just cleanin' up a bit afore supper, I am. Some o' the fellers, they eat first and then wash, but I figure I been breathin' coal all day long, an' I don't much fancy swallowin' it, too, that I don't." He soaped the left half of his belly, scrubbing away at the grime there with the washrag.

In a rather faint voice, Kathleen Flannery said, "But, Mr. McGaffigan—haven't you got a bathtub?"

"If I did, Miss, you think I'd be doin' this?" McGaffigan's voice had been mild, even affable. Now it turned sharp. "Dang few miners hereabouts with bathtubs, Miss, or toilets either. Can't afford such. These here houses are back to back, is what they are, with others just like 'em built against the far wall there. Us, we get to look out on the street, but we got to go round the corner to visit the loo. Them others back around there, they have themselves a short walk, but they get to look at the backhouses and the rubbish pitch all year long. You had your druthers, Miss, which'd you sooner do?"

Kathleen didn't answer. She looked green. Bushell had read, had heard of the conditions in which the miners lived. Running up against the reality was like a kick in the face.

"You're not a wealthy man, then?" he said.

McGaffigan stared at him, then laughed raucously. "Oh, sure and I am. This here is just me summer home, you know. Come winter, the missus and me, we takes an airship to our Florida mansion, and brings the young 'uns with us."

Bushell smiled, enjoying the miner's pungent sarcasm. "One for you. But if you haven't the money for a better house, how did you come by the train fare for your trip to New Liverpool? How did you manage to pay your hotel bills, you and all your friends?"

McGaffigan's face went hooded, wary. "All the lads roundabout, we been pitching in sixpences and shillings and the odd half a crown as we could, all these past months," he said at last. "Do it with enough of us, do it long enough, and in the end you have yourself a fair pile o' brass." Methodically, he began to wash his back. The water in the basin was now as black as he had been. Bushell marveled that it would still clean him. Pale skin did emerge from under the coal dust, though.

Samuel Stanley said, "If you all clubbed together to pay for your journey, you'll have the accounts of the money you collected, I expect. Who keeps those? We wouldn't mind having a look at them."

"Don't recall offhand, I'm afeared," McGaffigan answered casually, as if he'd been asked what he had for supper night before last. "D'you happen to remember the feller's name, Maggie?"

"No," his wife said, in the same sharp tones she'd used at the front door when she'd denied he lived there at all. "I never heard it, that I know of." She smiled a quick, false smile.

Kathleen Flannery exhaled sharply through her nose. That meant she had to take a deep breath a moment later, which made her look even less happy. Bushell didn't so much as bother looking over at Stanley. He could read his adjutant's thoughts, knowing they matched his own: Percy and Maggie McGaffigan were both liars, but the man of the family at least brought a certain amount of skill to the game.

"Thank you so much for your help," Bushell said dryly.

Percy McGaffigan's eyes kindled for a moment; not only could he use irony, he also recognized it when he heard it. He finished washing himself, dried his muscular upper body, and put back on a long-sleeved, collarless cotton shirt that, like everything else in the mean little house, had seen better days.

"Is that all?" his wife asked. "Our supper's just about ready."

"Only a couple more questions," Bushell told her before turning back to Percy. "Where does the Michael O'Flynn who went with you to New Liverpool live?"

"Red Mike, you mean? He's out on Colliery Road—number 29, I think, unless I misrecall."

"That *is* a help," Bushell said, meaning it this time. "One more thing, and we'll leave you be for the evening: do you know a man from up in the Six Nations named Joseph Kilbride? If you do, have you seen him in the last few days?"

"I know a Daniel Kilbride, but he was born in Charleroi, same as me," McGaffigan answered. "Poor devil had his leg crushed in a cave-in a couple-three years ago. He's been on the dole ever since, tryin' to raise a family on ten quid a week. Now I've got it hard, like all us working blokes do, but oh, Mother Mary, I pity the likes o' poor Daniel—and too bloody many like him there are, too."

Bushell thought he was telling the truth, but doubted his own judgment. To check it, he asked Maggie McGaffigan, "Have you seen this Joseph Kilbride?"

"That I haven't," she said. "I never heard o' the man, nor wanted to, neither." The pride and relief with which she spoke convinced Bushell that here, at least, she wasn't lying.

He left the McGaffigans' home neither elated nor cast down; he hadn't expected to come away with much in the way of new information, and so wasn't unduly disappointed when he didn't. It got very quiet when he and his companions came out onto Lantern Way. The children in the street stopped their games and stared at them. So did the couple of miners who'd carried chairs out onto their lawns to try to escape the heat—and, no doubt, the smells—inside their houses.

"They'll all grill the McGaffigans as soon as we're out of sight," Stanley muttered out of the side of his mouth.

"How can you imagine such a thing?" Bushell said, as if incredulous. Stanley chuckled softly. Bushell was looking across Lantern Way, not at the men there but at the houses. While those on this side leaned to the left, those on that leaned to the right, so as to be parallel to them. He wondered how many tunnels, and how deep, had been gnawed in blackness through black seams of coal under Charleroi, and how many had fallen in upon themselves to make the very ground ripple and buckle and the houses built upon it list like ships on a stormy sea or drunken men.

Kathleen Flannery also spoke in a low voice, but one filled with fury: "Any man who lives like this but isn't a Son of Liberty, he's the crazy one."

"Something to that," Sam Stanley said. "If you've got nothing, you go with anything that offers you hope of better."

When a man of manifest conservatism like Stanley could speak such sentiments, the squalor of Percy McGaffigan's home, of Percy McGaffigan's life, had to have bitten deeply into him. But Bushell shook his head. "If your roof leaks, you don't burn down your house to fix it." He kicked at a clod of dirt. "Oh, maybe you do, if you're twenty-five or so and don't know better. But then you have to live in the ruins you made yourself, and that teaches you something—or it should."

"There's more wrong with McGaffigan's house than the roof," Kathleen said, "and you may take that literally or metaphorically, as you please."

Bushell raised an eyebrow. "The idea, Dr. Flannery, is to convince me that you're not a Son of Liberty, not that you are."

"If you don't know by now that I'm not—" She stopped and glared at him. "But I don't turn a blind eye to misery or injustice, unlike some people I could name."

"You want to think before the next time you say something like that to an officer of the Crown." Bushell spoke so quietly, Kathleen had to lean forward to hear what he said. When she did, she rocked back as if he'd slapped her.

Samuel Stanley pulled out the map they'd got from Chief Lassiter. "Let's see whether we're closer to Rothrock's house or to Red Mike O'Flynn's," he said, changing the subject the best way he could find.

It worked. "Here, let me have a look at that," Bushell said. In his army days, he'd learned to have an enormous amount of respect for maps. With them, you could do anything. Without, you'd wander in the desert like the children of Israel, and likely never come to the Promised Land.

Kathleen Flannery bent over the map, too. She stabbed out a red-painted fingernail. "There's Coker Drive," she said. "It's only a couple of blocks over, and then a couple down toward the river, too." She grimaced. "I'm going to have tired feet tonight."

"We'll all have tired feet tonight," Bushell said, accepting the tacit truce. "All right, we'll go talk with Mr. Anthony Aurelius Rothrock. Let's see if he sings a more interesting song."

Rothrock's house was also on a block built back to back. Unlike McGaffigan's, it faced not Coker Drive itself but the alley behind it, giving him and his family a charming view of lavatories and dustbins. Someone had put naphthalene in the outhouses, so the reek that came from them was half barnyard, half mothballs. It was stronger if marginally less unpleasant than straight sewage would have been.

Where McGaffigan's house listed to the left, Rothrock's leaned forward, so that the wall at the base of the roof overhung the door by a startling and rather alarming amount. As he had in Doshoweh, Bushell wondered what an earthquake would do to the place. Then he thought again of all the tunnels worming under Charleroi, and decided the whole town might well plunge into the abyss.

From what he'd seen here, he wondered if that might not be the best thing that could happen to it.

He knocked on the door; like McGaffigan's, Rothrock's house was innocent of bell. The door didn't open. Instead, a middle-aged man with a walrus mustache, a stubbly chin, and a surly expression stuck his head out the window and glowered at him and his companions. "Who the hell're you?" he growled, the slur in his speech arguing he'd been home long enough to knock back more than a couple of drinks.

"Are you Anthony Rothrock?" Bushell asked.

"Who the hell're you?" the fellow repeated, scratching under the left shoulder strap of his dirty white vest—he wore no shirt over it. "A man's home's still his castle, ain't it? That's what the law says. You come round here bothering me, I'll set the law on *you*."

"I'll take that chance," Bushell said, and displayed his Royal American Mounted Police badge. "Not let's try it again—you are Mr. Rothrock?"

"Yeah, I'm Tony Rothrock," the fellow said unwillingly. "What's it to you?" His eyes narrowed. "You got a warrant, Robin Redbreast?"

"No," Bushell said. "We only want to ask you a few questions."

"Shove off," Rothrock told him. "I don't have to say nothin' to you, and I don't aim to say nothin' to you. You can go take a hike—far as I'm concerned, you can jump down the main shaft of Mine Number One. Take the big smoke with you when you go, too. You want to leave the redhead, that's jake by me." He leered at Kathleen Flannery.

Bushell waited for her to go up like a steamer with a punctured boiler. Instead, she turned to him and said in a low voice, "Would you like me to go in there and question him? I will, if he'll let me—and if you don't mind."

That wasn't really what she was asking. What she wanted to know was, *Do you trust me?* It was a question Bushell wished he didn't have to confront so bluntly, because the only answer he'd found was, *I don't know.* He kicked at the boards of the tiny porch in front of Rothrock's door. They were as bare of paint, as cracked and faded and defeated, as any he'd seen in Buckley Bay.

"Go ahead, then," he said—suddenly, without warning. Before the look of surprise could do more than begin to form on her face, he turned away from her and said, "She can come in, if you'll let her."

The miner seemed startled for a moment, too. Then he laughed. Bushell did not find it a pleasant sound. "Oh, aye, she can come in, all right, that she can." He disappeared from the window.

By her expression, Kathleen hadn't fancied that laugh, either. Quickly, before the door opened, Bushell said, "If you're not out in five minutes, I'm coming in after you. Shout if you need me." She just had time to nod before Rothrock, with drunken, scornful courtesy, waved her inside and shut the door in Bushell and Stanley's faces.

The two RAMs drew back a few steps from the doorway. Bushell did not want to retreat any further, not only for fear of missing a cry for help from Kathleen but also because the outhouses Rothrock's home faced were hardly pleasant company. "Are you sure you know what you're doing, Chief?" Stanley asked in a low voice.

"Not even close to it." Now Bushell kicked a the grass of the narrow strip of lawn. It was as tired and dejected as the porch boards. "I hate having to depend on anybody but me, especially someone who's not a RAM, especially someone whom—" He broke off.

"God knows what she's talking about in there with him," Stanley said, obliquely completing the thought for him.

Bushell lighted a cigar. People coming to use the plumbing facilities stared at him and Stanley. So did the harried-looking women who dumped rubbish in the bins. Those hadn't been emptied any time recently, and added their sickly-sweet reek to that of the lavatories.

"You know, if I lived in the middle of the other side of these back to backs, I think I'd sooner pitch my tea leaves and such in the gutter than haul them all the way around back here," Stanley said.

"By the look of some of the gutters we've seen, you've got what it takes to make a first-rate Charleroi housewife," Bushell answered.

Stanley drew back in dismay. "You've said some hard things about me over the years, Chief, but I don't think I deserved that." He rolled his eyes. "Lord, what Phyllis would say if she saw these places—"

"Poor people live like this," Bushell said. "If you're not poor, you don't have to go round the corner to throw away your rubbish."

"Mm, that's so," Stanley admitted. "But from the look of things, not all the ones on this side take much care of the places they're in, either." He had simple, straightforward, straitlaced notions of right and wrong. One look at the sad, frowzy homes on this side of the block said he also had a point.

Bushell smoked for a bit, then crushed his cigar under his heel. He pulled out his pocket watch and glumly studied the dial. "What is she doing in there?" he muttered.

"More to the point, how long are we going to let her keep doing it?" Stanley muttered.

"I'll give her another two minutes," Bushell said, glancing not only at his watch but also at the steadily sinking sun. "If she hasn't come out by then, I'll . . . go in." He grimaced. He wasn't in control, and he didn't like it.

He paced back and forth, his short choppy strides showing the worry he wouldn't acknowledge in words. A couple of seconds before the deadline he'd set himself, the door to Anthony Rothrock's house opened. Kathleen bounded off the little porch; her pleated skirt flew up enough to show a length of shapely calf.

Rothrock stood in the doorway. "Come back anytime, darling," he called, and blew a kiss after her. Laughing a loud, half-drunken laugh, he slammed the door shut.

One of Bushell's eyebrows twitched. "Darling?" he echoed.

If looks could kill, Kathleen's eyes would have started a massacre. Her cheeks were flushed—not embarrassment, if Bushell was any judge, but fury. Through tightly clenched teeth, she said, "Take me away from here this instant, or I shall go back in there and kill that man."

"What did he do?" Samuel Stanley asked, the usual, easy good nature dropping from his voice like a discarded mask. His big hands curled into fists. "Maybe we'll take care of it for you."

Kathleen shook her head, strands of auburn hair flipping back and forth as she did. "No, nothing like that—nothing so overt. Just take me away from here, please. Can we go back to the hotel?"

Bushell had wanted to track down Red Mike O'Flynn, but another glance at the sinking sun said that was probably not a good idea. He didn't care to try finding his way through the back streets of Charleroi in the dark, and he didn't think those streets would prove any too safe, especially to well-dressed strangers. "We'll go back," he said resignedly.

"Lassiter will be calling us, anyway," Stanley said with the air of a man trying to make the best of things.

Kathleen did not wait for them to finish talking themselves into it. She simply headed back toward the street and left it to them to follow. Bushell had to push himself to catch up with her. "Did you learn anything from the charming Mr. Rothrock?" he asked, and was rewarded with another murderous glare.

"Chiefly what tyrants men can be," she snarled, adding, presumably for his benefit, "not that I haven't already had lessons along those lines."

Not loquacious under any circumstances, Bushell maintained a prudent silence now. Kathleen stamped back toward the Ribblesdale House, looking neither to the left nor the right. After half a block, Sam Stanley, who came as close to being neutral as anyone available, worked up the gumption to ask, "Er—what did Rothrock do, exactly?"

"For starters, he chased his wife and daughter upstairs, and if he wasn't a gorilla about it, I've never seen one," Kathleen said, hunching over and clenching her fists to show how the miner had acted. "Didn't Chief Lassiter say he beat her? I believe it, I'll tell you that. The poor woman was terrified of him, and the little girl—a pretty little girl—too."

"Did you learn anything from Rothrock?" Bushell asked again.

Kathleen continued as if he hadn't spoken: "Then he sat me down on the filthy sofa in the front room, and then he sat down beside me. *Right* beside me." Her nose went into the air. "He smells."

"Go on," Bushell said. She was going to tell the story her way or not at all.

"He didn't—put his hands on me," she said. "That much I give him. It is all I give him. He got up, went to a little alcove under the stairway, and came back with a bottle of whiskey. Just in front of the couch, he struck a pose like a circus strong man and said, 'You like a real man, don't you—not one o' them toffs?' I wanted to laugh in his face . . . but I was afraid." She kicked at the ground; the admission plainly shamed her. "When I didn't say anything, he sat down next to me again, even closer than he had before." She ran a hand down the right side of her skirt, as if to wipe away the memory of Rothrock's presence.

Bushell tried again. "Does he know Joseph Kilbride?"

"As best I can tell, he doesn't know anything, the alphabet quite possibly included," Kathleen answered. "He would swig from the bottle, breathe cheap whiskey into my face, and tell me what a ladies' man he was." Even in the fading light, Bushell watched her turn red. "He went into some detail."

"If you expect a coal miner to have the manners of a baronet, you're apt to be disappointed," Samuel Stanley observed.

"Did Rothrock say anything about who the miners' treasurer was and where we can find him?" Bushell asked, persisting in what looked as if it were going to be a losing fight to get information out of Kathleen.

She shook her head. "He said he saw me at the governor's mansion, and that he fell in love with me then." She flushed once more. "I'm paraphrasing." She muttered something uncomplimentary to Anthony Rothrock, coal miners, and, by extension, the entire male sex. "I fear it was a useless and unpleasant conversation. He wasn't interested in answering my questions, and I wasn't interested in . . . what he was interested in."

"Thanks for making the effort," Bushell said with a sigh. "I do appreciate it." Everything she'd said had been in perfect keeping with what he'd seen of Anthony Rothrock: drunken, boorish, lecherous. Whether it had any relation to the truth, only she and Rothrock knew.

"Miserable, filthy place," Kathleen said. "A monster of a husband, a frightened wife—God help their poor daughter, is all I can say." She cocked her head to one side, fixing Bushell with that measuring stare once more. "Don't you think there should be Daughters of Liberty, too, dedicated to getting women free of beasts like Rothrock? A movement like that might sweep the Empire, not just the NAU."

"If you want men—and women—to stop acting like beasts, you need to talk to a priest, not a police officer," Bushell said. "We don't deal in miracles."

"You've grown hard, Colonel," she said after a moment's thoughtful consideration.

Bushell didn't answer: what point to responding to self-evident truth? After a couple of paces, Samuel Stanley said, "If you don't get hard on the outside, you can't do this job."

Kathleen thought that one over, too, then nodded judiciously. "But what if you get hard on the inside, too?" she asked.

"You have to be a little soft in the head to want to join the police in the first place," Bushell said. But a quip wasn't a real reply, and he knew this one was a shield to keep him from having to come up with a real reply.

They approached the train station and the Ribblesdale House close by. "You know," Stanley said, pointing toward the hotel, "compared to the way the rest of Charleroi lives, we don't have it so bad there."

"You're right," Bushell said, "and if that's not a judgment on the rest of the town, I don't know what is." He paused, his gaze swinging back toward the station. "We ought to talk to the ticket sellers here tomorrow. If Kilbride wanted to get out of town, he'd have to have bought a ticket."

"If, of course, he was ever here," Stanley said with a heartiness he obviously did not feel. "He could have got off in Pittsburgh, say, instead of riding as far as his ticket would let him. If he did something like that, he could be anywhere in the NAU by now."

"Oh, no!" Kathleen Flannery said; that chance evidently hadn't occurred to her.

It had to Bushell. "Yes, that's a cheery thought, isn't it?" he said. Now he looked toward the Ribblesdale House. "I wonder if the dining room has wild goose on the menu?"

In the dining room, along with a few other patrons, sat Jerry Doyle and Michael Shaughnessy. Stanley eyed them with something less than delight. "I wouldn't mind cooking *their* goose," he murmured. Bushell nodded.

When he and his companions walked in, Shaughnessy sniffed ostentatiously, then said, "What's that I smell?"

"Must be the odor of rectitude," Doyle said.

"No, it's Robin Redbreast, sure as the devil," Shaughnessy said. He sniffed again. "Either that or polecat." He and Doyle brayed laughter. They both had whiskey glasses in front of them. By their mirth, they'd already done some drinking.

Bushell took no outward notice of them, but found a table and sat down. Samuel Stanley sat across from him. Stanley's face was calm, but a deep rumble rose from deep in his chest, as if he were a tiger reacting to the chatter of monkeys in the jungle. Kathleen Flannery said, "The job you RAMs do is harder than I'd thought."

"*Most* people think well of us," Stanley said pointedly.

"And as for the ones who don't—" Bushell shrugged. His eyes flicked to the reporters from *Common Sense*. "I'll spend sleepless nights fretting over *their* good opinion."

"Of course you will," Kathleen said, in the same solemn tones he'd used.

He raised a warning forefinger. "See what you get for associating with us low types? You're in danger of becoming an ironist."

Kathleen made as if to flee the table. Now she, Bushell, and Stanley laughed. Doyle and Shaughnessy stared over at them. No doubt they thought they were the butt of the joke. That make Bushell feel better than he had in some time.

After supper, he went up to his room and took a shower. He'd been relieved to discover the room boasted a showerbath; given the less than luxurious nature of the Ribblesdale House, he'd feared he'd find a single bathroom down at the end of the hall.

He was toweling himself dry when the telephone rang. He rubbed at his mustache in wry amusement; the way things had been going, the call should have come while he was in the showerbath. Wrapping the towel around his waist, he hurried over to the nightstand. "Hullo? Bushell here."

"John Lassiter." The local constabulary chief's big, deep voice could hardly have belonged to anyone else. "I've tracked down the Michael O'Flynn you're looking for."

"So have I," Bushell said. "Red Mike O'Flynn, on Colliery Road."

He waited for Lassiter to congratulate him on his cleverness. Instead the chief sounded puzzled: "That's not what I got from Stephen at the mine. He told me it was Michael F. O'Flynn, powderman, who I happen to know is a black Irishman—and who lives at 51 Brattice Street. Who told you it was Red Mike?"

"McGaffigan," Bushell answered. "Somebody's lying. Finding out who might be—interesting." He dug out a notebook and pencil, then snorted—he reminded himself of Jerry Doyle. "Can you give me their telephone numbers?"

"Colonel, these chaps are lucky the months they scrape together enough brass for rent and food both," Lassiter said. "That's how it is in Charleroi. I'm not saying that's how it should be, necessarily, but that's how it is. There'll be no phone in either of those houses."

"Damnation," Bushell said. "Well, Chief, will you send a constabulary steamer over to the hotel here? If I can't telephone them, I'll have to take a steamer to both Michael O'Flynns and find out which one of them was really out in New Liverpool."

"And whether McGaffigan or Stephen Niles is lying," Lassiter said. "I can't believe Stephen would. He's always been—"

Though Lassiter couldn't see him, Bushell made a chopping motion with his right hand. "In this bloody case, saying 'I can't believe' is the best way I can think of to make something come true. Are you going to send me that steamer?"

"Five minutes," Lassiter promised, and hung up.

Bushell told Stanley where he was going, then hurried downstairs to wait in front of the Ribblesdale House. A northbound train rolled out of the Charleroi station, a plume of black smoke rising against the fading twilight. The steamer pulled up. A red lamp on its roof proclaimed its status. The constable who was driving leaned over to open the kerbside door. "Colonel Bushell? I'm Sergeant Vining. I'll do what I can for you."

"Thanks." Bushell slid in. "Are we closer to 29 Colliery Road or 51 Brattice Street?"

"Colliery Road," Vining answered.

"Then go there," Bushell said.

"Right you are, sir," Vining said. Bushell leaned forward in his seat, as if to urge the steamer to a greater turn of speed. At last, one place or the other, he'd get some answers.

Colliery Road was narrow and winding and full of potholes. Most of the street lamps along it had been broken. Sergeant Vining peered through the windscreen. About halfway down a long block, he stepped on the brake. "There you are, sir," he said, pointing. "That one on the left is number 29."

Bushell got out of the steamer and walked up to the door. The racket of several children playing together or trying to kill one another—Bushell couldn't quite tell which—floated out through the open window next to it. He knocked on the door. When nothing happened, he knocked again, harder this time.

The door opened. A young man with carroty red hair and mustache and wearing a sleeveless vest and denim trousers with holes at the knees stared out a Bushell. "Who the devil might you be?"

"I might be anyone." Bushell showed his badge. "I am Colonel Thomas Bushell of the Royal American Mounted Police." The redheaded man gaped in blank surprise. "Are you Michael O'Flynn, called Red Mike?"

"That I am," O'Flynn answered. "And what would you want with me?"

"Were you in New Liverpool on the night of 15 June?"

"New Liverpool? In Upper California, d'you mean? That I wasn't. I've never been further than Pittsburgh in all my days, and I've not been out of Charleroi this year, nor the last one, either. Why on earth do you care to know that?"

"To see who's lying to me—today," Bushell said. He turned and hurried back to the constabulary steamer, leaving Red Mike O'Flynn standing in the doorway staring after him. "Brattice Street," he told Sergeant Vining. "Red Mike here says he's never been out past Pittsburgh, and I believe him, so that means Percy McGaffigan's been telling tall tales. I do wonder why."

"Maybe you'll find out," Vining answered. "Brattice Street's about five minutes from here. Number 51 you want, isn't it?"

"That's right."

Brattice Street was a step up the social ladder from Lantern Way and Colliery Road. More houses had steamers in front of them, and fewer leaned either forward or sideways. More of the street lamps worked, too. It still wasn't the sort of place where Bushell would have wanted to live, but he might have contemplated the prospect without giving suicide at least even money as the better choice.

Sergeant Vining came to a stop in front of number 51. "Here, I'll come with you, sir," he said, and got out. "If this fellow's a right villain, who knows what he'll try? I should have thought of that before."

Bushell wondered how much help Vining would be in case of trouble. Constables dealt with vagrants and drunks and burglars. When it came to the Sons of Liberty . . . when it came to them, the Royal Marines hadn't been as much help as they might have. But any reinforcement was better than none.

If this Michael O'Flynn was a villain, his children didn't know it. They were raising Cain inside the house when Bushell rang the bell: this was the first miner's house with such an amenity he'd visited.

A blonde who might have been pretty if she hadn't looked worn to death opened the door. "Yes?" she said, staring in surprise from Sergeant Vining to Bushell and back again. "I thought you'd be my husband." Four or five children of assorted sizes peered out from behind her.

"Michael O'Flynn's not here?" Bushell said, making sure he had the right house. When the woman nodded, he showed his RAM badge and demanded, "Where'd he go?"

"Why, he took a friend to the train station," Mrs. O'Flynn answered. "And is there anything wrong with that, I'd like to know?" She set her hands on her hips. "Now you see here, sir, my husband's not done a thing, and I'll thank you to remember it."

"That's telling him, Mother," said the oldest child, a boy of about thirteen.

"I didn't say he had," Bushell answered. "He did go to New Liverpool, to the governor's mansion there, didn't he?"

"What if he did? It wasn't against the law, and not even a RAM can make out that it was." By the way she said *not even a RAM,* she gave Bushell the distinct impression she lacked the admiration for his corps most citizens of the NAU felt. Taking a deep breath, she went on, "And taking Mr. Kilbride to the train station isn't against the law, either, so why don't you just go home?"

"I didn't say it was against—" Bushell's wits caught up to what his ears had heard. "Mr. Kilbride?" he said. "Mr. Joseph Kilbride? Older man, looks like he's taken a few too many rights to the chops?"

"He does not," she said indignantly. "No such thing. He's—distinguished, Mr. Kilbride is. Collects art, he does, and all like that."

"Does he?" Bushell said. "And how does such a—distinguished—man know your husband?"

"He sympathizes with the hard life coal miners have, Mr. Kilbride does,"

Mrs. O'Flynn answered. "More than you can say for most officers of the Crown, too," she added with a venomous glare.

"You may find others with a different opinion," Bushell said. He turned to Vining and snapped, "Come on, Sergeant, what are you dawdling for?" Without waiting for a reply, he hurried back down the walk to the constabulary steamer.

Vining followed; being well trained, he didn't start expostulating till he got into the motorcar and saw Mrs. O'Flynn slam the door in what she obviously took to be triumph. So did Vining. "Aren't you going to wait and pinch Mike?" he asked in incredulous tones.

"Sergeant, I don't give a damn about O'Flynn," Bushell said. "I want Kilbride. He gives me a straight trail to *The Two Georges*; O'Flynn doesn't. Get me to the train station right now."

The constabulary steamer was a middle-class Henry. Vining did his best to drive the way Shikalimo performed in his high-powered Supermarine. By the time they got to the station, Bushell regretted his request—he was glad to arrive in one shaken piece.

"What can I do for you now, sir?" the constabulary sergeant asked as he squealed to a stop.

"Nothing, by God," Bushell said, in lieu of telling the man he was a public menace. "You wait here while I talk to the ticket seller." He got out of the steamer and headed for the ticket booth before Vining could come up with any convincing arguments for joining him.

The man in the booth was the same sour-faced chap who'd denied the existence of a good hotel in Charleroi when Bushell and his companions came to town. He looked up from the newspaper he was reading and said, "Told you the Ribblesdale House weren't worth a damn. Now I reckon you're going to blame me on account of it."

"Only if you're the chef there," Bushell said, which won a startled snort from the fellow. He went on, "Did you sell a ticket to a man answering this description?" and painted the best word picture he could of Joseph Kilbride.

"It ain't nobody's business but mine and his whether I did or whether I didn't," the ticket seller answered. "How come you get to go poking into people's business?"

"Best reason of all—they pay me for it," Bushell answered, and displayed his RAM badge. He'd done that so often lately, he wondered if he ought to have it mounted on his forehead, perhaps with a pair of tenpenny nails.

He watched the ticket seller study the badge, study him, and very visibly decide what to say. In the Pennsylvania coal country, most people were not automatically eager to help the duly constituted authorities. At last, though, in reluctant tones, the fellow said, "Yeah, I sold him one. What's he gone and done to have you Robins after him?"

"You're not the first person to ask me that," Bushell said. "Where's he going?"

The man inside the grilled cage looked out at him, then chuckled rheumily. "Bet the first fool who asked didn't get a straight answer, neither. I ought to make you trade me one for one, but you'll sweat me if I try—and besides, that feller's as bloody-minded as they come; you can tell it by lookin' at him. He's headin' for New York City, he is."

"Is he?" Bushell said. "We'll have to see if he gets there. What time did that train pull out of here?"

"Hour and seventeen minutes ago," the ticket seller told him. He didn't look at any timepiece Bushell could see, but sounded very certain all the same. If pressed, he probably could have answered to the second.

"He'll have been through Pittsburgh already, then," Bushell said musingly.

"Stops after that are Greensberg, Torrance, Altoona, Tyrone, Huntington, Lewistown, Harrisburg, Lancaster, Downington, and Paoli before you get into Philadelphia," the ticket seller said, again without consulting any visible reference.

"Had this job a while, have you?" Bushell murmured. He went back to the constabulary steamer and told Sergeant Vining, "I'm grateful for your help. Now I'm going back to the Ribblesdale House—I'll walk, thank you very much," he added hastily, before Vining could offer to drive him there.

When he got back to the hotel, he rapped on Samuel Stanley's door and told his adjutant how close he'd come to nabbing Kilbride. Stanley's eyes glowed. "We can still get him," he said.

"Don't I know it," Bushell said. "I'm going to call Sir Horace and have him arrange to pull Kilbride off the train before he even gets to Philadelphia, let alone New York. Then we'll see what we shall see."

"Sounds fine," Stanley said. "He got away from us once, he got away from us twice, but let's see him do it three times. Better yet, let's not."

Bushell went back to his own room and placed a long-distance call to Sir Horace Bragg's home in Victoria. It took longer to go through than he thought it should have; both the hotel operator and the operator at the Charleroi exchange seemed startled that anyone inside Charleroi knew anyone out of town. But at last the phone rang. "Hullo? Bragg here."

"Sir, I have a call for you from Colonel Thomas B—" the operator began.

"Yes, yes, of course," Bragg said impatiently. As the operator clicked off, he continued, "Hullo, Tom. Haven't heard from you in a few days. What's up?"

Briefly, precisely, Bushell told him what was up. "This could be a major break, sir," he finished. "If we can pull in Kilbride, he might lead us right to the heart of the plot."

"You're right," Bragg agreed, more enthusiasm in his voice than Bushell usually noted there. "I'll have men posted in all those stops your side of Philadelphia. Here, give them to me again so I can write them down. If we don't put manacles on Kilbride, he's not on that train. I'll ring you directly we have word."

"That's first-rate, sir," Bushell said. "I'll be looking forward to your call."

He thought about going downstairs to celebrate with a drink. He thought about going downstairs to celebrate with several drinks. He could hear Jameson calling to him, a lilt more tempting than any a colleen from the Auld Sod might turn his way. Odysseus had had himself tied to the mast so he could listen to the Sirens sweetly singing. If Bushell heeded Jameson siren song, he'd fling himself into that coppery sea and drown. He made himself get out of his suit and into his pyjamas, made himself get into bed and pretend to read, made himself turn off the bedside lamp and stretch out in the darkness.

Try as he would, he could not make himself sleep.

Or so he thought. The chime of the telephone bell made him jerk as if it were a bullet cracking past his head. He pulled the chain that turned the lamp on again, then glanced at his pocket watch. A quarter of three! The phone rang again. He picked up the handset. "Bushell here."

"Hullo, Tom." Sir Horace Bragg's voice dragged with weariness; he undoubtedly hadn't been to bed at all.

Hearing Sir Horace made Bushell's own weariness drop away. "Have we got him, sir?" he demanded excitedly.

"No," Bragg answered: a world of disappointment boiled down to a single word. "We went through that train four different times. When we searched it, nobody answering Kilbride's description—no one even close to Kilbride's description—was aboard. He must have left it at some earlier stop."

"Pittsburgh," Bushell said. "It has to be Pittsburgh. You should—"

"—Set some men going through it?" Bragg asked. "Is that what you were going to say? It's already being done. I don't know what luck they'll have, though. That's a big, busy train station. It'll be hard to spot someone there, and by now Kilbride could be on his way to—"

Bushell interrupted in turn: "—Anywhere."

Lieutenant General Sir Horace Bragg let out a long, somber sigh. "I fear that's true. They've outfoxed us again, dammit. I don't know about you, Tom, but I'm bloody sick of it."

"Oh, yes," Bushell said. "But no matter how sick of it I am, I'm going to run Kilbride and all the Sons of Liberty to earth, and then the shoe will be on the other foot."

Bragg sighed again. "I wish I had your confidence."

It wasn't confidence. After all the setbacks he'd suffered, Bushell had no reason to feel confident. "I'm just stubborn, that's all," he said. "Either that'll be enough, or else—" He broke off. He didn't fancy even hypothetical consideration of *or else*.

"We're all doing everything we can," Bragg said: "You and I and the whole corps of RAMs. Whether it will be enough, though . . . We haven't got a lot of time."

"I know that," Bushell replied grimly. "Before long, the *Britannia* will sail for Victoria, and then Charles III will make his speech about the virtues of unity— at which time our chief symbol of unity had better be there behind him."

"As I said, everyone's doing everything he can," Bragg answered.

"I know," Bushell said. "But if we come up short, losing *The Two Georges* or having to ransom it won't be everyone's fault. It'll be mine."

▼

Bushell sat bolt upright in bed. "God in heaven, I am an idiot!" he said before he was more than half awake. The early-morning sun was sifting its way through the curtains in front of the window. He looked at his watch again. It was a little past six.

He telephoned the Charleroi constabulary headquarters and got the promise of a steamer in fifteen minutes. He used the time to get dressed and hurry downstairs. Once there, he went over to the front desk, got a sheet of notepaper and an envelope from the clerk, and scrawled a few quick sentences telling what he was up to. He handed the clerk the sealed envelope, saying, "Give this to Mr. Stanley—the Negro gentleman traveling with me—directly he comes down."

"Certainly, sir." The clerk stuck the note in a pigeonhole.

The constabulary steamer pulled up a couple of minutes later. To Bushell's relief, Sergeant Vining was not at the wheel. "Take me to Michael O'Flynn's house on Brattice Street," he told the constable who was. If anyone knew where Joseph Kilbride really intended to go, O'Flynn was likeliest to be that man.

"Yes, sir," the constable said, and slid out into traffic. After a moment, though, he asked, "Is it O'Flynn himself you need to speak to?"

"If I'd wanted to talk to Percy McGaffigan, I'd likely have asked you to go to his house instead," Bushell answered.

"Yes, sir," the constable repeated. "But O'Flynn will be down in the mines by now, not all snug in his bed."

"So early?" Bushell said. "How long is a shift in the mines?"

"Seven, seven and a half hours," the constable said. "But that's just work *at* the coal face. Then there's the travel to it, which can be a mile, or two, or three, going along underground. The miners don't get a ha'penny for that, and it takes 'em a goodish while to manage: not all the tunnels are tall enough to walk upright in, you see."

"So I do," Bushell said slowly. "Yes, you'd better take me to the mine, then." The more he heard about what miners had to endure, the better he understood why their politics inclined toward the radical. What they had now was disastrously bad.

The rattle and clank of the coal-breaking and coal-sorting machinery dinned in his ears as the constabulary steamer glided to a stop in front of the offices outside the upper opening of the mineshaft. The constable said, "They'll be able to tell you in here where in the mine O'Flynn is working today."

Bushell took out his badge as soon as he got out of the steamer. It worked its usual magic on the clerks in the office, a set of men who wore their white shirts, collars, and ties with an air of special pride, as if to proclaim to the world—and to themselves—that they weren't miners. "I'll have him located for you in a moment, sir," one of them said, flipping through a large box of cards. "O'Flynn, Michael F. That would be Level D, Corridor 3. We'll have to send a man down to bring him out. It will take some time."

"I haven't got time to waste," Bushell said. "Get me a guide and a helmet or whatever you use, and I'll go down there after him."

The clerk stared at him in something approaching horror. "But, sir, you'll ruin your suit!"

"Worse things have happened," Bushell answered. By the look on the clerk's face, he couldn't think of any offhand.

He was, however, good at doing as he was told. He found Bushell an aluminium helmet with a battery lamp, then said, "Let's go over to the infirmary, sir. One of the miners there should be able to take you where you need to go." He seemed confident the infirmary would have patients in it.

And so it did. A gray-haired fellow who was getting a gashed arm sewn up and bandaged said, "Yeah, I'll get him down there." He looked Bushell over. "Let him see how the other half lives, what working for a living is really like."

"Thanks." Bushell stuck out his hand. "Tom Bushell."

The miner shook hands with him. His grip was as strong as the stone with which he labored. Bushell squeezed back, hard enough to gain some small measure of respect. "Rufus Fitzwilliam," the miner said. He picked up his helmet from the medicine cabinet where it rested and set it on his head. "Come on, let's go to the cage."

Bushell followed him to the lift that took men down in to the mine. It did look like a cage, with a plank floor, and sides and top of steel mesh. A tall man would have had to stoop to stand upright in it. "Level D," Fitzwilliam called to the operator. To Bushell, he said, "Usually we're all jammed in here like tinned herrings. I head down with just two in the box, it's like going on holiday."

"If you say so," Bushell answered. Halfway through the sentence, the floor of the cage dropped away from beneath his feet. His stomach tried to crawl up into his throat. Doing his best to keep his voice casual as he plunged down into the lightless shaft, he asked, "How deep are we going?"

"Level D? Oh, about fifteen, sixteen hundred feet, something like that," Fitzwilliam answered casually.

It seemed less, partly because the lift was descending so fast. Increasing air pressure made Bushell's ears pop several times. Without warning, the cage slowed abruptly; the floorboards pushed hard against the soles of his feet. For a horrid moment, he imagined he felt the planks giving away. Then the cage stopped and the sensation, if it had been real, vanished.

Rufus Fitzwilliam reached up and flicked on his helmet lamp. Bushell imitated him. Fitzwilliam bent down and unlatched the door to the cage. "Come on out," he said, chuckling slyly. "You're not one of those chaps who go all balmy for fear of being shut in, are you?"

"No," Bushell answered, to the miner's disappointment. Under any normal circumstances, that was true. But, when he stepped out into the mine and thought of better than a quarter of mile of rock above his head, suspended only by the stone walls of the tunnel and by stout support timbers, he had to wonder if he'd told a lie.

His lamp and Fitzwilliam's cast pale beams through the gloom. Globes were strung along the roof of the tunnel, too, but so far apart that they shed only a dim light.

Bushell looked around. Except for Fitzwilliam, he saw no one. "All right, where's O'Flynn?" he asked.

Fitzwilliam laughed. "We have us some traveling to do first, Mister RAM." He pointed into the black pit of a tunnel mouth. "He's about a mile and a quarter, maybe a mile and a half, down that way."

"Lay on, Macduff," Bushell said. When the miner stared at him in incomprehension, he waved for him to lead the way. The bluff gesture helped hide his own dismay. When you thought of what miners did, you thought about them going down into their shaft and digging out the coal. What you didn't think about—unless you were a miner, Bushell supposed—was what happened after you'd dug out all the coal from right around the bottom of the shaft.

The Charleroi constable had talked about travel time to the work, but what he'd said hadn't really sunk in. Now it did. And a mile and a quarter or a mile and a half deep underground was not the same as a mile and a quarter or a mile and a half along a smooth sidewalk with trees all around and a breeze in your face.

Fitzwilliam stepped into the tunnel down which he'd pointed. "Watch your head, Mister RAM," he said. "While you're at it, watch your feet, too."

Bushell followed him into the tunnel. He hadn't gone more than twenty feet before he banged the top of his helmet on the ceiling. He did it again a couple of paces later, and then again a couple of paces after that. Ahead of him, Rufus Fitzwilliam was moving along easily. "This tunnel isn't tall enough to stand up in," Bushell called to him.

"Just noticed that, did you? You're not the tallest feller I've ever seen, or you'd've found it out sooner." Fitzwilliam's stooping gait didn't interfere with his speed at all. Bushell did his best to imitate it. Before he'd gone very far, a knotting in his thighs warned that it required practice—practice he'd never had. He suspected he'd spend the next few days shambling around like a chimpanzee with the rheumatism.

And, despite everything, he kept banging his helmet on the rough stone just above him. "What did miners do back before they wore helmets?" he asked.

"Oh, I expect we was just a bunch of knotheads in them days," Fitzwilliam replied with a chuckle.

Bushell would have laughed, too, but he tripped over a rock the size of both fists and staggered, flailing his arms wildly to keep from falling on his face. The tunnel wasn't very wide, either; he caught the back of one hand a painful whack against the jagged rock of the side. He held the hand in the beam of his helmet lamp to see if it was bleeding. It was.

"Told you to watch your feet," Fitzwilliam called back over his shoulder.

"Lots of people tell me lots of things," Bushell answered, panting a little. He was getting a crick in his neck to go with the ache in his thighs. He'd come only a few hundred yards, but already he felt worse than he had at the end of his hike through the woods of the Queen Charlotte Islands. Then something moved in the tunnel, something that wasn't him or Rufus Fitzwilliam. "What the devil's that?"

"A mouse, is all," the miner said. "You'll see 'em every now and again. They fall down the shaft, they're too little to smash themselves when they hit bottom. Wish us miners could say the same thing."

Not much later, they came to a stretch where Bushell could walk upright for fifty yards or so. The relief was indescribable. But then the roof got lower again, and lower, and lower. Before long, he was waddling forward like a duck; it was either that or get down on all fours. Rufus Fitzwilliam took it utterly for granted.

Bushell wondered if he'd have any legs left by the time he got to Michael O'Flynn. He rather hoped not; if they fell off, he wouldn't have to feel them any more.

When the ceiling got higher, Fitzwilliam showed off by taking perhaps ten yards at a waddling, arm-swinging run. Bushell was barely able to stagger on, let alone run. Any trade had its tricks, and he knew none of the ones that worked here.

Noise came echoing up the tunnel from ahead. It got louder till it grew into a dreadful din of saws grinding through rock and pneumatic hammers pounding away at it. Bushell set his teeth and hoped that meant they were getting closer to where O'Flynn was working. If it didn't, it probably meant he'd died and gone to hell.

Moving shapes in the lamplight up ahead were not demons armed with pitchforks, so they had to be miners. One of them turned and spotted Fitzwilliam and Bushell. Seeing Bushell's unminerly apparel, he called to Fitzwilliam: "Who you got there? Some big steam from the company?"

"Not today, Henry," Fitzwilliam answered. "This here's a RAM. He's looking for Mike O'Flynn—wants to ask him some questions."

"A RAM?" Henry's voice rose in surprise. He waved to Bushell. "Come on, buddy. I'll take you to Mike. He's tending the coal-cutter."

That machine looked like an enormous, electrically powered bandsaw. It had teeth that would have done credit to a shark. One of the miners shifting it to make a new cut smiled unpleasantly at Bushell and said, "How'd you like to have it bite you in the leg?"

"Given the choice, I'd rather be in Philadelphia," Bushell answered. "Are you Michael O'Flynn?"

"No, he's right—" Before the miner could say there, the coal-cutter started up, and its hideous racket made speech impossible. It ground into the black seam of coal. Clouds of coal dust spurted out over the crew at the cutter—and over Bushell. For a little while, everyone was too busy coughing to worry about any-thing else. Great chunks of coal and gray shale crashed to the floor of the tunnel, making it shake beneath Bushell's feet.

The coal-cutter stopped. The silence that slammed down afterward was al-most like a blow. Into it, one of the miners said, "I'm Mike O'Flynn."

"I thought you were a powderman, not a slicer," Bushell said, pointing to the infernal device.

"A damn fine one I am, too," O'Flynn said. A couple of other miners nodded to show they agreed with the self-assessment. He went on, "That means I've got the sense to know when to use the stuff and when to leave it alone. Use it here and we'd be wearing that roof." He gestured up toward the rough stone just above his head. "Now—my wife told me you came by the house last night. What the hell do you want to know bad enough to come down here and ask me about it?"

Bushell looked at the other miners, who'd gathered round to listen. "Is there any place we can talk just between ourselves?"

O'Flynn shook his head. "I'm not afraid of my chums' hearing what we have to say. Are you?"

"No," Bushell answered. If O'Flynn and his chums took it into their heads to make him have an "accident," there wasn't much he could do about it, the more so as he'd left his pistol behind in a suitcase. *Stupid*, he told himself: he'd done what he'd warned Felix Crooke against. Too late to worry about it now. The best way to keep the miners from getting the idea was to go on as if it had never oc-curred to him, either. He said, "You're the Michael O'Flynn who went to New Liverpool to picket the governor's mansion?"

"Yeah, that's me." O'Flynn studied him. "I saw you there, didn't I? After Tricky Dick got his head blown off, I mean. Is that what this is about? About *The Two Georges?*"

"Yes and no," Bushell said. "Has Joseph Kilbride from Doshoweh been visit-ing your home?"

"Yeah. I took him to the train station last night—my wife told me she told you that already. What's it to you, anyhow?"

"Where did Kilbride tell you he was going?" Bushell asked.

"What's it to you?" O'Flynn repeated. "Nothing against the law about hav-ing somebody over at your house, is there? What's he done? What do you *say* he's done?"

"He's involved in running rifles into the NAU. I have evidence for that," Bushell said, stretching a point only slightly. "The people who run guns are in-volved on way or another with stealing *The Two Georges.*"

"I don't know anything about that," Michael O'Flynn declared.

"I didn't say you did," Bushell said. "But you do now." He glanced from O'Flynn to the other miners. They looked solemn, thoughtful: not everyone in the Pennsylvania coal country was an Independence Party man or a sympathizer with the Sons. The call of King-Emperor and country was heard here, too, even if not so loudly as in most of the NAU. Bushell pressed ahead: "So. Where did Kilbride say he was going?"

O'Flynn licked his lips. After he'd done it, they were the only color in a face blackened by coal dust. At last, reluctantly, he answered, "He told me he was heading up to Boston for a while."

"Is that a fact?" Bushell's voice was soft, toneless, the better to conceal the elation he felt. But he had to nail down what O'Flynn had given him: "Why did you take him to a train that was bound for New York, then?"

"I figured he'd change trains in Pittsburgh," O'Flynn said. "How come? Didn't he?"

"He bought a through ticket to New York, anyhow," Bushell replied.

"News to me," O'Flynn said with a shrug. "I dropped him at the station, dug his bags out of the boot, and went on home."

"How did you get to know Kilbride?"

"We met in a saloon here, a couple-three years ago," the miner said. "He was down here selling this and that, and we got to talking. He doesn't say a whole lot, but he's smart, Kilbride is—you can tell. And he cares about miners; you can tell that, too. And, every so often, he'd send me some good hooch. When he wired me asking if he could stay a couple of days, I said sure. Why not?"

"He didn't tell you he was in any sort of trouble while he stayed with you?" Bushell asked.

"Not a bit of it," Michael O'Flynn answered. "I had no idea till my wife told me you came round last night. And now you're down here." He shook his head. "Any man who comes down here when he doesn't have to is plain crazy, you ask me."

"Well, there you are, Mr. O'Flynn," Bushell said. The miner cocked his head to one side, not following him. He didn't try to explain. When he'd ridden down the lift with Rufus Fitzwilliam, his thought had been to get answers from O'Flynn as fast as he could. The more he saw down in the mine, though, the more he thought that everyone down in this pit was crazy, whether he had to be here or not.

"You going to arrest Mike here?" one of the other miners asked, in a tone that warned Bushell would be sorry if he answered yes.

But he'd already decided to answer no, and did. Percy McGaffigan was another matter, though he'd leave him to men who came behind. When he thought about how many problems he was leaving for men who came behind, he felt acutely embarrassed. Were he one of those men, he would have hated him. When weighed against the direct trail—what he devoutly hoped was the direct trail, at any rate—to *The Two Georges*, though, everything else was trivial.

He turned to Rufus Fitzwilliam. "Take me back to the lift, please."

"Right y'are." Fitzwilliam chuckled. "We'll see how the legs hold up when you've traveled out and back."

The legs barely held up at all. By the time Bushell finally came up into the sunlight again, he was walking as if he'd been galloping a horse for twenty-four hours straight after never getting on a horse till that moment: a slow, bowlegged hobble. When he had to go up a couple of stairs, he took them sideways, crab-fashion, that being the only way in which he was physically capable of ascending.

He was also, he discovered, a hell of a mess. When he checked into a hotel in Boston, its cleaning staff would not look on him with delight. Even now, the Charleroi constable seemed less than enthusiastic about having him in his steamer. "Back to the hotel," he said. The constable might have been thinking about asking him questions, but didn't.

Back at the Ribblesdale House, Samuel Stanley was full of them. He waved Bushell's hasty note in his face and berated him for going off alone. "Off into the mines, you mean?" Bushell said, hobbling up to his adjutant. "I assure you, Sam, you didn't miss a thing. Now, if you'll excuse me, I'm for the showerbath." He thought of McGaffigan and all the other miners who got far filthier than he was and had to try to clean up with a basin's worth of water.

"Go ahead," Stanley said. "You're blacker than I am, and you didn't start out that way. But what do we do after you get back to your proper color?"

"We go to the train station," Bushell answered, "and get tickets for Boston."

# XI

LOOKING AROUND BOSTON MADE BUSH-
ell despair of ever finding Joseph Kilbride there. It wasn't that no one would recognize Kilbride; they had the photograph of him back from Chief Lassiter, and
local RAMs and local constables were taking copies of it to every hostelry Boston
boasted—and it boasted a lot of them.

But Boston was a great city in its own right, and Kilbride had a multitude of
places where he might stay that had nothing to do with hotels. And Boston was
also one of the places where sentiment against the British Empire ran strong.
Someone who quietly sympathized with the Sons of Liberty could keep Kilbride
under wraps indefinitely.

"It's liable to be useless, Sam," Bushell said as they walked back into the
Parker House. "All he has to do is sit tight. Time's on his side, not ours. The
King-Emperor will be in the NAU before long, and if we haven't got *The Two
Georges* back by then . . ." He made himself say it: "They'll ransom the bloody
thing and keep the Sons in business for the next hundred years."

"We'll catch him," Stanley said. "Somebody at the train station will remember him, or the hackman who took him wherever he went, or—"

Bushell made a slashing motion with his right hand. "Odds are, one of his
charming friends picked him up when he got off the train, just so he wouldn't
have to take a cab." He was bound and determined to be gloomy, and would let
no ray of hope penetrate that gloom.

The Parker House was the oldest hotel in Boston, which meant it was one of
the oldest in the NAU. It had recently been refurbished in gaudy Rococo Revival
style, full of gold leaf, ornate woodwork, and walls and ceiling painted with
damsels in long, flowing gowns. Kathleen Flannery's lip curled, ever so slightly, as
it did every time she walked into the hotel.

As soon as he was well into the lobby, Bushell's lip curled, too. The quality—
or lack of same—of the place's decorations, though, had nothing to do with his
reaction. Springing up from a tufted, overstuffed sofa and hurrying his way came
Michael Shaughnessy and Jerry Doyle.

"Welcome to Boston," Shaughnessy said, as if he really meant it.

"What are you doing here?" Bushell asked. Even as he asked it, he knew the
question wasn't altogether fair. If the two reporters worked for *Common Sense*,

232

they likely lived in Boston. But being in Boston was not the same as being in the lobby of the Parker House.

Smiling, Shaughnessy answered, "Why, the very same thing we were doing in Charleroi: watching you bumble about and waste the ratepayer's hard-earned money. It'll make quite an interesting little study for the magazine, that it will."

"How did you know where to find us?" Samuel Stanley asked.

Jerry Doyle stuck his tongue in his cheek. "We have our ways," he said airily, and then added, "and we don't have to tell them to the Crown's hounds, either."

Any of several people in Charleroi could have put the men from *Common Sense* on their trail: the ticket seller at the train station, the desk clerk at the Ribblesdale, or one of the miners with whom Bushell had spoken. He wasn't much concerned with how Doyle and Shaughnessy had learned he was in Boston, or even at the Parker House—if someone here recognized him (and he was all too recognizable these days) and passed the word on to the Sons of Liberty, it would get to *Common Sense*, too.

"Impeding an investigation is a crime," he remarked, "but of course you fine, upstanding chaps would never do anything like that."

"Of course not," Doyle agreed; he could rise to irony, where Shaughnessy was just choleric. "We didn't bother you even a little bit down in Charleroi, now did we? Answer true."

The true answer was that they really hadn't bothered him in Charleroi. He didn't care to admit that, however. And, before he could say anything, Michael Shaughnessy put in, "We'll be watching you closer here, though, and not just us, either. You'll never know when the folk you're dealing with are friends of *Common Sense*, so you'd best be on the up and up every waking moment."

"Is that so?" Bushell purred. Jerry Doyle looked ready to haul off and belt his partner. Bushell didn't blame him. Doyle had done his best to publish his harmlessness, and now Shaughnessy was making out that *Common Sense* wasn't so harmless after all.

Samuel Stanley caught that, too. "You know, Chief, these gentlemen certainly sound like people who want to impede our investigation," he said happily.

"Don't they?" Bushell agreed. He glanced over at Doyle, who was shaking his head, as if to say such a thought had never entered his mind. Bushell went on, "They're only trying to do their jobs, though." At that, Doyle must have got a crick in the neck, so swiftly did he shift from shaking to nodding. Bushell took no notice of him: "If we want to get them off our backs, telling them to go away won't work. They don't take orders from us, they take orders from their publisher. If we want to get anywhere with them, we have to talk with him."

Michael Shaughnessy laughed in his face. "If you think Mr. Kennedy will hear a word that comes from your lying mouths, you can go and think again. He's been standing up to the lackeys of oppression his whole life long, and made *Common Sense* what it is today."

"Reason enough to blame him, don't you think?" Bushell said. Shaughnessy blinked; before he could answer, Bushell continued, "Do you want to know the truth, Mr. Shaughnessy? I don't much care whether he heeds me or not. But for most of *my* whole life long, I've wanted to let him now how much I—mm, shall we say *admire?*—him. And now you're given me the chance. Thanks very much. I never expected you to do me such a favor."

He stepped forward, seized Shaughnessy's hand, and vigorously pumped it before the startled reporter could snatch it away. Then, trailed by Samuel Stanley and Kathleen, he made for the bank of lifts, leaving the two men from *Common Sense* staring after him. Their dismayed confusion was as enjoyable as anything that had happened to him since *The Two Georges* disappeared.

▼

Boston had its share of modern buildings, whose architects tried to make up in curlicues and contrasting patterns of stone and brickwork what they lacked in imagination. Walking past one, Bushell turned to Kathleen Flannery and, pointing, said, "Is it my bad taste, or it that very ugly?"

"It's certainly very busy," she answered after judicious consideration. "That's not quite the same thing, but it's close."

He looked ahead. "Now that's more like it," he said enthusiastically. "It has to date from before the days of the Union."

"That's Faneuil Hall," Kathleen said. "You're right; it was built in the 1740s. Boston has more colonial architecture left than any other city in the NAU. It's a good deal—cleaner in line, isn't it?"

"Just a bit, yes," Bushell said, his voice dry. Verticals, sharp angles, straight lines—who needed more, except some overeducated tomfool who wanted to impress a client with his own cleverness?

"I like it," Sam Stanley said. "It looks like a building where you'd go to get something done, not a gingerbread house or a fruitcake."

With dark red brick and white marble trim, the office building across Dock Square from the noble Faneuil Hall did look like a gingerbread house. That was where *Common Sense* had its headquarters, though, and so it was where Bushell reluctantly betook himself.

The painting of a bald eagle behind the receptionist's desk did not show the bird in a static, almost overstuffed pose, as it appeared on the Independence Party flag. Instead, the eagle's eyes blazed and its beak gaped wide and fierce: it looked, in fact, a good deal more ferocious than its kind really were.

The receptionist, an attractive blonde with her hair in a shingle bob and her cheeks red with rouge, said, "Welcome to *Common Sense*. How may I help you further the cause of freedom?"

As he had so often in this case, Bushell took out his badge and displayed it. "I *am* furthering the cause of freedom," he said. By her expression, the receptionist did not agree. Her opinion worried him not a bit. He said. "I want to see Mr. Kennedy. I'm sick and tired of his running dogs sticking their noses into my investigation, and I expect him to call them off." He relished using the rhetoric of the Sons of Liberty against *Common Sense*.

"One—one moment, sir," the receptionist said, reaching for the telephone. "Let me speak to Mr. Kennedy's secretary. Your name is—?" Bushell gave it, and those of his companions. The receptionist dialed a number and talked in a low voice on the phone for a few minutes. While she did that, Bushell studied the alphabetical listing of *Common Sense* employees on the wall near the picture of the eagle. The publisher's office was on the sixth floor. The receptionist hung up. With a bright smile, she said, "Mr. Kennedy will be able to see you at eleven o'clock this morning."

"That's nice," Bushell said, and started for the lift down the hall. "I'm able to see him now."

"Sir," the receptionist called after him, "didn't you hear me? Mr. Kennedy won't be able to see you until—"

"Oh, I heard you," Bushell said, stepping aside to let Kathleen precede him into the lift car. "I'm just not listening to you." The lift's sliding doors cut off the receptionist's protests.

In the Charleroi coal mine, Bushell had taken a lift that dropped him into the bowels of the earth. This one rose far more sedately, and carried him to what was, if not the earthly paradise, a good first approximation for it.

Somewhere in the background, a phonogram softly played Handel's *Water Music*. Bushell's feet sank deep into the thick, luxurious pile of the carpet. The secretary who guarded the way into the office whose doorway read JOHN F. KENNEDY, PUBLISHER made the receptionist in the lobby seem dowdy by comparison, something Bushell would not have imagined possible. Her perfume teased his nose.

She frowned when he identified himself. "I distinctly told Roxanne Mr. Kennedy was not available till eleven this morning."

"What a pity—we must have misunderstood," Bushell said. "Since we're here, maybe he'll see us now."

That could have sounded contrite. On the surface, it did. But when the secretary studied Bushell's face, she realized he wasn't asking a favor. He wasn't waiting, either. He went to the door of John Kennedy's office, opened it, and went in.

Kennedy was in a meeting with two men and two women, the oldest of them less than half his age. He was smiling; they were all laughing. "That will give them something to think about, Mr. Kennedy," one of the women said in a low, throaty voice that struck Bushell as more appropriate for the boudoir than the office.

"Then it's wasted, Dorothy, for I doubt any of them can think," Kennedy said, his own New England–accented voice strong and younger than his years. That got more laughter. But then his associates—*Bright Young Things*, Bushell mentally tagged them—turned their heads to the doorway. So did he. For a moment, anger sparked in his green-blue eyes. "Who the devil are you?" he demanded.

"Colonel Thomas Bushell, Royal American Mounted Police." As he had so many times, Bushell showed his badge. "I have some questions about *The Two Georges.*"

"And you think you'll get answers from me?" Now Kennedy sounded amused. "Good luck to you."

"You don't have to tell him anything, Mr. Kennedy," one of the Bright Young Men said fiercely, "except to go away."

If Kennedy did that, Bushell knew he had little recourse. But the publisher of *Common Sense* waved a hand, a gesture full of careless confidence. "I'll talk to him. Why not? I have nothing to hide." He projected so much charm that even Bushell, who knew better than to trust him, wanted to believe. "Go on," Kennedy told his colleagues. "We were about finished here, anyway, weren't we? I'll be all right. I may even convert this fellow here to—common sense."

The Bright Young Things left the office one after the other, each glaring in turn at Bushell, Stanley, and Kathleen Flannery. A couple of them muttered under their breath. Luckily for them, Bushell ignored the mutters.

"Well, come in, Colonel," Kennedy said in that resonant voice, coming to the door and extending his hand. "Please introduce me to your friends—especially the charming lady here."

With a mental sigh, Bushell shook hands with the publisher. Kennedy's grip was firm, though he had to be well into his seventies. He did his best to deny his age, partly helped by nature, as with his voice, and partly by artifice: his hair showed silver at the temples, but the rest was a not altogether convincing redbrown. His teeth were whiter and more perfectly even than any not supplied by a dentist. With its peaked lapels and wide-legged pants that hung straight from the waist, his suit might have belonged to a university undergraduate—but few undergraduates would have had the taste to choose his Donegal tweeds . . . or the money to afford them.

He shook hands with Samuel Stanley, then made a production of meeting Kathleen Flannery: he pressed her hand between both of his before raising it to his lips. "Always a pleasure to make the acquaintance of such a fair flower from the Old Sod," he said, overlaying the New England accent with a brogue obviously donned for the occasion. When he moved back to let Kathleen enter his office, he didn't move quite far enough, so that they brushed against each other as she stepped in.

Where his clothes did not, his office seemed made for a captain of industry. The only missing touch was a print of *The Two Georges* behind his desk. Instead, he had a picture of uniformed RAMs wading into a crowd of striking coal miners sometime in the early days of the century. No one who looked at it could doubt the artist's sentiments; the RAMs were portrayed as bestial brutes, some of them grinning with ghoulish glee as they belabored the saintly-seeming miners with truncheons.

"Tea?" Kennedy asked, nodding to a silver service in the corner of the office. "Or would you rather have coffee? I prefer it myself—less British."

"Just business," Bushell said.

The publisher shrugged. "As you like." He took a cigar from a humidor, held it up to get permission—and to admire it—and then lighted it. The smoke he blew made Bushell's mouth water; they didn't grow tobacco like that anywhere in the British Empire, worse luck. After a couple of lazy puffs, Kennedy asked, "Well, what is it that's so important it won't wait till eleven this morning?"

"Conducting any investigation is hard," Bushell said. "Conducting one with reporters dogging your heels is worse; they enjoy printing things you'd sooner see quiet a while longer. Conducting one with reporters working to make you fail . . . a little of that goes a long way."

"I can see that it might," Kennedy said. "But what has it got to do with me?"

"I knew you were going to say that," Bushell told him. "Do you know how I knew?"

"No, but since you're going to tell me, I have the feeling I will," Kennedy answered.

Bushell's smile was hard and bright and cold, like February sunshine in Boston. "Because one of your demon reporters told me that was what you'd say. He tells us all sorts of interesting things about you. Would you like to hear some of them?"

"One of Shaughnessy and Doyle, do you mean?" Kennedy shook his head. "I don't believe it, not a word. They're good lads, honest lads, both of them, and I won't let your lies come between me and them."

"One of your reporters, I said," Bushell answered. "I named no names, and I didn't intend to. But if you think you can spy on the Royal American Mounted Police as we go about our business, why shouldn't you expect us to spy on you as you go about yours?"

Kennedy glared at him. Bushell had been on the receiving end of some fearsome scowls in his time, but this ranked among the leaders. It was both full of hate and restrained, an unsettling combination. The man would make—probably did make—a bad enemy. Thanks to *Common Sense*, he'd been a bad enemy to the Crown for close to half a century.

Perhaps trying to defuse the moment, Kathleen Flannery said, "I think I'd like a cup of tea after all, please, Mr. Kennedy."

The publisher went from glowering magnate to kindly host in the space of a heartbeat. He had charm in abundance when he wanted to, no doubt of that. "My pleasure," he said, rising from his seat. "It'll be Irish Breakfast, of course, but then you won't mind that, being Irish yourself. Do you take sugar, Dr. Flannery?—Kathleen, if you'll let me? No? I shouldn't be surprised; you must be sweet enough and to spare on your own. Would you care for a biscuit with it? I have vanilla wafers there that go very nicely."

"No, thank you," Kathleen said. "Just the tea, please."

Kennedy filled a bone-china cup from the samovar, then lifted a silver pitcher of milk from the ice-filled bowl in which it sat. Bushell had been wondering if he assumed everyone drank tea Russian style, but no, evidently not. The publisher carried cup and saucer over to Kathleen Flannery. "Here you are," he said, patting her on the shoulder.

"Thank you," she replied, her voice quiet.

After fussing over her a while longer, Kennedy went back behind his desk. "Where were we?" he asked Bushell, sounding affable enough. "Oh, I remember—you were telling me lies about my reporters."

"No, you were telling me lies about not knowing what they're up to and why," Bushell answered with another of those wintry smiles. "Me, I'm not a reporter; so I'm more likely to be telling the truth."

"A RAM a truthteller?" Kennedy shook his head; his wattled jowels wobbled slightly. "That's funny enough for a joke, or would be if it weren't so sad."

Samuel Stanley bristled. "What the devil *have* you got against the Crown and the British Empire?" he demanded. "What's the Empire ever done to you— aside from making you rich, I mean?" He waved a hand around to call attention to the splendid quarters in which they were conversing.

"The Empire hasn't made me rich." Anger sparked in Kennedy's eyes, too. "I made myself rich, and the way I did it shows the Empire's not so beloved nor so perfect as some blind fools think. America would be better off with its chains broken."

"Nothing's perfect," Bushell said, uneasily remembering the slums of Charleroi and the low, dark tunnels underneath them.

"The Empire does things pretty well, though." Stanley set his right forefinger on the back of his left wrist to remind Kennedy what color he was. "Britain freed the black slaves all through the Empire—even the southern provinces of the NAU, where the masters bawled like branded calves, screaming they couldn't raise their cotton without us. For that alone—"

Kennedy slammed a fist down on the desk. "Yes, England freed the black man—and left the Irishman in chains. Oh, we were free in law: free to starve when the potato failed. One of my several-great-grandfathers was down under seven stone when he dragged himself aboard ship for what he hoped might prove a better life. They made him a factory hand here in Boston instead of the farmer he had been, but he kept right on starving."

Bushell stood up and dug in his trouser pocket. "And you're still starving to this day." He found a shilling and tossed it onto Kennedy's desk. Silver rang sweetly off polished walnut. "Here, you poor man, buy yourself a crust of bread."

The publisher looked at the coin without picking it up. "Give me another one of those, and I'll save both to put on your eyes after America is free," he said softly.

Bushell threw another shilling on the desk. "Save them for yourself."

"One fine day—oh, and it will be a fine day—the Crown will go into the bonfire," Kennedy said. "And when it does, it will light our country—America, *our* country—and all who serve it, and the glow from that fire can truly light the world."

"My country," Bushell answered, "is the British Empire, ruled by His Majesty the King-Emperor, Charles III. If the rest of the NAU didn't feel the same way, the Independence Party would win elections and no one would need to read *Common Sense*."

"Elections are bought," Kennedy said with a scornful sniff. "That works—for a while. But those who make peaceful revolution impossible will make violent revolution inevitable."

"Mr. Kennedy—" Bushell let it drop. The publisher had composed so many editorials for his magazine, he even talked like one. You'd make Kennedy's brother the archbishop a Baptist before you convinced him the British Empire did more good than harm, and persisted for that very reason. Perhaps a straight search for information might yield something. "Do you know a Joseph Kilbride, Mr. Kennedy?"

"The art collector? Yes, I've met him," Kennedy answered. "Why?"

"Do you know his present whereabouts?" Bushell asked, not responding to the counterquestion.

"He lives in the Six Nations, doesn't he?" Kennedy made a dismissive gesture. "I don't know him at all well, I'm afraid."

"I didn't ask if you knew where he lived," Bushell said. "I asked if you knew his present whereabouts."

Kennedy rewarded him with a hooded look that pleased him more than the glares he'd earned before: he'd been intended to take that as a fully responsive answer. The publisher spoke carefully now: "No, I do not know his exact whereabouts. I do know I have not seen him or talked with him in two or three years, so I'm afraid I can't help you further." He took a pocket watch from a waistcoat pocket. "Have you got a lot of other questions, Colonel Bushell? I have another meeting in five minutes. If there are more, perhaps we could resume this afternoon with my solicitor present."

"Fascinating how someone who despises good British law is so quick to shelter behind it," Bushell remarked to no one in particular. With his solicitor present, Kennedy would say nothing of any consequence, and would have the best legal advice his money could buy justifying that nothing. The man had developed skating on thin ice into an art, but he'd never yet gone through. Sighing, Bushell said, "I think that's all."

Kennedy got to his feet. Just for a moment, he looked smugly patronizing: a prominent men who'd fended off an impertinent busybody who had almost—but not quite—managed to become an annoyance. Then the friendly, smiling mask slid back into place, and Bushell, against his will, found himself smiling back. Whatever else you said about the man, he did have charisma.

Kennedy extended his hand again. "I don't wish you ill, Colonel, not personally."

On that basis, Bushell clasped it without hesitation. "No, not personally, Mr. Kennedy." An open enemy, unlike the hidden terrorists who called themselves the Sons of Liberty, could deserve respect.

Kennedy shook hands with Samuel Stanley, too; Stanley also seemed to accept him as a declared foe but not necessarily a villain because of that. As he had when they were introduced, the publisher lingered over Kathleen Flannery. "A pleasure to meet you, my dear," he said. "I'd like to see more of you, if you'll be in Boston long."

"I don't know," she answered. "I expect I'll be very busy, however long I am here."

"What a pity." Kennedy finally let go of her hand. He held the door open so she, Bushell, and Stanley could leave. "Good luck, Colonel," he told Bushell, "but not too much of it."

Someone was sitting on the couch by the secretary's desk. Bushell glanced over at the man. Had this been the cinema, the fellow would have been Joseph

Kilbride. Bushell had no idea who he was, but Kilbride he wasn't. Bushell clicked his tongue between his teeth in regret, then headed for the lift.

He and his companions spent the rest of the morning at the Boston RAM offices on Parliament Street. That proved as frustrating as the interview with Kennedy had. Like Pennsylvania, Boston was a stronghold of the Sons of Liberty, but if any of the local Sons had anything to do with the plot to steal *The Two Georges* or any knowledge of it, the RAMs hadn't been able to prove it.

They hadn't found any sign of Joseph Kilbride, either. He might have dropped off the face of the earth—or Michael O'Flynn might have been lying, down there in the coal mine.

When church bells chimed noon, Bushell threw his hands in the air. "Where can we get something to eat?" he asked Major George Harris, the RAM who'd been helping in what looked more and more like a fruitless search.

"Try Durgin-Park, out in back of Faneuil Hall," Harris suggested. He was a Bostonian himself, and talked like one: the name of the eatery he proposed came out as an almost unintelligible *Duhgin-Pahk*. After he said it often enough for Bushell to understand him, he added, "They'll fill you up there, and they won't leave you broke."

Bushell looked at his companions. They nodded. "Why not?" he said. The three of them went out into the humid heat and walked over to the restaurant. He almost left when he found they had to queue up to get into the upstairs dining room, but didn't know anywhere else to go. The queue proved to move swiftly. Before long, he, Stanley, and Kathleen were sitting at a long table with a dozen other hungry souls.

The place was as far from elegant as could be imagined—and by all appearances deliberately so. Large, noisy fans stirred the warm air. Steam pipes rattled and wheezed overhead. The waitresses came in two varieties: surly and wise-cracking.

But the Boston baked beans with salt pork, the corn bread, and the roast beef were uniformly excellent, and, as Major Harris had promised, they gave you enough to feed a regiment. Bushell didn't know how he managed to find room for Indian pudding, but the cornmeal-and-molasses mix found a corner nothing else was filling. "I wonder what Shikalimo would think of it," he mused.

"Don't know," Samuel Stanley said."Have you got a wheelbarrow? Dump me in it and roll me back to the hotel."

"No rest for the weary—nor even the obese," Bushell answered with a smile. "Back to the RAMs, and then on to the Boston constables." He turned to Kathleen Flannery. "You see what a dramatic, exciting life we lead."

She nodded without saying anything. She hadn't said much since they left the offices of *Common Sense*. That worried Bushell. Had talking to John Kennedy made her wonder if she was on the right side after all? Was she really on the right side after all? He'd thought so; he'd been—almost—convinced. Now he started wondering again.

By about two that afternoon, Bushell was convinced he wouldn't learn anything more from the RAMs. He and his companions went down the street to the central constabulary station. When he got there, he wondered if he'd ever seen so many Irishmen all in the same place before. They fell over themselves trying to be helpful; he had no complaint on that score. Even so, he couldn't help wondering if one or another of Boston's finest might not occasionally slip a shilling into a telephone at a public box and ring up *Common Sense*. He tried not to let the thought worry him.

However friendly and solicitous they were, the Boston constables had not set eyes on Joseph Kilbride. The number of people who might have been harboring him ran into the hundreds, if not the thousands. Checking out each one would take a long time, time the investigation did not have. "And the worst of it is, there's sure to be plenty of men without even the littlest record who'd do a Son a good turn," a constabulary lieutenant said morosely. "If we do land this Kilbride item, it's as likely to be by luck as by design."

"The same pleasant thought had crossed my mind, yes," Bushell said. "But all the luck we've had on this case has been bad." He'd worried about getting stuck on the Queen Charlotte Islands without any idea of where to go next. If you had to get stuck somewhere, Boston was a more pleasant place to do it, but the idea of getting stuck now, with time growing short so fast, chilled Bushell's blood.

He was glum and quiet when he, Sam, and Kathleen went back to the Parker House. Not even the prospect of supper at Parker's, the restaurant attached to the hotel, did much to cheer him, though Major Harris had implied that you'd die happy if you shuffled off this mortal coil right after a meal there.

When he and his companions walked into the dining room, the maître d' handed Kathleen Flannery a red rose and Stanley and him a cigar. Had it been done showily, he would have thought it theatrical and cheap (though the cigar was anything but cheap). As it was, the man gave the impression that the flower and tobacco were gifts due anyone entering his domain, to be taken for granted. Such understated luxury made Bushell nod in approval: this was how the best places did things.

The waiter brought over butter and a wicker basket of rolls. Bushell stared at them. One eyebrow rose. He looked up at the waiter. "These wouldn't be—"

"Parker House rolls? Why, yes, sir, as a matter of fact they would. This is where they got the name."

Whatever you called them, they were good. Bushell ate one and sipped at a glass of Jameson. When the waiter returned, he ordered medallions of lobster Parisienne. Samuel Stanley chose Dover sole, while Kathleen ordered scrod. "It's something you can't get anywhere but Boston," she said.

"Oh, you can," Bushell said, "but they call it young cod anyplace else."

He took another sip of his Irish whiskey and admired the dining room. They'd had the sense to leave it alone when the Rococo Revival swept through the rest of the hotel. The walnut-paneled walls, well over a century old, complemented the earth tones of the decor. You didn't want to hurry anything here, not even drinking. Fine English hostelries were supposed to have an atmosphere like this. Bushell hadn't thought its like existed on this side of the Atlantic.

"Boston has more than three hundred years of history behind it," Kathleen said when he remarked on that: "time enough for tradition to have taken root here. Oh, set against London, three hundred years isn't much, but it's very old compared to most of the NAU."

"Practically prehistoric when you set it against New Liverpool," Bushell said. "The Empire's only been in the southwest a little more than a hundred years. Hardly anything left of old Franco-Spanish Los Angeles, either: street names, not much more."

Kathleen nodded. "I saw that. I think it's a pity. If you don't remember the past, how can you hope to make sense of the present?" She looked down at her gin and tonic. "Spoken like an art curator, I know."

"It makes sense, any which way," Bushell said. Samuel Stanley raised his mug of John Adams ale in salute and agreement.

The waiter came back with their suppers. Deft as a surgeon, he boned Stanley's sole right at the table. "Something more to drink, madam, sirs?" he asked.

Kathleen Flannery nodded again. "Maybe a little later for me," Bushell said; his glass remained a quarter full. Sam Stanley looked at him as if wondering if he was well. He grinned at his adjutant. Maybe he wasn't perfectly predictable after all.

With the first taste of lobster, worries about predictability vanished from his head. For the next little while, a rapturous silence enfolded the table. When at last plates were empty, Stanley raised his mug again: "To two fish and a lobster that did not die in vain." They all drank, Bushell finishing the last couple of drops of Jameson he still had left.

Instead of signaling for another, he chose a glass of port to go with the tray of cheese and fruit the waiter brought after clearing away the dishes that had held the entrees. After a glance toward Kathleen, Bushell and Stanley lit the cigars the maître d' had given them. Bushell savored the fine, rich smoke. "The animal part of me is about as content as it could be," he said.

"Amen to that," Samuel Stanley declared. "I don't remember the last time I had a finer meal. All the same, though, I'm going to cut things short, if you'll forgive me. I want to go upstairs and ring up Phyllis. It's been too long since I've talked with her."

Bushell waved indulgently. "Go on, Sam. I just hope she knows what a lucky woman she is, to have you still *wanting* to talk with her after all these years."

Stanley laughed at that. He rose, dipped his head to Kathleen Flannery, and hurried out of Parker's. Bushell sampled a ripe Stilton, then took another sip of port.

He glanced over at Kathleen, who had fallen back into the silence that had gripped her since she left the offices of *Common Sense*. "If you're content, Dr. Flannery," he remarked, "you conceal it very well."

She had a glass of port in front of her, too. It was more than half full. She lifted it and knocked it back as if it were a shot of rotgut. Bushell flinched; discontented or not, she had no business treating the lovely stuff that way. "Why on earth shouldn't I be, Colonel?" she said. "It's not every day, after all, that I have the privilege of abandoning my own will and following someone else's."

"We've been over that ground before," he said. "If you're going to help with the investigation—and you have helped, and I thank you for it—you need to come along with Sam and me so—"

"—So you can take me to be pawed like a cut of meat, and a cheap one at that," she broke in.

"Going in to talk with Tony Rothrock was your idea, not mine," Bushell said, "and you told me he hadn't pawed you, just made himself otherwise offensive. If we'd known differently, we'd have—"

Kathleen interrupted him again: "Rothrock? I'm not talking about Rothrock. I'm talking about John Kennedy this morning. Didn't you notice *anything*, Colonel?" By her tone, her opinion of his skill as an observer had just dived like a submersible.

"I saw he was attentive to you, but—"

"Attentive!" Kathleen said, loud enough to make people a couple of tables over look her way. Bushell resigned himself to never getting a word in edgewise, which had happened before in conversations with Kathleen. She went on, "I've not been treated like that in—oh, a very long time," and then added, in what was not quite the *non sequitur* it first seemed, "I shall have my father cancel my subscription."

Bushell scratched his head. "How did I miss this? I was in the same room with you, and I didn't notice anything out of the ordinary."

"You wouldn't have," Kathleen said. "For one thing, you weren't looking for anything like that, and for another, he's smooth. Usually, those unwelcome approaches are much more blatant."

Instead of salving Bushell's pride, that irritated him further. He made his living by noting what others failed to see. Now he had failed. "What the devil did he *do*?" he asked, and then held up a hand before Kathleen could answer. "Wait." He called up the mental image of them going into Kennedy's office. "You were introduced to him, and he took your hand."

Kathleen nodded. The expression on her face said she'd just turned over a flat rock and found something slimy and pallid underneath. "He certainly did . . . and as he clasped it, he used his middle finger to offer an invitation which I was not in the least interested in accepting."

"Did he?" Bushell rubbed at his mustache. "That's crude." He ran the mental cinema forward a few frames. "You brushed against him as you walked past. I didn't think anything of it at the time, but I do remember that."

"No, he brushed against me," she corrected. "I wouldn't have thought much of that, either, except for what had just happened before, but he pushed his hips forward so that he brushed against my backside. It put me in mind of a dog in the street, if you must know."

"Then what happened?" Bushell took a certain morbid delight in seeing Kennedy in a less than favorable light, and by talking about it Kathleen was venting some of the fury she'd bottled up all day.

"When he came around with the tea and put his hand on my shoulder, he just happened to slide it under the material of my dress and onto my skin. Purely a matter of chance, of course." Her snapping eyes gave the lie to her words.

"Why didn't you call him on it?" Bushell asked. "That was what, the third time by then?"

"What would the point have been?" she said with a bitter shrug. "I couldn't prove anything, and all he would have done was apologize—most handsomely and most insincerely, I have no doubt. I've heard such before—"

"Have you?"

"Oh, yes." Kathleen's nod was emphatic; she was feeling the port. "Apologies of that sort aren't worth having, and demanding them only makes you an enemy." She laughed, briefly and bitterly. "Now you're hearing the secrets of women in the professions. Any one of us could tell you the like."

"Really? The first assumption is that because something isn't talked about, it doesn't happen. I suppose I ought to know what that one's worth, being a policeman—of sorts. But, as you said, I've never looked for anything of the kind. Perhaps I should."

"Yes, perhaps you should," Kathleen said sharply. Then she bit her lip. "I'm sorry. I don't mean that personally, or at least not in the way it must have sounded. Heaven knows we've had our disagreements—"

"Really?" Bushell's voice was bland. "I hadn't noticed."

She started to explode, then pointed an accusing finger at him instead. "No, you won't get my goat that way; you've done it too often already. As I was saying—" She waited for him to interrupt her again. When he didn't, she went on, "We've had our disagreements, but you've been a gentleman about them."

"And the distinguished publisher of *Common Sense* was not?"

"No," Kathleen said, like a judge passing sentence. So, in a way, she was. The world was a smaller, quicker, more complicated place than it had been in the days of the two Georges or of Victoria, but the old standards of behavior still had some life in them. A man against whom the public rendered a verdict like the one Kathleen had delivered on John Kennedy would never again be taken seriously as a shaper of opinion.

At any other time, the prospect of that happening to the publisher would have filled Bushell with fierce glee. So it did now, but only in a small part of his mind. He said, "You've not had much luck with the male of the species, have you, Kathleen? Your fiancé and this and—"

"In the scheme of things, this was just a nuisance." She cocked her head to one side, studying him. He hadn'd used her Christian name before. After a moment, she went on, "As for the other, he was handsome, he was persuasive, and I—" She shrugged. "I was foolish."

"If they built enough gaols to hold all the foolish people, the outside world would be a pretty empty place. Lord knows I'd be wearing the broad arrow myself." Bushell was not usually a man in the habit of hesitating, but now he paused. After what he'd known with Irene had collapsed like a block of flats in a strong earthquake, he'd been hesitant (he wouldn't use the word *frightened*, even to himself) about revealing much of himself to—leaving himself vulnerable to—anyone else. When he did speak again, it was almost abstractly: "I've often wished we'd met under other circumstances. It would have been—interesting."

"You use that word to serve such a lot of ends," Kathleen remarked. She looked down at her hands. "There have been times I wished the same thing myself."

"Have there?" Bushell said. "I must say, you've hidden it very well."

"So have you," she answered. "I suspect our reasons aren't very different."

Bushell raised an eyebrow. "Is that so? You were afraid I sympathized with the Sons of Liberty, too?"

Kathleen stared at him, then started to laugh. "Oh dear, Tom," she said after a moment. "You did get me that time."

He set his hand on hers. "Not yet," he said.

The waiter had been coming up to their table, no doubt to ask if they wanted anything else. He was well trained; seeing what looked to be unfolding ahead of him, he abruptly found something else to do. The unsleepingly observant part of Bushell noticed him sheering off out of the corner of his eye. He was forgotten an instant later.

"Well," Kathleen said, as if it were a complete sentence. "Let me go powder my nose. I'll be back directly." She got up. "And then—" That also might have been a full thought.

No sooner had she headed for the door than the waiter appeared as if by magic, this time bearing the check: not only well trained but efficient. Bushell rewarded that efficiency with a tip larger than he usually paid. The waiter returned, scooped up the banknotes with a murmured word of thanks, and vanished once more.

Kathleen took longer to return than Bushell had expected. He drummed his fingers on the tablecloth. Had she decided he was as irksome as Kennedy and picked a discreet way of avoiding him, as she'd been discreet in the publisher's office? Had she—?

She came back into Parker's then, and his worries evaporated. He got up and walked over to her. When he offered her his arm, she took it as if it were the most natural thing in the world. They went over to the bank of lifts opposite the registration desk. "Fourth floor," Bushell told the operator.

"Yes, sir," the fellow said, touching a forefinger to the shiny leather brim of his cap. His eyes twinkled. He'd taken Bushell and Kathleen—and Samuel Stanley—down to Parker's for supper. The two of them hadn't been arm in arm then.

The fourth-floor hallway was long and quiet, the carpet thick and soft under Bushell's shoes. The electric lamp fixtures protruding from the walls resembled the gaslights they'd replaced in the early days of the century.

Stanley's room was closest to the lifts, Bushell's next to it, and then Kathleen's. They both smiled when they walked past Bushell's room. Kathleen took the key to hers from her handbag, set it in the lock, and turned it. The door opened. She went in. Bushell followed her. He closed the door after himself and made sure it was locked.

Kathleen turned on a lamp by an overstuffed chair. The shade was of thick parchment. The light that came from the lamp was brighter than any candles could produce, but the shade gave it some of that rich, buttery quality.

Slyly, Kathleen asked, "What would Doyle and Shaughnessy say if they knew the chief investigator in this case was alone in a hotel room with someone he'd suspected of sympathizing with the Sons of Liberty? It sounds like a compromising position to me."

"I don't much care what other people say," Bushell answered with a shrug.

"Yes, I had noticed that," Kathleen answered as he took her in his arms.

▼

Some time later, Bushell leaned up on one elbow and studied Kathleen by the warm light of that one lamp. She stirred under his gaze, as if lying on a bed naked and lazy in the afterglow were somehow more intimate than the act itself. Maybe, to her, it was: while you were actually making love, you weren't thinking about what you were doing and what it might mean. That came afterward.

He stroked her hair, smiled crookedly, and nodded. Then he gave a gasp of theatrical exhaustion, flopping limply back onto the linen sheets.

Kathleen reached out and poked him in the ribs. She happened to hit a ticklish spot; he wriggled and tried to get away. She laughed. "If you let yourself, you can be a very foolish man."

His head whipped around, as if in alarm. "My secret's out! You can blackmail me forever now. I'm putty in your hands."

"Hardly putty," she said, looking at him from under half-lowered eyelids. Then she poked him again. Her finger slid into a shallow groove in his flesh that ran along one rib. "What's this?"

"I'd say it was an old war wound, except, of course, we've never been at war with the Holy Alliance." Bushell's raised eyebrow told how seriously he expected her to take that. He shook his head in some bemusement. Going out onto the frontier showed you how very much the safe, contented Empire was really worth . . . but when you came back with that new understanding, you found you didn't quite fit into safety and contentment any more.

After a moment, he went on, "It was a worthless little skirmish down near the border with Nueva España—which side of the border we were on depends on whether you like British maps or the ones the Franco-Spaniards print. Of course, if you get killed in a worthless little skirmish, you're as dead as if it were a real war. One of my men got hit. I was a raw subaltern, green as paint, but I knew I had to go out and pick him up. So I did—and I got this. Sam Stanley brought us both back alive."

"A couple of inches farther in"—she ran her hand up toward his heart—"and it might have killed you."

"Really? The thought never crossed my mind." He waited half a beat, then added, "And if you believe that, I have in my suitcase a fine perpetual-motion machine and an elixir to turn lead into gold."

She stretched languorously. "After tonight, nothing you say you have would surprise me too much." She glanced over at him out of the corner of her eye.

He cupped her left breast in his hand. Her nipple grew hard against his palm. She arched her back and made a small noise deep in her throat. He caught her to him. Her mouth was seeking his as his sought hers. "Well!" she said a little later, when their lips separated for a moment: the second time that night she'd freighted the word with more than it was meant to bear. She amplified it: "So soon?"

"Hush," he said roughly.

Despite that admonition, the second time was slower, less urgent than the first had been. Bushell wondered if his body would betray its promise to him, but it didn't. When Kathleen's breath came quick and short and she quivered beneath him, he said "Yes!" to her or himself or possibly God, and yes it certainly was.

"Well," Kathleen said for the third time, and then, in a much more pragmatic voice, "You're squashing me."

"The romance is over so soon, is it?" he said, had had to pull back in a hurry before she could bite him in the shoulder. Their skins, slick with sweat, slid against each other as he went back to his own side of the bed.

Kathleen leaned over, kissed him gently on the lips, curled up beside him, and, in what couldn't have been more than ninety seconds, fell asleep. He watched and listened to that happen in some bemusement: legend claimed it was a male prerogative. He snorted—softly, so as not to bother Kathleen. He should have known better than to expect her to pay any attention to legend.

He lay on his back, fingers interlaced behind his head, staring up at the ceiling, trying to find patterns in random roughnesses of plaster. Even if he hadn't been celibate these past few years, he hadn't gone to bed with a woman who might also matter to him outside of bed, either, not till now.

That thought brought fright with it, fright hardly less than he'd known with bullets flying at Buckley Bay. He could see into the future, could see himself giving her his heart—and see her breaking it, a month from now, or a year, or five years, or fifteen. He'd been through that once. Next to it, a bullet that slid along a rib was a small wound. After a while, the bleeding stopped and the scar grew old and pale. You could prod that scar, as Kathleen had, and never feel a thing.

The other, though—A man who laid himself open to being twice wounded in love was a fool. But what was a man who, having been wounded once, forswore love afterward?

"A different kind of fool," Bush murmured, and then, after a moment, "A bigger fool."

Kathleen stirred and muttered at the sound of his voice. He lay still again, waiting for her to be quiet. Was what he'd said right, or was he just trying to convince himself? He had trouble being sure. At last, though, he nodded. Oh, if you lived your life in a shell, nothing could hurt you, but it was cramped and drab and lonely in there. Yes, you ran risks if you came out, but the world outside the shell was a nicer, freer place—and the company was better.

He slid out of bed and began to dress. The motion made Kathleen stir again. Lying there asleep, she looked absurdly young. Bushell sighed and shook his head. He wondered if he ought to wake her so she could put on whatever nightclothes she wore—and chuckled wryly as he realized he had no idea what those were. Silk negligee? Cotton nightshirt? Flannel pyjamas? So much he still had to learn about her.

He decided he didn't have the heart to disturb her. She was sleeping too contentedly, and he knew from too many long and wakeful nights how precious that was. He slipped toward the door. He started to set his hand on the knob, then turned back and blew Kathleen a kiss. No one saw it, not even her.

▼

"You're alarmingly cheerful this morning," Samuel Stanley said as he and Bushell waited for the lift to take them down to breakfast.

"Am I?" Bushell thought about that for a couple of seconds. "Well," he said, and smiled right in Stanley's face. His adjutant gave him a suspicious look; neither of them was normally at his best without a couple of cups of tea inside him.

Stanley peered down the hall. "The illustrious Dr. Flannery seems to be sleeping in this morning," he remarked. "She's just as likely to be up ahead of us, from what I've seen since Doshoweh."

Bushell nodded. "How's Phyllis doing?" he asked. That and the arrival of the lift served to distract Sam from thoughts of Kathleen Flannery.

Down in Parker's, Bushell was pouring milk into a cup of Darjeeling when Kathleen stood in the entranceway, looking around to spot him and Samuel Stanley. Both RAMs got to their feet as she came up to the table. Bushell pulled out a chair for her. "Thank you," she said brightly.

"My pleasure," Bushell answered, not least to see how she'd react. If she wanted to pretend in public that nothing had happened in the nighttime, that was her privilege.

Stanley grumbled something unintelligible down into his teacup, then spoke to the world at large: "Two grinning loobies at the table with me, no tea in 'em, no eggs, no bacon. If I didn't know better, I'd say both of you were smoking something you shouldn't be."

"You can check my cigar case if you like, Sam," Bushell said. Kathleen snorted a not quite ladylike snort.

The waiter came, took breakfast orders, and vanished as quickly and smoothly as if he'd fallen through a trap door. Samuel Stanley gulped down his tea, poured himself another cup, and pondered the peculiar breakfast riddle posed by companions who were not scowling and speaking in monosyllabic grunts. Sam's ruminations were quite visible. He was, Bushell realized, very likely to come up with four when he added two and two. What would happen then would be . . . interesting—one way or another.

Bushell was cutting a small, spicy pork link in half when Stanley let out a low, soft whistle. Being more inclined to meet difficulties head-on than to wait for them to come to him, Bushell asked, "Are you planning a second career as a steam locomotive, Sam?"

"Who, me?" His adjutant's face was the picture of innocence. "There's got to be more money in it than in what I'm doing now. I was going to say more travel, too, but that's not necessarily so, not when you think about how far we've been lately." Stanley didn't want to make an immediate issue of it, then. *Just as well,* Bushell thought, and ate the rest of the little sausage.

A few minutes later, Kathleen said, "Excuse me, please," and got up from the table. As she walked past Bushell on her way out of the restaurant, she let her hand rest affectionately on his back for a moment.

Samuel Stanley let out that low, thoughtful whistle again. Bushell glanced over at him, one eyebrow raised. Stanley began, "None of my business, but—"

"How right you are," Bushell cut in, hoping to nip things in the bud.

It didn't work. Stubbornly, Stanley went on, "If you'd met her in the regular way, I'd be cheering you on. I think she's good for you, and I think she's good people. But that's just it—I *think* those things. I don't *know* them. Are you sure of what you're doing, Chief? I mean, considering that—" Now he did stop.

"Considering that she's still a suspect of sorts," Bushell finished for him. "Is that what you mean?" Sam nodded, looking unhappy. Bushell said, "No, I'm not sure, and do you know what? I'm damned glad I'm not."

His adjutant frowned. "I don't follow."

"Every time I've been sure in this stinking case, I've been wrong," Bushell said. "So no, I'm not sure about Kathleen. I'm going to do whatever I do, and we'll just have to bloody well see how it works out in the end. If it doesn't—" He drained his own teacup. He knew too well that things didn't always work out to order. If this one didn't he wouldn't need to worry about Kathleen, or about the rest of his career, or about much of anything else, either.

He waited for Sam to scream at him, or take the more-in-sorrow-than-in-anger tone he used when he'd caught Bushell obviously in the wrong. Instead, to his amazement, his adjutant nodded. "You put it that way, Chief, all right. If you don't bet, you can't win."

That so closely paralleled Bushell's own thinking of the night before that he stared at Stanley. Before he could answer, Kathleen came back, her light green silk frock flowing about her as she walked.

She pointed a finger at him as she sat down once more. "The two of you have been talking about me again, haven't you? You dummy up like a couple of schoolboys whenever I get close enough to hear." Without pausing to let either Bushell or Stanley answer, she went on, "I suppose I'll just have to give you something to talk about, then, won't I?" She leaned forward and brushed her lips against Bushell's. Her eyes sparkled with amusement. "What do you think of that?"

"I," Bushell said solemnly, "like it."

Samuel Stanley took a slow, deliberate sip of tea. "The only times I've been sorry I was born a Negro," he declared, "are the ones when people can't see me blush."

Kathleen stared, convinced for a moment he was serious. In a severe voice, Bushell said, "You, sir, have been associating with me altogether too long."

The laughter from the table made heads turn all through Parker's. Bushell couldn't have cared less.

▼

Boston's muggy heat made the walk from the hotel to the RAM offices oppressive, even if it wasn't very long. Bushell envied Kathleen her cool silk dress. In his suit and waistcoat, cravat and fedora, he felt as if he were wearing his own portable steam bath.

Samuel Stanley was also sweating. He paused briefly to fan himself with his hat. Setting it back on his head, he said, "I think I may buy myself a straw boater. That might help fight the humidity a little."

"I was thinking the same thing," Bushell answered, "but if I do get myself a straw, the next clue we find will take us straight to Newfoundland, and I'll need a greatcoat instead."

"Things have worked out that way, haven't they?" Stanley said with a theatrical sigh. He touched the brim of his dark homburg. "First decent reason I've heard for keeping this."

Fans at the RAM offices stirred the sticky air without doing much to cool it. Indoors, though, Bushell and Stanley could take off their hats, which helped a little. Major George Harris greeted them with spread hands and a mournful expression. "Still no sign of your Kilbride, I'm afraid."

Bushell bit down on his cigar so that it jerked in his mouth. "I feared as much, the moment I came into town. Boston's too big; it has too many places to stay; and it has too many people who like the Sons of Liberty too well. What do we do next?"

Harris spread his hands. He was a slim fellow in his late thirties who wore muttonchop whiskers that didn't suit the shape of his face. "We keep looking, Colonel. I don't know what else we can do. If you have any suggestions beyond that, I'd be delighted to hear them."

"I'd be delighted to make them, too." Bushell tugged his shirt cuff away from his wrist and peered toward his elbow. "Nothing up my sleeve, worse luck."

"We have to do it the hard way," Samuel Stanley said. "Good old-fashioned police work, nothing else but."

The cigar jerked again. "We haven't got time for good old-fashioned police work," Bushell said. "The King-Emperor's yacht sails before long. The politicos will pay ransom to get *The Two Georges* back, sure as the devil they will."

"You're too right about that," Stanley said. He started to add something, then paused and scratched his head. "Matter of fact, I'd have expected more ransom demands—or at least threats—by now."

"Do you suppose the Sons have made some and they're keeping them quiet in Victoria?" Harris asked. "They wouldn't be proud of paying, even if—maybe especially if—they had to."

"It could be so, but I doubt it," Bushell said. Surely Sir Horace would have told him if the Sons had sent any messages either to RAM headquarters or to Sir Martin Luther King. When he went on, though, he picked a more publicly plausible reason: "If the Sons were making demands at the capital, they'd be making them in the newspapers, too."

"Yes, that's true," Harris said. "They've always been better at getting ink than they deserve. Pack of—" He glanced over at Kathleen Flannery; you could see him decide not to talk like a police officer. Instead, he went on, "In aid of which, any more thoughts on how you fared at *Common Sense* yesterday?"

"All things considered, quite well," Kathleen answered before either Bushell or Stanley could speak. Bushell raised an eyebrow; his adjutant coughed. Ignoring them both, Kathleen finished, "There was a good deal to consider, though."

"Er—yes." Major Harris sounded unenlightened. Bushell sympathized with him; he'd had that feeling after conversations with Kathleen, too. Valiantly, Harris tried to stay with her, asking, "Got some useful information, did you?"

"Not a bit," she said, her voice cheery.

Harris looked more bewildered than ever. Seeming to give up his questions for Kathleen as a bad job, he turned to Bushell and said, "We can put Kilbride's name and picture in the paper ourselves. If he's here, someone must have seen him."

Stanley looked worried. "I don't know about that," he said. "The ransom note they sent us said we weren't supposed to go after *The Two Georges*. If we did, something bad would happen to it. Having the Sons destroy it would be almost as bad as paying them their fifty million pounds."

"Officially," Bushell said in a musing voice, "officially, mind you, we don't know that Kilbride's involved with the theft of *The Two Georges*. Officially, we just suspect him of being involved with running Russian rifles from the Queen Charlotte Islands down to New Liverpool. If we were on the lookout for a gun runner, don't you think that would be news important enough to make the local papers?"

Harris's eyes gleamed. "That's perfect, Colonel. We'll play it exactly like that, as if we didn't have any other cares about him."

"Are you sure it'll be all right, Tom?" Kathleen Flannery asked anxiously. "The Sons of Liberty will know Kilbride's involved with more than the rifles. Won't they assume we know as much, too? And if they do assume that, what will they do to *The Two Georges*?" Keeping the painting safe plainly remained uppermost in her thoughts.

George Harris reached for a sheet of foolscap and a pencil and scribbled a note to himself. As he did so, he glanced over at Kathleen from under lowered lids. Bushell could all but read Harris's mind: she hadn't called him by his Christian name the day before. RAMs were trained to notice such things.

"I don't think they'll destroy *The Two Georges* till they're sure they won't be able to ransom it," he said. "If they were going to do that, they would have done it already. Am I sure it'll be all right, though?" He shook his head. As he had with Sam Stanley, he answered, "In this case, I'm not sure of anything. There's too much that doesn't add up yet."

"Do we dare take the chance, then?" Kathleen said.

"In my judgment, we haven't got any other choice," he said, and waited to see if that would make her boiler burst. She bit her lip but finally nodded. Whether that had anything to do with the previous night, he couldn't guess. He didn't know her well enough yet. *Looks as if I'm going to, though*, he thought, *and she me*. He hadn't felt that particular nervousness since he was in his twenties. He'd been comfortably intimate with Irene, and with no one else since he'd divorced her. He contemplated shells—and coming out of them.

"I'll plant the story in the *Globe*," Major Harris said. "That's our solid Tory paper, and I know the perfect fellow to ring up. The *Pilgrim* would likely give it the right slant, too. If it's all the same to you, though, I'll steer clear of the *New England Courant*. It's not that *Common Sense* owns the miserable rag, but it takes that kind of line."

"I leave the details in your hands," said Bushell, who hated leaving details in anyone's hands but his own. "You know Boston; we don't."

Harris scrawled more notes. "Let's see," he said, obviously thinking aloud, "do I want to ring Bill Tobin or Gabriel Pruitt over at the *Pilgrim*? Bill will run anything that has a juicy crime angle to it, but Gabe's less likely to ask me a pack of questions I can't conveniently answer."

That was a calculation with which Bushell could help. "Go with the fellow who doesn't ask questions," he said at once. "You're right—we can't afford to answer them."

"Good enough, Colonel. I'll tend to that directly," Harris said. "And, as I told you, I'll talk with Michael Young at the *Globe*, too. There won't be any difficulties with him; he's our unofficial mouthpiece in this town."

"Useful sort of fellow to have around," Bushell observed. He had his own pet reporters in New Liverpool—not that that had done him much good, since he hadn't had any good, or even interesting, news to give them after *The Two Georges* disappeared.

"That he is," Major Harris agreed complacently. "And what will you be doing while we wait to see if the stories flush our bird?"

"You mean, aside from gathering moss?" Bushell said, which got him a chuckle from Harris. "I expect I'll be on the telephone a good deal myself. Have you someone's desk I could usurp for the afternoon?"

"Two desks," Sam Stanley corrected. "I can split that load with you, Chief. We've left a trail all the way across the NAU."

"Three desks," Kathleen Flannery said. "I've been out of touch with my own colleagues since I left Doshoweh, and they may have come across something that hasn't reached the RAMs."

"I hardly think that's likely, Dr. Flannery," Major Harris said. He glanced toward Bushell, confident his fellow RAM—his fellow man—would support him.

"I don't know whether it's likely or not," Bushell said, "but it's already happened once with Kathleen." There—now he'd used her Christian name in public, too, and yes, Harris had noticed, and yes, Harris was drawing his own conclusions. Now that Bushell had shared a bed with Kathleen, he was in a way less eager to back her than he might have been before, for he knew he wasn't disinterested. Nevertheless, he was scrupulous about giving credit where due, so he went on, "Kilbride's an art collector, too. She may just come up with a line on him where we can't."

George Harris looked as if he'd bit into a lemon while expecting an orange. He put the best face he could on it, though, saying, "I'll see what I can find for you. If you'll wait here for a few minutes—"

By the look and smell of it, the room he got for the three of them probably belonged to sergeants or other such easily displaced types. Though they were gone, the memory of their cheap cigarillos lingered in the air. Their desks were old and battered; one of them had a paperbound novel stuck under a leg to hold it level. Some of the photographs on the walls, Bushell judged, were of suspects from cases that belonged to the RAMs here. Some were of crime scenes. And some, lovingly clipped from magazines, were of pretty young ladies—women, anyhow—wearing a good deal less than they might get by with in public.

Kathleen glanced at those, let out a loud sniff, and turned the battered desk chair in which she sat down away from the wall, letting her look out the window instead. As far as Samuel Stanley was concerned, the pretty girls might as well not have been there; he had eyes only for Phyllis. Bushell gave one smiling brunette a thoughtful and thorough inspection before he sat down and placed a call to Jaime Macias in New Liverpool.

He'd got used to waiting for a long-distance call to go through. When you made long-distance calls from places like Prince Rupert and Charleroi, you had to get used to waiting. But Boston was an important commercial hub, and had plenty of long-distance lines. Only a couple of minutes after Bushell picked up his telephone, the one on Macias's desk rang.

"Good to hear from you, Tom," the constabulary captain said when Bushell identified himself. "I was meaning to try to get in touch with you, because I have some news for you—"

George Harris burst into the sergeant's room. "Hold on a second, Jaime," Bushell said.

"Just got word," Harris exclaimed. "We've spotted Kilbride, over in Back Bay."

Bushell brought the handset back up to his mouth. "Jaime, I'll have to talk with you later," he said, and hung up.

# XII

▼

"THERE IS A GOD IN ISRAEL!" SAMUEL
Stanley exclaimed, slamming down the telephone in his hand.

"To say nothing of a British colonial undersecretary  holding the Sultan's
pasha to the straight and narrow," Bushell added less reverently. He turned to
Major Harris. "When and how did the tip come in?"

Harris pulled out his pocket watch and held it close to his face so he could
peer at the second hand speeding round its own little dial. "I got it three minutes
and—twenty-five seconds ago, now. Boston constable spotted the bugger—I beg
your pardon, Dr. Flannery—recognized him from the photograph you'd brought,
rang back to his station, and his lieutenant phoned me straightaway."

"Was he going to try to make the arrest himself?" Bushell demanded. "He
won't be armed, poor devil, and the Sons of Liberty pack a bigger punch than
anything a city constable will be expecting."

To his relief, Harris shook his head. "No, sir. The constables know he's our
fish. The chap who spotted him—McGinnity, his name is—is hanging back,
making sure the villain doesn't come out of the shop he's gone into."

"What sort of shop is that?" Bushell said, but then waved the question aside.
"Never mind. Take us back to the Parker House so Sam and I can get our pistols,
and then to—Back Bay, did you call it?"

Harris nodded. "Otherwise known as the Fens—reclaimed land, you know,
the same sort of thing the Dutchmen have done." He seemed to remember Kathleen was in the room, too. "You'll want to stay here, of course, Dr. Flannery, until
we bag the elusive Mr. Kilbride."

"In a pig's ear I will," she replied politely. "Having come this far, I do not intend to be held away from anyone who may know where *The Two Georges* is."

"Now really, Dr. Flannery—" Harris began. "I'm sure Colonel Bushell will
tell you this is no place for—"

"Let her come along, Major," Bushell said. Harris stared at him as if he
couldn't believe his ears. Kathleen's face lit up like a sunrise; from the glad surprise she showed, she hadn't expected him to back her, either. Samuel Stanley
could have given the Buddha lessons in inscrutability.

"Now really, Colonel," Harris repeated; evidently *now really* was what he
said when he meant, *Are you out of your mind?*

Bushell also repeated himself: "Let her come along." Kathleen's grin made

254

her look very fresh and young; it made him feel like grinning, too. He didn't. The reasons he wanted her with him weren't all flattering to her, not by a long chalk. In case he was wrong, disastrously wrong, about her, he didn't care to leave her here with a telephone and no one keeping an eye on her. If she knew where to call, she could do the case a hideous amount of damage.

"Colonel, I trust you know what you are about," Major Harris said in a tone that belied the words. "I wash my hands of the responsibility for injecting a civilian into the middle of a police investigation. Let me call a steamer to take you to your hotel and then to the scene." He executed a military about-turn of alarming precision and stalked away.

"Well, well." Bushell make hand-washing motions. "I didn't know Pontius Pilate had joined the RAMs."

Sam Stanley tried to suppress a snort and ended up with a coughing fit instead. When he could speak again, he said, "Go easy on him, Chief. He'll do what you told him to do, and that's what counts."

Major Harris reappeared. "If you will come with me, Colonel, Captain . . . Dr. Flannery." He might have carved her name from ice. He wasn't looking at her, though; he was looking at Bushell. *Giving your lady friend a thrill, are you, and a chance to see how brave and clever you are?* his eyes said.

Bushell tried to make his own face answer, *It's not like that, dammit.* He didn't think he had any luck getting the silent message across. He couldn't say it out loud, either, not without getting into more hot water. Shrugging, he followed Harris down to the underground carpark: space for such amenities of modern life was far tighter here than in New Liverpool.

"This is Sergeant Scriver," Harris said, nodding to a fellow at the wheel of a Morse steamer that had seen better days. "He'll take you to the Parker House, and then on to Back Bay. *I* shall go there directly." He did another about-turn, this one as sharp as the last; he must have been practicing.

"You bit him like a flea, didn't you?" Scriver remarked, not sounding altogether dismayed at seeing Major Harris irked. "Pile on in, folks; the teakettle's all nice and hot and ready to roll."

Scriver pulled up in front of the Parker House a couple of minutes later. Bushell and Stanley got out. A valet came over to warn Scriver away from the restricted parking area. He routed the functionary with his badge.

Bushell belted on his pistol, then hurried back to the bank of lifts to go downstairs again. He'd moved as fast as he could, but found Sam Stanley there before him. Stanley was tugging at his jacket, trying to make it do a better job of concealing the telltale bulge on his hip. He wasn't having much luck.

"I already gave up on that," Bushell said. "We'll have to look like a couple of bandits till we get out to the motorcar."

They did, too; both the lift operator and the elderly woman in mourning black who was already in the car drew back in alarm and stared at the two RAMs with frightened eyes. Bushell recognized the temptation to draw his revolver and put a round through the ceiling of the lift as the ignoble impulse it was, which didn't stop him from enjoying it.

He enjoyed almost running into Michael Shaughnessy halfway across the lobby much less. Whatever you cared to say about his politics—and Bushell might have said a great deal, however little of it would have been complimentary—the reporter had sharp eyes. "Armed, are you?" he said, spotting the pistol under Bushell's herringbone coat. "And whose funeral are you off to arrange?"

"Yours, maybe, if you don't move aside," Bushell answered. He didn't sound as if he relished the prospect, whatever he might have thought. But he didn't sound as if he'd shrink from it, either.

Shaughnessy got out of his way in a hurry. The man from *Common Sense* scowled, perhaps angry at his feet for being faster to heed Bushell than the rest of him had wanted. "You're worse than Bonaparte's dragoons," he shouted, shaking his fist. "Doing a tyrant's bidding was all they knew, but you—"

"Why, Mr. Shaughnessy," Bushell said, his eyes wide and innocent, "haven't I heard you apply that name to His Majesty the King-Emperor? You use his laws to protect yourself, and at the same time want to overthrow him? What a surprise when you find you can't do both at once." He strode out the door, ignoring the people Shaughnessy's shout had startled.

Sergeant Scriver made a turn into oncoming traffic that had Bushell cringing and laughing at the same time—police officers everywhere drove as if they were exempt from the traffic laws they upheld for everyone else. Blaring horns and rude gestures expressed the Bostonians' opinion of the maneuver.

Ignoring the unsolicited editorials, Scriver steamed past Kings Chapel, a stately church that had gone up in colonial days, then swung left onto Beacon Street. The turn was not a neat perpendicular, as it would have been in New Liverpool or Doshoweh or even Charleroi. The streets of downtown Boston seemed to have been laid out by someone who'd never heard of neat perpendiculars. They intersected one another at seemingly random angles and, for good measure, changed name every block.

When Bushell remarked on that, Sergeant Scriver laughed out loud. "From all I've heard, nobody ever laid these streets out, Colonel. They used to be cattle tracks, till one day they paved 'em." He sounded serious. Boston was old enough that the story had a chance of being true.

Once they rode past the broad meadow of the Boston Common, the streets did begin to follow a grid pattern that made some sort of sense. Back Bay, though, was a newer part of the city, which lent some backhanded support to Scriver's tale.

At the western edge of the Common, the sergeant swung south on Arlington to Boylston and then west again. "We've got ourselves a couple-three miles to go," he said. "Address Major Harris gave me is Lansdowne near Ipswich, way out in the Fens." He sighed. "Not much good happens in that part of town, and hasn't for a long, long time."

He turned right onto Lansdowne and pulled to a stop in the middle of a block full of shops that looked dedicated to one purpose and one purpose only: separating the none-too-discriminating customer from whatever small store of shillings he might possess without giving him anything worth having in return. Bushell stared in pained disbelief at the bright red socks on display in a haberdasher's window. Who would wear such things, and why?

George Harris, looking altogether too dapper to belong on Lansdowne Street, came up to Scriver's motorcar. "Kilbride was observed going into Yawkey's Tea Shoppe"—he pronounced the last word as if it had two syllables, so the name of the place nearly rhymed—"by Senior Constable McGinnity, as I told you back at the station, Colonel. He has not been observed to leave."

"Has the place got a back door?" Samuel Stanley asked.

"It does, but the alley on which it opens has only one egress"—Harris pointed to show where that was—"and McGinnity has been able to keep it and the front entrance to the tea shop under observation at the same time." Now the RAM pronounced *shop* in a normal fashion.

Bushell glanced over at McGinnity, who was leaning against a lamppost trying to pretend he wasn't doing anything in particular. The pretense wasn't worth much: if you needed a stage Irishman to play a constable, McGinnity would have been your man. He was big and beefy, red-faced and knobby-cheekboned, with red hair now drifted with gray. Throw in his uniform and he was about as inconspicuous as a chimp in church.

In thoughtful tones, Bushell asked, "Could Kilbride have gone into the Yawkey's place, out the back door into the alley, and then into another shop on Lansdowne here?"

Harris glanced over to Senior Constable McGinnity. He might not approve of having Kathleen Flannery along here, but he was no fool. "That would complicate our lives, wouldn't it?" He glanced back over his shoulder. "We'll have the manpower to find out, though."

Several constabulary steamers rolled to a stop. Big, burly men in uniform piled out of them. By their looks, a fair number could have been McGinnity's cousins. More motorcars pulled up at the corner of Lansdowne and Ipswich. The men who got out of them wore suits and waistcoats. Bushell had seen several of those fellows at the RAM station.

"All right, we can search the area," he said. He unbuttoned his jacket so he could get at his revolver in a hurry. Sam Stanley had already done the same thing. Bushell said, "Let's have a look at Yawkey's Tea Shoppe, Sam."

"Right, Chief," Stanley said.

"You want backup?" Harris asked quietly.

He'd had all the backup in the world at Buckley Bay. "We'll go first, anyhow," he answered, and started down the street. Stanley matched him stride for stride. Harris waited behind him, respecting his judgment. Kathleen Flannery, on the other hand, started after him. Hearing her footsteps on the paving slates behind him, he turned around. "Go on back, Kathleen. This is what they pay us to do. It's not your job."

"It's my painting," she said stubbornly. "I won't get in your way, but I want to do whatever I can to help."

Bushell exhaled through his nose. "The last time I went after the Sons of Liberty, I watched a good man get killed before my eyes because he didn't take them seriously enough. I'm not keen to run the same risk twice. Now will you go back, or shall I get a pair of manacles from Senior Constable McGinnity?"

Kathleen glowered fiercely, but halted. Bushell wouldn't have bet that she was going to. He and Stanley walked past a chemist's, a bakery, an ironmonger's shop, and a cabinetmaker's establishment that looked too fine for the neighborhood. A very fat, very blond man was examining the inlay work on a table by the front window.

A tavern, a tobacconist's, a fish market . . . Yawkey's Tea Shoppe was only a few doors away now. Bushell heard the sound of a woman's pumps clacking up the street after him. Samuel Stanley sent him a glance that said only one thing: *I told you so.*

"God damn it," he muttered under his breath. He didn't know whether he was angry at Kathleen for not listening to him (though when had she ever listened to him?) or at Major Harris for not keeping her in better check (though Harris undoubtedly figured she was Bushell's problem). Then he realized he didn't have to divide things up. He could be angry at both of them at once—and he was.

If he caused a scene on the street, he was liable to spook Kilbride—assuming Kilbride wasn't spooked already, a dubious proposition at best. Ignoring Kathleen also gave him the chance to savor his anger and let it grow. He stalked on toward the tea shop.

He'd just set his hand on the door latch when Kathleen stopped. That made him turn around where anger hadn't—had she had a sudden rush of brains to the head? He supposed stranger things had happened, though he was hard-pressed to think of one offhand.

Kathleen was staring into the window of the cabinetmaker's shop. *She can't possibly be shopping*, ran through Bushell's mind, though he didn't know what else she could be doing. After a moment, she started running again, not back down toward the steamer that had brought her, but up Lansdowne toward Bushell. Scowling, he turned away from her and started to go into the tea shop. "Wait, Tom!" she called urgently. "Please wait!"

"Why the devil should I?" he demanded as she came panting up to him. "I told you to—"

"To hell with what you told me," she said. She'd calculated that nicely; hearing her swear startled him into brief silence. She took advantage of that to go on, "That fat man in the front of the cabinetmaker's—I know him." She corrected herself: "I've seen him before, anyhow. I don't know who he is, but I've seen him."

Bushell believed her. He'd noticed the fat man himself. If you'd seen him once, you'd remember him. Whether that meant anything was a different question. "Where did you see him?" he asked.

Kathleen didn't even take any vindictive pleasure in dropping her bombshell: "At the showing of *The Two Georges* in Victoria, just after it got here from London, and then again when the exhibition moved up to Philadelphia." She surprised Bushell by laughing. "In a cutaway, he looks rather like a penguin that's swallowed a watermelon."

Bushell brushed at his mustache with a forefinger. Then, almost absentmindedly, he leaned forward and kissed Kathleen half on the mouth, half on the cheek. "And how will he look in a different suit?" he said, his voice musing. "One decorated with the broad arrow, I mean."

"Shall we go find out, Chief?" Stanley said.

"Yes, I think we'd better," Bushell said. "We're liable to come up with Kilbride at the same time, too, with only a little bit of luck." He turned to Kathleen. "Will you please wait here now?"

"After I've come this far? Not bloody likely." Again, her deliberate vulgarity surprised Bushell, but it didn't make him change his mind. The only way he could keep her back, though, was to have Sam hold her, and he didn't want to do that. Shoulder to shoulder with Stanley, he started down Lansdowne toward the cabinetmaker's. He hoped Kathleen would at least have the sense to walk behind the two of them rather than alongside.

He didn't get much chance to test that hope, because he'd taken only a couple of strides when the fat man came out onto the pavement. He looked down the street toward Kathleen. "He recognized her, too," Stanley said softly.

"So he did," Bushell answered, his voice just as quiet. Of itself, his right hand slid to the butt of his revolver. The fat man had his right hand jammed down in to the right outer pocket of his jacket. Bushell wouldn't have liked that under any circumstances. After the gun battle at Buckley Bay, he liked it even less.

The fat man looked at him and Stanley and Kathleen, and at the carloads of RAMs behind them at the corner of Lansdowne and Ipswich. He turned his head, a quick, nervous gesture, and spotted the Boston constables down toward Boylston. Even at a distance of thirty or forty yards, Bushell saw him lick his lips: his tongue was very wet and pink.

"Sir, we'd like to talk with you," Bushell said, taking another step or two toward him. "Do you know a man named Joseph Kilbride?"

"I don't have to talk to you," the fellow answered, his voice a foghorn bass. "I don't have to do anything you tell me to, not one damn thing, do you hear me?"

"Careful, Chief," Stanley muttered out of the side of his mouth. "He's as ready to go as a handful of fulminate."

"Don't I know it," Bushell whispered back. He raised his voice and spoke to the fat man again: "Take it easy, pal. Nobody's going to—"

"I'm not your pal!" the fat man shouted. He looked back over his shoulder at the constables. They'd moved toward him while his attention was fixed on Bushell. He made as if to retreat back into the furniture shop.

"Hold it right there!" Bushell said sharply.

Instead of obeying, the man yanked his hand out of his pocket and hurled what looked like a large, dun-colored egg at Bushell. "Grenade!" Samuel Stanley shouted, yanking out his pistol and throwing himself flat at the same time.

Bushell used his forearm to knock Kathleen Flannery to the pavement. She screamed. He didn't care. He dove down on top of her, shielding her with his body. As it had in the Queen Charlotte Islands, time seemed to stretch like taffy. He drew his own revolver, clenched left hand on right wrist as prescribed in the manual of arms, and aimed the weapon at the fat man.

Stanley fired. The grenade exploded. Instead of stretching, time suddenly crumpled in on itself, so that everything happened at once. Bushell squeezed the trigger. The revolver roared and bucked in his hand at the same instant as what felt like a couple of red-hot needles drilled into his right leg and Kathleen screamed again.

The fat man jerked as if stung. He performed an awkward pirouette, his arms flailing to help him keep his balance. Stanley fired again. So did Bushell, at almost the identical moment. One of those shots—Bushell was never sure which—caught the fat man in the side of the head. He crashed to the pavement, surely dead before he hit it. Bright red in the summer sun, a pool of blood spread beneath him and poured over the kerb into the gutter.

Bushell's ears rang. The stench of smokeless powder was thick in his nostrils. His heart pounded crazily. Kathleen Flannery writhed beneath him. All unbidden, his thoughts went back to the night before. How different that had been! He scrambled to his feet. "You all right?" he asked, including both her and Sam in the question.

"Yes, I'm fine," Stanley said. "God in heaven, gunplay twice now—three times, if you count Tricky Dick." He rose too and, revolver still in hand, walked toward the body of the fat man.

Kathleen took stock of herself. The green dress was filthy and had a hole above one knee. Her elbow was scraped raw, and a fragment of grenade casing had scored a bleeding furrow along one arm. "I'm all right," she said, as if she didn't quite believe it herself. "Thank you, Tom." Then her eyes went to the corpse on the pavement. "Oh, God," she whispered. She'd seen violent death twice now in a matter of weeks, twice more than the average civilian saw in a lifetime. Still whispering, she asked, "How are you, Tom?"

"I'll find out." Bushell's trousers were out at the knee, too. He wasn't sure he would be able to put weight on his right leg, but it held him as he walked, though blood ran down into his shoe. He pulled up his trouser leg. Like Kathleen, he had gashes from grenade fragments, but they didn't look deep or serious.

He reached down and helped her to her feet. Almost absently, he asked, "Now do you see why I asked you not to come with me?"

She nodded, but then she said, "If I hadn't, you never would have recognized the fat man, would you?"

"No, I don't suppose we would," Bushell admitted. His tone of voice changed as he added, "I'm glad you're not badly hurt." He didn't care to think about what might have happened had they been standing up when the grenade went off.

He followed Sam Stanley toward the fat man's corpse. All along Lansdowne Street, shopkeepers had come out of their establishments to see what the gunfire meant. They stared in disbelief at the body on the pavement. Had they heard gunfire more often, they would have had the sense to take cover instead of running out to investigate. Bushell envied them their quiet, secure little worlds.

Major Harris was also approaching the cabinetmaker's shop. "Have you got a weapon?" Bushell called to him. When he shook his head, Bushell waved him back: "Then get out of the line of fire." Whoever ran the cabinetmaker's hadn't come out with the rest of the local merchants. Bushell did not think that boded well.

Stanley had not gone right up to the dead body; he'd halted where nobody could shoot at him from the doorway of the cabinetmaker's. The door was slightly ajar. Bushell glanced at Stanley. "We go in?" he said. It sounded like a question, but it wasn't.

"We go in," Stanley said with a nod. "We've got the guns, looks like we'll need them, and it doesn't look like anybody else thought to bring any."

"Nobody believes it till it happens in his backyard." Bushell tried to remember what he'd seen about the layout of the cabinetmaker's shop when he walked past it on his way to Yawkey's. He said, "I'll go in first and break to the left. You're taller than I am; that'll give you a shot over my shoulder."

"Got it." Stanley shook his head. "And I thought I was done with combat. On three?" He didn't wait for Bushell to agree, but started counting: "One, two . . ."

Yelling like fiends, they ran for the door. Bushell hit it with his shoulder. It flew open. He dashed inside. Behind the counter stood two men. He recognized Joseph Kilbride's tough Irish face, twisted now into a grimace of hate. "Hold it!" he screamed.

Kilbride was already holding it—a grenade like the one the fat man had thrown. He'd pulled the pin; he was holding the detonator down with his thumb. He drew back his arm. Bushell remembered a Franco-Spanish grenadier springing up from behind a rock, somewhere near the Nuevespañolan border. The man standing beside Kilbride—perhaps the proprietor of the shop—dropped to the floor.

As Kilbride's arm started to come forward, Bushell and Stanley both fired. One slug hit Kilbride in the chest, the other in the flattened bridge of the nose. He let out a grunt of astonishment and toppled. His grenade fell beside him— and beside the man who'd taken shelter in back of the counter. A moment later, the grenade detonated. Casing fragments rattled off the walls and ceiling. A bubbling shriek burst from the throat of Kilbride's companion, then faded.

Pistols still at the ready, Bushell and Stanley ran around the counter to see what they could do to keep the fellow from expiring on the spot. As soon as they saw him, they looked at each other in dismay. The grenade had fallen by his face and neck. Fragments must have cut his carotids, for he was bleeding like a butchered hog.

"We'll never save him," Bushell said. "No point to trying."

Stanley looked down at his face once more—or rather, the shattered bone and burnt and diced meat where his face had been. "You're right, Chief," he said in a faraway voice. "Lucky for him that we can't, too."

Bushell made himself turn away from the horridly compelling sight. He waved the barrel of his revolver toward the open door to the back room. "We'd better see if we've missed anyone," he said, adding, "It would be nice if we had someone left alive to question, don't you think?"

"Could be useful, yes," Stanley answered, matching him dry for dry. "Shall I go first this time?"

"I'm still shorter than you are," Bushell said. "One, two . . . " They ran through the doorway one after the other.

Instead of powder and blood and the latrine stink of bowels loosed in sudden death, the back room smelled of sawdust and varnish and turpentine—clean, friendly odors that grated on Bushell's keyed-up senses. He spun wildly, looking for an enemy who was not there. Sam Stanley kicked over what was going to be a tabletop that leaned against the wall. No one crouched behind it.

Bushell went to the door leading to the alley. He opened it and peered outside. No one waited with a gun or another grenade. The alley was as empty as it might have been at midnight.

"I think that's everybody," Bushell sounded disbelieving, even to himself. He closed the alley door again and locked it.

"I think you're right." Stanley shook his head. "Dear sweet Lord, what a mess we have here." With a soldier's practicality and a baring of teeth that was not a grin, he added, "We came out on the right end of it this time, too."

Bushell was about to nod when voices came from the front of the store. He and Stanley stared at each other. Neither Kilbride nor his chum could possibly be breathing—could he? One thing Bushell remembered from his army days was that human beings could be devilishly hard to kill. Even so—

"Impossible," he mouthed to Stanley. His adjutant nodded, but then waggled his hand back and forth, downgrading the word to something like *damned unlikely.*

Moving quietly as they could, they went back to the door that had admitted them to the room on the alley. Bushell's gun barrel went into the doorway before he stuck out his head.

"Major, you're very brave, but you're also very foolish," he said, standing straight and showing himself. George Harris had just come into the shop by the street entrance, a constabulary truncheon clutched in his right fist. Bushell pointed the index finger of his left hand at the RAM. "Bang! You're dead."

Harris shrugged. "The chance one takes in this business now and again." Bushell admired his nonchalance, if not his good sense.

Behind Harris crowded a couple of other RAMs, a couple of uniformed constables, and Kathleen Flannery. One corner of Bushell's mouth turned down. As he'd told her, mixing it with villains was not her business. Then his expression cleared, to be replaced by one of mild surprise. Villains might not be her business, but after last night he definitely was.

She pushed her way up to stand at Major Harris's elbow. None of the police officers seemed to have the nerve to stop her. Bushell understood that down to the ground. "Are you all right?" she demanded, and started to shove past Harris.

"Not a scratch on me or Sam, except from where we hit the pavement," Bushell assured her. He held up a hand. "You don't want to come any farther, Kathleen. It's—not pretty back of the counter there."

For a wonder, she heeded him. Major Harris did come up to look at the carnage. He went faintly green. "Good heavens," he murmured. "We've not seen anything like *this* in a good many years." He ran a finger under his collar, as if to loosen it. "I tell you frankly, I could have gone a good many more years without it, too."

"There is that," Bushell agreed. "Here we have the late Mr. Kilbride." Nodding at the other corpse, he added, "Could Constable McGinnity tell us if this is—or rather, was—the proprietor of the establishment here?"

Major Harris looked at that body, then averted his eyes. "At the moment, I doubt whether his mother could tell who he was. McGinnity may perhaps know him by his clothing, though, so we'll find out about that."

"Careful there!" someone out on the sidewalk exclaimed, at the same time as someone else was going, "Watch out!" That sounded interesting—and alarming—enough to send Bushell and Stanley out to see what was going on. The RAMs had been searching the pockets of the fat man. One of them held in the palm of his hand a khaki-painted metal spheroid a bit bigger than a cricket ball. "Grenade," he said unnecessarily.

"Russian Army model," Samuel Stanley put in.

"If you say so," the Boston RAM answered with a shrug. "Far as I'm concerned, it's bad enough no matter who made it." For him it was just evidence of depravity, not evidence in a case.

His colleague had found a wallet in the fat man's left hip pocket. He opened it. "Here's his permit to operate a motorcar," he said, drawing forth one of the documents within. "Gives his name as Eustace Venable; his home address is in Georgestown, province of Maryland." He pawed through the wallet. "A little stack of business cards in here, too: Eustace Venable, Fine Cabinetry, and another Georgestown address, with a telephone number."

"Georgestown." Bushell tasted the word. "Right next door to Victoria. Why does that not surprise me?" He glanced up to the heavens, as if expecting a choir of angels to come down and announce he ought to be surprised.

Instead, Sam Stanley said quietly, "We should have known the trail would lead us there sooner or later."

"That's true," Bushell said. The King-Emperor was coming to Victoria— coming all too soon now. Bushell still had no idea whether *The Two Georges* was in or around the capital, but it seemed inevitable that some of the people who had stolen it would be there.

"Begging your pardon, sir," someone said behind him. He turned. It was Senior Constable McGinnity. The big Irishman went on, "Sir, I think that's Mr. Cavendish in there, though with him so torn up and all I've the devil's own time being sure."

"His papers and his fingerprints will identify him for certain," Bushell said. "Do you know whether he's got a wife or children?"

"Neither the one nor t'other," McGinnity answered. "He lived by his lonesome, Mr. Cavendish did. I've heard tell he was—you know"—a delicate shrug of the shoulders conveyed what Bushell was supposed to know—"but I can't say for a fact that that's so."

"If he was, he won't have let the other Sons find out," Bushell said. "They're harder on that sort of thing that the Crown's law courts ever dreamt of being."

A couple of constables came toward the cabinetmaker's shop along with a red-faced, gray-haired man with broad shoulders. One of them said to Bushell, "Sir, here's Mr. Yawkey from the tea shop back yonder. Reckoned you might be interested in having a word or two with him."

"Why, so I might," Bushell said, as if the notion hadn't crossed his mind till that moment. But his air of nonchalance fell away like a discarded cloak when he rounded on Yawkey. "So—you and Joseph Kilbride were friends, eh?"

"You might say so," Yawkey answered. "We've always got on well, anyway."

Bushell rubbed at his mustache. He hadn't expected such a forthright admission. Maybe Yawkey would sing like a crooner on the wireless. "And what did your friend"—he fought hard to keep an ironic twist off the word—"talk about when he dropped in on you today?"

"Why, tea, of course," Yawkey exclaimed, his shaggy eyebrows rising in surprise at the question. "What else?"

"Tea?" Bushell echoed, taken aback.

"Sir, if a man comes into a tea shop to ask after shoe-blacking, wouldn't you say he's in the wrong place?" Yawkey inquired with exaggerated patience; he'd evidently decided Bushell was on the slow side. "I've been selling tea to Joseph Kilbride for more than twenty years. He came in to ask after some Orange Pekoe."

Bushell muttered something under his breath. If all you thought about was Joseph Kilbride the Son of Liberty, you were liable to forget Joseph Kilbride the grocer. "Has he been traveling to Boston to buy from you in person for all that time?" he asked after pausing to think.

Yawkey shook his big, blunt-featured head. "Up until three or four years ago, we dealt entirely by post. But he's come into Boston several times now. I enjoy his company." He chuckled at Bushell's expression. "Oh, I'd guess he's not the easiest sort for most to get along with. But him and me, we were both in the prize ring a time or three, and we tell stories long into the night. Him and Phineas Stanage, the brewer down in Victoria, it's the same thing with them."

So Kilbride hadn't got his nose bent by accident then. But that was only a small part of what went through Bushell's mind. "Three or four years?" he murmured, as much to himself as to Yawkey. Business trips into Boston would have given Kilbride a perfect cover for any other visits he made here. And Stanage wasn't just a brewer; all the RAMs in Victoria knew perfectly well he was a Son of Liberty, though nobody had been able to prove a thing—not till now, anyway.

"I can give you exact dates, if you like," Yawkey answered. "I'll have 'em all written down in my account books."

"I may take you up on that," Bushell said, his voice still abstracted. Had the plot to steal *The Two Georges* been ripening for four years? Or had Kilbride got involved in it only lately? He couldn't ask the man now.

Samuel Stanley said, "Why did you let Kilbride go out your back door and down the alley?"

"We spent a deal of time in the storeroom in back of the shop," Yawkey answered. "He was buying in bulk and seeing for himself what all I had back there. Let me think back, so I can tell you just how it was. . . . We'd come close to finishing when he went to the front for a moment. Then he came back and just sort of asked if he could stroll out that way. I told him there wasn't anything to see in the alley but rubbish bins, but I didn't think much about it at the time."

"He must have spied McGinnity being inconspicuous," Stanley said to Bushell, who nodded.

"Can I go back to my shop now?" Yawkey asked. "I'm the only one minding it, and I'm apt to be losing trade standing around here making chitchat."

"A couple of more questions," Mr. Yawkey," Bushell said. The merchant's brows came down like shutters; he wasn't used to hearing no. Bushell pointed over to the cabinetmaker's shop in front of which they all stood. "How long has Mr. Cavendish been in business here?"

"Him?" By the tone, Yawkey's opinion of the late cabinetmaker was not high. Part of the reason emerged in his reply: "He's a Johnny-come-lately, he is: bought the place from old Fred Jenkins maybe four years back. Hasn't done any too well with it, either," he added with a certain somber satisfaction.

"Isn't that interesting?" Sam Stanley said, and Bushell nodded again. If the timing was coincidental, it made for a very large and robust coincidence.

"Did Joseph Kilbride ever go into Cavendish's shop before or after he came to yours?" Bushell asked Yawkey.

"I never saw him do it, but I don't know what that proves. I'm better at minding my own business than my neighbors'."

Most of the time, people who said things like that were lying through their teeth. Bushell got the feeling Yawkey was telling the truth. He said, "That's all for now. We may have more questions for you later."

"If you do, ask 'em in the shop," Yawkey said firmly. "Good day to you." He stumped on up Lansdowne Street as if it had been made for no one but him.

Major Harris came out of the furniture shop. "We'll need a statement from you, Colonel, and one from Captain Stanley, and one from Dr. Flannery, too. The forms must be observed, as you know."

"Oh, indeed they must," Bushell said. "In triplicate." It would be a long afternoon's journey into night. And the Boston papers would have a field day, too. Three men killed in the course of an investigation? Gunfire? Hand grenades? Newsboys would be shouting extras on the street corners tomorrow morning— no, more likely tonight. Well, soonest begun, soonest done. "Let's go," he said.

▼

Sitting on the edge of Kathleen Flannery's bed, Bushell blew a smoke ring toward the ceiling. She made silent clapping motions, which set her bare breasts bobbing prettily.

Bushell didn't feel like applause. He walked over to the bottle of Jameson he'd ordered from room service, poured a glass three-quarters full, and then, after due reflection, used silver-plated tongs to add a couple of ice cubes.

Standing there naked by the chest of drawers on which he'd put the bottle, he said, "Victoria," and then drank. It was not a toast. It was nothing like a toast. It was more on the order of getting the taste of the word out of his mouth.

But neither the whiskey's complex, smoky flavor nor the burning it set up in his belly could take away that taste. No matter what happened here in Boston, no matter what the local RAMs and constables turned up, his trail, as best he could see it, led straight on toward the capital of the NAU.

He hated the idea.

Kathleen watched him gulp down the glass of Jameson, pour himself another, and pour that one down, too. "Fix me a drink, please," she said. "With some water, not just ice."

"I thought you'd sooner have gin," he said.

"I would," she answered, "but this will be all right. After the grilling in the RAM offices, anything this side of chloroform would be all right."

He grunted, took another crystal tumbler from its silver tray, put in ice and poured Jameson over it, then had to walk into the bathroom for some water. When he came back and handed Kathleen the glass, she murmured a word of thanks and patted the mattress beside her.

Bushell sat down. She sipped her drink. Her eyes widened slightly. "You didn't put in much water."

"You didn't ask for much," he said. After a moment, he pointed a finger at her. "I know what you're doing." Two fast knocks of Jameson hadn't fuzzed his thoughts, but they might have made him less reticent about letting her know what those thoughts were: "You're distracting me."

"Why, Colonel Bushell, sir, I certainly do hope so," she said, and stretched just enough to make his eye travel the whole long, smooth length of her: a length marred at the moment by gauze pads and adhesive tape on both knees, a forearm, and one elbow. Bushell was similarly decorated.

He grunted again, this time in amusement. "Not what I meant—and you know it," he added, stabbing out that accusing forefinger once more. "If I'm making drinks for you, I can't very well be making any for me, and if I don't make them for me, I can't very well drink them, and if I don't drink them I can't very well get drunk—now can I?"

"No," she answered, a little angrily. "And why should you want to, anyway? The only people I knew who turned the name Victoria into a swear word were the Sons of Liberty—till you."

"And do you know what else?" he said after mulling that over. "We have the exact same reason, too." He waited for her to gape at him, and was not disappointed. Then he explained: "The Sons think Victoria, just by existing, puts a control on them they don't want to accept."

"Yes, of course they do," she said. "But if there's any man in the NAU more loyal to Crown and Country than you, I haven't met him."

"For which I thank you," Bushell said, even if he wasn't altogether sure she'd meant it as a compliment. "And as long as I'm in Prince Rupert or Doshoweh or Charleroi or even here in Boston, I'm the man who's in charge of getting *The Two Georges* back for Crown and Country, too."

He wondered if she would understand what he was driving at. She did: a point for her. "I see," she breathed, nodding slowly and thoughtfully. "When we get to Victoria, you won't be able to handle the case your way any more. You'll be under orders from your—commandant, is that the right title?"

"That's the right title," Bushell agreed. "Lieutenant General Sir Horace Bragg and I are old friends, but that makes things worse, not better. When Sir Horace gets orders from the governor-general, he has to hit me with them twice as hard as he would otherwise, just to let people know his friend isn't getting any special treatment. I understand why he does it, but that doesn't make life easy for me."

"A man of antique virtue," Kathleen said. Was she being ironic? He couldn't tell. She drank from the tumbler again. "That's not bad," she murmured, her voice judicious. "Different from Scotch. But what sort of orders that you won't like is the governor-general likely to give Sir Horace to pass to you?"

"Arrangements for paying ransom for *The Two Georges* comes to mind," Bushell answered bleakly.

He wondered how she'd take that; given her position, she was liable to want the painting back at any price. What she said, though, was, "Sir Martin Luther King strikes me as having more spine than that."

"If we were speaking only of Sir Martin, I'd say you were right," Bushell answered. "But his chief of staff is Sir David Clarke, and Sir David has all the spine of your average—actually your rather subpar—blancmange."

Kathleen's eyes glinted; maybe it was the Irish in her reacting to the prospect of a feud. "You don't sound as if you like Sir David Clarke," she observed, drawing out *like* to exaggerate the innuendo in her words.

"As a matter of fact, I don't," Bushell said. He regretted those two drinks; without them, he wouldn't have spoken so much of his mind. Now, unless he got lucky, he was going to have to say a lot more.

He didn't get lucky. "And why is that?" Kathleen asked. Sure enough, she did scent a feud, and she wouldn't be happy—more to the point, she wouldn't shut up—till she found out what was going on, and why.

Bushell got up from the bed and poured himself another tumbler of Jameson. In spite of Kathleen's disapproving look, he drank it down in a couple of swallows. Two drinks weren't enough to ready him for what he had to tell her. By the time he was through with the sordid story of Irene and Sir David, he'd had more than three, also.

He smiled crookedly at Kathleen. "Now you know how I come by the uneven tenor of my ways."

"So I do," she said, and then went on in a meditative voice, "When I found out Kyril had another fiancée, at least I didn't do it by finding him in bed with that other fiancée. I hadn't thought my situation had much to recommend it, but I see I had something to be thankful for after all."

"That's true." Bushell's words came out clear enough, but slightly lower than they should have, as if emerging from a wind-up phonogram whose spring was starting to wear out. Ever so casually, he scratched at the tip of his nose. He couldn't feel it. Yes, he'd had considerably more than three drinks.

He waited for Kathleen to say something sympathetic, or possibly—and even better—something unkind about Sir David Clarke. But the way she cocked her head to one side and studied him made him remember how much less she'd drunk than he. She asked, "Why do you suppose your wife—your ex-wife, I should say—chose to be unfaithful to you?"

That was a question he'd avoided asking himself for years; what had happened was far easier to understand than why. He didn't like facing it now. Slowly, he answered, "I took her for granted, I expect. You don't think that can possibly happen, not when you first meet, but it does—unless you know enough to watch out for it. And I won't deny being married to what I do, either." He turned and patted the side of the whiskey bottle; a lot of the whiskey was out of it and inside him. The crooked smile came back. "*In Jameson veritas.*"

"Maybe," Kathleen said. "And maybe your Irene wasn't altogether blameless, either—in fact, she couldn't have been, or she wouldn't have been doing what you caught her doing."

Absurdly, that angered Bushell for a moment. He'd concentrated all his fury on Sir David Clarke. In clinging to his memories of happier times with Irene, he'd forgotten—he'd made himself forget—he hadn't walked in during the middle of a rape. Women had been deceiving their husbands for as long as men had been straying from their wives. But he hadn't strayed, he hadn't wanted to stray, and he hadn't let himself think Irene would have.

"I certainly don't think well of Sir David for taking advantage of your situation, whatever the reasons for it," Kathleen said. Bushell nodded, glad for the chance not to think about Irene. Kathleen went on, "How could he be Sir Martin's chief of staff with that on his record?"

"Three reasons." With drunken precision, Bushell ticked them of on his fingers: "First, he did marry her. Second, chief of staff is not an elective post, of course. And third," he finished reluctantly, "he's good at what he does." One side of his mouth twisted into a wry smile. "Irene certainly thought so."

"Good you can joke about it," Kathleen said.

Bushell stared owlishly at her, then went back and listened to what he'd just said. "I did, didn't I?" he said in some surprise. "It's the first time I ever have, I'll tell you that. That calls for another drink." He picked up the bottle of Jameson, looked at it, and set it down. "As a matter of fact, maybe that calls for *not* having another drink."

"Yes, maybe it does," Kathleen said, with so much enthusiasm that Bushell knew she thought he'd already had one—or several—too many. Perhaps ill-advisedly, she asked, "And what is Sir David so good at?"

"Besides adultery, do you mean?" Bushell said. Snide comments about Sir David Clarke didn't count as jokes to him—nor, evidently, to Kathleen, either. She sat quietly, waiting for his answer. After a bit of thought, he said, "What he's good at, what he's good for—however you like—is keeping his boss out of trouble, making sure Sir Martin doesn't do anything to offend any large number of his constituents. In small doses, that's all well and good. But Sir David thinks—or I think Sir David thinks—that if a small dose is good, a large one will be better. If Sir Martin listened to him all the time, he'd be so bland he couldn't possibly lead us anywhere. He'd follow whichever way the people blow, and the people, given half a chance, blow every which way."

"He's more interested in having Sir Martin look good than in having him be good, you're saying," Kathleen remarked.

Bushell looked at her in an admiration that had nothing to do with the physical charms she still displayed so invitingly. "That's just what I'm saying. It's just what I would have said, as a matter of fact, if I had my wits about me." He smiled that lopsided smile again. "Must be love."

"If you weren't drunk, you wouldn't talk foolishness." Kathleen was brisk almost to coldness. He remembered life had bruised her, too. She went on, "Tell me that when you're sober and I'll—I'll think about believing it."

Thinking about being sober made him think about the morning, and about black coffee and paracetamol. By the way he felt now, he knew how he'd feel then, and how little the pain relievers would help. Well, he'd been through that before, too, more times than he cared to recall. "I think I'd better get back to my room and get what sleep I can," he said.

"Good," Kathleen answered. "For a moment there, I thought you had no common sense left at all."

"Hrmp," he said in mock dudgeon. He'd draped his clothes neatly on a chair. As he walked over to it, Kathleen rose from the bed to go over to the chest of drawers. He reached out and swatted her lightly on her bare backside when she bent to open a drawer. She straightened with an indignant squeak. "There, you see?" he said. "If you insult me, I beat you."

"And here I'd been thanking God I left Anthony Rothrock behind in Charleroi," she said, pulling out a pair of cotton pyjamas comfortable and sensible for someone traveling by herself. She looked at him out of the corner of her eye. "Shall I scream for the police?"

"If you do, you'll probably find an officer close by," he answered. They both laughed, as easy with each other as if they'd been together a long time. Bushell took that for a good sign. *Now*, he thought, *if the damned case would only give me one . . .*

▼

Several large, muscular men stood in front of the lifts when Bushell, Stanley, and Kathleen Flannery walked over to them to do downstairs for breakfast. They did not have the look of men waiting for a car themselves. After a moment, Bushell recognized one of them. "Hullo, Scriver," he said. "What's all this in aid of?" He spoke as softly as he could; the paracetamol he'd gulped in his first waking action hadn't yet started taking the edge off a headache that bored through his skull like the electric bandsaw slicing into a seam of coal deep down under Charleroi.

The RAM who'd driven him to Lansdowne Street answered, "We're here to keep the reporters away from your room, sir. Major Harris asked the hotel to stop incoming calls last night, too, to give the three of you some rest. But you'd better know there's a great ravening pack of newspapermen down in the lobby, just waiting for you to show your faces."

Bushell groaned. "They would be there, wouldn't they?" Samuel Stanley said. "Death by gunfire, hand grenades—all sorts of juicy things to put on the front page."

"Right," Bushell said in a tight, controlled voice. The prospect of facing the press never sent him into transports of delight. Facing them with a hangover, and with them standing between him and several cups of black coffee— He groaned again. What did Marlowe have the devil say in *The Tragical History of Doctor Faustus? Why, this is hell, nor am I out of it:* that was the line. At the moment, he had considerable sympathy for the devil.

"Shall we go back and ring down for room service?" Kathleen asked.

Bushell thought of the devil again, this time as tempter. Reluctantly, he shook his head—only a little, because it hurt. "Go ahead, if you like," he told her. "You're not officially part of the case. Me, I'd have to face them sooner or later anyhow. It might as well be now." With a martyred sigh, he turned back to Scriver. "Tell Major Harris I only regret I have but one life to lose for His Majesty."

"Er—right sir," Scriver said. "It won't be so bad as that."

"No—it'll be worse."

"I'll come with you," Kathleen declared, in a tone that said she didn't want him to go down there and die alone. It touched him absurdly; he wasn't used to having anyone but Sam cover his back.

A bell clanged and a light came on to signal the arrival of the lift. Scriver and his companions let Bushell, Kathleen, and Stanley board ahead of them, then climbed on themselves. On his little stool in one corner of the car, the operator muttered something about crowding. When no one paid him any attention, he sighed, closed the doors, and let the lift descend to the lobby.

More RAMs guarded the bank of lifts down there. Bushell idly wondered how a genuine guest of the Parker House was supposed to get up to his room. He found out when one such guest used his doorkey as a talisman to get him past the warders of the way up.

Bushell had hoped he wouldn't be recognized the instant he stepped out of the lift. That hope proved forlorn. "There he is!" half a dozen voices cried from all parts of the lobby, and reporters stampeded toward him. The Boston RAMs got in front of him like rugby forwards battling to keep the nasty devils on the other side away from the three-quarterback with the ball.

Getting from the lifts to Parker's was a pretty fair approximation of a scrummage. Elbows flew; some of the reporters were as big and burly as the RAMs. Neither Jerry Doyle nor Michael Shaughnessy was, but the two reporters from *Common Sense* made up in stridency what they gave away in pounds and inches.

"How does it feel to be a murderer of innocents?" Shaughnessy screamed into Bushell's ear.

"I don't know," Bushell answered. "If I ever try it, you'll be the first to hear."

"Most places I go to, innocents aren't in the habit of carrying hand grenades," Samuel Stanley said.

"Or throwing them at people," Kathleen added. Shaughnessy sent her a pained look, perhaps because she'd abandoned a cause he thought she held, or perhaps because the foot Bushell was stepping on belonged to him.

"Why were you armed when you went in search of Joseph Kilbride?" a reporter asked, notebook poised to receive Bushell's pearls of wisdom.

"If you're trying to arrest a gun runner, there is some small possibility that he might have a gun—or some other bit of nasty pyrotechnics—concealed about his person," Bushell answered.

"Pyro—" the reporter muttered, and sent Bushell a wry grin. "Why the devil didn't you pick a word I can spell?"

"Why the devil can't you spell the words I pick?" Bushell retorted. The reporter was only a little more than half his age. He rubbed it in: "Sorry state our schools have got to these days, isn't it?"

"I did that story *last* week, pal," the reporter said, not a bit put out. "You're what's news today."

Another newshound said, "What's the connection between Kilbride, Venable, and Cavendish on the one hand and *The Two Georges* on the other?"

"We're still investigating that," Bushell answered, a reply that had the twin virtues—as far as he was concerned—of being true and altogether uninformative. He'd hoped none of the reporters would make the connection, but what you hoped for and what you got too often had only the most distant relationship to each other.

"What's this I hear about your firing at poor Kilbride without even the slightest reason for it?" Jerry Doyle shouted.

"What is it?" Bushell said. "It sounds like a lie to me."

His voice an angry growl, Samuel Stanley added, "I suppose you think we dropped the hand grenade that blew Cavendish's face to bits. I hate to tell you, Mr. Doyle, but hand grenades aren't standard RAM issue—and how would we know to have them handy after Venable flung the first one at us?"

"*If* that happened," Doyle said stubbornly.

"Of course, *if*," Bushell agreed, reaching out to pat the man from *Common Sense* on the shoulder. "And *if* the sun goes down tonight—just on the off chance, mind you—it'll get dark in Boston."

"Give it up, Jerry," one of the other reporters told Doyle, his tone half amused, half sympathetic. "It really happened, and there's damn all you can do about it but take your lumps and come out fighting the next time."

Doyle frowned and didn't say anything. Michael Shaughnessy did: "If it was a RAM told me the sun was setting, I'd step outside before I believed him."

If *Common Sense* claimed the sun was setting, Bushell was ready to take that for proof it wasn't. He didn't bother saying so. For one thing, he and the men from John Kennedy's magazine would have sounded like a pack of five-year-olds. "If you say this—" "Oh, yeah? Well, if you say that—" For another, the RAMs had finally waded through the press of the press to the entrance to Parker's. Given the choice between arguing with reporters and getting some hot coffee outside, Bushell didn't think twice.

Some of the reporters did get into Parker's, but only as customers. The waiters there were more zealous in keeping them away from Bushell's table than were the RAMs. "Sirs, ma'am, if you come in here, we assume you want the chance to take things at your own pace and enjoy your meal," one of them said.

"I like this place," Samuel Stanley declared in ringing tones.

After breakfast, Major Harris laid on a RAM steamer to take Bushell and his companions to the local headquarters. That frustrated the reporters who'd hung about while they ate. Newsboys hawked dailies on every corner. One headline read, BUSHELL STRETCHES TRAIL OF GORE FROM SEA TO SHINING SEA.

He pointed to it and asked the driver, "That would be the *New England Courant?*"

"Yes, sir," the local RAM answered. "Heard of it already, have you?"

"How could I keep from hearing about such a fine patriotic paper?" Bushell asked. The driver chuckled.

When they got to the RAM headquarters, Major Harris met them again and said, "I expect you'll want to telephone Victoria from a more secure line then you could hope to get at the hotel."

"Yes, just so," Bushell agreed. Fear of listeners on the line wasn't what had kept him from ringing up Sir Horace Bragg the night before. He'd unburdened himself to Kathleen instead. Rather than dwelling on what that might mean, he asked Harris, "Have you already made a preliminary report to the capital?"

"Oh, yes, sir, that I have." Harris stifled a yawn. He'd probably been up till all hours. "But you know more of the picture—and you can take that any way you please—than I do. The commandant'll be glad to hear from you, I'm sure he will. Why don't you just come along with me?"

He took Bushell and his companions to the same room they'd occupied the afternoon before when word came that Joseph Kilbride had been spotted. As she had then, Kathleen Flannery sniffed at the photographs of scantily dressed women and then ostentatiously ignored them—not the sort of art of which she was a connoisseur.

The connection to NAU RAM headquarters in Victoria went through quick as boiled asparagus (*ah, the classics,* Bushell thought). When he identified himself, the RAM operator said, "Yes, *sir!* I'll ring you straight through to Sir Horace's office."

That didn't take long, either. "Office of Lieutenant General Sir Horace Bragg, Commandant, Royal North American Mounted Police, Sally Reese speaking," his secretary said, apparently without pausing for breath. Bushell moved the handset farther from his ear; as usual, Sally spoke as if she held a megaphone in front of her mouth.

He identified himself again, then said, "I'd like to speak to Sir Horace, please."

"I'm sorry, Colonel Bushell," Sally blared, "but you can't."

"It's urgent," Bushell said. "If he's in a meeting, please pull him out. I'll take responsibility."

"It's not that, Colonel," she answered, still at the top of her lungs. "I know he's always ready to talk to you, but he's not here this morning. He called in first thing to say he wouldn't be. He broke a tooth on a chicken bone last night, and he's going in to the dentist to get a crown put on."

"Oh," Bushell said, and touched his own jaw in sympathy. The miserable flesh of which men were made had a way of interfering with even the weightiest affairs. "He's lucky to have got an appointment on such short notice. Must come of being the commandant."

Sally Reese's shrill giggle reminded him of a saw blade biting into a nail. "That's the very same thing I told him myself, Colonel, the very same thing. This is to do with that horrible mess up in Boston yesterday, isn't it? Do you want I should transfer you to Brigadier Arthurs? He'd be glad to take your report, I know he would."

"No, never mind," Bushell said. Benjamin Arthurs was a sound enough man, but Bushell didn't care to put any more people than he had to between himself and the case. Like every RAM in the NAU, he had Sir Horace Bragg over him, but he wanted the chain to run directly from Sir Horace to him without developing intermediate links. To propitiate Sally Reese, he went on, "I really have little to add to Major Harris's report, and I'll ring back this afternoon to make sure I bring Sir Horace fully up to date."

"Well, I suppose it's all right, then." Bragg's secretary was loudly dubious, but not dubious enough to make an issue of it. "I'm sure he'll be looking forward to hearing from you. Good-bye for now." She hung up.

Samuel Stanley had got off his telephone in time to listen to the last part of Bushell's conversation. "You're going to call Victoria this afternoon?" he said in some surprise. "I thought sure we'd be—"

"—On our way to Victoria by then?" Bushell interrupted. "Of course we will, Sam; don't be absurd. And when we get in to the capital, I'll be so apologetic, it would make a dog lose his lunch to watch me. I had to get on the train or the airship or whatever the devil we'll get on. I couldn't possibly stay around the office to telephone. Oh, please, Sir Horace, won't you find it in your heart to forgive me this once?" He let out an alarmingly convincing sob.

Kathleen had been talking with one of her associates, not paying much attention to Bushell or Stanley. She looked up in surprise and concern at that sob. Bushell winked at her. She stared, then stuck out her tongue and went back to her own conversation.

Sam Stanley laughed, but quickly sobered. "Sir Horace isn't going to buy it, Chief. He's no fool"—*whatever else you can say about him*, his eyes added silently, letting Bushell ignore him if he so chose: and he did—"and he'll know just what you're up to."

"I don't care," Bushell said, so gleefully that now he startled his adjutant. "What he knows and what he can prove are two different beasts."

A slow smile spread across Stanley's face. "That's no pipsqueak lieutenant talking," he said. "You sound like any sergeant who'd been around the block with his superiors too bloo—ah, blinking many times. My hat's off to you." His hat was already off, sitting on the desk in front of him. He lifted it in salute, then set it down once more.

"Where d'you think I learned such things?" Bushell said. "Once upon a time I was straight and true as could be, and they put me in your hands, and you—you twisted me." He showed how with his hands; he might have been wringing out a washrag. Then he picked up his own hat. "Thanks, Sam."

"Any old time," Stanley said. "Who's next on your list?"

"I thought I'd call Shikalimo," Bushell answered. "He's the mover and shaker in the Six Nations, not the RAMs. I want to see if he's found anything at Joseph Kilbride's house yet."

"Yes, that will be interesting," Stanley agreed. "If we're lucky there—" His shoulders sagged. "We haven't been lucky so far, not this case."

Bushell glanced over toward Kathleen Flannery. She was concentrating on her telephone conversation, paying him no heed whatever. "Oh, I don't know," he said quietly. "It all depends on how you look at things." He contemplated that as if it were some new cocktail, then nodded in slow approval. "Yes, it all depends on how you look at things."

He called the Doshoweh constabulary station. Shikalimo was already on his way out to Kilbride's house. Bushell muttered in frustration, then remembered that Jaime Macias had been on the point of telling him something interesting when Major Harris brought work Joseph Kilbride had been spotted. But when he telephoned New Liverpool, he found that, despite the early hour back there, Macias, like Shikalimo, was out on a case. "Can we have someone else help you, sir?" the constabulary operator asked.

"No, that's all right; I'll ring back tomorrow," Bushell answered, and hung up. "Can't get hold of anyone this morning," he grumbled in not-quite-mock indignation. "The constables are all out working for a living, and Sir Horace no doubt wishes he was."

He had to explain that to Samuel Stanley, who clapped a hand to his jaw. "I'd sooner be working, if you gave me those choices," Stanley said. "And speaking of which, how are we going to get to Victoria?"

"Let's check the schedules," Bushell answered. "I'm sure there'll be plenty of trains; it's just a question of whether they have airships leaving at a convenient time—and how long we'd have to spend floating above the airship port before we could land." The time wasted over Astoria remained burned in his memory.

That turned out not to be an issue. Trains ran almost as fast as airships, and so many of them traveled the crowded Boston–New York–Philadelphia–Victoria corridor that he had only to pick a departure time that would let him and his companions finish up their work here, collect their belongings and check out of the Parker House, and reach the railway station. A young, eager lieutenant made the arrangements and volunteered to chauffeur them to the station.

When they left the RAM offices, newsboys were still shouting about the bloody events on Lansdowne Street, but they had another headline to cry, too: KING-EMPEROR PREPARING TO SAIL FOR VICTORIA. One of the papers—Bushell didn't notice which one—ran a subhead just below: TWO GEORGES STILL MISSING.

He turned to Stanley. "We're running out of time."

# XIII

▼

$\mathbf{T}$HE SUN WAS SINKING IN THE WEST WHEN the *Union Lifeline*, air brakes chuffing, pulled into Victoria Station. Several times during the eight-hour journey, Bushell thought about the yacht *Britannia*. When it sailed for Victoria, it would travel far more slowly than the train, and have to come much farther, but it would reach the capital all the same.

A captain in dress reds met them at the station. He introduced himself as John Martin. "Welcome to Victoria, Colonel, Captain," he said to Bushell and Stanley. Then he seemed to notice Kathleen was not standing at Bushell's side merely on the off chance a cab might materialize out of thin air somewhere nearby.

Bushell remembered he hadn't told Sir Horace he'd included Kathleen in the investigation. He smiled to himself. The next few days were liable to be . . . interesting. He thought of how she teased him for all the—interesting—ways he used that word, and his smile got wider.

He said, "Captain Martin, let me present you to Dr. Kathleen Flannery of the All-Union Art Museum." He waited for them to clasp hands and exchange polite phrases, then went on, "Dr. Flannery has greatly helped the investigation. Since she was curator of the traveling exhibition of *The Two Georges*, she has at least as great an interest as we do in safely recovering the painting."

There. The cat was out of the bag. Captain Martin was three grades and fifteen years his junior, so he had to smile and make the best of it. When word got back to Sir Horace Bragg, though . . .

Well, that could wait. His voice grew brisk: "I presume, Captain, you've made arrangements for us to stay somewhere besides this train-station corridor?"

"Uh, yes, sir," Martin said. "It wasn't easy, but I managed to book two rooms at the William and Mary." That again reminded him of Kathleen. "If Dr. Flannery is with the All-Union Museum, I presume she'll have digs of her own here in town? With the King-Emperor coming soon they're—blasted hard to come by."

"I do," Kathleen said, "but I've worked so well with Colonel Bushell and Captain Stanley that I'd hate to be separated from them at this crucial stage of the case." She batted her eyes at Captain Martin. "Do you think you could by any chance manage to arrange one more room at the William and Mary?"

The captain looked quite humanly harassed for a moment, then regained his

275

professional impassivity. "I'll see what I can do when we get there, Dr. Flannery," he answered, his voice wooden.

She set a hand on his arm. "Oh, thank you very much," she purred. The good Captain Martin, as most males would have, thawed like an icicle on a warm spring day. He picked up her bags and led the way toward his motorcar. As soon as his back was turned, Kathleen winked at Bushell.

"*Not* cricket," he murmured to her. She winked again. *If I laugh out loud,* he told himself, *if I howl like a wolf or giggle like a loon, Martin will either decide I've lost my mind or figure out what's funny.* Neither choice looked good. He kept quiet. It wasn't easy.

Victoria lay along the southern shore of the Potomac, on the other side of the Long Bridge from Georgestown, Maryland (local historians, Bushell had learned in his earlier stay at the capital, said Georgestown had formerly honored only one George, but pluralized itself after George III and George Washington reached their historic accord). In a way, it was an artificial city: it had gone up when the separate colonies fused into the North American Union, and would wither if ever government should leave it. Bushell peered out across the carpark at the scores of gleaming marble buildings dedicated to administering the broad expanse of the NAU. Victoria seemed in no danger of withering any time soon.

It had some of the advantages of artifice. Its streets, for instance, were laid out in a sensible grid: none of the twisting ex-cowpaths that had grown into Boston boulevards. Along with trolleys and an efficient underground, they let you get around with ease in the capital.

Bushell knew where the William and Mary was: only a block and a half from RAM headquarters. He'd made the trip from Victoria Station to headquarters scores of times, either in a cab or in his own motorcar. Despite his years in New Liverpool, going uptown felt intimately familiar. Here came the North American Mint, the great Telephone Exchange Building, the—

"Hullo!" he said in surprise, pointing to a large new structure with a yellow brick façade. "What the devil's that?" The reality of change had taken a swipe at his memories.

"The Imperial Asylum for the Insane and Feebleminded," Captain Martin answered. "Opened only a few months ago. You may hear someone say, 'Ahh, send him to the Yellow Brick,' if he thinks a chap's boiler hasn't got all the steam pressure it might."

"I did hear that when I was here last month," Bushell said. "Didn't know what it meant, but they're always coming up with new slang."

"I hadn't heard it," Kathleen said, "but I've spent a lot of time lately on the road, either with *The Two Georges* or searching for it—and we're a fairly stolid lot at the Museum, too."

"One day soon it'll go out on a wireless broadcast, and then people will be saying it from one end of the NAU to the other," Samuel Stanley said.

"Yes, and as soon as they are, Victoria will come up with something new," Bushell said. "Wouldn't do to have *hoi polloi* learn the insiders' secret language, now would it?"

"Feeling cynical tonight, Tom?" Kathleen asked.

"No more than usual," Bushell said. His eyes flicked to Captain Martin. The RAM's ears didn't flick to attention, but they might as well have. That casual use of his Christian name would get back to Sir Horace, too. *Well, if it does, it bloody well does.*

The William and Mary Hotel sprawled inside elegantly landscaped grounds. A light-skinned Negro clerk clucked in distress when Captain Martin tried to arrange a room for Kathleen Flannery. "That will be difficult, sir," she said. "I'm surprised Mr. Bushell and Mr. Stanley were accommodated."

"It has to do with the search for *The Two Georges*," Bushell said.

"Sakes alive, why didn't you say so?" The woman shuffled through a file box of registration cards like a professional *vingt-et-un* dealer at a casino in the south of France. By the time she was through, she'd gone from a frown to a smile so white and wide and dazzling that Bushell wondered whether her teeth were her own. "I've got you in room 527 now, Mr. Bushell, and you're in 529, Mr. Stanley—and Dr. Flannery, I've put you in 525. We'll worry about where the marchioness stays when she actually gets into town. I hope that's all right?"

"Couldn't be better," Bushell said solemnly. He turned to Kathleen. "Well! The marchioness will be *most* vexed, I'm certain."

Kathleen snorted at his languid, affected drawl. The desk clerk giggled. "You are a wicked man, Mr. Bushell," she said severely, shaking a finger at him. He bowed in gratitude. She giggled harder.

Captain Martin said, "I'm glad that's worked out. Someone will be by tomorrow to take you and Captain Stanley—and Dr. Flannery—wherever you need to go. Don't hesitate to ring me if there's anything I can do." He brushed a finger against the brim of his cap and hurried off.

"We'd better get up to our rooms right away," Bushell said. "We're only just around the corner from RAM headquarters. As soon as he gets back there, I expect my telephone to start ringing." The registration clerk ran the little chime that sat on the front desk. The bellman who had been hovering in the background swooped down on the travelers' bags.

Bushell unpacked with practiced ease and speed. His suitcases were not so full as they had been when he set out, either; he'd gone through a lot of clothes in chasing after *The Two Georges*. He'd have to do something about that—in his copious spare time. He laughed at the absurdity of the notion.

After he'd moved things out of cases and into drawers and closet, he rang room service and ordered a couple of buttered scones, jam, and a pot of blackcurrant tea for an evening snack. Then he sat down on the bed and stared at the telephone. The watched pot stubbornly refused to boil. "If you're going to be that way about it—" he said, and, when it still didn't ring, he stripped off his clothes and headed for the showerbath.

He thought the cheerful splash of hot water would be plenty to tempt the phone to life, but he got to finish bathing in peace. He was toweling his hair dry when the telephone finally rang. Wrapping the towel around his middle, he hurried over to the nightstand. "Hullo? Bushell here."

"Hullo, Tom. Welcome back to the capital," Sir Horace Bragg said. "You've taken a roundabout route getting here, haven't you?"

"You might say so, sir, yes," Bushell answered. "I've left so much behind along the way, too—I only hope none of that turns out to be crucial."

"One of the things you've left behind you is a trail of blood," Bragg said. "The papers are screaming their heads off. We've never had a case like this before, and I hope to heaven we never have another one like it again."

"Amen to that," Bushell said. "We weren't the ones who blew off the back of Tricky Dick's head, though. We weren't the ones who fired first at Buckley Bay, either. And I promise you I didn't throw the first grenade at the late, unlamented Mr. Venable. No, not unlamented: I take that back. I wish he were alive—or Kilbride, or Cavendish—so I could ask questions. Lots of questions."

"Yes, and the papers are screaming about that, too." Lieutenant General Sir Horace Bragg often sounded harassed, or at least dyspeptic, even when he wasn't. When he was, his voice turned downright lugubrious. "One of the dailies here ran the story under the headline, 'Dead Men Tell No Tales,' which doesn't make us look good."

"To hell with the papers," Bushell said, and was briefly glad Lieutenant Thirkettle couldn't hear him committing such blasphemies. "I want *The Two Georges*. That Venable comes from Georgestown, just over the river from here. Are your people turning the place upside down yet, grilling everybody who ever met him?"

"They will be, as of tomorrow," Bragg said. "I still don't know as much about this business in Boston as I'd like." His tone sharpened. "I would have expected, Tom, that you have rung me last night with a full report."

"I tried to reach you this morning, sir, but you were already at the dentist's." Bushell felt guilty about not telephoning the RAM commandant, but less than he'd expected. And if Bragg wasn't getting investigators into Georgestown till tomorrow, he wasn't as energetic as he might have been, either.

"Well, let that go, then," Sir Horace said, though by the sound of his voice it was far from forgotten. He paused, coughed, and then resumed: "What's this I hear about your associating Dr. Flannery with the investigation?"

"Oh, yes, sir, I'm very glad I did that," Bushell said brightly. "She was the one who identified Joseph Kilbride for us back in Doshoweh, and she was the one who spotted Venable in the cabinetmaker's shop, too. Without her, we'd be much farther from *The Two Georges* than we are." *I have other reasons, too, but those are none of your business—sir.*

"You can't possibly trust her," Bragg said. "I still find her involvement in the case suspicious, and to say that putting her on the investigatory team is irregular merely serves to weaken the power of language."

"I worried about it, too," Bushell said, which was true. "I had her join Sam and me not least to keep her from haring off on her own." That was also true. "The help she's given us, though, has justified the step I took."

"Most irregular," Bragg said, like a judge passing sentence. *If we don't come up with The Two Georges, you'll be my scapegoat because of this.* Bushell could hear the threat in his voice. He sighed. Had Sir Horace despaired of finding the painting? It sounded that way. Or maybe commanding the RAMs had finally made him come to think like a bureaucrat, not a soldier, with procedure ranking ahead of everything else, even results.

*He's old.* Bragg couldn't have had more than a year or two on Bushell, but he sounded like a man ready for his cane and slippers. The thought saddened Bushell, who felt a long way from the boneyard himself. He said, "We'll find it yet, sir. No new ransom demands, are there?"

"Eh? No." Bragg hesitated, then said. "See here, Tom, are you involved with the Flannery woman?"

"I want to get a good night's sleep tonight," Bushell said, "and maybe you can tell me what's on the agenda for tomorrow."

"You didn't answer my question," Bragg said. Bushell didn't answer again. After a silence that stretched for more than a minute, Sir Horace sighed. "If you walk a tightrope long enough, Tom, sooner or later you fall off." Bushell still didn't say anything. Bragg sighed again. "First we meet with Sir Martin Luther King. He's scheduled us for two hours, starting at ten. He's been following your work with great attention, I assure you."

"I believe that," Bushell said. "He's a politician, and he's got the shadow of the King-Emperor's visit hanging over him, too."

"Right on both counts," Sir Horace said. "I thought you'd spend the afternoon at headquarters—unless you plan on going out and shooting someone then."

Bushell rubbed at his mustache, which was unruly from the showerbath. Sir Horace waxed sarcastic only under great strain. "It's not on my calendar, so I guess I can let it go," Bushell said, even as the image of Sir David Clarke appeared in his mind for a moment.

"Heh, heh," Bragg said, just like that. "Well, keep tomorrow night open, too, if you'd be so kind. There's a reception laid on at the Russian embassy." He muttered something under his breath; Bushell thought he heard *damn Russians.* In an ordinary voice, Sir Horace went on, "We'll go there, too, and to all the other receptions and parties and banquets the ambassadors and ministers and chargés will be putting on before the King-Emperor's visit. We'll probably learn damn all at any of them, but we have to make the effort."

"The Russians," Bushell said dreamily. "Russian rifles, Russian roubles, Russian grenades. . . . Do you know, sir, I'm almost tempted to be undiplomatic when I get inside the Russian embassy. But, of course, I'd never do anything like that."

"Of course not," Sir Horace Bragg said. He might have been trying to sound hearty, but *uneasy* better described his tone. "I'll send a driver around for you and Captain Stanley—"

"—And Dr. Flannery," Bushell reminded him.

This time, the silence was on Bragg's end of the line. At last, Sir Horace said, "Very well, Tom. And Dr. Flannery. The driver will swing by a little before ten. On your head be it." He hung up, which effectively kept Bushell from getting in the last word.

He ran a hand through his hair. It was mostly dry by now; to make it lie flat, he'd have to oil it more heavily than he liked. He got up off the bed and started back to the bathroom. He hadn't taken more than two steps when someone knocked on the door.

"About time with the bloody scones," he muttered, and turned toward the doorway. He'd have been astonished if the room-service waiter hadn't seen patrons wearing nothing but a towel. He opened the door. For a moment, he and Kathleen Flannery stared at each other. In accusing tones, he said, "You're not room service."

Her eyes sparkled. "I could be," she said. "It depends on what you ordered." She stepped into the room, closed the door behind her, and undid the towel.

▼

The governor-general's residence, familiarly known as America's Number Ten, lay across Victoria from the William and Mary Hotel. The RAM driver who took Bushell and his companions there, a stolid veteran named Kittridge, refrained from pointing out all the scenic wonders they passed en route. For that alone, Bushell would gladly have promoted the sergeant to any rank this side of brigadier.

Maybe Kittridge remembered him and Sam from the days when they'd worked out of the capital and knew they knew the sights. He got the feeling, though, that Kittridge would have been as taciturn if he'd come from Mars rather than New Liverpool.

They purred down Union Avenue—otherwise known as Embassy Row—on the way to the residence. Far and away the two biggest buildings there housed the Franco-Spanish and Russian legations: the fleur-de-lis of the Holy Alliance and the Russian tricolor and two-headed eagle flew only a couple of blocks apart, separated, appropriately enough, by the smaller missions of several of the German states. "Miserable Russians," Bushell muttered, glancing toward the ornate brick pile they inhabited.

Sam Stanley was thinking along with him. "What, just because they'd fit into a building half that size if they didn't send so many spies over here?"

"Something like that," Bushell answered. Sergeant Kittridge still didn't say anything, but he did nod so vigorously that the waxed tips of his handlebar mustache quivered.

America's Number Ten was a two-story structure of white marble, with long north and south wings and a colonnaded main entrance. Exchanging small talk outside that entrance as Kittridge stopped the steamer were Sir Horace and Sir David Clarke.

Clarke clasped Kathleen's hand for what Bushell thought was an unduly long time when she got out of the motorcar. He wondered whether that was simple mistrust of Sir David, or whether what Kathleen had said of her experience with John Kennedy made him more alert to such things. "Ah, Dr. Flannery," Sir David said. "Sir Horace was telling me how you and Colonel Bushell had joined forces. I wondered how he meant that." His smile was broad and pleasant.

"Nastily, I suspect," she answered, which froze that smile on his face and made Bragg look even glummer than usual.

"It's just ten now. We shouldn't keep His Excellency waiting," Stanley said, doing his best to spread oil on troubled waters.

Bragg also seemed willing to make peace. "By all means," he said. Bushell shrugged and nodded. Without a word, Sir David Clarke turned and led them into the residence.

"Some splendid paintings on the walls here," Kathleen murmured.

"Yes, you can trace the history of the NAU as you walk down the halls," Bushell agreed. Colonial days gave way to the emancipation of the southern Negroes, the expansion across the prairies and then to the Pacific, the rise of factories, all punctuated with portraits of governors-general past. There was Jackson, looking grim enough to enforce the freeing of the slaves prescribed in London; there was short, roly-poly Douglas, under whom the NAU had spilled west over the Rockies; and there was Martin Roosevelt, shown at the controls of his personal airship. Rumor said he'd sometimes taken pretty girls up into the sky with him, but rumor said lots of things.

"I was thinking of the art, not the history," Kathleen said.

"I know," Bushell replied. "There's room for both." Kathleen considered that, then nodded. Bushell smiled, pleased they'd found something over which they didn't have to argue.

Over his shoulder, Sir David Clarke said, "We're meeting with Sir Martin in the Green Room. Don't be surprised when you find it's appointed in blue, because—"

"—Politicians have a habit of saying one thing and doing another," Bushell put in.

Clarke looked pained. "Because it was done deliberately, I was going to say, to show the mother country she hasn't got a monopoly on eccentric institutions."

"Why have I got the feeling our British cousins could figure that out for themselves?" Stanley said. Again, though, he spoke disarmingly.

A servant in black tie opened the door to the Green Room, which was, as Sir David had said, done in shades of blue. Sir Martin Luther King rose from his chair and walked over to the newcomers. "Welcome, gentlemen, Dr. Flannery," he said. He nodded to Sam. "You would be Captain Stanley. I don't believe we actually met when I was in New Liverpool."

"No, Your Excellency, we didn't." Stanley extended his hand. "I'm delighted to meet you now, though."

"As all of us have said throughout this sorry affair, I wish it were under more pleasant circumstances." Sir Martin's deep, rich voice filled the Green Room. Even here, in a gathering altogether unpublic, his every gesture seemed—not calculated, precisely, but a little stagier than it might have been, showing how conscious he was of eyes upon him. "Shall we get to work?" he said, indicating chairs with a smooth motion of his hand. "We haven't much time, as I'm sure you know. His Majesty's yacht sails tomorrow, and arrives—all too soon."

"And still no further ransom demands from the Sons of Liberty?" Bushell asked.

"Only a silence as of the tomb," Sir Martin answered. "They're playing their cards very cagily indeed: calculating how best to force us to go along with their demands when they do finally make them."

"When they do, we'll have little choice but to comply if we want *The Two Georges* back again," Sir David Clarke said. "Our own investigations seem better at strewing corpses over the landscape than finding the missing painting."

Bushell contemplated one corpse not currently strewn over the landscape, and what a pity that was. He declined to rise to Clarke's bait, though, saying, "We've made considerable progress tracking down the Sons involved in the theft, even if we don't yet have the painting itself. The chap who tossed a grenade at me yesterday, for instance, came from Georgestown." He turned a mild and thoughtful eye on Sir Martin's chief of staff. "You live in Georgestown, don't you, Sir David?"

That pierced Clarke's armor of affability. "I resent the insinuation, Colonel," he said coldly.

"Am I to take that as an affirmative?" Bushell asked.

Sir Horace Bragg said, "Disunion among us gives aid and comfort to our enemies. Russian rifles, Russian gold, now Russian grenades as well—and the Russians are masters of long, deep-seated plots. The Empire would do well to worry more about the Russians."

"So you have said these past weeks—repeatedly," Sir Martin Luther King observed.

"I don't think we worry enough about the Russians, either, Your Excellency," Bushell said.

Bragg gave him the first warm look he'd had from his commandant and old friend since he got to Victoria. "Thank you, Tom," he said. A moment later, he got to his feet and took a small bottle of paracetamol tablets from his trouser pocket. "Excuse me just for a second, if you please. This miserable tooth is killing me." He left the room.

Sir Martin Luther King turned his narrow, clever eyes toward Bushell. "It may be that you and Sir Horace are perfectly correct about the Russians, Colonel," he said. "Nevertheless, you must know the fable of the boy who cried wolf. I am sick to death of Sir Horace's harping on the Russians. He is as tiresome about them as he used to be about his family's past and vanished glories. I finally had to let him know that, since those glories were based on a plantation deriving its wealth from Negro slavery, his tales did not strike the chord with me for which he might have hoped."

"Oh, dear," Bushell said. He glanced at Sam Stanley, who nodded. "Oh, dear," he said again. "He does want to restore the family's former position, for which you can hardly blame him." He'd never thought he'd feel awkward defending Sir Horace, but he did now. Bragg had been . . . *gauche* was the politest word that sprang to mind.

"His remarks were, shall we say, not the most effective way of having his name placed on the Honors List Sir Martin submits annually to His Majesty the King-Emperor," Sir David Clarke observed. Bushell wanted to resent that, but found he couldn't, not even coming from Clarke. If Sir Horace had in mind ending his days as Baron or even Baronet Bragg, offending the man who recommended names for such titles was not the way to go about it.

Bragg come back then, cutting the thread of conversation as with a knife. "I am sorry," he said. "I think that dentist of mine should have been a butcher instead. He promised the pain would go away in a few hours, but my guess is that he was just trying to be rid of me." He chuckled dolefully. "Of course, the procedure hurt him not a bit."

"You should have bitten him, sir," Samuel Stanley said. "That would have taken care of that."

"If I ever submit to his ministrations again, Captain, I assure you I will keep the option in mind," Bragg answered.

"We all sympathize with Lieutenant General Bragg, I am sure," Sir Martin Luther King said, "but we have not come together here this morning to discuss dentistry. What I want to know is, what impact have recent events in Boston had upon the likelihood of recovering *The Two Georges*? I tell you frankly, gentlemen and you, Dr. Flannery, if that chance seems to me unlikely and the Sons of Liberty make their ransom demand as His Majesty Charles III is approaching Victoria Harbor, I shall have little choice but to comply."

Kathleen Flannery said, "Your Excellency, couldn't you ask His Majesty to postpone his visit until we've recovered *The Two Georges* one way or another? After all, if the Sons killed to steal one symbol of the unity of the Empire, mightn't they also think of making an attempt on the King-Emperor's life?"

"As a matter of fact, Dr. Flannery, at Sir David's urging I sent His Majesty a telegram of this purport the other day," Sir Martin answered. "That information, by the way, is not to leave this room." He waited for everyone to nod before continuing, "He replied most promptly, and declined most firmly: he said he should become an object of reproach rather than admiration throughout the Empire if he let concern for his personal safety deflect him from his chosen course."

"Oh, good show," Bushell said softly.

As usual, Sam Stanley had a more pragmatic turn of mind. "I wish he would have made an exception, just this once," he said. "I wouldn't have thought any less of him for making my life easier."

"Exactly what was in my mind," Sir David Clarke said. "Sir Martin predicted he would refuse." He glanced at his boss with bemused respect. *He has no courage himself, so he marvels that Sir Martin recognized it in someone else*, Bushell thought.

"We may take it as settled that His Majesty will depart London on the appointed day," Sir Martin Luther King declared, "and that no one save the almighty God on high will delay him from reaching Victoria, also on the appointed day." As he did every so often, he fell back into the cadences of the minister of the Gospel he had been.

"We may also take it as settled that we'd better have *The Two Georges* back by the appointed day—or else we start falling on our swords," Sir Horace Bragg said.

"That's correct," Sir David Clarke agreed. "We must obtain the return of the painting by the time the King-Emperor reaches us, and obtain it by whatever means prove necessary." He talked like a bureaucrat, not a preacher, but here his meaning was perfectly clear even so.

Sir Martin said, "*Sub rosa*, I will tell you gentlemen—and you, of course, Dr. Flannery—that I have directed the minister of the exchequer to gather together the sum of specie the Sons of Liberty demanded in their note. If ransom becomes necessary for the return of *The Two Georges*, it shall be paid. I find this course odious but in the last resort unavoidable."

"We'll have to make sure we don't come down to the last resort, then," Bushell said.

"Unfortunately, while we've heard a great many promises to that effect, we've seen little that actually appears to lead toward the recovery of *The Two Georges*," Clarke said.

"Did you hear that?" Bushell exclaimed. "It's the last straw. Now he's accusing me of talking like a politico!"

Samuel Stanley looked up at the ceiling. Sir Martin Luther King looked down at his hands. Lieutenant General Sir Horace Bragg rubbed the side of his jaw. Kathleen let out a tiny yip of laughter that might—almost—have been a cough. And Sir David Clarke gaped like a netted bluegill, eyes wide and staring, mouth fallen open. Bushell had gone after him plenty of times before, but never with such genial absurdity. What was the world coming to?

Bushell didn't quite wink at Kathleen. "Must be love," he said.

Her expression was unreadable.

If Sir Martin had sounded like a preacher a few minutes before, Sir Horace seemed downright pontifical as he declared, "Given the new evidence Colonel Bushell and his colleagues have amassed—evidence suggesting that *The Two Georges* may well be somewhere here close by the capital—I firmly believe we shall yet regain it in time for it to grace His Majesty's arrival, and that we shall do so without having to pay a single sovereign in ransom."

"A sovereign indeed," Bushell said. "Considering that the King-Emperor will soon be here in Victoria—"

"We have been considering that possibility," Bragg reminded him. "I'm confident that, given our heightened concern, we shall be able to protect the person of Charles III adequately while he is on American soil."

"We never have found out how the Sons—or even if the Sons—learned just when His Majesty was coming to Victoria," Samuel Stanley observed.

Sir Horace spread his hands in manifest regret. "I've investigated vigorously, but the Sons are a tight-knit band, and difficult to penetrate. You and Tom—and, I gather, Dr. Flannery—came up against three in Boston who must have been of high rank. Had any of them survived the encounter—"

"We probably wouldn't have," Bushell said. "But yes, that was unfortunate. We did get some leads to Georgestown that may prove profitable, though." He wished Sir Horace had immediately sent RAMs out to probe the property and affairs of the late Eustace Venable instead of waiting a precious day. Bragg might be—no, no *might be* about it: he *was*—a good administrator, but he left something to be desired as a man to head up a field investigation.

Sir David Clarke caught Sir Martin's eye. "Your Excellency, if I might speak with you for a moment—"

"Certainly," the governor-general replied. As he rose, he said, "Excuse me," to the RAMs and Kathleen. Clarke steered him out a side door in whatever chamber lay beyond it.

Bragg sighed and looked even more like a kicked basset than usual. "That's the way it goes here in Victoria," he said in a low, furious voice. "They pretend to listen for a while, then they go off by themselves and tell us what we're going to do and how we're going to do it."

"I wouldn't have your job for all the gold in the Bank of England," Bushell told his friend. "I've probably said that once or twice already, haven't I?"

Before Sir Horace could answer, Clarke and Sir Martin Luther King came back into the Green Room. "Here is what we have decided," Sir Martin said. "You will of course continue the search for *The Two Georges* up to the very moment of the King-Emperor's arrival. But if a ransom demand reaches us from this time forth, we shall—regretfully—comply with it in every particular, save only that we shall not require you to call off your search while payment is being arranged. In an ideal world, I would not proceed in this fashion. In an ideal world, though, *The Two Georges* would not have been stolen. Have you any questions, gentlemen? Dr. Flannery?"

No one spoke. Bushell glanced over to Sir David Clarke. The policy the governor-general had laid down was the one Clarke had espoused from the beginning. Was that triumph in Sir David's eyes or something else, something more serious? For the life of him, Bushell couldn't tell.

▼

Walking into the RAM headquarters for the NAU felt strange to Bushell, as it had every time he'd visited since going out to New Liverpool. The place of course remained familiar in broad outline, but his memory for which corridors led exactly where had faded. Even when his memory of what had been was accurate, it did not always gibe with what was now. Some faces were familiar; some he thought he should have known but could not match up with names; some, like the paint on the walls and the carpet underfoot, were new and strange.

The same sense of dislocation bedeviled Sam Stanley. "I wish they'd have moved to a new building," he said, staring around. "Then I'd be honestly sure I was lost."

Before Sir Horace Bragg got close to his offices, a worried-looking young major bearded him: "Sir, we're having trouble getting the warrants we need to search this Eustace Venable's home and business establishment. Something went wrong last night, and the friendliest judges got tied up in their morning casework before we got the chance to petition them."

Bragg clapped a melodramatic hand to his forehead. "Good God, Manchester, more delay?" he groaned. "We can't afford that."

"We don't have to, sir," Bushell said. He opened his briefcase and drew forth the signed blank search warrants he'd been given in New Liverpool. "Fill out a couple of these and we'll find out what we need to know."

Sir Horace stared at the blank warrants with commingled awe and doubt. "You must have a judge out there on the West Coast who's a lot more than just friendly to us, Tom." Bushell nodded, pleased to have pulled a rabbit out of his hat right under his friend's nose. Bragg went on, "I don't know about trying to use them here, though. If we get challenged—"

"I'll take the chance, sir," Major Manchester said eagerly, peeling a couple of warrants off the top of the sheaf Bushell was holding. "The key thing is speed now, that and gathering the evidence. These will give us just the chance we need to do it." He pumped Bushell's hand. "Thank you, sir. You're a lifesaver, that's what you are." He hurried down the corridor, waving the warrants and shouting for a typist to insert the relevant information on them.

"He looks promising," Bushell said. "Give him the ball and he runs with it."

"That he does." Bragg still sounded slightly dazed. He gathered himself. "Tom, you and Captain Stanley haven't got formal wear for tonight's gathering at the Russian embassy, have you?"

Bushell shook his head. "No, sir. I thought I'd packed clothes for all occasions, but I didn't figure I'd need a monkey suit." Stanley nodded agreement to that.

"It'll have to be dress uniforms for both of you, then," Bragg said. "Those are always acceptable. Why don't we go over to Accoutrements and get you fitted out?"

"Is that still Chalky Stimpson's bailiwick?" Bushell asked in some concern.

"Yes, but there's no help for it. Come along," Sir Horace said inexorably.

"Chalky Stimpson?" Kathleen sounded as if she knew a joke was lurking there somewhere, but couldn't find it.

"He's our tailor," Bushell answered. "He's been the tailor here since the days of William the Conqueror, as best I can tell. He's—how the devil do I say it politely? Chalky's thorough, that's what he is. You'll need to amuse yourself for a while, because once he gets Sam and me in his clutches, he won't let us out any time soon."

"Isn't that the sad and sorry truth?" Stanley agreed mournfully. "I had hoped to go over to Georgestown myself, but if I'm in Chalky's web—" He shook his head. "They'll have to do without me."

"And me," Bushell said. He turned to Sir Horace Bragg. "Can't we just snatch dress trousers and tunic that come close to fitting off their hangers for tonight? We'd look good enough—"

Sir Horace overrode him: "I've been to too many of these formal affairs. 'Good enough' isn't. You don't measure up at one, you don't get invited to another. Remember, Tom, embassies are extraterritorial; we can't make anyone let us in. They have to think we're interesting, or we stay off their grounds and twiddle our thumbs out on the pavement. We have plenty of people who can investigate the late Mr. Venable. We don't have plenty who can hobnob with the diplomats."

"As if anyone ever accused me of being diplomatic." But Bushell threw his hands in the air in surrender. "All right—on to Chalky."

Marcus Aurelius Stimpson—so the sign on his door proclaimed him to be—might not have been in Victoria since 1066, but he probably had been there longer than Bushell had been alive. He was a thin, pale man somewhere between sixty-five and eighty-five—Bushell wondered if anyone knew exactly how old he was. He had been tall; he was now somewhat stooped, but the gray eyes behind bifocals were still keen, and so were his wits, at least in his chosen field of endeavor.

"Ah, Bushell," he said. "Been a while, hasn't it? You were a forty regular. You'd be a forty-two now, I'd say. They feed you well out in New Liverpool, do they?"

"Hullo, Chalky," Bushell said. "*You* haven't changed, anyhow."

"Haven't the time for it," the tailor answered. His gaze swung toward Sam. "And Stanley; I might have known the two of you would hang together. Yes, you're still a forty-four long; don't worry about it."

Stanley smiled. "I wasn't really losing sleep."

"Chalky, they'll both need dress uniforms for tonight," Sir Horace Bragg said.

"It's not enough time," Stimpson grumbled. "Everything is rush, rush, rush these days; people don't take pains to do things properly." He heaved a long sigh. "Well, we'll see what we can manage, so we shall."

He started with trousers and tunic in the two RAM's approximate sizes, then used measuring tape and pins and scissors and the tailor's chalk that had given him his enduring nickname to make alterations. His sewing machine was an ancient model powered by a foot pedal; it would have taken a bolder man than Bushell to suggest that he trade it for one with an electric motor.

"Here." The tailor thrust trousers at Samuel Stanley. "Try these." Stanley dutifully donned them. "Turn around," Stimpson snapped, sounding like a drill sergeant. After Sam turned, the tailor clicked his tongue between his teeth. "No, not quite right. Take 'em off, take 'em off. We'll fix 'em." So Stanley stripped to his drawers once more, while Stimpson surveyed Bushell with a critical eye.

He made several passes on each pair of pants and each tunic. Bushell tried to short-circuit the process halfway through by peering down at himself and exclaiming in tones of wonder, "This is perfect, Chalky! Couldn't fit better!"

"Of course they could," Stimpson said with messianic certainty in his voice. "Come on, strip off—don't dawdle." *Clack, clack, clack* went that antiquated pedal-powered sewing machine. The next time Bushell was suffered to try on the dress uniform, even he had to admit it did fit better . . . but still not well enough to suit Chalky Stimpson.

Lieutenant General Sir Horace Bragg, of course, had in his closet a uniform meeting Chalky's exacting standards. That meant he could—and did—go off to do something useful with his afternoon. Every so often, Bushell pulled the pocket watch from his discarded waistcoat, looked at it, sighed, and put it back.

At last, though, even Stimpson pronounced himself satisfied. "Now I've one more thing to get for the both of you," he said.

"Chalky, you've done too much already," Samuel Stanley said in some alarm. Bushell was just getting a cigar lighted, or he would have beaten his adjutant to the punch.

Behind the bifocals, the tailor's eyes twinkled. "But don't you want the clubs you'll need to beat back all the pretty ladies?"

Sans clubs, Bushell and Stanley made their way to Sir Horace's office. Sally Reese greeted them there. "Hullo, Colonel," she bellowed at Bushell. She wore bifocals, too, along with too much rouge and hair dyed defiantly black. "That redheaded little hussy left this here for you." She thrust an envelope his way, not caring in the least that half the floor now knew her opinion of Kathleen Flannery.

"*Dear Tom,*" the note inside the envelope read in a clear, flowing script, "*I've begged a ride back to my place. Since your famous tailor can't work his magic on me, I've gone in search of something for the night's fes-*"

*tivities that hasn't seen the inside of a suitcase too many times over the past few weeks. I'll be back at the hotel to go to the embassy with you."*

She'd signed it *Kathleen*. A word in front of the signature was too thoroughly scratched out for Bushell to decipher, try as he would.

"Thank you, Sally," he said mildly.

"For what?" she blared. "I never throw anything away, you know that, but I wish I made exceptions, yes I do."

"For being so sweet, of course," Bushell replied, so persuasively that she took it for a compliment.

▼

Back at the William and Mary, Bushell knocked on the door to Kathleen Flannery's room. No one answered. He waited a moment, then knocked again. Still no answer. "Uh-oh," Samuel Stanley said. "That means she's already down in the lobby waiting for us, and we'll never hear the last of it, either."

"If I thought you were wrong, I would argue with you," Bushell answered.

Sure enough, Kathleen walked up to them when they came out of the lift. "Took you long enough," she said, but then, relenting, amended it: "This afternoon, I mean, with Chalky What's-his-name. Let's see what he's done to you." She studied Bushell with the serious attention she might have given a Whistler or a Finlay. "Well. I suppose the wait might have been worth it."

"Thanks," Bushell said. "That's the outfit you brought from home, eh?" He nodded in approval. "You'll do. You'll definitely do." The dress was of maize-colored silk, with a V neck and a sheer organdy collar. It had a pleated skirt with horizontal plaits on the sides, and looked summery enough to be comfortable in Victoria's humid heat. Kathleen set if off with topaz earrings and a pendant that drew the eye to the neckline.

She needed a moment to realize he used understatement in his compliments as elsewhere, then smiled broadly. "Shall we beard the Russian ambassador in his den?" she said.

"I'm given to understand he already has a beard suitable for all ordinary purposes and some extraordinary ones as well, but by all means." Bushell glanced at the clock opposite the lifts. "We're right on time." Offering his arm, he strode toward the hotel's street entrance.

His confidence was justified. Less than a minute later, a steamer driven by Captain Martin pulled up in front of the William and Mary. He opened the door for Kathleen. Bushell and Samuel Stanley got in after her. They glided off toward the Russian embassy.

The guards at the door outside the embassy wore ceremonial uniforms patterned after those of the Life-Guard Dragoons of Tsar Alexander I. Surveying them standing there stiff and motionless, Bushell consoled himself with the thought that their dress uniforms were even more uncomfortable than his. They wore long, heavy coats of dark green wool, with matching trousers reinforced with leather. Over their green tunics they had red shirtfronts held not only with buttons but also with a white satin sash. Their shakos had both plumes and tassels. Sweat gleamed on their broad, ruddy faces.

Their only concession to modernity was carrying bayoneted bolt-action rifles instead of sabers. Bushell glanced toward those rifles and then toward Sam Stanley, who nodded. They'd seen essentially identical Nagants in New Liverpool and up at Buckley Bay.

Inside the embassy, Sir Horace Bragg was talking with a Russian in tailcoat and knee breeches. Sir Horace looked up and saw Bushell and his companions. He waved, then turned back to the Russian. "Here they are now, Mikhail Sergeyevich," he said. "Colonel Bushell, Captain Stanley, Dr. Flannery."

"Very well, Lieutenant General Bragg," the Russian answered with a nod, checking off three names on a list—evidently he was chief of protocol or something of the sort. After he'd made his checks, he dabbed at his broad, bald forehead with a linen handkerchief: St. Petersburg did not prepare a man for the climate of Victoria.

"Come along, come along," Bragg said to Bushell. "We'll make our way through the reception line and then mingle and see what we can learn." He sent Bushell a hooded glance. "Be circumspect, Tom."

"What big words you use, sir," Bushell said with a grin. Bragg's demeanor did not significantly lighten.

But for the fact that a large number of conversations were being carried on in French—and even a few in Russian—the rituals of the reception were remarkably similar to those at Governor Burnett's residence in New Liverpool. Bushell made his way down the line of dignitaries, shaking hands and murmuring polite phrases as he did so. A small gap in the line developed behind him; the Russians had a way of lingering over Kathleen's hand that surprised him not at all.

At the end of the reception line stood Duke Alexei Orlov, the Tsar's ambassador to the North American Union. Orlov's magnificent silver beard spilled halfway down his chest, concealing some of the decorations that he wore. Bushell sometimes thought that, if a Russian noble got out of bed on the same side three days running, the Tsar would pin a medal on his chest to celebrate the achievement.

"I am pleased to meet you, Colonel," Orlov said in good English. "I have been following your exploits with great interest in the newspapers. I wish you the best of good fortune in recovering The Two Georges from the uncultured bandits who so wickedly stole it."

"Thank you, Your Excellency," Bushell said. "Having met Russian guns, grenades, and gold during those exploits, making your acquaintance brings things full circle, in a manner of speaking."

Sir Horace Bragg had already gone through the line, but was hovering not far away. He frowned. Duke Orlov laughed. The shining waves of his beard bobbed up and down. "It is a pleasure to complete your experience, Colonel," he said. Bushell dipped his head, acknowledging the man's unflappability.

A servant came by with a tray of champagne flutes. Bushell took one and sipped. He made for the nearest table, to deposit the glass as unobtrusively as he could.

Behind him, a man spoke in French: "Ah, Colonel, I see you have a discriminating palate. That sweet Crimean swill the Russians lyingly call champagne is fit only for the fattening of hogs."

Bushell turned, replying, also in French, "I think you have reason, monsieur," as he did so. His eyes widened slightly. "Pardon me, but are you not—?"

The Frenchman bowed. "I do indeed have the honor to be *Comte* Philippe Bonaparte, ambassador of His Majesty François IV Bourbon, King of France and Spain and their territories over the sea to your North American Union."

Bushell bowed back. The count was a short, slim, swarthy man in his midfifties, with wavy hair dyed black as Sally Reese's and a chin beard and mustaches whose points were waxed sharp enough to draw blood. He wore a white shirt with a stiff front, wing collar, and black butterfly cravat, and over it a jacket cut like an English tailcoat but, rather than being somber black, made of bright blue velvet embellished with gold thread. His flared trousers were also of blue velvet, his pointed-toed shoes of white patent leather.

As Duke Orlov had, Bonaparte said, "I tell you that I wish you a speedy recovery of your stolen treasure, Colonel."

"That's generous of you, monsieur, when your country would be better served if the Sons of Liberty managed to bring chaos to the British Empire." Bushell stuck up a forefinger. "Wait. Because you tell me this does not mean it is true."

Bonaparte bowed again, his eyes twinkling. "Few men discern subtleties even when their proper language is being spoken. It is the rare individual indeed who hears them in a tongue not his own. You are a gentlemen of considerable resource, Colonel." He laughed in elegant, insincere self-deprecation. "And I, alas, am but a poor diplomat who has proved not diplomatic enough. I tell lies for politeness' sake and I am found out."

"Sometimes you may have to do things for reasons of state that you would not do in your own person," Bushell said.

"If you understand this, Colonel, you understand a great deal," Bonaparte said, more seriously than he had spoken till then.

Kathleen Flannery, having at last escaped the receiving line and the elephantine attentions of Duke Orlov, came over toward Bushell. Like him, she took a glass of sparkling wine from a passing servant; also like him, she found one sip more than sufficient. "That's pretty bad," she said in English, and then switched to French more fluent than Bushell's: "*Monsieur le Comte*, I am pleased to see you again."

"*Mademoiselle Docteur* Flannery, I am always pleased to see you." Bonaparte kissed her hand. He might have been a stock silly-ass Frenchman in a cinema farce, except he really did radiate the charm a comic Frenchman only thought he had. "I am given to understand you and Colonel Bushell have associated yourselves in the search for *Les Deux Georges*."

"We have associated ourselves, yes," Kathleen said.

Bonaparte glanced from her to Bushell and back again. "How am I to construe this, if I may make so bold as to inquire?"

"Why, however you like, of course," Bushell said. "You will anyhow."

"This is an excellent answer," Bonaparte exclaimed, spreading his hands wide to show how fine it was. "Excellent! How is it that you are a mere colonel of police, Monsieur Bushell, when you show wit in even your common utterances, when your commander—you will, I trust, forgive me—while he may be sound enough, cannot be described as anything but stodgy? Perhaps it is that in the British Empire wit is a hindrance rather than an advantage?"

"How is he supposed to answer that without getting into trouble?" Kathleen asked.

The Franco-Spanish ambassador bared his teeth in what was not quite a light, amused grin. "I have not the slightest idea, Dr. Flannery. I leave it up to the colonel's ingenuity."

Bushell knew he was expecting a frivolous reply, and so answered seriously: "I think it is that we respect competence more than wit, monsieur. To us, wit seems dangerous, for it suggests solid abilities a man may in fact fail to possess."

"Well said." Kathleen nodded vigorous approval.

But Philippe Bonaparte shook his head. "I regret that I must disagree with you in particular and, if you are correct, with the British race as well. The competent man can be far more dangerous than the witty one. No one detects his malfeasance till too late, for nothing about him is worthy of notice. The wit, on the other hand, always draws attention to himself. Because he is under so many eyes, he has no choice but probity."

Bushell rubbed at his mustache. "I'm going to have to think about that one before I decide whether I agree with it."

"Colonel, I assure you that I have reason," Bonaparte said. "Perhaps life has not demonstrated as much to you, but it shall, as it does to everyone." He bowed. "And now, if you will excuse me, I must demonstrate to the wider world how charming and sociable I am. Do be certain I wish you my personal best in your efforts to recover your missing work of art."

"Interesting fellow," Bushell remarked thoughtfully. "More to him than you'd guess from that gaudy jacket. I wonder just how he meant that." He chuckled. "You see? There I go again, putting substance ahead of sparkle."

"You'd be a failure at the Court of Versailles," Kathleen said.

"I do hope so," Bushell said. "And speaking of failures—" He glanced at the two abandoned glasses of sparkling wine. "They must have something better somewhere. Shall we investigate?"

"That's what we're here for," Kathleen answered.

The investigation was hardly one to go down in the annals of the Royal American Mounted Police. A red-faced Englishman came out of the next room holding a tall glass with whiskey in it. "I deduce the presence of a bar," Bushell said happily.

"Astonishing!" Kathleen exclaimed. "A lesser mind would have been incapable of it." They both laughed.

Sure enough, in that next room three bartenders struggled mightily to hold thirst at bay for a host of dignitaries. Bushell's laughter dried up. There at the bar stood Sir David Clarke, talking animatedly with a Russian a head shorter than he was. As far as Bushell was concerned, Sir David was the triumph of surface over substance—*he* would have been a smashing success at Versailles or St. Petersburg or wherever flattery and fawning held the keys to advancement.

As a matter of fact, he *was* a smashing success here in Victoria—and what did that say about the NAU?

Rather than contemplating such an unpleasant question, Bushell made his way through the crowd toward the fortified position the bartenders held. Kathleen Flannery followed in his wake. He suspected that the soles of his shoes took the gleam off some patent leather, but he got stepped on himself a couple of times, too, so that game was even.

"Jameson over ice," he said when at last he reached the bar, "and . . . a gin and tonic?" He glanced back over his shoulder at Kathleen to make sure that was really what she wanted. She nodded. "A gin and tonic," he repeated, more firmly.

"*Da,*" the bartender said, and built the two drinks with offhand skill. Bushell had heard that the Russian embassy brought its entire staff, right down to the lowliest sweeper, from the *rodina*, the motherland, the better to keep spies from gaining access to whatever secrets it held. The tale was evidently true.

He knocked back his Irish whiskey and called for another one. Kathleen looked from the empty glass to him and back again. She didn't say anything. She didn't have to say anything. She'd barely tasted her own drink.

"It will be all right," Bushell assured her. Maybe he was assuring himself, too.

The bartender set the second glass of Jameson in front of him. Instead of disposing of it all at once, as he had the first one, he sipped sedately. Kathleen didn't say anything. He liked her better for that. Had she made approving noises, the imp of perversity that dwelt in his breast might have made him get drunk for no better reason than to show her she couldn't make him do everything she wanted.

He took a step back from the bar. Someone else instantly usurped his place. He would have liked nothing better than finding someplace to sit and chat with Kathleen, but this was liable to be his only chance inside the Russian embassy, and he had to make as much of it as he could. When he turned to tell her that, he found her in earnest conversation with a heavyset fellow who spoke French with a Russian accent. They were both talking about *Les Deux Georges.* Bushell sipped at his drink. Evidently, he didn't need to tell her anything.

"Good evening, Colonel." Sir Devereaux Jones made his way through the crowd toward Bushell. "Congratulations on your progress toward recovering *The Two Georges.*"

"I could wish I'd made more, but thanks all the same," Bushell answered. As Tory Party chairman, Sir Devereaux naturally put the best possible face on things. That came with his job, just as running miscreants to earth came with Bushell's.

"You're too modest," Jones said now, as much to the room as a whole as to Bushell. In less public tones, he went on, "Allow me to introduce you to my wife. Alexa, this is Colonel Thomas Bushell, of whom you've seen so much in the papers."

Alexa Jones, a striking blond woman in her early forties, extended a slim hand. "I'm very pleased to meet you, Colonel," she said. By her soft accent,

Bushell guessed she was from Georgia, or perhaps one of the Carolinas. "You've certainly had an exciting time on the trail of *The Two Georges*."

"Much more exciting than I wanted," Bushell answered. "I greatly prefer cases where the villains do something stupid right at the start, so we can scoop them up without ever leaving our desks."

She laughed more than the joke was worth, proving herself a politico's wife. Sir Devereaux Jones laughed, too, but not for long. "Very important to the Union, very important to the Empire, that we get the painting back safe and sound, Colonel," he said. He glanced over toward a couple of members of the Whig shadow cabinet, whom the Russians, in what Bushell thought at best questionable taste, had also invited to the reception. "Not that all the esteemed members of the, ah, loyal opposition would concur, their own interests being affected here, too."

"I understand," Bushell said, hearing what Jones wasn't adding: *very important to the Tory Party*. To him, that was of small consequence. "If *The Two Georges* is destroyed, we lose something precious and unique." He dropped his voice. "And if we pay ransom for it, we lose our peace of mind from now till I don't know when. But then, I daresay you'll have heard my views about that."

"I have had them reported to me in detail, Colonel," Jones replied, deadpan. His wife started to say something, then prudently held her tongue. The two people who would have told Sir Devereaux about Bushell's opinions were Sir Martin Luther King and Sir David Clarke, neither of whom was likely to have been an objective witness.

Jones steered Bushell away from the thickest part of the crowd. Under a somber-faced icon in a frame encrusted with pearls, he said, "Do you think you've been led here as a ruse, or is *The Two Georges* somewhere nearby?"

"That is the question," Bushell said, doing his best to sound like a melancholy Dane. "We've certainly suffered the slings and arrows of outrageous fortune—"

"—And you've taken up arms against a sea of troubles," Jones put in, not to be outdone. "But, the Bard aside—"

"The Bard aside, Sir Devereaux, my opinion is that *The Two Georges* is somewhere not far from here. Whatever the Sons of Liberty intend to do with it is tied to the King-Emperor's arrival in Victoria. And if they were only playing for the fifty million pounds, wouldn't we have heard more about arranging a ransom for the painting?"

Sir Devereaux Jones drew a snuffbox from the inner pocket of his tailcoat. The lid to the box was an enamelwork miniature of *The Two Georges*, brilliant as a jewel. He flipped it open, took a pinch of powdered tobacco, and placed it between his gum and cheek. Then he held out the snuffbox to Bushell, who shook his head. Jones flicked the lid with his thumb; it snapped shut. He put the box back into his pocket.

"That's—a disturbing thought, Colonel," he said at last, his broad face tired and worried. "Having the painting stolen was quite embarrassing enough—"

"More than embarrassing enough," Bushell said.

"Indeed," Sir Devereaux said. "I admit that paying ransom for its return strikes me as being equally unappetizing."

"I hope to God you've told that to Sir Martin," Bushell said. "All he's been hearing is that paying is the only thing he can do."

"And the reasons he's been hearing that is that not paying and having *The Two Georges* destroyed is also a consummation devoutly not to be wished," Jones replied. "I assure you, Colonel: weighing advantages is much more pleasant for a working politico than trying to decide which disadvantageous course has the fewest repugnant consequences. And now you've given me something more to worry about, which may prove even more unfortunate than either of the two previous unpleasant possibilities. I'll remember you in my nightmares." With great determination, he made his way toward the bar, using his wide shoulders to advantage in forcing his way through the crowd.

A string quartet that had been playing arrangements of Russian folk melodies suddenly switched first to "God Save the King" and then to "To Anacreon in Heaven," the old tune to which the NAU's national hymn was sung. Bushell strode back into the room that held Duke Orlov's receiving line: if he could get a chance to speak to Sir Martin Luther King without Sir David Clarke there to whisper into the governor-general's other ear, he would seize it.

Sir Martin and his wife were working their way down the receiving line. Bushell took a strategic position near the end of it. He saw Sir David Clarke appear in the doorway, drawn as he had been by the charge in the musicians' tunes.

A waiter carrying a tray laden with flutes full of nasty Russian sparkling wine came by. "You, there!" Bushell said. The waiter paused but looked blank. Bushell thought fast. "*Parlez-vous français?*" he asked.

Intelligence and comprehension filled the Russian's face. "*Certainement, monsieur.*"

"*Bon.*" Bushell explained what he wanted, pointed discreetly toward Clarke, and pressed a folded red twenty-pound banknote into the fellow's free hand. The way the waiter made it disappear was marvelous to behold. He made his way toward Sir David, who was beginning to approach the receiving line himself. At precisely the right moment, the waiter tripped over some prominent man's foot—or so it seemed, at any rate. He stumbled. Crystal flutes flew off the tray. They made sweet, tinkling music as they shattered on the floor. The wine a good many of them had held drenched Sir David Clarke.

"*Merde!*" he exclaimed into sudden horrified silence: even under the most trying of circumstances, he didn't quite lose his aplomb.

Servants converged on him as if drawn by a lodestone. Some dealt with the broken crystal; others dabbed at him with thick, thirsty cotton towels and, apologizing profusely, led him away for more comprehensive repairs. Conversation picked up again; someone close to Bushell said in English, "Pity we can't send *our* help to Siberia when they blunder so spectacularly, what?" A woman laughed. Bushell sighed. Here and there, you could probably still find people who thought emancipating Negro slaves had been a bad idea, too.

Taking advantage of his stratagem, he approached Sir Martin as the governor-general finally succeeded in emancipating himself from Duke Orlov. King took a glass of sparkling wine from a servitor who hadn't spilled his. He drank it all down, which bespoke either remarkable diplomacy or a lamentable palate.

"What is the latest word, Colonel Bushell?" the governor-general asked, perhaps seeking to forestall him.

It was a good ploy. "I regret I know little more than I did this morning, Your Excellency," Bushell admitted, thinking unkind thoughts about Chalky Stimpson and the inordinate amount of time the RAM tailor had fussed over him.

"No?" Sir Martin's narrow, almost Oriental eyes hooded over. "A pity. We have little time in which to learn. And now, Colonel, if you will excuse me—" His wife on his arm, he swept away.

Bushell had won the battle but lost the war. He consoled himself by remembering how Sir David Clarke had looked with Russian champagne dripping from him. That had been worth twenty quid, even if it hadn't let him have the talk he'd wanted with Sir Martin Luther King. His shoulders moved in a tiny shrug. Sir Martin was prejudiced against him anyway.

He headed back toward the bar. One more drink wouldn't hurt anything. Kathleen might not approve, but Kathleen, he saw, had gone someplace else. Sam Stanley wasn't anywhere close by, either. Having watchdogs around wouldn't have stopped him from doing anything he intended to do, but he was slightly miffed to find them falling down on the job.

He got himself another Jameson and then, as if to prove something to people who weren't watching him as they should have, carried it away with him without sipping from it. He headed farther into the embassy, intent on seeing whatever the Russians were willing to let him see and whatever else he could get away with.

They'd set up a buffet, with delicacies ranging from mushrooms to caviar to pickled herring displayed on glittering ice. Sir Horace Bragg and Sir Martin Luther King both contemplated it. They stood only a few feet from each other, but each man resolutely pretended the other did not exist. Had it not been likely to hamper the investigation, that might have been funny. Contemplating it, Bushell decided a knock of Jameson wouldn't hurt him after all.

He held himself to that one sip, though. Holding his nearly full glass as if it were a talisman, he pressed on. One room down a hallway was fitted out as an Orthodox chapel. The icons there were displayed not as *objets d'art* bit as objects of reverence. Some of them, nonetheless, were very fine art indeed. He stepped into the chapel to admire an image of the Virgin and Child. The Virgin's eyes did not meet his or the Christ child's; they stared off to one side, as if at a holiness and certitude only she could perceive.

With a tiny part of his mind, he heard someone—a woman, he thought—come down the hall and pause in the doorway. Absorbed in contemplation of the icon, he did not turn around.

"Tom?" she said. "It is you, isn't it?"

With a quick, almost convulsive gesture, he raised the glass of Jameson to his mouth and gulped it down. By the time he'd finished swallowing, he had himself back under control. He turned, slowly and deliberately, "Hullo, Irene," he said. "How are you tonight?"

# XIV

▼

IRENE CLARKE—FORMERLY IRENE BUSH-
ell—stood poised in the doorway, as if uncertain whether to go up to him or to flee. "I'm fine," she said after a moment's hesitation, and then, "You're looking very dashing in your dress uniform."

He laughed harshly. "Score one for Chalky Stimpson," he said.

"My God," Irene exclaimed. "They haven't retired old Chalky yet?"

She wouldn't have heard much about the RAMs since her marriage to Bushell . . . ended. He tried another laugh on for size. "Age cannot stale nor custom wither his infinite embroidery," he paraphrased.

The allusion went past Irene. As she often did when momentarily confused, she reached up and patted at her hair with the palm of her hand. Bushell remembered the gesture as if he'd last seen it the day before. But it hadn't been yesterday; it had been years. Reminded of that, he looked at her as she was now, not with the eyes of memory. She was a little heavier than she had been, he decided. Gray frosted her dark brown hair. She wore more powder and paint than she had, the better to hold Father Time at bay.

Still— "You look lovely tonight," Bushell said, not lying too much.

"Thank you." She started to smile, but then her red-painted mouth drew into a thin, hard line. "I would have liked hearing that sort of thing more often when we were married."

"Too late to worry about it now, wouldn't you say?" Bushell answered. "You made bloody sure it's too late. Besides, I expect Sir David pays you compliments all the time . . . whether he means them or not."

"Don't you start that," Irene said, her gray eyes snapping. She'd started it herself, but noting such things was not her long suit. She went on, "David has taken good care of me over the years—better than you ever did, that's certain."

"Sir David takes care of all sorts of things. It's what he's good for." A little too late—as he'd been too late in everything about their marriage, including realizing anything was wrong with it—he tried to be conciliatory. "I'm glad you're happy."

"Happy? I should say so." She tossed her head, another habit he remembered achingly well. "I've seen the *world*, Tom. I've been to London and Paris and St. Petersburg and Vienna. I've seen Rome and Athens and Constantinople and Delhi and Honolulu. And David's a knight, of course, and he's bound to get a higher title later." She stared at Bushell with a mixture of scorn and pity. "No knighthood for you yet? No, I'd have heard. None likely, either, I'd say."

Bushell shrugged. She'd been something of a social climber when she was his wife; being married to Sir David had evidently nourished that character trait. He said, "As long as I know I'm doing my job well, I don't care whether I have a *Sir* in front of my name."

"I know *you* don't," she said with a dismissive wave—almost a push—of her hand. "But what about your, ah, friend with the red hair? Pretty little thing, even if she is rather young."

What about Kathleen? Bushell didn't know, but he was damned if he was going to tell that to Irene. "You've got no business taking that tone with me," he growled. He wished he hadn't been to the bar before he ran into his former wife. He'd moved into a hotel the very day he'd found her and Sir David Clarke together; after that, their conversation had been entirely through solicitors. He had things—years' worth of things—he'd never told her. With whiskey in him, with her standing in front of him, all the stored-up anger was liable to come spewing out. He hadn't known how much there was, not till now, not till it heaved against all the restraints he'd built to hold it back, bubbling upward like lava under a volcano that had been—had been—dormant.

"Why not?" Irene said. She kept her voice down, remembering where they were, but she sounded angry, too. *That's pretty funny,* he thought: her *angry at me.* "Why not?" she repeated. "We're both in the same place at the same time for once, so you can listen to me for a change."

"And what the devil is that supposed to mean?" Bushell demanded.

"Just what it says," Irene answered. "You were never there when we were married, that's for certain. If you weren't on the road, you were at the office, and if you weren't at the office, you were sitting in front of a typewriter, pounding out endless stupid reports no one would ever read. You never gave me the notice you'd pay a florin slug fished out of a stamp-selling machine, not unless you were hungry or you wanted to go to bed with me—sometimes not even then."

"That's a lie," Bushell said, though it had an unpleasant ring of truth. "I did work for a living, you know. I still do, as a matter of fact."

"God help your pretty little friend, then," Irene said.

"Leave Kathleen out of it. She's none of your business—you made bloody sure of that, didn't you?"

Irene tossed her head. Under her makeup, she flushed; that shot had got home. "I had to do something, didn't I, to remind myself I was alive. Better than waiting for you to notice me, that's for sure." She made a small, purring sound, deep in her throat. "A lot better, let me tell you."

He wanted to slap her face. Remembering they were years divorced and in public came hard, hard. He shuddered with the effort of not taking a step toward her. "What was the point of talking about my work with you, Irene?" he asked wearily. "You never paid any attention when I did, so I thought I might as well not bore you. All you wanted to talk about was—"

"Life?" she suggested. "Whatever you call it, it was more interesting than the dusty things you were always puttering over."

"It was my life," Bushell said. "It *is* my life."

"That's what I said: God help—Kathleen, did you say her name was? What a boring, useless life it was. It's no wonder that I—" Irene stopped.

"That you what?" Bushell demanded. He still found himself knowing, as if by instinct, when Irene wasn't saying something that mattered. She might not have thought he was paying attention to her, but he was, even if not in ways she would have wanted.

"Don't you badger me," she said. "It's none of your affair." She laughed, unpleasantly. "Certainly not that. Boring." She gave an emphatic nod, as if that proved the truth of her description. Then she threw more fuel on the fire: "What a gray way to pass the days. Do your work, write your reports, go through forty years, and what do you get? A pension. A gold pocket watch. A funeral, because you hadn't noticed you were already dead. So what? I wanted someone who would stay interesting, someone who was going somewhere, someone who would take me with him. I found someone like that, too."

"Oh, yes, you found Sir David," Bushell said. "You welcomed him with open arms, in fact—and open legs, too." Irene gasped; that one stung, too. Bushell went on, "You just wanted to live out your silly dreams, even though you knew they were silly. RAMs mostly don't get knighted, no matter what they do, and you know why. The work is like an iceberg: nine tenths of it never comes up above the waterline to be noticed."

"What about your dear chum, Lieutenant General Sir Horace Bragg?" Irene said.

Bushell didn't fancy the way she flung the question at him. "There are exceptions to everything," he answered, trying to take no notice of her tone. His private opinion was that Bragg had got the knighthood by stubbornly going after it till at last it fell into his lap. That was how Sir Horace got everything. A couple of more deserving men might have been up for consideration, but no one would have made the merits he did have more visible to the right people.

"Do you remember the party we had for him when his name went onto the list?" Irene asked. A nasty glow kindled in her eyes.

"Yes, I remember," Bushell said shortly, as if he were in the witness box, trying to admit as little as possible to a barrister. "So what?"

"So what, is it?" she snapped. Something—unshed tears?—roughened her voice. "After I put up with so much from you, that's all I get? So what? God damn you to hell, Tom Bushell, I'll tell you so what." She took a deep breath. "Do you remember that party? Do you?"

"I already said I did." Rubbed raw by her tone, he fired back at her: "And I'll tell you what else I remember: I remember what a shockingly bad hostess you were. You kept disappearing, and I can't imagine where you got to." Amazing, he thought, how annoyances from years before could suddenly spring to life again when watered.

He'd thought—he'd hoped—the gibe would anger her even more. To his surprise, she threw back her head and laughed. She *was* plumper; he took a certain malicious glee in noting the onset of a double chin. But she was still angry, too: she said, "Then you haven't got much imagination, have you? I'll tell you just where I was: I was helping Sir Horace celebrate his knighthood with some-thing better than cocktails and canapés." She twitched her hips to leave him in no possible doubt about her meaning. A reminiscent smile spread over her face. "Quite a lot better, if you must know."

"I don't believe you," Bushell said automatically.

"I don't care," Irene answered. "It's true whether you believe it or not."

To his horror, Bushell did believe it. Just as he'd always known when Irene was leaving something out of what she was saying, he'd also always known when she was telling nothing but the truth, no matter how crazy it sounded. He heard that ring of truth in her voice now, he felt it in his belly—and how he wished he didn't.

She sniffed. "I don't know how you've hung on so long in police work, Tom, when you can't see the nose on your face. All these years, and you haven't changed a bit. It's too bad. I'd hoped you might have. It could have been—inter-esting."

Dully, he realized he'd borrowed his odd use of that word from her. He also realized she'd been thinking about putting horns on Sir David with him, just as she'd put horns on him with Sir David—and with Sir Horace? The revelation shook him as if the unsteady ground of New Liverpool rocked beneath his feet.

Irene twitched her hips again. "Do you want me to tell you *all* about it?" she asked.

"No," he said, his voice not angry now, but absentminded: he might have only half heard her. He looked straight through her toward the far wall. He wasn't ignoring her existence; he'd just forgotten about it. Her mouth narrowed again. She'd seen that faraway look in his eyes during their married days. It meant he was thinking hard about a case, generally to the exclusion of her. She'd made it all too plain she'd had too much of that then. She turned and walked away. Bushell's eyes never wavered.

"Lieutenant General Sir Horace Bragg," he said in slow, quiet wonder. "I can't believe it." He'd known Horace Bragg for going on thirty years now. He couldn't imagine his old friend being able to keep that kind of secret from him. And he'd never had the slightest inkling of it, not even after he'd found out Irene was being unfaithful with Sir David Clarke. Good God! If anyone had helped him get through the dark times after his marriage burned like an airship full of hydrogen, Horace Bragg was the man.

He blinked, then chuckled softly. He was less angry with Irene now, knowing what she'd spewed out at him, than he had been while they were quarreling. With the quarrel past, it felt over, done, abruptly years old, not immediate, harsh, painful. Maybe taking up with Kathleen really had soothed some of his bitterness there—or maybe he'd needed to get that last fight out of his system. Maybe Irene had, too.

But what the devil was he to do when he saw Sir Horace, which he was li-able to do in a matter of seconds and would certainly do no later than tomorrow morning? How could he keep working with Sir Horace to recover *The Two Georges*?

He squared his shoulders. Thinking of it that way helped put matters in perspective. He'd served with plenty of men for whom he didn't care: he was, after a fashion, even cooperating with Sir David Clarke, whom he despised. He tapped his left hand against the side of his thigh. He still thought Sir David the likeliest conduit through whom the Sons of Liberty might have learned of the King-Emperor's plans to visit the NAU, but he had only suspicions, no evidence to support them.

But this would be different from cooperating with Sir David. He'd never liked Clarke, even before the man took Irene away from him . . . or she departed, however that had been. He and Sir Horace, though—

Something else struck him. He hadn't seen Cecilia Bragg here at the embassy. She'd always been the self-effacing sort; Sir Horace might not have brought her along tonight. But he'd brought her to Bushell's house that night years ago. Bushell remembered kissing her on the cheek as she and Sir Horace came through the door.

Where had Sir Horace kissed Irene, later that night?

Bushell shook his head. He couldn't afford thoughts like that, not now. He glanced back at the icon of the Virgin. He had no great piety, but couldn't help wishing Irene had found a different place to tell him what she'd told him. Then it occurred to him that even a pious man would agree no man—or woman—save only the Virgin's Son was without sin. Maybe the little chapel hadn't been the worst place for such news after all.

He went out and walked back to the bar. He stiffened when he saw a red coat there, but Samuel Stanley was wearing it. Sam, who was holding a pint pot, glanced over at him as he ordered another Jameson. "Haven't seen you in a while," Stanley remarked. The unspoken question *How many of those have you had?* lay behind his words.

"I'll drive you back to the William and Mary, if you like," Bushell replied, answering what his adjutant had asked rather than what he'd said.

"We'd disappoint the poor fellow waiting out there for us if you did," Stanley said, but let it go at that. He glanced toward the bartenders to make sure they couldn't overhear before lowering his voice: "Learn anything worthwhile?"

"Oh, a couple of things," Bushell said. Stanley brightened. Then Bushell added, "They haven't got anything to do with the case, though, worse luck. How about you, Sam?"

"Me? I've learned pickled herring goes right well with ale, and I've learned I ought to brush up on my French: I know I'm missing half of what goes on around me. That hasn't got anything to do with the case, either. I was hoping you'd have better news—you must have been poking into odd corners."

"Oh, I was," Bushell said, "and I ran into some odd people, too." He let it go at that. Running into Irene would have been trying enough without what she'd told him. With that news . . . he knew he needed to do a lot more thinking.

Sam Stanley straightened to a semblance of attention, just ostentatiously enough to show Bushell he was doing it. Bushell could think of only one reason why Sam would do such a thing. He turned to find Sir Horace Bragg approaching.

"Here we are all together, a flock of Robin Redbreasts," Bragg said, his jovial tone contrasting oddly with his usual dolorous expression. "We can give the damned Russians something to stare at."

"Yes, sir." Bushell brought the words out with an effort, as if he were much drunker than he was in fact. How could Sir Horace have taken Irene to bed when he and Bushell had already been friends for half a lifetime? Friends didn't—or friends shouldn't—do things like that. And how could he have gone on about his business afterward as if nothing had happened? It was a puzzlement.

Bragg leaned close to him. "Any luck?" he whispered, breathing Scotch and tobacco into Bushell's face.

"No, sir," Bushell answered, as woodenly as before.

Sir Horace set a hand on his shoulder. He almost shook it off in unthinking rejection, like a horse twitching its ear to be rid of a fly—that was the hand that had cupped Irene's breast, squeezed her bum, and then clasped his own hand in friendship. *Years ago, all years ago*, he reminded himself, and stood still. "We'll get the bastards tomorrow, then," Bragg said. He sounded very sure of himself. "It's heading toward midnight now, though. We should break away if we're to be good for anything in the morning. This affair will go on till all hours." His bushy eyebrows came down in stern disapproval. "Why not? Most of the people here don't have to work for a living, not really."

"I suppose not," Bushell said—he *could* come out with more than two words at a time. The more he tried, the easier it became: "Let me find, uh, Kathleen." He'd almost said *Irene*. To cover the near-slip, he went on, "Your driver will be wanting to get home, too, I expect."

Bragg tried to fit a smile onto the narrow, bony contours of his face. "You always did take good care of the men in your command, Tom."

"It's the mark of a good officer," Samuel Stanley observed. Half a beat too late, he added, "Sir."

"Come on, Sam, you can help me round up the lady," Bushell said in his best facetious tones. He wanted nothing more than to get away from Sir Horace Bragg, and, after that last dig, Stanley needed to escape the commandant.

Bushell found Kathleen near the buffet, discussing early nineteenth-century art with Comte Philippe Bonaparte. "I hold you personally responsible, Colonel, for depriving me of the company of this charming young lady," Bonaparte said.

"I'll survive," Bushell said dryly. The Franco-Spanish ambassador chuckled. Bushell went on. "I have to say, *Monsieur le Comte*, that I may owe you an apology."

"For taking Dr. Flannery away?" Bonaparte asked. "Other than that, you have done nothing to cause offense, I assure you."

"No, not for that," Bushell answered. "I've been thinking. You may have been right about the trouble a merely competent man can cause." Kathleen Flannery looked a question at him. He pretended he didn't notice.

▼

Maybe Lieutenant General Sir Horace Bragg had actually got himself a good night's sleep. Maybe he'd just fortified himself with several cups of coffee or strong tea. Whichever was the case, he seemed alert, energetic, and enthusiastic when Bushell and his companions walked into RAM headquarters the next morning.

"Here—come see," he said, directing them to a storeroom where RAMs were methodically going through a couple of file cabinets' worth of documents. "We pulled these from Eustace Venable's home and cabinetry shop yesterday. We haven't seen everything there is to see, but you were right, Tom—he is definitely linked to some men in and round Victoria who are known to be affiliated with the Sons of Liberty. We'll pay them visits today."

"That's—first-rate, sir," Bushell said. Regardless of whether Sir Horace had taken Irene to bed, his minions looked to have come up with important evidence. If dealing with the evidence meant dealing with Bragg, too, Bushell was willing to make the sacrifice. Solving the case was more important than whether his friendship survived. A huntsman's eagerness stirred in him. "I want to go along on one of those raids."

"So do I," Samuel Stanley said.

"Me, too," Kathleen added. Before Bragg could say anything, she went on, "Pity you didn't send your men to Venable's house and shop a day earlier, Sir Horace. Then they could have been raiding while we were at the embassy banquet last night."

The RAM commandant, who had been lighting a cigar, suffered a coughing fit. When he'd stopped hacking, he said, "I do regret that, Dr. Flannery. Of course you may accompany Colonel Bushell and Captain Stanley. I have no doubt that you will discover something they overlook." The irony was thick enough to slice. Kathleen didn't care. She looked smug. She'd goaded Sir Horace into giving her exactly what she wanted. And, as far as Bushell was concerned, she'd been dead right about when the RAMs should have gone out to Eustace Venable's residence and business.

"Where do you propose sending us, sir?" Stanley asked. He had no interest in quarreling with Bragg. All he wanted to do was to help push the case forward in whatever way he could.

"Based on the evidence we found at Venable's shop, we've obtained a warrant to search the home of Phineas Stanage," Bragg answered. Now it was his turn to be smug.

Bushell jerked as if stung by a wasp. "Stanage!" he said. "We never could touch him before. Not enough evidence, the judges kept saying—he's a sharp devil, and a careful one. But we've got it now, by God! Kilbride was visiting with him, that tea-seller up in Boston told me. If Venable is—was—connected to Stanage, too, odds are good he's up to his neck in the *Two Georges* case."

Sam Stanley looked at Bragg with respect perhaps grudging but no less genuine for that. "If you've talked a magistrate into granting us a search warrant for Phineas Stanage's house, sir . . . we ought to break things wide open."

"Let's hope so," Bragg said. Bushell nodded in understanding. He and Sam had both thought the case was about to break wide open several times, only to be disappointed. Here in Victoria, Sir Horace must have been sliding from exhilaration to gloom along with them. Now he added, "Stanage isn't the only chap we've tied to your cabinetmaker, either, Tom." He spoke several other names, two or three of which were familiar to Bushell.

"They're all guilty as sin, no doubt. Let somebody else bag them, though." Bushell's face went predatory. "Stanage is the one I want. Cut off the head and the body dies."

"Pity you didn't find anything leading you back to John Kennedy," Kathleen remarked. Yes, she could hold a grudge: Bushell took note.

For the first time, Sir Horace Bragg looked on her with something other than glowering disapproval, no doubt because it was the first time she'd said in his presence anything with which he agreed. "That *is* a pity," he said in musing tones. "Well, no matter. I presume you want to be after the foe."

Bushell nodded, replying with a couplet from Pope's *Essay on Man:* "'One master-passion in the breast, / Like Aaron's serpent, swallows all the rest.'"

Kathleen smiled; maybe she recognized the quotation. Bragg obviously didn't. He wasn't one for poetry or classics—law books suited him better. A *competent man*, Bushell thought. Philippe Bonaparte notwithstanding, competence was useful and more than useful in a police officer. But could you truly understand *what* if you'd never thought about *why*?

He put aside such musings as unprofitable as he went out to the steamers that would take him and his companions, along with several local RAMs, to Phineas Stanage's home. The locals were armed. Bushell nodded again, this time in grim approval—Bragg was taking no chances.

Bushell had seen Stanage's home before, when RAMs surveyed it in the hope of discovering something actionable there. The oaks in front of it and the magnolia to one side were taller than they had been years ago. Sometime in there, Stanage had changed the paint on the two-story building from white to light blue. Otherwise, all was as it had been.

No, Bushell found one more difference: now he didn't have to watch the home from afar. Along with the rest of the RAMs and Kathleen Flannery, he marched up to the front door. The knocker was a shiny brass eagle. He took primitive pleasure in making a racket with it.

The door opened. A servant in a long black skirt and frilly white shirtwaist stared out at the RAMs. "Oh, God," she said.

One of the local officers brandished the search warrant. In a fine bureaucratic drone, he said, "By authority of His Majesty's court here in Victoria as symbolized in this warrant, we are authorized to search the property and premises of Mr. Phineas W. Stanage. Please stand aside, Miss, and let us perform our duty."

"Mr. Stanage, he isn't going to like this," the servant predicted.

"What a shame the warrant doesn't cover his opinions," Bushell said. He stepped over the threshold. The servant got out of his way.

He—and no doubt the other RAMs with him—took a certain malicious glee in going through the home of a Son of Liberty. By the time they'd been inside for a couple of minutes, the place looked as if a tornado had hit it. The contents of drawers were dumped out onto the floor, then the drawers themselves, then furniture cushions. After that, chairs and sofas got overturned so the RAMs could make sure nothing was lurking in their linings.

Kathleen watched in amazement as what had been a neat and orderly establishment was turned inside out. The maidservant who'd admitted the RAMs and the rest of the staff watched, too, in something more like horror. Bushell felt a certain amount of sympathy for them. Once the RAMs had left, they were the ones who would have to clean up the mess.

Phineas Stanage arrived about half an hour after the RAMs went to work. Bushell presumed one of the neighbors had called him. He was a corpulent man in his mid-fifties, with a close-trimmed white beard and gold-framed bifocals. He wore a suit of Donegal tweed that Bushell wouldn't have minded having, and looked like what he was: the chairman of a prosperous brewing company.

He took one look at the chaos in the front hall and bellowed, "This is an outrage!" He proceeded to embellish and elaborate upon that theme for several minutes, with ever-increasing heat and sulfur content. Bushell listened in considerable admiration. Whatever Phineas Stanage was now, at some point in his life he'd been a soldier, a sailor, or a scatologist's assistant.

When Stanage started repeating himself, Bushell whistled a couple of bars of "Yankee Doodle." "That's a filthy lie!" Stanage shouted.

"Is it?" Bushell said. "Eustace Venable didn't think so. Do you want to tell me about your dealings with him?"

He hoped Stanage would be furious enough to do just that. But the brewing magnate said, "I wouldn't tell you my name without my solicitor present."

"Good to hear someone knows it," Bushell murmured, which set Stanage spluttering anew. It was not an informative sort of spluttering; after a minute or so, Bushell stopped listening to it.

A call came floating down the stairwell: "We've started up here on the first floor, sir. All sorts of lovely things to take apart and paw through." Bushell glanced at Phineas Stanage. The man's cheeks and forehead were noticeably redder than they had been when he first reached his home. Would he fall down in a fit of apoplexy? Bushell wouldn't have missed him, but he stayed resolutely—and irately—upright.

Sure enough, when Bushell went upstairs he found Sam Stanley and a couple of other RAMs tossing clothes out of Stanage's closets and going through the papers in three tall oak filing cabinets. Kathleen had joined the sport, too. The cabinets had presumably been locked before the RAMs got to them, but any search team brought along someone gifted in the art of making locked things open.

"Anything juicy?" Bushell asked in hopeful tones.

Stanley made a sour face. "We haven't found anything yet. I don't care for his politics, I don't care for the people he associates with"—he gestured toward some of the file folders strewn on the floor to show how he'd drawn his conclusions about those—"but nothing out-and-out illegal, not yet."

"I don't know about that." A local RAM held up a copy of the scurrilous pamphlet about the imperial princesses that Titus Hackett and Franklin Mansfield had printed in New Liverpool—*paid for with Russian roubles*, Bushell remembered. "If this isn't obscene, what is?"

Regretfully, Bushell shrugged. "I don't know, Captain, but a jury decided that it wasn't."

The local RAM rolled his eyes. "Juries do strange things sometimes." Every RAM in the room nodded solemn agreement to that.

Phineas Stanage came clumping up the stairs. He clapped a melodramatic hand to his forehead. "Good God! The minions of the Grand Inquisitor in Madrid couldn't do worse than this!"

"You're wrong in two particulars," Bushell answered. "Inquisitors wouldn't bother with a warrant, and they'd take you apart at the same time as they would the house."

"Only a barbarian, a Cossack, would boast that something could be worse," Stanage retorted. One of the RAMs searching on the ground floor knocked something over with a crash. Stanage groaned and dashed down there to find out what the newest catastrophe was.

Kathleen Flannery pointed to the file cabinets. "Do those drawers come out?" she asked. "He might have hidden something behind one of them."

"Next item on the agenda, ma'am," a RAM said, and whipped out a long-shanked screwdriver. He attacked the file cabinets, one after the other. Out came the drawers. He set them on the floor, none too gently. Then he peered into each cabinet, shining a little electric touch to make sure he missed nothing. "If he has stashed anything away, he didn't do it here," he said in disappointed tones.

"Who says he didn't?" Kathleen reached out and plucked free a folded sheet of paper that had been taped to the back of one of the drawers. With a flourish, she presented it to Bushell. The gleam in her eyes said she had a sharp comeback waiting for Lieutenant General Sir Horace Bragg.

"Well, well, what have we here?" Bushell said. The other RAMs and Kathleen crowded round to see what they had there. Bushell unfolded the paper, holding it at arm's length so he could read whatever message it contained. That message, eight typewritten characters' worth, did not make immediate sense:

HM 1608 DC

"What the devil does that mean?" asked the RAM who'd dismantled the file cabinets.

"I can figure out part of it, I think," Kathleen said. Everyone looked at her. She colored a little, but went on, "His Majesty is coming to Victoria on the six-teenth of this month—the sixteenth of August—isn't he?"

"So he is," Bushell said, nodding approval: three fourths of the riddle solved in one fell swoop.

"Nicely done," Samuel Stanley agreed, just as quietly. At the praise from him, Kathleen's face lit up like a sunrise. It brightened even further when the RAM with the screwdriver clapped his hands together twice. She could pull her weight here, and was proving it to everyone.

Bushell stared at the last two characters, the ones Kathleen hadn't deci-phered. In a musing voice, he went on, "We have what. We have when. What does that leave?" He often used Sam for a sounding board; now he noticed he was talking to Sam and Kathleen both. Before either of them could speak, he answered his own question: "Who was sending the message, maybe."

"Who's DC?" Kathleen asked.

"Haven't you ever heard of Defore Christ?" asked the RAM with the screwdriver. Kathleen gave him a disgusted look. Bushell didn't blame her, but saw something she missed: the banter meant the RAMs had accepted her as one of their own.

And, with a light like the sun breaking through on a cloudy day, he knew who DC might be. Without another word, he folded the paper again and put it in his inside coat pocket. He wondered if Captain Patricia Oliver could match the typewriter on which the message had been produced. If she couldn't, he'd suggest some possible comparisons.

Samuel Stanley nudged him. "You don't think—?" He stopped, his eyes widening. "You do think."

"Do you know what, Sam?" Bushell said. "I hope I'm wrong." That surprised him. For years, he would have liked nothing better than to see Sir David Clarke held up to public obloquy. Now that the chance appeared before him, he found it was liable to cost more than it was worth. Betraying your sovereign was a much darker business than stealing another man's wife. He didn't want to imagine even Clarke capable of it.

Kathleen realized who DC might be a few seconds after Bushell and Stanley. "I hope you're wrong, too, Tom," she said, "for—for everyone's sake."

"For everyone's sake, I'm going to arrest Mr. Phineas Stanage," Bushell said. "We'll see what questioning him back at RAM headquarters will get us."

When Stanage found out he would have to go with the RAMs, he put on a display of cursing that made his previous efforts sound uninspired. Bushell showed him the paper that had led to his arrest. "You are an idiot, a cretin, a moron, a one hundred percent unadulterated jackass," Stanage boomed. "That, if you must know, is the password I have to furnish at the Bank of London, Victoria, and Alexandria to gain access to my safety-deposit box. My solicitor can arrange to prove that for you. He can also arrange a suit for false arrest, and I have no doubt that he shall."

"You'll come along with us anyhow," Bushell answered, which produced more bravura blasphemies from Stanage. Inside, though, Bushell worried. Bank records were hard to alter, and he'd never heard of the Bank of London, Victoria, and Alexandria's being connected to the Sons of Liberty. On the contrary: it was, so far as he knew, a solid, conservative financial institution.

"Don't let it bother you, Chief," Sam Stanley said as they drove back to RAM headquarters. "Let him sue all he likes. There'll be enough in those papers of his to keep him in hot water for years." He sounded as if he relished the prospect.

"I know," Bushell answered. "But there's one particular kind of hot water I want him to be in." He looked at the sheet Kathleen had found, then shook his head. "No, no one would believe this didn't have something to do with *The Two Georges,* not even a judge . . . I hope."

Several teams of RAMs had already returned from their raids when Bushell and his companions got back to headquarters. They cheered when they found he'd come back with something worth pursuing; most of them had had little luck. "From what we found by looking, you'd think the miserable Sons were all deacons and altar boys," a disgruntled RAM complained.

Bushell took the paper with the single typewritten line on it to Captain Oliver. He explained where he'd found it and what he thought it was. "Very good," she said with a brisk nod, and examined the line. "Yes, that's a Quiet Writer, a popular brand here in Victoria. I use one myself, as a matter of fact."

"And Victoria's the typewriter capital of the NAU, along with every other kind," Bushell said. "How can you be a bureaucrat if you don't have a typewriter? That makes things harder."

"Not necessarily." Patricia Oliver reached into a desk drawer and pulled out a jeweler's loupe, which she set in front of her eye to look at the characters more closely. "Yes, I thought so. The C rides slightly above the line, and the H slightly below. And there is—I think there is—a slight flaw in the left-hand stem of the M. If this comes from any machine Sir David Clarke was likely to be able to get his hands on at the governor-general's mansion, we should be able to identify it."

"Good. I hoped you'd say that." Bushell paused for a moment. "If he has a typewriter at home, you might want to check that, too. Discreetly, of course."

She took off the loupe and glanced up at him. "So discreetly he never finds out about it? So discreetly a judge never finds out about it?" Bushell didn't answer. He made a point of not answering. Patricia Oliver gave him a knowing smile different from the one she'd used in the Grosvenor Hotel bar on the other side of the continent. "That might be arranged . . . discreetly, as you say. If we learn anything interesting from it, I expect we'll be able to bring it to the attention of the proper authorities . . . discreetly, again."

"Fine," he said. "I thought you'd be able to manage something along those lines. Getting type samples from machines you want to check must be hard sometimes."

"Sometimes," she agreed. "One way or another, though, I generally manage to get what I want." When Bushell didn't rise to that, she said, "I must introduce you to my husband one day while you're here."

"I'd like that," Bushell said. "I suspect he's a luckier man than even he knows."

Patricia Oliver laughed. "You're so quiet most of the time. That makes you twice as dangerous when you do let fly." An expression he couldn't quite read replaced the amusement on her face. "I gather your current . . . friend wasn't hampered by the inconvenient presence of a bit of jewelry?" She spread the fingers of her left hand. The diamond on the fourth one sparkled: a large stone, and a fine one, if Bushell was any judge.

"No, Kathleen's not married," he said steadily.

"Not yet," Patricia murmured. More directly to him, she went on, "I hope you end up happy, however that turns out."

Bushell hadn't thought about being happy in a long time, not as a continuous as opposed to a momentary condition. He found the notion unlikely. "I suppose stranger things have happened," he said, and left before Patricia Oliver found a reply.

More teams of RAMs were coming in, bringing with them little evidence but a lot of unhappiness. "By what my gang found, you'd think the bloody Sons knew we were coming," growled a major with a beard that didn't quite hide a scar on his right cheek.

He might not have meant his words literally, but they produced an appalled silence from his colleagues. Then, from the doorway, Sir Horace Bragg said, "I heard that." The local RAMs were appalled all over again; several of them seemed to be looking for places to hide. Bushell didn't blame them. Sir Horace might be good at holding things in, but when he lost his temper, the results could be memorable.

Remembering what Irene had flung in his face, Bushell realized just how good Bragg was at holding things in. For one frightening instant, Bushell teetered on the edge of throwing himself at the man who had cuckolded him and then gone on about his business as if nothing had happened. His right hand twitched, starting to make a fist; the muscles in his shoulder bunched, as if he were about to throw a punch. Making himself ease away from that animal rage was one of the harder things he'd done. *Not now, dammit,* he told himself fiercely. *No matter how good it would feel, not now.*

Bragg, oblivious—as Bushell had been oblivious for so long—looked around with his large, sad eyes and said, "Williams, I fear you may be right."

"My God, sir," said the scarred major—Williams, evidently. "That would mean the Sons have a source—here." He turned through 360 degrees, as if to scan everyone's face to try to spot the traitor.

"The day before yesterday," Bragg said, biting his lip in anger, "I had the distinct displeasure of sacking a pair of Royal American Mounted Policemen at our Richmond office, on the grounds that they had cooperated with the Sons of Liberty there to impede investigation of several local crimes of which various Sons were suspected. This cooperation had apparently been going on for some time before it drew notice. If it happened there, it's not beyond the bounds of possibility that it could be happening here. I have instituted an investigation to determine whether that is in fact so."

Now every RAM was looking at all the others. No one bore the mark of Cain on his forehead. Bushell rubbed at his mustache. If the RAMs couldn't trust their own friends in the investigation, that would make things a lot harder. You wouldn't want to share what you'd learned. You'd hold it and keep it to yourself. And if Fred over there might usefully have combined it with something he knew . . . well, too bad.

"Sir, I hope you find the—" The presence of Kathleen and a couple of RAMs of the female persuasion inhibited Bushell in his choice of words, but he packed as much temper into that silence as Phineas Stanage had into a whole string of incandescent obscenities.

"So do I," Sir Horace said wearily. "I heard on the wireless this morning that the *Britannia* has set sail for the NAU. We haven't much time left."

The gathered search teams broke up after that, some to examine the meager haul of evidence they'd found, others to pursue new leads. Bushell went off to find a telephone. The busier he kept himself, the less chance he'd have to think about what Bragg had said. He didn't want to think about that. He couldn't do anything about it anyhow, except to be careful to whom he spoke. Trying to get *The Two Georges* back before Charles III arrived and trying to make sure Victoria was safe for him when he did arrive would keep him busy enough, or rather more than busy enough.

He rang Captain Jaime Macias back in New Liverpool. A few days before, Macias had been on the point of telling him something important, and he still didn't know what. *Time to find out,* he thought.

The connection went through smoothly. Given Victoria's massive telephone exchange building, he would have been surprised and annoyed if it hadn't. And, for a wonder, Jaime Macias was at his desk. "Tom!" he said when Bushell reached him. "Good to hear from you, friend. By what I see in the papers and hear on the wireless, you're not having a dull time of it."

"That's a fact," Bushell agreed. "This case has given me a whole new appreciation of what a lovely word *routine* is, let me tell you. You sit at your desk, you sift through the clues, you go out and arrest the villains, and you fling them into gaol where they belong. That's the way it's supposed to work. Having the buggers greet you with bullets and grenades isn't."

"Adventures are nasty things that happen to other people, eh?" Macias suggested. They both laughed.

Bushell said, "Last time I managed to get hold of you, you sounded like a man on the trail of something good. I never did find out what—that was when I got to make the acquaintance of Mr. Eustace Venable, or rather of his hand grenade. So what's the word?"

"We have a little more checking to do, to make the case as gastight as a coronium bladder in an airship, but in another few days, we're going to drop on the chap who shot Tricky Dick. We've got him under twenty-four-hour surveillance now; he won't get away. We need to nail a last couple of things into place before we get out the warrant."

"That *is* good news," Bushell said, leaning forward on the desk as if to go after the villain himself. "How'd you come to suspect him?"

"We went over every bloody square inch of that brush-covered knoll across from the governor's mansion about a dozen times," Macias answered, his voice full of remembered weariness. "Not far from where we think the gunman fired, we found a good, clear footprint of a size eleven and a half shoe. And ever since then, we've been following up on Sons of Liberty whose gaol records show they have size eleven and a half feet."

"Good Lord," Bushell said in profound respect. "Talk about needles in haystacks! And you found a match, did you? Who is he?"

"His name is Zack Fenton," Macias said. "He's not your typical Son, by any means: he has a Nuevespañolan common-law wife, for instance. Only political arrest was for disorderly conduct at an Independence Party rally a few years ago, at which time pamphlets from the Sons were discovered on his person. But he has served two stretches of time for poaching on the property of His Majesty's Wildlife Parks."

"He'll know how to handle a rifle, then," Bushell said, nodding even though

Macias could not see him. "Good circumstantial evidence. If you can get someone to put him at the scene of the crime at the right time, he's yours."

"That's what we're working on," Jaime Macias answered. "He's supposed to
have been at a card game, but one of the chaps there is starting to go, 'Well, he
might have stepped out for a little while, but maybe he didn't, too'—you know
what I mean?"

Bushell nodded again. "Oh, yes. I don't think there's a police officer in the
NAU who hasn't heard that song a time or six. Make this Fenton's chum sweat—
if you can break the case open from that end, it'll do me a good turn on this one.
Let me know whenever something happens. If you can't catch me here at headquarters, I'm staying at the William and Mary."

"The William and Mary," Macias repeated, probably as he was writing it
down. "All right, Tom, you'll hear from me as soon as I know anything."

"Thanks, Jaime. Good luck—and be careful." Bushell had given that warning to a great many officers since *The Two Georges* disappeared. He still lived in
the hope that people occasionally listened to what he said, though he hadn't evidence of it to take before a judge.

He got up and started off to carry the good news to Sir Horace Bragg. Before
he made it to the door of the office he'd borrowed, the telephone rang. He
frowned, wondering if the call could be for him. Only one way to find out.
"Hullo? Bushell here."

"Colonel Bushell?" a RAM operator asked, confirming that precious few
people listened to him. When he'd declared his identity once more, the man
said, "Colonel, I have Sir David Clarke on the line for you."

"The devil you say!" Bushell exclaimed. He was hard-pressed to think of
anyone less likely to want to talk to him. "Ring him through, ring him through."

"Colonel?" Yes, that was Sir David's pleasant baritone. Bushell admitted he
was himself. Clarke went on, "Colonel, why have a squadron of RAMs been tapping at the typewriters in the governor-general's residence for the past hour? I
don't think they've missed a one of them."

"Good," Bushell answered. "They'd better not. As for why—" He hesitated,
weighing the pros and cons of telling Clarke what he'd found. To see what reaction he'd get, he explained.

A long silence followed. At last, Sir David said, "Colonel, I've given you reason to dislike me." He sighed. "Good God, I've given you reason to hate me, and
I know it." He paused, waiting for Bushell response. Bushell didn't say anything.
Sir David sighed again, then went on, "I will be damned, sir, if I know what reason I've given you to think me a traitor to my country."

In Clarke's shoes, Bushell would have said exactly the same thing in exactly
the same tone of voice. Was the chief of staff a good enough actor to put that injured outrage into his words? Did Bushell dare think he wasn't?

Telephoning him had taken more nerve than he'd supposed Clarke owned.
Damn it, he didn't want to paint the man who'd taken Irene from him in any
color but black. He tried to strike a businesslike note, saying, "You understand,
Sir David, that, having found the lead, we must pursue it."

"Colonel, my first thought was that you had planted that lead, intending to use it to destroy me," Clarke answered.

Bushell looked up at the ceiling. "Had I thought of it, and were the matter on which it bore less urgent, I might have done just that."

"The second part of your explanation is the one that matters," Sir David Clarke said, and Bushell found himself nodding, as he had for Jaime Macias. Agreeing with Sir David was a new and disagreeable experience. The governor-general's chief of staff went on, "I believe you are willing to put your country above personal animus, as I am, so I also believe you when you say you are not trying to frame me. But someone is, by heaven. I held the date of the King-Emperor's arrival in strictest confidence until its release was authorized. Think of me as you like, but that is the truth."

"Let everything be exactly as you say," Bushell replied. "Once I found the piece of paper in Phineas Stanage's file cabinet, I'd still have to see whether it matched a typewriter to which you had easy access."

"I suppose you have someone out burglarizing my home even as we speak," Clarke said bitterly. Since Bushell did—or at least hoped he did—he kept his mouth shut. Sir David sighed once more, then continued, "All right, Colonel, I see your point. But I remind you that I am not the only one with access to that information. Even if you didn't frame me, someone else certainly has."

"We'll look into that possibility, too, I assure you," Bushell answered. He'd meant that to come out cool and matter-of-fact, but it sounded more sincere than he'd thought it would. He drummed his fingers on the nicked wooden surface of the desk. He couldn't quite figure out how he'd come to believe Sir David Clarke, but he had. "We'll look into everything, or as much of everything as we can in the time we have left."

"Irene has always said you were evenhanded to a fault," Sir David said. It was the first time he'd ever mentioned Irene to Bushell save to bait him. "I suppose I shall have to hope she was right." He hung up.

After a moment, so did Bushell. He sat staring at the telephone for a few seconds, then got up and went off to see Sir Horace Bragg. The commandant listened to his summary of the conversation with Sir David Clarke and dismissed it with a wave of his hand. "What do you expect him to say, Tom?"

"What he said," Bushell admitted. "Not a word different. The way he said it, though—I've done a lot of interrogations, and if he's a liar, he's a bloody good one."

"He's a politico. Of course he's a good liar," Bragg said, which was hardly a thought alien to Bushell.

"We'll check the typewriters first," he said. "That will tell us something, even if not as much as we'd like." He regathered his enthusiasm. "It isn't really what I came in here to talk about, anyhow." He told Sir Horace of what he'd learned from Jaime Macias. "We may get help from that side of the case, sir."

Bragg's bristly eyebrows came down in a fearsome frown. "Good God in the foothills, Tom," he burst out, "I might could have thought you had more important things to worry about than who blew the head off Honest Dick the Steamer

King. It's a goddamn sideshow: that's all it is, nothing else but. You've been moaning how you haven't got time for this and you haven't got time for that, but somehow you have got time for something that hasn't got anything much to do with where *The Two Georges* is. Drop it, that's all I can tell you. Let the New Liverpool constables do their job. You do yours."

Bushell stared at the RAM commandant. He couldn't remember the last time his old friend (*who'd laid his wife*—but there was a piece that didn't fit into the jigsaw puzzle) had been so flustered by a case. Sir Horace didn't slip back into the North Carolina accents of his youth unless he was very upset.

Cautiously, Bushell said, "Sir, it looks to me as if what they're doing back in New Liverpool is liable to be important to what I'm doing here."

"It doesn't look that way to me," Bragg declared. "Even if they do catch Tricky Dick's killer, that's not going to give us *The Two Georges*. Do you hear me?"

"Yes, sir, I do—" Bushell began.

Before he could say anything more, Sir Horace seemed to deflate before his eyes, like a balloon with a coronium leak. Bragg leaned forward and buried his face in his hands for close to a minute. When he straightened, he seemed more himself. "I'm sorry, Tom," he said. "I shouldn't have flown off the handle like that. Trying to come up with that miserable, stinking painting has taken twenty years off my life, I swear it has. I haven't slept. I've been eating like a pig, too, trying to make up for it."

That sounded like the Horace Bragg Bushell knew. The RAM commandant was, if anything, skinnier than ever.

Bragg went on, "I did mean what I said, though. The murder case isn't your responsibility; it belongs to this Muñoz—"

"Macias," Bushell corrected automatically.

"Whatever his name is," Sir Horace said with an impatient wave. "You have more important things to do. Seeing whether Sir David Clarke is a traitor to the Crown springs to mind, for instance."

Most of the time, Bushell would have risen to that like a trout to a fly. Now— "I've got that well under way, sir," was all he said. Bragg nodded, apparently satisfied. Bushell himself was rather less so. Some of the triumph of proving the man he hated a villain had evaporated in the conversation he'd had with Clarke. And Sir David turned out not to have been the only man with whom Irene had betrayed him. Sitting across the desk was another one.

Sir Horace proceeded down the track of his own train of thought: "If we can disgrace Sir David or show that he's a villain, maybe Sir Martin will listen to a man of sense instead."

"That's possible, sir," Bushell agreed. "Sir Devereaux Jones seems to have a good deal of common sense buried under the politico's exterior he wears."

"Perhaps." By the way Bragg said it, Sir Devereaux Jones was not the man of sense he'd had in mind. In grudging tones, he admitted, "I suppose anyone would be better than that scoundrel Clarke. After what he did to you—"

"Yes, sir." Bushell got to his feet. "If you'll excuse me—" He managed to smile at Sally Reese as he went past her, but it wasn't easy. How could Bragg tax him about Sir David's iniquity when his own matched it? *Simple*, Bushell though. *He doesn't think I know about his.*

▼

The dining room of the William and Mary was so packed, anyone should have had an easy time getting close enough to spy on someone else. But it was also so noisy, no one at one table could make sense of what anyone at the next table said. You had trouble enough hearing what anyone at your own table said.

Over crab cakes and sweet potatoes in a glaze of molasses, cinnamon, and ginger, Bushell took advantage of that relative anonymity to say, "I don't know what's wrong with Sir Horace. His heart just doesn't seem to be in this case. If he were a musician, he'd always be coming in a beat late."

He didn't say anything about Irene. What had happened there was relevant to his friendship with the RAM commandant, but not, he thought, to tracking down *The Two Georges*.

"I've noticed the same thing, Chief," Samuel Stanley said after swallowing a bite of crab. "I kept my mouth shut, doubting I could be just. But if you see it, too, I'd say it's really there."

"I'm afraid it is," Bushell said. "When I tried to tell him about what Captain Macias is digging up out in New Liverpool, he told me to leave Macias alone and concentrate on what's going on here in Victoria. That's not like him, Sam; he's always been one for sweeping in all the evidence from wherever it shows up. He taught me that, for heaven's sake."

"Maybe the safety valve is stuck on his boiler," Kathleen Flannery said. "Sometimes, if too much piles onto people, they do blow up. This isn't the best time for him to do it, though."

The understatement there was enough to make Bushell raise the glass of Jameson to his lips. "You're right, of course," he said. "Sam and I have known Sir Horace for—a long time now, and I don't think either one of us has ever seen him act anything like this."

"Not even close," Stanley said emphatically. "Either the steam pressure in there is way too high, or else he's playing some game of his own."

Bushell realized what Stanley meant was, *Or else he's a villain.* The suggestion should have shocked him more than it did. Also speaking obliquely, he said, "I know how we can find out."

"Good," Stanley said, and turned the subject. "What news about Sir David Clarke?"

"He called me this afternoon and denied everything," Bushell answered, "but I wouldn't have looked for him to do anything else, not after a swarm of RAMs took typewriter samples from America's Number Ten. As best we can tell, though, none of those samples matches up with the one on the note we found at Phineas Stanage's home. Neither do samples from the typewriters at Sir David's residence. A couple of points for him, but nothing conclusive."

"How did you get typewriter samples from Sir David's home?" Kathleen asked.

Bushell paused to take another bite. After he'd swallowed, he said, "I may have had better crab cakes in Baltimore, but I wouldn't swear to it. These are pretty tasty." He sipped his drink.

When Kathleen realized that was all the reply she'd get, she started to say something angry. Bushell raised his hand in warning, just a little. She looked thoughtful. Then her face cleared. "Oh," she said. "That was unofficial, then." Bushell still didn't answer, but she seemed to have found out what she wanted.

▼

Later that evening, lying beside Bushell up in his room, Kathleen said, "Why won't you talk about what your people do unofficially?"

"Because if I did, I'd have to admit we do things unofficially," he answered, "and if you admit to doing things unofficially, they almost become official."

"But it's only me," Kathleen said. "If you can't talk about unofficial things with me, with whom can you?"

"Don't wheedle," he told her, and watched her eyes kindle. Before either of them could take it any further, the telephone rang. "Saved by the bell," Bushell said, and reached across her to answer it. His arm brushed her bare flesh, distracting him as he picked up the handset. "Hullo? Bushell here."

"Tom?" A woman's voice, familiar but—

He stiffened. "Irene." Her name came out altogether flat. Kathleen's eyebrows flew up. "What do you want?"

"Were some of your men here this afternoon?" she asked. "David told me what they were doing at the residence then, and what—what you suspect him of." She spoke in low, hurried tones; he got the idea Sir David didn't know she'd rung him. "Were they here, Tom, checking the same thing? I can't prove it, but I'd swear I left the study window latched, and some of the papers by the typewriter there look neater than they ought to."

"Searching a home without a warrant is illegal, Irene," he said.

Kathleen nodded at him, apparently conceding the point that some unofficial business stayed unofficial for a reason. Then she found a way to be very distracting. *Stop that,* he mouthed at her. She shook her head and kept on.

"Pooh," Irene said; in his mind, the part that wasn't being distracted, Bushell could see the flip of her hand that would accompany the word. She went on, "Don't forget, I used to be married to you. I know RAMs don't admit to everything they do."

"Then you should know I won't admit to any of this," Bushell answered. He wasn't likely to forget they'd been married, either, however much he sometimes wished he could. Irene was doing her best to pretend they hadn't flayed each other at the Russian embassy, which was more sensible than the way she often acted.

Irene said, "David hasn't done any of the terrible things you think he has, Tom. He wouldn't. He couldn't. He loves the Empire with everything that's in him. I know you don't see eye to eye with him about policy. And I know—" She sighed. "I know you hate him, and I know why you hate him. I can't do anything about that, not any more. But if you go after him because you hate him and not because you've got evidence against him, you'll waste effort you ought to use tracking down the real villains."

She still knew how to put the argument so it would hit him hardest. Absently, he wondered if she had the same knack with Sir David. Picking his own words with care, he said, "We have some evidence that looks as if it may be against him. We're trying to find out if it really is. We have to do that. I'm not treating him any differently because he is . . . who he is . . . from the way I would if . . . if you and I were still married to each other."

"All right," Irene answered after a moment's hesitation. No doubt she regretted that fight now. So did Bushell. What she'd flung at him then complicated his life in ways he didn't have time for. She paused again, then said, "I believe you. I've always said—when I'm not angry I've always said—that, whatever else you are, you're a just man."

"Yes, Sir David told me as much this afternoon."

"Did he?" Irene said. "He didn't tell me he'd spoken directly to you. Well, you are, Tom. It wasn't enough for me, but it is still true." She paused once more, then used a quick whisper to say, "I've got to go now. He's coming." Her voice got louder: "Yes, of course I'll ring you tomorrow, Madge. Good night." She hung up.

Bushell had to shift to do the same. "Enough," he said to Kathleen. This time, she listened to him. He laughed. "Of all the doings I'll never be able to put in the memoirs I'm never going to write, the past few minutes go to the top of the list."

"That's nice," Kathleen said equably. "Time shouldn't just pass; things should *happen*."

"On the whole, I agree with you," Bushell said. "I could have done without several of the things that have happened over the past few weeks, though."

"Well—possibly," Kathleen said. "But would we have ended up together without them, and, if we wouldn't have, would you have done without them?"

The only way to answer that was by avoiding it, a course Bushell took without hesitation: "If you want to play with might-have-beens, find one of the hacks who churn out those scientific romances the Sons love so well. Me, I have enough trouble figuring out what's real to waste time worrying about what isn't." She took a deep breath. He saw she wasn't going to let him get away with that. To forestall her, he said, "Now I have a question for you."

"Do you, now?" she said. She was probably most dangerous when she sounded most Irish. "And what might that be?"

"This: when you left me that note yesterday, you blacked out a word in front of your name. What was it?"

She sat up and drew away from him. That they were naked together on the bed suddenly seemed irrelevant; it was almost as if they'd just met for the first time. "I didn't expect you to ask me that," she said quietly. "The word was *love*." She thrust out her chin, as if to say, *What do you make of that?*

"I thought so," he answered. "Why did you black it out?"

"Because you've used it twice, once when you were drunk and once for a joke, and it frightened me both times," Kathleen said. "Because I've seen you still carry scars from . . . your former wife. Because after I wrote it, I was afraid that if you saw it, it would scare you away."

"It's safe enough now," Bushell said. "We're in my hotel room, so I can't very well run."

But sometimes you couldn't hold up a quip for a shield and expect it to ward you from all human feeling. Bushell wished he had a bottle of Jameson handy. Had he had one, though, he probably would have crawled into it. He'd been shocked and horrified at Buckley Bay. Now he was frightened. He knew what kind of wounds he was risking, how deep they cut, how long they lasted.

He looked at Kathleen, who was warily looking back at him. She knew about those wounds, too—oh, maybe not to the full bitter extent he did, but enough. He could wound her, if he chose to. She'd given him the chance, and now she sat waiting to see what he would do with it.

"We made love before we said we were in love," he said slowly. "Bodies, sometimes, are simpler than brains. They just do things; they don't have to try to understand what things mean. And when, before, with other people, things didn't mean what we thought they—"

He ran down in the middle of his sentence, something he rarely did. After a moment, he saw it didn't matter. He'd agreed they were in love, he hadn't been joking, and he hadn't run out of the hotel room—though he hoped Kathleen never found out how tempted he'd been.

"Now we see where we go from here," Kathleen said.

Bushell nodded. This felt different from what he'd been like when he first met Irene: less ferocious, less giddy. But he got the idea it could indeed go places. As for what those places might be— "If we don't find *The Two Georges*, we can head into exile together."

She looked at him. "If we don't find *The Two Georges*, will we want to have anything to do with each other . . . afterward?"

"Now there's a question." He got up, walked over to his jacket, and took his cigar case from the inside pocket where it rested. He made a ritual of getting the cigar started. Only when surrounded by wreaths of fragrant smoke did he turn back to Kathleen and remark, "You know, I had reasons enough already to want to get the bloody thing back."

He'd hoped she would laugh. Instead, she answered, "One more never hurts." He thought that over, then nodded again.

▼

Sir Horace Bragg looked up from the papers that, piled high on his desk, seemed to build a wall between him and the outer world. He smiled his lugubrious smile across that wall and said, "Good morning, Tom. You look ready to whip your weight in tigers today. I wish I could say the same."

"What now, sir?" Bushell asked.

"Stanage's solicitor got him out on a writ yesterday evening."

Bushell made a face. "So that was his safety-deposit box password, eh? I wonder how long it has been. I'd give you long odds the judge never asked." He and Bragg silently commiserated about the unfathomable ways of judges. Then he went on, "I had a good idea last night, or I think so, anyhow. I want to hear how you like it."

"I'm all ears," Sir Horace answered, reaching up to touch one of the rather fleshy protuberances in question. He wasn't saying anything about Bushell's conversation with Jamie Macias or his own reaction to it. *Probably trying to pretend it never happened*, Bushell thought.

He said, "All the evidence we've developed in this case makes the Russians look to be the people feeding the damned Sons of Liberty gold and guns, doesn't it, sir?"

"Can't argue with you there," Bragg said. "We've been over that ground again and again. Haven't come up with anything I know of to make us suspect the Holy Alliance or somebody more unlikely like the Prussians or Austrians."

"No, sir," Bushell agreed. "Not a scrap. But one of the things we've been worried about is whether stealing *The Two Georges* was an end in itself or part of a bigger plot, one that would endanger the King-Emperor when he gets to Victoria."

"As a matter of fact, Sir Devereaux Jones rang me up with that very concern not ten minutes ago," the RAM commandant said. "He seemed genuinely alarmed, and he's not a man to concern himself with trifles."

Bushell had said the same thing the day before, but let that go. He'd succeeded in putting a flea in Sir Devereaux's ear, all right. "It occurred to me that, if there will be an attempt on the person of Charles III, the Sons of Liberty may well need to get some weapon or piece of apparatus from the Russian embassy at the last minute. One way to keep that from happening would be to seal off the embassy grounds for the duration of His Majesty's visit, let no one in or out during that time."

"Duke Orlov would scream blue murder," Sir Horace observed. "That's not the sort of slight a diplomat will take lying down."

"To hell with diplomacy," Bushell said, not the first time he'd voiced such a sentiment. "Keeping the King-Emperor safe counts for more, if you ask me."

"Oh, I agree with you," Bragg said. "Don't mistake me for a moment. All right, we'll do it that way, and let Sir Martin or the foreign secretary pour oil on troubled waters. I won't be sorry not to have the Russians sneaking around during the imperial visit, and that's the God's truth."

"That's very good, sir." Bushell hoped the glad surprise he felt didn't show in his voice. He dismissed as foolishness his fear that the RAM commandant was somehow involved in the theft of *The Two Georges* and whatever plot might be hatching against Charles III. The Russians, he was convinced, were part and parcel of that plot; if his old friend was part of it, too, he would have come up with any number of good reasons to leave the Russian embassy open. Instead, he'd agreed to close it down.

Sir Horace had passed the test. It was the best news Bushell had had for days. The only problem with it was, it left the leak to the Sons of Liberty unaccounted for. He made a mental note to go after that leak, not that he had much hope of finding it unless the villain, whoever he was, made a mistake: when you asked a leaker if he was leaking, he wasn't likely to say yes.

Bragg must have been following that same melancholy train of thought. His forehead corrugated into a badland of wrinkles. "I wish to heaven I could find out how the devil the Sons got word of our raids. When I do—if I do—someone's head is going to go on the block, and that's the God's truth, too. If the Sons have infiltrated the RAMs, nothing and nobody is safe anymore."

"I know," Bushell said, glad once more to find Sir Horace thinking along with him. "How's your tooth, sir?" he asked sympathetically.

Bragg rolled his eyes. "Don't speak of it. I may have to go back to that quack of a Pendleton sometime in the next few days to get the nerve killed. That doesn't sound so bad, does it, not when they put it that way? What they don't tell you is that it means drilling a good, deep hole in your head. I think half the torturers in the *Okhrana* started out as dentists."

Bushell, who had been through the procedure, nodded vigorous agreement. He said, "Have you got any idea who the turncoat might be?"

"I wish I did," the RAM commandant answered, his voice even more melancholy than usual. "And speaking of turncoats, have they managed to match that note from Stanage's to a machine handy for Sir David Clarke? Safety-deposit box password, my—" His snort said his opinion of that was the same as Bushell's.

"No, sir," Bushell answered. "From what Captain Oliver says, it doesn't seem to be any of the ones in America's Number Ten."

"Maybe one he has at home, then," Sir Horace suggested.

"Neither of those, either," Bushell said. "Unofficially speaking, of course."

"Really? You do sail close to the wind, don't you, Tom? And I've said that before, haven't I?" Bragg sighed, then held out his hands, palm up. "It doesn't signify, anyhow. Sir David could lay hands on a fresh typewriter as easily as he could lay hands on—" He didn't take that any further.

"So he could." If Bushell's voice came out cold, Sir Horace would attribute that to his still-smoldering anger at Sir David Clarke. And that anger was there, and likely would be for as long as Bushell lived. But now he was angry at Sir Horace, too, not only for bedding Irene but also for trying to manipulate him.

He looked across the desk at the man he'd long thought his friend. *I'll work with you till we get* The Two Georges *back. After that, we're quits.* Had Sir Horace shown the slightest reluctance to shut down the Russian embassy while the King-Emperor was in Victoria, they would have been quits already.

Bragg's eyes were deep and dark and moist: sad spaniel eyes. If you looked into them, you'd swear you could see all the way down to the bottom of his soul. Bushell had thought he'd done just that. Only went to show you couldn't tell by looking.

"One way or another, things will work out," Bragg said. "We'll whip the villains yet."

"Yes, sir," Bragg said. *After that, we're through.*

# XV

▼

LVERY DAY, THE WIRELESS BROUGHT WORD of the progress of the yacht *Britannia*. The dailies printed front-page maps that showed nothing but the mother country, the eastern coastline of North America, and a dot on the Atlantic Ocean. Every day, the dot moved closer to the coastline.

The Jack and Stripes of the NAU normally fluttered from a plethora of poles all over Victoria. Great Britain's Union Jack was far from rare, either. In the days before Charles III reached the North American capital, workmen spread red-white-and-blue bunting, either striped or in crosses, over every available vertical surface. If a man had to stand too long waiting for an omnibus, he risked being decorated.

Hawkers with trays or handcarts sold little flags and other allegedly commemorative items on every other streetcorner. One hair salon offered to dye patrons' locks in the colors and pattern of the Union Jack. From what the papers said, it stayed open almost around the clock to keep up with demand.

Bushell viewed the story with amused tolerance: mankind kept coming up with new foibles. (The first time he saw one of the dye treatments, a couple of days after the story broke, he viewed the results with amazement, but that was another matter.) He took a slightly dimmer view of the hawkers, many of whom were petty grifters who probably wouldn't be averse to picking a customer's pocket if opportunity beckoned.

And he worried about the swarms of workmen prettying up Victoria, and especially the routes along which the King-Emperor would travel. "Damn it, Sam," he burst out as he and Stanley combed through papers seized under search warrant, "how the devil are we supposed to keep an eye on all of them? Some of them have to be Sons. They could be planting bombs behind the bunting, they could be picking the manhole cover from which a rifleman will pop out, they could be doing—anything."

"That's true," his adjutant said, and then paused for the ritual of lighting a cigar. "And do you know what you can do about it?" he went on once he'd puffed out a good cloud of aromatic smoke. "Nothing, near enough, not by yourself. They've got plenty of other RAMs to worry about things like that, Chief. You can't carry the whole world on your shoulders."

"No, eh?" Bushell said with a wry grin. "When did they go and change the

319

rules again?" After that, though, he buckled down and attacked the papers once more. But, for all he gleaned from them, they might as well have been written in Hindustani.

That evening's reception was at the Austrian embassy. The Hapsburgs' ambassador to the NAU, *Graf* Friedrich-Maria von Hötzendorf, was a short, thin, weary-looking man with impressive mustachios, a stiff brush of iron-gray hair, and eyes even more sorrowful than those of Sir Horace Bragg.

"I wish you good fortune, Colonel, in your quest to recover your missing imperial treasure," he told Bushell in fluent but gutturally accented French as the RAM went through the reception line. "In your large realm here, the miscreants who absconded with it have all too many places in which to keep it concealed."

"As I know all too well," Bushell replied.

Only after he'd passed on to bow over the hand of the ambassador's wife did he fully appreciate the longing Hötzendorf had packed into *large realm*. Austria was a European power but, because of its position on the map, would never be a world power. It intrigued against the Holy Alliance in the Italian states, and against the Franco-Spaniards, the Prussians, and the Russians in the Germanies, but its only real avenue for expansion, toward the southeast, was blocked by the British protectorate over the Ottoman Empire. When Hötzendorf contemplated a nation that stretched from Atlantic to Pacific and was but a part of a larger empire, he had to contrast that with the straitened horizons of his own homeland. No wonder he looked sad.

Duke Alexei Orlov and *Comte* Philippe Bonaparte had gone into the Austrian embassy by the time Bushell, Stanley, and Kathleen Flannery arrived. Envoys from the minor German states danced attendance on the two powerful envoys; the Bavarian minister, for instance, hung a pace and a half to the left and rear of Bonaparte, as if he were a wife following her husband in some backward part of India or China.

As they had at the Russian embassy, diplomats gave Bushell their sympathies and good wishes. All the same, he got the feeling that here they thought more about their ancient, almost ballet-like maneuverings against one another than they did of the affairs of a latecomer to the game like the NAU.

Kathleen Flannery saw the same thing. "We won't learn anything here tonight," she said.

"Not from the ambassadors, anyhow," Bushell agreed. "You never can tell what our own people might give away, though."

He was watching Sir David Clarke being charming to the wife—the young, pretty wife—of the *chargé d'affaires* from some minor German principality. As people sometimes will, Sir David sensed that eyes were on him. He kept glancing around till he spotted Bushell. He smiled: a wide, political smile made to conceal whatever was going on behind it. Bushell's answering upturn of lips should have displayed a hunting tiger's fangs, not merely human teeth.

Sir Horace Bragg came up, a glass of white wine in his hand. "By God, Tom," he said, "I shouldn't want to be on the other end of that look."

Sir David evidently did not like it, either. He gulped down his drink and purposefully headed toward Bushell. "You see," Bushell murmured to Kathleen.

Then he nodded to Clarke, affably enough now, waiting to learn whether the governor-general's chief of staff was far enough gone to create a scandal in front of most of Victoria's diplomatic corps. If he wasn't, Bushell intended to give him a helping hand.

Clarke thrust out a forefinger, saying, "Have you discovered anything entitling you to stare at me in that fashion, Colonel?"

The question was too much to the point. Bushell hadn't—nothing, at least, pertaining to *The Two Georges*. Out of the corner of his eye, he saw Irene come back into the room, perhaps wondering what had detained Sir David. Spotting him with Bushell, she hurried in their direction, alarm on her face.

Before Bushell could say anything, Sir Horace spoke in his place: "A man who has covered his tracks may look innocent, but that doesn't prove he is."

Sir David's eyes widened slightly. *"Et tu, Brute?"* he said to Bragg. "I thought you shied away from slander yourself." He turned to Bushell. "As long as I'm flinging Latin about, here's a tag you ought to remember: *quis custodiet ipsos custodes?"*

Sir Horace understood the thrust of that as well as Bushell did. His sallow cheeks went red. "'Who will watch the watchmen'?" he growled. "I'll watch you, you son of a—" He took a step toward Clarke. Bushell got between them in a hurry—this wasn't the scandal he'd had in mind starting.

Irene reached them just then. Bushell thought of how the scene had to look through her eyes: her ex-husband keeping her former lover from hauling off and punching her husband. The absurdity of it hit him harder than Sir Horace had wanted to hit Sir David. In spite of himself, he started to laugh. Bragg and Clarke both stared at him as if he'd taken leave of his senses.

"We're all letting this rot our brains," he said. "Let's have a drink and try to remember we're supposed to be on the same side."

Sir Horace Bragg calmed himself at once. "You're right, Tom," he said sheepishly. "The strain is telling on everyone, me included."

"It must be," Sir David Clarke said. "Without it, I can't imagine Colonel Bushell inviting me to have a drink with him." His eyes flicked to Bushell. "If I sound surprised, Colonel, it's only because I am."

Thinking about it, Bushell was surprised, too. He shrugged. "I said it, Sir David," he answered. "I'm not going to back away from my word." He raised an eyebrow and raised his voice: "Unlike certain politicos I could mention." He'd said things like that before, commonly with intent to wound. Now he was joking, and made that plain.

Irene was not only surprised but also, by the look on her face, greatly relieved. "What has come over you, Tom?" she asked.

He set a light hand on Kathleen Flannery's arm. "Must be love," he answered, not joking at all. Kathleen stiffened. She couldn't have been easy about being used as a weapon against his ex-wife. Bushell realized he'd also told Sir Horace Bragg what he'd asked a couple of days before. The RAM commandant's shaggy eyebrows flew upward.

Irene saved the moment, saying, "I hope you'll be happy together," sincerely enough that, if it happened not to be the complete truth, no one could call her on it. Then she had another inspiration: "What about that drink?"

Bushell hadn't said anything about drinking with her. Having agreed to drink with Sir David, though, he could hardly get up on his high horse now. "Onward!" he said, as if leading a cavalry charge on the Northwest Frontier, and headed off in a soon-successful search for the bar.

None of the gossip he soaked up along with several drinks over the course of the rest of the evening amounted to much. With detached amusement, he watched Sir David start another conversation with that German *charge's* attractive young wife, and watched Irene draw him away from the woman with an ease that bespoke considerable practice.

"I didn't think we'd learn anything much there," Kathleen said as Sergeant Kittridge drove her, Bushell, and Sam Stanley back to the William and Mary.

"Oh, I don't know," Bushell answered thoughtfully. "I found out a thing or two about myself, which is worth doing."

"Ah, but will it help you solve the case?" Stanley asked.

Bushell made a sour face. "That's another question altogether, worse luck for me."

▼

RAM headquarters and the streets of Victoria and Georgestown by day. The glittering social whirl of the embassy circuit by night. A little sleep, stretched by endless cups of tea and coffee and a great fragrant bonfire of cigars. A dot on the newsprint Atlantic, moving inexorably closer to the Chesapeake Bay and the capital.

"They're a step ahead of us, maybe two," Bushell said wearily, pouring milk into yet another cup of Irish Breakfast. "We've only got a couple of days left, and they're still ahead of us."

"No ransom demand yet," said Samuel Stanley, whose own cup of tea sat gently steaming in front of him. He shook his head. "When you haven't got much in the way of good news, you look hard for the silver lining, don't you?"

"That you do." Bushell sipped at his tea. "Maybe they won't ransom it after all. Maybe they'll pour paraffin on it in front of America's Number Ten and light it off. Or in front of the All-Union Art Museum, say, when His Majesty's in there giving his address in front of a blank wall."

"What a horrid idea," Kathleen said. She didn't have a desk in the office she shared with the two RAMs; Sir Horace took the position that granting her such a boon would in some way force him to recognize that she was there. Bushell had liberated a table no one seemed to be using. She had papers piled high on it. Sir Horace, in his mercy, had not complained about her using official Royal American Mounted Police foolscap and pencils.

The telephone on Bushell's desk rang. He tensed. Any message right now was liable to be bad news. Maybe the Sons of Liberty wanted their fifty million pounds after all. He picked up the handset. "Hullo, Bushell here."

"Colonel Bushell? This is Operator Perkins, down in Communications. I have a long-distance call for you from New Liverpool: a Captain Macias. Shall I ring him through, sir?"

"By all means." Bushell covered the mouthpiece with his hand and spoke to Sam and Kathleen: "It's Macias." Both of them showed the same relief Bushell felt. No ransom demand, not yet, nor news even worse.

After a couple of clicks and a loud *pop*, Jaime Macias came on the line. Across a continent and a static-filled telephone line, his excitement came through loud and clear: "We've got him, Tom! We dropped on the villain not half an hour ago. And with everything we found when we did, Mr. Zachariah James Fenton will hang higher than Haman."

"By God!" Bushell said. He spoke again to his colleagues. "He's pinched the villain who shot Tricky Dick." Kathleen let out a war whoop; Stanley slammed his hand down on his desk, making a noise like a gunshot. Through the racket, Bushell returned to the telephone: "You have the weapon, too?"

"We have a Nagant we think is the weapon, at any rate," Macias said. "Ballistics will let us know about that before long: before the day is out, with luck. But that's not half—that's not a tenth part—of all we have."

"Tell me," Bushell urged, but then broke in before Macias could speak. "No. Wait. Let me guess. You've got boxes with lots more Nagants in them, enough Russian roubles to start up what would be about the third-largest bank in New Liverpool, and maybe, if God is kinder to us than He has been lately, a proved connection to the *Okhrana*. Stinking Russians—"

"Exactly what I was expecting to find when we served the warrant and made the arrest," Captain Macias said. "Not exactly what we found, though. No, not exactly." He sounded like a stage magician distracting his audience with a clever line of patter so they'd be surprised when he pulled a rabbit out of his hat.

"All right, Jaime, I'll bite," Bushell said, willing to be surprised. "What exactly did you find?"

Over the wire, he heard shuffling-paper noises; Macias was going to tell him *exactly* what he'd found. The New Liverpool constable said, "We found . . . let me see . . . forty-eight Lebel revolvers, thirty-five Eibar revolvers, and twenty-seven Astra Modelo 200 pistols, each with its appropriate ammunition in large quantities—I'm assuming you don't need the precise number of boxes and rounds for each, or I would give them to you. We also found twenty-nine Lebel military rifles with bayonets and three Chauchat light military machine guns, again with large quantities of the cartridges those two weapons share."

"You found enough for a small war—no, a medium-sized war," Bushell said, almost dazed. "And all Franco-Spanish stuff?" He scratched his head. "That doesn't fit in with anything else we've turned up."

"Everything in that house but for the one Nagant and the unexpended rounds in its magazine is from the Holy Alliance," Macias said. "And I'm not done with the list, either. In gold and silver currency, we found the sum of £219,827,15 shillings, ninepence, ha'penny, most of said currency being in the form of livres d'or or pesos: again, from the Franco-Spanish Empire."

"Two hundred twenty thousand pounds?" Bushell let out a low whistle. Sam Stanley jerked in his seat and stared at him. Kathleen sprang to her feet. Bushell waved her down—by the sound of things, Macias still wasn't through. "What else have you got?"

"Subversive literature in large quantities, both the usual sort the Sons turn out and some in Spanish calling on people who've come to New Liverpool from the Franco-Spanish provinces of Nueva España to rise and restore the land to its rightful owners and the true faith—"

"I wouldn't have thought you'd find both those kinds of documents in the same house," Bushell observed.

"I wouldn't have thought it, either, but find them I did," Macias said. With the air of a man producing a fifth ace, he said, "And I also found 943 pounds, 8¾ ounces of purified extract of coca leaf, number one quality, shipped into the NAU in sealed coffee tins from the province of Nueva Granada."

"Half a ton of coca extract?" Bushell whistled again. So did Stanley, the second he heard. "That's enough to keep half the coca-sniffers in New Liverpool happy for—a long time, anyway." Some people used coca extract like snuff, the only trouble being that it wasn't mild like snuff, and had been illegal in the NAU since the early days of the twentieth century. Coca-sniffers would pay through the nose to get it, though, which probably explained a lot of the money Macias had found.

"Half a ton," Macias confirmed. "And all the firearms . . . I've never imagined the Sons having such good connections with the Holy Alliance. They . . . aren't usually what you'd call fond of Franco-Spaniards in general and Nuevespañolans in particular. I'm not fond of them, either," he added.

Bushell wondered whether he was speaking as a constable or as a man of Nuevespañolan blood. That didn't matter. What did matter was the news Macias had. "Anything else?" Bushell asked.

"Nothing yet," Macias answered. "Fenton and his common-law wife are denying everything at the top of their lungs—they had no notion any of that stuff was in the house, they say." The constabulary captain snorted. "They won't convince a jury with that tale, not for a minute they won't. But so far they're refusing to say anything till they've spoken with a solicitor, and we're going to hold them for the full legal forty-eight hours before we let them do that. If they do decide to open up while we're grilling them, you'll be the first outside New Liverpool to hear."

"Thanks, Jaime," Bushell said, and hung up. He looked to Sam and Kathleen. "A break at last—and a big one." He frowned. "I wish I knew what it meant, though. After all the Russian connections we've unearthed, this one doesn't fit."

"It probably also doesn't get us any closer to *The Two Georges,*" Kathleen said. "I know it's important for us to catch the man who shot Honest Dick, but that's not the half of the case we need right now."

"You're right," Stanley said in mournful agreement. "They're too smart to have told the shooter much, I'm sure."

"Yes, that's so." Bushell rubbed at his mustache. "It must be why Sir Horace didn't want me to spend time on the Tricky Dick end of things. Even if it did crack open, it might not help us soon enough. But this is still something he has to hear straightaway."

He dialed Bragg's office number. "I'm sorry, Colonel," Sally Reese blared in his ear. "You can't talk with Sir Horace right now. He's gone to the dentist again this morning—that crown just isn't right. He said he didn't sleep a wink last night, and he's getting it seen to."

"This is important, Sally," Bushell said.

"I understand that, Colonel, but I can't make him be here when he isn't, now can I?" Bragg's secretary laughed her loud, scratchy laugh.

"No, you can't do that," Bushell admitted. He rubbed his forehead. Bragg had mentioned the dentist's name a few days before, he was sure of it. He snapped his fingers in triumph. "He goes to Dr. Pendleton, doesn't he?"

"Yes, he does," Sally Reese laughed again. "I think he swears at him more than he swears by him, but he's kept going back all these years."

"Give me Pendleton's telephone number, then," Bushell said, reaching for the pencil he'd used to make notes on what Jaime Macias had told him. "If Sir Horace isn't under general anesthetic, he needs this news now."

"Well, since it's you as asks," Sally said. "Let me go through my pile of cards here. I'll have it for you in a jiffy, yes I will."

"You're a sweetheart, Sally," Bushell said with all the charm he had in him. In his ear, Bragg's secretary giggled like a schoolgirl. From behind her table, Kathleen Flannery made as if to retch. Bushell stuck out his tongue at her.

"Here it is," Sally Reese said, ignorant of the byplay on the other end of the line. "It's AGincourt 4873."

"Unless he's unconscious, Sir Horace will want to know what I've got to tell him," Bushell assured her. "And if he is unconscious now, he'll be sorry he was when he wakes up."

"All right, Colonel. You sound like you know what you're talking about." Sally Reese slammed down the phone. She did even that with unnecessary vigor. Before he rang the dentist's office, Bushell paused a moment to dig a finger into his ear. Kathleen looked puzzled. Samuel Stanley, who'd had more dealings with Bragg's longtime secretary, chuckled softly.

Bushell dialed the number Sally Reese had given him. A woman's voice came on the line: "Offices of Dr. Spencer Pendleton, member of the Royal North American College of Dentists and Oral Surgeons. How may I help you?"

The best way for her to have helped a man with a bad toothache, Bushell thought, would have been to shorten the introduction. He let that alone, though, merely giving his own name and title and saying, "I need to speak to Lieutenant General Sir Horace Bragg immediately."

He waited for the receptionist to tell him Bragg was trapped in the chair and unavailable. He'd settle that in short order. But the woman answered, "I'm sorry, Colonel, but Sir Horace isn't here."

"Really?" Bushell said, sitting up straighter. "Has he already left? That means he'll be back at the office soon."

"I'm afraid you misunderstand, sir," the receptionist said. "He's not been in this morning. He has no appointment scheduled, he has not asked to be seen on an emergency basis, and, if you'll forgive me, I've no notion why you believe he would be here."

"Why?" Bushell said. "To get something done about the crown Dr. Pendleton put on him last week. He's done nothing but complain about it ever since."

"Sir?" If that wasn't honest bewilderment in the receptionist's voice, she belonged in front of a cinema camera. "Sir Horace wasn't in here last week to have a crown fitted or for any other reason. Let me check to be absolutely certain—" Bushell heard flipping pages, presumably from Dr. Pendleton's appointment book. The receptionist came back on the line: "No, sir, the last time Sir Horace saw Dr. Pendleton was last February 19, to have him replace a filling that had fallen out of a bicuspid. He's not been here since."

"You're sure of that?" Bushell demanded.

"Sir!" The receptionist remained polite, but unmistakable frost came into her voice. "Our records are most exact, I assure you. If there's nothing more—" When Bushell didn't answer, the woman hung up as emphatically as Sally Reese at her best.

Bushell gently replaced in its cradle the handset he was holding. He sat staring at the telephone. Samuel Stanley, of course, had heard only his side of the conversation with Dr. Pendleton's receptionist. "Sir Horace is on his way back here?" he said. "When did he leave the dentist's?"

"He didn't," Bushell answered. "He wasn't there. He hasn't been there since February, as a matter of fact."

Stanley and Kathleen exclaimed together at that. "Where the devil has he been, then?" Sam burst out.

"If I knew, I would tell you," Bushell said. "I don't know. I just don't know."

"Do you suppose he keeps a mistress?" Kathleen asked.

Samuel Stanley burst into rude, raucous laughter at that idea. Flustered, Kathleen looked down at the table. Bushell held up a hand. "It's—not as unlikely as you think, Sam," he said slowly.

"Oh yes, it is," Stanley said, laughing still. "That miserable, dried-up—" He cut himself short, no doubt remembering—a couple of words too late—Bushell's friendship with Sir Horace.

But Bushell hadn't spoken to defend Bragg. "It's not as unlikely as you think," he said again, and then did something he'd thought he'd never do: he repeated what Irene had said at the Russian embassy about Sir Horace.

"Good God," Kathleen whispered.

"Good God is right," Sam Stanley said in an altogether different tone of voice. "I was *at* that party, Chief. The *nerve* of the man—not just for doing it, but for doing it *there*. I wouldn't have guessed he had it in him, not in a thousand years." He probably would have elaborated on that theme had Kathleen not been in the room, and had Bushell's ex-wife not have been involved in the affair.

"I wouldn't have, either," Bushell said. "I *didn't*. But then, Irene turned out to be . . . susceptible to men with titles. I didn't find out about that till later on, either." Sounding dispassionate about the breakup of his marriage came easy by now; he'd had practice. Not having to hide internal anguish, though, was new.

"What do we do now?" Kathleen asked. "Come up to him when he does get here and say, 'We know you didn't go to the dentist, so where were you?'"

"If he's visiting a kept woman at a time like this, he ought to be horsewhipped," Stanley said, sounding as if he wouldn't mind being the fellow cracking the whip. Then he looked thoughtful. "Do you suppose Sally knows? If she does, would she tell us?"

Bushell shook his head. "If it's true, and if she does know, she'll deny it to her dying day. She thinks the sun rises and sets on Sir Horace. And if we do ask her, it's sure to get back to Bragg." He listened to himself in surprise once more. He'd never spoken—he'd never thought—of Sir Horace by his unadorned surname.

"Sir Martin ought to know about this," Kathleen declared.

"So he should," Bushell said. "There's a problem, though. If I ring up America's Number Ten, or even if I hop in a steamer and go over there, they won't just escort me into the Green Room or wherever Sir Martin happens to be. I'll have to get past the top flunky, who happens to be—"

"Sir David Clarke," Samuel Stanley finished for him.

Kathleen winced, but said, "You'd better do it."

"You're right, worse luck," Bushell said with a sigh, and picked up the telephone. He rang the governor-general's residence, asked to be connected to Sir Martin Luther King, and, sure enough, found himself talking to Sir David.

"Yes, Colonel?" Clarke said coolly. "I trust this is of some importance?"

"I think so, yes," Bushell answered, fighting understatement with understatement. In an abstract way, he was tempted to tell Sir David what Irene had told him—Clarke might have worried about Sir Horace Bragg from time to time, but never, Bushell was sure, in *that* way. But the public good sometimes meant forgoing private pleasure, and so he stuck to business: "I need to speak to Sir Martin at once—I have new evidence about who is, or may have been, leaking information to the Sons of Liberty."

Sir David Clarke asked the question Bushell had known he would ask: "And that person is—?"

"I'll tell Sir Martin. I won't tell you," Bushell said. Clarke was still a suspect in his own right, which meant that, if Bragg was involved, too, they might have been working together. Alerting Sir Horace was the last thing Bushell wanted.

"You're going to tell him it's me," Sir David said. "No matter what I try to do to convince you I am no traitor, you refuse to believe me, and you carry on this vendetta as if you were from the Kingdom of the Two Sicilies, not the NAU. Deny it if you can."

"I—" Bushell shut up. Even denying it would have given Sir David enough information to let him draw his own conclusions—if he didn't reckon the denial an outright lie.

After the silence had stretched for half a minute or so, Clarke said, "Good day, Colonel," and hung up the telephone.

"I knew this was going to happen. I couldn't tell him," Bushell said, recounting the conversation for Samuel Stanley and Kathleen. "I *couldn't*. He does remain our principal suspect at the moment."

"Right now, Chief, I'd say we have two principal suspects," Stanley remarked.

"And I'd say you may well be right," Bushell craved a drink. If Sir Horace was in league with the Sons of Liberty, that was a betrayal worse then Irene's. "But if Bragg is working with the Sons," Bushell went on, thinking aloud, "why is he so willing to shut up the Russian embassy when the King-Emperor gets into Victoria? I'd worried about him before, but you know that set my mind at ease again."

"True," Stanley said, drumming his fingers on the desktop.

"But what if the Russians haven't got anything to do with the theft of *The Two Georges*?" Kathleen Flannery said. "I know both of you have been focusing on the Russians since Tricky Dick got shot, but look what they found in the house where they arrested his killer. Maybe the Holy Alliance planted the other evidence to make you look away from France and Spain."

"Mm—maybe," Bushell said. "That's as much as I'd give it." He glanced over to Sam Stanley, who nodded. Having concentrated so long and hard on the Russian connection, both men were reluctant to abandon it without overwhelming evidence to prove they should.

"Where *do* we go from here, though?" Stanley said. "We can't trust Sir Horace, who's over us, and we can't trust Sir David, who's between us and Sir Martin. What does that leave? Not bloody much, if you ask me."

"Oh yes, it does," Bushell said. "It leaves *us*. All right—we can't trust anybody over us. But I can think of a couple of people here I'd trust: that Major Manchester, for one. The way he jumped on those warrants I pulled out of my briefcase was a joy to watch. Williams, too—the fellow with the beard and the scar. Remember how he wondered about a leak here at RAM headquarters? They'll know others we can count on, too."

"Sergeant Kittridge," Stanley said, his face lighting up. "Always ask a sergeant about officers if you want a straight answer."

"We're forming a cabal," Kathleen said in tones of wonder.

"That's just what we're doing," Bushell said, and picked up the telephone.

Major Manchester was the first one to get to the office they were using. Bushell would have been surprised had it worked out otherwise—Manchester, whose Christian name proved to be Walter, seemed to rush headlong into everything he did. He fidgeted impatiently when he had to wait for his two colleagues to arrive.

Sergeant Kittridge (his first name, Bushell learned on asking, was Ted) arrived next. Whatever he was thinking, his face showed none of it. Bushell wouldn't have wanted to play cards against him. He took out a cigar case, used his eyebrows to get permission from Kathleen Flannery, and lit up a cheroot so vile that Bushell wished she hadn't granted it.

A minute or so later, Major Williams walked in. He nodded to Ted Kittridge, whom he evidently knew well, and introduced himself as Micah to Major Manchester. Then he rounded on Bushell, asking, "Well, what's all this?"

Bushell got up and shut the door before answering. That bit of theatrics earned him stares from all three newcomers. Then he borrowed Kathleen Flannery's word: "This, gentlemen, is a cabal."

More stares. Walter Manchester found his tongue first: "What kind of cabal?"

"One to get *The Two Georges* back in spite of everything," Bushell answered.

"What's everything?" Williams asked, at the same time as Manchester was saying, "Why do we need a cabal for that?" Sergeant Kittridge, who spoke as if he had to pay a shilling for every word he used, stood quietly, smoking and listening.

Bushell explained, telling the Victoria RAMs of the evidence that pointed toward Sir David Clarke—Williams already knew some of that—and what he'd just learned about Sir Horace Bragg. As he set it out before strangers, it seemed much less substantial than it had when he was hashing it over with Sam and Kathleen. He finished, "As far as I can see, we can't trust either one of them. Let's go on as if they weren't there any more and do this job the way we know it ought to be done."

He waited. Having thrown the dice, he had no idea what he'd do if they turned up a losing number. After three of the longest heartbeats of his life, Major Manchester said, "I'm with you, Colonel. When you came up with those warrants after the judges had gone to chambers, I knew you were somebody who could get things done."

"Count me in, too," Micah Williams said. "That operation we ran against the Sons last week—that was a shame and disgrace, nothing else but. And we've just been running around since. If we can't do better than this, we don't deserve to find *The Two Georges*." When he frowned, his scar pulled one corner of his mouth out in a sinister grimace. "Count me in, but there's not much time left."

Everyone looked at Ted Kittridge. The sergeant stubbed out his cheroot, then said, "Captain Higgins and Lieutenant Custine will lend a hand, I expect."

"Good choices," Major Williams said, nodding. He turned back to Bushell. "We can come up with men who'll want to be turned loose against the Sons—no doubt of that, Colonel. But how are we going to get search warrants on the quiet?"

Walter Manchester let out what sounded alarmingly like a giggle. He pointed to Bushell's briefcase. "The man is armed—and dangerous." Williams lifted a questioning eyebrow. Bushell opened the briefcase and displayed the warrants he'd been carrying since New Liverpool. Both of Micah Williams's eyebrows rose then. Sergeant Kittridge lighted another cheroot. This one sat at a much jauntier angle than its predecessor had.

"If we can get the men, we can legally do the job," Bushell said. "Well, legally enough, anyhow. The other question is, what job do we do? I haven't got an unlimited number of these"—he pointed to the warrants—"and we ought to hold a couple in reserve to follow up on whatever we find in our first sweep. We have to make that one count."

"You know what I'd do if it was up to me?" Williams said. "I'd go back to a lot of the places we hit last week. Those buggers—beg your pardon, ma'am—they had to know we were coming. We only found what they wanted us to find, not one thing more. If we hit 'em when they aren't looking for us, though—"

Bushell weighed that. After a few seconds, he nodded. "We'll do just that, then. I wouldn't mind finding out what Phineas Stanage really has in his files, I'll tell you that."

"But that paper I found taped to the file-cabinet drawer—" Kathleen began.

"May mean exactly what it says, or may have been planted there to make us think it means what it says," Bushell said. "By the end of today, if we're lucky, we'll have some idea which."

"If we haven't got some ideas by ten o'clock in the morning, day after tomorrow, it won't matter any more," Samuel Stanley said. "That's when the King-Emperor gets here."

▼

Sergeant Kittridge drove Bushell, Stanley, Kathleen Flannery, and Lieutenant Toby Custine back to Phineas Stanage's house. "Can't wait to have a go at this blighter," Custine said, for the third or fourth time. "Can't wait." He was very young, very blond, very enthusiastic. Bushell thought Kittridge had made a shrewd choice with him. Point him at a target, turn him loose, and he'd bring it down.

When Bushell knocked on the door to Stanage's, the same maidservant who'd answered before opened it. She drew back in dismay when she recognized him. "Oh, dear sweet suffering Jesus, not again," she moaned. "We're just starting to get picked up from the last time."

Bushell displayed the warrant. "Afraid so, Miss. Now if you'll stand aside and let us do our job—"

"I can't stop you," the woman said bitterly, "but Lord, I wish I could."

The RAMs swarmed into Stanage's house. Bushell wondered how long they'd have today till the brewing magnate showed up in full wrathful glory. Or maybe, hearing the RAMs were back again, he'd flee instead.

One advantage of searching a place for the second time was that you had some notion of where things were. Bushell headed for the file cabinets up on the first floor. They were locked. Toby Custine produced a little leather case from an inside coat pocket. Out of the case he drew some highly specialized metal tools.

Glancing over to Bushell, he said, "I wanted to be a safecracker when I was a boy, but my dear old father convinced me that, while I'd take long holidays with a trade like that, they wouldn't be at places I much fancied visiting."

"Your dear old father was a man of sense," Bushell said solemnly.

"So he was, so he was," Custine replied. "That once, anyhow, I listened to him." He got to work with his lock picks. In moments, the file cabinet opened. Whether or not he'd fancied larceny as a career when he was young, he would have been good at it.

"Hullo!" Sam Stanley said, reaching in and snatching out a folder. "This wasn't here last time we came calling."

"Are you sure?" Bushell asked. "He had a lot of Independence Party material then, too."

"Yes, and that's how all of it was labeled—INDEPENDENCE PARTY, I mean," Stanley said. "Not a folder in the bunch just said INDEPENDENCE."

Lieutenant Toby Custine muttered something pungent under his breath. Aloud, he said, "Looks like you were right, Colonel. If this wasn't here the last time you came through the place, somebody'd tipped Stanage off beforehand."

"Let's see what we've got," Bushell said. Samuel Stanley set the folder on a nearby table and flipped it open. Staring up at him was a scribbled note from Eustace Venable to Stanage. The note was headed PHIN and had nothing to do with cabinetry, nor was the tone that of artisan to client:

> It's ready and waiting. I'll be heading up to Boston tomorrow to talk things over with Joe. He and the boss have cooked up three or four different ways to play it. I want to know for certain which one they intend using. Will inform you when I learn.

"Not much there you could take to court," Custine observed.

"That's true," Bushell said, "but it puts old Phin in the picture all the same— and if Joe isn't Joseph Kilbride, who is he?"

"Who's the boss?" Custine asked.

Sam Stanley started going through papers. "Maybe these will tell us."

But they didn't. Phineas Stanage's correspondents had been maddeningly— and, in their shoes, sensibly—elliptical. Nowhere was there an overt mention of *The Two Georges*: the letters talked about *it* and *the thing*.

One of those letters came from Michael O'Flynn in Charleroi. Bushell clicked his tongue between his teeth. "I hope Chief Lassiter has him locked up good and tight. Have to make sure about that—in a bit. First things first."

"I know what happens next," Stanley said. "We head off to Stanage's brewery and find out he's not there. He'll have left for Astoria twenty minutes before we show up, and he'll be back in six weeks."

"Not this time, Sam," Bushell predicted. "He won't go far from the capital, not two days before Charles III gets here." Toby Custine nodded vigorous agreement. Of course, Bushell realized after the words were out of his mouth, for Stanage to be in and around Victoria was not necessarily the same as his being in his office waiting for the RAMs to scoop him up. He tried to pretend he hadn't had that thought—things were starting to go his way now, after so long favoring the villains.

He went downstairs. Ted Kittridge proved to have an unexpected talent for devastation; Stanage's living room looked as if a Cossack cavalry *voisko* had galloped through it. Kathleen Flannery was lending spirited help, using a sharp little knife to slit furniture linings so she could peer inside. Stanage's servants stood watching and wringing their hands.

"Anything we need to know about?" Bushell asked. Kittridge and Kathleen shook their heads. "Let's go then," he said, and turned to Stanage's domestic staff. "Thank's for your help this morning."

"You took a big chance there, Chief," Stanley said as they piled back into the RAM steamer. "If old Phineas had some Nagants that we didn't find stashed in his basement, one of the footmen might have shot you."

"Mm, something to that, I shouldn't wonder." Bushell checked a sheet of stationery he'd taken from the home. "The Josiah Stanage Brewing Company, Ltd., is on Tilden Way. That's not far from here, is it, Sergeant?" He'd been away from Victoria long enough to make him distrust his memory for directions.

"Fifteen minutes," Kittridge said, and put the motorcar in gear.

It turned out to be more than twice that long; a nasty accident snarled

Tilden Way only a mile or so from the brewery. Constables were busy taking statements from those in a condition to give them. Red lights flashing, an ambulance sped off with a couple who weren't. Wreckers labored to pry apart the vehicles that had come together. Firemen spread sand on spilled paraffin.

Bushell drummed his fingers on his thigh as they crawled along. They'd got trapped in traffic before they discovered how bad the wreck ahead was. "Nothing we can do but wait," Stanley said. Bushell grudged every second that sped past; he knew he had none left to spare.

Once past the wreck, Sergeant Kittridge practically flew to the brewery, a large brick building with advertising signs painted on all four sides:

JOSIAH STANAGE & CO.,
PROUD BREWERS OF BALD EAGLE ALE, YANKEE STOUT, AND FREEDOM BEST BITTER.

"Bilgewater," Kittridge declared. Bushell didn't know whether he meant the political sentiments proclaimed by the brand names or the quality of the beers produced inside those walls.

The rich, nutty odor of malted barley clogged the air. Stanley laughed. "You can get a buzz just breathing," he said, and inhaled deeply.

A guard in a red-coated uniform that looked a lot like a RAM's stood in front of the entrance. "Help you gents?" he asked, adding, "And you, ma'am?" a moment later.

Bushell and his male companions flashed their badges. As had often happened before, their display of glittering metal blinded the guard to the fact that Kathleen bore no such talisman. The not-quite Redbreast touched a forefinger to the bill of his cap in a not-quite salute and held the door open so the newcomers could enter the brewery.

A series of questions to employees within led them to Stanage's office. Bushell would have guessed that to be on the topmost floor, so the magnate could look out a window and savor the view—or perhaps just watch lorries hauling barrels of nice, profitable beer off to be quaffed.

Instead, though, Stanage quartered himself in the basement. His secretary, a gray-haired woman who looked even sterner than Sally Reese, glared at people with the temerity to interrupt her typing. "No, you can't see Mr. Stanage now," she snapped, and started clattering away at a letter once more.

"It's urgent," Bushell said, showing his badge again.

"I don't care," the woman said. "You still can't see him." She paused. He got the idea she hoped he'd shout at her, so he didn't. Faint disappointment in her voice, she went on, "Reason you can't see him is, he's not here."

Samuel Stanley grunted. Bushell had heard that same sound of surprise from a soldier hit by a rifle bullet: it was the sound you made before you felt the pain. He already felt it, and asked, "Well, where is he?" Maybe he'd been wrong. Maybe Stanage had decided to get out of town.

But the secretary said, "He's up in Georgestown, across the river. There's a gathering of commercial travelers today." She sniffed in loud, sharp disapproval. "Excuse for a pack of nasty men to get together, tell filthy stories, and pour down the demon rum, if you ask me. I'm a good Christian woman—I've told Mr. Stanage as much, right to his face I have."

Bushell didn't doubt it. He knew a first bit of sympathy for Phineas Stanage. Stifling it, he said, "Where is this gathering being held?"

"I told you: in Georgestown." When that wasn't enough to send Bushell on his way, she grudgingly pawed through a file cabinet. "Here we are: the Worshipful College of Victuallers"—she pronounced it as it was spelled, not the right way—"at 427 Armritsar Way. Ugly name for a street."

"Thank you for your unsolicited opinions," Bushell said. He hadn't more than half turned before she was pounding away at the typewriter again.

They got back into the battered blue Reliable that Kittridge was driving. Bushell pulled out his pocket watch. "It'll be after one o'clock when we get there," he said unhappily. "Less than two days now before His Majesty's yacht comes into the harbor."

"Less than half a day from the ransom deadline the Sons set when they took *The Two Georges*," Kathleen added, even more unhappily.

"If they were going to ransom it, we would have heard by now," he said, and hoped he was right. "They have something else in mind. They must."

"Burning it in front of the All-Union Art Museum, for instance," she said. "You were talking about that before, and I've feared something like it all along."

He shook his head. "I don't think they'd throw over the chance at fifty million pounds for the sake of a gesture."

"They're fanatics," Kathleen said bleakly. "What do fanatics care about money?"

The steamer rolled onto the Long Bridge as Bushell answered, "Of course, a lot of the Sons are fanatics. But the leaders of this scheme are plenty shrewd. Fifty million would let them pay for any number of outrages. If that's not what they're after, then they have good reason to think they can get something more."

"Or, of course, they might be holding off the ransom demand to the last possible moment to give us less chance to set a trap for them," Samuel Stanley said. Bushell nodded. It wasn't how he read the situation, but it was far from impossible.

Traffic on the bridge slowed down as the steamer neared the checkpoint on the Maryland shore. "Bulk tobacco?" a green-uniformed inspector asked Kittridge. Maryland had a hefty tobacco tax; Virginia didn't. The revenue inspectors searched motorcars at random to discourage smuggling.

Kittridge showed his badge. The inspector nodded, drew back, and waved him through. Kittridge reached into the glove box for a map to guide him to Armritsar Way. They got to the Worshipful College of Victuallers at 1:07. Toby Custine pointed to the building across the street: an Independence Party headquarters. "Why doesn't that surprise me?" he said.

Another steamer that had seen better days came down Armritsar Way from the opposite direction and parked in front of the headquarters building. A burly man with a beard that didn't quite cover his scar got out of it. "That's Major Williams," Bushell and Stanley said together.

Kittridge pulled over to the kerb. Everyone got out of the motorcar he was driving. Lieutenant Custine called to Williams and his companions. "What are you people doing here?" Williams demanded. "You come to shake down this place, too?" He jerked a thumb toward the Independence Party building.

"No, we're after Stanage at the victuallers' hall," Bushell answered, pointing toward his own target. "Had some luck, did you?"

"I should say so!" Williams boomed. "The stinking Sons hadn't a clue we were coming, not this time. Now I've got clues—so many of 'em, I wish I could be four places at once."

"Same here," Bushell said. "What's going on with the charming Independence Party people? They aren't in the habit of going out on a limb."

"Well, they bloody well have now, or at least this batch of 'em has," Williams said. "All sorts of lovely correspondence between them and proved Sons about *it* and how they were going to exploit *it*—not a word of what *it* is, worse luck, or where *it* is, either, but I've drawn my own conclusions, and now I'll see if I can't get these people to color 'em for me."

"Sounds like what I'm doing with Stanage and his crowd." Bushell thumped Williams on the shoulder. "Let's go get 'em." He had another thought: "If we make arrests, we'll take 'em to the Georgestown gaol. The less we alert the powers that be, the better."

"Right," Williams said. "Colonel, I wasn't sure anything was rotten in Denmark till I went out this morning. Now—I don't want anyone over you getting wind of any of this." He laughed, down deep in his throat. "If you hadn't been the one who put me on to it, I wouldn't tell you about it, either."

"Good," Bushell said. He rounded up his companions by eye, then headed across Armritsar Way to the Worshipful College of Victuallers.

The fellow who greeted him there certainly hadn't lacked for victuals. The white linen suit he wore had enough material for a four-man tent, or maybe two of them. His pink, pink skin was fine as a baby's. "Help you folks?" he asked, then wheezed in another gulp of air.

"Phineas Stanage and the party from the Stanage brewery works," Bushell said.

"Dining room two," the fat man answered, pointing.

Dining room two was a raucous place, full of well-hopped good cheer. Bushell understood at once how Stanage's secretary had acquired her distaste for such gatherings. The room was blue with cigar and pipe smoke, and bluer with coarse language. His head swiveled this way and that. He didn't see the man he was after. He tapped a commercial traveler in an ugly houndstooth jacket. "Where's Stanage?"

"Phin?" The man didn't take him for a police officer. "He stepped out a few minutes ago. Not for lunch, by Jesus!" He patted his abdomen, as if to say no sane man would leave the victuallers' hall for food or drink.

"Check the jakes," Bushell told Lieutenant Custine. "Check with that human airship out front, too, and see if he's left the building."

Custine hurried away. Bushell wished he had more manpower with him. If he could have descended on this place with a host of RAMs instead of a carful . . . he was all too likely to have given the game away.

But he heard cursing down the hall that was altogether different from the ge-

nial sort accompanying the commercial travelers' tales of conquests over customers or pretty girls. One corner of his mouth quirked upward as he recognized
the style: Phineas W. Stanage was unhappy with his world.

"Crackbrained idiotic fornicating Cossack *Okhrana* inquisitors!" he bellowed
as Toby Custine led him back into the dining room. The RAM lieutenant had
clapped manacles around his wrists.

"Here, what have you done to good old Phin?" one of the commercial travelers shouted. An angry chorus rose from the company.

"Arrested him," Bushell answered. The chorus grew louder. In a few seconds,
some half-drunk fool would lead a charge to rescue good old Phin. Bushell hadn't
the men he'd need to stop such a charge. Before it could start, he went on, "For
conspiracy to steal *The Two Georges*, and for conspiracy to commit murder by
firearm."

"It's a lie, a filthy, stinking, goddamned lie," Stanage roared, sounding very
much like a man who'd boxed for pay for a while before taking up the family business. But the men who sold his brews were suddenly silent. Some of them might
have sympathized with the Sons of Liberty, but most were probably Tories: commercial travelers were seldom inclined to embrace innovation of any kind.

"Take him away; get him out of here," Bushell muttered to Custine, who
started Stanage down the hall. Stanage tried to kick him in the shins. Custine
skipped out of the way and shoved the brewing magnate, hard. Stanage almost
went over on his face. To his sales force, Bushell said, "This day's festivities are
over. You've had your luncheon and you haven't had to listen to all the speeches
that were coming up. Count yourselves ahead on the bargain: instead, you've got
the rest of the day off. Enjoy it."

He waited. If he wasn't lucky, he'd have a riot on his hands. Well, he told
himself, that would get the Georgestown constables over here in a hurry. But
luck, for once, was with him. The first commercial traveler who spoke up said, "I
hope you get the painting back, pal. If Phin knows somethin' about it, go on and
make him sweat." A new chorus rose, this one of agreement. If anyone in the
dining room held a differing opinion, he made sure he held it close.

You had to have discipline if you were going to survive traveling from town
to town and drumming up sales wherever you could. Once it became clear to the
assembled multitude that no one was going to try breaking Stanage free of the
RAMs, the men gulped down a last few bites, upended their pint pots, and
started filing out toward Armritsar Way.

Most of them were chattering about what they'd just seen, and most of those
were professing loud and sometimes profane (though not so ingeniously profane
as Phineas Stanage) hope *The Two Georges* would soon be back in proper hands.
In that milieu, the strapping, black-haired fellow who kept quiet and kept his
head down while he tried to edge away from Bushell succeeded only in making
himself conspicuous. Bushell might not have paid him any mind he had tramped
along with his comrades. As it was, he took a second look.

"Mr. O'Flynn!" he exclaimed gleefully. "You'll come along with us, too."

The miner from Charleroi tried to bolt, but a commercial traveler half his size leveled him with a tackle that would have drawn a red card on any football pitch in the Empire. Bushell jumped on him and manacled his hands behind his back.

As Phineas Stanage had, O'Flynn tried to kick. "Naughty," Bushell said, and bounced his face off the tile floor of the hallway, not so hard as he might have done. "As I said, you'll come along with us." He yanked the miner to his feet.

Because of the struggle, he didn't get out to the street as fast as he might have. When he did, Major Micah Williams greeted him with a glad cry. "Thanks for the bonus," the bearded, scarred RAM said. "I never expected Christopher Cole to walk by me bold as brass. I was going after him later on."

"Who's Christopher Cole?" Bushell said, and then, "Never mind. He was a villain masquerading as a commercial traveler, was he?" Williams nodded. Bushell went on, "I nabbed one of those, too. Nice little gathering Stanage had here, wasn't it? And a nice cover, too; he could meet the other Sons and plot anything he liked with no one the wiser."

"He could write it off his taxes, too," Samuel Stanley said. "If that's not adding insult to injury, I don't know what is."

"One more charge to throw at him," Bushell agreed. "Something will have to stick." He turned to Williams. "How'd you do?"

"Got my man," the major answered. "Cameron Moffett is another one we've suspected for years without being able to lay hands on proof. I found it earlier today, and now I've found him." His face darkened with anger. "The Sons must have had a pipeline into our office for years, too, same as they did down in Richmond. This time, thanks to you, we really did catch them napping."

Several man had emerged from Independence Party headquarters to argue with the RAMs who'd come with Williams. Bushell glowered at them. They were all plump, prosperous, middle-aged, with the sleek look of solicitors to them. He could understand why a Michael O'Flynn might wish the NAU different from what it was. But the Union and the British Empire had done things for these men, not to them. Where was their gratitude?

The breeze picked up; it flipped the homburg off one of the Independence Party men, then flung awry the few straggling strands of hair he'd combed over a wide expanse of scalp. That floating, wispy hair was what drew Bushell's gaze to him. One eyebrow rose. "Well, Major," Bushell said softly, "I think you've just returned the favor you say I did you." He raised his voice: "Mr. Johnston! How good to see you again."

Morton Johnston started. If the Independence Party leader from New Liverpool thought it was good to see Bushell, his face didn't know it. For a moment, before the lawyerly mask dropped over his features, he looked uncommonly like a boy caught with his hand in the biscuit tin.

Bushell waved to him. "Why don't you come over here, Mr. Johnston, and tell me what you're doing three thousand miles from home."

Johnston did come over, gathering himself as he did so. "I haven't got to tell you a bloody thing, sir, as you know very well. But I shall tell you: I am here to help my colleagues plan protests against the tyrant's visit to our shores."

It was a plausible answer, plausibly delivered. But Johnston hadn't been glad to see Bushell, not even slightly, and it was the day before the deadline the Sons of Liberty had given for ransoming *The Two Georges*, two days before Charles III arrived. Bushell asked, "If I ring up your headquarters in New Liverpool and ask them where you are, what will they tell me?"

Had Morton Johnston been in Victoria on legitimate Independence Party business, he would have told his fellow enthusiasts exactly where he was going, and why. He might have told them where he was going, but lied about his reasons. But when he took a couple of seconds too long to come up with any sort of answer, Bushell concluded he hadn't told them even part of the truth.

"I shall make that telephone call, Mr. Johnston," he said happily. "Meanwhile, you can come along to the station and answer some questions for us."

"Am I under arrest, and if so, on what charge?"

Lieutenant Toby Custine had ducked into the Independence Party building. He came out in time to hear Morton Johnston's question. In a studiously neutral voice, he remarked, "Three of the clerks in there say Phineas Stanage visited you this morning, and that the two of you spent some time alone together."

"Vile, treacherous dogs!" Stanage roared. Johnston said nothing, but the glare he sent though the plate-glass window was homicidal in intent if not in effect.

"On a charge of conspiracy to aid in the commission of a felony, namely the theft of *The Two Georges*," Bushell answered.

Now Johnston found a bellow to match Stanage's: "You'll never hang that on me!"

"Maybe I will, maybe I won't," Bushell answered, "but I'll have fun trying." He turned to Ted Kittridge: "Ring up the Georgestown constables, Sergeant, and have them send some motorcars here. We've gathered in a bigger haul than I thought we would."

"Right," Kittridge said, still speaking as if words were at a premium. Bushell had expected him to go back to the Worshipful College of Victuallers and use the telephone there. Instead, he strode into Independence Party headquarters. The clerks and functionaries there were going to get an earful of the doings of their superiors. Bushell hoped they enjoyed it.

Enough RAMs were on the scene to make sure the prisoners didn't try to escape. Bushell took Lieutenant Custine off to one side and said quietly, "Those Independence Party people are fanatics. How the devil did you get three of them to point the finger at Stanage and Johnston?"

"It was simple," Custine said with a wink: "I didn't. But the reactions we got from those two were most satisfactory, don't you think?"

"You'll go far, Lieutenant," Bushell predicted. He thumped the younger man on the back. Custine grinned from ear to ear.

Within a couple of minutes, several Georgestown constabulary steamers rolled up. The constables who got out of the gold and black checked motorcars stared in considerable curiosity at the crowd of RAMs and suspects waiting for them. "What the hell is going on here?" demanded a burly fellow with a lieutenant's pips on the shoulder boards of his khaki uniform.

"These charming individuals"—Bushell pointed to Stanage, Johnston,

O'Flynn, and the rest—"are charged with conspiracy to abscond with *The Two Georges*, among other things. We'd like to interrogate them and hold them at your gaol, Lieutenant—"

"Hammond. Maxwell Hammond," the Georgestown constable said. Bushell introduced himself. After the formalities, Hammond said, "See here, Colonel, why don't you just take them back to Victoria and grill them over your own fire?"

"Come along with me, Lieutenant." Bushell walked slowly down Armritsar Way. Hammond followed, his heavy features frowning and suspicious. When they were effectively alone, Bushell went on in a low voice, "I'm not taking them back because I don't want my superiors or the politicos at America's Number Ten to know I've got them. If I have to draw you a picture, I will."

Maxwell Hammond stared at him. "Good God," he said, also quietly. "What is the world coming to?"

"Whatever it thinks it's coming to, I don't aim to let it," Bushell answered. "Are you with me, or not?"

"Oh, I'm with you, all right." Hammond rumbled laughter. "Never thought I'd help a RAM put one over on his own people. Like a dream come true, this is." Local and provincial constables often envied RAMs their resources and authority. Taking advantage of them now had to feel sweet to Hammond, who labored almost in the shadow of the NAU headquarters for the Royal North American Mounted Police.

Far from allergic himself to tweaking the nose of authority, Bushell said, "Enjoy it."

"Oh, I shall. I shall." Hammond turned and hurried back to his men. By the grins that broke out on their faces, he was telling them what Bushell had told him. They hustled the prisoners into their motorcars and sped away. The two steamers full of RAMs followed.

"Better not lose 'em," Sergeant Ted Kittridge muttered under his breath. "Damned if I remember where the Georgestown constabulary station is at."

It proved to be a grimy building in a grimy part of town, far from the elegant district where Sir David Clarke made his home. Kittridge's call had alerted the constables at the station, and they awaited the newcomers' arrival with obvious impatience. The gaoler, a tall, skinny Negro named Olmsted, patted down the prisoners, turned out their pockets, and put their personal effects—including belts, shoes, and cravats—in paper bags. He required them to sign itemized receipts he'd prepared.

"This is an outrage!" Morton Johnston cried.

"Law doesn't say you have to be happy about it," Olmsted answered imperturbably. He'd heard it all, no doubt more times than he could count. "Law does say you have to sign, so we can show the court we kept all your goods safe."

"I know the law, you—" But Johnston stopped there. He might know the law, but he'd never before been in its clutches. He was smart enough to see that antagonizing a man who meted it out here was less than wise.

Bushell turned to the gaoler. "Put them in separate cells. In fact, can you keep them far enough apart from one another that they won't be talking back and forth?"

"Oh, yes, sir, we'll take care of that," Olmsted answered. "Gaol's not what you'd call crowded right now. Maybe the usual lags are on their best behavior." He laughed to show how likely he thought that was. "Or maybe they're waiting for more toffs to show up when His Majesty comes into Victoria so they'll have more fine stuff to steal."

The paperwork that went with arrests was mind-numbing. Here the forms were even more complicated than usual, precisely because the RAMs were using constabulary facilities under the jurisdiction of the sovereign city of Georges-town to house prisoners arrested not because of city ordinances but as a result of the violation of All-Union statutes. By the time the last *i* was dotted and the last *t* crossed, twilight was settling outside.

A constable went out and came back with a pasteboard box full of greasy, newspaper-wrapped packets of fish and chips. "This side has vinegar, the other one doesn't," he said, pointing to show which was which. "Take your pick."

After all the fine meals Bushell had eaten lately, vinegar-sour fried fish and potatoes were like a slap across the face with a cold, wet towel. He gulped them down, then lifted a mug of strong tea in salute. "To dyspepsia!" he said.

He rang up the William and Mary and asked if any messages had come in for him. "Yes, sir," the hotel operator said. He heard papers being shuffled. "One from Sir Horace Bragg . . . another from Sir Horace Bragg . . . and a third from— Sir Horace Bragg. The last was not fifteen minutes ago. Do you require the number for a reply?"

"No." Bushell hung up. So Bragg wondered what he was up to? Well, he wondered what Bragg was up to, too, and wouldn't ring him right back. Instead, he dialed RAM headquarters and asked to be connected to Major Walter Man-chester.

"I'm sorry, he's not at his desk," the RAM operator answered. "Who's ring-ing, please?" Warily, Bushell gave his name. "Oh, very good, Colonel," the oper-ator said. "He gave me a number where you could reach him: it's FLodden 2127."

"Thanks." Even though he hadn't been in Victoria for some years, he knew what that number was: the central station for the Victoria city constables. Major Manchester must have made arrests of his own, and must have been as leery as Bushell of bringing his prisoners back to RAM headquarters.

Bushell rang the FLodden number and spoke briefly with Manchester, let-ting him know where he could be reached. "We did catch 'em napping," the ma-jor said, as Micah Williams had. "I'll ring you directly I squeeze anything worth knowing out of these chaps."

"Right. I'll do the same for you." Bushell set the phone down. He wondered if he'd done the right thing by telephoning into RAM headquarters. Word that he'd done so was liable to get to Bragg. Still, no one there knew how to reach him. If the men he'd recruited into the cabal—and the men they'd recruited— kept quiet, they could operate unsupervised a while longer. God willing, they wouldn't need much more time. Under his breath, Bushell muttered, "We'd bet-ter not."

The only thing left to do was use the time he'd bought as best he could. The interrogation room had old, battered furniture and walls that needed painting. It stank of stale sweat, stale tobacco, stale coffee. In his expensive tweeds, Phineas Stanage looked out of place there, like a petunia in an onion patch.

"Let me call my solicitor," the petunia growled.

"We can hold you forty-eight hours first," Bushell said, "as I'm sure you know perfectly well." Stanage grunted. Bushell said, "What were you doing, meeting with Michael O'Flynn?"

"Who?" Stanage said. "Never heard of him."

"How did a Charleroi coal miner get invited to a gathering of commercial travelers from your brewery?"

"Since I never heard of him, how can I tell you that? For all I know, he sneaked in for a pint or two and a bite to eat."

Bushell glowered. He'd feared Stanage would be tough. "What was Eustace Venable talking about when he said he was going up to Boston to see Joseph Kilbride about *it?*"

"Probably a cabinet I'd ordered from him," Stanage answered in offhand tones. "And who's this Kilbride item? I don't recall Venable's ever mentioning anyone by that name."

The note the RAMs had found referred to *Joe*. Bushell glowered harder. Stanage *was* tough. Contemptuously, Bushell said, "Don't play stupid games with me. You tell me you don't know Kilbride and I'll call you a liar to your face. The two of you ran in the same pack."

"Well, what if I have heard of him? So what? I don't know *that* Venable was going up to Boston to see him. If he was, I don't know *why*. And I haven't a clue about what *it* is."

"It's *The Two Georges*, Mr. Stanage," Samuel Stanley said, his voice quiet, reasonable. "We know that. You know we know that. Why not make it easy on yourself and tell us what you know?"

Stanage laughed at him. "You dumb smoke, I've had enough nosy police officers poke their snouts into my business to know when I'm getting whipsawed between the rough one and the sweet one. Go peddle your papers."

Stanley walked over to him and backhanded him across the face. "Which one am I now?" he asked, quiet still.

Phineas Stanage's head snapped back. His cheek glowed red. "I've had tougher louts than you work me over, too," he snarled. "Try some more. Maybe you'll bugger the job and leave marks my solicitor can see and take to a judge."

"You may as well give it up," Bushell told him. "Sir David Clarke's spilling his worthless guts at RAM headquarters right now." An artillery unit would sometimes let fly a few shells to see what response they drew. *Firing for effect*, the gun bunnies called it. Bushell was firing for effect now.

Stanage shrugged. "I've not done anything, so he can't hurt me."

Like a dreadnought's armor, he turned every question fired at him. The hands of the loudly ticking clock on the wall went round. It chimed the hours, one by one. When midnight came, Samuel Stanley said, "This is the deadline the Sons gave us. Still no word, though—I hope."

# XVI

▾

No WORD WE'VE HEARD, ANYHOW." BUSHELL didn't want to call back to RAM headquarters to confirm that, or to America's Number Ten, either. "So we go on." He turned to Lieutenant Hammond. "If nobody else is grilling Michael O'Flynn, fetch him in here."

"Right," Hammond said, and, to Stanage, "Come along, you." The brewing magnate went with him. He looked as worn as Bushell felt, but hadn't yielded anything. Maybe that was because he didn't know anything, but Bushell didn't believe it for a minute. For once in his life, he wished he were an *Okhrana* man, to feel easy about using more than a slap in the face to squeeze answers from prisoners.

Michael O'Flynn looked sleepy and rumpled when Hammond brought him into the interrogation room. He nodded to Bushell, then glanced around the room at the other RAMs and constables. "One of me and a lot of you this time," he remarked to Bushell. "All right, have your innings."

Bushell nodded back, not quite happily. Down a quarter-mile under Charleroi, O'Flynn and the other miners could have done anything to him; if they all told the same story afterward, they might well have got away with it, too. They'd let him do his job and go back above ground. Did he owe O'Flynn anything for that? Nothing he would ever have admitted. Even so . . .

"What are you doing in Georgestown?" he demanded.

"Visiting my cousin," O'Flynn answered. "His name's Dermot Coneval; he sells ale for Stanage Brewery."

They could check that. Bushell had the bad feeling it would turn out true. The Sons had shown enormous skill at nesting their lies in defensible truths. He said, "You just happened to be here now, the same way you just happened to have driven Joseph Kilbride to the Charleroi train station."

"That's right," O'Flynn said. "Pure chance, every bit of it."

"That's your story?" Bushell stood up and stepped closer to the miner, leaning over him and staring down. O'Flynn waited for the hand or the fist or the sap he so plainly expected. *Go ahead*, his eyes said. *Renege*. Both Bushell's hands stayed by his side. "I say you're a liar."

"You can say it," O'Flynn answered. "I'm not calling the shots here." He laughed wryly. "Not hardly, not me."

"I say you're a liar," Bushell repeated, "and I say I can prove it. You don't un-

derstand the fix you're in, O'Flynn. We haven't just netted up you little fish.
We've got Sir Horace Bragg himself." *Fire for effect.* "He's down at RAM headquarters, leaking like a cheap roof in the rain."

"Who?" O'Flynn said. "I never heard of any Sir Horace Whoozis." Bushell
thought he was telling the truth again, but had trouble being sure. Everything
the Sons of Liberty did fit into intricate patterns, and when you tried sorting out
what was true and what wasn't, as with O'Flynn's cousin, you found yourself wandering bewildered after something briefly glimpsed in a maze of mirrors.

"Why did you try to run away from me, then?" he asked. On something like
that, he had hope of a straight answer.

O'Flynn looked at him as if he'd just come out of the—what did they call the
local bedlam house?—the Yellow Brick, that was the name. "Wouldn't you?" the
miner demanded.

"Not if I hadn't done anything," Bushell replied.

"The more fool you," O'Flynn said. "You should see poor Percy McGaffigan
after Chief Lassiter and his bully boys got done pounding on him. He's lost four
teeth, the sorry devil, and he's limping still. I've got a family, too, I do. I didn't
want to go home to 'em all crippled up."

"Who's this Lassiter?" Lieutenant Hammond asked, and then let out a huge
yawn.

"Charleroi constabulary chief," Bushell told him. He shook his head, not
just tired but also frustrated. O'Flynn was answering too well. No matter how
well he answered, though, he was in too deep to be believable. Bushell swung
back to him. "You're telling me you *happened* to know Joseph Kilbride, and you
*happened* to know Phineas Stanage—"

"I never told you I knew Phineas Stanage," O'Flynn shot back. "I told you
my cousin works for him, and he does."

"And you just *happened* to be there with Stanage, and on the day Stanage
went over to talk with another damned Son?" Bushell shook his head. "It won't
wash, O'Flynn. Not a jury in the world would buy it, even for a minute."

"Then they'll put the broad arrow on me, but not for anything you can prove
I deserve," Michael O'Flynn replied. Like Hammond, he yawned. "Can you let
me go back to my cell now? I was asleep when your Cossacks came and got me."

"He talks like a Son," Sam Stanley observed.

"So he does," Bushell said. "He's had more sleep then either one of us, too."
As he had with Stanage, he hammered away at O'Flynn. The coal miner projected an air of stubborn ignorance. Without getting rough, Bushell had no hope
of penetrating it. Finally, when the noisy wall clock showed it was nearly six, he
gave up and sent O'Flynn away.

He walked into the hallway himself. Kathleen Flannery sat dozing in a chair.
Ted Kittridge was sitting, too, working on a cheap cigarillo and yet another cup
of coffee. No matter how strong and black Bushell drank it, he could feel it
wasn't helping him hold his eyes open any more. If he didn't sleep a little now,
he'd collapse soon. Stanley looked to be in the same straits.

Bushell sat down next to Kathleen. He started to close his eyes, then jerked them open again. "Turn on a wireless, somewhere where the Sons can't listen to it," he told Lieutenant Hammond. "If word comes that *The Two Georges* is ransomed, we'll—hell, I don't have the faintest idea what we'll do, but I want to know." Hammond nodded. Bushell's eyes did close.

Next thing he knew, someone was shaking him. He jerked in startlement and almost fell off the chair. "I'm sorry," Kathleen Flannery said. "Here. Try some of this." She held a mug full of coffee under his nose.

The rich, earthy smell filled his nostrils. "An angel of mercy, only slightly disguised," he said, taking the mug. "No wonder I love you." Even in the dim light of the hallway, he saw Kathleen flush. He gulped down half the mug. It was as bad as constabulary-station coffee usually is, but it was hot and strong, which also counted. He finished it in another couple of long swallows, then said, "What time is it, anyhow?"

"A little past ten," Kathleen said.

Bushell got up. An ache in the small of his back said he'd been sleeping in that awkward position for a while. He rubbed at his eyes. If Kathleen hadn't wakened him, he might have gone on sleeping quite a while longer. "Any word of anything?" he asked her.

She shook her head. "No news of a ransom on the wireless, no reports from Major Manchester, nothing."

"I'd better ring him," Bushell said, and went off to use the telephone in Lieutenant Hammond's office.

"I was just going to phone you," Manchester said when the connection went through. "We had to be awfully persuasive"—Bushell suspected he wouldn't have cared to find himself on the receiving end of that persuasion—"but we've had a break. One of the lads I dragged in says *The Two Georges* was in a storage cubicle, somewhere not far from here. No matter how persuasive we got, though"—yes, that was a euphemism—"he didn't know where, and neither do any of the other buggers we have here."

"And there are only about ten thousand of those bloody cubicles around—if the painting is still in one, which it's liable not to be," Bushell said, resolutely refusing to be optimistic. "Still, it's something. We'll see what we can get out of the dear lads we have here." He glanced up at the clock in Hammond's office: half past ten now, a few minutes later, actually. "The Ides of March have come, but they have not yet gone," he muttered.

Micah Williams had been interrogating Cameron Moffett. He came out of the chamber looking depressed, so Bushell had a go at the Independence Party man. Moffett, who was large and beefy and looked like one of Morton Johnston's distant cousins, proved to be the sort who did not easily yield ground.

He shook a well-manicured forefinger in Bushell's face. "This is character assassination you're engaged in, sir, nothing else but—character assassination and interference in the affairs of a legitimate political party, to say nothing of illegal and amoral suppression of dissent."

"I thought you said it was nothing but character assassination," Bushell answered. Moffett stared at him. "Never mind," he growled. "I didn't come in here to waste my time listening to your drivel. If they don't hang you, you'll spend the rest of your natural life in gaol. Sir David Clarke has told us everything he knows, and he knows plenty."

"That toffee-nosed little weasel?" Moffett jeered. "Past getting the unmentionables off half the women in this town, he couldn't tell manure from mayonnaise." That was also Bushell's judgment, but he did not find it reassuring to have a Son agree with him.

Bushell turned away so Moffett wouldn't see him scowl. He'd tried that gambit or the one with Sir Horace Bragg on every prisoner he'd questioned, and every man had been convincing in his rejection of it. The Sons were getting information and protection from somewhere high up, though. Past Sir David and Sir Horace, Bushell couldn't imagine any other one man well enough positioned to give them both. Sir Martin Luther King? The notion was absurd. Sir Devereaux Jones? No, he didn't have enough clout to know of upcoming searches in time to warn the Sons of Liberty about them. Besides, any Negro who backed the Sons belonged in the Yellow Brick.

Medium-ranking RAMs might have heard of the searches and passed the word to the Sons, as had happened in Richmond. But medium-ranking RAMs wouldn't have known of Charles III's impending visit soon enough to get that word to the Sons in time for them to steal *The Two Georges* and demand its ransom. It all added up to—nothing that made any sense.

If you believed Cameron Moffett, he didn't know anything, he'd never known anything, and he wouldn't know anything if he lived to be a hundred and twelve. Bushell didn't believe him, but couldn't shake him, either.

It was nearly four when he gave up and sent Moffett back to his cell. At some time in there, someone had gone out for more fish and chips. They'd saved him a portion. It was long since cold, and greasy enough to lubricate a steamer's differential. He ate it anyhow.

"Still no word?" he asked Sam Stanley, who was smoking a harsh-smelling cigarillo he must have borrowed from Ted Kittridge.

"Still no word."

"Have we gone through the prisoners' effects for keys that might lock up storage cubicles?"

"Oh, yes." Sam looked pained. "But you know how those places operate, Chief. You buy your own lock and you put it on the door. So long as you pay 'em your fiver every month, or whatever the freight is, you're fine. If you don't pay, they haul out the bolt-cutters and fling your stuff in the street. So the villains have a good many keys that *might* be the right one, but so what? How do we find out?"

"Damn good question," Bushell took out his own key ring. "Hell, I've got a couple of keys that *might* be the right ones myself—except they aren't. I'd wager you have, too."

"Oh, yes," Stanley said again, even more mournfully than before. "If we can catch a break some other way, we have a chance of learning which key is the right one—if any of them is—but that hasn't happened. The only break we've had—and believe me, I count my blessings—is that Sir Martin hasn't had to shell out fifty million quid to get the bloody painting back yet."

"Or if he has, we don't know about it," Bushell said. "That'll do—for now."

They went on with the interrogations. It got dark outside. Bushell wished for a chance to sleep, to bathe, to change the clothes he'd had on for a day and a half now. Lieutenant Toby Custine did fall asleep, right in the middle of a question he was putting to Stanage. Bushell and Maxwell Hammond got him to his feet and half dragged him out to one of the chairs in the hallway. He woke up enough to mutter an incoherent protest, then was gone again.

The clock chimed ten, eleven, twelve. "Deadline's past," Samuel Stanley muttered.

Bushell shook his head. "The deadline's not past till His Majesty makes his speech tonight without *The Two Georges* on the wall behind him." He rounded on Cameron Moffett. "You might as well tell the truth for a change. That'll give you some chance of seeing the outside of a penitentiary before you're ninety-one."

"You can go to the devil, you bloody tyrant," Moffett returned. "You have to let us call our solicitors this afternoon, and after that we'll be free men again—the way all Americans should be free."

The clock chimed one, two, three. The round of interrogations resumed. Hammond brought in Morton Johnston. In spite of a rumpled suit and stubble on his cheeks, the Independence Party man from New Liverpool remained an imposing figure. "How did I miss you before now?" Bushell said, fighting back a yawn.

Snug in his cell, Johnston had had more rest. "I don't know and I don't care," he snapped. "The rest of your band of desperadoes has harassed me more than enough to make up for your absence."

Bushell did yawn, half exhaustion, half contempt. "That was then, Johnston. This is now. Things have changed since the last time we put you through the wringer—you'd better believe they have."

"How?" Johnston retorted. "Have you tortured a false confession out of one of my fellow detainees?"

"We don't need *their* confessions, not any more," Bushell answered. "We certainly don't need them to sink *you*. Down in Victoria, Sir Horace Bragg is talking, and when he's through there won't be a Son free from here to the Pacific."

Morton Johnston went white. "No," he said in a voice that meant anything but *no*. "I don't believe you."

The RAMs all looked at him. None of them looked at Bushell, none of them looked at one another, fearing any change of expression would give the game away. Bushell, having finally broken through, wished he knew more than he did. Showing ignorance now would prove to Johnston he was running a bluff. He picked words with great care, and took even greater care to ensure that they sounded artless, casual: "Yes, you can come off it now: when the head goes, the body dies. The head's in the Victoria gaol, and we've got our lads heading to the storage cubicle to pick up *The Two Georges* right this minute."

Lieutenant Hammond stuck his head into the interrogation chamber. "Telephone for you, Colonel, from the Victoria gaol."

He couldn't have delivered a better-timed message if he'd tried for a year. "That must mean they have the painting back," Bushell said happily. "We'll leave you alone for a few minutes, Johnston, let you think about just how much trouble you're in." He gathered up his colleagues by eye. They all got up and came out with him. He closed the door on Morton Johnston.

Without a word, Samuel Stanley set a hand on Bushell's shoulder for a moment. But Bushell had no time to savor the breakthrough. He hurried to Maxwell Hammond's office and picked up the telephone. "Bushell here."

"Walter Manchester." The RAM major spoke in a quick, worried voice: "Colonel, I hate to tell you this, but I just got the word myself: the ransom demand went in at a minute before midnight. Has to be paid by eight this morning, or else. I'm sorry. If I'd known sooner, I would have called sooner. Word just got here."

"Damnation!" Bushell exploded. "And the King-Emperor's due when? Ten?"

"His arrival's been moved up," Manchester said. "Security, don't you know? He'll be here at nine now."

"Damnation," Bushell said again, this time dully. He looked at the clock in Hammond's office. It was a little before four. "The payment is going forward?"

"I don't know that for certain, but I gather it is." Manchester sounded disgusted.

"All right, Major, thank you. I'll do what I can." Bushell hung up. He sat staring at the wall—through the wall—for half a minute. Then he grimaced, as if a regimental surgeon were about to probe for a bullet without anesthetic. He picked up the telephone and rang America's Number Ten. When the operator answered, he said, "Put me through to Sir David Clarke—at once."

"I'm sorry, sir, but—" the operator began.

"Tell him it's Colonel Bushell. He'll speak to me."

"One moment," the operator said doubtfully. Bushell drummed his fingers on Maxwell Hammond's desk. Then the operator came back on the line. "Go ahead, Colonel."

Bushell did, without preliminaries: "Buy me an hour, Clarke."

"I'm afraid that's impossible, Colonel," Sir David answered, matching his directness. "You heard Sir Martin's declared policy at the same time I did: if you had not recovered *The Two Georges* before a final ransom demand arrived, he would pay the required sum. You have not, it has, and he will."

"I've never begged any man for anything in my whole life," Bushell said heavily, "and God knows I'd start with somebody else if I had a choice. But I don't. So . . . I beg you, Sir David, buy me an hour. Buy me two if you can. I'm *that* close. I might not even need the hour—but I might. The one thing you can do is talk. So talk. Buy me that hour, I don't care how."

There was a long silence on the other end of the line. At last, Sir David said, "I'll . . . try, Colonel. I can't promise anything. We're to deliver a lorry bearing the sum to New Leicester Square, and then—"

"Arrange boiler trouble," Bushell broke in. "Arrange a punctured tyre. Arrange *something*, for heaven's sake."

"I'll try," Clarke said again, more firmly this time. He coughed, then went on, "This can't be easy for you, Colonel. I respect your courage and your patriotism, and I—"

"To hell with that." Bushell slammed down the phone. Getting *The Two Georges* back had become his hunt for the great grey whale in the famous novel of the same name, and he knew it.

He went out into the hallway and quickly briefed the other RAMs, Kathleen, and Lieutenant Hammond. "How do you want us to play it?" Sam Stanley asked.

"Just back me," Bushell told him. "Johnston should be done to a turn about now."

When he and his colleagues walked back into the interrogation room, Morton Johnston sprang to his feet. "Now see here," he said, his jowls quivering in indignation real or manufactured. "I demand to—"

"Sit down," Bushell said. "Keep quiet." He didn't raise his voice. Nonetheless, Johnston, bluster pierced, sank back into his chair. Bushell glanced over at the officers and Kathleen as if they were medicos who'd agreed he had to give Johnston the bad news. Give it he did, in offhand, casual tones that brooked no contradiction: "It's all over now. We have the painting back, we have the blundering fools you Sons sent into New Leicester Square, we have Bragg's confession to send you up personally on a charge of treason and conspiracy with the Holy Alliance." That was a shot in the dark, but a good one, and he added to it, again in the most matter-of-fact way possible: "And we have Zack Fenton out in New Liverpool, too."

"My God." Johnston buried his face in his hands. When he looked up again, his features were an overfed mask of tragedy. "I was always afraid Bragg would give us away in the end," he said, drawing in a long, shuddering breath.

"Oh? Why's that?" Bushell asked.

Before Johnston could answer, Sam Stanley said, "The old family estates, eh?"

"You'd know, wouldn't you, being the color you are?" Johnston said bitterly. "Of course, the old family estates. When the Crown made the planters turn their Negroes loose, a lot of good men were ruined."

"A lot of good men were freed," Stanley answered.

And a lot of things Sam had said, things that hadn't made sense to Bushell, suddenly became clear. "Lord!" he burst out. "You said back in New Liverpool that Bragg wouldn't mind seeing the plantation days come back again, but I never dreamt you meant it literally."

"I didn't think you did." Stanley sighed and spread his hands. "What can I tell you?" He might have known Bragg's opinion of Negroes, but how was he supposed to say anything like that to a man who counted himself Bragg's friend? Bragg hadn't given Bushell any sign that he held those views, but then, he wouldn't have. For how many years had he been leading a double life?

No time to worry about that now. Bushell turned back to Morton Johnston.

"So you'll talk now, will you? It might keep them from putting a noose around your fat neck. Of course, it might not."

Johnston licked his lips. "What does anything matter any more? It's all ruined. Go ahead, ask your questions."

"As if we can rely on everything you tell us," Bushell said scornfully. "How do we know you won't try feeding us more lies?"

The Independence Party leader drew himself up with dignity more pathetic than impressive. "I am a solicitor, sir."

Sam Stanley let out a raucous laugh. "Proves the colonel's point, doesn't it?"

Morton Johnston looked indignant. Bushell flicked Sam a warning glance. He didn't want Johnston mulish and defiant; he wanted him soft and squishy as a blancmange. Afer a moment's thought, he told the lawyer, "I'm going to test you: I'll give you a question where I already know the answer. If you give me that answer back, I'll pass on to my superiors that you were cooperative. As I say, it may help you. If you lie to me—" He made hand-washing motions.

"Go ahead," Johnston repeated in a voice like ashes.

"All right." Bushell worked to keep his voice light, easy: "Give me the name of the storage facility where you people had hidden *The Two Georges*."

Anguish crossed Johnston's plump face. "I don't know it. I'm from New Liverpool, remember? As God is my witness, Colonel Bushell, I don't."

Bushell shrugged and turned to Lieutenant Hammond. "Take him back to his cell. We'll deal with him in the ordinary way."

"Wait!" Johnston howled as the Georgestown constable strode toward him. "I don't know the name of the place, but I know where it is." He send Bushell a beseeching look. Bushell nodded to Maxwell Hammond, who stopped. Rapidly, almost babbling in his haste to get the words out, Johnston went on, "It's down by the docks, on the Victoria side of the river—not far from where the *Britannia* will land. Don't ask me if there's any connection to that, because I don't know, truly I don't." He stared anxiously at Bushell.

"Take him back to his cell, Lieutenant," Bushell said to Hammond. "He may as well get used to it, for he'll be in one for some time to come. He'd have got out sooner if he'd gone through the trapdoor of a gallows, but I don't suppose that will happen now." Morton Johnston sagged with relief; he seemed to become shorter and wider, as if his bones had turned to jelly. When Hammond led him away, he went with willing step.

As soon as the door closed behind him, Kathleen Flannery threw her arms around Bushell's neck. "We have it!" she exclaimed exultantly.

"We may have it," Bushell corrected. Even the feel of her against him could barely penetrate the grey haze of exhaustion in which he moved. Nerves and coffee and cigars kept a man going only so long. He could feel how close to the edge of the cliff he walked. The clock said it was a little past four. He'd last long enough. He had to last long enough. Slowly, he went on, "There are a good many storage places down by the docks. Finding the right one will take time—time we haven't got."

He went back to Lieutenant Hammond's office and rang America's Number Ten again. This time, he had no trouble getting through to Sir David

Clarke. "They've agreed to another hour," Sir David said without preamble. "If I ask for anything more, they say they'll touch a match to the painting. I believe them."

"All right. You did what you could," Bushell answered, and then surprised himself by adding, "Thank you."

"You're welcome." Clarke also sounded surprised.

Bushell hung up, then called Maxwell Hammond. "Have you got a city directory for Victoria here?" he asked. Hammond yanked open a desk drawer, pulled out a fat paperbound book, and dropped it in front of Bushell with a thud. "First-rate," Bushell said. He flipped to the index, then to the section on storage facilities. "Half these places didn't exist when I was working out of Victoria," he muttered as he scribbled down names and addresses. He suddenly seemed to remember Hammond was there. "Go round up all the keys that are liable to open a storage cubicle."

"Right." Hammond paused for a moment at the doorway. "We're going to have to be lucky, you know."

"Really? That never occurred to me," Bushell said. The Georgestown constable stared at him, shook his head, and hurried away. When he returned with the keys, Bushell took them, stuffed them in his pocket, and said, "Keep sweating the other Sons. Let 'em know how much we know. With luck, one of 'em'll give you the name of the storage facility they're using. I'll ring you every so often. If you get it out of them, you'll let me know."

"I do the work, you RAMs get the glory," Hammond said, not altogether in jest. "Seems like that's the way it always goes."

"Cut the shit," Bushell said succinctly. "You haven't got jurisdiction south of the Potomac anyhow. And if we get *The Two Georges* back without having to ransom it, there'll be glory enough to go around, I promise you."

Hammond considered, then slowly nodded. "How persuasive with these bastards you want me to get?"

"Don't ask me questions like that." After a moment, Bushell went on, "I owe one to O'Flynn. Otherwise—" He made the same hand-washing gesture he'd used in front of Morton Johnston, but added, "Don't get stupid, either." Hammond nodded again.

Before setting out into the cool quiet of the wee small hours, Bushell made sure everyone in his steamer and Micah Williams's was armed. Though Kathleen was entirely unofficial, he tried to get her to draw a revolver from the constabulary armory. She refused, saying, "I'd be more dangerous to myself with it than without it." When he tried to argue, she stuck out her chin and looked stubborn. He shrugged and let her have her way.

The streets of Georgestown and then of Victoria were as quiet and empty as those of New Liverpool had been the early morning after *The Two Georges* was stolen. Bushell tried not to think of that early morning, and the night before it. With luck (and how right Hammond had been to say he'd need it!), he'd soon make it as if that night had never happened.

Sergeant Ted Kittridge pulled up in front of the Precious Treasures Storage Corporation, Ltd., at a little past five. The eastern horizon was bright with sunrise soon to come. Bushell paused to scribble the name and address of the storage corporation on one of the last few blank search warrants.

He bounded out of the steamer with pistol drawn. His head swiveled every which way. If the Sons of Liberty wanted to fight to keep *The Two Georges*, they had plenty of cover here. But the only person who came up to see what a couple of carloads of RAMs descending on his storage center meant was a grey-bearded night watchman who carried an electric torch with failing cells and who exuded a powerful odor of cheap whiskey.

Bushell showed him the hastily prepared warrant. After shining the flickering torch on it, the watchman touched a forefinger to the shiny brim of his cap. "Go right ahead, pal," he said, breathing more whiskey fumes into Bushell's face. "Hope you find what you're looking for."

"Not half so much as I do," Bushell said.

Samuel Stanley carried the keys they'd taken from the Sons of Liberty at the Georgestown station. Bushell had to hope one of those keys would open the cubicle where *The Two Georges* was hidden. He didn't have time to test anything else. Picking locks was too slow. Even bolt-cutters would be too slow when there were so many locks that had to be checked. If he was wrong in his hope, the NAU would be out about fifty million pounds, and he and Kathleen Flannery out a career apiece—small change in the register of history, but not to him.

He took the keys from Sam, kept one himself, and gave out the rest, one to a RAM, as far as they went: except for the last, which he handed to Kathleen for luck. "Now we go down the cubicle doors, one at a time. If your key turns a lock, sing out."

He could tell at a glance that his first key would not fit the first lock, a stout Harvard. He tried it anyhow, a measure of his desperation. When it wouldn't go in, let alone turn, he hurried along to the next cubicle to test it there. Again, no luck. On to the next. Then the other key-bearers formed a line behind him, Kathleen bringing up the rear.

The sun rose, almost blinding him, as he was trying his key in the last lock. He waited for the others to try theirs, too, then did his best not to sound discouraged. "We go on to the next storage company," he said. Then he pulled out his pocket watch, grimaced, and put it back. Almost six o'clock. Not much time left at all now.

Seeing the telephone in the night watchman's office reminded him to ring back to the Georgestown constabulary station, in the hope of cutting short the search from storage firm to storage firm. But Maxwell Hammond had no good news for him: "Colonel, we've been working hard since the minute you left, but we haven't got anything out of any of 'em. Maybe they really don't know." He made the admission as if he hated it.

"Keep working." Bushell slammed down the phone.

He expected building traffic to slow the steamers as they headed for Bedrock Storage, Ltd., but he got there quickly through streets still almost deserted. "Holiday today," Ted Kittridge reminded him when he remarked on that. He thumped his forehead with the heel of his hand. For once, Charles III's arrival was bringing him something other than trouble.

The watchman at Bedrock Storage resembled the one at Precious Treasures, from shiny-brimmed cap to grizzled beard to whiskey aroma. The only differences Bushell could see were that he'd put away his torch since the sun was up and that he was Negro rather than white. He looked at the hastily written search warrant Bushell gave him, said, "I hope you folks find whatever you're looking for," and leaned back against the side of the building. As Bushell passed him by, he drew a pint flask from his hip pocket, raised it to his mouth, tilted his head back, and swigged noisily.

Bedrock Storage had more cubicles to check than Precious Treasures. It was almost seven before the RAMs and Kathleen discovered none of their keys opened any of the locks on those cubicles. Bushell's shoulders slumped when he went into the storage-company office to telephone the Georgestown constables. Again, Lieutenant Hammond had no good news to give him. He went back out to his comrades.

"It's all up to us," he said. "We can check one more place, maybe two, and then we turn into pumpkins. I've got half a dozen on this list." He took it out of his inside coat pocket. "I'm going to read them off. If any of you can think of a reason we should go to one instead of another . . . I'd be awfully glad to hear it. All right? Here: Crown Jewel Storage, Douglass Storage Cubicles, Keep Keepsakes Safe (don't ask me to repeat that one), Adler Cubicles, NAU Special—something, Kathleen?"

"Maybe." She bit her lip. "It isn't much, but—"

"Spit it out," Bushell said harshly. "Nobody else has any bright ideas. Whatever it is, it can't hurt now."

"All right," she said. "*Adler* means *eagle* in German."

"Does it?" Bushell said. He had French and Spanish and some Russian, but he'd never found a reason to learn German. "After all the eagles we've seen in this case—maybe one more?" He looked around at the other RAMs. "Anybody have a better idea? Anybody poke a hole in this one?" Nobody spoke. Bushell stuck the list back into his pocket. "Let's go. Adler Cubicles, on Calhoun Street down close by the Potomac."

As he had before, he prepared a search warrant as Sergeant Kittridge drove the steamer to the new target. He had only one more warrant left in his briefcase, too. Out of time, out of paper . . . out of luck? Wouldn't be long before he knew.

He got to Adler Cubicles at 7:11. Maybe that was luck. When he saw the bald eagle daubed on the front wall of the place, he began to think it was. His eyes flicked up to the roof. If this was the place, the Sons of Liberty were liable to have riflemen up there. He didn't spot any. Even so, when he got out of the steamer, he crouched behind the wing for a moment, pistol in hand, wondering if he would draw fire.

He didn't. The only thing that happened was that a fat, bald clerk with a neat little mustache came out of the front office and said, "Hullo! Are you filming a cinema here?" Behind steel-rimmed spectacles, his eyes sparkled with excitement.

"In a word, no." Bushell presented him with the search warrant.

His eyes got even wider and brighter. "My goodness!" he said. "What are you looking for? Are people moving great piles of contraband tobacco again? I re-member last year when—"

Bushell didn't care a farthing for the clerk's reminiscences, and the only thing talk of contraband tobacco did was to remind him he wanted a cigar. Still wary, he pushed forward into the long, narrow courtyard around which the stor-age cubicles themselves were placed. His colleagues followed and fanned out in a skirmish line, but everything seemed quiet and peaceful.

Hardly daring to believe the tranquility he found, he reholstered his pistol and took out the key he'd got from Samuel Stanley. He walked over to the cubi-cle with a tarnished brass 1 screwed into the plywood door, put the key in the lock, and tried to turn it. It would not turn.

The other keyholders lined up behind him. They tried one by one to open the cubicle. They all failed. Bushell went on to the second cubicle, then to the third, then to the fourth. . . .

He was on the seventy-eighth when, from two behind him, he heard a sound he had begun to believe he would never hear: a soft click. His head whipped back to the right. Lieutenant Toby Custine stood in front of cubicle 76, his mouth gaping foolishly wide, staring down at the lock that had just come open.

Kathleen Flannery stood between him and Bushell. "Mother Mary," she whispered.

"From whom did your key come, Lieutenant?" Bushell asked as everyone converged on the storage cubicle.

Custine glanced down at the tag taped to the key. "From O'Flynn, sir," he answered in a slightly dazed voice. He took off the lock and opened the door to the cubicle.

Kathleen screamed and threw her arms around his neck. Bushell was not the least bit jealous. Had Kathleen not beaten him to it, he would have hugged Cus-tine himself. There against the back wall of the storage cubicle leaned *The Two Georges* in its heavy, elaborately carved gilded oak frame.

A lamp with a dangling chain hung from the cubicle's ceiling. Kathleen yanked that chain. The lamp came on, filling the shadowy cubicle with harsh yellow light. Kathleen knelt by *The Two Georges*. "This *is* the painting, not a copy," she said at once. She cocked her head and studied it. "It seems to be in good condition, too. It seems to be." She sounded as if she hardly dared be more certain than that.

Samuel Stanley pulled out his pocket watch. "We did it, by God," he said, "and with a good hour and five minutes to spare, too."

That reminded Bushell he had other things left to do, things he'd almost for-gotten in the desperate race to find *The Two Georges*. "The ransom!" he ex-claimed. "I've got to block it." He dashed out of the storage cubicle and up to the company offices. The clerk was on the telephone, telling someone named Marge about what was happening. He got off an instant before Bushell yanked away the handset and brained him with it.

Bushell rang America's Number Ten. The operator put him through to Sir David Clarke at once. "Don't pay the bastards a ha'penny," he barked when he heard Sir David's voice. "If anybody shows up in the square, arrest him. We've got *The Two Georges* back, and it's not harmed."

Out of the corner of his eye, he noted the clerk's stunned expression: the fellow evidently hadn't known everything that was going on. "Colonel, I wouldn't have believed it," Sir David said. "I'll pass your wonderful news to Sir Martin immediately. I can't afford to wait a moment—he's about to leave for the *Britannia's* berth. He'll greet the King-Emperor with a glad heart now. On his behalf, let me say that you have the Union's gratitude. And, for whatever it may be worth to you, you have mine as well."

"Never mind that," Bushell said. "The important thing is to have the painting behind His Majesty when he speaks tonight, and we've done it." He glanced up. "Now I'd better get off the line. Here comes Kathleen. She'll need to talk to the people at the All-Union Art Museum to arrange to get *The Two Georges* back where it belongs in time for the speech."

Kathleen took the phone from Bushell as peremptorily as he'd taken it from the storage-company clerk. She dialed a number. When someone answered, she exclaimed, "We've got it!" Bushell could hear the shout of joy on the other end of the line. She gave her colleagues at the museum the address of Adler Cubicles, said, "Good," and hung up. She turned to Bushell. "The lorry to take the painting home will be here in half an hour. Home!" She laughed at herself, and seemed to sag slightly. "You know what I mean. I'm so tired. I must look a fright, too. I've been *living* in these clothes."

"You'll always look good to me," Bushell said, which made her smile. He rubbed his bristly chin. "You don't need a shave, that's one thing. Another is, as long as *The Two Georges* looks all right, nobody's going to notice you."

"Mm, I daresay you're right," Kathleen answered. "Now whom are you ringing?"

"Major Walter Manchester, the RAMs he has with him, and the Victoria constables," Bushell said. "That lorry of yours is going to have itself a nice, strong escort on the way to the All-Union Art Museum. Now that we've got the painting back, I don't aim to let it be stolen again."

"I hadn't even thought of that." Kathleen rubbed her eyes. "I have the feeling I'm only thinking about half as well as I ought to be."

"I know what you mean," Bushell said. "Let me just ring Manchester here, and then we can go back and stare at the painting till they take it away." When he got through to the major, Manchester bellowed in his ear, almost as if he were a male Sally Reese. Bushell finished giving him the news and turned to Kathleen. "Reinforcements on the way."

She nodded, then rubbed her eyes again. "I'll be so glad when this is all over. After tonight, I intend to sleep for about a month straight."

"What a wonderful idea," Bushell said. He headed back toward *The Two Georges*. In spite of the other RAMs standing in front of and inside the storage cubicle, he feared something dreadful would happen to the painting if it left his sight even for a moment.

The little bald clerk tagged along. He was all but bouncing with excitement.

"*The Two Georges* was here all the time, right under my nose? I can't believe it. Marge won't believe it. I want to see it, just so I can tell her I did."

Bushell found it hard to imagine this eager nonentity a Son of Liberty, but he managed. He let the man have the briefest of glimpses, ready to jump on him if his hands went into his pockets. Then he said, "Go back to your office. You can take a better look when they load it onto the lorry, and you can see it at the All-Union Art Museum. No more now."

Looking like a kicked puppy, the clerk turned away. Kathleen said, "Don't feel bad, sir. If you come to the museum, have me paged." She gave him her name. "I'll see that you and, uh, Marge are admitted free of charge, and I'll shoot you both to the front of the queue to view *The Two Georges*."

"That's very kind of you," he said, and walked off a happier man.

"That *is* very kind of you," Bushell said.

Kathleen shrugged. "It's safe. It's been safe here. No rats in the cubicle, the roof doesn't leak—he deserves something for that, even if he didn't know what was in cubicle 76."

"We did it," Sam Stanley said again, when Bushell walked into the cubicle. "You make sure we aren't going to be out fifty million?"

"You'd best believe I did," Bushell replied with feeling. "Sir David and I were even civil to each other. Will wonders never cease?"

"Two miracles in one morning." Stanley didn't sound as if he was joking. Bushell looked at him sharply. He didn't look as if he was joking, either.

Every so often, Bushell's hand would fall to the butt of his pistol. He had trouble believing the chase was over at last, *The Two Georges* recovered, the Sons of Liberty thwarted. He kept expecting an attack, kept waiting for gunfire to break out, bullets to fly, men to fall.

The courtyard was very quiet, very peaceful. The day gave every promise of being hot and muggy, like most August days in Victoria. A pigeon flew down and landed on the concrete in the middle of the courtyard. It peered at the RAMs out of one orange eye. When it decided they weren't going to throw it any crumbs, it took off again. The wind whistled through its wings.

Constabulary steamers started pulling up in front of Adler Cubicles at a quarter past eight. The tight knot inside Bushell began to ease. It would take an army to get *The Two Georges* out of safe hands now, and the Sons of Liberty, whatever else they were, were not an army.

"You know what I'm going to do as soon as that lorry from the museum steams off with *The Two Georges*?" he said to Sam as Victoria constables jostled one another to get a look at the famous painting.

His adjutant nodded. "The same things I am: you're going back to the William and Mary, you're going to hop in the showerbath, you're going to shave, and then you're going to go to sleep."

"Your boiler still has full pressure in it, however tired you are," Bushell answered. "That's the list, item by item. Sleep." He spoke of it longingly, as Lancelot might have of the Grail.

So many constables and RAMs pounded his back that the continued impacts might have sufficed to keep him awake. He felt drunk without Jameson, a happier buzz than he ever got from Irish whiskey. At 8:35, a couple of minutes later than promised, the All-Union Art Museum's lorry pulled into the courtyard of Adler Cubicles. Malcolm Desmond and Walter Pine, Kathleen's assistants on tour with *The Two Georges*, sprang from the cab along with a couple of stalwart workmen in overalls and cloth caps. They hugged Kathleen, pummeled Bushell some more, and got the painting into the back of the lorry.

"Sir Martin will be able to give the good news to His Majesty, too," Bushell said. "I got hold of Sir David just before the governor-general was going to leave for the docks. Sir Martin's probably spreading the word to all the politicos waiting for the *Britannia* even as we stand here."

"Very likely," Stanley agreed. "He'll probably take all the credit for getting *The Two Georges* back, too. That's the way politicos op—" He broke off when he saw the expression on Bushell's face. "What's the matter, Chief?"

Bushell pointed at him. "You didn't tell anyone Sir Horace was the number one villain in this piece, did you?"

"What?" Stanley stared. "Of course not. Nobody told anybody outside the cabal. If we'd told, it would have got back to Bragg and given the game away."

"That's right," Bushell said. "We were smart. But we were too smart. Nobody except the people in the cabal knows Sir Horace is a villain, right? Which means nobody's going to keep him from being there when the King-Emperor lands, right? God in heaven, he's commandant of the Royal American bloody Mounted Police. And here comes Sir Martin Luther King, singing hosannas because we've got *The Two Georges* back and didn't have to pay a farthing for it. *What's Bragg going to do then?*"

Samuel Stanley's eyes got very big and wide. So did those of Sergeant Ted Kittridge, who was standing nearby. "Jesus," Stanley said. "He's probably carrying a pistol, too. He would be—to keep His Majesty safe from the Sons of Liberty."

Without another word, all three men turned and sprinted for the steamer that had brought them to Adler Cubicles. Bushell heard several questioning shouts from in back of them, including one from Kathleen. He ignored them all. No time for questions now. Maybe no time for anything.

They piled into the steamer. Kittridge maneuvered his way through the blockade of constabulary motorcars like a footballer picking his way through a defense toward a shot on goal. Then, that done, he jammed the pedal to the floorboard. "How long?" Bushell asked.

"We'll be cutting it fine," Kittridge answered. "Too fine."

"They'll have a perimeter around the landing dock sealed off," Stanley said. "That'll help us—once we get to the perimeter."

Around it, traffic moved, but spasmodically. A lot of people had headed toward the docks in hopes of getting a glimpse of the King-Emperor. Signs saying that wasn't going to be possible turned back some of them. Charles III was arriving an hour earlier than had been announced, too, and that didn't hurt. The roads were more crowded than usual, but not impossibly so.

All the same, time stretched very tight for Bushell. He'd known that feeling before, but only in combat. Now he sat here, unable to do anything useful, while about a week went by. He pulled out his pocket watch. The week turned out to be seven minutes, not seven days. While he was looking at the watch, the second hand moved at its normal rate. The instant he put it back in his waistcoat pocket, everything slowed down again.

Kittridge grunted and pointed ahead through the windscreen. Bushell nodded. There stood a roadblock, with armed RAMs in dress reds behind it. They waved away the steamer in front of Kittridge's, then stared suspiciously at the nondescript motorcar with the three dirty, unshaven characters in it. One of the RAMs came up to the driver's side window. "Sorry, gents," he said, "no traffic past this point."

Ted Kittridge spent a word: "Emergency." He displayed his badge. Bushell and Sam Stanley already had theirs out.

The RAM shook his head. "No traffic of any sort past this point, on Lieutenant General Bragg's orders. We're to be alert for infiltrators, he says, and you blokes don't look a hell of a lot like RAMs to me."

Bushell started to reach for his pistol, though he knew that was likelier to touch off a firefight than get him through. But to be stopped so close was intolerable. He could see the *Britannia* ahead, and the gangplank leading down from it to the dock.

Just as his right hand closed on the butt of the pistol, another RAM said, "Let 'em through, Harry. I know Sergeant Kittridge. If he says something's an emergency, you can believe it is."

Harry looked stubborn. "*I* don't know him, and I'm damned if I'm going to take chances with His Majesty's safety." Up there by the imperial yacht, a band struck up "Hail to the King-Emperor." A tiny figure that had to be Charles III walked down the gangplank. Another tiny figure that had to be Sir Martin Luther King stepped forward to greet him.

Bushell slapped Kittridge on the shoulder. "Ram it!" he said.

The steamer sprang forward. The barrier—a red-painted plank atop two red-painted sawhorses—went over with a crash. Tyres screaming, the motorcar raced toward the *Britannia*, perhaps a quarter of a mile away. Shouts rang out behind.

Between them and the imperial yacht were another, similar barrier and more RAMs in dress uniform. "If they shoot us, we won't get the job done," Samuel Stanley said. It was more comment than protest.

"Tell me something I didn't know." Bushell held his badge out the window, hoping the RAMs would take it as a talisman.

Kittridge never slowed down. *Wham!* The spurting steamer hit the barricade like an icebreaker smashing a floe. Broken timber flew to either side. Bushell hoped it didn't hurt any of the RAMs who scattered before him, but he went by too fast to be sure.

"Where do you want to go?" Kittridge demanded, accelerating still. Heads among the assembled dignitaries were turning now. That second barricade smashing had drawn people's notice. A couple of the more alert were springing to their feet.

"As close to His Majesty as you can get," Bushell answered. "Try not to run anybody down here. We'd be talked about."

"Right." Kittridge used a couple of precious syllables' worth of laughter.

Everything ahead swelled as if a cinema camera were moving in fast for a tight shot. There stood His Majesty Charles III, head turned toward the onrushing motorcar but features schooled to calmness even so. There beside him stood Sir Martin Luther King, looking quite humanly astonished. And there, coming up to protect, or rather as if to protect—

"It's Bragg!" Stanley yelled.

Lieutenant General Sir Horace Bragg did indeed carry a revolver on his hip, along with his dress sword. He drew the pistol as Kittridge screeched to a stop not ten feet away. "Halt or I'll shoot!" he shouted, his Carolina accent broad and harsh.

Bushell and Stanley flung themselves out of the steamer before it stopped rolling. Bragg's face worked horribly when he recognized them. Bushell sprinted toward him, shouting, "He's the one! He led the plot, he—"

With a wordless scream of hate, Sir Horace fired at him at point-blank range—and missed. The report of the pistol and the crack of the bullet past his ear almost deafened Bushell. He'd been in enough combat to know how hard it was to shoot straight when your heart pounded and your hand shook.

Bragg whirled, swinging the muzzle of the pistol toward the King-Emperor. Before he could shoot, Bushell jumped on his back and dragged down his arm— no time for him to yank out his own weapon. They crashed to the ground together in a cursing, clawing heap. Bragg tried to knee Bushell in the crotch. He twisted to one side just in time and took the blow on the hip, all the while hanging on to Bragg's pistol arm like grim death.

"Let go of the gun," Bushell panted. Bragg snarled an obscenity and rabbit-punched him. He grunted in pain. His grip weakened. Shouting in triumph, Bragg jerked the pistol free. He fired—just as Samuel Stanley landed on top of him and Bushell.

Stanley cried out, in pain rather than triumph. But his weight knocked the pistol from Bragg's hand. Bushell kicked at it. It spun out of Bragg's reach. The RAM commandant howled like a lost soul.

Lost or not, the RAM commandant fought on. As Bushell had back in New Liverpool the night *The Two Georges* was stolen, he tried to draw his ceremonial sword and use it as a real weapon.

A muscular man, a long-faced fellow in his mid-forties, clamped both hands on Bragg's wrist and kept the sword in its scabbard. "Thanks," Bushell gasped. After a moment, he added two more startled words: "Your Majesty."

"My pleasure," Charles III said, and sounded as if he meant it.

The dignitaries and uprushing red-uniformed RAMs swarmed onto Sir Horace Bragg and pinned him as much by sheer weight of numbers as by skill and prowess. Bushell didn't care how the job was done, so long as it was done. Still woozy and sick from the rabbit punch, he rolled away and sat up.

Sam Stanley had his right hand clenched tight around his left forearm. Blood dripped through his fingers. His lips were skinned back in a grimace that showed all his teeth. "Damnation," he muttered. "All those years as a RAM made me forget how much I didn't like getting shot." He shook his head. "The memory comes back mighty fast, though."

The RAMs dragged Bragg away. Several of them looked as if they wanted to drag Bushell and Stanley after him, but when the King-Emperor came over and set his right hand on the shoulder of one and his left on that of the other, the RAMs subsided—except for one who undid a clasp knife and came up to Stanley, saying, "Let me cut away your shirt and jacket, sir, so we can have a look at that wound."

"Just a second," Stanley told him. He glanced up to Charles III. "Your Majesty, please step back. Can't know what this fellow's going to do if he gets close to you, not after Sir Horace."

"I'm no traitor!" the RAM cried indignantly.

"I'll cover you even so," Bushell told him, freeing his own pistol from its holster. He too looked toward the King-Emperor, and went on in pointed tones, "After His Majesty withdraws."

"What sort of monarch am I, to have my subjects order me about?" Charles III demanded in what Bushell hoped was mock indignation.

"A live one," he answered, and the King-Emperor stepped away from Stanley.

The RAM with the knife did as he'd said he would, quickly and skillfully. "Through and through," he said, stating the obvious. "Can you move your arm, sir?"

Stanley tried to rotate it, winced, and shook his head. "I've got a bone broken in there, sure as the devil."

"Afraid you're likely to be right, sir." The RAM took out a white handkerchief and began bandaging the wound. It quickly became obvious he'd need more material than one handkerchief could provide. Bushell gave him his. The King-Emperor also drew an immaculate square of linen from his breast pocket and handed it to the RAM.

Sir Martin Luther King came up. Bushell blamed him not in the least for missing the brawl; he was far from young and, as a former minister, had trained in the arts of peace rather than those of fighting. His deep, rich voice more than a little shaken, the governor-general said, "Your Majesty, allow me to present to you Colonel Thomas Bushell and Captain Samuel Stanley of the—of your— Royal American Mounted Police."

"In a manner of speaking, we've already been introduced, wouldn't you say, Sir Martin?" Charles III answered. He turned to the two RAMs and said, "Thank you, gentlemen."

In a different tone of voice, that would have been perfunctory. As Charles III said it, it covered all the ground needed and then some. Not even Bushell's cynicism was proof against the living centerpiece of the Empire. "It was a pleasure, Your Majesty," he said, and Sam Stanley, wounded arm and all, nodded. Bushell went on, "If it hadn't been for Sergeant Kittridge there"—Kittridge had got out of the steamer when the fight started, and now was one of the men holding Bragg down—"we never would have got here on time."

"Sergeant, I thank you, too," Charles III said warmly.

Ted Kittridge sprang to his feet, and to stiff attention. "Your Majesty!" he said. He was still sparing of words, but looked about to burst with pride.

To Bushell, the King-Emperor said, "Just before this—unpleasantness—began, didn't Sir Martin mention your name in connection with the recovery of *The Two Georges?*"

"We do have it back, Your Majesty," Bushell said. "It should be at the All-Union Art Museum in a few minutes; it's on its way there now." What Sir Martin had said of him he did not know, and so did not speak to that.

The governor-general said, "Sir David Clarke rushed out to my limousine with the good news as I was about to depart to meet His Majesty here. He spoke most highly of you, Colonel, and I was delighted to relay his praise to the King-Emperor."

Charles III nodded to confirm that the praise had indeed been relayed. Sir Martin Luther King's narrow, slightly slanted eyes were inscrutable as he studied Bushell. Bushell understood that. He'd have bet it would have taken more than getting *The Two Georges* back safe and sound to squeeze praise for him from Sir David.

"You never can tell, Your Excellency," he said, and then glanced over to Sir Horace Bragg. "You never can tell."

First faint in the distance, then swelling rapidly, came the urgent clang of an ambulance's alarm bell. To Bushell, Sir Martin said, "You will of course honor us with your presence at the All-Union Art Museum, having made it possible for the happy event there to proceed as originally planned."

But Bushell shook his head. "Your Excellency, you'll have to do without me. Making sure Sam is all right comes first. After that—" He shrugged vaguely. At the moment, the prospect of lying down on a real bed in real pyjamas and sleeping felt far more attractive than listening to a speech from anyone, the King-Emperor included.

Sir Martin Luther King's nostrils flared slightly; one eyebrow might have risen a sixteenth of an inch. Without perceptibly changing his expression, he sent Bushell a clear message: *you're making a mistake.* Bushell didn't care. He'd made enough mistakes on this case already. What did one more matter now?

And then Charles III nodded to him. "Stout fellow," he said. "Your mates come first."

"Yes, sir," Bushell agreed enthusiastically. The governor-general was a politico, and thought in terms of protocol. The King-Emperor was a ruler of men, and, by the way he talked, remembered his own regimental service. Sir Martin could run a country, and did a capable job of it. Charles III was more than capable at inspiring the Empire.

The ambulance skidded to a stop behind the steamer Ted Kittridge had driven. Photographers who'd captured on film the seizure of Sir Horace Bragg now spent more flashbulbs as a couple of husky young men in white service caps, white jackets, and black trousers jumped out through the wide doors at the vehicle's rear.

They were carrying a light stretcher. When Stanley saw it, he tried to wave them away. "Put that back," he said. "I don't need it." He started to get to his feet.

"Stay there on the ground, sir!" one of the young men said, almost as sharply as if he were covering Stanley with a firearm.

The other medical assistant knelt beside him and examined the bandage the RAM had put on his arm. He nodded grudging approval. "Not a bad job. Here, just let us set a light splint on the injured member till we can get you in hospital for a proper setting."

The assistant who'd told Stanley to stay down went back to the ambulance and returned with a couple of thin boards and some cloth strips with which to tie them. As he got to work, Charles III came over and said, "I want you to see that this man gets the very best of care."

"Everybody we treat gets the best of care, pal," the medical assistant said without looking up. His partner kicked him in the ankle. When he did see who had spoken to him, he went pale. "Uh, Your Majesty, I, uh—"

"Never mind," the King-Emperor said. "Your answer was as it should have been." The medical assistant went back to work. His hands were shaking so much, he had to try two or three times before he could get the ties as he wanted them.

"Here, sir, if you'll slide onto the stretcher—" his partner said, and Stanley did. As the two men lifted him, that same one asked, "Have you got anyone to go with you to hospital?"

"Right here," Bushell said, taking a step after them.

"Good enough." The medical assistants slid Sam Stanley into the back of the ambulance, then climbed up after him. One of them waved Bushell forward. "Mind your head, sir. It's a bit cramped in here."

"Chief, you're going to have to ring Phyllis, let her know I'll be all right," Stanley said. "If the wireless was carrying His Majesty's arrival, she may already have heard I got shot."

"I'll take care of it," Bushell promised.

The ambulance driver backed the steamer away from the motorcar in which Bushell and Stanley had arrived, then started toward the hospital, alarm bell clanging. Inside the ambulance, it echoed and reechoed like a warning for the end of the world.

One of the medical assistants took a hypodermic syringe from a compartment set into the side wall of the ambulance. "Would you care for an injection of morphia, sir?" he asked Stanley.

"Why not?" Sam said. "It hurts, and I'm no hero."

The two assistants looked at each other. "With all due respect, sir, I wouldn't say that," the one with the syringe answered as he slid the tip of the needle under Stanley's skin.

"That's better," Stanley said a couple of minutes later, as the drug took effect. He sounded dreamy, far away.

When the ambulance pulled up at the side entrance to the Victoria Memorial Mercy Hospital, the swarm of doctors and nurses waiting for it also argued that, regardless of whether Stanley thought of himself as a hero, the rest of the world did. Some of the assembled medicos also had words of praise for Bushell.

"Never mind me," he snapped. "See to him." He jerked a thumb toward the stretcher that held his friend. "I've got to ring his wife. What will you be doing to him?"

"We'll have to open up that arm," a physician answered. "Any fragments of bone or bullet in there are potential foci for infection. We'll clean them out as thoroughly as we can, reduce the fracture while the wound is open, and so forth. Should be straightforward enough."

He spoke with easy confidence. Why not? It wasn't his arm. Bushell let it go: better a confident medico than a doubtful one, as far as he was concerned. "All right. Lead me to a telephone."

That produced a small bureaucratic contretemps: allow an outsider to make a long-distance telephone connection from within the hallowed precincts of the hospital? But if the outsider was a hero, even the dragon of bureaucracy slunk back into its cave, vanquished. Installed in the posh office of an assistant director, Bushell rang Phyllis Stanley.

"Oh, thank God it's you, Tom!" she exclaimed when she recognized his voice. "Edna Allston from next door was listening to the broadcast, and she just rang me in hysterics. What happened? How's Sam?"

"He'll be all right," Bushell answered. "They're operating on his arm now, but it doesn't look like a bad wound. They're just cleaning up in there. He'll be fine." He hoped he was telling the truth. He thought he was; he'd seen men with far worse injuries pull through. But septicemia was a risk, and nothing to sneeze at.

Phyllis knew that, too, in spite of his optimistic tone. "I'll pray," she said quietly. "Now—how did it happen? Edna's a sweet lady, but her fiddle is short a couple of strings."

Bushell explained how they'd recovered *The Two Georges,* which made Phyllis Stanley exclaim again. Then he told her who had headed the conspiracy to steal the painting. A long silence followed.

At last, Phyllis said, "I have to tell you, Tom, I'm not surprised. You look in Sam's dossier. All the good fitness reports have your name on them. All the ones full of faint praise—you know the kind I mean—those are Sir Horace's, from the days when he supervised both of you. If it hadn't been for those, I think Sam would have a higher rank today. Sir Horace—he was always smooth, but he doesn't fancy Negroes, not even a little. You could tell."

"Maybe you could tell," Bushell said. "I couldn't tell. Why didn't you tell me? Sam said the same sorts of things, too, but only after we found out Bragg was the villain. If I'd known what you just told me, I might have figured that out sooner."

After another pause, Phyllis replied, "He was your friend. He was your superior, too, and Sam's. Would you have listened?" Without letting him answer that, she went on, "Anyhow, stirring up that kind of trouble has a way of costing more than it's worth. This may be a pretty fine country, but it's not a perfect one."

Now it was Bushell's turn to think for a while before he spoke. "*Pretty fine* is about as much as human beings can hope for, don't you think? But all right, I take your point. Sam told me the same thing not long ago, as a matter of fact. Still, though, a dossier with *saved the life of His Majesty Charles III* in it will look, oh, fairly good come the next promotion review. You have to think of these things, Phyllis, so you know how to spend the extra money that'll be coming in soon."

"Thomas Bushell, you are impossible? If I were in Victoria right now, I'd—" Phyllis gave up and started to laugh. "Kiss you right on the cheek," she finished.

"Promises, promises," Bushell said. Phyllis laughed louder. He went on, "I'll ring you back directly Sam comes out of the operating room."

"Thank you," she said, and hung up.

That promise meant he had to mollify the assistant administrator's secretary, who seemed to feel that, while his using the telephone once was a possibly forgivable breach of etiquette, using it twice clearly violated one if not several of the more obscure canons of the Council of Nicaea.

The secretary had his revenge by leading Bushell to a waiting room that not only stank of carbolic acid but was so bare, so stark, so grim that any prisoner interrogated in it would have had good cause to complain to a judge through his barrister on grounds of inhumane treatment. The magazine rack held three ragged periodicals, none of them anything Bushell cared to read, none more recent than the previous December's issue.

A little less than an hour later, a nursing sister escorted Ted Kittridge into the waiting room. The sergeant nodded but wasted no precious words explaining why he'd come—if Bushell couldn't figure it out, too bad. Instead, Kittridge lit up a cigarillo. The look the nursing sister turned on him would have petrified a basilisk. He seemed to find it mild and benignant. Defeated, and incredulous at being defeated, the nursing sister retired in disorder.

Except for the pungent smoke, waiting with Kittridge was like waiting alone. Bushell stared at the glossy white paint on the far wall and waited for something—anything—to happen. After an hour or so, something did: a doctor in surgical whites came through the door. Bushell bounced to his feet. "How is he?"

"Pretty well, all things considered," the medico answered. "The bullet cracked the radius, but didn't splinter it—must have hit at an angle and ricocheted away rather than smashing right through. He should recover full function in the hand, or close to it, at any rate."

"Good news," Bushell said. Kittridge nodded again, and lighted another cigarillo. The medico's glare had no more effect on him than had the nursing sister's. Bushell went on, "When can I see him?"

"Another couple of hours, I'd say," the surgeon answered. "He's still anesthetized now, of course, and we'll be giving him more morphia when he regains consciousness. But as I told you, absent a wound infection, he should do very well."

"Good news," Bushell repeated. "I'll ring his wife and let her know." He stretched, noticing for the first time in several hours how worn he was, then shook his head in slight bemusement. "By God, I really do think that wraps things up."

# XVII

▼

Bushell got off the line quickly after letting Phyllis Stanley know Sam had come through the surgery well. That gave the assistant director's secretary an agreeable surprise; by his expression, he'd thought Bushell aimed at bankrupting the hospital with his extravagant telephone habits.

His suspicions returned when Bushell asked for the use of a razor, shaving soap, and a showerbath in an unoccupied room, and redoubled when Ted Kittridge not only asked for the same things but blew smoke in his face doing it. His plaintive cries were, however, overruled, and he went off to sulk in his tent while the two RAMs bathed in the advantage of their heroic stature.

Putting back on the suit he'd been wearing so long irked Bushell, but not enough to make him want to go over to the William and Mary for fresh clothes. After he'd seen Sam would be time enough for that.

"Sir?" A nursing sister approached him—warily. When she seemed satisfied he wouldn't bite, she went on, "Dr. Duncan says you can see Mr., uh, Stanley for a few minutes, provided you don't tire him."

"Oh, too bad," Bushell said. "I'd been planning to take him out for a run around the block." The nursing sister stared, shook her head, and reluctantly let him follow her to Samuel Stanley's room.

The chamber smelled of carbolic acid, even more strongly than the waiting room had. Arm swathed in splints and bandages, Stanley looked up at Bushell. His eyes were large and round and staring. "Hullo, Chief," he said in a distant voice: he was awake, and alert enough to know who Bushell was, but still woozy from the medications they'd given him.

"Hullo, Sam. I told Phyllis you were all right."

"Oh, she'd be sure of that any which way. She knows I was born to hang." Stanley giggled, not the sort of sound Bushell was used to hearing from him.

"You're feeling no pain," he observed.

Stanley shook his head. Each back-and-forth motion seemed to require a separate effort of will. "It's there," he said. "I know it's there. It's just that it's there and I'm—over here." He raised his right arm and waved it around to indicate some immense distance. Then he giggled again.

Bushell didn't know what to make of that. Standing here in the white room, looking at the white bandages, reminded him of how close they'd come to failing, too. He didn't want to think about that, so he said, "I wish you'd been plainer about what you thought of Bragg."

"That tight-arsed, Negro-hating old statue?" Stanley couldn't have been a great deal plainer if he'd tried for a week. With his head buzzing from anesthetic and morphia, he didn't care what he said. "You liked him, though. I never could figure that out, but what the hell? I just thought, *Nobody's smart about everything,* and went on about my business."

"Nobody's smart about everything," Bushell repeated. "Bragg damn near was. Even after we found out he was the villain, he almost—" He didn't want to say it. The British Empire hadn't suffered regicide in more than three hundred years. God willing, another three hundred would go by before the Empire had to worry about it again.

"Put that vile thing out this instant, do you hear?" a nursing sister said out in the hall, her voice unwontedly loud and angry. When Ted Kittridge came into the room a moment later, he did so sans cigarillo.

He stopped a couple of paces in from the doorway and stood looking toward Stanley. "Glad you're going to be all right, Captain," he said, more words than Bushell had heard from him in all the time they were waiting.

"I suppose I am," Stanley said. "Glad you were driving. Glad we got there in time. Glad—" His smile was broad and foolish. He seemed to know it, saying, "Listen to the medicine talking."

Kittridge waved that aside—wordlessly, as usual. The nursing sister came in and said, "That will be enough of that, gentlemen." She was short and thin and elderly—and no one in his right mind would have thought even for an instant of disobeying her. Under her stern, bespectacled gaze, Bushell and Kittridge left the room.

Once out in the hallway, Bushell asked her, "Have you got a cafeteria in this place?" As if to punctuate the sentence, his stomach growled like an irritated mastiff. He hoped the nursing sister didn't hear it.

"Yes, sir," she said. "Ground floor, west corridor, most of the way back from the street."

Bushell made it to the cafeteria without too much trouble. Ted Kittridge accompanied him. They filled their trays and found an empty table: not hard, since most of them were empty. As soon as he dug in, Bushell understood why. "This is worse than what they feed you in the army," he said, being unable to come up with any stronger dispraise on the spur of the moment.

"And you don't have to pay for that," Kittridge agreed, dismayed into using a complete sentence.

After he'd eaten as much as he could stomach, which didn't take long, Bushell once more bearded the assistant director's secretary in his den. That worthy, assured Bushell did not intend to strain the hospital's accounts by ringing long-distance yet again, grudgingly vouchsafed him the further use of a telephone.

He dialed the number for RAM headquarters. When he identified himself, the switchboard operator shouted in his ear, then managed more coherent congratulations. "Has Major Williams got in yet?" he asked.

"Not half an hour ago, sir," the operator answered. "He's one of the men questioning the traitor now." His voice showed cold fury. No longer was Lieutenant General Sir Horace Bragg the longtime, well-respected commandant of the Royal American Mounted Police. He'd found a shorter, harsher label, the one he'd take down in history.

"Ring me through to him," Bushell said.

"Stay on the line, sir. Someone will have to call him out of the interrogation room, which may take a minute or two."

Bushell stayed on the line. Within the promised interval, Micah Williams picked up a telephone. "Here's to cabals, Colonel," he said; his gruff voice had a purr in it, like that of a lion that has made a kill. Then, quickly, the purr changed to concern: "How's Captain Stanley?"

"He should be all right. He's come through surgery, and I've spoken with him."

"Thank God for that," Williams said. "I thought you and he and Kittridge had lost your minds, running out on us like that. But you knew what you were doing, all right, and thank God for that, too."

"It was a damned near-run thing even so," Bushell said. "What has Bragg got to say for himself?"

"Not much," Williams answered. "Why should he talk? They're going to stretch his skinny neck already, so he hasn't got a thing to gain by speaking up. The bugger actually seems smug about what he's done, as if he were proud of himself, as if he hadn't lost the game."

"Well, he bloody well has," Bushell said. "After His Majesty speaks tonight at six—hell, by now, I suppose, what with the news going out over the wireless—it'll be worth a man's life for anyone to find out he's a Son of Liberty."

"And a good thing, too, says I," Micah Williams answered. "Of course, I've been saying it's a good thing these past twenty years, same as you. But now people will listen when we say it."

"If that happens, it will be pretty fine," Bushell said before returning to the business at hand. "Have you found out yet where Bragg was when he said he was at the dentist's?"

"Not yet," Williams said. "We'll grill him through the full forty-eight, though, before we let him ring his solicitor. We'll see what comes of that. It worked with the villains we rounded up in Georgestown, even if we did have to squeeze 'em like a bid-whist player trying to get a last trick out of a hand."

Bushell thought of something else. "How's Sally Reese taking this?"

"I wasn't here, of course, when news of what happened down by the docks came in," Williams said, "but they tell me the shriek she let out frightened people on three different floors. She's crushed, Colonel—flat as a griddle cake. Somebody—I think it was Patricia Oliver, but I'm not certain—took her home a little while ago."

"Whoever it was should stay with her for a while, make sure she doesn't slash her wrists or stick her head in the gas oven," Bushell said. "I was afraid you'd say something like that. She's just had her world cave in. And what about Cecilia Bragg?"

"I don't know about her," Micah Williams said. "We're going to have to question her, I suppose, and find out whether she knew anything. Lord, what an ugly mess this will be when all's said and done."

"Isn't that the sad and sorry truth?" Bushell agreed. "My guess is that Bragg kept things from her, the way he did from everyone else." He remembered what Irene had told him of that party he'd thrown for Bragg on the occasion of his knighthood. "He was always good at that. But you never can tell. Cecilia might have been good at it, too. As you say, we'll have to sweat her to know."

"Yes, sir," Williams said. "What are you going to do now, sir?"

"Me?" Bushell was only just beginning to think about that. "Get some sleep, maybe, and see how Sam is doing after that, and then—I don't know. Maybe I'll get one more ride from Sergeant Kittridge and come back to headquarters to help you people sort through things."

"If it hadn't been for you, sir, we'd be out fifty million pounds, and God only knows what would have happened to His Majesty."

"Stubborn counts," Bushell said. "Sometimes I think it counts more than anything else."

Micah Williams laughed. "You're talking to a police officer. Tell me something I didn't know."

"Never mind that," Bushell said. "If you can't tell me something I didn't know, I'm going to ring off and see if they'll give me someplace where I can close my eyes for a while—and see how big a fit they pitch when I ask for it."

To his surprise, almost to his disappointment, the powers that be in the hospital didn't pitch a fit. Instead, a nursing sister led him to a room currently without any patients. When he walked in, he understood. There on one of the beds lay Ted Kittridge in his stocking feet, derby down over his face to hold daylight at bay. From under the derby came more than respectable snores.

Bushell got out of his own shoes and lay down on the other bed. He feared Kittridge's racket would keep him awake. And so it did—instead of falling asleep in thirty seconds, he tossed and turned for sixty, or perhaps even ninety.

▼

The first thing he noticed when he woke up was that the light had changed: the sun had traveled across the sky and was no longer shining in the window. The second thing he noticed was that Sergeant Kittridge was sitting up in the other bed. "What time is it?" he asked, hearing how blurry his own voice sounded.

Kittridge took out his pocket watch. "Quarter of five," he answered. He glanced over at Bushell. "You snore . . . sir."

"So do you," Bushell said. Both men chuckled. Bushell swung his feet down onto the floor. He went on, "I feel much better now. I'm all the way up to ancient and decrepit."

"Uh-huh," Kittridge said—as much a grunt as a word. Sam, now, would have given an answer worth having. Sam, though, wasn't in hospital to catch up on his rest, though Bushell hoped he was able to do that, too.

Bushell's backbone crunched and creaked as he bent to pick up his shoes. "You suppose they'll throw us out on the street if we try to see Sam again?"

"No," Kittridge said: an economy of expression difficult to match.

Under other circumstances, Bushell might have contemplated grabbing a bite to eat before he went to visit his adjutant. Given the quality of the hospital cafeteria, he decided to do without. He clapped a hand to his forehead. "Lord, if that's what they serve the guests and the doctors, what do the patients get?"

"Slop, I expect," Kittridge answered.

The broth and stewed prunes on a tray set on Stanley's bed fit Kittridge's definition well enough. "I want a beefsteak," Stanley said, "a big, juicy beefsteak. Beef builds blood. Doesn't that quack of a dietitian know anything about how to feed a man?"

"Me, I wouldn't fancy a hospital beefsteak unless my shoes wanted resoling," Bushell said. "But even if they gave it to you, how would you cut it?"

Sam mournfully contemplated his wounded arm. "If I had a good, true friend, I suppose he might give me a hand," he said. "It would take a mighty good friend, but—"

Bushell laughed. "You don't want a friend. What you want is a slave."

"No, no, that's Bragg," Stanley said, laughing, too. But he quickly sobered. "He really does, you know. If the Sons ever got their way, I wouldn't care to be the color I am, not in the North America they'd give us."

"It's fifty million pounds and one painting further from happening than it was this morning," Bushell said. "Now we need to find out if it was Russia backing the Sons all through this plot, or if the Holy Alliance was trying to pull a fast one on us."

"Could be war," Ted Kittridge said. "Could be a big war."

"Abetting the assassination of a sovereign?" Bushell weighed the gravity of the charge. After a moment, he nodded. "You might be right."

There hadn't been a big war, a world-bestriding war of the kind Kittridge meant, since the eighteenth century, not long before the North American Union came into being. Since then, the British Empire had been too strong for any other power to challenge head-on. But an Empire cast into confusion by the murder of its chief and perhaps by an uprising of the Sons of Liberty might have been vulnerable to attack from a foreign foe. Bushell weighed the odds. "If there's war now, we'll win it."

"Hell, yes," Kittridge said. "Would have anyway. For sure now."

"The Sons who really make me angry are the rich ones," Stanley said, following his own thought. "Bragg was doing fine where he was—why does he think he needs his plantation back? Joseph Kilbride, Stanage, Morton Johnston: they're all rich. They've got no business conspiring with foreign kings, wanting to tear down the Empire that let them do so much."

"That's right," Bushell said vehemently. "I can understand why somebody like Michael O'Flynn might become a Son. You earn your little wage setting powder charges way underground, never sure whether the roof's going to come down on your head or the mine will blow up . . . you live like that, any change looks good. Maybe Eustace Venable had his reasons, too: a cabinetmaker's not going to be able to retire rich at forty-five, no matter how good his work is. But some of the others we've hauled in—" He shook his head.

"Rum old world," Kittridge said. Bushell and Stanley both nodded. There wasn't a police officer in the British Empire—there probably wasn't a Franco-Spanish inquisitor or *Okhrana* man in Russia—who didn't sing that song a dozen times a week.

"And the rich ones use the poor ones, and most of the time it's the poor ones who get caught," Stanley said. "Even now—what was the word Williams used for Bragg, Chief? He's still smug? Is that it? I don't care how smug he is. The Mint doesn't stamp out enough sovereigns to hire the solicitor who could get him out of the prisoners' dock now, because there's no such man."

"Good thing, too," Bushell said. "He'll get what he deserves, and he deserves—" He didn't go on. His own anger at Bragg was as much rooted in his betrayal of friendship as in his betrayal of country, but if a man could do the one, it was easier to see how he might also do the other.

"Sorry it worked out this way, Chief," Sam said, guessing some of what was going through his mind.

"I'd sooner have put Sir David's head up on the wall, and that's a fact," Bushell said. "You can't always get everything you want, though, and we did pretty damn well here." He hesitated, then made a grudging admission he'd never expected to hear from his own lips: "And Clarke isn't—quite—the bastard I always thought he was."

Samuel Stanley turned to Sergeant Kittridge. "Take this man back to his hotel, Ted. He's spent so much time in hospital, he's come down with softening of the brain."

Bushell snorted but didn't argue. Without a word, Kittridge led him off to the carpark alongside the hospital. The local RAM turned the key to ignite the burner; he'd killed the pilot when he pulled into the carpark. Bushell leaned back in his seat and waited for steam to come up in the boiler. Idly, he took out his pocket watch and glanced at it. Maybe he'd be back at the William and Mary in time to catch His Majesty's speech on the wireless, or maybe he'd have a proper supper at the hotel restaurant and walk over to RAM headquarters afterward.

Kittridge had time enough to smoke one of his odorous little cigarillos down to the butt before steam pressure built to the point where they could get rolling. Bushell lit a cigar of his own in self-defense, but the smoke from Kittridge's was pungent enough to overcome the milder tobacco he favored.

He rolled his window all the way down when the steamer got moving. The breeze got rid of some of the cigarillo stink, but replaced it with the hot, muggy air of Victoria in high summer—a bargain, perhaps, but not the best one he'd ever made.

He was close to dozing, in spite of the rest he'd had back at the hospital. Like a gourmand looking for a snack to fill up a tiny empty space after some gargantuan repast, he worried at the question of why Horace Bragg remained smug after his plot had utterly failed. Was he proud of taking a brewer and a coal-mine powderman and a cabinetmaker down into ruin with him? That seemed a perverse sort of pride, indeed.

A street-corner trafficator ordered a halt. Kittridge obeyed it, then reached into his waistcoat pocket for the case where he kept the dock-scrapings he called cigarillos. Bushell eyed the move with what he hoped was well-concealed resignation.

Suddenly he jerked the door of the motorcar open, jumped out, and ran over to a red public telephone box near the corner. Kittridge shouted something at him. Ignoring his fellow RAM, he fed a shilling into the coin slot. When an operator came on, he said, "Ring me the All-Union Art Museum."

"I'm sorry, sir," the operator said after a moment. "All lines are engaged at the moment—hardly surprising, what with His Majesty's visit and the excitement of the day. Perhaps you'd do better to try another time."

"The excitement of the day's not done," Bushell snarled. He slammed down the phone and dashed out of the box without getting his shilling back.

Ted Kittridge was still sitting at the corner, though the trafficator's arms gave him the right—indeed, practically commanded him—to move. Klaxons blared behind him; irate, sweaty drivers leaned out their windows to discuss his ancestry. As far as he was concerned, they might as well not have existed. He glanced toward Bushell with mild curiosity on his face. "What's up?"

"Where's the All-Union Art Museum from here?" Bushell demanded. "The map inside my head's all twisted around."

"You want to go to the museum?" Kittridge asked. Bushell nodded vehemently. "Not the hotel?" the sergeant persisted, picking now of all times to be talky.

"No, I always say I want to go one place when I mean the other," Bushell answered. "Don't you?" Kittridge considered that, grunted out an economical bit of laughter, and sent the steamer spurting across the intersection just as the trafficator arm swung up to bar his way. The drivers behind him who hadn't got across shouted more curses. The drivers on the cross street, who had been about to roll through the intersection themselves, blew savage blasts of protest on their horns.

As far as Kittridge's demeanor showed, he might have had the boulevard to himself. After a couple of minutes he glanced over at Bushell and asked, "What's wrong now?"

"Maybe nothing," Bushell said. "I hope to God nothing, as a matter of fact. But if we've got a Son in gaol who's a dab hand with blasting powder, and if the late, unlamented Eustace Venable was a master cabinetmaker, and if *The Two Georges* has that big, fat, fancy frame around it—"

"—And if Bragg doesn't give a damn that they're going to hang him," Kittridge said, thoughtful enough to expend a whole sentence to complete Bushell's thought. On top of the first, he added a second: "We'd better hurry."

"Yes," Bushell said, and let it go at that. The ten minutes they'd spent waiting to get up steam pressure suddenly felt like a squandered eternity. If he was right, and if they got to the museum a couple of minutes too late to do anything about it—what would he do then? The only thing that occurred to him was, *Crawl in a bottle and never come out.*

Kittridge scraped a lucifer against the dashboard and used it to light another cigarillo. The sulfurous smoke from the lucifer was better than what came out of the cigarillo, as far as Bushell was concerned. Kittridge took a couple of puffs, coughed, and then asked, "What if you're wrong?"

"Then I'm going to look like the biggest damn fool the world has ever seen, and I'll do it in front of all the millions of people listening to His Majesty's speech on the wireless."

"Charles'll forgive you," Kittridge said, blowing out another cloud of vile smoke. "He'd better, considering."

"He may forgive me," Bushell answered. "Nobody else will."

▼

The All-Union Art Museum was a neoclassical building with a marble stairway leading up to a colonnaded front modeled after that of the ancient Roman Temple of Concord. Bushell and Kittridge reached the grounds surrounding the museum at 6:13. Bushell hadn't heard any ambulances or constabulary vehicles clanging their way to the site or, worse, away from it, and took that as a good sign. He needed all the good signs he could find.

By then, he was used to barricades manned by red-uniformed RAMs. This time, Kittridge didn't have to crash through any of them. The RAMs waiting at the roadblocks stumbled over themselves shoving them aside and waving his steamer forward. "You're a hero," Kittridge said as he rolled up to the entrance. "See what it gets you?"

"Into more trouble," Bushell answered. He got out of the motorcar as soon as it stopped. So did Kittridge. They bounded up the steps together, as he and Sam Stanley had on the way up to the first floor the night *The Two Georges* was stolen. He wished Stanley were at his side now. Had it not been for Sam, though, he might not have made the connection between the knowledge the Sons of Liberty had and the remaining danger to Charles III.

*Provided, of course,* he told himself as, panting, he pulled at the heavy glass-and-bronze doors to the museum, *there is any remaining danger.* If there wasn't.... He shook his head. He'd been through that already.

Just inside the doors, more RAMs stepped forward to block his path. When they found out who he was, they went from wary and hostile to eagerly helpful in the space of a heartbeat.

"Yes, sir," one of them said. "His Majesty is speaking in the Heritage Room. Down that corridor, turn left, and then right at the first door. Here, let me come with you and clear a path."

Bushell didn't argue, but set off for the Heritage Room at the best pace he could manage. It was almost 6:20 now. If there was a bomb in the frame around *The Two Georges*, the Sons wouldn't have set it for much after six. They'd know the King-Emperor would start to speak right on the hour, for the benefit of the wireless broadcasts that would beam his words across the NAU, all through the British Empire, and around the world.

The RAM guards at the door to the Heritage Room were not carrying pistols. They had Lee-Enfield rifles with bayonets fixed, and brought them up as Bushell, Kittridge, and the RAM from the front entrance bore down on them. At that RAM's urgent gesture, they lowered their weapons. "What the devil's going on?" they demanded, almost in chorus.

"Trouble," Bushell answered. One way or another, that was true. Either the King-Emperor was in trouble or Bushell momentarily would be.

He thumbed the latch and yanked the door open. The sudden sharp noise made heads turn all through the Heritage Room. Up at the podium, Charles III never faltered, but continued with his address: ". . . bound to one another by ties of blood and friendship, of unity and amity, we go forward together and . . ."

Press photographers, gaudy security badges pinned to their jackets like decorations from minor German powers, stood against the walls of the Heritage Room. Flashbulbs popped as Bushell and Kittridge trotted to the front of the hall. One went off almost in Bushell's face. Ignoring the blast of light, he hurried past the photographers.

Charles III went on with the speech until the very moment Bushell came up beside him. Among the dignitaries seated behind the King-Emperor was Kathleen Flannery, who looked lovely in a gown of shining, dark green silk Bushell hadn't seen before. She got to her feet, saying, "What—?"

Bushell leaned forward so the microphone would pick up his words. "I'm sorry," he began, thinking, *I'll be sorrier if I turn out to be wrong*, "but you must clear the hall at once. We have"—*some*—"reason to believe an explosive device may be concealed in the frame of *The Two Georges*."

He'd used the euphemism on purpose, to try to hold panic to a minimum. But people didn't take long to realize *explosive device* was just a five-syllable synonym for *bomb*. They didn't quite stampede out the doors at the back of the Heritage Room, but they weren't perfectly chivalrous, either.

Bushell turned to Charles III, who showed no inclination to leave. "That means you, too, Your Majesty. Especially, that means you. If there is a bomb and if it goes off and catches you, the Sons win in spite of everything else we've done today."

The King-Emperor considered that, looked unhappy, and finally nodded and retired, much less rapidly than most of his subjects. Kathleen said, "Why do you think—?" Again, she didn't finish the sentence.

"I'll explain later," Bushell said. *One way or another*, he added to himself. "Go on now—get out of here while you can." When she looked mulish, he told her, "The King-Emperor listened to me."

"It's not the King-Emperor's museum," she said, and didn't budge.

"No point getting blown up to no purpose. This is your life we're talking about," he said, and shoved her toward the RAMs staring in from the hallway. "Get her out of here." Ignoring Kathleen's vehement protests, the RAMs did just that.

"Help me get it down off the wall," Bushell told Ted Kittridge. They lowered *The Two Georges*. Bushell examined the frame, front and back. It looked fine. *It would*, he thought. *Venable was a hell of a cabinetmaker.*

Raising his voice, he called to the RAMs who had taken charge of Kathleen:

"Have we got an explosives expert handy?" Nobody said anything or came forward. He rubbed at his mustache. "Looks like it's amateur night," he said to nobody in particular.

He took out his pistol, unloaded it, and used the barrel to tap at the frame. It sounded like solid wood. He tapped again, a couple of inches farther along the oak. That sounded like solid wood, too. Seeing what he was doing, Sergeant Kittridge took the cartridges out of his own weapon and started tapping at the other side of the frame.

Tap, tap. *Thunk, thunk.* Tap, tap. *Thunk, thunk* . . . Bushell turned the corner on the frame. Tap, tap. *Thunk, thunk.* Tap, tap. *Thunk, thunk.* Tap, tap. *Thunk* . . . *thok.*

Bushell paused and tapped at the second place again. *Thok.* The sound was distinctly different. He glanced over to where the picture had hung on the wall of the Heritage Room. That part of the frame would have been right behind the King-Emperor, and about chest-high.

He stared at the frame. It still looked fine. He put on his reading spectacles and brought his head so close to the gilded wood, his eyes crossed. Was that a hair-thin straight line that didn't belong in the rococo exuberance of the carving? He couldn't be sure. He ran his thumbnail across it. He couldn't be sure there, either.

"Only one way to find out," he said, and, reversing his pistol so he held it by the barrel, brought the butt down on the picture frame as hard as he could.

Wood chips flew. He smashed at the frame again, and again. Without warning, he broke through into a hollow cunningly concealed in the very heart of the oak. Wires ran from a timing device to a large sausage of explosive a couple of inches away. He reached in and tore their connections loose.

That done, he lifted out the timer. It was based on a small alarm clock. He glanced down to see the hour for which the clock had been set, then pulled out his pocket watch.

He wasn't the only one looking from the face of one timepiece to that of the other. "Cutting it close," Ted Kittridge remarked.

"Five minutes, I make it—all the time in the world." Bushell got to his feet. He caught Kittridge's eye. "Let's hang it back up so His Majesty can finish his speech."

▼

The door to the interrogation room at RAM headquarters opened. Horace Bragg came in. Without being told to, he sat down in the hard chair reserved for prisoners. The pyjama-like suit of coarse cloth with the broad arrow on it hung like a tent from his gaunt frame.

From under bushy brows, he stared across the table at Thomas Bushell. Something—the vital spark—was gone from his eyes. Bushell had seen that before, in other prisoners who had given up.

"Hullo, Tom," Bragg said. Something had gone out of his voice, too. He sounded as if he saw the hangman's noose looming large in his future—and he had reason to sound that way.

"Hullo," Bushell said, and then formally, for the record: "As you have indicated of your own free will the wish to speak, I must inform you that this is not required, and that what you say may be used against you in a court of law." A colored clerk recorded his words and Bragg's; he wondered if the Negro's presence was salt on his friend's—his former friend's—wounds.

A bit of impatience came into Bragg's voice: "I ought to know that rigmarole, Tom; I helped revise it, after all. Go on. Ask your questions."

"Then you also know I'm required to go through it with you," Bushell answered. *We don't want any possible errors a smart barrister might exploit.* He didn't say that out loud; Bragg would be able to figure it out for himself. Instead, he did as Bragg had said and asked his questions: "Where were you when you claimed to be visiting your dentist?"

"Where do you think I was?" Bragg tried to smile, as if that were no more than light badinage, but he managed to keep the corners of his mouth pressed upward for only a couple of seconds.

"I think you were with *Comte* Philippe Bonaparte," Bushell answered. "We've found a waiter in a cafe just off Embassy Row who says he saw the two of you together there at times when you were supposed to be in the chair getting your crown."

"If you already know the answers, why ask the questions?" Bragg said, a little sullenly.

"Because sometimes they give us new answers," Bushell said. "Suppose you had assassinated the King-Emperor? What then? What did you hope to gain from all this?"

"Freedom," Bragg said. "A new chance to make America what it was meant to be, not tied to the apron strings of an island full of busybodies far across the sea. In the chaos, we would have seized the moment and—"

"Lost," Bushell put in.

"When the risings began—"

Bushell interrupted again: "What risings? Who on earth besides your handful of fanatics ever wished the Empire and the NAU anything but good?"

"Risings for freedom, all across America," Bragg said. "We've endured this tyranny for two centuries and more, endured its robbery for a century and a half."

"Robbery? A century and a half ago?" Bushell scratched his head. Then his eyes widened. "Good God, Sam was right all along—you *are* still angry the Crown freed the slaves way back then, even if your however-many-times-great-grandfather got paid off for them."

"It *was* robbery," Bragg insisted. "Yes, he got a pittance for the Negroes, but how could he go on working his land without them? How the family suffered afterwards—" He waved a scrawny hand. "But that isn't what you asked. Of course there would have been risings. Some the Sons would have aided, yes, but others, hundreds of others all across the land, would have erupted and spread like wildfire. From Drakestown to Victoria—"

"You would have been hunted down like dogs," Bushell said. "Oh, there would have been risings, all right—risings against the regicides." He wondered how the mining country would have gone, but refused to give Bragg the satisfaction of saying so out loud. There would have to be changes in Pennsylvania and Franklin and Virginia; he'd realized that much. And in almost all the NAU— "There wouldn't have been enough constables and RAMs to keep the mobs from lynching every Son they could catch."

"We would have had help," Bragg said. "The Holy Alliance would have—"

"Lost," Bushell said again. "And even if you'd won, you wouldn't have got free. You'd have been a Franco-Spanish cat's-paw instead of a piece of the British Empire. Damned if I can see any improvement there."

Horace Bragg let out a long sigh. "No, I suppose not. I had such hopes for you, Tom. You always seemed so—American, so ready to be free. But you never would take off the King-Emperor's dog collar, not even when you were left all alone after you divorced Irene. That bloody well drove me mad, let me tell you." He shook his head. "Finally I had to send you away."

Bushell stared at him. New answers indeed! Had Bragg seduced Irene to try to wreck his marriage and make him more vulnerable to recruitment by the Sons of Liberty? Bushell wouldn't ask that with the clerk listening; he didn't need it in evidence. But it made more sense than any reason he'd come up with till now. As for the other— "You had to send me away? Why? For fear I'd notice what you were up to?"

"Of course," his former friend answered, eyes widening as if no other reply were imaginable.

"How long *have* you been working toward—not this exact scheme, maybe, but something like it?"

"My whole life," Bragg said simply.

Bushell wondered if he'd ever really know the man on the other side of the table at all. He got to his feet and walked out to the two RAMs who waited in the hall. "I'm done with him," he said. "Take him back to his cell."

▾

When Bushell was summoned to America's Number Ten now, it was not to the Green Room, nor to confer with Sir David Clarke. A servant in the livery of the previous century conducted him to Sir Martin Luther King's administrative office.

If Governor Burnett's desk back in New Liverpool had been a dreadnought, aeroplanes might have landed or taken off on the surface of the one Sir Martin Luther King used. The governor-general rose from behind it to shake Bushell's hand.

"Just take a seat here, Colonel," he said, waving to a velvet-upholstered chair with elegant Chippendale lines. "I expect my other guest to arrive shortly."

About five minutes later, the same servant escorted into the office *Comte* Philippe Bonaparte. The Franco-Spanish ambassador was wearing a suit of Savile Row cut, but a Savile Row tailor would sooner have sliced his wrists with a pair of pinking shears than turn out a suit of crimson velvet with gold embroidery on the lapels and collar of the jacket. The worst thing Bushell could find to say about the ambassador's cravat was that it made the rest of the outfit conservative by comparison.

"Good day to you, Sir Martin," Bonaparte said in fluent if accented English, half bowing to the governor-general. He turned to Bushell with a broad, friendly smile. "And here we have the man of the hour! It is an honor to see you again, Colonel."

"*Comte* Bonaparte," Bushell said with the same expressionless tones he might have used to begin an interrogation.

The ambassador from the Holy Alliance started to take the seat next to Bushell's. "I did not invite you to sit, *Comte* Bonaparte," Sir Martin Luther King said, ice in his voice. He hadn't risen to shake hands with the diplomat, either.

"So you did not, Your Excellency," Bonaparte said, straightening. "I assumed, however, you did not summon me here for the purpose of insult only." His eyes glittered. "Perhaps I was wrong."

"Perhaps you were," Sir Martin said. "I summoned you here to inform you that, as you have become *persona non grata* to the North American Union and the British Empire, I request and require you to leave our territory within forty-eight hours of this moment."

"On what grounds?" Bonaparte cried.

Sir Martin nodded to Bushell, who continued his flat recitation: "On the grounds that you conspired with Sir Horace Bragg and other Sons of Liberty to raise a rebellion against the lawful government of the North American Union, and that this conspiracy involved the theft of *The Two Georges* and the attempted assassination of the King-Emperor, Charles III."

"Of this last I knew nothing," Philippe Bonaparte replied. "It was the inspiration of Bragg and his fellow—what is the word they use?—patriots; yes, that is it. As for the other—" He shrugged a Gallic shrug. "It is my duty to enlarge my country's prospects, just as it is the duty of the British ambassador in Paris to do likewise for your Empire."

"And if the British ambassador is caught meddling as your sovereign deems he should not, he is expelled," Sir Martin said. "You have been caught at something rather worse than meddling, sir. Count yourself lucky we content ourselves with your expulsion and do not go to war."

"You would not," Bonaparte said. "It would send the whole world up in flames."

"That did not concern you when you gave aid and comfort to the Sons of Liberty," Sir Martin Luther King replied. "My opinion is that the prospect of losing concerns you more than the prospect of war."

"You are of course entitled to your opinion." Bonaparte gave the governor-general another half-bow; even expelled, he lost none of his urbanity. After a moment, he added, "And speaking of opinions, mine was never that this effort had—or deserved—a large probability of success." He turned to Bushell. "I gave you a warning, you will recall, during the reception at Duke Orlov's."

"If that was a warning, you'd been ambassador to Delphi before you came to the NAU," Bushell said. Bonaparte nodded to show he appreciated the classical allusion. Bushell went on, "If you didn't think your plot deserved to succeed, why the devil did you cover up what you were trying to say? Why didn't you just come right out and tell me—tell somebody—what you meant?"

"But I could not do that, *Monsieur!*" Now Bonaparte sounded genuinely shocked. "I had my duty to my own sovereign and to his requirements of me to consider first. Within those limits, I told you everything I possibly could. Does not your Empire, your duty, come before your own personal feelings?"

The shaft hit close to the mark. Had Bushell paid less attention to his duty and more to his personal feelings, he might well have remained married to Irene—and how would that have affected his chances of dealing with the theft of *The Two Georges?* The very way he framed the question showed how deep a hold duty had on him.

"All right, *Monsieur le Comte,*" he said. "There is some truth in what you say."

"Some, perhaps, but not enough," Sir Martin Luther King said. "Our Lord said, 'Render therefore unto Caesar the things which are Caesar's; and unto God the things that are God's.' Doing one's duty renders unto Caesar, but doing what is right renders unto God."

"It is not to be doubted, Your Excellency, that you must have been formidable as a man of the cloth, even if you suffered the misfortune of Protestantism," Bonaparte said. "There must of necessity, however, be a difference between the views of a man of the cloth and those of a man of the world. Is this not so, Colonel Bushell?"

"It's so," Bushell said, not caring to agree with the Franco-Spanish ambassador—the *ex*-Franco-Spanish ambassador—but not about to lie, either. "I wish it weren't."

"I also wish it were not so," Sir Martin Luther King said. "As a man of the world, *Comte* Bonaparte, I repeat to you that you now have something less than forty-eight hours to remove yourself and your personal effects from the territory of the North American Union. I do not say *au revoir,* sir. I say good-bye."

"I obey under protest," Bonaparte said, and turned to go.

"So long as you obey," Sir Martin said to his retreating back.

▼

The taxi pulled to a halt halfway down the block of attached homes. The driver pointed. "There you are, sir—number 41," he said, then glanced at his meter. "That'll be four pounds, three and sixpence."

Bushell gave him a fiver and walked toward the door through evening twilight without waiting for change. Like all the other homes on the block, number 41 was neat and well kept—a far cry from the grim dwellings of the miners in Charleroi, even if built to the same basic principle.

Before Bushell could ring the bell, Kathleen Flannery opened the door. She looked cool and comfortable in a flower-printed shift of thin cotton. "Come in," she said, smiling.

"Thanks." Bushell hung his hat on the tree just inside the door—a lone fedora among cloches, pillboxes, berets, a couple of broad-brimmed picture hats, and others of styles whose names he'd never bothered to learn. Then he kissed her. She prolonged the kiss. His arms tightened hungrily around her.

When they separated, she waved him down the short front hall. "Go on, sit down—make yourself at home."

"Don't mind if I do." Bushell paused in front of the sofa to look around before he sat. Books, prints, a phonogram and wireless receiver in a cabinet of blond wood, furniture upholstered in a green, lustrous fabric, rusty-brown carpet a few shades darker than Kathleen's hair. He nodded once, decisively. "I like this place. It looks like you."

That made Kathleen peer around the room, as if seeing it in a new light. "It does, doesn't it?" The breeze from an electric fan on a bookcase tugged at her hair. Probably without noticing what she was doing, she smoothed it down as she said, "Do sit down. I'll be right back." She went into the kitchen. Her heels tapped on the tiles there. Bottles clinked together. Ice cubes clattered musically into glasses.

She came back with two drinks, handing Bushell the amber one and keeping the clear one with a slice of lime for herself. "Thanks," he said again, and sipped.

"Is it all right?"

"Jameson," he said. "Ice. Hard to go far wrong." A stack of cork-bottomed coasters with medieval-looking paintings of knights on them stood at a corner of the polished oak coffee table. He picked one up, examined it, set it down, and put his glass on it. After a moment, he passed her one, too.

"The clerk from Adler Cubicles came by today—with Marge," she said. "I shot them to the front of the queue, the way I said I would." She paused to drink from her gin and tonic. "Marge was very impressed."

"At seeing *The Two Georges*, or at the VIP treatment?"

"Both," Kathleen said. "I got the idea she didn't believe he could deliver. When he did, it left her speechless."

"That must have made the clerk even happier than he was already."

Kathleen's scowl would have been more effective had it been less severe. Bushell smiled back at her, bland as butter. The scowl faded. "You are an impossible man," she told him. "I believe I've mentioned that once or twice already."

"I believe you may have," he agreed. "I do try." He wondered if that would draw another glare, but she gave him a thoughtful nod. He sipped the Jameson, set the glass on the coaster again. "We're well matched."

"I think so. I'm glad you do, too." Kathleen peered down into her gin and tonic, as if the little bubbles that rose and burst there told her something she needed to know. Without raising her head, she asked, "How long are you going to stay in Victoria, Tom?"

Bushell took out his cigar case. "Do you mind?" he asked. Kathleen shook her head, again brushing back a lock of hair that got in front of her eyes. The ritual of getting the cigar lighted gave him something to do with his hands, and gave him half a minute or so in which not to answer her question. After he'd savored the first mouthful of smoke and blown it out, he said, "It'll be a while yet. Brigadier Arthurs needs . . . all the help he can get."

"He's trying to hose out the Augean Stables," Kathleen said. "He knows you're clean."

"There is that," Bushell said, and let it go. Normally, he might have been pleased to turn the conversation from the personal direction in which it had veered to his work. Brigadier Benjamin Arthurs, however, left him sad. The man was earnest, affable, and not very bright. Bushell wondered if Horace Bragg had aided his rise precisely because of that blend of qualities. Arthurs had spent several years not noticing a thing. Now, all at once, he was supposed to purge the Victoria RAM office of whatever Sons of Liberty Bragg had infiltrated into it. At least he realized he was out of his depth—or perhaps he'd had orders from the governor-general's residence. Bushell didn't know, or want to know, about that.

Kathleen finished her drink and set down the empty glass. She started to say something, stopped in surprise, and began again: "I was going to make us both another one, but I see you've not finished your first."

"I can fix that," Bushell knocked it back. But as he handed her the glass, he said, "I haven't been as deep into the bottle lately, seems like. Will you get angry if I call you a good influence?"

"Probably," she answered. "I sound angry, don't I? With *The Two Georges* back, the strain's off everyone." She got up, went into the kitchen, and returned in a couple of minutes with fresh drinks.

Bushell savored the Irish whiskey for the way it tasted, not for the thick, transparent wall it built between him and the world. He hadn't drunk like that for a long time, not since . . . his married days. But the thought of Irene didn't make his belly knot, didn't make his brain and his mouth crave the smooth, musky taste of Jameson. "Must be love," he murmured.

Kathleen slammed her glass down onto the coaster. "You say that. You even mean it—I think. And so?" She stared a challenge at him.

Now he wished he hadn't lighted the cigar so soon. Down along the disputed border between the NAU and Nueva España, the soldiers of the Holy Alliance had the charming habit of sowing fields with land torpedoes and then covering them up so cleverly you never knew they were there . . . till you walked on one.

He picked up his own drink. All at once, his hand and his mouth remembered the urge he thought he'd escaped. Deliberately, he contented himself with a small sip. Wherever he put his foot, something was liable to blow up on him.

"I don't know," he said, after the pause had stretched longer than it should have.

Kathleen's mouth drew down into a thin, bitter line. "It's been fun, Dr. Flannery," she said, putting words in his mouth with irony sharper than a scalpel. "I'd like to go on having fun as long as I'm in Victoria, Dr. Flannery, and after that I'll be off to New Liverpool, Dr. Flannery, and it'll be all done. So long, Dr. Flannery."

"That would be easiest," Bushell said. She gave him such a withering gaze, he looked for a better word, and found one: "That would be—safest."

"Everything we've been through, and you talk about—safety?"

He nodded, and then did finish the drink after all. The wall of whiskey kept the world from coming in—and him from coming out. Facing Kathleen was terrifying in a way facing bullets had never been. In combat, you just reacted. Here . . . "Falling in love with a police officer isn't a good idea."

"Since I've already gone and done that, it's a bit late to worry about it, wouldn't you say?" she answered. "And he says he's fallen in love with me. But—" She shrugged.

"Falling in love is easy," he said harshly. "What comes afterwards isn't." He imagined coming home one afternoon and finding Kathleen in the arms of another man. The mental picture was shockingly vivid. And why not? He'd been through that once. Did he dare risk it again?

"Do you think I don't know that?" she answered, and he remembered he wasn't the only one with sorrows in his past. "But if you run away from it for fear of what might happen afterwards, what's the point of doing it at all? What do you have from me that you couldn't find on a street corner for a ten-pound note?"

He blinked. Women were seldom so forthright. One thing he'd found about Kathleen was that she was seldom anything she was supposed to be. "Do you know," he said slowly, "that's a damn fine question."

"I wouldn't mind a damn fine answer, then," she said, which made him notice he'd used a word he didn't normally employ in feminine company.

"I haven't got one," he admitted. That didn't seem enough, either to him or, obviously, to Kathleen. He looked with longing toward the glass he'd emptied. "If we go on as we have gone on," he said, eyes on the ground for land-torpedo tripwires at every word, "then you're right: we ought to see how long we can go on."

"And how long would you like to see us go on?" Kathleen asked.

"If I'd known this was what you meant by 'coming to court,' I'd have brought a barrister," Bushell replied. He wasn't used to being on the defensive; his style was to push hard himself. But when it came to matters this intimate, he found himself barely able to move at all. Did that justify Kathleen's prodding at him? Maybe it did, if you looked at things through her eyes.

"I'm sorry," she said; maybe she was trying to look at things through his. But then she shook her head. "No, I'm not sorry. It's something I need to know, because it'll tell me more about how you really feel."

"You're right," he told her, which, by the way her hand groped for and missed her drink, surprised her more than anything else he could have said. He went on, "I'd like to see us go on for—years." He couldn't say *forever*, not even now; it felt too much like asking for trouble. "I don't know yet if we can, but I'd like to see it."

"All right." Now Kathleen hesitated. "You don't—have anyone waiting back in New Liverpool?"

"The way that Lozovsky blackguard had a lady friend waiting back in Tsaritsin, you mean?" he asked. Kathleen nodded. He shook his head. "No, nobody like that." He spoke with assurance, for about the first time since he'd sat down on the sofa.

Kathleen noticed as much, too. "That's good. I didn't think so, but . . . it's hard being sure."

"Lord, isn't it!" Bushell exclaimed. For that moment, he and Kathleen understood each other perfectly. He looked around the room. His eyes narrowed slightly. "I just noticed—you haven't got a print of *The Two Georges* here. All these other lovely things, but not that one."

"Of course I do," she said, and then, a moment later, "I keep it in the bedroom."

"In the bedroom?" he echoed, surprised himself now—it wasn't a painting he would have hung there. "Well—*de gustibus non disputandum.*"

"You don't believe me," Kathleen said indignantly.

"I didn't say that."

"You meant it." Kathleen jumped to her feet. "Come with me, then. I'll show you." She headed for the stairs, not looking back to see whether he followed or not.

Follow he did. He was only a couple of paces behind her when she flicked on the bedroom lamp and waved him in ahead of her. A fine print of a Fragonard hung on one wall, and a smaller reproduction of Greuze's portrait of Sophie Arnould on another, but— "There's no *Two Georges* here."

"You're right," Kathleen said from behind him. "I lied."

"Why?" he asked, turning.

Mischief filled her face. "Can you think of a more—decorous—way for a lady to invite a gentleman into her bedroom?"

"Can't be a gentleman *all* the time," he said, and took her in his arms.

▼

The telephone rang. "Oh, God, what now?" Bushell said, spinning his swivel chair away from the typewriter wherein sat a report recommending the dismissal from the Royal American Mounted Police of Drinkwater, Lieutenant Obadiah J., on the grounds of allegiance to an organization aiming at the subversion of the North American Union and the British Empire. "Hullo? Bushell here."

"Colonel Bushell?" a female voice said. "One moment, please. His Excellency the governor-general desires to speak with you."

*What's gone wrong now?* Bushell wondered. The thought had hardly formed before Sir Martin Luther King came on the line: "I'm sorry to disturb you, Colonel, but could I ask you to come to my residence as soon as may be convenient for you?"

In plain English, that meant *immediately*, and Bushell knew it. "Is this something we could possibly do by telephone, Your Excellency?" he asked, with hope but without any great expectation of success.

"I'm afraid not," Sir Martin answered. "Some matters are too important to be entrusted to such means."

*Fewer than you think.* But Bushell didn't say that out loud. Maybe the governor-general was like a horse shying at shadows—and maybe something dreadful really had erupted. After the past few weeks, how could you be sure? "I'm on my way," Bushell said, and hung up.

He was heading for the bank of lifts when he came upon Ted Kittridge walking in the same direction, a couple of thick manila folders under one arm. "Where are you off to with those?" he asked.

"America's Number Ten," Kittridge answered sourly. He hefted the folders. "They think they're smarter than we are."

"If they were half as smart as they think they are, they'd be right," Bushell said. Kittridge let out a brief chuckle. Bushell went on, "I'm on my way to the same place, matter of fact. Somebody's had a brainstorm, or thinks he has. Can I take up some space in your steamer?"

"Why not?" Kittridge chuckled again. "What with the last couple of rides we had, I oughtn't to let you near it. But they turned out right, so—"

Once they were in the motorcar, he lighted another one of his poisonous cigarillos. Bushell already had his window down, the better to stir the hot, soupy air of Victoria summer. Some of the smoke blew away. Some, unfortunately, didn't. As he had before, he fired up a cigar of his own to fight the stink.

At the entrance gate to the governor-general's residence, RAMs in dress reds meticulously checked Bushell's badge, then Kittridge's. They saluted and waved the two men through. "Better than crashing a barricade, eh?" Kittridge said. Bushell nodded. For Kittridge, that was an amazing show of loquacity.

When the steamer pulled up to the residence, Sir David Clarke came out to meet Bushell, who started worrying in earnest. If Sir Martin sent out his chief of staff, he did think something was going on. Whatever it was, Clarke was tight-lipped about it, saying only, "Come with me, Colonel."

Bushell came. Kittridge followed along behind, carrying those manila folders. "What's all this in aid of?" Bushell asked. "Sir Martin didn't want to say much over the telephone."

"I really think I'd better let His Excellency make the required explanations," Clarke answered, glancing back over his shoulder at Sergeant Kittridge. That set Bushell worrying again. If Clarke didn't care to talk in front of a man who'd helped save the King-Emperor's life not once but twice, whatever was going on had to be horrid. Either that, or the governor-general's chief of staff deserved a clout in the teeth for slighting Kittridge—and, with Clarke, that was always a possibility.

The office to which Kittridge had to deliver his precious folders was only a couple of doors down from Sir Martin's sanctum. "Meet you downstairs," he told Bushell, who nodded.

Before they went into the governor-general's office, Bushell tried again: "Anything you can tell me? I hate walking in blind."

Sir David Clarke pointed to the closed door. "As I said, Colonel, Sir Martin will fully inform you inside." *Damn you, Clarke,* Bushell thought. Only the memory of the hour Sir David had wheedled out of the Sons of Liberty kept him from grabbing the chief of staff and shaking the truth out of him right there in the corridor.

He might have done it in spite of that memory, but Clarke's hand was already on the latch. He relaxed, yielding to the inevitable. This wouldn't be the first time he'd gone into a briefing cold, and likely wouldn't be the last, either.

The door opened. The hum of conversation inside Sir Martin Luther King's office quieted. Hearing any talk at all in there startled Bushell, who'd been expecting to confront a grim-faced Sir Martin alone. What with the governor-general's urgent efforts at maintaining secrecy and those of his chief of staff, with whom could he be conferring?

"Go on in, Colonel," Sir David said.

Bushell took two steps into the office, then stopped dead. That was when Samuel Stanley, his left arm still splinted and supported by a sling, handed him a glass of champagne. "Ha! We did fool you, Chief," he said, his expression triumphant. "I can see it in your face—and Kathleen owes me a fiver. She guessed you'd tumble to it."

Bushell almost dropped the champagne flute. He felt like a man who'd been hunting for reverse and by mistake found top gear instead. He stared around the room. There was Kathleen, next to Sam. There was Brigadier Arthurs, pink-faced, white-mustachioed, looking like everyone's favorite if ineffectual grandfather although decked out in full dress uniform. There flanking him stood Micah Williams, Walter Manchester, and Toby Custine; they wore dress reds, too. Off against the other wall, there was Irene . . . Clarke. She waved to him and said something he didn't catch because coming toward him, hands outstretched, were Sir Martin Luther King and Charles III.

"Your Excellency," Bushell said, and then, a moment later, "Your Majesty." The ceremonial uniform Charles III had on outdid those of the RAMs as the sun outshone the moon. Bushell wondered how he stayed standing with all those decorations weighing him down. And the blade on his belt was more like a broadsword than the usual dress saber.

Magically relieved of file folders, Ted Kittridge came into the governor-general's office. Bushell rounded on him. "You were part of this plot," he said severely.

"Plot?" Kittridge tried, without much success, to look innocent.

"If Colonel Bushell can uncover the deep-laid plans of the Sons of Liberty, we must expect him to see through ours as well," Sir Martin Luther King said. People laughed and clapped their hands.

Bushell shifted the glass of champagne Sam Stanley had given him back to his right and raised it high. "His Majesty, the King-Emperor!" he said. Everybody who had a glass—except His Majesty, the King-Emperor—drank to the toast. Making it was, so far as Bushell knew, the only act proper at any and all times throughout the British Empire.

Then Charles III raised his champagne flute. "Colonel Thomas Bushell!" he said, and people drank again, amid more applause.

Servants went around filling glasses. Kathleen came over to Bushell. Even if she had lost her bet with Sam, she looked smug. She put a hand on his arm. "Congratulations, Tom," she said.

"All in a day's work," he answered. Her expression said he hadn't managed to bring that out as pat as he'd hoped. Toasting the King-Emperor in person and having him toast you back knocked the props out from under the most thoroughgoing cynicism. He tried a different tack: "You had something to do with congratulations' being in order, you know."

She shook her head, brushing the hair back from her face with that familiar automatic gesture. "This is your time. Enjoy it."

"Yes, ma'am!" he said, and gave her a smart salute. She made as if to pour champagne on his shoes.

"Go ahead, Chief—you *should* enjoy it," Sam Stanley said, knowing that didn't always come easy for Bushell. "You've earned it, by God." His wounded arm was mute testimony to the price of earning it, but when he saw Bushell's eyes go to it, he shook his head. "I'll be fine—see?" The fingers of his left hand stuck out from the bandages that wrapped the splints. He wiggled them, to show he could.

Sir David Clarke drifted over to a spot a few feet away and politely waited for Bushell to notice him; his manners, as always, were impeccable, even if the same word did not apply to the rest of his behavior. After everything that had happened, Bushell found it impossible to snub him. When he nodded, Sir David said, "I do hope you won't mind my having brought Irene. She was quite insistent, so much so that I found it impossible to say no. She is . . . fond of you."

"It's all right," Bushell said. "We're all on the same side today."

Clarke's handsome face lit up in a broad smile. "Well said!"

If he thought that meant Bushell forgave him, he remained mistaken. Bushell was, though, willing to grant him neutral status, at least for the day. Considering his feelings toward Sir David a little while before, that in itself was, if not a miracle, as close to one as mankind commonly had the privilege of seeing.

Samuel Stanley said, "I wish Phyllis could have been here to see this, Tom, but they only told me about it last night. You can't get from one coast to the other in less than a day, not unless you're a military pilot in a hot aeroplane."

Bushell almost asked, *Been here to see what?* He stopped with the question unspoken, feeling foolish. How many commoners had the King-Emperor toast them at a reception in their honor? *Not bloody many,* he thought, and stood straighter with pride.

He found a different question to ask Stanley: "How long will you have to wear that thing?" He pointed to the boards and bandages that stabilized his friend's arm.

"Not too much longer," Sam answered. "I may even miss it." When Bushell let out a highly dubious snort, he explained, "As long as I have it on, I can clout villains without waiting to grab for a sap." He lowered his voice. "And if I get the chance to talk with Brigadier Arthurs for five minutes alone, by this time tomorrow there'll be a regulation ordering every RAM in the NAU to put on splints for the good of the service."

Bushell laughed, then thought better of it. He wouldn't have given odds of worse than three-to-two against Stanley's being right. "He means well," he said, also quietly.

"Oh, his heart's in the right place," Sam agreed, "but he hasn't got the head he needs for the job. Bragg, now—Bragg had the head, but not the heart. We found out about that. It was worse than the brigadier's way, at lot worse. The service needs somebody with both." He turned a mild and speculative eye on Bushell.

"Listen, Sam, if you think I'm going to let them chain me to the commandant's desk, you're out of your—" Before Bushell could finish, he was interrupted by someone affectionately rumpling the hair at the back of his neck. He spun around, annoyed Kathleen would take such a liberty at a gathering like this. But it wasn't Kathleen; it was Irene. He didn't know whether to be angry or sad. No point to anger, he decided, not today. He sighed and said, "Thank you for coming."

"I wouldn't have missed it," she answered. "I am proud of you, Tom, in spite of . . . everything." Her voice trailed off the same way Sir David's had.

"Thanks," Bushell said again.

Then he got a glimpse of Kathleen, who glared daggers at Irene's back as his ex-wife walked away. "She has no business touching you like that," Kathleen hissed. "*No* business."

"No, but she thinks she has," Bushell said. "Right of prior possession or former possession or whatever you want to call it. It doesn't mean anything to me. I know when I'm well off."

That got through to Kathleen. "You'd better," she said, and gave a grudging nod.

Charles III cleared his throat. Instantly, every head in the room swung toward the King-Emperor. He said, "One of the pleasures of my post is that, on occasion, its privileges are commensurate with its duties. This is one of those happy occasions: beyond the ability of most men, I have the power to reward favors given me." His voice took on a tone of command beyond any a mere field marshal could assume: "Colonel Bushell, Captain Stanley—attend me!"

"Me?" Sam said, his eyes widening. "I thought it was him." He pointed to Bushell.

"*I* knew it was both of you," Kathleen said. "You ought to give me my fiver back."

Bushell still didn't know what *it* was, but when his sovereign ordered that he attend, he obeyed. Then Charles III drew that impressive sword. As light glittered off the polished steel of the blade, Bushell understood. "Kneel, gentlemen," the King-Emperor said.

Kneeling, Sam whispered, "It was supposed to be you."

Bushell contrived to tap his friend's splinted arm through the sling as he went to his right knee. "Battlefield commission," he whispered back, staring down at the carpet.

"A happy occasion indeed," Charles III said, "and a most appropriate one, to create two new Knights Commander in the order of chivalry reserved for those dwelling in this broad western land, the Most Illustrious Order of the Two Georges." The sword touched first Bushell's shoulder, then Stanley's. "Arise, Sir Thomas! Arise, Sir Samuel!"

Cheers rang out as the two new knights got to their feet. Bushell looked from Sam to the King-Emperor to Sir Martin, to Irene just for a moment, and last of all to Kathleen's delighted face. He had never been prouder to be an American.